TURNING THE HERD

Then Red rode up to the herd, gun high over his head, to yell and shout. Larry took his cue from that and did likewise. Sterl, riding back a hundred feet, followed suit. Cedric and Drake, with the drovers farther back, let loose with guns and lungs.

The front of the great mob, like the sharp edge of a wedge, roused to lunge and thud away from the din. It headed away from a direct line toward the river. That relieved Sterl. The turn was not enough, but it had started. Cattle, like sheep, blindly followed the leaders. Every few seconds Sterl would fire his gun and whoop. Dust clouds began to lift. The trampling of many hoofs, the knocking of horns, the increase in hoarse bawling, indicated the start of the milling Sterl was so keen to accomplish. Something like a current ran all the way back to the rear. That frightened Sterl. He yelled and fired and waved his sombrero. They had the apex of the mob quartering away from a direct line to the river bed. But the river took a bend to the east there, and looked less than two miles away!

Suddenly from the far side of the herd waved a trampling roar that drowned yells and gunshots. Sterl's piercing yell was a whisper in his ears. He had heard that kind of roar. His blood ran cold....

The Great Trek

ZANE GREY®

LEISURE BOOKS   NEW YORK CITY

A LEISURE BOOK®

June 2008

Published by special arrangement with Golden West Literary Agency.

Dorchester Publishing Co., Inc.
200 Madison Avenue
New York, NY 10016

ISBN 10: 0-8439-6062-0
ISBN 13: 978-0-8439-6062-4

The name "Leisure Books" and the stylized "L" with design are trademarks of Dorchester Publishing Co., Inc.

Printed in the United States of America.

10 9 8 7 6 5 4 3 2 1

Visit us on the web at www.dorchesterpub.com.

The Great Trek

Foreword

by Loren Grey

When my father made his first visit to Australia in the fall of 1935, it was on a pioneering expedition for big game fish, particularly the giant man-eating sharks known to frequent Australian waters. At the time, deep sea fishing, though not unknown there, was in a relatively primitive state compared to angling in New Zealand—which he had made famous during his travels there in 1921, 1927, and 1929—and at Catalina Island, Florida, and other Atlantic waters. Just a short time after he arrived, he was rewarded by the capture of a world record one-thousand-thirty-six pound tiger shark, landed right in the middle of the shipping lanes just three miles off the entrance to Sydney harbor. Of course, the attendant publicity was huge and did not appear unduly diminished by the fact that about three weeks later Lyle Bagnard, one of Dad's employees, landed a one-thousand-three-hundred-sixty-five pound tiger shark, which, of course, broke Dad's world record. Although Dad graciously consented to pose with Lyle for the publicity shots, perhaps not surprisingly no mention of Lyle's catch appeared in his book about this first visit, AN AMERICAN ANGLER IN AUSTRALIA.

In all respects—except for the one just mentioned—his trip was a huge success. In addition to his fishing records, he also starred in a full-length movie called WHITE DEATH, a name he had given to the great white shark. It was never a commercial success, but added to the lore about the world's greatest living man-eater.

Dad also quickly became aware of another great frontier in Australia, the nature of which was virtually unknown to most Americans—the vast central desert of this great continent to which the Australians referred in their laconic manner simply as "the Outback."

Although Zane Grey never crossed this great wilderness completely, he traveled far enough inland to see that it very much resembled his own American desert in many respects except, of course, for the bewildering array of strange and exotic species of animals and plants to be found there, as well as the enigmatic presence of virtually the last Stone Age man left in the world—the Australian aborigine. Everything about this strange land enthralled him. It was not long before his imagination led him to the dream of writing a great Australian frontier epic revolving around the attempts by Australian cattlemen-drovers, as they were called, with the help of American cowboys to drive a huge herd of cattle across the northern desert to the verdant Kimberley Mountains on the northwest coast, where gold had been discovered and beef was in short supply.

The result is this huge sweeping saga which in many ways is one of his finest. But as so often had happened in his frequent publishing woes with the moguls of Harper, when this book was completed in 1937, it was not on their agenda. It was too foreign, too strange, too "unlike" the Zane Grey which, literally, had kept them solvent during the Depression years. Instead, came WEST OF THE PECOS, RAIDERS OF THE SPANISH PEAKS, and KNIGHTS OF THE RANGE, all well written, tried and true oat-burners which gave them no risks and helped to improve their bottom line which, as most of us know—or should know—is the religious deity of all business. This new novel not only had the handicaps mentioned above, but to the editors at Harper, it was also much too long.

It was 1944 before they finally got around to considering publishing it, five years after my father's death. But even then, though the Depression was only a memory, small was still big. With inflation and the higher costs of paper, to make money and keep the same prices, books had to be much shorter. So the editors chopped and chopped, and, when they were done, they chopped some more. The book ended up practically a novelette, being less than one-third of the length of the original story. Most of his great descriptions of the Australian wilderness were cut out and even some of the fine plot was thinned. Surprisingly, the resulting "foreign" book sold very well to American readers, which made everybody happy but me. Mother and my brother, Romer, who ran the family affairs didn't seem to mind, but for a while I was mad. In the ensuing years, as a result of many such experiences as heir, with my sister, to the Zane Grey estate with the mighty house of Harper, I have never become much happier with what I have seen as the cavalier manner with which most Harper editors have treated Zane Grey and all of us who followed him since the beginning, all the way back to 1910. I have many files with letters from them where they, figuratively, patted Zane on the head like a small, wayward child, telling him this book is too much of this and that book is too little of that. Of course, having dealt with editors about my own writings—which editors always seemed to know more about than I did—I got used to it. Today they still act the same way, but they want Zane Grey—or at least say they do—on their catalog list *without* changes now, even though on reprints we have seen to it that they only get ten percent of the royalties earned by the books instead of the usual fifty percent split. At least in this sense we have had some revenge. And now, for the first time in many years, we have other options.

This story is now is being published by Five Star Westerns in its entirety for the first time, as THE GREAT TREK. And as new material surfaces (which is still happening even after all these years—if you don't believe this, come and look at my garage!) and the stature of Zane Grey as a major voice in the legends of the West grows, there will be other unrevised novels appearing for his readers to enjoy. I think it is about time.

Loren Grey
Woodland Hills, California

Chapter One

Across the blue Tasman Sea, smooth and heaving on that last day, the American adventurers eagerly watched the Australian horizon grow bold and rugged, changing from dark to pale green, its ranges spreading far-flung and wide, significant of a vast wild country beyond.

"Red, it's land . . . land," Sterl Hazelton said, his gray eyes dim from watching and remembrance of other land like that, from which he must forever be an exile.

"Shore, pard, I seen it long ago," replied Red. "This heah sea gettin' level an' that sight jest about saved my life. Sterl, I've gone places with you years on end, but no more ridin' ships for Red Krehl. Not even for you."

"But Red, old friend, let me remind you how I begged you not to come," replied Hazelton earnestly.

"What kind of talk is thet? Do you think I'd ever let you go to hell alone? Only I'm sorry it wasn't that Argentine country we've lit out for. Them pampas plains . . . the *gauchos* an' grand hosses . . . an' dark-eyed Spanish *señoritas.*"

"As if dark eyes and blue eyes hadn't ruined us enough?" Sterl muttered bitterly.

"Pard, this heah Australia begins to loom up kinda big, at thet. But it's English. . . . An' whoever heerd of an English gurl lookin' at a cowboy?"

"Red, someday you'll get enough girl to do you for good and all, as I got."

"Shore I can stand a lot, Sterl. Air my eyes pore or is thet shoreline standin' kinda cliff-like an' gold?"

"Yes, pard. Walls of gold, like an Arizona cañon, with a great break there in the middle. The mate told me that was Sydney Heads, entrance to the finest harbor in the world."

"Yeah? Wal, I'm from Mizzourie. He's gotta show me. Sterl, anythin' thet reminds us of Arizonie an' Texas is gonna be bad."

"It sure is. Like home! We've been on this blasted sailing ship for a thousand days, it seems, and now we are reminded of home. I wanted this country to be new and strange."

"Wal, it shore looks big an' wild. Kinda eases away thet orful pain I've had. Pard, this heah sea-sickness is wuss than gun-shots."

"Funny I didn't get sick," mused Sterl. "But you've worn out your stomach with nine cups of coffee every meal, and gallons of hard liquor between times."

"Say, if I had a bottle on this ship, I wouldn't be near dead now. Sterl, let's have one orful drink before we hunt for jobs."

"Sounds good, but it's not sense."

"But we never had no sense no how," Red protested. "You takin' the blame for thet gun play? An' me fool enough to let you!"

This time Hazelton did not reprove his friend and shut him up about the fatal step which had bound them for a far country. But outside of Red's incredible loyalty he had no part in the killing that had made Sterl an outlaw. Red might be driven, if not per-suaded, to go back to America. This idea had developed and waited in Sterl's mind, and now with the ship making time across that rippling blue and white sea, due before midday in Sydney, it was time to try the plan out on Red.

How high the gold-rimmed cliffs loomed! Sterl thought of the Verde, of Oak Creek Cañon, of Cañon Diablo, of many lesser Arizona cañons he had known so well. If Australia was full of craggy, colored walls like these, how would he ever forget? The pang was there in his breast and the endless leagues across the Pacific had not seemed to ease it. But Sterl had never suffered a regret for his sacrifice. A rolling stone gathered no moss. He knew in the depths of his heart that Nan Halbert could have steadied him, changed his wandering trail life, ended his drink-

The Great Trek 7

ing and gun-throwing, if it had only worked out that way. She had loved him, too, as well as his cousin, Ross Haight. Ross, the gay handsome blade, lovable and sweet-tempered, except in his cups, the only child, pride and hope of an ailing father with lands and herd to bequeath. Ross, who had in a moment of passion shot a man who certainly had deserved it, but which deed had put the range hounds of justice upon the track of the killer! Sterl had taken upon himself that guilt, which to him was not guilt. His family had been gone so long that he hardly remembered them, except his schoolteacher mother who had loved and taught him. There had been only Nan. And what could he have done for her, compared to what Ross could do? It was the big thing that singularly appealed to him. And it all rolled back in poignant memory to the last scene where Ross had confronted him and Red that last night, passionate and desperate in remorse and shame.

"But Sterl!" he had rung out, "Nan believes you killed this man! Dad believes . . . and everybody else. How can I stand that?"

"For her sake! She loves you best. Go straight, Ross. . . . Good bye!"

And Sterl had raced away into the blackness of the Arizona night, soon followed by the loyal Red, who could neither be eluded nor driven.

"Red, you remember what Ross forced upon you to give me?"

"Shore I remember," replied Red, looking up with interest. "I had a hunch it was money. An' as I knowed you was about broke. . . ."

"Yes . . . money. I never opened that packet till we got to Frisco. Ten thousand dollars!"

"Holy mavericks!" Red ejaculated, astounded. "So much money! Where'd Ross get it?"

"Must have told his father. Well, you know we outfitted in Frisco and bought tickets on this ship. Red, I'm asking you to take half this money and go back home."

"Yeah! The hell you air?" Red retorted scornfully.

"Yes, pard, I'm begging you."

"An' why for?" queried Red. "'Cause you don't want me with you?"

"No . . . no. It'd be grand to have you . . . to be pards, riders together . . . gamblers with adventure. But for your sake!"

"Wal, if it's for my sake, don't insult me no more. Would you leave me, if you was me an' I you? Honest Injun, Sterl?"

It seemed quite impossible to look into those blazing blue eyes, that lean face red as flame, and tell such a lie. Krehl was always good to look at, but, when eloquence or passion possessed him, then he shook Sterl's nerve. Reluctantly he had to reply in the negative.

"Wal, what's eatin' you then? Anyone would think I hadn't any romantic feelin's or love of adventure. Why, I always had you skinned to a frazzle."

"All right, I apologize. Stay with me, Red. God knows I need you."

"I should snicker to snort you will. No matter where we haid up, some girl will go for you an' there'll be trouble. Hasn't thet always been so? Twice on the Chisholm Trail, Waco an' thet Red River Ranch, if you remember, again in Abilene, an' time an' again in Arizona, toppin' off with thet turrible case on Nan Halbert. What'd become of you but for me, pard?"

"¿Quién sabe? Boy, we're getting somewhere. Look. There's a big ship steaming along under the left wall, from the west. And another way off there to the north."

"Gosh, they shore look grand. I never seen ships a-tall till we got to Frisco. What's thet smoke out heah?"

"Another steamer, hull down they call it. And that long, black rolling cloud of smoke comes from her funnels."

"Hull down? For cripe's sake, is she sinkin'?"

"Red, didn't you ever hear that the earth is round?"

"Not thet I remember. The school I went to for six weeks in Mizzourie didn't know it, I reckon. All thees ships a-comin'! This Sydney must be a real man-sized burg, huh?"

"Big city, Red, so the sailors tell me, and I'm going to take you out of it *muy pronto*."

"Suits me, pard. But what air we gonna do? We don't know nuthin' but hosses, guns, an' cattle."

"I read that Australia is going to be a big cattle country."

"If thet's a fact, we're ridin' pretty," Red returned with satisfaction. "But mebbe I won't be glad to get my feet on good old solid ground."

They lapsed into one of their frequent silences while the ship sailed on, her canvas bellying, her yards and bones creaking. Under the bow below where the friends reclined, the water gurgled and splashed, at long intervals lifting the ship to a heaving swell.

Sterl saw the two steamers turn and head into the wide portal between the great rocky heads. And the third, that had been hull down, rose as if by magic out of the sea, to bear down upon the sailing vessel. She was a huge liner, flying the Union Jack, a roaring, hissing hulk, massive as a mountain, and somehow pregnant and magnificent with the potency of foreign lands. She made Sterl think wonderingly of what little he knew of the world. And she passed the sailing ship, slowing down to meet the pilot boat that stood out from the heads.

Soon the mile-wide gateway to Australia offered the sailing ship a lonely entrance. Sterl got up to gaze with intense and inexplicable interest. The moment was far-reaching, and it baffled him. Red made some loquacious remark about the lighthouse high upon the western head. The cliff sheered up hundreds of feet, a seamed and scarred face of yellow rock, like any age-old cañon wall, and at its base the white surge broke with hollow roar.

Australia's far-famed harbor opened up to Sterl's sight, a long curving bay with many arms cutting into the land. Here and there red-roofed houses stood out markedly from the bright green. Miles inland, around a broad turn where ships rode at anchor, the city of Sydney stood revealed, strange to the Westerners, foreign and stately, gray-walled, red-roofed, a broad and undulating area of edifices.

In due course, while Sterl and Red packed their bags, the ship eased alongside a dock, and tied up, to the cheery chant of glad sailors. Going down the gangplank, Red manifested an unsteady gait, and, when he staggered out upon the deck, he walked like a man who had one leg shorter than the other. Sterl would not have bragged about his own steadiness. They were accosted upon the dock, led into a shed, where after a brief examination they were free. One of the stevedores directed them to an inn up the street, where soon they had a room and were relieved of their heavy bags.

It was early in the afternoon. Krehl voted for seeing the sights. But Sterl disapproved, for that meant looking upon drink.

"Pard, we must get our bearings and rustle for the open range," Sterl said, and he meant to abide by that.

Whereupon they had their first Australian meal, about which they disagreed, and then set out to ask two cardinally important questions—where was the cattle country and how could they get there?

"Outback," replied more than one person, waving a hand that, like an Indian's gesture, signified vague and remote distance. In the reply of others they interrogated, that queer word stood forth with prominent significance.

"Outback?" echoed Red, growing exasperated. "Where'n'll is thet?"

They wandered too far uptown, and the shops, the crowds of people, the lithe red-cheeked, clear-eyed girls, all so different from those in San Francisco, began to intrigue Sterl and wholly possessed Red.

"Red, this isn't getting us jobs," Sterl observed, reluctantly turning.

"Aw, pard," remonstrated his comrade poignantly. "Thet one looked at me twice. An' the second time she smiled."

"I saw her. High-stepper who took you for a hick from America."

"Come on, you everlasting lover of all women!"

Back on the waterfront they resumed their search and asked questions of everyone who would listen. Civil and courteous, these Australians, thought Sterl, but not interested in tramps from foreign countries. At last a big man, ruddy of visage, looked them up and down and smiled when he said: "Yankees?"

"Yes. It must be written all over us," admitted Sterl, with an answering smile.

"You asked for information about the cattle country. Are you drovers?"

"Drovers?" echoed Sterl, puzzled, while Red looked belligerent.

"Horsemen . . . drivers of cattle?"

"Oh! You bet. Plain Arizona and Texas cowboys. We eat up hard work. Where can we get jobs?"

"Any station owner will hire you. But I advise you to go to Queensland. Big cattle mustering there."

"Where and how far?" Sterl queried eagerly.

"Queensland is upcountry. Five hundred miles up the coast and inland three or four hundred more."

Sterl looked blankly at their informant. He received another subtle intimation of probably endless distances in this Australia. But Red was equal to the occasion.

"Wal, only about a thousand miles. Nothin' a-tall. My pard an' me don't care how far we have to walk, so long's we're shore of jobs."

"That's absolutely sure. But you can't walk," replied the man, who had taken Red seriously. "Board the freighter *Merryvale* down the dock. Sails at six today. Brisbane. Queensland is your stop. Good luck, cowboys."

"Thanks, mister," returned Sterl soberly. "It was kind of you."

Sterl led his comrade down the waterfront to where the big freighter was tied up at the center of busy shipping activities. He soon found an officer who said they could buy passage to Brisbane. And then Red Krehl broke out: "My Gawd, pard! You cain't be heartless enough to drag me on thet sea again? I won't go. You can jest go to hell without me. Aw! I tell you I'm seasick this heah minnit. I'm gonna look on red likker."

Nevertheless, despite Krehl's reiterated exposition of his woes and determination to desert his friend, they were passengers on the *Merryvale* when she steamed out between Sydney Heads. He had, however, procured a bottle before leaving the waterfront, and Sterl was glad to help him drink its contents. Red raved and groaned about being seasick, but his reproaches were untenable because he did not suffer at all.

Next morning they awoke to find the sea calm, with the steamer tearing along not five miles out from a magnificent and picturesque shoreline. Evidently this fact made a vast difference to landlubber Red, and it was a most unexpected and pleasing factor for Sterl. Never had he been more sure of what had made him a range rider—love of the open, of color and beauty, of the wild and the free, of waving prairie grass and rugged purple steppes, of ghastly desert and calling phantom mountain, of the raw and the physical in nature. It had been born in him. And as he leaned over the rail of this steamer to gaze at a white-wreathed shoreline, for leagues on leagues to north and south, at the rolling green ridges rising on and upward to the high ranges, he sustained a singular and revivifying intimation that beyond these calling dim mountains there might await him the greatest and most insuperable adventure of his life.

"Dog-gone it!" Red was drawling. "I wanta be mad as hell, but I jest cain't. Gosh, pard, that's grand country. I wonder what's beyond over there . . . Outback, as they call it. I've a hunch somethin' is comin' to us. Talk about wild range. No farm, no ranch, no town, far as we can see. I hate to knuckle to it, but even Texas cain't beat that."

"Texas is grand, you old horned-toad!" declared Sterl. "This country is green, bright, rare, rich green, new to me."

"Must rain a lot, leastways along this heah coast. But Sydney was hot an' dry. We wasn't there longer'n a jack rabbit's jump, but I felt it. Lemme see. . . . Must be May . . . spring, by gosh, an' thet's great."

"May, aye, Red, but not spring. It's fall."

"Aw, how can it be May an' be fall?"

"Red, your ignorance is terrific. We're south of the equator, where the seasons are reversed. When it's summer at home, it's winter here."

"Yeah? Wal, I reckon I'll never get thet through my haid. Any more'n I can savvy what thet sailor told us about it bein' summer all the year up heah. If thet's so, I'm shore gonna like this Australia."

It was a bright, sunny day, warm and pleasant, with the sea glassy and smooth, and running a long, low swell. A flock of gulls followed the ship. Fish and porpoises sported upon the blue water. Far to the north the smoke of a steamer drifted along the horizon.

Sterl and Red spent all save mealtime upon deck, and it appeared that the farther north they traveled the more attractive grew the mainland. At last, when night fell, they sought their bunks, tired out from gazing and conjecturing.

Next day, if anything, the weather was even finer, and the view of shore and island magnified all the properties that had been so satisfying. The sailors, having little work to do, were friendly and talkative. Red sighted his first whale and nearly fell overboard in his excitement. "Gosh, he shore was a buckin' broncho. How'd you like to ride him, pard?"

In the afternoon the skipper, a fine old sea dog, invited them to come up on the bridge with him. Sterl took advantage of the opportunity to tell him their plan. He was interested and communicative.

"Boys, you are in on the ground floor, if you can stand the heat, the dust, the drought, the blacks, the floods, the fires, besides harder work than galley slaves."

"Captain, driving cattle on the Texas plain wasn't just a picnic," replied Sterl.

"You'll think so, after droving upcountry here."

"Boss, I reckon we've been up ag'in' all you said 'cept the blacks," Red inquired, deeply interested. "Jest what air these blacks?"

"The black men. Natives of Australia. Aborigines."

"You mean niggers?"

"Some people call them niggers. But they're not Negroes. They are black, all right. Shiny black . . . dead black as coal. There are innumerable tribes of these Australian natives, most of whom live as they did in the Stone Age, and further back, perhaps thousands of years."

"Wal, can you beat that?" Red exclaimed, vastly perturbed. "Boss, what about these black men? Bad medicine, mebbe?"

"Cannibals. They eat you."

Red's expression was something to laugh at, and Sterl indulged himself. But he was surprised, too, and shocked as well. He did not entertain Red's southern Texas hatred of Negroes.

"Boss," went on Krehl, "I've had my fill of fightin' greasers, rustlers, robbers, an' redskins on the Texas trails, but gosh! All of them put together cain't be as wuss as black men . . . cannibals who eat you."

"Right you are, Red," declared Sterl. "That's a new one on cowboys. Captain, you're sure putting the wind up on us, as you Australians say. But tell a little about cattle and ranches . . . I mean stations."

"Well, I've only a general bit of knowledge," returned the skipper. "Cattle raising is not so new. There are stations up and down New South Wales, and eastern and central Queensland. Gradually cattlemen are working Outback. Five years or so ago the drovers ventured to muster mobs of cattle into the Northern Territory. I've heard of the terrible times they had. But I can't give you any specific details. I do know, however, that no drovers have yet ventured way beyond the Outback of Australia . . . into the unknown interior . . . called the Never Never Land by the few explorers who did not leave their bones to be picked by the black men and bleach on the sand. That Never Never Land must be the most wonderful and appalling upon the earth."

"Never Never Land?" Sterl mused, deeply stirred. "Like our prairie land, or the *Llano Estacado,* or Death Valley, only I venture to guess vastly magnifying all the distances, hardships, and dangers of our country."

"Pard, thet's kinda hard to believe," said Red, shaking his head. "No places I ever heerd about an' ventured into was as bad as they was painted. But thet always makes you the keener to see for yoreself."

"Well, boys, you are in for an adventure," continued the skipper. "There's some big movement on out from Brisbane. We have consignments of flour, harness, wagons on board that prove it. You make me wish I was a lad again, without the call of the salt sea in my blood."

Toward sunset that day Sterl gloated and mourned over a panorama that brought stingingly home to him the glory of Arizona.

There were clouds above the lofty range that turned gold and purple, at last to take fire. A flame slanted down over the billowy green slope, transparent and changing, that lost its red only when blocked by a stretch of sandy shore and long curved white line of breakers. A headland projected far out into the sea, tipped by a sentinel lighthouse. The similarity here to any Arizona scene lay in the vividness of the sunset hues, burning, transforming, and at length dimming. The transparent purple veil dissolved off the mountain range, and quickly it seemed the day was done.

The *Merryvale* docked at dawn far up a muddy river on the west bank of which stood Brisbane. After breakfast Sterl and Red labored ashore, dragging their burdens of baggage, curious and eager as boys half their age. Brisbane did not impress them with its bigness, but it sparkled under a bright sun, and appeared alive and bustling. They found a hotel and, leaving their baggage, sallied forth on the second lap of their adventure.

In less than an hour they were directed to a merchandise store which was filling orders for a company of drovers making ready to leave Downsville, a cattle town in Central Queensland for points unknown.

Sterl got hold of the manager, a weather-beaten man who had
seen service in the open.

"We are two American cowboys," Sterl began swiftly. "Is there
any chance for jobs Outback?"

"Chance? Young man, they'll welcome you with open arms.
Report is that the drovers can't find bushmen enough to start.
Bing Slyter is here with his teamsters. He's one of the drovers,
and he's buying supplies for the Danns and the other drovers. I'll
find Slyter for you."

Sterl turned to his shining-eyed comrade. "Red, we're in luck.
Right off the bat!"

"Wal, so it 'pears. But let's take it cool an' easy."

"How can we? This deal opens up big . . . makes me breathless."

In a moment they were greeted by the manager, and faced a
big man whose wide shoulders made his height appear moderate.
If he was an Australian bushman, Sterl thought, he surely liked
the type. Slyter had a strong face cast in bronze, a square chin,
and eagle eyes that pierced like daggers.

"Good day, young man," he said in a voice that matched his
size. "Watson here tells me you're American cowboys, looking
for jobs."

"Yes, sir. I'm Sterling Hazelton, from Arizona, and this is Red
Krehl, from Texas. I'm twenty-five, and he's a year younger. We
were born in the saddle and have driven cattle all our lives. We
rode the Chisholm Trail for three years. That's our recommendation."

"It's enough, after looking you over," returned Slyter in boom-
ing gladness. "We Australians have heard of the Chisholm Trail.
You drove mobs of cattle across Texas north to new markets in
Kansas?"

"Yes, sir. Five hundred miles of hard going. Sand, bad rivers,
buffalo stampedes, electric storm where balls of fire rolled along
the ground, storms with hailstones big enough to kill a man,
fighting Indians and rustlers."

"Rustlers? We call them bush-rangers. Cattle thieves just

beginning to make themselves felt. One reason we drovers are leaving central Australia. I'll give you both jobs. What wages do you ask?"

"Whatever you want to pay will satisfy us," replied Sterl. "We want hard riding in a new country. We will give our best."

"Settled. If it's hard riding you want, you'll get it. And I'm fortunate to get you. We drovers are undertaking the greatest trek in Australian history. Seven-thousand-five-hundred cattle, three thousand miles across the Never-Never!"

Sterl felt stunned at that ringing statement. But Red drawled in his cool and easy way: "Boss, that's nothin' a-tall to us. Jest all in the day's work! But it shore sounds sweet."

"Mister Slyter," burst out Sterl, "such a drive is unheard of. Three thousand Texas longhorns made hell on earth for a dozen cowboys. But this herd . . . this mob, as you call it . . . across that Never Never Land, if it's unknown and terrible as they say . . . ? Why, man, the drive is impossible, unthinkable. Please excuse me, Mister Slyter, but I know this cattle trail game."

"Hazelton, we can do it, and you're going to be a great help. I was discouraged before I left home. Just couldn't find teamsters and drivers who would undertake it. But Leslie said . . . 'Dad, don't give up. You'll find men. Besides, I'm going to be one of your drivers.' Leslie's a grand kid."

"You're taking your family on this trek?" Sterl queried aghast.

"Yes. And there'll be two other families."

"You Australians don't lack nerve," smiled Sterl. "I remember only two drives, when we had women. And they were worse than buffalo stampedes."

"Boys, we'll have much to talk about, and plenty of time later. I've no time now. Do you need money to outfit?"

"No, sir. We have money. But we need to know what to buy."

"Buy here, then. Cheaper and far more goods to select from. Rifles, and all the ammunition you can afford. Tents, blankets, and mosquito nets, clothes, boots, socks, some tools, a medicine kit, bandages, gloves . . . a dozen pans, some bottles of whiskey, and about a ton, more or less, of tobacco. That goes furthest

with the blacks. You needn't stint on account of room. We'll
have wagons and drays."

"But, Mister Slyter," exclaimed Sterl, in amazement. "Buy all
that stuff? We don't want to stock a store."

"Haw! Haw!" laughed the drover with impressive humor.
"Boys, this great trek will take two years. Two years droving
across the Never Never Land to the Kimberleys!"

"Indeed, it will be never!" cried Sterl, staggered at the import.

"*Whoopee!*" yelled Red.

Chapter Two

The remainder of that stimulating day Sterl and Red spent in
a big merchandise store, making purchases for a two years'
trip beyond the frontier.

Cowboys always loved to mill around in a store full of horse
equipment, guns and ammunition, rider's garb, tools, and range
articles. Sterl never remembered possessing money to buy one
tenth of what he longed for. This wonderful occasion made up
for all past longings. Red, in his boyish eagerness, was like a bull
on a rampage. "Gosh! Look at thet English saddle. Could I stick
on thet, pard. Them gadgets on the front . . . pretty slick. Must
be to hold you on. Fine leather, though, an' workmanship."

The English rifles also intrigued the cowboys. Sterl had
brought along his Winchester .44 from which he would not have
been separated. And he had five hundred shells for it. But he had
a vague idea these would be inadequate for such a long and perilous trip. He bought two of the English rifles, of a caliber advised by the merchant, and a thousand shells for each.

These purchases broke the ice of old accustomed frugality,
and introduced an orgy of spending. "Well, pard, what do we
care about money?" drawled Red. "We're rich, an' anyhow we
ain't never gonna come back from this drive." They bought all

Slyter had advised, and more besides. Sterl had a weakness for bright scarves and pocket knives, while Red went berserk over socks. "You see, pard, never before in my life did I have more'n one pair. I used to wear 'em till they fell off an' then go barefoot." Lastly, Sterl laid in a store of candy and fancy things that might be handy to trade to the blacks, if no better use presented. More than once he wondered what this Slyter's daughter, Leslie, would be like. Sterl attributed that to Red's outspoken curiosity.

The bill for this prodigious load of purchases amounted to over a hundred pounds—five hundred dollars in American money. Sterl looked aghast at the bill. Red's jaw dropped in consternation. "Holy Mackeli, pard, thet's orful. I'll turn in most of what I bought. I must 'a' been loco."

"You'll do nothing of the kind," Sterl declared quickly. "It's more fun, buying this stuff, than I ever had before. You were a plumb circus. Red, think how fine it'll be using all this, way out in a strange country. If we can only pack it!"

It took a dray to transport their outfit to the yard on the outskirts of town, where they had been directed to go. Late in the afternoon they had all their purchases stowed away in the front of one of the big new wagons, with their baggage on top, and the woolen blankets spread. Before that task, however, they had changed their traveling clothes to the worn and comfortable garb of cowboys. Sterl had not felt so good for weeks. It was all settled. No turning back! The wild and unknown called irresistibly. Red seemed unutterably happy, and that meant more to Sterl than he had realized. He had a job that struck fire in him. He owned more things dear to a rider's heart than ever before altogether. He had money, however hateful it had seemed to accept it. Early that day, visiting the two banks, Sterl had changed his American money into Australian pounds. The bulk of it was far less. And this fortune, to him, reposed in a leather money belt around his waist, where he could always feel it. Never until that sunset hour, with their task done, had Sterl felt stable, beyond vacillation and grief. Nan Halbert was happy. She would never know how that happiness had come from him. Ross had depth and fineness. All he had needed was this jolt to make a man of him. Sterl gazed with dim sad eyes out over the gold green hills. That time of contending tides of trouble was past. He would be glad, presently, and forget.

They had scraped acquaintance with one of Slyter's teamsters, a hulking, craggy-visaged chap some years their senior. He imperturbably announced that his name was Roland Tewksbury Jones. Red's reaction to that cognomen was characteristic.

"Yeah? Have a cigar," he said, producing one with a grand flourish. "My handle is Red. Seein' as how I couldn't remember yore turrible name, I'll call you Rol, for short. In our country real names never get anywhere. On the Texas trails I knowed a lot of Joneses, in particular Buffalo Jones, Dirty Face Jones, an' Wrong-Wheel Jones. I'll tell you about them shore-fire Westerners some day."

Roland evinced a calm speculation as to what manner of man this Yankee cowboy was. He accepted Sterl's invitation to have dinner with them, and after that he invited them to go to a pub for a drink. They all had several drinks, and returned to their wagon where they found a fire blazing and the other teamsters busily unloading the supplies. Sterl looked for Slyter, but that individual did not appear.

Red averred he was so tired he could not wag any longer. The day had been harder for Sterl than fifty miles over a rough trail. Still, the fire felt so good and the bustling work about them so interesting that they stayed up until they almost fell standing. Then, spreading their canvas and blankets under the wagon, as they had done thousands of times, they composed themselves to rest and sleep. Sterl's last waking sense was to hear Red: "Where'n'll air them muskeeters they hollered about?"

Sterl slept infinitely sounder out in the open, on the hard ground, than he had for a month on soft beds. Indeed, the sun was shining brightly when he awoke. Red appeared dead to the world. Sterl mildly kicked him and called: "Comanches!" Red stirred, but did not come out of it until Sterl shouted: "Point the herd, Texas!"

Red opened his eyes, blinked, and stared at the wagon bed roof and at Sterl, then, comprehending, he said: "Mawnin', pard. That'll do about Texas."

They rolled out to perform hurried ablutions. Teamsters were leading horses out of the paddock; others were tying tarpaulins over the wagons. Jones addressed Red: "You have time for breakfast, if you move as fast as you said you did in Texas."

The cowboys took the hint and hurried off, with Red growling: "What you make of that, pard? The English galoot? I never said nothin' about bein' fast nowhere."

Sterl sensed considerable strife and no little humor in Red's adapting himself to the Australians. As for himself, Sterl resolved to go slow, to be friendly without encouragement, to bridle his tongue. Once out on the trail he had no misgivings as to how Red and he would be taken by their hosts.

Returning to the wagons and teamsters, Sterl saw that they were about ready to start, two teams to a wagon. He had an appreciative eye for the powerful horses. Jones called for them to hop up. Sterl found a seat beside the driver, while Red propped himself up behind. Inquiry about Mr. Slyter elicited the information that the drover had left at daylight in his light two-horse rig. Jones took up the reins and led the procession of drays and wagons out onto the road.

It was an exhilarating moment. Evidently Red nearly burst, holding in a cowboy yell. Sterl labored under a stress of feelings, prominent in which was that old heart-swelling call of the wild.

Soon the town was left behind out of sight. A few farms and gardens lined the road for several miles. Then the yellow, grass-centered road led into a jungle of green and gold and bronze. Right then began Sterl's education in Australian bush. Even if Jones had not been civil, which he was, Sterl could not have refrained from asking questions. They had ten days or more to drive, mostly on a level road, good campsites, plenty of water and grass, meat for the killing, mosquitoes in millions, and bad snakes.

"Bad snakes?" echoed Sterl in dismay. He happened to be not

over-afraid of snakes, and he had stepped on many a rattler to jump out of his boots, but the information was not happy.

"Say, Rol, I heahed you," interposed Red, who feared neither man nor beast nor savage, but was in mortal terror of snakes. "That's orful bad news. What kind of snakes?"

Sterl sensed Jones rising to the occasion. "All kinds and thick as hops. Black and brown snakes most common, and grow to eight feet. Hit you hard and are not too poisonous, though they kill people often. Tiger snakes mean and aggressive. If you hear a sharp hiss, just turn to stone right where you are. Death adders are the most dangerous. They are short, thick, sluggish snakes, easy to step on, and rank poison. The pythons and boas are not so plentiful. But you meet them. They grow to twenty feet and can give you a right smart hug."

"Aw, is that all?" Red queried disgustedly, who evidently was impressively scared, despite his natural skepticism. But Sterl saw no reason to doubt the teamster's matter-of-fact assertions. Before they had traveled far, Sterl had his interest in Australia increased. And he grasped that his knowledge was growing by leaps and bounds.

The thick golden-green grass grew as high as the flanks of a horse; cabbage trees and a stunted brushy palm stood up conspicuously; and the gum trees, or eucalyptus, made a forest of new color and beauty. They grew in profusion, from saplings to sturdy trunks, shell-barked and smooth, some of them resembling the bronze and opal sycamores of America, and others like the beeches and laurels. Here and there stood up a lofty spotted gum, its straight trunk symmetrical and round, branchless for a hundred feet, and then spreading great curved limbs above the other trees to terminate in fine, thin-leaved, steely-green foliage.

Soon, as they penetrated inland, birds began to attract Sterl even more than the timber. A crow with a dismal and guttural caw took Sterl back to the creek bottoms of Texas. Another crow, black with white spotted wings, Jones called Australia's commonest bird, the magpie. It appeared curious, friendly, and had a most melodious note—a carol that grew upon Sterl. It was deep and rich—a lovely sound—*cur-ra-wong . . . cur-ra-wong.*

"Red, this magpie has your Texas mockingbird skinned to a frazzle," said Sterl, turning enthusiastically to Red.

"Thet?" barked his comrade insulted. "Thet noise! What's eatin' you, pard? There ain't nothin' beautiful about that. Jest a squall. If I had my gun out, I'd take a peg at some of them."

Jones glanced disapprovingly at Red and warmed to Sterl's praise.

"See you must like birds. So do I," he said. "Australians ought to, for we have hundreds of wonderful birds. The bell bird has a heavenly song. And the lyre bird in the bush can imitate any song or sound he hears. Leslie Slyter loves them. She knows where they stay, too. She'll take you at daybreak to hear them."

Here Red Krehl pricked up his ears to attention. "Wal, now," he said condescendingly, "thet there liar bird, he jest appeals to me. I'll ask Miss Leslie to take me out to heah him."

Sterl gave his comrade a sly and knowing glance, as if he were as transparent as crystal. Anything in the world, even to digging post holes, if it could be relegated in the slightest to femininity, Red clasped to his breast.

Presently the road led out of the jungle into a big area of ground cleared of all except the largest tree, which gave it a park-like appearance. On a knoll stood a house made of corrugated iron. Jones called it a cattle station. Sterl looked for cattle in vain. Red said: "Shines out like a dollar in a fog."

The teamster was bewildered anew at Red's singular language, but he didn't voice it.

Grass and brush densely covered the undulating hills. Sterl concluded Australian cattle were equally browsers and grazers. The road wound to and fro between the hills, keeping to a level, eventually to enter thick brush again. Sterl made the acquaintance of flocks of colored parrots—galahs, the driver called them—that flew swiftly as bullets across the road, and then a flock of white cockatoos that squalled and squawked in loud protest at the invasion of their domain. When they sailed above the wagon, wide wings spread, Sterl caught a faint tinge of yellow, and he thought they were exquisite birds despite their raucous screech.

"Humph! Reckon they're English, all right," Red declared cryptically.

Sterl had glimpses of furry animals fleeting through the grass that skirted the road. And he saw a long lizard or a snake. This inland region was growing more colorful and alive every mile. They crossed the first brook, a clear, swift, little stream that passed on gleaming and glancing under the wide-spreading foliage. A blue heron and a white crane took lumbering flight.

They came into a wide valley, rich in wavy grass and studded with bunches of cattle and horses. "Ha! Some hosses. Pretty nifty, pard," Red said. Next to girls, horses always gladdened that cowboy's eye. Far up the valley a tin roof caught the glare of the sun. It belonged to another station, Jones said.

All over this valley dead trees, bleached and ghastly, stood up and spread gnarled branches futilely into the air. Sterl observed that these dead gums had been ringed around the trunks with an axe. No doubt the idea was to get rid of the shade and let the sun nourish the grass.

At the end of this valley, where the road turned and climbed slightly, Sterl looked back to see three of the following wagons in sight. They were all making good time over this narrow, grass-bordered road. As Jones slowed up along a bank higher than the wagon bed, Sterl heard solid, thumping thuds, then a swish of grass, and Red's stentorian—"*Whoopee!*"

Sterl wheeled in time to see three great, strange, furry animals leaping clear over the wagon. They had long ears and enormous tails. He recognized them in the middle of their prodigious leap, but could not remember their names. They cleared the road, to alight with thumps and bound away as if on springs.

"*Whoa!*" yelled Red. "What'n'll was that? Did you see what I see? Have I got 'em, pard? Lord! There ain't no such critters."

"Kangaroos," said the teamster. "And that biggest one is an old man 'roo, all right."

"Oh, what a sight!" Sterl exclaimed. "Kangaroos . . . of course. One of them almost red. If thet wasn't great! Jones, it struck me they sprung off their tails."

"Kangaroos do use their tails. Wait till you get smacked with one."

The trio of queer beasts stopped some hundred rods off and sat up to gaze at the wagon.

"Are they good to eat?" queried the practical Red.

"We like kangaroo meat when we can't get beef or turkey or fowl. But that isn't often. No end of game."

"Gosh!" Red ejaculated. "I'm gonna have my rifle handy in the mawnin'. Pard, we didn't figger on huntin'. An' I was wonderin' what we'd do with all them shells you bought."

"What's that?" Sterl shouted suddenly, espying a small, gray animal, hopping across the road.

"Wallaby. A small species of kangaroo."

"Aw! Where?" interposed Red, craning his neck. "I didn't see him."

More interesting miles, that seemed swift, brought them to an open flat crossed by a stream bordered with full-foliaged, yellow-blossoming trees, which Jones called wattles. Sterl mutely gazed at them, as if they were an unreal picture. Red, however, was more interested in gray forms, bobbing about.

Jones made a halt here to rest and water the horses, he said, and let the other wagons catch up. Sterl got out to stretch his legs, mindful to be cautious about snakes. Upon his return, Red was making friends with the other teamsters, always an easy task for the friendly, loquacious cowboy. These Australian drivers appeared to belong to a larger, brawnier type than most American outdoor men, and certainly were different from the lean, lithe, narrow-hipped, round-legged cowboy. They built a fire and set about making tea, "boiling the billy," Jones affirmed. Sterl sampled the beverage and being strange even to American tea he sagely and humorously said: "Now, I savvy why you English are so strong."

"I should smile," Red drawled, making a wry face. "Stronger'n aquafortis. I shore could ride days on thet drink."

The afternoon journey was a repetition of the morning, the only difference existing in an exaggerated sameness for some miles and in others a monotony of green and dearth of life. Only one other station was passed. Densely wooded hills at last spread away to permit of another green valley, marked at the far end by a huge tree that must have been a landmark for leagues around. Upon arriving at this monarch, which stood on the bank of a creek, Jones drove into a cleared space under the enormously spreading branches and called a halt for camp.

"Wal, Rol, what air there for me an' my pard to do?" queried the genial Red.

"That depends. What can you Yankees do?" Jones replied simply, as if really asking information.

Red took that query dubiously. He cocked a blazing blue eye at the teamster and drawled: "Wal, it'd take a lot less time, if you'd ask what we cain't do. I reckon, though, I'd better make you acquainted with our gifts. Outside of possessin' all the cowboy traits such as ridin', ropin', shootin', we can hunt, butcher, cook, bake sour-dough biscuits an' cake, shoe hosses, mend saddle-girths, plait ropes, chop wood, build fires in wet weather, bandage wounds an' men with broken bones, smoke, drink, play poker, an' fight. I reckon Sterl an' I can do about anything 'cept wash pots an' pans an' dig fence post holes."

"You forgot one thing, I've observed, Red, and that is you can talk," replied Jones, still sober-faced as a judge.

"Yeah? I reckon I ain't so pore at that, either," Red rejoined, just a little crestfallen. "But fun aside, what can we do?"

"Anything you can lay a hand to," answered the driver cheerily.

Sterl set out to do something useful, but outside of helping unhitch the team he did not get anywhere. One by one the other wagons rolled up. These teamsters were efficient and long used to camp tasks. The one who evidently was cook knew his business. "Easy when you have everything," he said to Sterl. "But when we get out on trek, with nothing but meat and tea, and damper, then no cook is good."

Suddenly a wild yell from Red startled Sterl, and, running

around the wagon, he saw the cowboy making prodigious leaps. He stopped, his red hair standing up like a flame, and his language was blasphemous.

"What'd you see, pard?" called Sterl.

"Snake! Long as my laig. He made a pass at me. Hit my boot. I'm gonna kill thet *hombre*."

"What color?" Jones asked.

"He was blue-black. Slim an' long. Did he slip through the grass? Come on, Sterl, let's waylay the son-of-a-gun. You go first, pard. You never been bit by a snake. He was in there."

Diligent search, however, failed to discover the serpent, much to Red's chagrin. "Rascal might crawl in my bed."

Sterl and Red had time to put up their tent and unroll their beds before they were called to supper. It proved to be a good, wholesome repast, the first appetizing repast the cowboys had enjoyed since their arrival in Australia.

"Cook," said Red, "thet grub was so darn' good I gotta help you wash up."

Sterl got out his rifle and, loading it, strolled away from camp along the edge of the creek. The sun was setting gold, lighting the shiny-barked gums and burnishing the long, green leaves. He came upon a tree fern where high over his head the graceful, lacy leaves drooped down. That was Sterl's first sight of a giant fern. The great gum tree, too, came in for a share of his reverence and admiration. All riders of the bare ranges loved trees. This red gum, as the guide had named it, was by far the most magnificent tree Sterl had ever seen. It stood over two hundred feet high, with no branches for half that distance, and then they spread wide as large in themselves as ordinary trees. The color was a pale green with round pieces of red-brown bark sloughing off. In one lofty notch Sterl saw a bushel of slivers of bark that had lodged there.

All at once Sterl's keen eye caught a movement of something. It was a small, round, furry animal, gray in color, with blunt head and small ears. It was clinging to a branch, peering comically down at Sterl. It did not look afraid. Then Sterl espied another one, farther up, and then another way out on the same branch, and at last a fourth, swinging gently upon a swaying tip. Sterl yelled lustily for Red and Jones. They answered, and directly came running through the grass and brush.

"Look, Red. Up in the tree. . . . Jones, what are those queer little animals?"

"Native bears. Koala bears," said the teamster, when he had located them. "Queensland bush alive with them."

"Bears! Well, I'll be darned," Sterl shouted, delighted.

"Pard, pass me yore gun," said Red.

"Ump-umm, you blood-thirsty cowboy! They look tame."

"They are tame," rejoined Jones. "Friendly little fellows. Leslie has some for pets."

"Do you have other Australian bears?"

"No. The koala is the only one."

"Jones, we have bears in Arizona that weigh over a thousand pounds and can kill a steer with one blow of a paw. Grizzlies are bad medicine. I'm sure I like your little Koalas much better."

They returned to camp, over which twilight soon settled down, and night made the campfire pleasant. The teamsters, through for the day, sat around smoking and talking. They made a robust, ruddy-visaged group. Campfires in Australia seemed to have the same cheer, the same opal hearths and flying sparks, the same drawing together of kindred spirits that they had on the ranges of America. The great Southern Cross stood almost straight above Sterl, an aloof and marvelous constellation that proved to him, despite the campfire, that he was an exile in a foreign land. How much farther his thought might have drifted did not materialize, owing to a dismal chorus of wild barks from the darkness.

"Holy Mackeli!" burst out Red. "What next? Heah's a flock of dawgs."

"Dingoes," a teamster said.

"Dingoes. Haw! Haw! Another funny one. Any dingoes about heah? An' jest what air these dingoes?"

"Wild dogs. They overrun Australia. Hunt in packs. When hungry, which is often, they're dangerous to man."

"Sterl, didn't our coyotes come from wild dawgs?" asked Red.

"No. I've heard that our domesticated dogs descended from coyotes and wolves. Listen, isn't that a dismal sound? Not a yelp in it. Nor any of that long, wailing, sharp cry we range riders love so well."

"Say, will them durn' dingoes keep thet up all night?" Red asked.

"You'll get used to them."

"Wal, I kinda like it at thet. Shore is wild an' lonesome. Sterl, let's go to bed. Come to think of it, we forgot about our mus-keeter nets."

"A little too cool tonight to be bothered," Jones said. "We'll run into some farther Outback. And on the Never Never there are mosquitoes that bite through two pairs of socks."

"Gee! I never even have one pair. But thet's nothin' a-tall, Rol. We have muskeeters in Texas thet can drill through a cop-per kettle. Fact! I heahed about one cowboy who struck 'em bad one night, when he was left alone. A flock of them big, white-winged 'skeeters flew down on him. Smoke an' fire didn't help none. By golly, he had to take refuge under a copper kettle thet the cook had. Wal, the sons-of-guns bored through the kettle. The cowboy took his gun an' riveted their bills on the inside. An' damn me, if them 'skeeters didn't fly away with the kettle."

Red's listeners remained mute under the onslaught of that story, no doubt beginning a reversal in serious acceptance of all the cowboy had said. Sterl followed Red toward their tent.

"Knocked 'em cold, hey pard?" whispered Red in great glee.

"You knocked 'em, Red, but I couldn't swear it was cold."

"Good night, Yanks," Jones called. "Breakfast early tomorrow. We leave at daylight. Long drive."

"Red, old bedfellow, you could always make friends easily. You're just a no-good, likable cuss. But for cripe's sake don't start any of your Texas cowboy tricks on these Australians."

"I reckon not, pard," Red responded soberly. "I'm shore leery of them. But all the same I like them. Gosh! I'm skeered of sleepin' in this heah tent. Why, an elephant could get in. I reckon I ain't gonna sleep a wink."

But Red was slumbering soundly not long after he stretched out with a grateful groan. Sterl was weary, too. His eyes shut as if glued. Still he was aware of the strange Australian sounds. And his consciousness knocked at the door of the past, which he had closed forever. There were ghosts coming down the dim aisles of memory, when he fell asleep.

He awakened at the crackling of fire without. Dark, moving shadows on the yellow tent wall told that the teamsters were stirring. But daylight had not come. Boots and coat were all Sterl had to put on to be fully dressed. He rolled over Red, saying the while—"The day's busted, old-timer."—which elicited murderous reply from his comrade.

Sterl parted the tent flaps and went out to find it dark as pitch beyond the blazing fires, air cold, stars like great, white lanterns through the trees, fragrance of ham and tea wafting strong.

"'Morning, Hazelton," was Jones's cheery greeting. "Was just going to yell that cowboy call . . . 'Come and get it!' We'll have a good early start."

Sterl observed with satisfaction that there was hot water to wash in, a fact which Red greeted with exultation. In a moment they were kneeling at the spread tarpaulin, where all conversation ceased as if by magic.

In the gray of dawn Jones drove out, leading the caravan. Sterl could not recall when he had faced a day with such exuberance. This far country, this extraordinary contrast to all he had known, began to earn a singular response. Red could not fool him with his dry complaints. The cowboy was trying to hide his glad surprise.

A long, gradual ascent through thick bush offered no view, but the melodious carol of magpies, the squall of the cockatoos, the sweet songs of thrush and other birds were worth the early rising. The stars paled and died, the gray lightened, the brightening in the east grew rosy, and soon it was day.

Topping the long ascent Jones drove out of the bush into the open. "Kangaroo Flat," said the teamster. "Thirty miles. Good road. We'll camp at the other end tonight, unless you cowboys go gun berserk."

"Gun berserk?" shrilled the ever-touchy Red, apparently insulted. "What the hell you mean?"

"Lots of game to shoot at," Jones replied mildly.

"Aw, that's fine. Holy Mackeli, pard, air you seein' what I see?"

Sterl was, indeed, and quite speechless. The scene was lovely in the extreme. A soft, hazed valley, so long the far end appeared lost in purple vagueness, stretched out beneath them, like a sea burnished with golden fire. It was so fresh, so pure, so marvelously vivid in sunrise tones. The enchanted distances struck Sterl anew. Australia was prodigal with its endless leagues. He imagined he gazed through a crystal-clear, painted veil. As the sun came up above the low bushland, a wave of flame stirred the long grass and spread on and on. The cool air blew sweet and odorous into Sterl's face, reminding him of the purple sage uplands of Utah.

"Wal, heah we air, pard, an' I gotta admit it's pretty nifty," Red said, which encomium from him was, indeed, flattering.

Down on a level again their view was restricted to space near at hand. A band of dingoes gave them a parting chorus where the bush met the flat. Rabbits began to scurry through the short, gray-green grass and run ahead along the road, and they increased in numbers until there appeared to be thousands.

"One of Australia's great pests," said Jones.

"Yeah? Wal, in that case I gotta take some pegs," replied Red, and he proceeded to raise the small caliber rifle and to shoot at running targets. This little rifle and the thousands of shells had been gifts from Sterl, and the cowboy had at once put his enjoyment into effect. Sterl could see Red did not hit any of the rabbits. Deadly shot with a hand gun, as were so many cowboys, Red could not hit a flock of barns with a rifle. Sterl's unerring aim, however, applied to both weapons.

That was the beginning of a wonderful day, in which time

stood still or flew swiftly by, Sterl could not tell which. Some miles out on the flat, kangaroos made their appearance, sticking their heads out of the grass, long ears erect, standing at gaze watching the wagon go by, or hopping with their awkward, yet easy, gait along ahead. In some places they slowed the trotting team to a walk, and, here, Red began to yell at them and shoot at their long tails, to both of which they appeared oblivious.

The sky was dotted with waterfowl. Jones explained there were water courses through the flat and a small lake in the center, where birds congregated by the thousands. With the sun soaring on high and the light growing brilliant, the winged and four-legged life of that grassy expanse took on what appeared to be an incredible manifestation of the fecundity of nature.

The cowboys were used to sterile ranges where, for days, there would be a dearth of life, and where herds of buffalo, bands of antelope, and colonies of jack rabbits and coyotes were few and far between. Whereforth this fertile and fecund meadow was a joy to behold. Sterl reverted to the boy in him and Red to the savage. The wagon rolled along the level road that wandered from a straight line at times to go around sedgy low places and streams, and behind it crawled the other wagons and drays, spread far apart.

While looking back, Sterl's quick eye caught a broken column of smoke rising from the bushland in the rear.

"By golly! Red, look at that. Like Indian smoke signals."

"Shore, I was wonderin' about that. How about it, Rol?"

"Black men, signaling across the flat. Look over there. They know all about us twenty miles ahead. The aborigines talk with smoke."

"All the same desert stuff," Red announced. "Dog-goned small world."

Far ahead, somewhat to the left, toward which the road appeared to turn, Sterl made out two dim, broken columns of smoke, miles apart. He studied them with foreboding interest.

"Jones, I've a hunch these black fellows are going to cross our trail," he said soberly.

"Yes, you've reason to. Stanley Dann, who's mustering this big trek, says the abos will be our worst obstacle."

"Has Dann made a trek before?"

"No. This will be new to all the drovers."

"Do they believe there's safety in numbers?"

"That is one reason for the large muster of bushmen and cattle."

"Like our wagon trains crossing the Great Plains. They have caravans with as many as two hundred wagons. This ensures reasonable safety from the Indians. But driving cattle is a different thing. The Texas trail drivers found out that ten or twelve cowboys and up to three thousand head of longhorns moved faster, had fewer stampedes, and lost fewer cattle."

"Ours will be a great trek," rejoined the teamster ponderingly.

At noon Jones made a halt at a water hole and waited for the other wagons to come up. The cook had hauled a supply of firewood, which augured for the importance of brewing tea. The halt, the rest, and a bite of lunch seemed regular to Red, although he was not used to that kind of travel, but this solemn and evidently necessary "boiling the billy" intrigued and interested him exceedingly.

"Say, what'd you *hombres* do if you ran out of tea?" he asked bluntly.

"We've never suffered that misfortune yet," replied Jones.

"An' you're gonna muster a mob of seven thousand steers, drove 'em three thousand miles over Never Never Land where there ain't never no water, no whiskey, no air you can breathe, never nothin' but heat, dust, 'skeeters, an' cannibals?"

"Red, it sounds ridiculous, spoken out like that, but it's just what we are going to try to do," returned Jones gravely.

"Uhn-huh. No . . . not . . . never! But I gotta hand it to you all for nerve," concluded Red.

After a short rest the cavalcade proceeded onward across the rippling sea of colored grass. Sterl's satiated sense of pleasure soon had a revivifying shock. The road passed along streams and pools where thousands of wildfowl lent animation and varied hues. Jones appeared to have quite a fund of bird knowledge. The herons were not new to Sterl, but white ibis, spoonbills, egrets, jaribu, and other wading fowl afforded him lasting wonder and appreciation. The storks particularly caught his eye. Their number seemed incredible. Many of them let the wagon pass by within a few yards. They were mostly gray in color, huge crane-like birds, tall as a man, and they had red on their heads, and huge bills. The problem of the enormous amount of food they consumed had a solution in the action of these waders. These waters, however, must be extremely prolific of frogs and fish.

Beyond the wet center of the flat both birds and beasts thinned out. Sterl exchanged places with Red, and, drowsy from excessive looking, he went to sleep. He was awakened by yells. Sitting up, he found Red waving and wild. Sterl saw that he must have slept quite a while, for the blue gleam of water, like a mirage, showed dim and far back along the road. All the wagons were in sight. Almost the same instant Sterl attended to his excited friend.

"Ostriches! Black ostriches!" Red yelled, beside himself. "Whoever'd thunk it? Dog-gone my pictures! Sterl, wake up. You're missin' somethin', or I'm shore loco."

Wheeling to the fore, Sterl did not need Red's extended arm to sight a line of huge, black bird-creatures, long-necked and long-legged, racing across the road. They were certainly ostriches, and they made the dust fly. Sterl found himself calculating on the possibility of running down these fleet birds with a fast horse and lassoing one. It could have been done.

"Emu," said the teamster laconically. "You run over them Outback."

Sterl watched the emus go out of sight in the heat-hazed distance. Next thing to inflame the dynamic Red was a band of dingoes that boldly raced close—sleek, nimble, tan-colored, vicious dogs. Red emptied the magazine of his rifle at them, the last shot of which elicited a wild howl from one.

Mile after mile Jones drove on, until at length even the sensitive, imaginative Sterl began to feel the dominant note of endless

distances that brooded over this sunny land. It grew upon him.
And he received his first intimation of the absolute need for patience. This was like the *mañana* land of the Mexicans, the land
where it is always afternoon. After sober reflection Sterl was glad
the hours bade fair to stretch out to treble their normal length
and his life in Australia, if it did not come to an untimely end, be
prolonged indefinitely, surely long enough to blot out the mess he
had made of it in Arizona.

"As I'm a born sinner, heah comes a bunch of hosses!" Red exclaimed, pointing. With the Texas cowboy on the lookout there
was not much chance of anyone beating him to sight of moving
things. On the range Red had been noted even among hawk-
eyed riders and *vaqueros* for his keen sight.

"Brumbies," Jones declared.

"What? What you say?" shouted Red. "If they're not wild
hosses, I'll eat 'em."

"Wild, surely. But they're brumbies," said the Australian.

Red emitted a disgusted snort. "Brumbies! Who in the hell
ever heahed of callin' wild hosses such an orful name? Ain't you
English supposed to have originated the English language? I can
stand for a lot, Jones, but wild hosses air wild hosses anywhere.
Once in our outfit we had a grub-line rider who called every
band we run into broomtails. Broomtails! Imagine that to a
Texas hoss-lovin' *hombre!* By gosh, I had finally to lick that feller,
an' he was a tough nut to crack."

"Red, it was sort of a silly name . . . that broomtail," responded Jones with his rare grin. "Brumbies is quite as bad. I suggest we have an interchange and understanding of names, so you
won't have to lick me."

"Wal, I reckon I couldn't lick you, at thet," Red retorted
quick as a flash to meet friendliness. "You're an orful big chap,
Rol, an' could probably beat hell out of me *pronto*. So I'll take
you up."

"What does *pronto* mean?"

"Quick. Right now. I heahed you say pad. In my country a pad
is what you put under a saddle to ease yore hoss. What is it heah?"

"A pad is a path through the bush. A narrow, single track."

"Uhn-huh. But thet's a trail, Rol. Say, you're gonna have fun ediccatin' us. Sterl heah had a mother who was a school-teacher, an' he's one smart *hombre*."

While the horses trotted along, the harness jingled, the wheels creaked, the sun slanted toward the far horizon, the brightness changed to gold and rose. It was some time short of twilight when Jones hauled up at the edge of the bush, which had beckoned for so many hours. A bare spot on the bank of a deep, slow-moving stream attested to many campfires.

"Made it fine before dark," Jones said with satisfaction. "I was sure you cowboys would run hog-wild across the flat and hold us up."

"Hog-wild? Wal, I don't have to have thet translated. But, Rol, when you spring a lot of names on us thet mean two things, you'd better smile."

"Look!" interposed Sterl, coming out of his trance to point at the forms that had transfixed him. They were natives, of course, but a first actual sight was stunning.

"Black man, with *gin* and *lubra*, and some kids," said Jones.

"Holy Mackeli!" Red ejaculated. "They look human ... but ... ?"

Sterl's comrade, with his usual perspicuity, had hit it. The group of natives stood just at the edge of the bush on the far bank of the stream. Sterl saw six figures out in the open, but he had a glimpse of others back in the bush. The man was exceedingly tall, thin, black as coal, almost naked. He held a spear upright, and it stood far above his shaggy head. A scant beard covered the lower part of his face. His big, bold, somber eyes glared a moment, then with a long stride he went back into the bush. The women lingered curiously. The older, the *gin*, was hideous to behold. The *lubra*, a young girl, gained immeasurably by contrast. She appeared sturdy and voluptuous. Both were naked except for short, grass skirts. The children were wholly nude, with distended potbellies their distinguishing features. A harsh voice sent them scurrying into the bush.

"Saw that old black on my way in," Jones said. "He's not too bad. But there are some mean ones in his tribe."

"I'd hate to meet that long-laiged *hombre* in the dark," rejoined Red.

"Hope they come around our campfire," Sterl added with zest.

He had his wish, at least so far as the black man was concerned. After supper, about dusk, the native appeared, a towering, unreal figure. He did not have the long spear. The cook gave him something to eat, and the native, making quick dispatch of that, accosted Jones in a low voice.

"Him sit down alonga fire," Jones replied, pointing to Sterl.

The black man slowly approached the fire, then stood motionless on the edge of the circle of light. He made an imposing figure, strange and wild. Presently he came up to Sterl.

"Tobac?" he asked in a low deep voice.

"Yes," replied Sterl, and offered what he had taken the precaution to get from his pack. At the exchange Sterl caught a good look at the native's hands, to find them surprisingly supple and shapely. He next caught a strong body odor that was unpleasant. Red's expression proved that he was a victim of various sensations.

"Sit down, chief," said Sterl, making signs for the aborigine to take a seat beside the fire. He accepted and, folding his long legs under him, appeared to sit on them. Red gave the black some cigarettes. The cigar Sterl had given him was evidently a new one on the native. But as Sterl was smoking one, he quickly caught on, and, lighting it with a blazing faggot, he began to puff. Sterl adopted the method cowboys always used when Plains Indians visited the campfires. He manifested a silent dignity. But in the bright light he certainly did not miss any detail about this aborigine. The mere fact that he was sitting beside an Australian black man—a descendant of the oldest race of human beings, a cannibal, was a tremendous stimulus to curiosity. The black man was old; no one could have told how old. There was gray in his shaggy locks, and his visage was a map of lines that portrayed the havoc of elemental strife. It was, indeed, the most remarkable face Sterl had ever studied. The American Indian was new in the scale of evolution compared to this relic of the Stone Age. Sterl divined thought and feeling in this savage, and he felt intensely curious.

Jones left the other teamsters to come over and speak to the native.

"Any black fella close up?" he asked.

"Might be," replied the black.

"They watchem smokes all alonga bush?"

Either the aborigine was not communicative or his absorption with the cigar precluded any response, for he maintained silence to that remark and another direct inquiry that Jones put to him. Presently he arose and stalked away in the gloom.

"Queer duck," Red said reflectively.

"He sure interested me," replied Sterl. "All except the smell of him. Rol, do all these blacks smell that bad?"

"Some worse, some not at all. It's something they grease themselves with."

"Wasn't he funny with thet big cigar?" queried Red, his red face wreathed with smiles.

They conversed a while longer, hoping the blacks would come, but, as they did not, Red followed Jones to bed, and then Sterl, tired out in body if not in mind, soon sought his blankets.

The next day was a long trek through bush, without incident or much to see, and the following day turned out monotonously similar. On the fifth, however, they reached the blue hills that beckoned to Sterl. The wagon road wound into a region of numerous creeks and fertile valleys where parrots and parakeets abounded and kangaroos were remarkable for their scarcity. They passed by one station that day and through one little sleepy hamlet of a few houses and a store, and outlying paddocks where Sterl espied some fine horses. If it were a cattle country, the cattle were not in evidence. Camp that night offered a new experience to the cowboys. The cook was out of beef, and Jones took them hunting. They did not have to go far or shoot often. It was exciting, because any kind of hunting was that for Sterl; still for one with his unerring skill, it seemed murder. The meat had a flavor that Sterl thought would grow on him, and Red avowed it was equal to porterhouse steak or buffalo rump. But that ever-hungry cowboy had been known to relish chuckwallas on the desert.

They had a two-day dry trek across sparsely timbered country, which fixed for good in Sterl's mind the haunting sense of a far-flung country, of the inestimable distances to back of beyond, and the tremendousness of Australia.

When at last, two noons later, Jones drove out of the jungle to the edge of a long slope that afforded a view of Slyter's valley, it was none too soon for Sterl Hazelton. Without action, with nothing to do but look, the long leagues had grown arduous, despite the never-ending procession of birds and beasts.

"That road goes down to Downsville," Jones said, pointing, "a good few miles. This road leads to Slyter's station. Water and grass for a reasonable sized mob of cattle. But Bing has big ideas."

"Rich, warm-looking valley," rejoined Sterl. "That golden wattle blossoming everywhere. Heavy bush topping these hills. More of that red-flowering eucalyptus! I see water shining. And down there the open range. What say, pard?"

"Wal, if Slyter leaves this heah valley, I'll hole up an' stay," Red replied, which remark from him was, indeed, expressive.

Jones headed down the gentle winding road, followed by a dray loaded with flour. The other wagons kept on to the right. Presently Slyter's gray-walled, tin-roofed house came into sight, picturesquely located on a green bench with a background of huge eucalyptus trees, and half hidden in a bower of golden wattle. The hills on each side spread wider and wider, to where the valley opened into the range, and numberless cattle dotted the grassy land. The whole scene was so verdant and compelling that Sterl's heart swelled, and his love of a ranch seemed renewed.

Along the brook, farther down, a bare-poled fence of corrals came in sight and then a long, low, log barn, with a roof of earth and green grass and yellow flowers, instead of the ugly galvanized iron.

"Home!" sang out Jones. "Eight days' drive! Not so bad. If we just didn't have that impossible trek to face!"

"Wal, Rollie Tewksbury Jones!" Red declared gaily. "You air human, after all. Fust time I've heard you croak."

Sterl leaped down to stretch his cramped legs. Red called for him to pick out a campsite up from the low ground a little, while he helped the teamsters unhitch. To that end Sterl mounted the green bench to the barn. There was a roof that extended out from the wall, upheld by sapling posts. Door after door opened upon stalls, clean, smelling of hay, then a store room, and finally a cabin with bunks.

Sterl walked on, intending to find a place for the tent under those yellow-blooming wattles. As he passed the corner of the cabin, his face turned the other way, trying to locate who was running, a person collided violently with him, almost knocking him over. He turned to see that someone had been knocked almost flat. He thought it was a boy because of the boots and blue pants. But a cloud of chestnut hair, tossed aside, disclosed the tanned face and flashing hazel eyes of a girl. She raised herself, hands propped on the ground, to lean back and look up at him. Spots of red came into her clear cheeks. Lips of the same hue curled in a smile, disclosing even, white teeth.

"Oh, miss! I'm sorry," Sterl burst out in dismay. "I wasn't looking. You ran plumb into me."

"Rath-thur!" she replied merrily. "Dad always said I'd run into something some day. I did. I'm Leslie."

Chapter Three

With surprising agility the girl leaped erect, showing herself to be above medium height, lithe and strong, with a rounded form no boy's garb could hide.

"You're Dad's Yankee cowboy . . . not the red-headed one?"

"I'm Sterl Hazelton," he returned, taking the hand she offered. It had a rough palm and a hard grip. "Glad to meet you, miss."

"Thanks. I'm glad, too. Dad has been home four days, and I could hardly wait." She was frank and vivid and looked up at him with wonderful, clear eyes that took him in from head to foot, and back again.

"I came up here to find a place for our tent. All right to put it there, under this tree?"

"Of course. But we have a spare room in the house."

"No, thank you. Red and I couldn't sleep indoors."

"Let us go down. I want to meet Red. Did you have a good trek Outback?"

"It was simply great. Such a strange, big country! Birds and animals galore! I never looked so hard and long before. The time just flew."

"Oh, how nice! You're going to like Australia," she pronounced it *Ausstraallia*.

"I love it already. And Red, who's from Texas, can't hide from me how he likes it, too."

It chanced that they came up to Red when his back was turned, as he was lifting bags out of the wagon. Sterl discovered zest in the moment. "Red, a lady to meet you." Sterl saw him start, grow rigid, then slowly turn, to disclose a flushing, amazed face. "Miss Slyter, this is the other Yankee cowboy, my pard, Red Krehl. Red, our boss's daughter, Miss Leslie."

Then, as his face blazed, he gave Sterl one meaning glance, and turned to the girl his cool, gallant self again.

"Wal, I shore am glad to meet you, Miss Leslie," he drawled, as he doffed his sombrero and shook the hand she proffered.

"Thank you, Mister Krehl. I've been looking forward to meeting you cowboys," she said, gazing up at him with wholesome interest.

"Yeah? Of course, my pard heah had the luck to meet you first."

"I don't know about the luck," she replied, laughing gaily. "It wasn't for me. He knocked me flat."

Red stared out of his flashing blue eyes, so expressive of his mischievous spirit. "Aw, he did? Sterl would do somethin' to impress himself on you."

"Oh, Miss Leslie, this cowboy is likely to think anything. Red, I was walking past the cabin. She came running. I heard but didn't see her. And she ran plumb into me."

"Pard, you shore needn't explain," rejoined Red resignedly. "You didn't give me no even break. It was a double-crossin' cowboy trick."

"Boys, you must talk English," Leslie cried archly, and though plainly nonplused at Red's vernacular, a becoming blush attested to the fact that she divined the contention for her favor.

At this juncture Slyter, stalwart and vital in his range garb, stamped down upon them. "Roland, you made a fine drive. Didn't expect you till tomorrow. Well, cowboys, here you are. Welcome to Australia's Outback. We saw you coming, and I sent Leslie to meet you. How are you, and did you like the short ride out?"

"Mister Slyter, I never had a finer ride in my life," Sterl averred.

"Boss, it shore was grand," added Red. "But short? Umpumm. It was orful long. I see right heah we gotta get so we can savvy each other's lingo."

"That will come in time, Krehl. Listen, all of you. I'm just back from Downsville. Allan Hathaway leaves tomorrow with six drovers and a mob of fifteen hundred cattle. Woolcott has mustered twelve hundred and will follow. Stanley and Eric Dann go next day with ten drovers and thirty-five hundred head. They plan to travel slowly, and we are to catch up with them. That leaves Ormiston, three drovers and eight hundred head. He wants to drove with us. I don't know Ormiston, and I'm not keen about joining him. But what can I do? Stanley Dann is our leader. He's ordering the trek. Our mob is about mustered. We won't have an accurate count, though. But I'm underestimating my mob at a thousand head. Now all that's left to do is pack and start."

"Oh, Dad! I'm on pins and needles!" Leslie cried, jumping up and down and clapping her hands. Her hazel eyes held an intense and beautiful light. "If only Mum can make a choice of what to take! She's weeping over so much she wants to take and cannot."

"Boss, that's good news. We can be ready," declared Jones.

"Slyter, how many riders . . . drovers have you?" Sterl queried.

"Four, not counting you cowboys. Here's Leslie, who's as good as any drover. I'll drive our covered wagon, and Bill Williams, our cook, will drive the other. Roland, you'll drive the dray."

"Seven riders, counting Miss Leslie," Sterl pondered.

"I see you think that's not enough," spoke up Slyter. "Hazelton, it'll have to do. I can't hire any more drovers in this country."

"Boss, how about yore remuda?" interposed Red anxiously.

"Remuda? What's that?"

"Excoose me, boss. Thet's Texas lingo for hosses. How many hosses will you take?"

"We've mustered the best of my stock. About a hundred. The rest I've sold in Downsville."

"Dad has the finest horses in Queensland," Leslie spoke up proudly.

"None too many. But are your horses hard to handle?" rejoined Sterl.

"Spirited and fiery, but well broken. They will drove right along with the mob."

"That'll be a help. Cowboys always keep two riders with the remuda."

"Well, men, I'm glad to get that off my mind," concluded Slyter with a laugh. "Roland, send Bill up to get supper for all of us. We might as well begin the big family mess. Hazelton, you boys come up when you've unpacked. Leslie, let's go back to Mum."

Leslie gave Sterl a parting flash of glad eyes that the vigilant Red did not miss.

"Pack the tent, pard, an' I'll foller with our bags," he said.

Sterl labored up the grassy bench, conscious of a queer little sensation of pleasure, the origin of which he thought he had better not analyze. But Red, the fox, had caught the cause even before Sterl had felt it. He dropped the heavy canvas roll into the likeliest spot, and sat down in the gold glow from the wattle. The adventure he had fallen upon seemed unbelievable. But here was this golden-green valley, with purple sunset-gilded ranges in the distance; there was bow-legged Red staggering up the gentle slope with his burdens. He reached Sterl and, depositing them on the grass, wiped the sweat from his red face, and said: "Queer deal, eh, pard?"

"I should snicker to snort, as you say sometimes."

"Wal, if you're jest wishin' I could be back on the Brazos, I wouldn't wish it. I'd rather be heah with you, pard."

"Thanks. But you look most damn' serious."

"I feel kinda serious. Don't you?"

"Maybe that's what is wrong."

"Pard, I've a hunch these fine Australian men have no idee what they're up ag'in'. They're takin' their families. Leastways, Slyter is, an' this Stanley Dann. Must be one fine *hombre*, accordin' to Jones. Takin' his only daughter, too. Beryl Dann. Purtiest lass in Queensland, so Rol says. Wal, it'd be hard enough an' tough enough for us without a couple of girls. . . . This Leslie kid. About sixteen, I'd say. But a woman, an' full of all a woman has to make men tremble. Pard, even if you hadn't seen her first, I'd pass, 'cause I seen her look at you, as I've seen other girls look."

"Red, don't be a sentimental jackass, not out here in Australia," replied Sterl severely. "These people are English. Why, this Leslie is like a boy. Outspoken . . . wholesome. She's English, I tell you."

"Wal, what'n'll is the difference if she is?" retorted Red. "Shore I'm a sentimental jackass. But I'm no fool about women. An' you know it, pard."

"Would you advise giving up this trek?" asked Sterl half hopefully.

"Hell, no! Leave this Slyter in the lurch? Not me. An' you know you wouldn't. Pard, I'm jest kinda sick in the gizzard at the most turrible mess we ever rode into. An' thet's sayin' a lot."

"By thunder, you can say a lot anytime. Let's put up the tent and unroll our beds. It'll be dark when we get through supper."

They had advanced halfway through their task before Red spoke again, and this time it seemed he was thinking aloud. "Wonder what this Beryl Dann is like. Gosh! A flock of girls is bad enough. But jest one . . . orful pretty . . . out alone in this Never Never. . . . Red, you're a ruined man!"

Sterl entertained the same idea; indeed, he had been ruined before he left America, but this Australia bade fair to give ruin to the bright face of danger, the zest of strife.

Red contrived to rope up the mosquito nets so that they could be let down when needful and rolled up with the tent. And he said: "Pard, I've an idee. You know I'm handy with canvas. Wal, I'll sew a canvas floor in this tent, with buckles in front, so we can keep out the varmints."

"Dog-gone it, Red, are we getting soft?" queried Sterl dubiously.

"Soft-haided, you mean? Wal, you always was, an' I'm gonna do it this . . . what they call it? . . . this trek."

"I meant soft physically, you dunce."

"Wal, if we air, you can bet yore sweet life it won't be for long. This Never Never will make the *Llana Estacado* an' the *Jornada del Muerto* look like green pastures."

Presently, just before dusk, they were called to supper. Sterl was struck with the wonder of the falling shadow, the stealing on of the golden dusk, the strange bird songs, of which only the sweet melancholy *cur-ra-wong, cur-ra-wong* was familiar. Here again the strangeness emphasized the reality of a far country.

They were ushered into a big, plain living room, where a fire burned in a crude, stone fireplace, and a long table with steaming, savory foods invited keen relish. Slyter introduced the cowboys to his wife, a buxom, pleasant woman who appeared to be a fitting pioneer mate for him. She wore havoc on her broad face that Sterl had seen on the faces of Western ranch women. Evidently Leslie inherited her fine physique, but not her coloring.

However, when the girl came in, Sterl hardly recognized her in a dress. She did not look slim or provoking, but appeared infinitely prettier. Her frank, winning gaiety offset her mother's silence. Probably Mrs. Slyter anticipated the rigor and gravity of the coming trek. Red brought a smile to her face, however, by saying such a supper would be something to remember when he was hungry way out on the Never Never. Sterl averred that Red had eaten enough to last through the whole trek.

"Wal, Sterl, I reckon I didn't see you puttin' away from the table," retorted Red.

"Boys, in the morning, first thing I want you to look over the horses," Slyter said. "After that, we'll ride over to town. Dann is keen to talk with you before he leaves."

"Miss Leslie, what was that you said about yore Dad's hosses?" Red asked.

"Dad breeds the finest stock in Australia," she replied. "That's where his heart is. And mine, too. We raise cattle to buy or trade horses, so everyone says. The chief reason Dad wants to cross the Never Never is because he has learned that in the far northwest, in the country of the Kimberleys, there is a perfect climate, grass and water beyond a drover's dreams."

"Sounds sweet. What air the Kimberleys?"

"Mountain ranges. Stanley Dann's brother, Eric, has seen the Kimberleys. If what he claims is true, they are paradise. He was one of the drovers who went on the Gulf trek several years ago. Then he went on to see the Kimberleys. But that trek was not across the Never Never."

"I savvy. Then the three-thousand-mile drive we're undertakin' is jest a short cut?"

"It is, really. But that sounds strange. The whole idea thrills me through and through."

"Shore. I can see why for a boy. But for a girl. . . ."

"I'm tired of that Downsville school. I've learned all the teachers know. I'm crazy about the trek. I love to ride . . . anything to do with horses. Then I couldn't let Mum and Dad go without me."

"Yeah? But can you ride, Miss Leslie?" went on Red, drawling quizzically.

"Please don't call me miss. Ride? I'll give you a go any day, Mister Cowboy."

"Please don't call me mister. 'Course, I wouldn't race you. No girl in the world could beat a Texas cowboy, if she could beat a Texas cowgirl, which I sure doubt. Sterl, tell her what you think about it."

Sterl had been listening smilingly to this dialogue, and, thus importuned, he replied: "I wouldn't risk any guesses or wagers."

"You'd better not. My horses are the fastest in Queensland. We'll miss the races this fall. I'm sorry about that. All the fun we ever have here is racing."

"Yore hosses. You mean yore Dad's?"

"No, my own. I have ten. You boys show a kind of a superior something when you speak of horses to me. I'm just waiting to show you!"

"We're from Mizzourie, Leslie, an' shore have to be shown."

Soon after that the boys said good night and left for their camp, groping through the dark. It was starlight, but the great gum trees shaded the way. Dingoes were barking somewhere, and some kind of a waterfowl was booming. The air was cold now and bore an unfamiliar fragrance along with the tangy eucalyptus. They found their tent, crawled in, and, removing coats and boots, they sought their separate beds.

"No 'skeeters around here," observed Red with satisfaction. "Pard, did you look Leslie over tonight?"

"I saw her, but I didn't look twice."

"Shore a fine looker in that blue dress. In them ridin' pants she 'peared a little bit bowlaiged. She was born on a hoss all right. An' what strong hands she has, an' arms an' shoulders! Mark my words, Sterl, she's a hosswoman, an' like as not a wonder. . . . Did you notice she was a little less free with you than with me?"

"No, pard, I didn't."

"Wal, she was. But thet isn't goin' to keep me from takin' my chance. Aw, I don't entertain no big hope of cuttin' you out. I never could win any girl, when you was around."

"Red, you can have them all," Sterl declared, settling himself to woo sleep.

"Yeah? Wal, you're uncommon generous all of a sudden. Dog-gone it, you give me the willies ever since you lost Nan. She wasn't the only sweet an' beautiful kid in the. . . ."

Red's voice trailed off in Sterl's consciousness and died away. When Sterl awoke, he could feel that he had slept and rested for long hours, surely the greater part of the night. The tent was so dark he could not see his hand before his eyes. Not the faintest sound disturbed the silence. Sterl lay awake until the darkness turned gray. The first sound to announce the coming dawn was the sweet notes of a thrush. That seemed to awaken other song-sters. A swish of heavy wings above the tent roused Sterl's cu-riosity. He heard squeals down by the creek and that same booming cry. Crows began to *caw*, and then the lovely *cur-ra-wong* thrilled through Sterl. Then other birds burst into song until the air was full of melody.

Sterl half-dozed off into a musical dream from which he was disrupted by Red. It was daybreak. The station life had awakened. Roland called them to breakfast, which Bill served before sunrise. In short order, then, they were off for the paddock, laden with saddles, bridles, and blankets. It proved to be quite a walk down along the creek. Another barn marked the opening to the level valley. Cattle were bawling; horses were whistling. A heavy dew glistened upon grass and brush. Down the lane, riders, mounted bareback, were driving a string of horses into a corral. The barn proved to be a long, open shed of stalls.

Presently Sterl and Red were perched upon the top bar of the corral fence, as they had done perhaps thousands of times on Western ranches, directing keen and experienced eyes at the drove of dusty, shaggy horses. They proved to be fat, full of fire and dash, superb in every requirement so critical an audi-ence might require. They came of a rangier, heavier, more pow-erful stock than the ordinary Western horses, and in these particulars markedly superior to the plains mustang. Sterl doubted that any horses in the world had the speed, the endurance of the Río Grande-bred mustang. Nevertheless, he sustained an agreeable surprise at the general excellence of these Australian horses.

"Wal, come out with it, you locoed hoss-fancier," drawled Red, crossing his legs and lighting a cigarette.

"Wonderful bunch, Red, that's all," declared Sterl.

"Gosh-durn-it! I never seen their beat. Did we have to come way out heah to see English stock beat the socks off ours?"

"But, Red, they have to have speed and stamina," returned Sterl weakly.

"Hell, you can see thet in every line. Hosses gotta be the same all over. We never knowed any but ornery-eyed, kickin', bitin' cayuses in all our lives."

"Red, I remember a few that you couldn't call that. Baldy, Whiteface, Spot . . . my old favorites on the Chisholm. And, Red, you couldn't demean, let alone forget, Dusty . . . that broke his heart and died on his feet for you."

"Shet up! I wasn't meanin' a hoss in a thousand. Lord, could I forget the day Dusty outrun them Comanches? Wal, pard, the past is daid, along with all them grand hosses. An' heah we air. I have no idee what hossflesh is wuth heah, but at home this bunch would fetch a fortune. Look at their eyes, pard. Not one mean, cross-eyed. . . . Wal, there is one I wouldn't trust."

Jones sauntered over, accompanied by a brawny young man whom he introduced as Larry. "Boss's orders are for you each to pick out five horses. Hurry now, for we have two days' work to do in one."

"Wal, Rol, they look so darn' good, I don't see any sense in pickin' a-tall. But it's fun an' tickles a cowboy's vanity. Sterl, toss you for first pick."

Red won, and his choice was the very black Sterl had set his heart on. Still in a moment he espied another that suited him, and chose that.

"Bays, browns, blacks, whites, sorrels, an' a couple blue roans.

An' there's a chestnut. Gosh, what a hoss! I pick him. Pard, I aim to have five colors, an' name 'em accordin'."

"Not a bad idea. Here's a sorrel for me. I'll name him after you, Red. But I don't see a black like that one you beat me to."

Leslie's rich contralto rang out from behind. "What's that about a black?"

"Hello. I wondered about you," replied Sterl.

"Mawnin', Leslie," Red drawled. "I kinda like you better in them ridin' togs. Not so dangerous lookin' to a pore cowboy. Looks like you been ridin' some, at thet."

Indeed, she did, thought Sterl, and could not recall any ranch girl who equaled her. Leather worn thin, shiny, metal spurs that showed bits of horsehair, ragged trousers stuffed in high boots, gray blouse and colorful scarf, her chestnut hair in a braid down her back—these charmed Sterl entirely, aside from the gold-tan cheeks with their spots of red, her curved lips like cherries, and her flashing eyes.

"Red got first pick on me," Sterl explained. "Snitched that black from me."

"Not too bad, you cowboys," returned Leslie, her glance taking in their choices. She was then silent, but an intensely interested spectator of the remainder of that horse-choosing contest.

"It's not so easy to choose the best ones, when they're all good," Leslie said. "Roland, you and Larry bring them over to the shed. The boys may want to try them, when we come back from town."

"Gosh, I wonder if I can fork a hoss after thet orful buckin' ship," drawled Red plaintively.

"Red, I've about concluded you are a terrific impostor," Leslie replied. "How about my judgment, Sterl?"

"Correct, marvelous, infallible!" ejaculated Sterl.

"Yeah? All right, double-crosser," Red sighed. "I see where I get off."

Leslie giggled. "You Yankees are the queerest talking people. But I believe you'll be good cobbers. Come now, I'll show you some real American horses."

"Lead me on, lady," said Red happily.

Sterl had prepared himself for a treat to a horse-lover's eyes, but, when he looked through the fence of a corral adjoining the shed, he could hardly credit his sight. He saw the finest horses he had ever seen in one bunch in his whole range experience. These were not shaggy, dusty, range-free horses, but well-groomed, sleek, and shiny Thoroughbreds in the pink of condition.

"Don't say anything," Leslie cried, delighted with the sensation she had created. But that did not keep Red from letting out his long cowboy yell.

"Leslie . . . who takes such grand care of these horses?" gasped Sterl.

"I do a good deal. It's all the work I have. But Friday does most of it. He's my black man. Dad sent him up town. Well, I'm disappointed. You might say something."

"I can't, child," Sterl returned feelingly. "Horses have been the most important things in my life. Even before guns! I know horses. I've loved several. . . . And these of yours! But are they really yours, Leslie?"

"Indeed, they are. Mine! I haven't anything else. Hardly a new dress to my name. A few books. But I'm happy with my horses."

"Leslie, haven't you any beaux?" Sterl asked lightly, not looking at her.

"I had. But Dad shut down on them lately. Too many fights," replied the girl seriously. "Not that I cared very much. Only I've been lonesome."

"Wal, young lady," drawled Red, "it ain't gonna be so lonesome from now on, if my hunch is correct."

"Oh, I won't be," she said happily. "My horses, the long trek, and two new friends. But. . . ." She broke off there, blushing. Sterl read her mind. There were other young men concerned in this long trek.

"That black horse," spoke up Sterl, pointing to a noble, racy beast to which his greedy gaze had continually returned.

"That's King. He's five years old. Bred from Dad's great dam.

King has won all the races the last two years. Oh, he's swift! He threw me last race. But we won."

"So you were up on him? Well!" Sterl rejoined, victim to a sensation of wonder and admiration. The girl was sweet enough without such call to a cowboy's love of horses, speed, nerve.

"Yes, I can ride him. But Dad says no more. At least not in races. He's too strong. Has a mouth like iron. And once running against other horses he's terrific."

"I'll have to put my hands on him," Sterl said.

"You're going to ride him, cowboy," replied the girl. "Let's go inside the paddock."

Red had straddled the top bar of the fence, and his silence was eloquent. Sterl had never seen him look any more rapt. Leslie opened a huge gate, and led the way inside. She called and whistled. All the horses threw up their heads, and some of them started for her. Then they all trooped forward, fine heads up, manes flying. Sterl needed no more to see what pets they were. Still they halted some yards from the fence, eager, whinnying, but not trustful of the strangers.

"Come up heah, pard," called Red. "They're skeered of you. Instinct! They know you're a hard-ridin' *hombre* from Arizona."

Sterl, thus admonished, climbed up beside Red. "Good Lord, Red, what have we fallen into? Look at them!"

"I'm lookin', Sterl. An' thinkin' thet, after all, there'll always be hosses."

Leslie walked away from the fence somewhat and coaxed. A spotted, iron-gray horse, clean-cut in build and unusually striking in his color, was the first to come to the girl.

"Jester," she called him, and got hold of his mane to lead him back to the fence. "One of my best. He's tricky . . . full of the devil, but fast, tireless. . . . Red, would you like to have him on the trek? It would please me. I think you'd be tricky enough to match him."

"Would I? Aw, Leslie, thet's too good of you. Why, he took my eye fust thing. But I oughtn't take him. You hit me in my one weak spot, Leslie. My heart!"

"Done. He's yours. Get down and make friends with him."

Red complied with alacrity. Sterl watched as he saw the cowboy's lean, brown hand, slow and sure, creep out to touch the arching, glossy neck. "Jester, you dog-gone lucky hoss! Why, I'm the kindest rider that ever threw his laig over a saddle."

"King, come here," Leslie called to the magnificent black. But it was a beautiful bay, a racer, that came at the girl's bidding. "Lady Jane, you know I'm going to ride you this morning, now, don't you?" She petted the sniffing muzzle and laid her cheek against the trim black mane. Then, most of the others, except King, came begging for her favor, dark eyes softly alight. She introduced them to the cowboys as if they were persons of rank— her favorite, Lady Jane, a beautiful mettlesome bay, Duke, a great rangy sorrel, almost red, pride and power in every line, Duchess, a white mare, an aristocrat whose name was felicitous, her distinguishing features long white and black mane and tail, Lord Chester, a trim gray that was hard to overlook, even in that band of Thoroughbreds.

King, the black, stayed behind with three other horses, and Leslie had to go fetch him. Closer at hand his magnificent physical qualities appeared more striking.

"King," Leslie said impressively. "This is an American cowboy, Sterl Hazelton, who is going to ride you . . . ride you, I said, you big devil, on our great trek to a new range."

Sterl had feared this very thing. Faced with it, he could not have refused the horse on any pretext or excuse imaginable. Still he protested. "Leslie, don't ask me to take him . . . your favorite."

"But he's not my favorite! I don't love him . . . well, not so much since he threw me. I can't ride him. And I don't care to have any of the drovers ride him. Please, Sterl."

"I only wanted to be coaxed," rejoined Sterl lamely. "Thanks, Leslie. It's just too good to be true. I had a horse once. . . ."

"Lead him out," Leslie said, then with surprising ease she leaped upon the back of Lady Jane. Red followed with Jester, and Sterl gently urged the black to join them. Red shut the gate on the whistling horses left behind.

"King, let's look each other over," said Sterl, as he let go the mane and squared away in front of the horse. King threw up his noble head, and his black eyes had a piercing curiosity. He sensed events. But he was not mean. He had never been hurt by a rider. He was not in the least afraid. Sterl put out a confident hand to rub his nose. Then he walked all around the black. He did that wholly out of tingling pleasure, not in doubt of any of the horse's points. Reluctantly, as far as appearance went, Sterl admitted that King uncrowned all the other horses he had ever ridden, and he had no doubt that this grand beast had the speed, the endurance, the fighting heart to match his looks.

"Saddle up, boys," Leslie said, slipping off. "Let's get this trip to town over. I don't mind showing you to the girls, because they'll be left behind, except Beryl Dann. And I just hate to introduce you to her."

Sterl did not voice his surprise, but Red blurted out: "An' 'cause why, Leslie? We're Yankees, shore, but not so pore."

"I'll be jealous," laughed the girl frankly. "I'd like you both for my cavaliers. Oh, Beryl is lovely, even if she is spoiled and proud. Her father is lord of the manor, so to speak."

In short order they were saddled up and ready to ride away. King pranced a little under Sterl, but a firm hand and voice, unaccompanied by touch of spur, quieted any rebellion he might have felt. Sterl sensed the tremendous latent power underneath that saddle.

"Pard, air we on a picnic or somethin'?" Red drawled, the blue blaze in his eyes.

"I guess. . . . Leslie, you had better pinch me."

"What for?" she asked curiously.

"To wake me up."

"Oh! I'd rather you kept on dreaming. Boys, it's nice to have you with me. You say such new and sweet things."

One branch of the road turned back past the house; the other, which Leslie took, crossed the creek and wound up the slope into the bush. The three trotted abreast. Wattle trees sent a golden shade down upon them, and again the red-blossoming eucalyptus changed it to red. It appeared to Sterl that singing currawongs followed them, and he remarked about these birds to Leslie.

"Bell-magpies," she said. "I love them almost as well as the kookaburras. Of course, you know them by now."

"I don't think so. I have a good memory."

"Oh, just wait!" exclaimed the girl heartily. "That reminds me, Dad won't let me take all my pets. I'll have to part with some of them. Oh, dear, more packing! But I'll find time to show them to you boys."

They rode on. Red appeared as one in a trance. Everything that pleased the cowboy here in Australia made Sterl glad, because remorse knocked at his heart that this comrade had forsaken the American range for this unknown country.

Thick bush began to thin out, soon evidencing the clearing axe of the pioneer. Another mile brought open country, green rolling hills and vales that looked to Sterl as if they had been over-grazed. In the distance blue ranges towered hauntingly. Presently Sterl saw horses and cattle, and columns of smoke, and at length a big, white house with the inevitable tin roof and great, tin water tanks under the eaves. He had not observed this around Slyter's house, but he had grasped that most of these Australian station owners had to catch their water. The road turned to permit better view down a long lane of trees to the town. Three huge wagons, one of them canvas-covered, with men packing them attested to another of the drovers' activities. Leslie explained that this was the Dann station, just outside of town.

"I was going to ride in after Beryl. But it isn't necessary. There she is," said Leslie, and, waving a gauntletted hand, she called. She was answered, and presently Sterl saw a fair-faced, fair-haired girl, distinguished by grace even in what evidently was the workaday dress of the moment.

"Pard, don't you reckon I oughta pull leather out of heah?" Red whispered in perturbation.

"I should smile you should," returned Sterl. "And me, too!"

"Stand to your colors, men," Leslie retorted, who certainly had heard. Somehow her tone stimulated Sterl and augmented his interest. Presently he was doffing his sombrero and gallantly bowing to a handsome girl, some years Leslie's senior, whose poise permitted a graciousness and hid curiosity, if she felt any.

"Beryl, let me introduce Dad's new hands, Mister Krehl and Mister Hazelton, cowboys from America. This is Miss Beryl Dann, of whom I have spoken. She is going with us."

Sterl made his pleasant little speech, in response to the girl's greetings, and then Red cut in with his Southern drawl, as cool and easy as if he had been home on the range.

"Wal, Miss Dann, I shore am glad to meet another Australian girl. I reckon two oughta be about enough. My pard heah, Sterl an' me, have been sorta worried over this long trek an' thought of backin' out. But not no more."

Beryl Dann was neither too dignified nor grown up not to be pleased and flattered by what Sterl divined was an extraordinary speech to her. He did not fail to feel the distance between the only daughter of a rich Englishman and American cowboys; nevertheless, she was as thoroughbred as she was attractive, and he liked her.

The girls fell at once into mutual excitement about the trek, what they could pack and what leave home, and how wonderful and terrible the prospect. Red leaned over, all eyes on the girl, whose fair face flushed and whose blue eyes showed she did not lack spirit. Sterl managed to get a word in, and presently recalled Leslie to herself.

"Oh, Beryl, we must ride on to town," she cried. "Dad is there waiting. Isn't it wonderful? I won't believe it until we're out on the trek. Then I'll be . . . be . . . I don't know what. Good bye."

As Sterl rode on with Leslie, he observed without looking back that Red did not accompany them.

"Did you like her?" queried Leslie, a dark flash of her hazel eyes on Sterl. She was a woman, like all the rest of the female creatures, still Sterl could not react to the situation with teasing duplicity, as one impulse prompted him to.

"Yes, of course," he said frankly. "Pretty and gracious, if a little haughty. I wonder . . . has she lived out here long?"

"Yes. The Danns have been here all of five years. But Beryl went to school in Sydney. She visits there often. If haughty implies she looks down upon me a little . . . well, you're right. But she's lovely. All the young men court her. Didn't you fall in love with her at first sight?"

"My child, I did not."

"Don't call me child," she flashed quickly. "I'm grown up. Old enough to get married!"

"You don't say. I wouldn't have thought it," replied Sterl teasingly.

"Yes. Dad thought so. He wanted to give me to a station man over here. But I wouldn't. Red has not escaped Beryl . . . that's obvious. Look back."

Sterl did so, to be amused as well as dismayed to see the cowboy still leaning over his saddle, gazing down upon the fairhaired girl.

"Sterl, I like Red," Leslie went on confidentially. "But I'd never let him see it. I don't know cowboys, of course. But I know young men who are devils after women. And he's one. I could feel it. But I guess you're different. You must be, not to fall head over heels in love with Beryl Dann. I'm glad you're like that. I had a brother once. How I needed him after I grew up! Sterl, I'm crazy to take this trek. But I'm frightened. There will be twenty young men with us. I know how they can be even trekking into Brisbane. Eight days! My mother and Stanley Dann's sister, Emily, the only women. Beryl and I. Won't it be terrible?"

"Leslie, I'm bound to admit it looks pretty serious for you girls. Your fathers never should take you."

"But I want to go. Beryl does, too. It means new homes, new friends, new lives. Sterl, I hope you'll be a big brother to me. Will you?"

"Thank you. I'll try," responded Sterl sincerely. The girl's frank wistfulness touched him deeply. "But I'm a stranger. How can you trust me so soon? I might be what Red calls no good a-tall."

"You might be, but I don't believe it. You're different. I see a shadow in your face . . . a far-off look in your eyes. Did you leave a sweetheart back there in America, whom you must go back to?"

"No, Leslie," Sterl said, disturbed.

"Oh, I'm glad. I was afraid . . . it was that. . . . I like you, Sterl. I'm not afraid of you. Mum says I'm a hoyden. But I'm sensitive. These Outback fellows court you on sight . . . hug and kiss you . . . or try to. They're not so raw in Brisbane and especially Sydney, so Beryl tells us. They're English gentlemen. But Outback it's a fight for love, girls, cattle . . . for life itself."

"Leslie, it's much like that on the Western ranges where I come from. I understand a little how a young girl feels."

"You are going to be a comfort, Sterl," she concluded happily. "Here we are, right in town. And there comes Red, putting Jester to a canter. . . . There's where I went to school. This is the main street. Stores and pubs. Do you drink, Sterl?"

"Oh, I take one now and then. But I'm not what you would call a drinking cowboy. Neither is Red, though he will get a hide-full, as he calls it, upon occasion to celebrate, whether joyous or grievous."

"I'm glad. All the men here drink like fish. It's an old English custom. And this town will be lively. It looks like all the two hundred inhabitants are out right now. Oh, I forgot something I want to tell you. Do you remember Dad mentioning a drover, Ashley Ormiston?"

"Yes. He is the man Mister Dann wants your Dad to throw in with."

"Sterl, I don't like the idea at all. This Ormiston is new to Downsville. You'll meet him today, so I don't need to describe him. But he has been very much in evidence ever since the races. I met him that day, and to be honest I was fascinated . . . thrown off my feet. He drove me home. He was worse than our young men . . . in his hugging and kissing. . . . Sterl, he . . . he insulted me that very first night. I didn't dare tell Dad. But I've tried to avoid him ever since. That's not easy to do. He visits us on Sundays, and Dad and Mum . . . the fools! . . . leave us alone."

"But why don't you tell your father?" queried Sterl in a voice that betrayed his anger.

"I dare not. Dad would kill him," she replied simply.

At that moment Red caught up with them. "Say, you, what'd you run off from me for?" he asked, apparently grieved.

Leslie laughed at him. "Let's tie up here," she said, halting. "Red, you forgot all about us. . . . Now, boys, I've got to buy things for Mum. You hunt up Dad. He'll be somewhere, waiting for you. Stanley Dann wants to meet you. It's important. Be good. Don't drink . . . or forget you're my cowboys."

She left them with a bright smile. Red did not appear to be aware of the curious people, or the wagons, or the charged atmosphere of the town. "Pard, dog-gone it, I gotta confess, I fell harder'n I ever got piled by a hoss in all my life," said Red with something of poignance.

"You did? Well! Over what or who?" inquired Sterl tantalizingly.

"Who'd you think, you dumb-haid? Gosh, she was nice. Sterl . . . hullo, what the hell have we run into heah?"

They had passed a corner to reach a point opposite a large store, in front of which had collected a crowd of people, mostly men but a few women and youngsters, all of whom were excited and frightened, trying to get out of the way of a conflict of some kind. Then Sterl saw a white man kick an aborigine into the street. He heard a woman cry out that it was Slyter's black man, Friday.

Sterl stepped out of the crowd off the pavement. The black was down. Then a white man, agile and powerful, leaped into the street to kick the black with vicious, resounding thuds, knocking him flat, accompanying his attacks with curses, prefixed to the word nigger. Striding over, Sterl placed a hard hand against the aggressor and shoved him back, far from gently.

The man straightened up, adding amazement to fury. He was

a dark-browed, handsome fellow of about thirty, garbed as a drover, heavily booted. Sterl had particularly observed the boots.

"What business . . . of yours?" he panted hoarsely.

"I just thought you'd kicked that black enough, unless his offense was heinous, which I doubt," declared Sterl deliberately.

"Who are . . . you?" demanded the other, his dark eyes burning. Sterl caught a strong odor of whiskey, the effect of which appeared further corroborated by the man's slight unsteadiness.

"No matter. I'm a newcomer."

"Damned meddling Yankee blighter," shouted the Australian, and with a back-handed sweep he struck Sterl a blow across the mouth that staggered him.

Recovering his balance, Sterl leaped forward. He gave his antagonist a sudden blow, low down, then swung his right fist hard and fierce between those malignant eyes, and felled him like a bullock under the axe.

Red jumped down to line up alongside his comrade. "Wal, pard, we're shore runnin' true to form."

The buzzing circle of people crowded into the street. Sterl, to his dismay, espied Leslie's pale face. Then her father dragged her back and strode out, accompanied by a tawny-haired giant, leonine in build and mien.

Slyter gazed at the prostrate man, who was groaning and stirring, and from him to the black.

"Friday. You're spitting blood. Who hit you?"

"Boss, that one fella," replied the black, and pointed to his brutal attacker.

"Damn, it's Ash Ormiston!" Slyter exclaimed.

"I see. Looks as if a horse kicked him. Here, you, what does this mean?" boomed the giant, wheeling upon Sterl.

Red intervened, cool and wary. "Watch that *hombre*, pard. He might have a gun."

"Krehl!" shouted Slyter. "Did you slug Ormiston?"

"No. Sterl did thet. But I'd have liked to."

"Stanley, these are my two American cowboys, Krehl and Hazelton."

"Drunk and rowing, eh?" queried Dann.

Sterl confronted Dann, and he was not in a humor to be conciliatory.

"No, I'm not drunk," he rang out. "It's your countryman, Ormiston, who is that. I came upon him kicking this black man, Friday. Kicking him in the face and chest with a heavy boot. I interfered . . . shoved Ormiston back. He called me a damned meddling Yankee blighter and hit me. Then I soaked him!"

"Friday, what you do alonga Ormiston?" asked Slyter gruffly. His brown visage showed a tinge of red.

"Black fella tellum bimeby," replied Friday, and stalked into the crowd, where Sterl saw Leslie try to stop him and fail.

Meanwhile Ormiston staggered to his unsteady feet, one of his eyes badly puffed and the other glaring with fierce passion.

"Where's that god-damn' Yankee who hit me?" he bit out.

Dann laid a restraining hand on him. "Man, you're drunk."

Sterl confronted him. "Go for your gun, if you've got one."

Ormiston violently threw Dann off.

Dann waved the crowd back. "Get off the street!" he yelled.

Chapter Four

If Ormiston had a gun concealed on his person, of which fact Sterl had an uncanny certainty, he made no move to draw it. Sterl's hand dropped back to his side.

"I'll not exchange shots . . . with a Yankee tramp," Ormiston panted, struggling to master his fury. A sickly green hue began to erase the red from his dark face.

"No. But you're not above kicking a poor fellow, when he's down," replied Sterl scathingly.

Red again slouched over to Sterl's side. "Haw! Haw!" His hard, mirthless laugh rang with scorn. "Orful particular, ain't you, Mister Ormiston, about who you throw a gun on? Wal, you got some sense, at thet."

"Dann, you're a magistrate here," Ormiston shouted. "Order these Yankees out of town."

"You're drunk, I told you," replied Dann from the sidewalk. "You start a fight, then fail to go through with it."

"No, I didn't. I only kicked that snooping nigger. This Yankee started it. I'll not engage in a gun fight with a foreign adventurer," replied Ormiston in hoarse haste.

"Yes, and you're a yellow dog," Sterl interposed coldly.

"Mister, why don't you pull thet gun I see inside yore coat?" drawled Red.

Ormiston appeared unable to control his rage at being shown up before this crowd. "Dann, order these Yankees to leave," he asserted stridently.

"No. You're making a fool of yourself," declared Dann. "Slyter has hired these cowboys to help him on the trek."

That information evidently completed the sobering influence upon the drover and acted as a check to the expression of tremendous wrath. "Slyter, is that true . . . you're taking these cowboys?"

"Yes, I've hired them."

"Will you discharge them? At my earnest solicitation?"

"No, I certainly will not."

"Then I refuse to take my drovers and my mob of cattle on Dann's trek."

Slyter looked aghast and upset at this decision, which no doubt would be grievous to Dann, but after a moment he burst out hotly: "Ormiston, I don't care a damn what you do."

The drover made a forceful and passionate gesture, then shouldered his way through the crowd to disappear. Slyter lost no time getting Sterl and Red, whom manifestly he wanted to leave and so dragged them with him across the pavement into a store. Dann strode after them. And there the four men faced each other.

"Gentlemen, I'm terribly sorry," Sterl began poignantly. "It's just too bad that I had to mess up your plans at the last moment. But I couldn't help it . . . I couldn't. Leslie told me about Friday caring for her horses. That influenced me. But in any case I couldn't have stood for such dirty, low-down brutality."

"Pard, don't feel so bad about it," drawled Red, coolly rolling a cigarette. "If you hadn't been so damn quick, I'd have busted Ormiston myself. We cain't help how things come out."

Dann stroked his golden beard with a massive hand, and his penetrating eyes studied the cowboys, while he evinced none of the agitation that possessed Slyter.

"It was unfortunate," Slyter began. "Ormiston had been drinking. But I'll swear the aborigine absolutely did not deserve that kicking. Friday is the best native I ever knew. He's honest, loyal, devoted to Leslie, who was good to his *gin* when she lay dying. Stanley, I had to take Hazelton's side in this matter."

Red eased forward a step in his slow way. "Mister Dann, if you don't mind, I'd like to put in a word. Slyter needn't apologize for my pard, an' stick up for thet black man. Shore, we're strangers in a strange land. But men air men the world over. I'd like to ask you, without meanin' offense, if there ain't Englishmen heah an' there who's jest no good a-tall?"

Dann let out a deep laugh that was convincing. "There are, cowboy, and you can lay to that."

"Wal, I'm glad to heah you admit it. You see, me an' Sterl have ridden the ranges for years . . . since we were kids. We know men. An' it's hard for a bad man, no matter how slick he is, to pull the wool over our eyes. If ever I met a low-down *hombre*, thet Ormiston is one. Mebbe it wouldn't have been so easy to see through him but for the drink. But I'll bet I'd've been suspicious of him in any case. No, Ormiston is jest no good a-tall . . . an' he come damn' near bein' a daid one."

"Tell me, Hazelton," spoke up Dann, his amber eyes full of dancing little glints, "if Ormiston had moved to draw the gun I know he always carries . . . what would you have done?"

"I'd have killed the fool," Sterl declared, "and for me it would have been murder. Mister Dann, we cowboys have had to live by our guns. Hard men at a hard time learn to draw a gun swift as lightning. It may not be a worthy gift, but on our frontier you need it to survive."

"Indeed! Did you see Ormiston was armed?"

"No. But I knew he had a gun. I read his mind. Now, Slyter, I think the thing for Red and me to do is to leave town at once."

"You will do nothing of the kind," Slyter rejoined stoutly.

"Boys, it's not to be thought of," added Dann. "Ormiston was bluffing. He won't quit us. Like all of us he sees a way to wealth. Deep as he is, I grasp that much. And we need him with us. The more drovers, the more cattle, the better our chances for success. He is the last man I could persuade to risk the trek."

"Mister Dann, I see the necessity for you. But if Red and I go . . . we'll clash with Ormiston. And I'll kill him, if Red doesn't beat me to it."

"Listen, you young roosters," went on Dann persuasively. "Outback there will be too much clash with the elements and the blacks for we drovers to fight among ourselves. We'll all be brothers before we reach the Never Never. Isn't that so, Bing?"

"It has been proved by other treks, none so great as this must be," replied Slyter earnestly. "If you boys are concerned about me or Stanley . . . just forget that and take the risk."

"Boss, we'll never let you down," Red said.

"We will go," added Sterl, and his tone was a pledge. "But gratitude and wonder about the drovers."

"Hazelton, I grasp that you think we have no true idea of what this undertaking means," responded Dann, with a seriousness that matched Sterl's.

"Stanley, I could say the same thing," said Slyter. "Are we wrong and is Hazelton right?"

"Stumps me. Maybe we allow ambition and greed to blind us. Maybe we idealize this trek."

"Have you ever driven cattle into a hard wilderness, months on end, against all the hard knocks a desolate country and forbidding nature can deal you?"

"No, Hazelton, we have never been on a real trek. But my brother Eric has. He slights the hardships either because he is callous, unfeeling, or because he doesn't want me to know. In fact, Eric has failed after several starts in Queensland, and he has been instrumental in fostering this great trek."

"Then you know little of actual contact with life in the raw, with hard men desperate in a hard time?" queried Sterl.

"In the way you mean I must admit . . . nothing at all."

"Are you asking my advice?"

"Indeed, yes."

"For God's sake, leave the women home!"

"Impossible. They won't stay behind," Dann asserted with finality.

"Well, I had that hunch. So did Red. Dann, in such times as I've intimated, a few of which I've lived through, when men are faced with primitive, savage things . . . greed, lust, blood, hate, starvation, thirst, fear, some of them become gods and most of them beasts."

Dann nodded his leonine locks. "It's too late now, even if I would back out. Hazelton, perhaps Providence sent you range men to help us. I believe so . . . I hope so. Slyter, I suggest that you let these cowboys join my drovers. Ormiston will then join you, I know, and with his drovers you will have eight."

"Stanley, I'm sorry. I won't accept, either," Slyter replied decisively.

"You are right not to. I was selfish. Ormiston can join me or stay back, as he chooses. Anyhow, soon all our cattle will be thrown into one great mob. Now, Hazelton, to get down to fundamentals. Tell us just what kind of range you have driven mobs of cattle over . . . how far . . . what kind of obstacles . . . how you worked."

"That's easy, gentlemen, and you can believe what I tell you," replied Sterl. "Some years ago, just after the Civil War, Texas was overrun with millions of longhorn cattle. The ranchers had no home market. A rancher named Jesse Chisholm conceived the idea of driving herds of cattle from southern Texas across the plains to Kansas. Red here was a boy of eighteen when the trail driving got into its great stride. I came on later. But we both had hard and terrible drives. Chisholm started out with over three thousand head of cattle and twelve riders. The distance was approximately five hundred miles. He made it in something over ninety days, losing four cowboys and two thousand head of cattle. But he sold what was left of his herd at so big a price that he made a huge profit. His success inaugurated trail driving in Texas. Millions of cattle have been driven up the Chisholm Trail, which is now a wide, deep lane across the plains.

"As for hardships . . . there are many. I'll name the important ones. In that early day there were all of fifty million buffalo that ranged from the Gulf in the south to the Dakotas in the north. This vast herd traveled south in the fall, and returned north the next spring. For years stampedes of buffalo were the worst obstacle the trail drivers had to overcome. Next to that were the attacks and raids of savage tribes. The Indians saw that the doom of the buffalo was inevitable, and, as they lived on the buffalo, it meant their doom, also. The Comanches were the fiercest tribe, next the Kiowas, the Apaches, the Cherokees, and so on. Seldom did any trail herd ever escape from an attack. There were many rivers to ford, some of them big and wide, often flooded. Thousands of cattle, with horses and riders, were lost every year in floods. In dry years there were long drives from water to water, often entailing great loss and suffering from thirst. Thunderstorms often stampeded herds. The electric storms struck everywhere, and balls of fire rolled along the ground, and streaks of fire ran across the backs of horses and cattle . . . these electric storms always stampeded a herd. Dust storms, sand storms were terrible to drive against. Trail drivers suffered from intense heat, and many were victims of sunstroke. In the fall and winter, *del norte*, the freezing gale that blew out of a clear sky from the north, was something the riders hated and feared. Lastly, there came the development of rustling . . . the era of the cattle thieves, which is in its heyday right now, and they caused more fighting and blood-spilling than the Indians. There, gentlemen, I've covered the main points in regard to what trail drivers had to meet."

"Wonderful! Wonderful!" Dann exclaimed, his eyes shining. "Jesse Chisholm was a man after my heart. A savior of Texas, yes?"

"Indeed, he saved Texas and built the cattle empire."

Red emitted a cloud of smoke, and drawled: "Boss, I rode for Jesse once. He was a great *hombre*. Harder than the hinges on the gates of hell! Sometime I'll tell you stories about him . . . one thing special, his jingle-bob brand, thet was so famous."

"Boys, I'll eat your stories up, when time permits," boomed the drover. "I thank the good Lord for sending you to Australia, and, Slyter, I thank you for fetching them here. Hazelton, one thing more. How did you drive your mobs?"

"We rounded them up into a great triangle, with the apex pointing in the direction we had to go. Pointing the herd, that was called. Two of the nerviest and hardest-riding cowboys had the lead at the point. The mass of cattle would follow the leads. Two cowboys on each side at the center of the herd, the rest at the broad base where stragglers and deserters . . . drags, we call them . . . have to be carefully watched and driven."

"Were you one of those cowboys who rode at the head and pointed the herd?" queried Dann, a warm light from his big eyes shining upon Sterl.

"No, but Red was, always. I was a good hand after the drags. Then, I could handle a rifle."

"Shake hands with me, cowboys," bellowed Dann, and his giant clasp nearly wrenched Sterl's hand, sinewy and hard as it was. Red bent double and let out a yell. "Aw, boss, I'm gonna need that mitt!"

"Slyter, I'll go home and cheer up my womenfolk with a word about these God-sent Yankee cowboys you found for us," Dann concluded. "I'll order my drovers to start my mob tomorrow, positively. I'll tell Ormiston come with us, or go to hell, as he chooses. . . . Meet us out on the trek. Good bye."

He was gone, his swift, heavy steps resounding. Slyter's keen gaze on the cowboys seemed to ask tribute for this pioneer Australian. It would have been forthcoming, without solicitation.

"Boss, he's another Chisholm, shore as we're born," Red said.

"Slyter, I like him," added Sterl warmly, "his heart matches his body. He's the leader for such a trek."

"Fine!" exclaimed Slyter. "You fired Stanley Dann as no one ever did before. Boys, go home and set your hands to things. Tell Leslie we leave day after tomorrow."

Slyter's tenseness, his pallor and thick voice silenced the cowboys and gave them another intimation of the colossal enterprise at hand. Sterl and Red were young, without attachments or duties, free to answer the call of adventure. Slyter and Dann and their partners were men of family, with great responsibilities. To abandon homes, to tear up ties by the roots, to risk the lives of loved ones along with their own, all for the chimera of fortune, to go forth to seek and find the pot of gold at the foot of the rainbow—what splendid courage, what faith, what greatness!

Sterl became aware that the store was full of curious people. He and Red were the cynosure of all eyes. Red enjoyed such attention, but Sterl hated it, especially, as had happened so often, when he had just engaged in a fight. He shivered when he thought how closely he had come to shooting Ormiston's leg off or worse; a sinister move on the man's part would have meant his death. Sterl felt the heritage of the hard life of a trail driver. How easily for the leap of tigerish blood that had been developed and fostered in him. He had hoped Australia had not bred the type of badmen whom he had been compelled to work among. But this Ormiston was a man to inspire instant hate.

Outside the store the crowd began to disperse. Leslie met them with her arms full of packages. Sterl promptly relieved her of some of them, while Red took the rest. Red made a drawling remark about being a pack horse, but Sterl, after one look at Leslie's white face and eyes blazing almost black, felt too dismayed to speak. Leslie had seen his encounter with Ormiston. If he were not mistaken, the girl betrayed singular manifestations of anger. He wondered if these Outback Australians, well-educated and poised as they seemed to be, had under their veneer the primitive instincts natural to such a wild, primitive country. Of course, they would. No race could escape its environment.

As Leslie walked along between him and Red, she had a hand on Sterl's arm. And it was not a light touch. They came to a point opposite the horses.

"Heah we air, Jester, a-gonna make a pack hoss out of you fust thing," spoke up Red, and Sterl knew the cowboy was talking to ease the situation. Sterl could see, too, how Red had a vigilant eye on all points. No surprising that trail driver at home or abroad! Red did not like the situation.

"Leslie, have you finished your buying?" asked Sterl.

"Not quite. But I'll not stay longer . . . in town," she replied in a thick, unsteady tone. She mounted her horse as Sterl remembered seeing Comanches mount. "Let me have a couple of packages."

Handing these to her, Sterl looked up into her face, impelled by its stress.

"Leslie . . . you were there?" he asked.

"Yes. I ran after you . . . to tell you something . . . I forget what . . . and I saw it . . . all."

"I'm sorry. Bad luck like that always hounds me."

"Who said it was bad luck?" she retorted. "I never . . . had such a thrill. But Sterl . . . you jumped at that chance to smash Ormiston . . . on my account!"

"Well . . . Friday's first . . . and then yours. Still I'd have interfered, if I'd never heard of either of you. I'm built that way, Leslie."

"You're built greatly, then. A thrill hardly does justice to what I felt . . . when you hit him. But, afterward . . . when it looked like a gun fight . . . I nearly fainted. And Sterl, I've seen gun fights, at the races . . . without being squeamish . . . it was . . . something else."

"So that's why you're so pale?" rejoined Sterl, endeavoring to speak lightly, and he turned to King. The black champed his bit and pranced a little, but gave Sterl no trouble. Red led off the street, saying: "Pard, this heah burg ain't Dodge or Lincoln, but I shore don't trust it."

The horses were skittish for a spell, but beyond the busy sector of the town they toned down, so that Sterl and Leslie could resume their conversation.

"Am I pale, Sterl?" she asked.

"Not so much now. But for a few minutes back you were white as a sheet. And your eyes black!"

"Sterl, I ran into Ormiston."

"And what did he say?"

"I'll never tell you," she replied.

"Why?"

"Because it's easy to see you . . . and Red, too . . . would be worse than Dad."

"Leslie, are you keeping secrets for Ormiston's sake or ours?" asked Sterl with constraint.

"Yours. I'll stave off that fight as long as I can. But, oh, I know it will come!"

"So do I. Well, Leslie, what did you say?"

"I don't remember everything. One thing, though, was what you called him . . . a yellow dog."

"Leslie! That will tickle Red. It's not calculated to make Ormiston love me any better."

"How he could hate you so fiendishly . . . all in a moment . . . is beyond me."

"I slugged him . . . dared him to draw . . . showed him up before all those people, and you. Wasn't that provocation enough to make his breed do murder?"

"Sterl, I mean the man is two-faced. I felt it just now. He's not what he made himself out to be to Mum and Dad and me."

"Don't doubt it," Sterl replied thoughtfully. "Do you think he'll make good his threat not to be on the trek?"

"I do not," said the girl positively. "Ash Ormiston couldn't be kept from going. I wouldn't say wholly because he's so keen after Beryl Dann and me."

"Beryl, too? Well! He's what Red would call an enterprising gent."

"He's deep, Sterl. And he doesn't love either cattle or horses. I can't explain what I feel. And I distrust his attitude toward the trek."

"Not a born pioneer, eh? Leslie, if he does go, I'll bet he doesn't last long."

"Oh, you'll fight!" she cried.

"Not that I'll provoke it. I'll say, though, if Ormiston joined one of our trail drives in Texas, he'd get shot *pronto*. Leslie, what had he against Friday?"

"He had enough. I should have told you that. One Sunday, several weeks ago, when Mum and Dad were in town, Ormiston came out and found me in my hammock. He made violent love to me. I was scared, Sterl. He . . . I . . . I fought him . . . and I must have cried out. For Friday ran up with his spear. It was all I could do to keep him from killing Ormiston."

"So that was it? No man, drunk or sober, could have the passion I saw Ormiston show without some cause. Leslie, you met Friday . . . tried to stop him. Did he say anything?"

"He said . . . Black fella killum bimeby! Friday will do it, too, unless somebody else does. These aborigines are wonderful people, Sterl. You'll think so, when you learn to know them."

"Is Friday going on the trek?"

"Dad wants him. To track lost horses. The blacks are marvelous trackers. Dad claims Friday is the greatest he ever knew. But Friday says, no. Maybe you can persuade him, Sterl. A black never forgets a wrong or fails to return a service."

"I sure will try. What a lot I could learn! Hello, there's Red beside one of those Dann wagons. Leslie, I'll bet he stopped to see Beryl again."

"Good-o!" squealed Leslie merrily. "Red's not letting any grass grow under his feet."

They soon reached Red, who evidently had waited for them.

"Howdy, folks," he drawled with a twinkle in his blue eyes. "Reckoned I'd wait for you."

"Red, you've seen Beryl again," declared Leslie.

"Me? Umpumm! I was jest watchin' them pack the wagon," returned Red innocently.

They rode on at a canter without any incident except the dropping of a package by Red, whose horse required some riding. And soon they arrived at the valley, to cross the creek and halt at the paddock.

"Boys, I'll go on to the house," Leslie said, dismounting. "I can carry these bundles. I'll be helping Mum for a while. Suppose you try out some of your own horses. And come up later for tea. Oh, yes, and to see my pets."

"Don't care if I do, unless I want to be spoiled riding King. Leslie Slyter, mark my words, you'll be to blame," declared Sterl.

"Wish I could spoil you, Sterl Hazelton," Leslie said, her eyes betraying what she seemed wholly unconscious of.

"Yeah? Wal, I can stand some, too," drawled Red. "Heah, gimme some of them bundles. Pard, I'll run along with Leslie, far as our tent. I've got a couple jobs to get done, one in particular, sewin' on thet canvas floor. There was some kind of a varmint come in last night, an' skeered me stiff."

"Opossum. They are as tame as cats. I like them, especially the furry, brown ones with the rings round their eyes."

Left to his own devices, Sterl went among the horses he had selected for the trek, which Roland had tethered in the shed, and set about the slow and pleasing task of making friends with them. He had always been one cowboy that did not deliberately ruffle the temper of horses the wrong way. And while he engaged in this friendly task, he mused over the momentous ride to town. He could no more keep things from happening to him than he could stop breathing. He recalled only one man, out of the many rustlers and hard characters who had crossed his trail, who had incited as quick a hatred as had this man Ormiston. After a little pondering Sterl decided that, if possible, he would keep out of the man's way, and as always be vigilant to avoid friction. Offsetting Ormiston's peculiar power to engender base and resentful feeling was thought of the inspiring presence of Stanley Dann. Here was a man. Sterl harkened to the chief drover's need. And Sterl did not pass by the fair-haired Beryl, with her proud, dark-blue eyes and the poise of her head. Leslie, however, occasioned him more sentiment than he thought could be possible for a cowboy who had broken his heart and ruined his life for another girl, whom he had renounced forever. Leslie was appealing in many ways, but the charm she had, which he found vague, sweet, and disquieting, was the fact of his apparent appeal to her, of which he felt she was wholly unconscious.

When the sun stood straight overhead, Sterl wended a meditative way down along the creek toward camp. Of one thing he felt unalterably sure—he was in the open again, away from the restraint of walls and ships, already in contact with Nature, with trees, birds, beasts, snakes, horses, about to ride out on this incredible trek, that menaced with all Australia's interior, primal perils. That was enough. That was all left him in life, this strenuous action of the natural man. Sterl discounted any lasting relation to these good white folks who needed him.

While gazing into a clear pool, watching the fish, he fancied he heard a loud, prolonged laugh. But there did not appear to be any of the men within sight or hearing. He was glad he had included some fishing tackle, and everything else he could think of, in that orgy of spending at Brisbane. As long as the wagons held up on that trek, some of these useful purchases would last.

Sterl found Red sitting before the tent, profoundly thoughtful and solemn. He did not even hear Sterl's approach.

"Say, cowboy, has that blonde girl locoed you? I can remember when you were all for brunettes."

Red apparently did not catch the import of Sterl's good-natured taunt. "Pard, did you heah anythin'?" he asked almost in a whisper.

"Hear? When?"

"Jest about a minnit ago . . . mebbe longer. I don't know. I'm dotty. Did I have any drinks up to town?"

"You sure didn't."

"Gosh, I'm shore I've got the willies. Sterl, I was in the tent heah, sewin' to beat hell, when somebody busted out in a laugh . . . the . . . snortinest laugh you ever heahed. Right heah outside the tent. 'Who'n'hell's laughin' at me?' I said, an' I was mad. But I kept mum. Pretty soon again . . . an' this time right on this spot . . . wusser, louder, somebody made orful fun of me. This time I spoke up an' said it wasn't jest safe for any *hombre* to give me a hoss laugh like thet. I was burnin' under my collar, an' figger'n who it might be. Wal, nobody answered me, till presently it busted out again. Pard, you never in yore life heahed such a loud brayin' ass laugh. When the smart-alec got through, I come out to bust him. Seen nobody. I looked down by the cabin, an' behind the tent. Not a soul in sight! An' I swore I had 'em bad. Then I seen a brown an' white bird, like one of our kingfishers, only a lot bigger, sittin' right ther on thet branch. I'd thought nothin' of it, if the damn bird hadn't looked at me so queer. Stuck his haid on one side an' looked out of devilish black eyes at me, as if to say . . . 'Heah's one of them Yankee blighters.' Then he flew away. An' heah's what's been drivin' me dotty. If thet bird didn't give me that hoss laugh, then yore pard has gone plumb stark ravin' crazy."

"Whew! Red, you look sort of bug-house at that," returned Sterl with concern. "Let's go up and ask Leslie."

On the way up the path under the wattles they met Leslie. Before she had time for more than her flashing smile, Red burst into the narrative of his perplexing experience. Sterl watched the girl's face. It still possessed its natural bloom. Red did not slight his tale or his exasperation and mystification, still he did not take too long. Before he had quite ended, however, Leslie's face began to transform and ripple and glow, until she burst into uncontrollable mirth.

"Aw, Leslie! I cain't see anythin' so funny about thet," the cowboy protested.

"Oh . . . oh! It was . . . Jack," she choked out.

"Jack who?"

"My pet kookaburra. Oh, Red! Such fun. I couldn't have . . .

hoped for more. It was my laughing jackass that gave you the horse laugh."

"Wal, I figgered he was a laughin' hyena, all right. But thet pet kooka somethin' . . . thet has me beat."

"Jack is a bird . . . a laughing jackass, Australia's most famous bird. He is a giant kingfisher."

"Aw! So it *was* thet bird? Thank Gawd! I reckoned my mind was gone. You see, Leslie, trailin' about for years an' years with this heah Sterl Hazelton is enough to drive any man dotty. An' I feared I was, shore."

"Leslie, I must make Jack's acquaintance," spoke up Sterl eagerly. "Surely you'll take him on the trek?"

"Right-o. Also Cocky and Gal, but I can't take my little bears. It breaks my heart. Come in to tea first." At the door Leslie whispered to Sterl. "I didn't tell Mum what happened up town."

Slyter had not returned, nor did his wife expect him. "I'm too terribly busy to chat," she said, after serving them and drinking a cup of tea. "Les, I wanted Friday to carry things down to the wagon. Have you seen him?"

"I'll find him, Mum."

"We'll help, Missus Slyter," interposed Sterl. "And I'd like a look at your wagon while it's empty. We must make a boat out of it, so it can be floated across the rivers."

"How thoughtful of you! That had not occurred to Bingham. By all means stop the leaks, and do anything more for us."

"We'll fix up a little room in the front of your wagon, behind the seat," went on Sterl. "I've done that before. A wagon can be made really comfortable, considering. All your baggage can be safely stowed to make space, and still be handy. On top of heavier stuff, of course, because the wagon will be loaded. Your cots can be placed on each side of the wagon with space between."

"Cots?" asked Leslie, puzzled.

"Yes, your beds."

"But you mean stretchers."

Red groaned. "Aw, Lord, it gets wuss an' wuss. Leslie, a stretcher is what they carried me in at Dodge, when I got shot up bad."

They all laughed, and Mrs. Slyter murmured: "Les, what was it your Dad said about these boys being sent?"

"Mum, it was God-sent! And I know it's true," Leslie returned warmly. But her eyes scarcely included Red in her encomium.

Suddenly they were interrupted by a piercing sound from outside.

"Thet son-of-a-gun again!" yelled Red wildly.

It was a discordant, concatenated, rollicking laugh that certainly would have fooled Sterl. Then from somewhere in the distance reverberated an answer, as wild and comical as that near at hand.

"Jack sassing other kookaburras," Leslie declared. "Come and see him."

They went outdoors. The black man, Friday, stood under one of the gum trees, looking up into the branches and holding out a queer stick with a white, oval end. In his other hand he held out a long spear.

"Friday has his *wommera*," said Leslie gravely. "That doesn't look so good for Ormiston."

Just then a large brown and white bird fluttered down from the tree to alight on the black's spear. "There's Jack," Leslie cried gladly, and she ran out. The cowboys followed. Sterl certainly looked the kookaburra over. He appeared to be a rather short bird, built heavy forward, with a big head and strong bill. He turned that head from side to side, peering out of black, merry eyes in a mischievous manner. Sterl thought that his queer laugh certainly fitted his looks. Red drawled: "Wal, I'll be dog-goned!" On Leslie's call, Jack hopped to her extended hand.

Sterl's attention shifted to the black man. Upon close view Friday appeared to be a magnificent specimen of aborigine. He stood well over six feet, slender, muscular, perfectly proportioned, black as ebony. He wore a crude garment around his middle. His dark visage held for Sterl an inscrutable dignity and mysticism in which qualities it resembled somewhat the American Indian.

Sterl went up to Friday and tapped him on his deep breast and asked: "Friday no hurt bad?" The native understood for he grinned and shook his head.

"Leslie, you ask him, or tell me how to ask him to go with me on the trek."

"Friday, white man wantum you go with him, far, far that way," said Leslie, making a slow gesture which indicated immeasurable distance toward the Outback. Friday fastened great black, unfathomable eyes upon Sterl. They seemed to project Sterl's instincts into the unknown future, giving the moment a singular significance. And he felt impelled to answer for them.

"White man come from far country, away 'cross big water," said Sterl, pointing toward the east and speaking as if to an Indian. "He need Friday . . . track horse . . . kill meat . . . fight . . . tell where pads go."

Sterl felt that never before had he been put to such a searching and incomprehensible test. Perhaps that was his imagination, always prone to exaggerate under stress. But he seemed to feel the elemental intelligence of this aborigine.

"Black fella go alonga you," replied Friday.

Leslie clapped her hands so enthusiastically that the kookaburra deserted her and flew up into the tree. "Good-o! I was sure he'd go, if you asked him," she cried. "Never fear, Sterl, you have made a native your friend. Dad will be happy. His only fear is for his beloved horses. Not for Mum or me!"

Red slouched over to Friday and handed him a cigar.

"Big smoke, Friday. White chief to black chief. Me same blood to boss, heah. Paleface heap much friend black man. Give tobac . . . plenty tobac."

Red's elocution was as funny as it was earnest. Sterl watched for the aborigine's reception of the cowboy's overture. He knew what to do with the cigar, for he bit off the end, which, however, he did not spit out.

"You close up boss?" he asked.

"Shore, Friday," replied Red eagerly.

"You um fadder?"

"Fadder? Hell, no! Gosh, do I look thet old? Him my brudder, Friday."

"Black fella im brudder your brudder," declared Friday loftily, and stalked away.

Sterl felt something poignant and far-reaching. They watched the black lean his *wommera* and spear against the porch and glide on out of sight. Red came out of his fascinated gaze.

"Pard, I'm tellin' you what you can't explain. Bet you a million *pesos* some power beyond our ken put you in the way of thet black man today."

"Right-o! And that's not all," Leslie pealed out enigmatically.

Chapter Five

It turned out that Leslie's freeing of her native bear pets was merely a spiritual act—a matter of saying good bye to them, for they were not confined. They lived in the trees of a small eucalyptus grove in back of the house. Sterl enjoyed the sensation of holding some of them, of feeling their sharp, strong, abnormally large claws cling to his coat. Nature had developed those claws to hold tightly and securely to the branches. The one that pleased Sterl most, and put the simple Red into ecstasy, was a mother bear that carried her baby in a pouch. The little one had his head stuck out, and his bright, black eyes said that he wanted to see all there was to see. Sterl had some vague idea of the natural history of these animals, but Red was the first to display his ignorance.

"Red, you know, of course, about marsupials?" said Leslie.

"Yeah? Wal, if you do, I shore don't know it. What's the idee?" he returned, scratching his red head in perplexity.

"It's only when I've read about animals in other countries that I realize how strange and different our Australian fauna are," said Leslie glibly, as if she knew her subject. "But I've been brought up with our marsupials . . . kangaroos, wallabies, opossums, wombats, and these darling little bears. I've made pets of all of them. Really, it's the easiest thing. The young of marsupials are born like those of cattle or horses, only very tiny, indeed. Baby native bears are scarcely an inch long when they're born. Then they are put in the mother's pouch and nourished there. It takes six months or more before the little beggar can come out and hang onto his mother's back. Now look here."

Gently but firmly Leslie drew the little bear from its mother's pouch and placed it on her back, where it stuck like a burr and appeared perfectly comfortable. Sterl never saw a prettier animal sight than that and said so emphatically.

"Marsupials!" Leslie said. "All sorts of them Down Under, from kangaroos to a little blind mole no longer than my finger."

"Well, I'm a son-of-a-gun!" exclaimed Red. "What's a marsupial?"

This started Leslie on a lecture concerning Australian mammals and birds. When she finished with marsupials, which carry their babies in a pouch, and came to the unbelievable duckbilled platypus which wears fur, suckles its young, lays eggs, and has a bill like a duck and web feet fastened on backward, she stretched Red's credulity to the breaking point.

"How can you stand there, a sweet pictoor of honest girlhood, and be such a orful liar?"

"Talk for yourself, cowboy," Sterl said with his blazing smile. "Leslie, how about that lyre bird Jones said you could show us? The most wonderful bird in Australia?"

"Right-o! Boys, if you'll get up early, so we can go into the bush at daylight, I'll promise you shall hear a lyre bird, and maybe see one. But they are very hard to see."

"It's a date, Leslie, tomorrow mawnin'. Right heah. Hey, pard?"

"You bet. And now let's get to work. I see Friday, packing bundles down the hill. We'll help Leslie, and then I want to fix up your wagon so that it'll be a boat, a boudoir, a sleeping room, and everything else."

"Good-o, magician! Come!"

The porch on the living-room side of the house was littered with boxes and bundles, bales and packs, half a dozen grips and two trunks. Sterl and Red laid hold lustily. They caught up with Friday, laboring and staggering under another trunk, smaller and flatter than those the boys packed down. Even Leslie, with a pretty heavy load for a girl, beat the black down to the wagon. Sterl was curious and reminded Red how they had seen a Navajo Indian carry a whole tree into camp. Just to satisfy himself, Sterl lifted the trunk Friday had fetched down. It was no load for any-one used to packing weights on his shoulder. The native was not accustomed to that kind of work. His wonderful physique de-noted a number of powers, but Sterl imagined he would not be able to budge a two-hundred pound sack of grain.

Presently Sterl left the others, carrying down the lighter stuff while he examined the wagon, which Slyter intended for his womenfolk and all their personal effects, and whatever other stuff for which there was room. It was a sturdy, big wagon with wide-tired wheels and high sides and a roomy canvas top stretched over hoops.

"How about water an' sand?" queried Red dubiously.

"Well, when they are too deep, the load will have to be light-ened. For deep water she'll float. Red, dig up a couple of chisels and hammers while I get rags or old sacks, anything to caulk these seams."

They set to work with a will, and in short order had the wagon bed so that it would not leak. Then, while Red began the same job on another wagon, Sterl devoted himself to fixing up some approach to a prairie-schooner, tent-like dwelling for Leslie and her mother. The girl was not only a capable worker, but her en-thusiasm was infectious. Sterl had her designate the bags and trunks, the contents of which would be needed *en route*, and these he put aside until he had packed the forward half of the wagon bed fully two feet deep.

"Now for the cots, Leslie," he said.

"Stretchers," she corrected smilingly.

"Not much. That makes me think of cripples and sick people."

When Sterl got these placed to the best advantage, he was elated. Then Leslie deftly made the beds. The rear half of the wagon was effectively transformed into a bedroom.

Slyter arrived with the drays and climbed off the driver's seat to begin unhitching. His face was dark, his brow lined and pondering. Sterl wondered what more might have been amiss. Later, when the immediate tasks on their wagon were completed, Sterl followed Jones to the barn, while Red returned to his canvas stitching.

"Roland, pack all the flour on top of this load and tie on a cover," said Slyter. "Hazelton, how's the work progressing?"

"We're about through. There's room in the back of your wagon for more stuff. Hope nothing more came off uptown?"

"Testy day. Just my personal business. I'm leaving Downsville poor as Job's turkey. You'll be interested in this. Ormiston sobered up and tried to square himself. Stanley accepted his good graces."

"Then Ormiston will go on the trek?"

"Yes. He said to tell you he had been half drunk and would speak to you when opportunity afforded. He asked me what guarantee I had that you cowboys were not tramps and adventurers from America . . . if you had any references."

"That was to be expected, Slyter," Sterl rejoined. "I was surprised that you did not ask for any."

"I didn't need any. Nor did Stanley Dann. If we Australians take to a man, that's enough. Ormiston was trying to sow seeds of discord."

"Thank you, Slyter. I'm sure you'll never regret your kindness to me and Red."

"Hathaway and Woolcott left about midday," went on Slyter. "Some of their drovers were drunk. One had to be thrown into a wagon. The Danns are all ready to leave at dawn. We'll start tomorrow sometime."

"How about water holes?"

"No fear. We've had a good few rains lately. There'll be plenty of water . . . maybe too much . . . and grass all the way out of Queensland. Rough going, thick bush, and blacks . . . that'll be all to hold us back. If we could travel straight, we'd make twice the distance every day's trek. But we must keep to level open country, where it's possible. Stanley Dann and his brother Eric had another hot argument. Eric was one of the drovers who made that Gulf trek. He wants to stick to that route. But Stanley argues we should leave it beyond the Diamantina River and head northwest more directly across the Never Never. I agree with Stanley. But there's no hurry. We've months to trek before we reach the Diamantina."

"Boss," called Red, coming over. "I see some good boards heah. Heavier'n hell, but they'll come in orful handy. Can we pack them somewheres?"

"Wherever you like," he answered. "Let's finish up here, so we can get a good night's sleep. Big day tomorrow."

Sterl had faded into deep slumber, from which he was awakened by a slap on the tent. A faint ray penetrated the canvas. "Hello," he called.

"Boss go alonga missy?" It was Friday's deep voice, heralding the day of their departure on the great trek.

"Be right alonga you, Friday," Sterl sang out, and threw back his blankets.

" 'Mawnin', pard," drawled Red, who was sitting on his bed, pulling on his boots. "Sterl, old socks, I'm doubtin' thet you got the fire you used to have. This is the day. I been awake long. Soon we'll be forkin' hosses to ride all the live-long day . . . all the live-long day!"

"Yes, Red, but not the lone prairie. No more the lone prairie. Still this bushland, this Never Never land. . . ." Sterl did not follow out his dreamy and prophetic thought.

It was dim, gray morning when they mounted the shadowy aisle leading up to the house. Cattle were bawling, horses were whistling, dingoes were barking off by the paddocks. Sterl was thinking that soon the birds would awaken, when right over his head, startling and pure and beautiful, rang out: *cur-ra-wong, cur-ra-wong!*

They found Leslie waiting with Friday. "Aren't you ashamed, you sleepy heads? You're late. Come. Don't talk. Don't make the slightest sound."

They followed Friday, a silent, moving shadow in the gray gloom. They walked through heavy grass. The east was brightening. Down in the valley, crows and magpies had melodiously begun the day. Fainter and fainter grew the bawling of cattle. Presently, Friday glided into the bush. He made no more sound than if he were the shadow he resembled. The way appeared to be a zigzag course to avoid brush and trees that loomed like giant, gray specters. Friday halted to listen. Leslie pointed to Sterl's boots, intimating he was too noisy. Red snickered. "Say, I been walkin' on aiggs," he whispered. Leslie put her finger to her lips with a "Shussh." They went on more slowly, halting here and there. Gradually the bush grew lighter. The day was breaking. Soft mist hung low under the pale-trunked trees. They came to a glade that led down into a ravine where water tinkled. The black man's movements and Leslie's intensity provided mystery and portent to the little adventure. Sterl felt them. The ravine opened out wide upon a scene of veiled enchantment. Small trees, pyramid-shaped, pointed up to the brightening sky, and they shone as white as if covered by frost. Great fern trees spread long, lacy, exquisite leaves from a symmetrical head almost to the ground. Huge eucalyptus sent marble-like pillars aloft. The fragrance attacked Sterl's nostrils with an acute, strangling sensation. Sterl heard a thrush breaking into song, and a distant *cur-ra-wong*. A bell-like note struck, lingering upon his ear. Friday halted, and Leslie caught Sterl's hand.

"Gosh, air we huntin' Injuns?" Red whispered very low.

Sterl was concerned with the black man's posture. He was a part of that bushland. As he lifted his hand with the gesture of an Indian, Sterl heard the lovely call of a thrush near at hand. Leslie put her lips right on Sterl's ear. "It is the lyre bird!" Then it seemed to Sterl that his tingling ears caught the songs of other birds, intermingled with that of the thrush. Suddenly a bursting *cur-ra-wong, cur-ra-wong* shot through Sterl. Could that, too, be the lyre bird? The note was repeated again and again, so full of wild melody that it made Sterl ache. It was followed by *caw, caw, caw,* the most dismal and raucous note of a crow, so striking in contrast with the sweet, deep-bellied *cur-ra-wong.*

"Don't you understand, boys?" whispered Leslie, bending her head between them. "The lyre bird is a mocker. He can imitate any sound."

That information added immeasurably to the zest of the moment. Sterl could not believe his ears. The beloved song of his Arizona mockingbirds was here transcended. But that sweet concatenation of various bird notes was disrupted by the bawling of a cow.

Red let out a stifled—"Aw!"—most eloquent of his regret to have the lovely concert broken.

Leslie squeezed Sterl's hand. "Not a cow, you tenderfeet! It's our lyre bird!"

But that marvelous imitation was not repeated. From off in the woods, quite a distance, sounded a mournful, rich note, like the dong of a bell.

"Another, lyre bird. Oh, but we're lucky," whispered Leslie. "Boys, would you like to try to see one? A chance in a thousand! And none, if you make the slightest noise."

After such injunction as that, and inspired to superhuman effort, Sterl and Red succeeded in following their guides with noiseless stealth. Daylight came into the forest while they were proceeding a very short distance in what seemed a long time.

The aborigine sank down on one knee to become a black statue, as if modeled by a great sculptor. Leslie softly dragged Sterl to his knees, and Red bent over them. Leslie's grip on Sterl's hand precluded need for her to point. Sterl knew that she saw the object of their search, and he marveled at the feeling she roused in him.

Across a little leafy glade he noticed low foliage move and part to admit a dark, brown bird, half the size of a grown hen-turkey. It had a sleek, delicate head. As the bird stepped daintily out from under the foliage, its extraordinary tail stood up erect and exquisite. It described the perfect shape of a lyre. Long, slender fern-like feathers, broad, dark, velvety brown, barred in shiny white or gray, with graceful, curling tips that bowed and dipped as the lyre bird moved. It was the epitome of the loveliness of the wild in Nature. Sterl, who from boyhood had always loved to watch birds, sustained a lasting reward for that lifelong habit.

The lyre bird pecked under the leaves, sent them scattering, and devoured a luckless grub or insect. Then with gorgeous tail swaying with an unbelievable grace it ran out of sight under the foliage. The watchers waited a moment, tense and hopeful, but the bird did not reappear or sing again.

"Now, what do you say?" Leslie asked, rising with Sterl's hand still in hers.

"Lovely beyond compare," responded Sterl feelingly. "To hear that lyre bird, then see him, gave me an exhilarating sense of happiness. Leslie, if Australia holds no more for me than acquaintance with its beautiful birds and strange creatures, I shall be repaid for . . . for all it cost me to come."

"Oh, Sterl! What a sweet and eloquent tribute! Thank you! And now, Red, what do you say?"

"Leslie, you mean to tell me that dog-gone lyre bird bawled like a cow?"

"It did, Red, honest and true. It can imitate the ringing stroke of an axe. I've heard that."

"Wal, I pass. I give up. I'm gonna go back on the old sagebrush mockers of Texas. Never love them less, mind you, 'cause mockin'birds have sung to me all my life. But for wonder, for music, wal, yore lyre bird has our mockers skinned to a frazzle."

"That must mean something," returned Leslie, giggling. "Come. We'll be late. And Dad will row. Let's run."

With lithe and long stride the girl slipped through the woods and vanished. The black followed. Red broke into his clumsy, cowboy-booted gait, and as he broke through brush ahead of Sterl, there suddenly came a crash and a thump. Red tumbled head over heels, as a half-grown kangaroo or a wallaby bounded away into the woods. He came up with a gun in his hand and fire in his blue eyes.

"Pard! Thet son-of-a-gun walloped me one with his hoof or his tail. It shore hurts. I'll bore him for thet."

Sterl laughed heartily and held his irate friend. "We better look before we leap. Next time it might be a big tiger snake."

"By golly, yes. Go ahaid, pard. My eyes air shore pore."

Their arrival at the house at sunrise was greeted by a terrific uproar from Leslie's kookaburra, Jack, and six others of his kind, all laughing together in a fiendish din.

They went in to breakfast; Roland and Larry were leaving, sober as judges. Bill Williams, the cook, was banging pots and pans with unnecessary force. Slyter looked as if he were going to a funeral, and his wife was weeping. Leslie's smile vanished. She served the cowboys, who made short work of that meal.

"Boss, what's the order for today?" Sterl queried shortly.

"Drake's mustering for the trek," Slyter replied gruffly.

Leslie followed them out. "I'll catch up somewhere. I'd go with you now, but Mum. . . . Ride King and Jester, won't you?"

Sterl found difficulty in expressing his sympathy. The girl was brave, although deeply affected by her mother's grief. It really was a terrible thing to do—this forsaking a comfortable home in a beautiful valley to ride out into the unknown and forbidding wilderness.

"Shore we'll ride King an' Jester," said Red hastily. "Now, Leslie, don't you shenanigan on us the last minnit!"

"What's that?" she murmured wistfully.

"Wal, thet's backin' out. Leavin' me an' Sterl to go alone. 'Cause, Leslie, I reckon now we'd never go but for you."

"Red, I'll never shenanigan . . . on the trek . . . or anything."

The, cowboys turned away and hurried down the hill. "Kinda tough, at thet," Red soliloquized. "Shore is a game kid. Wonder if Beryl is, too? Must be, 'cause she's givin' up a lot more."

After rolling the beds and tent, which they loaded in Roland's wagon, there was apparently no more to do save make for the horses. They saw Roland coming from the barn, leading the harnessed teams. "Roland is going to hitch up," said Sterl. "Looks like an early start."

"Shore. Slyter wants to hit the trail *pronto*. Wal, chaps, canteens, slickers, rifles. Thet's about all, pard. Heah, take yore own, an' let's rustle."

At the paddock they found Larry, leading out King and Jester. All the other horses were gone, except Larry's and Leslie's Duke which stood saddled, waiting.

"Howdy, Larry. You're sure moving," said Sterl. "Sorry we're late. Leslie took us to hear a lyre bird. And we saw one. I wouldn't have missed that for anything."

"'Mawnin', Larry," added Red. "Wait for us. We don't want to get lost out there."

"We'll all be lost in a few weeks."

"Yeah? Wal, misery loves company."

King surprised Sterl with his willingness to be saddled and bridled. He knew he was leaving the paddock, and he liked it. Sterl tied on the slicker and canteen and slipped into his worn leather chaps, conscious of a quickening of his pulse. Red, who was in the act of donning his, let out a telltale groan. Then Sterl took up his rifle and walked around in front of the horse. "Are you gun shy, King?" The black knew a gun and, showing no fear, stood without a quiver while Sterl shoved the rifle into the saddle sheath.

"Say, air you a mud hen, thet you go duckin' jest 'cause I've got a gun?" Red was complaining to his horse.

In another moment they were in the saddles, and, joining Larry, they rode out into the open valley.

"Larry, air you leavin' any girl behind?" Red drawled. "From the sick look you got, I've a hunch you air."

"Fact is, Red, I'm leaving two."

"You don't say? For cripe's sake, why didn't you fetch one anyhow?"

"Tried to. But neither would come."

"Dog-gone! Girls are fickle critters."

"Did you leave any behind in America?"

"Wal, I remember about six."

"Shut up, you Romeos," interposed Sterl. "This is a serious moment. None of us will ever experience it again."

"Pard, I been sayin' good bye to places . . . an' girls . . . since I was four weeks old," declared Red.

Ahead of them, about a mile out in the widening valley, a herd of grazing horses and beyond them Slyter's cattle added the last link to the certainty of the trek. Sterl's heart swelled. He felt for these courageous drovers. It was in him, too, this seeking and finding spirit, this great urge of the true pioneer.

Waiting this side of the horses were three riders, superbly mounted. Their garb and the trappings of the horses appeared markedly different from those of the Americans. Sterl had made up his mind about these riders of Slyter's; still he gave a keen scrutiny. Drake was middle-aged, honest and forcible of aspect, strong of build, which, however, did not indicate excessive labor on horseback. The other two, Benson and Heald, were sturdy young men, not out of their teens, and sat their saddles as if used to them. Larry's introduction was brief, and the space between horses precluded handshaking.

"Drake, we have Slyter's orders to report to you," Sterl added after the greeting.

"I've sent Monkton ahead to let down the bars," replied Drake. "We fenced the valley ahead, there, where it narrows. I'll join him. Benson and Heald will drove behind us, one on each side. You boys bring up the rear."

"No particular formation?"

"Just let the mob graze along at a walk. We'll keep right on till Slyter halts us, probably at Blue Gum."

Drake said no more and rode away to the left, accompanied by Heald, while Benson trotted off to the right.

"Huh! Short an' sweet. All in the day's work," complained Red. "I kinda wish these Australians would show some feelin'. Why, hell, this is wonderful. Larry, air you daid upstairs, too?"

"I don't know about upstairs, but I've got a pain here," he replied, putting his hand to his breast.

"Good-o. So've I. Wal, pard?"

"Red, you ought to be in front. But, no doubt, that'll come in time. Spread out, boys, to left and right corners. I'll take the center."

"*Whoopee!*" Red's stentorian yell pealed out, rolling down the valley, ringing in echo from hill to hill.

In another moment Sterl was alone. An old, familiar, stinging sensation beset him. How many hours, days, months had he bestrode his horse, along behind a herd of cattle? He lighted a cigarette. King pranced a little and wanted to go. Sterl patted the grand, arched neck and fell at once into his old habit of talking to his horse. "King, we don't know each other yet. But if you're as good as you look, we'll be pards. It's a long trek across the Never Never to those Kimberleys. Take it easy. I see you're too well trained to graze with a bridle on. You can unlearn that, King."

Sterl stilled the restless horse and sat his saddle motionless, waiting for the tremendous moment that was to be the start. He felt the swelling wave of emotion, daring to sweep over him. Impossible to escape from fact! He was to ride across a whole unknown continent, from which journey, if he survived it, he would never return. The climbing sun, glorious over the bushland, shone in his face from the east—from over the ranges he had ridden, from over the vast Pacific. Sterl faced the east. And he could not keep back a farewell whisper—"Good bye, Nan. . . . Good bye!"—which seemed final and irrevocable.

When he turned back again, prompted by the keen King, the long line of cattle was on the move. The great trek had begun. Red's mellow cowboy yell pealed across the wide space between them. He was moving. He waved a beckoning hand. Larry, on the other side, had started. Then, King, with a snort, leaped forward. Sterl pulled him from trot to walk. Once at the heels of the horses Sterl let out his answering call.

Leisurely the bank of horses grazed forward in the wake of the cattle. They were free. They knew it. Piercing whistles split the air; cows bawled lustily. But there was no milling, no crowding close together, no ranging wide of an excited steer, no running wild of any of the Thoroughbreds. It was as if this lazy grazing along had been their custom.

Suddenly Sterl's emotions reached a bursting climax, and his transfigured sight took in the scene.

It was bright, glittering, green-gold, with the many-colored mob of cattle and band of horses moving as if to rhythm. Only slow, puffing clouds of dust arose in spots. Flocks of blackbirds wheeled and circled; hawks soared above, dark spots against the blue sky; from the wooded slopes pealed the mellow *cur-ra-wong, cur-ra-wong* of magpies; the songs of other birds filled the air. Something majestic attended the slow beginning of this trek.

Sterl looked back down the valley. It was filled with a rich, thick, amber light. Fleecy, white clouds sailed above the green line of bush. The gold of wattles and the scarlet of eucalyptus stood out vividly even in the brilliance of the sun-drenched foliage. A faint and failing column of smoke rose above the forsaken farmhouse that seemed to have gone to sleep among the wattles on the slope. A glancing gleam of tranquil, reed-bordered pond caught Sterl's sight. All this color, all this pastoral beauty, this land of flowers and grass and blossoming trees, this land of milk and honey, so it seemed, was being abandoned for the chimera of the pioneer who, with strange vision, saw into the future. But this was the luxuriant season after full rains. Sterl could not picture what drought and heat might do to this paradise. Stanley Dann knew; Slyter knew. And they were leaving it for a far richer, far greater country, where they alone would be kings of vast ranges.

Chapter Six

Sterl espied the white, canvas-covered dray, driven by Bill Williams, climbing the hill road toward Downsville. And behind him rolled Jones, driving one of the wagons which soon passed out of sight, as if by magic. Three wagons appeared miles ahead, moving along, close together. But there was no sign of Leslie. She had gone on with the wagons. Sterl looked in vain for her, but he recognized eight of her Thoroughbreds. That pleased him, proving what a cowboy gift he possessed. He calculated, too, that the mob was traveling over two miles an hour. The long grass, reaching to their knees, made this progress possible. Already they had been seven hours on the trek. Only in the creek bottoms of Texas was there such verdure as grew prodigally on these downs.

Long since King had satisfied his appetite. He was full, lazy, drowsy. But there were the other horses ahead. He kept on without word or touch from his rider. No stragglers to round up! No drags lagging behind the herd! Sterl sat his saddle, dreamy, content, lulled by sensorial perceptions into the unthinking mood that was the open's chief charm.

He knew not how time passed, but sooner or later he awakened to westering sun, to the long halloo of his comrade, of halted cattle and horses. Stirring to see—a huge, dead gum tree, bleached and gnarled, marking a sunset-flushed stream—outcropping rock and jungle beyond—and to the right lanes of open country leading into the bush.

First camp! Sterl sighted it with singular joy. Cattle and horses made for the creek and spread along its low bank for a mile. When they had drunk their fill, some of the cattle fell again to grazing while many of them lay down to rest. The horses trooped back to their grazing. In Sterl's judgment both would require little night guarding on such pasture as that.

He let King quench his thirst, then rode down the creek into camp. Pungent wood smoke brought back other camp scenes. But no campsite he could remember had possessed such an imposing landmark as the great, dead, blue gum tree. On its spreading branches Sterl espied herons, parrots, a hawk perched on a top-most tip, kookaburras low down, and other birds he could not name.

The wagons were spaced conveniently, though not close together. Locating his own, Sterl dismounted to strip King and let him go. Then he hauled tent and beds out of the wagon and had begun unrolling them when Leslie approached like a slender boy rider in worn garb.

"Well, so here you are? I wondered if you'd ever catch up," Sterl said.

"I hadn't the heart to leave Mum today," she replied, her pretty face showing traces of recent sorrow. "I . . . would have been all right, but for her."

"Why, you're all right anyhow, Leslie. Don't look back . . . don't think back! Our first camp's a dandy. Where's Friday and your dad?"

"Both over there. Friday walked all the way, sometimes leading Duke. I rode a little. Mum came out of it all at once. Dad is just fine. He and Drake just had a pull at a bottle. And here come Red and Larry."

Sterl with Leslie crossed over to the center of camp, where Friday was packing water. Williams bustled about between fire and wagon, and Slyter, after rummaging under the seat of his wagon, brought a little book to Leslie.

"Les, one of your jobs is keeping our journal. Here you are. Don't ever miss a day. Keep date, distance trekked, weather, incident, everything."

"Holy Mackeli, what a job!" exclaimed Leslie. "But I'll love it. How far today?"

"A long trek. Sixteen miles?" Slyter said dubiously.

"And then some," interposed Sterl. "Ask Red. He's a wonderful judge of distance. Now, boss, how about night guard?"

"Three changes. Two men on for three hours. Eight to eleven, eleven to two, two till five. Which watch will you and Krehl like?"

"The late one, boss. We're used to the wee small hours."

"Aborigines seldom attack before dawn. But you'll have our black man Friday. Hazelton, you'll find him a tower of help."

"How about hobbling horses?"

"None of ours will need it. They won't stray away from grass like this. Keep them bunched, that's all."

Sterl returned to where he had left the tent and beds. Red walked up from somewhere, the happy blaze in his blue eyes. "Wal, you old snoozer, I seen you takin' catnaps on an' off. Gosh, wasn't it one old-time first day in a hundred? Nothin' to do but fork yore saddle an' browse."

They all agreed it had been a fine first day. And over dinner all congratulated themselves and each other for the day's accomplishments. Then it was time for sleep.

As he prepared his bed, Sterl listened to the swishy sound made by flying-foxes over his head and the bawl of cattle. Then Leslie appeared by his side. "Are you feeling better," he asked hesitantly.

"Red cheered me up with an argument, then a funny story. I'll be right-o tomorrow. Good night, Sterl."

"Pleasant dreams, pioneer girl," replied Sterl.

"Ain't a damn bit sleepy," said Red, joining up with Sterl as he walked tentward.

"Neither am I, pard. Excited, lively. But I'm bone-tired. Let's hit the hay."

The thud of horses' hoofs awoke Sterl before Larry called into the tent: "Two o'clock, boys. Roll out."

"Aw," groaned Red, "but a cowboy's life is ha-ard."

In a moment more they were outside. A campfire emphasized the black night. Friday knelt before it, drinking out of a tin.

"I'll pour you a cup of tea," Larry said, handing Sterl the halters.

"Tea? . . . I pass," growled Red.

"Better have one, Red. Let's fall into the habit. *¿Quién sabe?* We may need it."

"OK, pard. Wal, heah's my white hoss Larry fetched. Which one have you?"

"Don't remember him in the dark. Looks all horse." What an unusual and fine thing, Sterl reflected, to have a strange horse stand in the dead of night to be bridled and saddled by a strange man! "Well, horse," he soliloquized, "I've only got so much regard to divide up, but you'll have yours."

Ready to go, the cowboys repaired to the fire for the tea Larry had poured for them. It was scalding hot and strong as acid, but Sterl downed his. Red did likewise with the aid of fearful profanity.

"Larry, where's the mob?" queried Sterl.

"About a mile out, resting. Horses close by."

Sterl found his night hawk sight returning.

Red said: "Pard, we gotta learn these strange stars. We only know thet grand Southern Cross. Gosh! What a bunch of brilliant sky lanterns! But, hell, they don't make no cross!"

"Red, that great white cloud across the sky must be the Milky Way of the Southern Hemisphere."

"Got ours skinned to death."

The band of horses was huddled between camp and the mob of cattle. They were quiet, only a few grazing. The cattle had bedded down to make a huge, irregular, black patch on the grass.

"My Gawd, pard, shades of the old range!" Red cried poignantly. "Bury me on the lone prairiee."

"If you sing that, I'll murder you," hissed Sterl.

"What'll we do, Sterl? Circle or stand guard?"

"Circle, Red, till we get the lay of the herd."

Red rode on into the bright starlight, and the cold wind brought back the smoke of his cigarette. Sterl turned to walk his horse in the other direction. Old sensorial habits reasserted themselves—the keen ear, the keen eye, the keen nose, and the feel of air, wind, cold. The cattle and the horses were quiet. Strange, discordant barks of dingoes lent unreality to the wild. Sterl sensed only hunger in their utterance. Wide-winged birds or foxes passed over his head with a silky swish.

In half an hour Sterl heard Red's horse before he sighted it, a moving, ghostly white in the brilliant gloom. Presently the cowboys met, halting a moment.

"Fine setup, pard," said Red. "A lazy cowboy job!"

"All well on my side. Go halfway 'round and stand watch."

"Air kinda penetratin', pard. I reckon I'll mosey to an' fro," Red returned, and rode on.

When Sterl reached the end of a half circle, he was amazed to see a tall, black man, like an apparition, stalk up to him. How easily one of these aborigines could spear him or knock him off his horse with a boomerang! This black, of course, was Friday, free to exercise his trust as he saw it. Sterl hailed him, to receive an affirmative reply. Then the black reached him.

"Cheeky black fella close up," Friday said, striding on.

Sterl pondered that speech while he watched Friday to see just how far he could distinguish him. By straining his eyes, Sterl kept track of the black for a goodly distance. And thereafter he swept his gaze in wary half-circle. These aborigines would kill and steal beef. Sterl had been assured of that. Farther Outback such a night watch would be a perilous duty.

But nothing happened. The night wore on toward dawn. Friday did not return, although Sterl had a feeling that the black man was close. Once he saw Red strike a match. Sterl sat his saddle, got down to walk to and fro, mounted to watch another hour, and slowly, mysteriously the dreaming, darkest hour passed.

From the first faint lighting in the east there were gradual, almost imperceptible changes until the dim downs were clear, and the cattle began to stir. Sterl circled around to meet Red. "'Mawnin'," said that worthy. "J'ever see such a tame bunch of cattle? But I had a scare at thet. One of them flyin' bats hit me on the haid. How'd you make out?"

"Just killed time. This sort of work will spoil us. It's after five. Let's ride in."

Breakfast was waiting. Two of the wagons were already hitched up. Friday was in the act of loading the cowboys' tent and bedding into one of them. Leslie stood by the fire, drinking tea. She waved a gauntleted hand. Booted and spurred, with cheeks like roses, she looked, indeed, what Red had called her—an eyeful for a cowboy. While Sterl and Red hurried with their meal, Slyter drove off, with a cheery call for those behind. Jones soon followed Slyter's wheel tracks for the ford. Larry came riding up, leading three horses, one of which was Duchess, Leslie's favorite.

Red saw the girl swing up on her saddle with one hand, and he said: "Pard, I gotta hand it to that kid. If Beryl is like her, wal, it's all day with me."

When they rode out on fresh horses, the sun had just burnt red and glorious over the eastern bush, and the downs were as if aflame. Drake had the mob ready. Leslie and Larry were driving the straggling horses. Red loped across the wide flank to take up his position on the far right, and his long, pealing cowboy call to the cattle rang through Sterl. Friday came along with giant strides, carrying his spears and *wommera* in his left hand and a boomerang in the other. Leslie rode loping back to turn on the line even with Sterl. Then the four rear riders, pressing forward, drove the horses upon the heels of the cattle, and the day's drive was on.

The bustle and hurry before the start seemed to come to an abrupt end in the slow, natural walk of grazing cattle and horses. Sterl watched the black man, marveling at the human being who could set out on foot to cover thousands of miles. Friday would be a source of endless interest and education to Sterl. The picturesque girl, bareheaded, with the sunlight shining on her hair, was not too far distant for Sterl to watch and admire her in secret. For the rest there were the Thoroughbreds to draw his attention, and the colored mob of cattle, and the myriad of winged life about, the rocky and timbered slope on the left, and the wide, winding lanes of grass ahead, bordered by patches of scrub and ridges of bushland. The wilderness to the fore could not be too far, too wide, too hard for Sterl Hazelton.

Three times before afternoon, Leslie rode over to Sterl on some pretext or other, the last of which was an offer to share the bit of lunch she had brought.

"No, thanks, Leslie. A cowboy learns to go without. And on this trek in particular, I'm going to emulate your black man."

"I suppose you cowboys live without fun, food, or . . . love?" she queried flippantly.

"We do, indeed."

"Like hoo you do," she flashed. "Oh well, maybe you do. This is the third time you've snubbed me so far today. You're an old crosspatch."

Sterl laughed, though he felt a little nettled. The girl was distracting. She did interrupt the even, almost unconscious, ebb and flow of his sensorial perceptions. Presently, no doubt, as this lonely trek lengthened out, and the inescapable accidents and dangers of it brought them close together, depending on one another, she would be pretty nigh irresistible. Sterl resented the healing of his heart, the fading of sad memories, and the singular appeal of this virile chestnut-haired daughter of Australia.

"I've been called worse than that by sentimental young ladies," replied Sterl satirically. "Would you expect me to babble poetry to you or listen to your silly chatter?"

"Oh-h!" cried Leslie, outraged, reddening from neck to brow. And she wheeled her horse to lope far along the line toward Red.

"That should hold her a while," Sterl murmured regretfully. "Too bad I've got to be mean to her. But. . . ."

He forgot her presently. Mile on mile the slow progress was offset by new vistas. A flock of emus held his gaze for long. The trek crossed one dry stream bed and another flowing creek. There was no obstacle to hinder the cattle, and the horses might have been in their paddock. Once, from a slow heave of land, Sterl caught a glimpse of Dann's mob, far ahead, like a huge cloud shadow on the green.

A bit of open bush, where scrub and scattered gums made the

stock hard to locate, marked the flat country below the low eminence from which he could see afar. Progress there was slow. The drovers rode to and fro, keeping their charge intact. A league of rolling grassland led into a thicker area of bush. Once penetrated, it proved to hold a gray-green oval which was bisected by a winding line of wattle trees, a veritable snake of gold crawling across the meadow. Slyter had halted for camp at the foot of a ridge, running out like a spur from the rougher bushland. Manifestly a stream came from around that ridge.

It was no later than mid-afternoon with the sun still warm. A short trek, Sterl thought, perhaps owing to the fact of longer distance to water the next day. Cattle and horses made for the stream that turned out to be a river that could not be forded with wagons at the point Sterl reached it. Letting the horse drink, Sterl eyed the golden-lined wattles with appreciation.

In camp, Sterl was pitching the tent when Red and Leslie rode in, followed at some distance by Friday. The girl with head up and eyes forward rode by Sterl as if he had not been there. Red slid out of his saddle in his old inimitable way, and soon with a slap on the flank he sent his horse scampering.

"About ten miles, I'd say," he drawled. "Slick camp and a hefty river. Say, pard, what'n'll did you do to the kid?"

"Nothing," replied Sterl.

"Wal, you're a dad-blasted liar. Leslie was all broke up."

"She bothers me, Red."

"Ah-huh. I savvy. Same heah. But I'm feared the kid likes you an' hasn't no idee a-tall about it."

Sterl remained silent, revolving in his mind a singular realization prompted by Red's talk—that he had felt a distinct throb of pleasure. This would never do, yet how could he help it?

The cowboys finished their chores, then strolled over to the busy Slyter. Leslie sat near, writing in her journal.

"Boss, how come you hauled up so soon?" asked Red.

"Long trek tomorrow to next water."

"Where will we ford this river?" added Sterl.

"Below here. There's a shallow place. But the river is high.

Dann crossed ten miles or more below. If it had been the rainy season, we'd cross before camping."

"Any work we can lay a hand to?"

"No. Early camps like this make a trek good. There's two between Brisbane and Downsville, if you remember. Rest or find tasks of your own. There's always something. You can always hunt. Our main ration will be meat, you know. And the more game you kill, the less beef we need to use."

"Dog-gone! Pard, get the black and let's rustle."

Sterl turned to the girl. "Leslie, where is Friday?" As she did not appear to hear, he asked her again. Then she looked up. "Please do not annoy me, Mister Hazelton. I'm composing poetry," she said coldly.

Sterl kept a straight face until his back was turned. Red drawled: "Holy Mackeli, pard! Didn't she freeze you? Say, I hope you didn't insult her . . . or somethin'."

"How could I do that, Red?"

"Well, you needn't look at me like I was a skunk. You might have tried to kiss her, anyhow. Leastways, I've known you to do thet on short acquaintance."

"No, you brainless baboon. I asked Leslie if she wanted me to babble poetry to her and listen to her silly prattle."

"Haw! Haw! Wal, you did? No wonder she has her chin up. Dad-blast you, pard, I reckon thet's why wimmin lose their haids over you so *pronto*. I'll try that on Beryl."

"Umpumm, pard. Save Beryl's life or ride a chariot race for her."

"Damn if I don't!" Red ejaculated gleefully.

They got their rifles, and, finding Friday, they took him along. Upstream, around the corner of a ridge, they found thickets leading up to the bush. Red evinced great interest in the black's weapons. "Boomerang an' *wommera*? They're some tongue-twisters, pard. Pretty soundin', though. It'll shore be a circus to see him use them."

Chapter Seven

Day after day passed on the trek. Camp after camp left Sterl with some memory of location or incident. The late afternoon hour arrived, at length, when Slyter caught up with the Dann brothers and their partners. The place befitted such an important occasion. From here the drovers would push on together to the end. It was the gateway to a valley between mountain ranges. Giant eucalyptus trees towered loftily, their opal-lined trunks and lacy canopy of green bright in the westering sun. They stood far apart, stately and unsociable. Here and there blossoming wattle trees, like huge golden mounds, graced the verdant parks, through which a crystal stream ran babbling over rocky shoals. Sterl, growing more used to beautiful campsites, still protested this one was too good to be true.

Slyter led his mob to the left and hauled up on a wide curve of the stream. In the center, half a mile from Slyter, the Dann encampment, with its ten wagons and drays, its canvas tents bright against the green, its blue smokes and active figures, made an imposing sight in Sterl's eyes, like a plains caravan. Farther to the right showed the camp of Hathaway and Woolcott. Hundreds of horses grazed in between. Across the river flamed the enormous mob of cattle which the drovers had evidently thrown together. Twice as much stock as Sterl had ever seen at one time. It bore some resemblance to a herd of buffalo. Whatever the magnificent effrontery of these drovers, the bold challenge flung into the teeth of inland Australia, with its rivers and cannibals, its wastelands and jungles, its terrific heat and growth, the spectacle was one to wring sincere tribute from Sterl. This Stanley Dann possessed the qualities of the country.

With Slyter's mob and remuda placed to rest and graze, the drovers made toward camp by diverse routes. Sterl arrived first. More days passed than he could remember; the black horse, King, had completed his conquest over memories and exceptions the cowboy clung to. They had taken to each other. King recognized a gentle, firm, and expert master; Sterl reluctantly crowned the black for spirit, tirelessness and speed, and for a remarkable power in the water. After a first ford over slippery rocks Sterl put iron shoes on the horse and that made him invincible.

While Sterl was unrolling the tent, Red and Leslie rode in. Exposure and sun had given the girl a golden tan that magnified her charm. After that tiff the second day out, Leslie had persistently ignored Sterl. But this day, knowing as they all knew that they were to come up with the main company of drovers, she had manifested unmistakable signs of remorse and uneasiness. Sterl, however, gave her no encouragement.

"Pile off, Red, and go through the motions," called Sterl, and soon his comrade was helping, markedly reticent for him.

"Well, what's on your chest?" queried Sterl, desiring to express himself.

"Pard, I reckon it's over," Red said without his cheerful drawl.

"What?"

"Wal, this nice, long, easy drive. It'll be hell from now on."

"Let it come."

"Say, you cheer me up. Sterl, what do you think? Leslie has commissioned me to beg you to forgive her for bein' catty."

"Yeah? Red, you're sure a good friend to have on one's side, but you can tell Leslie to ask me herself."

"OK, pard. I won't give you away, but you'll forgive her, I'm shore."

"I have nothing to forgive. I was deliberately rude to her. And I'm sorry. A few sunny days on horseback changed my mood. Red, she's worried, now we've caught up with the big outfit."

"Shore is. An' so'm I. But once I get mad I'll be good-o, as Leslie says. All same for you?"

"Right-o, as Leslie says. It won't be long now. But Red, let's be wise. We're not on the Texas trails. And we can't judge these Australians as we would our kind. We may be testy, sore, suspicious *hombres*."

"Shore. An' we'll find human life jest the same heah, mebbe not so generally ornery, but individuals like Ormiston will make up for thet. He's got four riders, so Jones tells me, an' he didn't know 'em from Adam an' didn't like 'em one damn' bit."

"We'll look them over before we judge."

"OK. But tip me off. S'pose Ormiston tries to make a sucker out of you?"

"Red, old pard, you're not paying me any compliment."

"I know, Sterl. But you've been different out heah. Harder it 'pears to me. An' more than ever prone to keep to yoreself."

"Don't let it worry you, friend. All I need is a jolt."

Williams was a cook who not only spread appetizing and rationed meals in accordance with Slyter's orders, but he was expeditious. Before sundown that important day, supper had been disposed of, and Slyter had strode off to visit Dann accompanied by Drake and calling upon Sterl and Red to follow.

"Boss, take Red and let me stay in camp," suggested Sterl.

"No. I may need you. Stanley will ask for you. As for Ormiston . . . the sooner you meet him the better. I ask you to meet him on the grounds you would adopt in your own country."

"Thanks, Slyter. I'll come."

"Dad, please let me come with the boys? I want to see Beryl," entreated Leslie.

"Of course, my dear. I'd forgotten you."

"Red, you run along with Leslie," Sterl added. "I want to shave. Be with you in a jiffy."

While Sterl attended to his own semi-weekly task, Friday stood a little way off, an attentive observer. Sterl had curbed his natural tendency to be over-friendly and generous with the black, as he had often been with Indian scouts.

"Friday, many smokes today," said Sterl.

"Plenty black fella alonga here."

"Cheeky bad fellas, Friday?"

"Might be."

Presently Sterl sauntered along the streambank, under the giant gums, toward Dann's camp. How cowboys he remembered would have reveled in this strange spot with its colored songsters filling the air with bright plumage and mellow notes, its incredible towering trees with koala bears up in the branches, its crystal, murmuring stream that surely wound down the valley from a high waterfall in the distance, lastly the great mob of tame cattle that would have brought keenest delight, the score on score of wonderful horses!

Under perhaps the grandest monarch of all these eucalyptus trees, Sterl came upon the wagon and camp of Dann's sister and his daughter, Beryl. Leslie was talking excitedly with the girl, while Red stood, sombrero in hand, listening to the sturdy, comely Australian women. Sterl was introduced and greeted cordially. Beryl wore boy's garb, more attractive and not so worn as Leslie's. Her fair face had known the daily touch of sun and to her decided advantage. She was more than pretty.

"Doesn't it seem long since we all met, 'way back there in Downsville?" she asked. "I nearly died of homesickness for days. But now it's not too bad. I intend to be a drover, like Leslie."

"Wal, see heah, miss," Red interposed, "we shore need another trail driver."

"Oh, Beryl, it'd be lovely to have you ride with us sometimes," murmured Leslie.

Sterl added his persuasion, augmented by his gaze.

"How queer the way you cowboys carry your pistols!" Beryl exclaimed, pointing to the low-hanging sheaths well down the right thighs. "Dad's drovers stick them in their hip pockets, or under a belt."

"Wal, Miss Dann," drawled Red, "you see us cowboys gotta throw a gun quick sometimes, an' it needs to be handy."

"Where do you throw it?" she asked curiously.

"Aw, at jack rabbits or any ole varmint thet happens along."

"Miss Beryl, Red is teasing you," chimed in Sterl. "To throw a gun means to jerk it out, quickly . . . like this."

"How strange! Oh, so you can shoot quickly at your antagonists?"

"Exactly. And the cowboy who throws his quickest has a better chance to survive."

"Mister Red, then, was taking advantage of my ignorance?" she queried a little constrainedly.

"It's a way Red has to joke."

"Yeah?" drawled that worthy, his coolness matching Beryl's constraint. "Wal, there shore ain't any joke about the six notches on the handle of Hazelton's gun."

"Come now, Red, don't mystify the girls further," Sterl insisted. "Please excuse us, Miss Beryl. Our boss wants us in on the conference over here."

Sterl led his silent comrade over to a little group of men, standing in a half-circle back of Stanley Dann, who sat before a box doing duty as a table. Here the cowboys met the leader's partners, not including Ormiston. One glance and a handshake sufficed for Sterl's favorable impression. Eric Dann was the younger of the two brothers, short and strongly built, with rather stern, dark features. Hathaway was tall and florid, apparently under fifty years. Woolcott appeared fully sixty, a bearded man, with deep set eyes and gloomy mien.

"All of you have a look at this map," spoke up Dann, indicating a paper on the box. "Eric drew it from memory. And, of course, it isn't accurate as to distance or points. Still, it will give you a general idea of the country as far as the headwaters of the rivers that run into the Gulf of Carpenteria. This line traced here marks the road we're on and which we can trek fairly well. There will be breaks where sandstorms or floods have obliterated it. But we can always locate it again. This dark line, way up in Queensland, is the Diamantina River, an important obstacle in our way. This vast open space, without dot or line, represents the Never Never . . . some two thousand miles across, perhaps.

Beyond, to the northwest, this long area of black lines represents the Kimberleys, our destination . . . please God! You observe that they are northwest. Our direction is the same. Hello, Ormiston, you're just in time to give your opinion. You're already familiar with what I am outlining. Well, my brother wants to follow this old wagon trek beyond the headwaters of the Diamantina River and the Warburton, on north across the Gulf rivers, and then west to Syndham and the Kimberleys. There's no telling how much farther this route will be, probably a thousand or two miles. Too far! And just as hard. It's only good feature is that it has been traveled. Striking west beyond Diamantina to the Warburton, following that to its headwaters, and then striking straight west, will be a short cut, and save us, Lord only knows how much!. I call for a vote from each man present, except Drake. And I include these American cowboys, with your permission, because they have had extensive experience droving cattle across the plains."

The vote ended in a deadlock, Slyter, Sterl, and Red arraying themselves upon Stanley Dann's side, and the others standing by Eric. The leader showed no feeling whatsoever, but his brother Eric and Ormiston argued vigorously for the longer and once traveled route.

Sterl's perspicuity and intensity had had no greater test. He listened and bent piercing eyes upon this quartet, and at length his deductions were clear-cut, and he would have sworn by them. Eric Dann feared to take the great trek into the unknown. Ormiston had some personal reason for standing by Eric Dann, and he had influenced Hathaway and Woolcott.

"Very well. It hangs fire for the present," concluded Stanley Dann. "Perhaps the months to come will bring at least one of you gentlemen to reason."

If Ormiston tried to conceal his satisfaction, he failed to hide it from Sterl. His handsome, sun-browned face, clean-shaven, told nothing one way or another. But it was a man's eyes in which Sterl had learned to read secrets and greed and hate, and the thought to kill. That was a gunman's instinct.

"Hazelton, I don't impose upon you any colossal task," Stanley Dann said. "But I'm just curious to know what you think, if you'll commit yourself."

"Are there black men all over this Never Never Land?" countered Sterl.

"Yes, according to our few explorers."

"If they can be propitiated, perhaps we could learn from them, as the pathfinders in my country have learned from the Indians."

"Good-o," boomed the leader. "That's an idea . . . a new one, as far as we're concerned."

"These niggers are a mean, lying, unscrupulous race," Ormiston put in contemptuously.

"Perhaps because of the treatment white men have accorded them," spoke up Slyter.

Ormiston chafed under any opposition to his wishes, but for the moment he let well enough alone. He impressed Sterl further as a secretive, deep, and calculating character. After this conference Sterl felt recurrent and instinctive distrust in this man; and his deduction was that Ormiston would approach him. As it happened, when Ormiston confronted him, Sterl espied Leslie and Beryl accompanied by, a frank-featured blond young giant, nearing the group. Ormiston might have chosen this moment because he saw them coming. Garbed in drover's rough clothes, with trousers stuck in heavy boots, a gun at his hip, his bold face darker from exposure, he was a virile figure. Ormiston accosted Red first.

"Krehl, good day. Glad to see you again," he said agreeably, as he extended a hand.

"Howdy, yoreself," Red drawled with guile meeting guile. And he shook hands with the man.

"Sorry you are on the wrong side of the fence. But you're a stranger in Australia. I venture to predict you're too experienced an outdoor man to be long deceived by mirages, as you call them in your country."

"Hell, no. I cain't be deceived forever. This heah country is so grand I jest don't believe in your Never Never."

"It's a fact, however, and I hope you don't learn from bitter experience."

"Yeah? Wal, you're orful kind."

At this juncture, when Leslie with her companions came up to Slyter and Dann, Sterl knew absolutely that Ormiston had timed his greeting for their benefit whatever he meant to do, and the thing made Sterl burn under his cool exterior.

"Hello, Hazelton," called the drover in pleasant and resounding tones. "I'm glad to see you, too. I've wanted to meet you again, to tell you I regret the unpleasantness of our meeting at Downsville."

"I'm sure you regret it, Ormiston," replied Sterl, ignoring the proffered hand, and his piercing gaze met the drover's dark, veiled eyes. He was a capital actor, but he was too passionate to hide his real nature from Sterl.

"I didn't regret it because I booted that nigger," rejoined Ormiston, slowly withdrawing his hand.

"That is perfectly obvious," Sterl retorted, not without contempt. He saw the slight vibration of the man's powerful frame, an indication of the release of blood.

"Why do you think I regret it?" flashed the drover.

"Because you ran into the wrong man and got showed up," Sterl flashed just as quickly.

"No. I did regret it, because I was drunk."

"Drunk or sober, you'd be about the same, Ormiston."

This reply, stinging and cold, evidently drove home to Ormiston the fact that his overtures were repelled. He betrayed an intense irritation hardly controllable. Slyter had approached to within a few steps, and Dann, with the girls hanging to him, startled and dismayed, halted beside Slyter, while the others stood back.

"Nonsense," burst out Ormiston. "No man is responsible when he's drunk."

"Right-o. That's why you gave yourself away," retorted Sterl.

Ormiston threw up his hands with a gesture indicating the hopelessness of placating this hard-headed American. But there was a hint of genuine surprise in his well-simulated front of sincerity and, deep underneath the surface, a mastered fury. Sterl warned himself not to underrate this man.

"Cowboy, I approached you to express my regret . . . to apologize for the sake of this trek. To prevent discord!"

"If you're so keen on preventing discord, why did you incite it and foment it between our leader and his other partners?" Sterling's tone was contemplative. As he ended, he completed his few slow steps to one side. To any Westerner it would have been plain that Sterl wanted to get Ormiston out of line with the others. But the drover did not show he realized that.

"I'm not exciting discord," Ormiston returned hotly. "I come from North Queensland. I know something of the Gulf country. Eric Dann is right, and Stanley Dann is wrong."

"That might be true. But Stanley Dann is our leader. If you didn't want to abide by his leadership, why didn't you come out with that at Downsville?"

"I opposed it, and I was sure he could be prevailed upon to take the longer and safer trek."

"Ormiston, how do you know it's safer?" queried Sterl sharply.

"Eric Dann knows. And I believe him. Hathaway and Woolcott are convinced of it. That's enough."

"Not by a damn' sight! Not enough for you to split this outfit," Sterl declared deliberately.

"You insolent, cock-sure Yankee. . . ."

"Careful!" interrupted Sterl. "I stood your insults in Downsville. But we're out in the open now. Don't talk to me any more. Ormiston, you're not on the level. You've got something up your sleeve. You have a selfish reason for opposing Stanley Dann. Now put this in your pipe. You'll never get away with it."

Ormiston had turned livid to his very lips. His eyes glared. He appeared to struggle for speech.

"Umpumm, Mister Ormiston!" Sterl went on tauntingly. "You'll never get away from me! I've known some men who wanted to shoot me in the back. I called you in Downsville, and you showed yellow. I'm calling you here, not to throw your gun, for you won't do that. But calling you before Dann and Slyter. You've got some scheme inimical to the success of this trek. Go back or dismiss it . . . otherwise, you'll get my game. That's all."

Ormiston wheeled to the other men. "Dann, you heard him. This intolerable riff-raff . . . this Yankee. . . ."

"Ormiston, you started this," boomed the leader, as the drover choked. "It's between you and him."

"Miss Dann . . . I appeal to you," went on Ormiston, his voice shaking. "Your father has been . . . taken in by this . . . this interloper. Won't you speak up for me? We've begun this trek. Too late to turn back! But not too late to overcome disruption and failure."

"Dad! It's an outrage," Beryl cried, white of face and angry of eye, as she appealed to her father. "Will you permit this crude, low-bred American to insult Ashley so vilely . . . to threaten him?"

"Girl, go to your tent," ordered Dann sternly. "If you must take sides, you should take mine. Go, it's no place for you."

"But Dad!" cried the spirited girl. "It is. We're all in it. We're out here on this terrible trek."

"Yes, and it appears I shouldn't have brought you. At least try not to make it harder."

Beryl bent a withering glance upon Sterl. "Mister Cowboy, do not speak to me again."

"Suits me fine, Miss Dann," Sterl replied curtly. "I'm bound to help and defend your father. Certainly not to concern myself with a girl who's been made a fool of by a coward and a cheat!"

Miss Dann gave Sterl a stinging slap on his cheek. Then she drew back, gasping, as if realizing to what limit her temper had led her. With red burning out the white of her face she ran toward her wagon. Ormiston wheeled to three waiting men, evidently his drovers, and he stormed away with them, violently gesticulating.

Sterl watched them intently for a moment, then he turned away towards Slyter's camp. Stanley Dann called for him to wait, but Sterl hurried on. He wanted to be alone, first to hide his wrath over Beryl Dann's conduct, and, secondly, to piece into a whole the details of his certainty that Ormiston now loomed as a sinister figure.

"Hey, pard, why the hell do you run away from me?" complained Red, to the rear. "You know I cain't walk fast."

In spite of this Red did not catch up with Sterl until he reached the tent. Then both were to discover that Stanley Dann, Slyter, and Leslie had followed them.

"Heah they come, pard," Red whispered. "Come out of it. Rotten deal, but we got the cairds."

With a hard grip on Red's arm Sterl assured him of recovery and his gratitude for the comradeship and shrewd intimation. When Stanley Dann arrived with Slyter and Leslie, Sterl met them.

"Hazelton, don't run away from me, when I call you," Dann complained as he caught up.

"I'm sorry, boss. I lost my temper."

"Then you fooled me, because I thought you deliberately invited a split with Ormiston."

"Oh, he couldn't rouse my temper. It was Miss Beryl. She hurt my feelings. I shouldn't have spoken as I did to her. But it's hard not to tell the truth."

"One thing at a time. Let's sit down on the log here. I'm tired. And it wasn't the long trek."

They found seats, except Leslie, who significantly stood close to Sterl, her youthful face grave, her hazel eyes, darkly dilated, fastened upon him.

"Les, you better run over to Mum," Slyter said.

"Not much, Dad. You brought me on this trek. And if Beryl is going to share the fights and everything else, I am, too."

"Good-o, Leslie," Dann declared heartily. "You stay here. I'm going to need all the championship possible. Hazelton, you spoke right from the shoulder. Man to man! I can't understand why Ormiston stood it, unless he is a coward, which I suspect. What concerns me is this. Have you any justification for the serious insinuations and open accusations you visited upon Ormiston?"

"Yes, I have," replied Sterl.

"Very well. Tell me them, or explain them."

"Boss, they're all a matter of instinct. I've been years on the frontier. I've been in outfits where there were outlaws, desperadoes, rustlers, men who lived by crookedness. I have met hundreds of badmen. I have had to suspect some of them, outguess them, be too quick for them . . . or get shot myself. I learned to see through evil men. Not of late years have I made any mistakes. Ormiston might have fooled me for a while, if it had not been for the accident of my happening upon him kicking Friday. But not for long! Dann, there's no need for me to repeat what you heard me say to Ormiston. If I had had any doubt before I called him, I'd have been absolutely sure afterward. Now I know. He's playing a deep game, for what I can't figure out . . . yet. But I will find out."

"Hazelton, you impress me," pondered the leader. "When Ormiston and my own daughter appealed to me to resent your arraignment of him, I had only one reaction. You were opposing him in my interest. I couldn't take sides against that. It seems incredible . . . your effrontery . . . what you insinuated about him. Yet, you might possess some perspicuity . . . some insight denied to me and my partners. I have known of villains, and I have come in contact with a few, but I can honestly say I never have had dealings with even one. Men have trusted me, and I have trusted them, thank God. But this trek looms appallingly. That does not change me . . . frighten me in the least. I will make it. Still, I must think through every little and big detail, and miss nothing. It is my responsibility. And now I begin to see opposition, intrigue, perhaps treachery, blood, and death."

"Boss, you can be sure of all of them," Sterl rejoined earnestly. "And you can be as sure that my opposition to Ormiston is on your behalf. Otherwise, I'd have forced him to draw on me and shot him in the act."

Dann nodded his shaggy golden mane like a sleepy lion. "Krehl, suppose you give me your angle, unbiased by your friend," he said presently.

"Wal, if Sterl hadn't been heah, an' I had met thet *hombre* same as he did, we wouldn't be botherin' about Ormiston now, not a-tall," drawled Red caustically.

"Meaning?" Dann roared.

"Meanin', boss, thet when Ormiston rushed me like a bull, I wouldn't have risked my precious right hand on his mug, like Sterl did. I'd jest have bored him, had a couple drinks of red likker, an' forgot all about him."

"Men, but that's the red instinct to fight . . . to kill," declared Dann. "Is it something raw developed in you cowboys by hard years? Where is the conscience, the religion, the justification in such acts?"

"Boss, thet'll all come out in the wash," Red replied. "We say Ormiston is not good . . . thet he threatens the success of yore trek. If no wuss! An', so help me Gawd, he means wuss! Wal, give Ormiston the benefit of a doubt, an' leave it to me an' Sterl to find him out."

"Reason, intelligence, courage," the drover boomed. "These I respect above all other virtues. I am definitely committed to you cowboys in faith. You have my consent. Go slow. Be sure. That's all I ask. Slyter, can you add anything to that?"

"No, Stanley. That says all. It is a terrific problem. But we chose it with our eyes open."

"Yes, and nothing shall deter us. Hazelton, I was surprised and sorry, indeed, at the way Beryl took Ormiston's part. She is a headstrong, passionate child. Then, Ormiston has gotten around her. They have spent a good deal of time together, so my sister says. Anyway, Beryl has been pleading with me to give into Eric's and Ormiston's demand that we take the trek by way of the Gulf."

A silent acceptance of that statement attested to its significance. Red, only, dropped his gaze to the ground, and Sterl saw his lean, brown hand clutch until the knuckles shone white.

"Not that it influences me in the least," continued Dann, rising. "I wanted you to know, that's all. . . . I'll leave you now, as it is supper time. Slyter, come to my camp later."

Slyter arose also, shaking his head. "As if droving a mob of eight thousand cattle wasn't enough! Leslie, I'm glad to have these wild Yankee cowboys with us."

"Rath-thur, Dad," she replied, her voice deep, and she walked a few steps with him, then returned.

"Dog-gone you, Leslie, cain't you leave me an' Sterl alone a-tall?" complained Red, but a child could see that he did not mean that.

Leslie looked from him to Sterl with troubled, grateful eyes.

"Run along, little girl," Sterl said brusquely.

"Boys, you can't exclude me . . . altogether," replied the girl, breathing hard. "If Beryl is in it, so am I. And she is! She's on Ash Ormiston's side. He has been making love to her all along. She didn't exactly brag of it, but I could see. Besides, I know her. She had all the boys at home in love with her. She likes it. Cedric, that boy today. He came on this trek solely because of Beryl. He's an honest, fine lad. But he's a man . . . a bold, unscrupulous man with girls. Neither her father nor my dad can see that."

"Wal, my dear, we can see it," Red returned persuasively. "An' jest so long as he doesn't get nowhere with you, it'll be all right heah."

"I hate him . . . hate him," she declared, flaming. "And, oh, after today, I'm afraid I hate Beryl, too."

"Kid, now don't be in too big a hurry. I'm not as all-fired stuck on Beryl as I was, at thet. But let's give her a chance."

"Leslie, I want to talk seriously to Red," interposed Sterl.

"But . . . Sterl . . . won't you see me . . . later?" Leslie implored. "I know you've been angry with me for days. I deserve it. I'm sorry. I told Red to tell you I'd been a cat. . . . Everything seems to be messed up now we've fallen in with the other drovers. Dad is worried. I . . . Sterl, I couldn't bear to have you despise me any longer."

"Leslie, how silly! I never despised you . . . and I don't," Sterl replied with a smile. "I'll come after you later."

A light illumined her troubled face. She wheeled to bound away like a deer. For a moment the cowboys sat silent.

"Pard, shore you see how it is with Leslie?" Red queried.

"I'm afraid I do," reluctantly admitted Sterl.

"Wal, it's a hell of a good thing, if you're good to her. An' you'll have me jumpin' all over you, if you're not. I reckon Ormiston an' thet fracas over at Dann's air to blame. She's scared of him. I'll bet she didn't tell us all about thet *hombre*. Too innocent an' modest, mebbe, or afraid we'd kill him."

"Which is a safe bet," Sterl said darkly.

"Hell, yes! If we were in Texas, one of us would have bored him long ago. But we jest cain't do it heah, unless he's the aggressor. An' he's too yellow an' too smart to be thet. These Danns an' Slyter air square, upstandin' men who cain't think evil, let alone see it. They've got to find out. An' Lord knows what'll come off before thet happens. Why, Ormiston might fool them all the way."

"Red, what's his game?"

"Easy to say, far as the girls air concerned. Leslie had it figgered. Shore he didn't mean marriage with her. But he might with Beryl. If Dann gets to the Kimberleys with half his cattle, he'll be rich, an' richer *pronto*."

"He'll never get there with half his cattle," Sterl rejoined.

"Hell, no. But Ormiston might figger thet way."

"Red, we're concerned with his intentions. It's a cinch he'll never end this trek with us."

"I've got a hunch he doesn't mean to."

Sterl gave Red a searching gaze, comprehending, and indicative of swiftly revolving thoughts. "You red-headed cowhand! So your mind's beginning to function? Talk!"

"Ormiston is too deep to figger *pronto*, unless we jump at conclusions."

"All right. Jump."

"No, pard, this is ticklish bizness. I'm almost afraid to speak out to myself what I think. Aw hell, he's a louse an' a stinker! But all the same, he's one of those Australians, well-educated, like all of them, an' he's got some kind of standin'. Because he's made the Danns think so."

"As we know cattlemen, Ormiston is not hot enough for this trek?"

"Exactly. His passion is not the trek . . . this great pioneer drive across the Never Never . . . but what he can get out of it."

"Pard Red, as usual you've hit the trail. We're up against the deepest, hardest game we ever struck. Listen, let's try a trick that has worked before. Tip off Slyter and Stanley Dann that you and I will pretend to quarrel . . . fall out . . . and you'll drink and hobnob with Ormiston's drivers, in order to spy on Ormiston."

"All same goin' to the bad stuff, huh?"

"Yes. And Red, you sure can do it."

"Thet'll queer me with Beryl. Not thet I care about it now."

"No. It'll make a hero out of you, if through this you save her father."

"Dog-gone!" Red exclaimed, his face lighting. "You always could outfigger me. Why, it's a hell of a good idee. Only I hate to give up our comfortable tent."

"Give up nothing," Sterl replied forcefully. "In camp, at night, you can hobnob with those riders, and then sneak back to me."

"Settled, pard, an' the cards air stacked. Tomorrow night you an' me will have a helluva fight, savvy? Only be careful where an' how you sock me."

"Right-o. There's Friday. Red, I'm going to try to make that black understand our game."

"Go ahead. Another good idea. I shore like that native. I'll tell Slyter, an' then talk to Leslie a bit."

Friday stood on the brink of the riverbank. How magnificent he fitted into the wild scene! A golden aftermath of sunset hung in the valley; a full moon tipped the notch where the waterfall shone; the river ran amber and gold; waterfowl of bright plumage lined the sandbars; bird songs were so varied and commingled that there was contrast between discord and melody. The mile-wide grassy flat across the river was alive with cattle of different colors, and the smell of dust and manure was in the air.

"Friday, you sit down alonga me," Sterl said to the native. "Me bad here. Trouble," went on Sterl, touching his forehead. The black's big eyes appeared to engulf him with inscrutable interrogation. Again Sterl received an impression that the black was quick, intelligent, mystic in his interpretation. Sterl summoned all his wit and feeling as he made an impressive gesture that embraced the mob of cattle. Then he smoothed out a little bare spot of sand and made marks on it. "We here," he went on. "Long way, far up, big river. Long way farder big water . . . big gulf. Ormiston, and three drovers"—here Sterl held up three fingers—"want to go alonga gulf. Big boss, me, redhead, and Slyter want go along river, then cross this way . . . here . . . cross big land. No pads alonga here. Nobody know. Mebbe black fella know. Savvy, Friday?"

"Me savvy," replied the black, and, tracing the gulf line, he shook his head vehemently, then tracing a line along the big river and across the big land he nodded just as vehemently.

"Good, Friday," Sterl affirmed, strongly stirred. He would stake a great deal on this native. "You know country up alonga here?"

The aborigine shook his head. "Might be black fella tellum."

This thrilled Sterl to the core. He touched Friday on his black breast. If the native could learn from these wild natives *en route* how wonderfully that would help! "Friday, get black fella tell?"

"Might be. Some black fella good . . . some bad."

"Some white fella bad," went on Sterl intensely. "Ormiston bad. Him wanta go this way. No good. Him make some white fella afraid. Savvy, Friday?"

The native nodded. He encouraged Sterl greatly. If he understood, then it did not matter that he could talk only a little.

"Ormiston bad along missy," continued Sterl. "Alonga big boss's missy, too. Him make magic alonga Dann missy. Him wants me." And here Sterl struck his own breast. "Bad white fella. Afraid me. Afraid Red. Afraid Friday. Stab in back!" Here Sterl took out his knife and made as if to stab Friday from behind. "Friday, watchum all the time. Me watchum all the time. Savvy, Friday?"

The aborigine nodded his black head instantly with the mien of an Indian chief damning an enemy to destruction. "Friday savvy. Friday watchum. Friday no afraid. Bimeby black fella kill him!"

Sterl left Friday then and walked alone in the moon-blanched dusk. He thought he had cause to be elated. That black man was a tower of strength. His help would be inestimable. Sterl wondered if Friday had meant a black fellow would kill Ormiston, or if he would. Sterl inclined to the latter possibility, although Slyter had told him black men very seldom killed whites. In this case, however, there was profound incentive and persuasion.

Sterl forgot to call for Leslie, but, when she stole upon him, it was certain that she had not forgotten, and that with the moonlight on her rippling hair and sweet grave face and unfathomable eyes she was lovely.

"I waited and waited, but you didn't come," she said, taking his arm and leaning on him.

"Leslie, the talk I just had with Friday would make anyone forget. I'm sorry. But as you didn't, well. . . ." He looked down upon her with stirring of his pulse. In another year Leslie would be a beautiful woman, and irresistible. Long before that he divined she would cure his heartbreak. What a hopeless situation for a cowboy!

"You've forgiven me?"

"Really, Leslie, I didn't have anything to forgive."

"Oh, but I think you had. I don't know what was the matter with me that day. Or now, for that matter. Today has been a little too much for your cowgirl. Red told me about cowgirls. Oh, he's the nicest, cutest, strangest boy I ever knew. I adore him, Sterl."

"Well, I'm not so sure I'll allow you to adore Red," Sterl stated, half in jest, half in earnest.

"Oh, but you misunderstand me, Sterl. I don't mean love. I don't love Red."

"Yeah? What's the difference?"

"I think to love him would be the opposite of how I hate Ash Ormiston?"

"I savvy. And see here, Leslie, now that we've made up, and you're my charge on this trek. . . ."

"How did you guess I longed for that?" she interposed frankly.

"I didn't. But as you seemed upset this afternoon and put such store in my friendship, why I decided to sort of boss you."

"Sterl, I'll do anything you ask. Dad hasn't any time for me. He's so troubled over this trek. And Mum can't see me, either. She thinks I'm still a little girl."

"I started to ask sentimental and intimate questions, young lady. Would you mind telling me just what boys have been to you?"

"Not at all. They've been fun. Playmates, until a couple of years ago, when all of a sudden I changed. Then the tomboy fun somehow changed. All the boys there at Downsville made . . . well, advances. I didn't like being kissed and hugged. That is until Cedric came. I guess I liked his kisses. But Beryl soon cut me out, and that was the end of that."

Sterl did not need to hear any more about Leslie's adolescence and puppy love. She was as transparent as crystal water.

"Leslie, to change the subject, this trek we've started has got me buffaloed."

"Buffaloed? What on earth's that?"

"It's cowboy slang. Buffalo have a habit of stampeding. Millions of huge shaggy beasts rolling along like an avalanche."

"Then I'm buffaloed, too. Sterl, I was doing fairly well, outside of my fear you didn't like me any more. But since we got to this camp, and I saw Ormiston again . . . I'm just scared out of my wits. Silly me!"

"Scared of what?"

"Him. The trek. The split among the drovers. Beryl's insult to you. Of which way to turn. Oh, so much."

"Well, outside of Ormiston, I reckon there's plenty to be scared about. Ormiston, though . . . you needn't fear him personally, any more."

"But I do. You don't know Ash Ormiston," returned the girl somberly.

"It looks as though I am doomed to get pretty well acquainted with him," Sterl said grimly. "Keep out of his way. Always ride within sight of us. Never lose sight of me in a jam of any kind. Don't go to Dann's camp unless with us or your dad."

"Dad would take me, and forget me *pronto*. I can't stick in camp with Mum all these long evenings. Sterl, won't you please let me be with you often like this? I couldn't have slept tonight, if you hadn't."

"Yes, you can be with me all you want," promised Sterl, helpless in the current. "But we must go to bed early. Remember, I have night guard. That means you're slated for bed right now."

"Oh, you darling," she cried happily, and, kissing him soundly, she ran toward her wagon.

Chapter Eight

Slyter wanted to keep his mob of cattle intact, so that it would not be lost in the larger mob. It was inevitable. Sterl told him that sooner or later there would be only one mob. All the cattle except Woolcott's were unbranded.

Stanley Dann had foreseen this contingency, and his idea was to number the stock of each drover as accurately as possible, and, when they arrived at their destination, let each drover take his percentage of what was left.

Discussion of this detail was held at the end of the next day's trek, in a widening part of the valley, where the stream formed a large pool, like a lake. Leslie, whose duty was to give a name to each campsite, called this one Green Pool. Ashley Ormiston objected to the idea of percentage, and, when Stanley Dann put it to a vote, Red Krehl sided with Ormiston. This did not mean anything much for the moment, because both Dann and Slyter were in the secret of Red's apparent defection. It had other effects, however, inasmuch as it brought Beryl's favor and infuriated

Leslie. She was developing fast on this trip; she had a mind of her own, and she spoke it.

"Red Krehl, I'm ashamed of you," she burst out, when Red approached the Slyter campfire that night.

"You air. Wal, thet's turrible," drawled Red, in a voice which would have angered anyone.

"I saw you, after we halted today. You were with Ormiston's drovers. Very jolly! And after that conference at Dann's you were basking in Beryl's smiles. She has won you over for Ormiston."

"Les, you're a sweet kid, but kinda knot-haided an' dotty."

"I'm nothing of the kind. You've worried Dad, and Sterl is hurt . . . deeply hurt. I thought you were his pard, his devoted friend."

"Wal, Les, a man's feelin's get worked on out in the open. An' this country is gonna be tough. Me an' Sterl don't agree on some things."

"But Sterl is right. Any fool could see that."

"I must be one, then, 'cause I cain't see it."

"Oh, you've been drinking. I saw a bottle sticking out of your pocket. Drink changes men. It does Dad. And I ran from Ormiston, when he'd been drinking."

"You'd better run from me, *pronto*, or I'll spank the daylights out of you."

"You . . . you . . . !" Leslie was too amazed and furious to find words. She looked around to see how Sterl, and her parents took this offense. They could not help hearing. Mrs. Slyter called for Leslie to leave the campfire. Sterl sat with bowed head. Her father smoked calmly, his back to the fire. Leslie found her voice, and her dignity. "Mister Krehl, some things are evident, and one is that you're no gentleman. You leave my campfire, or I will."

Day came, and the guards trooped in to breakfast. Red did not show up at Slyter's camp until time to drive the herd across the stream. The wagons crossed only hub deep at a bar below camp. But the cattle were put to the deep water. The take-off was steep,

and many of the steers leaped only to go under. Splashing, cracking horns, bawling, the mob swam across, then waded out. The
horses, following in the deep trough cut into the bank, trooped
down to take their plunge.

It was well Sterl had an oilskin cover over his rifle as King
went in, up to his neck. The black loved the water. Leslie came
last. She bestrode Duke who hated water, but showed that he
could not be left behind. He pranced, he reared.

"Come on, Les," called Sterl cheerily. "Give him the steel."

"OK," trilled the girl, spirited and sure. She spurred the big
sorrel, and he plunged to go clear under, letting the swirling water come above Leslie's waist. She kept her seat. The sorrel came
up with a snort and swam powerfully. Leslie caught up with
Sterl, who had held King back. "Oooo! It's cold," cried Leslie.

"All in the day's ride, cowgirl," called Sterl.

"Dog-gone it, I wet my biscuits," was Leslie's reply.

They waded out on the heels of the herd, already stringing
ahead in line with Drake and his drovers. The rear-end of the
wedge was narrow, holding Sterl and comrades relatively close
together. Friday walked between Sterl and the girl. The horses
slowed down, their noses reaching for the grass, and then began
the long slow day's trek. Half a mile or more to their right, the
other mobs spread across the floor of the valley, a ponderously
moving mass. The course of the winding stream could be located
by the lines of stately eucalyptus trees. Kangaroos were conspicuous for their absence. A flock of blackbirds, rising, swooping,
settling, followed the cattle. Flocks of parrots sped overhead like
bullets with their whistling flight. Trees were white with
squalling cockatoos. Birds of prey sailed high in the air on the
scent for meat.

At last the sun rose high enough to be warm and to dry wet
garments. At noon it was hot. By the almost imperceptible increase in temperature and the changing nature of the verdure,
Sterl became aware of the tropics. He saw strange trees and flowering shrubs along with those he already knew. No mile passed
that he did not observe a beautifully plumaged bird that was new.

On a bare slope his sharp eyes located a herd of brumbies, as Jones had called them.

Leslie rode over to offer Sterl one of her wet biscuits. She had recovered from her shyness, or else in the broad sunlight and mounted on a horse that would jump at a touch she had something of audacity. Presently he chased her back toward her station, when with her eyes flashing back and her sombrero swinging, she sang out: "Sterl, what was it you called me last night?"

He waved her away, almost convinced of her developing coquettishness. He would play more than square with this kid, he thought, but he grew more aware of her captivating charm and freshness as the nights and days passed. He had no illusion about any cowboy, even himself. Yet he was disgusted with being wooed so easily from a lamentable love affair. He should hate all women. And then presently he forgot Leslie, and did not think of her even when he saw her, lax and dreaming in her saddle.

Afternoon was waning when Sterl sighted far ahead two large, colorful mounds, one scarlet, the other gold. And he had to ride another mile before he discerned them to be trees in blossom. The gold one was, of course, a wattle.

Sunset had come and passed when the main mob ceased to move, indicating that the drovers on the right had halted for camp. Slyter followed suit, and, when his lengthy herd had massed again, he loped in behind his comrades.

It was almost dusk when Sterl arrived, too late to see clearly the scarlet and gold trees. Jones, having come to appreciate Sterl's weakness, had halted his wagon in the lea of the flaming tree, at which Sterl gazed with wonder and admiration. Red sat his horse, waiting.

"Pard," he said, low-voiced, as Sterl halted close, "I'll eat with thet other outfit tonight. Meet you at the big campfire after supper. Spring the dodge then, but, as I told you, don't sock me too hard, or I'll get sore."

"Depends on how mean you get," replied Sterl with a mirthless laugh. "Red, honest Injun, I don't like the dodge."

"Hell, no! But, pard, it's for them, an' us, too," Red returned sharply. "It's our deal, an' I've stacked the cairds. Play the game, you!"

Red rode away at a swinging canter. That last from him stirred Sterl out of his lethargy. One of Red's great qualities was the virtue of never deviating from a set course of action once decided. Sterl felt justly reproved.

King, turned loose, made for the bare spot where Duke and another horse were rolling. With a heave King thumped down, and in one single motion he rolled clear over, and with another he rolled back, which quick and powerful act, in a cowboy's opinion, argued for a great horse. Friday helped Sterl pitch the tent. Darkness descended, and the cook pounded a kettle to call all to supper. Leslie omitted her usual custom of waiting on Sterl, then eating with him.

Stanley Dann's community campfire blazed brightly in the center of a circle of bronzed faces. In addition to the six partners there were present a score or more of the drovers. Dann had barbecued a beef. It hung, revolving, over a pit full of red-hot coals. The hour was the early evening before night guard. Sterl, purposely late, took in this scene, appreciative of its rugged beauty and significance. He observed other things, too, one of which, Ormiston's attention to Leslie, added a slumbering resentment to his mood.

In the merriment that prevailed Sterl's soft step was not heard, as he came up behind Ormiston to hear him say: "But Leslie, my sweet girl, surely you cannot hold that against me?"

Sterl could not see her face, but her silent acceptance of Ormiston's speech inflamed Sterl. He smothered an impulse to kick the man with all his might. Probably Red's arrival, more than his restraint, checked the precipitation of an issue that was bound to come. There were two drovers with Red, trying to hold him back, as he wrestled good-naturedly with them and broke out in loud, lazy voice: "Dog-gone it, fellers. Lemme be. Wasser masser with you? I'm a ladies' man . . . I am . . . an' I've seen some punkins in my day."

His companions let him go and kept back out of the circle of light. Krehl made a picturesque figure of rough life out on the range. How vividly he recalled to Sterl many and many a fire-spirited cowboy, under the influence of the bottle, humorous and harmless, unless inflamed. But Red was not drunk. And Sterl nerved himself to the pre-arranged split between Red and himself.

Red, however, shouldered Ormiston aside, to bend over Leslie, no doubt inspired by unexpected opportunity. "Les, I been huntin' you all over this heah dog-gone camp," Red said with a gallant tone.

"I've been here, Red," replied Leslie quickly, evidently glad to welcome him, drunk or sober. "Come, sit down."

"You shore air my sweet lil' girl fren'," Red returned gleefully.

What his next move might have been did not transpire, for Ormiston confronted him belligerently. Sterl's alert eye had caught the drover scrutinizing Red for the gun usually in plain sight. Tonight it was absent. Ormiston shoved Red violently. He had not seen Sterl, and here apparently was a golden opportunity, not by any means to be lost. "You drunken Yankee pup! This is an English girl, not one of your trail-drabs to mouth over."

Sterl did not risk Red's reaction to that. He leaped between them, facing Ormiston. "Careful, you fool!" he called piercingly, in a voice that silenced the others. "Haven't you any sense? Krehl has killed men for less."

Opposition to Ormiston, the sudden menace, checked any further motion or word toward Red.

"He's drunk," rejoined the drover presently. "His presence here, his familiarity with Leslie is insufferable."

"Yeah, it is, and I'll handle him," Sterl retorted. "But in your conceit don't imagine you can hide your familiarity any longer."

"What do you mean?" blustered Ormiston.

"You know what I mean." Sterl backed away from Ormiston, vigilant for any move on that worthy's part. The drover's gaze told volumes.

"Here, men," Dann boomed, striding over. "Can't we have one little hour free from work and fight?"

"Boss, there'll not be any fight," Sterl replied. "And Ormiston is not to blame this time, for any more than one of his two-faced cracks. . . . It's Red."

"Boss, I wasn't huntin' trouble," interposed Red sulkily. "Shore I've had a coupla drinks. But whasser masser thet? I ain't drunk. I jest said a playful word to Leslie, an' I gets insulted by Ormiston heah, an' then my pard. Dog-gone it, thet's too much."

"Well, Krehl, you don't look ugly to me," rejoined the leader and left them.

"Red, I'm disgusted with you," Sterl declared angrily. "This is the second time. I warned you."

"What'n'll do I care? You make me sick with yore preachin'. Jest 'cause I fell in with some real pards who ain't afraid of red likker, you get sore. I ain't a-gonna stand it no more."

"Cowboy, you'd gone to hell long ago, but for me."

"Shore. But I'm on my way again. We'll all be on our way, if we stick to the big boss's idee, an' trek off into thet Never Never."

"Red! You're not shifting to Ormiston's side?" protested Sterl, aghast.

"Shore am. Changed my figgerin', pard, an' if you don't like it, you can lump it."

Sterl worked himself into a manifest rage. Laying a powerful left hand on Red's collar, he jerked him so hard that the cowboy's red head shot forward and back. "Why you double-crossing, lowdown coward!" raged Sterl. "You fail us for a few drinks, for this slick-tongued Ormiston!"

"Wal, they ain't so pore. An' it shore looks like I got the decidin' vote," rang out the cowboy, with perfectly convincing elation.

Sterl let out a fierce cry of disappointment and wrath. And he knocked Red flat. Despite his promise not to hit him too hard, he feared he had done so.

Beryl Dann leaped up to run and drop upon her knees beside

Red. "Oh, he's terribly hurt!" She glanced up at Sterl, face and eyes flaming in the light. "You! You are the discord . . . the villain on this trek!"

Sterl bowed scornfully and left the campfire. Scarcely had he reached the cover of darkness, when Friday appeared at his side like a shadow out of nowhere. "Me watches close up," he said. "Ormiston he glad. Me tink it bad."

"Not bad, Friday. Me and Red friends. Work black magic on Ormiston. Fool Ormiston. Red all same find out what Ormiston wants. . . . Savvy, Friday?"

But this was one time when the black held silent. He stalked beside Sterl across to their campfire, which he replenished. Sterl sat down, still in the throes of controlled anger. But that seizure was being lessened by his satisfaction with the part he and Red had played so deceptively, and by a humorous concern in regard to what his comrade was going to say about that jolt on the jaw. Red was going to be outraged.

He appeared to be alone in camp, Friday having stalked off somewhere. It was still early, and, lighting a cigarette, Sterl settled down to smoke and think and listen, when rapid footfalls told that someone was coming on the run. He turned around to see Leslie appear out of the darkness, to make for him and grasp his arm with a strong hand, while the other pressed to her heaving breast. At that moment she appeared most distressingly pretty, wild, and desirable.

"Can't you ever walk like a lady should?" queried Sterl gruffly.

"I can . . . but not in . . . the dark . . . with Ormiston at large," she panted.

"After you again?"

"Yes, he is. . . . Bare-faced as . . . anything."

"Are you two-faced, same as Ormiston?"

"Oh-h, Sterl!"

"You have encouraged him."

"I . . . have not," she cried in distress.

"Leslie, I don't believe you," Sterl returned quite brutally. Somehow that little incident beside Dann's campfire had roused unreasonable jealousy. If she could hurt him, then he must like her, which Sterl resented.

"So you . . . think I . . . I could . . . lie to you?" she whispered huskily.

"Well, you're a woman, same as all the rest."

"Sterl Hazelton, I might be . . . ten times a woman . . . but I couldn't tell you a lie."

"And why not?"

The query nonplused Leslie. A dark wave of color changed the paleness of her face. "I . . . I just couldn't," she faltered.

"Yeah?" taunted Sterl, when he simply had to believe her.

"Sterl, I lied to Mum . . . and Dad about Ormiston. I was scared. . . . But I'd not lie to you."

"Very well, then, I apologize. . . . But you must confess that I had cause to suspect something . . . seeing him so close to you and hearing what he said."

"The devil! Yes, you had. He sat down by me, took hold of me, began his soft-soaping talk. . . . What could I do?"

"You could have got up and left. In the future you do that, or you'll find yourself in trouble with me."

"I promise . . . that, Sterl. Red said something today . . . that I didn't know it and you didn't know it . . . but I . . . I was your girl."

"The rattle-brained cowboy? Leslie, don't let him bamboozle you."

"What's bamboozle?"

"Make a little fool of you."

"Oh! Then, it isn't. . . . true?" she whispered plaintively.

Sterl could have shaken her, but there was an irresistible sweetness in her candor. "Of course, it's true, in a way, for this trek," he replied, trying to keep from putting his arm around her, rather than carefully choosing his words.

"Then I can be happy, in spite of your brutality to Red," she rejoined most earnestly, hanging to his arms and devouring his face with dark eyes of wonder and sorrow. "He was drunk, I know. But Red is so funny and so nice. Then I would have been glad to have him sit by me. Only Ormiston spoiled it. Why didn't you hit him, instead of your friend?"

"I was angry, Leslie. What happened after I left?"

"Oh, it would have tickled you. It did me. . . . Beryl has a tender heart for anyone hurt. And Red was hurt. She bent over him and almost cried over him. I bent over him, too, and I could see Red was not only hurt but glorying in it. He never looked at me with such eyes. Then it happened. Ormiston dragged us away from Red. He was perfectly white in the face and quivering with fury . . . jealous fury. Why, the madman thinks he can have us both! I wrenched free, for I'm strong, Sterl. But Beryl couldn't, and Ormiston led her away to her dad, who was watching. Then poor, dear Red sat up, his hand to his face, and he said . . . 'Leslie, tell thet pard of mine thet I'll get even for the sock he gave me. . . .' Others were coming, so I ran off."

"Poor, dear Red," muttered Sterl, and then he laughed. It was funny, too. "Listen," he continued, in sudden feeling. Then Leslie dropped her head, as if her neck muscles had collapsed. "Leslie!"

"When you whisper that way . . . I . . . I can't hear . . . any more," she returned in a betrayal of which she was not conscious.

"Don't be a little dunce," flashed Sterl, shaking her, remorseful with himself. "You're no kid any more, despite what Red says. You've got to be a woman . . . to use your wits to help us . . . to be cunning. Listen, can I trust you?"

She looked up wonderingly. "Yes, Sterl."

"That quarrel and fight with Red was all pretense. Red wasn't drunk. He was just making believe. Our plan is for him to make it look like he split with me . . . to hobnob with those drovers and spy on Ormiston. To find out what the *hombre* has up his sleeve. Leslie, we know Ormiston is crooked. I can't explain that. Neither can we prove anything, till we find out. Your father and our leader would not damn any man, much less a partner, on mere hearsay, on the suspicions of foreigners. Red and I have worked this trick before. It may take longer, more clever work here, but Red will do it. Now, I'm confiding in you because I won't have you believing me a brute."

"Who thought you were a brute? Oh, so Red wasn't drunk? How glad I am! I just adore him."

"Fine, as long as you can say it that way."

"Will Beryl be in on the secret?"

"No, indeed. Only your dad, Stanley Dann, and you."

"So that was it," mused the girl.

"That was what?"

"Beryl's sweetness toward Red. The cat! Ormiston has twisted her around his little finger, and now that she thinks Red has gone over to Ormiston's side, she's so sweet sugar wouldn't melt in her mouth."

"Right-o, Leslie. Now you overcome or hide those perfectly human feelings and practice deceit yourself. Oh, don't look like that. You can, for you belong to the feminine gender. Make friends with Beryl, at any cost. Be a ninny. Be the little softy who looks up to the proud Miss Dann. But you be cunning, sharp as a fox, and find out all that is possible about Ormiston through her."

"Oh, Sterl, how wonderful you are," she murmured, her big eyes worshipfully upon him.

"Yeah?" retorted Sterl, feeling foolish.

"Red is wonderful, too. You both could deceive anyone. So that's my part? Ohhh! But it's for Dad, for Mum, for Mister Dann, for you. Yes, I can do it."

"Good-o! I'll bet you turn out wonderful yourself. Run! Here comes Red. From the way he walks, I'd gamble he's mad! Good night, my Australian cowgirl."

Leslie rose to dart away while Red stalked into the firelight, his eyes like daggers, his hand to his mouth. He removed it to expose a swollen and bloody lip.

"Wal, you . . . liar!" he said. "You promised not to sock me, an' look what you did. No hoss ever knocked me that hard."

"I'm sorry, pard," replied Sterl, stifling a laugh. "Honestly, I didn't mean to. But I was riled before you came up. Then when I swung, you dumb-head, instead of ducking, you met it."

"I shore met it. But you're a better actor than me, 'cause you don't pretend nothin'. Why, my lower teeth air all loose, an' my lip is busted so I couldn't kiss Beryl, if she'd let me, which I think, by thunder, she would. Pard, thet is all thet was good about thet sock . . . the surprisin' way she came across. I never figgered thet. She was sweet as apple pie to me, an' mebbe Ormiston wasn't sore. Aw, no! But, Sterl, I don't like how he's got around her. Not one damn bit! Thet *hombre* has a way with wimmin. Kinda like a snake with a dove!"

"Well, I'm glad Leslie is more of a hawk. Red, what's your angle?"

"Pard, I ain't stuck on this deal a-tall," Red replied ponderingly. "I heah somebody comin'. Let's go in our tent an' hit the hay. Then I'll talk."

Sterl had to strain his eyes to make out Friday's prone form under the low-drooping wattle branches. Somehow he had come to liken the black to a watchdog. He felt how infinitely keener the aborigine was than any white man, and most likely far keener than any Indian scout Sterl had ever known.

Thirty-one days later, according to Leslie's journal, on the twenty-ninth of June, after a prodigious trek through a jungle pass, Stanley Dann called a halt for a rest and repairs, both to equipment and drovers and mob.

The trip had been the most expansive in acquired knowledge of natural things that Sterl Hazelton ever experienced. He had lost track of days until Leslie's appeal to help her with her journal staggered him with the actual brevity of a strenuous and full period which had seemed endless. About all that she entered in her journal were the dates and the number of miles and a few outstanding incidents.

Ormiston, with the two partners and drovers whom he dominated, broke out of the pass into the open, after a three-mile trek which took more than half the day. The Danns followed on his heels. Slyter's cattle and riders found the grass and brush trampled, the tree ferns and sassafras knocked down, the creekbanks cut into lanes, stray cattle and horses which they drove on, an easy trek except for the grades.

Sterl, the last rider to hold up the rear, halted King on the crest of the saddle between the lofty slopes and faced with a gasp the extraordinary scene that burst in glory before him.

"Umpumm," he soliloquized wearily. Long hours and excessive fatigue had dulled his faculties of reception and appreciation. Moreover a score of days up this astounding pass, with its labyrinthine jungle marvels and beauties, had left him unable to absorb the appalling loveliness of the rolling golden-purple open spreading boundlessly before tired eyes. He reverted to Red's cowboy repudiation of facts. "Dog-gone it, there ain't no such country!"

An hour's rest on the flat of his back, a bath and a shave, and change of clothes, restored Sterl to some semblance of his former self. Red was longer at these imperative details. The faithful and tireless Friday performed their chores meanwhile. Sterl then had a short talk with Slyter, cheerful and energetic again. Mrs. Slyter appeared none the worse for the long wagon rides and the many camps with their incessant tasks. But Leslie showed the wear of six weeks and more hard riding in fair weather and rain, across numberless fords, and through miles and miles of brush and jungle.

"Howdy, ragamuffin," said Sterl, coming at her call.

"I am, aren't I?" she replied ruefully, surveying herself. "I've got two other suits, but I'll mend these rags and make them go as far as possible. My, how spic and span you look. Very handsome, Sterl!"

"That goes for you, Les," he rejoined heartily. "How prettily you tan! And you've lost weight. All to the good!"

"Flatterer! I've had to ride myself nearly to death to extract that compliment from you. Good-o for this rest. It was high time. Oh, what a trek! Sterl, you must help me with my journal."

"Sure will. Let's see." It was then that Sterl discovered they had trekked only thirty-one days through these mountain ranges for an aggregate of one hundred and seventy-eight miles. "Not so good."

"My journal? Dog-gone! You don't help me. There's so little time, it's often dark and wet."

"I was referring to our trek, not your journal. It's very neat. Only there's so little. I saw Beryl's journal the other night. It has yours skinned to a frazzle."

"Yeah? She writes in the wagon. And Red helps her at night. That was another thing which made Ormiston jealous."

"Well, add a long footnote here. I can remember the important things."

"Put this down. Slyter lost two horses and some twenty-odd head of cattle. Bad crossing at the ford you called Wattle Rapids. You're good on names, Les. Flooded a wagon there, but no damage. Visited by only a few blacks. Growing unfriendly. Mosquitoes terrible at the Forks. Big tree-ferns. Grand mountain ash trees. Over two hundred feet high. Huge and fluted at base. Bad going last few days. Short treks. Wagons need of repairs and grease. Last day . . . today . . . the worst. Cattle tired and hungry. Horses fine. Riders the same, except Larry thrown and lamed. That's all, Leslie."

"Oh, good-o!" cried Leslie with satisfaction. "Sterl, I just couldn't take this trek, let alone do my journal without you."

"I forgot a couple of items. Leslie about stripped to rags and lost, say, five pounds."

"Umpumm, cowboy! I don't record that. You're getting as bad as Red."

"Just how bad is Red?" Sterl queried anxiously, being reminded of his worry about this friend. Red was a problem, but only where a girl was concerned. Apparently he had progressed further with Beryl than with the important work he had undertaken. According to Red he was not so far behind Ormiston in the race for the Dann girl's favor. Red's heart, however, always ran away with his head.

Supper, as usual on short day treks, came early this time, as happened often, without Red in attendance. Members of Slyter's group were always too hungry to mind the sameness of fare. They had a well-balanced ration of which dried fruits, served in different dishes, were especially relished along with game. Damper, tea, and beans were the other essentials, and on occasion Bill, the cook, managed some surprising pastry. Sterl had concluded that their diet offered a better nourishing and strength-sustaining food than what he had been accustomed to on American treks. Cowboys drank too much coffee, sometimes ten cups a day. Sterl and Red had learned to like tea, but they confined drinking it to two meals a day.

"Les, it'd pay us to walk up to that saddle at sunset, if you're not too tired," Sterl said, when he had finished supper.

"Good-o! I'm not tired," she replied happily. "I need to stretch my legs."

Slyter interposed to ask Sterl to go with him first to Dann's camp.

"Grand country, don't you think?" queried the drover, as Sterl accompanied him.

"It is, boss, beyond compare. But that pass through the ranges was no place for cattle."

"How are we doing?"

"Not so good, from a cowboy's standpoint."

"Nor from a drover's. But we've moving. Some places on this trek we'll be held up weeks, by drought or flood. We haven't talked with Stanley for ten days."

The Dann camp was bustling. Evidently supper had been served. One wagon had been jacked up, while the hubs had been partly unpacked; tents were in progress of erection; a brawny drover was splitting firewood. Red sat on the ground beside a hammock, in which Beryl was laboriously writing in her journal. Ormiston did not appear to be in evidence.

Dann, the blond, golden-haired giant, assuredly had his place in that camp. He greeted Slyter and Sterl in booming welcome.

"Heard my order that we hold up here a week?" he queried.

"Yes. Heald fetched it. I'm glad. A good few days will put us right again. Sterl agrees."

"Just had words with Ormiston. He disagrees. Says one day is rest enough. We want to make time. I told him he had my order.

He replied that he'd go on with Woolcott and Hathaway. At that I put my foot down, and told him that he wouldn't do anything of the kind. Reminded him that I was the leader of this trek. He left in high dudgeon."

Slyter demurred at Ormiston's continued antagonism. Sterl queried ponderingly: "Why does he try to block everything? Why? Any fool would know the cattle need rest, and there are needful things to do. Let's ask Red."

Sterl called to the happily engaged cowboy who did not hear him the first time. Then at Sterl's trenchant call he bounced up and came on the run, an awkward, bowlegged figure at that gait.

"What the hell? Injuns, or have I gotta dig post holes?" he growled, but his eyes belied his complaint.

Dann informed the cowboy of Ormiston's defection and asked if he could throw any light on it.

"Shore. Jest Ormiston's policy. He's gonna oppose you in all ways, 'cause it's stuck in his craw to fight you on the big issue."

"Policy, eh? It does seem like that. If I had known this man was so obstinate, so incapable of working with me, I'd never have made a partner of him. But it is nothing. Merely a flea bite. We are going through. I anticipated obstacles."

"Boss, I cain't give any reason yet for Ormiston's angle, except he's a mean cuss. I'm playin' my game slow. I'm shore, though, he'll never go through with that bluff."

"Immaterial to me whether he does or not. He'd surely wait for us to catch up."

Dann and Slyter withdrew, leaving Red to return to Beryl, accompanied by Sterl. She received Sterl with a rather distant hauteur. If anything Beryl had gained on the trek, in a golden tan, a little weight, and certainly in beauty. Sterl took advantage of the moment to tell her so. Her answering pleasure betrayed the jewel of her soul. Even if she hated a man, she could not help responding to a tribute to her beauty.

"Pard, will you mosey off somewhere, so I can help Beryl? You're a turrible distractin' cowboy."

"Don't be rude, Red. He may stay."

"Umpumm. Two's company. Besides I have a date with Leslie," replied Sterl.

"How is she? She hasn't been over for days. Tell her she must come, now that we have leisure ahead."

"Leslie's brown and fine."

Sterl returned to Slyter's camp, where Leslie eagerly awaited him. Letting her carry his rifle, he secured a long, stout stick, and they set out with Leslie firing rapid questions. The grass was knee-high, partly green and purple, mostly gold in color. Magpies were caroling. Once more the thick, pungent fragrance of eucalyptus filled the air. As the cattle had been driven to the right coming down from the saddle, the grass had not been trampled, and Sterl kept an eye out for snakes. Recently he experienced several close calls, one with a death-adder, and he thought it behooved him to be vigilant. Presently a movement of grass and a sibilant hiss startled them to jump back. Then with the long stick Sterl located the snake. It was a tiger snake as thick as his wrist, and nothing if not aggressive. Jones had informed Sterl that this species was very poisonous and during the mating season would attack a man. Sterl felt reasonably safe with the forked stick.

"Isn't he pretty? Tan, almost gold, with dark bars. Hasn't got a triangular-shaped head as our bad snakes have."

"Step back, Sterl. Let me shoot his head off," demanded Leslie who manifestly was not sentimental over snakes.

"Umpumm. What for? He might be a gentleman like our rattler, who won't strike you unless you step on him."

"This tiger is no gentleman, I can assure you."

Sterl gave the snake a poke. It slid away into the grass then, exposing six feet of thick body.

"You're very tender-hearted over snakes, aren't you?" queried Leslie with a subtlety. Sterl thought he had better not inquire.

It turned out that Sterl had chosen a fitting time to reach the saddle. As they surmounted the ridge, now a well-trodden road packed down by thousands of hoofs, they looked down into the magnificent mountain pass through which they had come. Sterl had not calculated at all upon a backward view. It had been the forward and unknown one that he had anticipated. But he stood spellbound.

From behind the sun shone golden and red, striking far on in the pass, leaving the descent of the saddle in shadow. In places the shining ribbon of stream wound through verdure, and on the far flat, flame trees were mounds of burning foliage, and the wedge-shaped sassafras trees glistened as with golden frost. But most striking of all was a waterfall Sterl had not seen on the way through, a lacy, downward-smoking cascade, leaping fall after fall in golden glory from the mountainside, full in the blaze of the sun.

"Sterl, not there . . . here!" cried Leslie, tugging to wheel him around. "That is pretty . . . reminds me of home. But this here . . . this purple land we are trekking into. . . . Oh, Sterl, how wonderful!"

Indeed, the scene to west and north struck Sterl with its appealing loveliness. Like most cowboys, always exposed to the phenomena of nature, always alert to the spectacles that had to be waited for and came but once, Sterl succumbed to silent transport. At first the scene was too blazing, or too glorious, to be encompassed. He rubbed his eyes, and the dimness returned. He felt Leslie clinging to him, as mute, as rapt as he, yet this was her native land. It was only gradually, as the blaze began to soften, that Sterl's sight cleared, and his mind grasped the details of this incomparable panorama.

"Oh, Sterl," whispered the girl. "The Kimberley country is like this! Where we are trekking to make homes!"

From the height where they stood, the glistening, grassy slope with tufts and flowers like bits of fire descended gradually to the camp, where tents and canvas wagon tops shone white, and columns of blue smoke curled up, and great gum trees towered, their smooth trunks opal-hued up to the immense spread and sweep of hoary branches, fringed with leaves that were thin glints of green against the golden sky.

These spreading gums were like pillars of an arch, a wide portal opening down into a softly colored vale, from which swells of land, covered with flowering trees, rose and fell away into a plain, spotted with flame-trees and wattles, which lured the gaze on over timbered ridges, on and on with dimming gold into the luminous purple that intensified and darkened into the never-ending vastness.

Sterl gazed until the purple encroached upon the gold, and the sun sank behind the western horizon. Then he became aware that Leslie was pressing close to his side, clinging to him, gazing up with dark, shining eyes.

"My Australia," she murmured. "Isn't it glorious? Don't you love it? Aren't you glad you came?"

"Yes, Leslie . . . yes," he said, his emotion naturally shifting to the sense of her beauty and nearness.

"You will never leave Australia?"

"No, child . . . never," he replied with sadness in his voice.

"You are my dearest friend?"

"I hope so. I'm trying hard to be . . . your friend."

"And my big brother?"

Suddenly there came a convulsion within his breast, a hot gush of blood that swiftly followed his surrender to her sweetness, to her appeal. "Not your big brother, Leslie," he said thickly, as he clasped her tight. "Stop these . . . these childish notions. You're a woman . . . sweet. No man could resist. . . . And you torment me." He kissed her passionately, again and again . . . until she lay relaxed and acquiescent on his breast.

"My God! Now I've done it," he exclaimed remorsefully.

"Sterl!" She drew back to gaze up with wondering eyes and flaming face. Then with a cry she turned and fled down the slope. Sterl watched her out of sight.

"Cowboy, that's what Australia has done to you," he said, and bent to pick up his rifle.

Chapter Nine

Day after day the great trek crept across the wilderness that Leslie had called the Purple Land. Day after day the smoke signals of the aborigines arose and drifted away over the horizon in that mystic telegraphy of theirs which betrayed to the pioneers how closely their daily movements and advances were marked.

Slyter, who knew the coast blacks well, maintained it was merely one band of natives telling another of the approach of the trek. Eric Dann averred a menace increased with their penetration into the interior. Friday grew mysterious and reticent, answering queries with a puzzling: "Might be."

Sterl, grown wise from his long experience with the American Indians, had learned not to question the black about his people. He had gathered that some aborigines were friendly, but most were inimical. Those who had never had contact with the whites were not to be trusted. Those who had were afraid and would not openly attack.

Stanley Dann had no fear of blacks or endless trek or flood or heat or drought. As the difficulties imperceptibly increased, so did his cheer and courage and zeal, and his unshakable faith in himself and comrades. On Sundays in camp he held a short religious service which all were importuned to attend. Sterl noted, as the days passed, and the spell of the wilderness encroached and worked upon the minds of the trekkers, that the attendance on these simple services gradually decreased. Faith did not fail Stanley Dann, but it lost its hold on the others, who retrograded toward the primitive. All day in the open, under the hot sun, in the teeth of rain and wind, in the solemn stillness of the vast purple earth, stretching away forever in its beautiful monotony, and all night under the star-fired vault of heaven, in the wild solitude, nights and days on end, weeks augmenting into months—all this time, with its need only of the senses, developing the physical while civilization had demanded but less and less, imperceptibly and inevitably took its victims back along the trail of evolution.

Sterl saw all this, understood it only vaguely. Always he had resisted the insidious charm, had fought it, and had won because the cause, the resistless contact with nature, had sustained a break before he became utterly a savage. On this endless trek, however, he had his doubts about a break in time. It would be too long before the home instinct could counteract this tremendous influence. A ceaseless fight to carry on, to overcome, to kill the beasts and aborigines, liberated the instincts and passions that made for internal conflict in Dann's band.

Ormiston had already succumbed to it, added to his greed and lust, which would lead to his death, soon enough Sterl hoped, to circumvent his evil schemes, whatever they were. Red would succumb to it, as he had done before, unless a genuine love for Beryl Dann proved too strong for this life in the raw. Even so, Red had it in him to be great. All the drovers were being affected, and Sterl felt that not many of them would turn out gods. The women, Sterl was certain, were hopelessly in the grip of nature. Being female, being responsible for the reproduction of the species, they were closer to nature, closer to the earth, and, therefore, prey to all primitive things.

Beryl responded slowly but surely to this urge. And in her its first effect was a growth of her natural instinct of acquisition of admirers. Every night at Dann's camp a half dozen or more young drovers vied with Ormiston and Red for her smiles. It was amusing and interesting at first, but came to be the only circumstance that had power to irritate Stanley Dann. He reared his displeasure on several occasions, notably after Ormiston badly beat the boy, Cedric. Red played his game differently from the other rivals. He was wise in knowledge of

what would come to pass. He confined his efforts to serving
Beryl, so that the girl seemed to rely upon him while being
piqued that he was not at her feet. Ormiston's inordinate jealousy grew. Always when he and Red were near Beryl at the
same time, there was a charged suspense in the very air. Beryl
reveled in it. Red bore a cool, careless demeanor that deceived
all but Sterl. Ormiston might have made Red's detective task
an easy one, but for the girl.

Leslie, being the youngest in the trek and a girl of red blood
and spirit, tumbled more rapidly than any of them in her relega-
tion to the physical. She loved horses, action, danger, achievement. She lost her fear. Sometimes she would let out a piercing
wild cry of sheer rapture. She had never been squeamish about
blood and death, circumstances that some way or another on
the trek were of daily occurrence. After that sunset hour in the
gateway of the pass, when Sterl, yielding to the loveliness of
their purple land, and the appeal of the girl, had so boldly embraced and kissed her into an awakening of love, she had
avoided being alone with him for weeks. But here shyness gradually fell away from her, like dead scales no longer of use, and as
the long trek went on through austere days and nights of time
and distance, she warmed anew to Sterl, naturally, growing less
ashamed as consciousness of it faded, until her need of him was
that of a mate.

But Sterl had never transgressed again, as at that mad and un-
restrained sunset climax, though there were times when he desired to almost overwhelmingly. Nevertheless, love had come to
him again. Her beauty and youth and charm had not all to do
with this saving thing. Her perfect adaptation to this strenuous
and perilous life, her call to the manhood in him, and his recog-
nition of her sterling qualities of strength and nerve—these constituted the greatest factor in his love. Yet in all his rides with
her, their hunts and walks, he never let himself dwell upon a future. For many of Stanley Dann's troop, and very possibly for
him, there might not be an earthly future.

"Plenty smoke," said Friday, one afternoon when camp had

been made on a dry stream bed, where only a few water holes, widely separated in deep holes, afforded drink for thirsty cattle.

Sterl and Slyter, together at the campfire when Friday spoke, scanned the horizon, where on the moment all was clear. Sterl had observed smoke throughout the day, to his eye no different from those of yesterday. But the black's somber eyes and deep voice made Sterl's flesh creep.

"Friday, what you mean?" queried Slyter anxiously. "We come far." He held up three fingers. "Moons . . . three moons. Plenty smokes. No black man. All same alonga tomorrow?"

"Black fella close up." The aborigine made slow, trenchant gestures to signify as plain as print that the smoke-signaling natives were traveling along with the trek, gathering more day by day. "Black fella go alonga us. Plenty black fella. Come more. Bimeby no more smokes. Spear cattle . . . steal!"

"How long, Friday? When?"

"Mebbe soon . . . mebbe bimeby."

"What do?"

"Watchum close up. Killum!" declared the black sonorously. He reminded Sterl then of a great Kiowa chieftain, noted for his oratory.

Slyter looked apprehensively at Sterl and threw up his hands. "We've been very fortunate. Here it is end of August, four hundred miles and more on our trek, with only minor mishaps. No black trouble. Nothing to worry about but the growing dissension among us. But this looks bad."

"It does, boss," Sterl agreed gravely.

"Let's go tell Stanley."

They found their leader, as had happened before, patiently listening to Ormiston. Sterl's keen eyes noted a graying of Dann's hair over his temples. Ormiston looked hard and fit, trained down, but not lean, a man used to activity in the open. He had brooding dark eyes that did not meet Sterl's.

Slyter briefly told them of Friday's sinister knowledge of an increasing aborigine horde on their track. Dann stroked his golden beard.

"At last, eh? We are grateful for this long respite," he said, his eyes lighting as if with good news. Dann never saw bad in anything.

"I asked Friday what do? He said . . . 'Watchum close up! Killum!' " concluded Slyter.

"Well! For a black to advise that!" exclaimed the leader ponderingly. "But I do not advise bloodshed."

"I do," declared Ormiston bluntly. "If we don't, this nigger mob will grow beyond our power to cope with it. They will hang on our trek, spearing cattle at a distance, attacking us in the early dawn hour, eventually driving us frantic."

Sterl wondered what was working in this man's mind to influence him thus. But it seemed a wise ultimatum. "Boss, I agree with Ormiston."

"What's your opinion, Slyter?" asked Dann.

"If the blacks spear our cattle and menace, then I say kill."

Dann nodded his huge head in sad realization. "We will take things as they come. Probably they will not be as bad as we fear. Merge all the cattle into one mob. . . ."

"I told you I'd not agree to that," interrupted Ormiston.

"Don't regard it as my order. I ask you to help me that much," returned the leader, with patient persuasion.

"Ormiston, listen," interposed Sterl. "I've had to do with a good many cattle drives, treks you call them. After a stampede or a flood, or a terrible storm, things that are bound to happen to us, cattle can't be driven separately again."

"That I do not believe."

"Yeah? All right," snapped Sterl. "What you believe doesn't count so damn' much on this trek. What we believe does. And if you don't throw in with us, we'll believe you have the same secret motive that you have in opposing our leader's plan to cross the Never Never!"

"Ha! Hazelton, you mean that's what you'll believe," retorted Ormiston, his lips ashen.

"I believe it now. These partners of yours can't go much farther in their incredible faith in you."

Ormiston gazed away across the purple veldt, his square jaw set, his eyes smoldering, his mien one of relentless opposition.

"What's more, I can change Woolcott's allegiance to you, if not Hathaway's," declared Sterl.

"Our differences are not the important issue now," Ormiston said finally. "That is this nigger danger." And without looking at his partners he stalked away.

"Slyter, we'll put double guards on watch tonight. Merge your cattle with my mob," ordered Dann.

Before dusk fell, this order had been carried out. Slyter's cattle had become so tame that only a very unusual and unexpected event could frighten them into a stampede. They merely went on grazing along with Dann's mob. Ormiston's mob included Woolcott's and Hathaway's and grazed across the stream bed a mile distant.

Supper at Slyter's camp was late that night, and Red Krehl the last rider to come in. He sat cross-legged between Leslie and Sterl. His dry, droll humor was lacking. It gave Sterl concern, but Leslie betrayed no sign that she noticed it. After supper, at the campfire, she plagued him about Beryl.

"Les, you're a cold, fishy, soulless girl, no good a-tall," finally retaliated Red.

"Fishy? I don't know about that. Sterl, should I box his ears?"

"Red, do you mean she's an angelfish?"

"I should snicker I don't. Back in Texas there's a little catfish. And can he sting?"

"Oh, I see. Red, I'd rather have you fighting than the way you are tonight," she returned more earnestly.

"All same me, too," chimed in Sterl.

"An' for why?" the cowboy retorted.

Sterl let Leslie reply to that. She said: "Red, three times before this you've been like you are tonight . . . and something has happened."

"Yeah? An' how am I tonight?"

"Cool. Aloof. Hard as flint. Your eyes glitter. And if you smiled, your face would break like glass."

"Right-o, pard, Leslie has grown as keen as a whip. I've told you what's on my chest. How about yours?" Sterl asked.

"Ormiston ordered me out of his camp just before I rode in heah."

"What for?" asked Sterl sharply.

"I ain't shore. Beryl has been kinda sweet to me lately in front of Ormiston. It ain't foolin' me none. But it's got him. Another thing. Her Dad makes no bones about likin' me . . . havin' me look after Beryl. Ormiston hates thet even more'n he does Beryl's playin' with her other beaux. I reckon he sees I'm someone to worry about."

"You are, Red. But I've a hunch your attention to Beryl has kept you from getting a line on Ormiston."

"Mebbe it has. All the same, shore as you're knee-high to a grasshopper, Beryl will give him away yet, or let out somethin' thet I can savvy."

"Is Beryl in love with him?" Sterl asked.

"Hell, yes," replied Red gloomily.

"Les, what do you think?"

"Hell, yes," repeated Leslie, imitating Red's laconic disgust. "Beryl's had a lot of love affairs I know of. But this one is worse."

"You're both wrong," rejoined Sterl. "Beryl is fascinated by a bold, snaky man. It's the time and the place. She's a natural-born flirt. But I figure she has depth. She's not shallow, only vain, and thinking of herself. Wait till she's had real hell!"

"Pard, you're a comfortin' cuss. An' sharp as a dagger about wimmin. I hope you're right. If hell's all Beryl needs, I reckon she'll get it *pronto*."

Friday loomed out of the shadow. He carried his *wommera* and bundle of long spears. "Plenty black fella close up. *Corroboree!*"

"Listen!" cried Leslie.

On the instant a wild dog howled. It seemed a mournful and monstrous sound, accentuating the white-starred, melancholy night. Sterl saw the lights of fires, away beyond Ormiston's camp. Then a low, weird chanting of many savage voices, almost drowned by the native dogs baying the dingoes, rose high on the still air into a piercing wail, to die away. It was a blood-curdling sound, and Sterl could not analyze its power to make a white man shudder. But the wilderness took on stranger meaning, of isolation, of immensity, of agelessness, of all that was inimical to white men.

"Leslie, is it a war dance?" Sterl asked.

"They dance, I know. . . . Friday, what mean this kind *corroboree?*"

"Black fella sit down alonga us ebry night. Bimeby plenty black fella. Spear cattle . . . steal everythink."

"Friday, will these black men kill us?" queried Sterl.

"Might be bimeby. Watchum close"

Slyter came to the fire, holding up a hand to silence the talk. As he turned his ear to the east, his weather-beaten visage betrayed a somber apprehension. He listened. They all listened. The howling of dingoes, the barking of native dogs, the chanting of the aborigines transcended any wild sound Stern had ever heard. The staccato, concatenated barks of coyotes, the lonely mourn of blood-thirsty wolves, the *roo-roo-roooo* of mating buffalo, the stamping, yelling war dance of the Indians—these were wild sounds of the open, but hardly to be compared to this Australian bushland chant of beast and aborigine. Sterl sustained a queer thought that the incalculable difference might have been cannibalism.

"Cowboys, how does that strike you?" asked Slyter grimly. "That comes from the black men, the oldest men on earth, in Australia, the oldest continent, the cradle of the human race."

"Not so good, boss," replied Red. "I don't want to be alone no more. Makes my gun hand itch."

"Slyter, I am amazed . . . distressed . . . scared," Sterl admitted darkly. "For me to feel all that at once takes some figuring."

Leslie added: "Something wonderful and terrible!"

"Daughter, would you like to be home again?" queried her father. "Mum has her hands clapped over her ears."

The girl gave him a wan, brave smile. For an instant this mystic evil had caused a regurgitation of feeling for home, for security, for what had been normal civilized life. But it faded swiftly.

"No. We're on the trek. We'll fight."

"Right-o!" ejaculated Slyter. "Les, you have a rifle, and Hazelton has made you a dead shot. If you see a black man spear a horse . . . kill him!"

It struck Sterl significantly that Slyter thought of his horses, not cattle.

"Get some sleep," he concluded. "Don't risk your tent tonight. Black men seldom or never attack before dawn. But we won't trust that. Sleep under your wagon. Drake is on guard with three men. He'll call you, when they come in."

At that, they all stood up to say good night. "Red, keep my horses bunched," said Leslie. "Gosh, Sterl, I'm glad you built that board fence around my wagon!"

The cowboys piled packs and bundles outside the wheels of their wagon, on the side toward the open. Then they crept under to stretch out on their blankets in their old cowboy custom without removing coat or boots. The night was warm, and would not cool off until late. Friday lay just outside the wheels. Red growled about the *corroboree* keeping him awake, but it did nothing of the kind. Sterl thought he would find it hard to get to sleep with that savage crescendo in his ears. Habit was too strong, however, when he composed himself to sleep. Then it seemed he had hardly secured forty winks, when Red rudely shook and called him.

"Come on, pard. I shore don't want to be alone in the dark no more."

They rolled out, dressed to ride, rifles in hand. Larry was saddling horses. Drake and his three drovers were drinking tea.

"A cowboy's life is hard," Red sang under his breath.

"What time, Drake?" asked Sterl.

"Long past midnight. Near two o'clock, my watch says."

"How was the guard?"

"Mob quiet. Horses resting. No sign of blacks. But we heard them on and off. Look sharp just before and at daylight. Good you have Friday with you."

They took time only for a cup of hot tea and to light cigarettes before they were mounted and off into the night, with Friday trotting ahead. Crossing the gray stream bed, they rode out into the starlit open. The first black patch on the blanched grass was Slyter's horses, resting and grazing, a contented remuda, Sterl thought, if there ever was one. Beyond, some distance, vague and dark, stretched the great mob of cattle, quiet enough considering their numbers.

"Boys," said Larry, "I'll drove the far end, up and down this side. Meet you here every once in a while."

Sterl told Friday and Red to stay there while he rode down along the other end. He passed Dann's horses, patrolled by one rider, and a mile further down came upon another horseman, who turned out to be Cedric. They greeted each other. Cedric had been on guard for an hour and reported all well. Sterl rode back to Red.

"Wal, pard, it'd be OK but for thet damn moanin' over there," reported Red. "Gives me the willies."

"Same as any other night, so far as the stock is concerned. But what do we know? Listen and watch, Red. Keep me and Friday in sight."

"OK. I bet my chaps thet whatever's gonna pop will be over there," rejoined Red, pointing toward Ormiston's position.

Sterl kept a hundred yards or so away from the mob and patrolled a short beat, letting King graze when he was inclined to, and ever and anon making sure he could see Friday and Red. At intervals low blasts of the *corroboree* waved out across the veldt. The campfires of the aborigines still glimmered. Dogs and dingoes had ceased their howling. Sterl's senses, strung to acute alertness, gradually toned down. Nevertheless, it would not have been easy for a rabbit to escape his vigilance. His state recalled the first time he had stood guard on the Texas range when Comanches were expected to raid. They had done so, too, matchless and fleet riders, swooping down upon the remuda to stampede it and drive off horses, leaving one dead Indian on the ground, victim of Sterl's unerring rifle. Sterl had been sixteen years old then, and that had been, his first blood-spilling.

The years had sped by, hardening him with their risks and pains, and fights and wounds, and killings, so that as he sat astride King on this wild Australian hinterland, with cannibals chanting off in the darkness, he felt that these black men had better give him a wide berth.

Every half hour or thereabouts, Sterl rode back to have a word with Red, during which interval Larry had come to report all was well at his end. On these trips Sterl came back by way of Slyter's horses. The only time Sterl accosted Friday, the black held up his hand: "Bimeby!"

Therefore, all the encroachments of the feelings roused by night, solitude, space in no wise lulled Sterl away from the dark potency of Friday's bimeby.

As the hours wore on the chanting of the aborigines ceased, and the *corroboree* fires glimmered fainter and fainter to die out. Just before dawn the air was cold and still. The cattle slept. The silence seemed uncanny. There was no dreaming, tranquil, long-drawn-out ending of the night. Sterl caught something from Friday, that, once sensing it, he felt in the air the stillness, the awakening of the cattle.

The first streaks of gray in the east heralded a rumble of hoofs, like distant thunder. How Sterl started up at that sound, his hair rising stiff, his skin cold and prickling! The mob of cattle belonging to Ormiston and his companions was on the run. Sterl galloped back to Red. Friday joined them.

"They're runnin', pard, but not stampeded," Red said, his lean head bent, his ear to the east.

"Slowing down, Red," returned Sterl, straining his hearing. "Friday, what happen alonga there?"

"Black fella spearum cattle," was the reply.

"Not so bad, thet. But a stampede of this unholy mob would be orful," declared Red. "Listen, Sterl. . . . they're rollin' again, back the other way."

"Saw a gun flash!" Sterl cried, and then a dull report reached them.

"Wal, the ball's opened," said Red coolly. "Take yore pardners."

Flashes from several points, wide separated, and booms of guns attested to the activity of Ormiston's drovers.

"Aw, hell! Our cattle are wakin' up, pard. Heah comes Larry."

The young drover came tearing up to haul his mount back onto sliding haunches. "Boys, our mob . . . is about to . . . break," he panted.

"Umpumm, Larry," replied Red. "They're jest oneasy. But if thet damn mess over there gets wuss, they might. . . . Keep quiet. Listen."

More bangs of guns in lessening number accompanied the roll of hoofs. Sterl calculated a thousand or more cattle were in motion, less than a third of Ormiston's mob. It began to diminish in volume as the gunshots became desultory. But the lowing of Dann's mob, the cracking of horns, the restless hoofs caused Sterl great concern, in spite of Red's assurance. The center of this disturbance appeared to be back along the sector from which Larry had just come.

"Sterl, I'll go with Larry," Red said, wheeling Jester. "Jest in case. You ride up an' down heah. If we don't get back *pronto*, come a-runnin'. But I'm shore it ain't nothin' much."

Loping up and down Sterl put in a few moments of extreme anxiety. But presently, when he halted King to listen, he found that the dull trampling from across the flat was dying out, and that the ominous restlessness of Dann's mob was doing likewise. There were no more gunshots. Gradually silence reigned again. A rapid thud of hoofs proved to be Red's horse, loping back.

"Lost my matches. Gimme some," said the cowboy, as he reined in beside Sterl. His lighting of a cigarette relieved Sterl. "They was movin' out up there, but easy to stop. Larry can hold them, if there's no more fuss. What the hell was goin' on, pard?"

"Friday says . . . 'black fella spearum cattle.'"

"Yeah? Wal, if they don't do any wuss than thet, we're a lucky lot of *hombres*. . . . Sterl, this mob of Dann's fooled me. They've been so tame, you know, not a-tall like longhorns, thet I reckoned it'd take a hell of a lot to stampede them. But umpumm!"

"We've got a lot to learn about Australian cattle, blacks, and white men, Red."

"Wal, the men ain't much different. Stanley Dann is another Chisholm, only not so hard. Slyter is one grand feller. Ormiston is a skunk. . . . Say, I'll bet two *pesos* he'll be interested in what came off over there."

"Yes. All quiet now, though. And it's daylight."

At sunrise they rode back to camp, finding breakfast ready and the drivers busily hitching up for the day's march. Slyter wore a grave aspect and listened intently to Larry's report, which plainly relieved him. Leslie, brown and red-cheeked, was there to write the report in her journal. Presently Slyter went out to meet Friday, who was approaching from the flat. They had all just finished breakfast, when a mounted messenger in the person of Cedric dashed up to inform Slyter that Dann wanted him and the cowboys at once.

"What has happened?" queried Slyter.

"Blacks killed somebody at Ormiston's camp," replied Cedric, then loped away.

Slyter himself was the only one who showed no surprise. Dominated by Stanley Dann he just could not believe calamity would overtake them.

"That's bad. I wonder who . . . ? Boys, let's go. Larry, I'll ride your horse. Fetch in horses for today's trek."

"Wal, it'll jest be too bad if Ormiston got a spear through his gizzard," drawled Red.

"No fear," Leslie replied with a caustic little laugh. "Dad, can I go with you?"

"Good heavens, child . . . no!"

"Friday, run alonga me," said Sterl to the black.

In a few minutes they reached the larger camp. Stanley Dann and Eric with Cedric and another drover were mounted, waiting for them. Sterl espied Beryl, watching them with big troubled eyes. She waved a hand to Red.

"Bingham," spoke up the giant calmly. "Ormiston just sent word that Woolcott had been speared by blacks."

"Woolcott! Cedric didn't tell us . . . ! I thought . . . ? Stanley, this is terrible. When . . . what?"

"No other word. I dare say, if Ormiston had wanted us he'd have said so. But by all means I should go. In the excitement I suppose Ormiston forgot or didn't think it was necessary."

"We all should go," rejoined Slyter.

"Wal, I should smile," Red drawled in a peculiar tone that only Sterl understood. The cowboy was thinking hard. His eyes had a glint. His mind had leaped, as had Sterl's, to instant speculation. Sterl knew that the keen cowboy would disregard anything except his own observations and deductions.

They set out on a trot for Ormiston's camp. Cedric followed a well-defined path of hoof tracks. The dry stream bed, with its fringe of trees, made a wide bend, around which the camp appeared, and beyond grazed cattle and horses.

The tall Hathaway, bewhiskered now and no longer florid, met Dann's group as they reined in near the wagons.

"A terrible tragedy, Stanley," he said huskily. "Woolcott insisted on doing guard duty, in spite of Ormiston's advice. The blacks attacked at dawn this morning. Speared Woolcott and his horse! We fired guns to scare them off. But too late!"

"Where is he?" asked Dann.

Hathaway led them beyond the campfire, where drovers were eating, to a quartet of men beside a wagon. Ormiston, haggard of face, turned to meet the visitors. Two of the group had shovels, and had evidently just dug a grave, as indicated by a pile of yellow soil.

"Dann, it's a gruesome business I'd hoped to spare you," said Ormiston, not without harshness. "Woolcott heard the blacks rowing, and he went on guard. I advised him, particularly, to stay in . . . that the blacks probably meant only a raid for beef. But he went . . . and got killed."

"Let me see Woolcott," boomed the leader.

"Bedford and Jack just fetched him in. . . . There!"

Woolcott lay on his side, a ghastly figure, limp as a sack, with a spear through his middle. Only the side of his gray visage was exposed, but it was enough to show the convulsions of torture that had attended his death. Sterl met the sinister antagonism in his mind with the visual facts, but they left him not wholly convinced.

"Where's his horse?" asked Dann.

"Out there," replied Ormiston with a motion of hand toward a low ridge. "We have the saddle and bridle. . . . This won't delay us, Stanley. Go on with the trek. We'll bury Woolcott, mark his grave, and catch up with you."

"Bury him without any service?"

"You needn't wait to do that. If you wish, I'll read a psalm out of his Bible, and bury it with him."

"I'd like that. We can do no less. Poor Woolcott! Men, do not let this dishearten you. It is our first catastrophe. There will be others, but we are going on."

"Wal, boss," Sterl called, as Dann appeared about to leave. "I want to see just what this black man spear-work looks like." Sterl slipped out of his saddle and motioned Friday to come from behind the horses.

"Me, too," drawled Red coolly, as he swung his long legs and stepped down. "Reckon it'll be my luck to get bored by one of them spears. An' I'd jest like to see how they stick in a fellar."

Sterl, stepping slowly out from the horses, made it a point to be looking at Ormiston when the drover espied Friday. Evil and forceful as Ormiston undoubtedly was, he was not great. Sterl had seen a hundred outlaws and rustlers who could have hidden whatever this man had to hide. One was a sudden flaming hate of the black or of all blacks, and the other a fleeting glimpse of startled fear.

Friday stepped close to Woolcott's prostrate body, and with sinewy black hand, wonderful in its motion, its lifetime of familiarity with that aboriginal weapon, he laid hold of the spear, to move it, to bend over.

Ormiston burst out: "All niggers look the same to me!" And with murder in his protruding eyes, he pulled a gun. Sterl, ready and quick as light, shot the gun out of Ormiston's hand.

Pandemonium broke loose. The drover yelled lustily. The horses, snorting, plunging, kept the riders busy for a moment. Friday backed away, probably frightened, though no sign of it showed in his inscrutable face. Sterl stepped back a little, smoking gun extended, lining up the shocked Ormiston with his drovers, Bedford and Jack. Red was at Sterl's side. Stanley Dann bellowed an order from behind.

"Ormiston, you and I will have real trouble over Friday yet," rang out Sterl. He had meant to cripple the drover, shoot his hand off, but the bullet had evidently hit the gun, to send it spinning away. Ormiston had been holding that stung member with his left. He gazed at it as if he expected to see blood and shot flesh. But his hand was intact.

"Next time you throw your gun, do it at me," Sterl added scornfully. "You'd have killed this black man."

"Yes . . . I would . . . and I'll do it . . . yet," shouted Ormiston, now purple in the face. "All niggers look alike to me."

"Ormiston, you're blacker at heart than Friday is outside."

Stanley Dann urged his big charger near to the belligerents. "What damned revolt is this?" he demanded.

Sterl explained in few words. Ormiston contended that sight of the black had incited him to frenzy.

"Let that do," boomed the leader. "Isn't Woolcott's death lesson enough? We must squash this dissension amongst us. Ormiston, I blame you most. To attempt to kill Friday was unwarrantable. Give Woolcott a decent burial. Put up a cross. Then come on with the trek. Back to camp, all!"

Dann, with Slyter and his brother, Eric, and Cedric, rode away. "Mosey along, pard," Red said curtly, "but don't turn yore back *pronto* to these *hombres*."

That idea had been far from Sterl's mind. He had not taken two backward steps before he bumped into King. The black had stood his ground. Sterl led him away. Passing Hathaway, who appeared extremely upset, Sterl called out that Red had meant no offense to him. Beyond the wagons Sterl leaped astride King and spurred him to the side of his comrade, already mounted. They soon overtook the long-striding Friday. Slowing down to accommodate the black, they rode a beeline for their own camp.

Slyter came in while Sterl and Red changed horses. The drover looked as if thought was a confusing faculty at the moment.

"Sorry, boss," said Sterl. "I'm always deepening those furrows in your brow. But you have eyes. You must have seen that Ormiston would have shot Friday. Anyway you heard him say so."

"I saw and I heard," declared Slyter, wagging his head. "I tried to convince Stanley that Ormiston meant to murder my black. But, no!"

"Let Dann take his own time."

Leslie bounced out from somewhere, like a handsome, lithe boy in rider's ragged garb. "Dad! You saw and heard what?" she cried, flashing-eyed and keen, not to be denied.

"Oh, Lord!" groaned her father.

"Leslie, put this down in your little book," Sterl said, and he made a swift, concise report of the incident.

She flamed even more readily than usual. "He would have shot Friday." Then she swore, the first time Sterl had ever heard her use a word of the profanity so prevalent in camp, and most often on the drawling cowboy's lips. When her father looked shocked and helpless, Leslie went on. "The louse! The dirty low-down *hombre!*"

"Haw! Haw! Haw!" rang out Red's laugh, this time with a deadly note. "Les, you're shore the makin's of one genuine American cowgirl."

"Boss, come here and listen," Sterl spoke up while he fastened the cinches on his rangy sorrel. "Red and I will start out on the trek. But we'll come back with Friday, and, after Ormiston is on the move, we'll ride around back there to look over the ground. Red and I can read tracks. And if it's too much for us, maybe Friday can see something. We'll catch up *pronto.*"

"Sterl, let me go," begged Leslie.

"No."

Ormiston had manifestly lost little time trekking away after the Danns. And it was Sterl's opinion that he would now drove his cattle to unite in one mob.

Woolcott had been hastily buried in a shallow grave without a headmark. A few pieces of lumber lay scattered about. Sterl had Friday carry stones to place on the grave, after Red and he had stamped the ground hard. Then they erected a makeshift cross, which could be seen at a distance and would last for years.

That done, with the black in the lead, they set out on foot, leading their horses, to find what signs they could of the tragedy. Half a mile out on the grassy flat, at the edge of rising, sandy ground, Friday located a dead horse.

"Pard, shore makes me sore the way this black man can see," complained Red. "Why, I reckoned I had eyes. They must be gettin' pore, or Friday is jest too damn' good."

"Red, I found that out long ago. Friday has the eyes of an eagle."

The dead horse was a bay, lying on its side, with a spear sticking up high. While Friday scrutinized it, laid gentle hold of it, the cowboys walked around the prostrate bay. They had seen thousands of dead horses—dead from every cause that accident and the elements and the brutality of man could bring about.

"Look, heah," said Red, presently, pointing to a bloody ear on the underside of the head. "Wait until Friday is through . . . then we'll turn this hoss over."

The black had pulled out the long spear and was scrutinizing it.

"Boss," he said to Sterl, "all same killum horse like white man." And Friday made one of his impressive gestures back toward Woolcott's grave.

"How, Friday? Show me?" Sterl queried intensely.

The black fitted the bloody spear to his *wommera*, and made ready as if to throw.

"No *wommera*. No black fella spearum white man! No black fella killum horse!"

"By Gawd!" ejaculated Red, not in horror, but in confirmation of something that had been sensed.

"Friday, let me have them," said Sterl in swift passion. He adjusted the spear to the *wommera* in his awkward way and, as Friday had illustrated, made about to throw. "No black fella throw spear? No killum Woolcott that way? No spearum this horse?"

"No . . . no, me tinkit!" replied Friday emphatically. His great eyes glowed like ebony balls on fire.

"How, then?" cried Sterl.

"Spear pushum in white man. Pushum in horse. No black fella do." And Friday took the long spear, to shove it into the horse, a deliberate and intelligent action.

"Heah, help me turn this hoss over," Red said. The three of them managed it, not without dint of effort. The cowboy got down on his knees to examine the bloody ear. The little stream of blood had dried. Red threw off a glove and thrust his bare hand into that ear. Suddenly he grew tense. When he looked up, it was certain that Sterl had an accelerated heartbeat and a mind in which whirling thoughts were centering—fixing. He had seen Red look like that before.

"Shot!" hissed the cowboy. Then again he bent over to move his hand. "Got my finger in a bullet hole. . . . Somebody shoved a gun in this hoss's ear an' shot him! Look heah!" As he pulled out his hand, there were black stains merged with blood on his forefinger. "Powder! Burnt powder!"

Red wiped his hand on the sand and grass, then completed the job with his handkerchief. He stood up, and, searching his pocket for tobacco and matches, he sat down to roll a cigarette. His tense, lean face, red as fire, and his luminous blazing blue eyes disappeared in a cloud of smoke.

Sterl addressed the watchful black. "Friday, look . . . see tracks . . . black fella tracks all around." Sterl himself could not see a single one except Friday's. Naturally there were boot tracks all around in every sandy spot. Sterl sat down heavily.

"Murder!"

"Pard, as shore as Gawd made little apples . . . it was murder," replied Red, blowing away the smoke. "Hell, we shouldn't be surprised. We knowed it all the time . . . only we was afraid to think. Thet . . . !" Red let out as if in relief a long string of vile names—the worst that the Western range afforded.

"Why . . . why?" queried Sterl passionately.

"What the hell why?" flashed Red, getting up. "It is! We don't care why. Did we ever care for low-down rustler motives? We had Ormiston figgered from thet fust minnit we seen him!"

"Stanley Dann will never believe it. Slyter, neither, though he is beginning to show faint signs of intelligence. Could we prove murder to these drovers, if we fetched them back here?"

"Mebbe, if they'd come. But Dann wouldn't come. Pard, I'm afraid he's leanin' to a belief we Yankees air too hardhearted an' suspicious."

"I had that thought, too," said Sterl soberly. "Red, you're figuring we'd better look out for our own scalps and let these drovers find things out?"

"I reckon I am, pard, though I ain't had time to figger much."

"Maybe you're right, Red. You're harder-headed than I am. Little sentiment about you in this kind of deal. But I find it, well, not easy to fall in with."

"Why so, Sterl?"

"If Ormiston is really as bad as he is . . . heavens! He'll not stop at anything. There's Leslie to think of . . . and Beryl. I can see no difference in the way he looks at either girl. He's a tiger."

"Leslie is yore lookout, pard, an' Beryl is mine. She's a vain little flirt . . . the damnedest proposition I was ever up against . . . but thet's no call for me not to save her, if I can. Besides, pard, I cain't help lovin' her, damn my fool heart."

Friday returned to say: "Boss, no black fella tracks alonga here."

The cowboys mounted, each taking a last glance at the dead horse, with its sinister meaning, then they followed Friday.

It was not far to where he came upon the black man tracks thick in every bare spot. He led the cowboys past dead campfires, merely a few charred sticks crossed, and on for several hundred yards to a trampled, blackened, sandy patch where a large fire had burned. A steer's head, skinned and split, needed not the scattered bones, all of them gnawed, and the bloody ground to mark the spot where there had been an aboriginal feast. What amazed Sterl was the completeness of it. No hide or hoofs left! Only a few bones divested of their marrow. From that spot foot tracks of a horde of natives led on in the direction of the trek.

Friday pointed to smoke signals so many miles ahead that they showed only faintly.

"Wal, thet'll be about all, pard," said Red. "Let's ride around across this heah flat, an' come up behind the mob on Slyter's side."

"While meditating that there are bloody *hombres* here, like those we thought we'd said good bye to at home?" Sterl asked bitterly.

"I reckon human nature is the same all over the world," observed Red.

Chapter Ten

That day's trek, owing to the larger mob of cattle becoming infused with the excitement which dominated Ormiston's, proved to be the longest so far. There were steers among them that had native spears sticking from their backs. When Dann halted for camp in a wide vale of grass with a lake in the center, dusk came on too quickly for the drovers to put the wounded cattle out of their misery, which Sterl supposed they would do.

That night the vote of argument went against Stanley Dann. The drovers contended that to kill the speared cattle would be playing into the native's hands. The decision showed lack of foresight, thought Sterl. The blacks would spear more cattle night after night, and all of these would die eventually, or become diseased and a menace to the mob and so would have to be killed.

Sterl's reply to Dann's interrogation carried little weight with Ormiston and his adherents. Sterl had said: "Sure. Kill the speared cattle, and shoot enough more for these blacks to gorge themselves for a month or two. Maybe then we could lose them."

At this camp Sterl had little inclination and not much opportunity to add to Slyter's worries by telling him that Woolcott had been murdered. But Slyter did confide in Sterl and Red that he had learned from the Danns of Ormiston's claim to Woolcott's fifteen hundred head of cattle for a gambling debt. Sterl was staggered, and the fluent Red rendered speechless for the moment.

"Hathaway verified it," went on Slyter. "Told me Ormiston, Woolcott, and those drovers, Bedford and Jack, gambled every night."

Later, when Slyter went about his tasks, Red came out of his dumb spell. "Pard, thet ain't so. It's another of Ormiston's damn' lies. Hathaway might believe it, I reckon. He always went to bed with the chickens. For months, almost, either I have seen Ormiston with Beryl, or I have been with them drovers, Jack an' Bedford. Cairds was never mentioned to me, an' you know I had a roll of English pounds thet would have choked a cow. I got a hunch they figgered on stealing it from me. An' there wasn't no hurry, 'cause where'n'll could I spend it out heah?"

"A-huh. So the plot thickens," mused Sterl.

"An' misfortunes ain't comin' singly. I was jest waitin' for somethin' to start."

Red had clairvoyant power, or hunches as he called them in his cowboy philosophy; and in this instance what he said proved to be in the nature of prophecy.

Leslie, in order to replenish the fire so that she could see to write, picked up a bundle of firewood that Friday had packed in and, having neglected to put on her gloves, she was severely bitten by what Slyter feared was the red-back spider.

Friday found the spider, which he gave an unintelligible name, and which Slyter pronounced to be one of the deadly poisonous species. While he applied what remedies were at hand, the black ran off to get one of his native cures.

The spider had been killed but not crushed. Sterl and Red examined it with attention, as evidently it was more dangerous than their well-known tarantula. This red-back had a body as large as a small marble, with a red band around it, and eight legs, two long ones in front, and the same at the back, with the four shorter ones between.

From the swelling of Leslie's shapely hand, and the pain which grew intense, it was evident, indeed, that the red-back bite produced somewhat the same symptoms and consequences Sterl had experienced in a rattlesnake bite and in other cowboys who had been bitten.

Leslie made light of it, especially after Friday returned to paste some herb concoction of his own upon the ugly wound. Sterl had found out that strong coffee was a better remedy for snake bite than whiskey. He plied the girl with coffee and walked her up and down for hours, keeping her awake until she fell asleep in his arms from exhaustion. Then he carried her to the wagon and laid her on her bed.

Soon after that the night guard changed, with Larry bringing in the horses. When they called Red, it was to discover that he was ill with chills and fever, the like of which had never before fallen to that cowboy. But he refused to stay in bed. The three men rode out together, preceded by Friday. They made connection with Cedric at the back end of the mob and Eric Dann at the front, when they separated as before to patrol their respective beats.

Sterl, once more alone, reverted to concern over Leslie's condition, and to the menace of the night. The only comfort he had was the presence of the black man. While Friday sat on a stone, motionless and alert, Sterl had no fear of being surprised.

The night was warm with sweet scents on the breeze. Wild fowl out on the lake uttered weird cries. He listened in vain for the howling of dingoes and native dogs, and the melancholy chanting. The mob quieted down into repose and another dawn wore around.

That day Red was so sick he could not sit his horse. Stanley

Dann claimed his ailment was intestinal and came from something he had eaten. Red swore and asked for whiskey. He rode on the dray, high on top of the great load of flour bags, where he went to sleep.

Leslie should not have ridden at all, but neither her father nor Sterl could dissuade her. "Shucks," she said. "I'm all right. I won't give into thet pesky old red-back!"

Sterl rode close to her that day, during which she fell out of her saddle twice. She was game, and she did not lose her sense of humor or even the new audacity that had developed on this trek.

"Red says I'm gonna be a genuine cowgirl, didn't he?" And on the occasion of the second sliding out of her saddle, which Sterl thought came from her falling asleep, she swayed to and fro in his hold, unable to mount without his aid. "Dog-gone it, Sterl," she said, when she was up, "if I fall off again, treat me to some of that . . . that medicine you gave me back at that one camp."

Two days of laborious travel followed. Before sunset of the first, the expedition stalled before a considerable stream with steep banks. Even when the mob, driven across in advance, had trampled out crude roads, it required eight horses to drag each wagon across. Leslie was still too weak to brave the treacherous current, and Sterl, mounted on King, carried her across in his arms. Midcurrent, she looked up and said softly: "I'd like to ride all the rest of the way like this."

"Yeah? Three thousand miles?" responded Sterl. "Well, you wouldn't have much consideration for King . . . and me."

"King? Oh, he can carry double. And you are so strong," she murmured, her eyes closing. Sterl thought she was falling asleep.

This little occurrence he registered as one of the dangerous incidents, if not misfortunes, that were multiplying.

Dry camp that afternoon awakened Sterl anew to the alarming probability that lack of water headed Stanley Dann's list of obstacles to the trek. So far it had been negligible. Camp stood picturesquely in a great open bush with huge gums wide apart, spinifex and mulga abounding, sassafras trees pointing skyward like inverted ice-cones, and flowering flame-trees burning in the sunset.

The drovers threw the mob in a huge circle, closely bunched. Ormiston pitched his camp a stone's throw from the Dann's; Slyter kept to his rule of isolation at some distance.

Friday anticipated a native *corroboree* that night, and it was forthcoming, with its accompaniment of dingo choruses and dog howls. No fires were visible off in the bush. Dann's order was to let the aborigines alone, unless they stole into camp to attack. Morning disclosed no close evidence that the blacks had killed cattle, but Slyter shrewdly claimed their leader could have found out he put Friday and the cowboys to hunting tracks.

All day the smoke signals rose far ahead, the sun burned hotter, the tiny flies swarmed invisibly around the riders' and drovers' heads. Ten miles or more onward through the deepening bush a small stream invited camp and rest. At dusk flying-foxes, like vampire bats, swished and whirred over the camps; opossums and porcupines had to be thrust out of the way; stealthy animals rustled in the spinifex almost within the circle of campfire light. Every piece of firewood hid a horde of ants, and, as they crawled frantically away in every direction, Bill, the cook, scooped them back into the fire with a shovel. But in spite of that they swarmed everywhere and bit everybody, which, although a trivial thing, Sterl thought, yet acutely added to the irritating discomfort and the sense of misgiving.

Then there was a large bug that came out of decayed wood, a blue-black bug over an inch long, which was not painful like the fierce ants, but decidedly more annoying in the vile odor it gave off when discovered. Slyter called it a cockroach. Friday gave it an unpronounceable name, but Red Krehl roared: "Jest a plain ole stinkin' American bedbug growed into a giant!" And Sterl was bound to admit that his cowboy comrade's description was felicitous. Snakes, too, became more common in the bush as the trek neared the tropics. Sterl espied a death-adder under his lifted foot, stepped on it before he could jump, and then leaped like a bent sapling sprung erect. Red, scared as he was, let out a yell of glee. "Aw, pard, it ain't a-comin' to us, not a-tall!" After that the friends did not take off their chaps at the end of the day's trek; and Sterl cut down an extra pair of his for Leslie to wear. The girl's extraordinary delight in them was equaled by the picturesque exaggeration of her charm. Red proposed to Beryl that he model a pair of his for her, which offer she received with pleasure. But Ormiston pooh-poohed the idea, she explained, and told Red he need not sacrifice his chaps. Sterl thought that more than usually a mark of the ascendancy the handsome drover was acquiring over Dann's daughter. "Wal," declared Red to Beryl, "if you're more afraid of Ormiston's ridicule than snake bite, why go ahaid an' get bitten. Shore would tickle me."

There were times when Red showed a side that puzzled and piqued Beryl to redoubling her charm over him. There would come a time, Sterl reflected, when the girl would fail with Red.

On and on the trek plodded to the north and west, its progress retarded somewhat by the bush, but scarcely hampered by the blacks who followed. Several nights Ormiston's drovers fired upon marauding aborigines, so they claimed; then so far as shooting was concerned, there might not have been any thieves bent on stealing beef. But there were, because Friday informed Sterl of it, and Sterl told Slyter. The news never got to Stanley Dann.

For weeks after Woolcott's death Ormiston kept mostly to his camp. He had even neglected Beryl, a circumstance Red had made the most of. Stanley Dann made the remark that Ormiston had taken the Woolcott tragedy very grievously. Dann had been gratified by the drover's throwing his cattle in with the main mob. The strained relation was certainly no worse, if it had not grown better. But Sterl was not deceived by Ormiston. Red had abandoned his plan of intimacy with Ormiston's drovers, and apparently worked a miracle in his transformation of behavior. He bided his time. He still clung to his belief that Beryl Dann would be instrumental in exposing Ormiston in his true colors.

The old track of the first and only cattle trek into that northland was easy to locate, though difficult to travel. This open bush appeared to be a plain, bounded by hills ranging in the same direction. On clear mornings purple mountains shone ahead. Pests and vermin and heat and failing water holes increased perceptibly every day's trek.

Finally the smoke signals gradually diminished in number until they were seen no more. The hungry horde of blacks, abreast of the trek for a month or more, had satiated their ravenous appetites and had gone, vanished like their mysterious smoke.

With the departure of the aborigines, relieving the guard duty and the ever-present menace, Sterl reverted somewhat to his absorption in natural phenomena. It was hard to be enthusiastic and vigilant with a blazing sun overhead, a swarm of black flies obscuring his sight, and the invisible little devils, biting like fire. Leslie had constructed a head-net which saved her face and neck. During the trek through the bad fly country the cowboys let their beards grow and wore silk scarves up to their eyes, and even over them at times.

Both Mrs. Slyter and the girl were in good health and spirits despite the hard work, ceaseless movement, and nervous strain. As for the last, however, Leslie could not have been said to possess nerves any more. She thrived on the spare rations, the days astride horses, the innumerable details of the trek. Sterl had since worn out his perturbation at the girl's speaking eyes, with their light for him. If it helped Leslie to feel about him as evidently she did, to sustain her courage and lend to romance, then Sterl was glad. He could well put off the distant day when they might come out of this hazardous trip alive.

One night Red returned to camp rather earlier than usual, and his look prepared Sterl for a disclosure.

"Pard, I jest happened to heah somethin'," he whispered impressively, leaning his falcon-shaped red head toward Sterl. "I was after a bucket of water for Beryl, kinda under cover of the bank where the brook was clean. Ormiston with Jack an' Bedford came along above. I heahed low voices, kinda sharp, before they got to me. Then, right above, Ormiston spit out . . . 'No, I told you. Not till we get to the headwaters of the Diamantina.'"

Sterl echoed his last four words. "Red, what do you figure from that?"

"Wal, it's plain as print so far. Whatever Ormiston an' outfit have in mind, it's to come off at the haidwaters of thet river. No doubt his men, those two *hombres* I've distrusted all along, want to pull off the deal sooner."

"Big stake in it for them," pondered Sterl.

"Shore. Money stake. Mebbe all the whiskey they can drink. Don't imagine thet wouldn't go a long way with those *hombres*. This thirsty trek has got their very flesh cryin' out for likker."

"Money stake? Ormiston wouldn't let everyone in on a big deal?"

"Right-o, pard. Wal, what is thet deal?"

"You tell me, Red."

"Hell, you used to have brains. Cain't you help me figgerin'?"

"I'll try. Suppose I analyze this in what we will call an Australian way. Then you give me your old cowboy range American slant."

"Hop to it, pard."

"Ormiston wants to be a partner of Stanley Dann's after the trek. Or get control of a big mob of cattle, and marry Beryl. He is working his deal so that his antagonism to Dann and his threatened split will induce Dann to give almost anything to keep him on the trek. Ormiston's drovers want a showdown for their labors on a speed-up of the break."

"You ain't calculatin' anythin' a-tall on our idee thet Woolcott was murdered?"

"Hardly. That is a sticker, I admit, but I am trying to find a motive more credible for those Australians."

"Umpumm! Hell, no! Not a-tall!" Red exploded. "Cain't you get it in yore dumb haid thet one or more of these Australians can be jest plumb bad?"

"Yes. But Stanley Dann or Slyter couldn't figure that way."

"No. An' thet's why they'll get it where the chicken gets the axe, unless we circumvent the deal. . . . Pard, listen to a little plain sense from a Texas *hombre* who's knowed a thousand bad eggs. Ormiston is a drover, mebbe, a cattleman, mebbe. He's been used to the open, what these people call the Outback. Thet we can be shore of. He's after Beryl, shore, but he's no keener after her than he was Leslie. She's in the deal. He's after cattle, all he can steal! It's a cinch he killed Woolcott, or had one of his outfit do it. Woolcott probably bucked. Wanted to go back to Dann. Their gamblin' debt can be discounted. Ormiston is workin' to persuade some of Dann's riders to side with him. I know thet. They jest damn' near approached me, which was what I was wantin'! Wal, muss thet all up an' figger. Ormiston has control of three thousand haid. He'll get hold of more, by hook or crook. An' he'll split with Dann at the haidwaters of thet river, take Beryl with him by persuasion or force, an' light out for some place he knows, or is figgerin' on. Thet, my son, is what old Dudley Texas says!"

"My God! Red. All same just another bloody rustler?"

"All same jest another bloody cow thief, like hundreds we've knowed an' some we've hanged. Only this bird is long on good English talk an' manners, an' short on rustler brains an' cunnin'."

"I can't believe it."

"Yes, you can. You do. But you're humped because he's Ash Ormiston of Australia. Hell, pard, if he had bucked you at home as he has heah, why he'd be daid!"

"Stanley Dann will never believe that until too late."

"Reckon not. We might talk Slyter into realizin' what it's all about. Queer deal, ain't it, pard?"

"Queer and extraordinary," returned Sterl with a hard breath.

"Wal, only thet last 'cause we're heah. The size of the herd, near eight thousand haid, is enough to make it turrible. Onheard of! An' the men involved . . . except you an' me . . . jest men who have run cattle for years without learnin' thet big herds in wild places breed easy money an' all thet goes with it."

"Red, we can't let it go . . . come to a head. We can't," Sterl declared.

"We jest can, my love-sick gazabo!" retorted Red. "For the present, I'm in love with Beryl wuss than I ever was with any other girl. An' with less hope. But Ormiston will have to kill me to get her. Savvy? An' I'll bet my all that you'll kill Ormiston before he gets anyways near takin' Leslie."

"You're talking facts now," said Sterl stridently. Then he eased up on the harsh speech. "Red, I haven't let myself believe I love that kid. But if I don't, I ought to."

"Thanks, pard. I reckoned you was already. No matter. A few more months on this trek will answer for that. An' I'm glad."

"Ours is the biggest issue. At the least it means the lives of these two girls, who have been forced into this raw country by blind fathers. To hell with the cattle! Let's go out and clean up Ormiston's outfit."

"You're gettin' mad too soon. No call for thet yet, as I can see. We'd queer ourselves with Allan Hathaway, who's a weak member, with Eric Dann, mebbe with Stanley. No, pard, we've stood this deal for months. Let's stand it some more, a lot more, before we get mad. Somethin' will happen one of these days, jest like that crack of Ormiston's I heahed today, an' always there's the chance Beryl will put us wise to Ormiston. She thinks he's a prince. Told me so. Prince? Good Lord! An' she's gone against her dad, as grand a man as ever had a daughter. I'm layin' low, Sterl. I'm playin' safe. I have eyes in the back of my haid, an', believe me, I'll know *pronto* if any of thet outfit tries to sneak up on me. Never was so sore, so keyed up in my life. Darn' if I don't almost like this set-up. It's somethin' to figger out. Pard, we've been in some tough places. This is shore the toughest. Let's never let it get the best of us."

"Red Krehl, did I have to come 'way out here to Australia to appreciate you?" demanded Sterl.

"Dog-gone if I know," replied Red in dubious surprise. "I reckoned you always had me figgered, pard."

"No, I'm afraid I didn't, Red," Sterl returned reluctantly. "Maybe it took this trek to make me. Maybe you sense things beyond my powers. . . . But, old-timer, I swear I'll rise to this thing as you have risen. And see it as you see it. And I'll take a long hitch in my patience, and whatever else it calls for."

Chapter Eleven

The trek plodded on day after day. And more and more Sterl felt himself slipping back to the level of the unconscious savage as represented so strikingly in the black man Friday, who had mental processes, it was true, but was almost wholly guided by his instincts and his emotions. It was a good thing, he reflected. It made for survival. Thrown against the background of the live and inanimate forces of the earth, he reflected, man had to go back. He discussed his mood sometimes with his companions of his campfires. Slyter laughed: "We call it 'gone bush.' I would say it denoted mentality!" Leslie gave proof to his theory by flashing: "Sterl, you make me think. And I don't want to think!" Stanley Dann said: "Undoubtedly a trek like this would be a throwback for most white men . . . unless they found their strength in God." Well, he himself had a job to do—to deal with Ormiston.

Stanley Dann eventually arrived at the conclusion that somewhere back along the trek they had crossed Cooper Creek, famed in the pioneer explorer annals. Any one of several streams could have been Cooper Creek. But he admitted that he had expected a goodly stream of running water. Long ago, Sterl thought, Dann should have been warned by a sun growing almost imperceptibly hotter that water would grow scarcer. So it had proved to be. Still, always in the blue distance, mountain ranges lent hope. The ranges were watersheds and from them perennial streams wore down to the grasslands.

Through this bush, the endless monotony of which the interminable glory and green and gold, the everlasting area of gum trees and mulga scrub and spinifex, wore so strangely on the trekkers that desert country would have been welcome, they never made an average of more than five miles a day. Dry camps occurred more often; two-day stays at water holes further added to the slowing up. But the drovers plodded on and on, and ever on, which was the realization of the dream of Stanley Dann.

In October the trek at last worked out of the "always-always-all-same-land," as Red Krehl had named it, on to the gradual slope of open grass leading down to what appeared a boundless valley in the west and purple mountains to the north. Water would come down out of them. A wandering thread of darker green, crossing to the west and losing itself in the vastness, promised a river or stream. The absence of game and fowl, however, had an ominous significance. Stanley Dann trekked fifteen miles that day, from dawn until dark, and then had to make dry camp. A second day ended almost as long a trek without coming to water. A third day's journey, prolonged to the point of exhaustion, brought the drovers to stream and jungle and looming ranges and was none too soon to save the cattle. They dammed the stream. Many of them drowned; others were mired in the mud; a few were trampled to death by the frenzied mob. The horses fared badly, though not to the point of loss.

"Make camp for days," was Stanley Dann's order, when mob and remuda had been droved out upon the green. The night watch was omitted. Horses and cattle and trekkers rested from nightfall until sunrise.

Day disclosed the loveliest site for a camp, the freest from flies and insects, the richest in color and music of innumerable birds, the liveliest in game that the drovers had experienced. But ill luck still dogged the trek, or, in Stanley Dann's version, just the daily vicissitudes to be expected.

Larry stalked to breakfast to inform Slyter that horses were missing from the remuda. This was serious for the horse drover. It turned out that some of Slyter's wagon teams had been driven off or had wandered away. Red's favorite horse, Jester, a gift from Leslie, and King and Lady Jane were gone.

"Friday told me no black fella close up," Slyter said. "So they can't be stolen."

"King never ran off before," rejoined Sterl.

"Not on this trek," said Slyter. "But he has. All the horses have a wild streak. Maybe brumbies led them off. Sterl, I suppose that you, being a cowboy, can track a horse?"

"Used to be pretty good," Sterl said. He got his rifle and started.

But he only lost himself in the deep bush, and continued to be lost for three days. Afterward, he looked back on this adventure with mixed feelings of chagrin and of glory in the experience. The chagrin rose from the fact that in an obscure stretch of jungle he mistook the faint tracks of a band of cassowaries for those of King's shod hoofs, nor realized it until he came upon a flock of these great, awkward, ostrich-like birds staring at him with protruding, solemn eyes. The rest he remembered afterward only in snatches: an open space where foliage and a cascade of the stream caught an exquisite diffused golden light breaking through blue rifts in the green dome overhead. Tiny butterflies, or flying insects, like sparks from a fire, vied with wide-winged butterflies in a fascinated fluttering over a pool that mirrored them, and the great opal-hued branches above, and the network of huge-leafed vines, and the spears of lacy foliage. Fly-catchers, birds too beautiful to be murderers, were feeding upon the darting, winged insects.

"Wal, if I gotta die," mused Sterl, quoting Red, "let it be heah!" And Sterl found a seat on a mossy rock to forget his hunt. Of the many trees that sent lofty branches above to reach out, twine, and roof this glade, there were four that were remarkable. The nearest to him was some kind of a gum, huge in girth, white as snow in that restrained light, spotless and branchless for over a hundred feet, where it split and spread in great gnarled arms with opal patches between areas of peeling brown bark that lost themselves in the green. Another was a gray tree, ten feet thick at the base, encompassed and lassoed and criss-crossed by a thick bulging vine, like a boa constrictor, that grew tightly into the trunk, all the way up in triangles and squares that left little of the tree exposed. And this giant of the jungle was dead, killed by the parasite. The third tree was one of which Sterl had seen a number, though none approaching the grandeur of this one. It was what Slyter had called a mountain ash, and from a fluted trunk twelve feet thick it sheered up branchless and noble to refuse to mingle its outspread top, high above the green dome. The fourth tree was like an enormous banyan, of which Sterl had seen pictures. It resembled the banyan in the way it sent down innumerable branches, all to become rooted and spread wide.

A splash in the water, and a movement of something alive, distracted Sterl's attention from the tree-tent he was examining. He saw a strange animal slide or draw out on the bank. It had a squatty body that might have resembled a flat pig, but for the thick fur on its back. It had a long head, which took the shape, presently, when Sterl located the eyes, of an abnormal and monstrous bill of a duck. Sterl stared disputing his own eyesight. But the thing was an animal and alive. It had front feet with long, cruel claws. Its back feet and tail were hidden in the grass. All of a sudden Sterl realized that he was staring at the strangest creature in this strange Australia, perhaps in the world, no less than Leslie's much-vaunted duck-billed platypus. Then, as never before, Sterl wished for his skeptic cowboy friend. If that queer cross between a duck and an egg-laying mammal had not slid back into the pool, Sterl would have watched it till dark.

Taking up the horse tracks again, Sterl reluctantly left the shining, silent glade and went on. Tree ferns high over his head, drooping fern leaves twenty feet long, appeared in spots where their crowns could catch the sunlight. And the deeper he penetrated upon the course he had decided upon, he began leaving a trail his black man friend could follow at a trot. Every few steps he broke the tips of brush or stripped the tufted grasses or crashed through the scrub.

He followed an irregular, flowing stream into level, rocky country where, if the jungle still persisted, its luxuriant growths were wanting. The great gum trees, however, spread on interminably. Light ahead and open sky prepared Sterl for a change in the topography of the bush. And a low hum of falling water was the voice of a waterfall. Out from behind giant trees he stepped to the brink of a precipice and to a blue, sun-streaked abyss that brought him to a standstill.

It was sunrise. The sun, gloriously red and blazing, appeared again to be in the wrong place. Sterl had to reconcile himself that this burst of morning light came from the east. No matter how badly a man was lost he dared not deny the sunrise. The abyss at his feet had the extraordinary beauty, if not the colossal dimensions, of the Arizona cañons he had known from boyhood. Sterl was an expert in cañon walls and depths. Up from his right seared a low, thunderous roar. By craning his neck he saw where the stream leaped off, turning from shining green to lacy white. It fell a thousand feet, struck a ledge of broken wall, cascaded over and through huge rocks, to leap from a second precipice from which purple depths no murmur arose. Walls opposite where Sterl stood, rust-stained and lichened, sheered down precipitously in shadow. On his own side the sun tipped the ramparts with rose and gold and blazed the great wall halfway down.

The space across the neck of this cañon appeared narrower, perhaps, than it really was. It widened away from that notch where Sterl stood. Far down the cañon green slopes met in a dark line, where outcropping crags of yellow broke the dark monotony. Above these crags a bulge of timbered slope brunted the cañon and split it. To the left it yawned into purple space, and to the right a smaller branch led Sterl's searching gaze to another waterfall, a wedge-shaped column of exquisitely sunrise-tinted white that fell down and down, like smoke, to disappear without a murmur.

"Well, Australia, as if I hadn't already seen enough!" was Sterl's tribute. It was hard for a lover of cañons to turn away from that superb sight, and Sterl did so reluctantly. But he was lost, seriously lost. He pushed on, turning away from this deceiving sun, marveling that such a huge break in the earth could occur on what had apparently been a level terrain with mountain ranges rising. It added another proof of the immensity and diversity of this hinterland.

Strange birds caught his attention, one of them a black parrot, and gigantic beetles, dragon-flies, spiders. He pushed on, resolutely opposed to the instinct and passion that had led him into the predicament. A gigantic snake in his path, however, stopped him agape, alarmed, his rifle thrust forward ready for an attack. But the mottled reptile, neck as thick as his arm, body as large as his thigh, glided away, lengthening out to fully twenty feet.

"Whew! He was a humdinger," burst out Sterl, wiping the sweat from his brow.

Sterl decided he would shoot a wallaby, or rabbit, or even a Koala bear, if he met with one, and have the meat in case he was held up in the bush another night. He saw three kinds of snakes, all of which slipped away out of sight. Once he had a shot at a bush turkey, running like a streak across an open place, but he missed to his chagrin. "Never could hit turkeys running crosswise," he grumbled. He passed nests of some kind, all of twice his height, and from one a big bird, to judge from the roar of wings he made, flew off unseen into the bush.

But Sterl did happen on a bird so beautiful in appearance and astounding in action that it halted him in his tracks. The spot was open to a little sunlight, carpeted with fine brown needles like those from a pine tree. The bird espied Sterl, but that did not change its strange and playful antics. It was bright with many colors, not quite so large as a robin or meadowlark. This fairy creature of the bush skipped and hopped around so friskily that Sterl had to look sharp and long to locate its lovely hues. But the most pronounced was a golden-yellow. There was brown, too, marked with white, and a lovely sheen of greenish-olive, like that on a hummingbird, and its under-part appeared to be gray. Its exquisite daintiness and sprightliness gave the bird some elfin quality, some spirit of the lonely bush. It seemed to Sterl that the lovely creature's dancing movements were a sort of playing with leaves and twigs. It saw him, assuredly, out of bright, dark eyes, and, for all Sterl knew, it might have been the incarnation of joy and life in that bushland. Then again he remembered Leslie's lecture on Australian wildlife. It was the golden bower bird.

The day passed like a dream, and he did not kill any meat to eat or find his way out of the bush. The thousand and one animate creatures he sighted made those hot hours pass. But sunset found him more honestly lost than ever, and, as nightfall approached, apprehension, with its attendant depression, fastened upon him. He could not remember a time when he had found building a fire so desperately hard. At last he accomplished it, just in time to have the smoke save him from being eaten alive by mosquitoes. He had to hold his head over the smoldering fire until he was almost suffocated, and then, when he bent aside to catch a breath, he would be assailed by the fierce, humming, long-billed, blood-sucking devils.

That turned out to be a terrible night, sleepless, without rest, miserable to the point of exhaustion. When it ended and day came, Sterl set out again, blinded, poisoned, and in a frightful condition. He could not travel fast, even if that had been wise. Sterl's consideration of his situation convinced him that he should halt and wait for Friday to find him. The black man would be far on his trail by now. He had not the slightest doubt of that. He should stop and wait. To go on might just prolong the stalk and the agony. Any moment he might fall over the rocks or into a hole, to break a leg, or otherwise injure himself so that getting back to camp would be a grievous, almost impossible task. To that end Sterl chose the first open spot near water that he came across. It was high noon and hot, even in the shade. He lay down to rest before gathering a store of wood for several fires, and almost at once he went to sleep.

He was roused by a voice and a hand shaking his shoulder. A black visage, beaded with sweat bent over him. Great black eyes pierced into his very being.

"Friday!" Sterl cried in a husky voice, and he struggled to sit up. "You found . . . me?"

"Yes, boss. Black fella tinkit boss sit down quick."

"No. Boss fool!"

Friday had his *wommera* and spears in one hand, a small bag in the other. "Meat," he said, and opened it for Sterl. Inside were thick strips of beef, cooked and salted, some hard damper, and a quantity of dried fruit. Sterl felt his mouth water, and the fragrance of the meat distended his nostrils. He tore a strip in two, and handed half to Friday. When had meat ever tasted so good?

"How far camp, Friday?" he asked between periods of mastication.

"Close up." And the black made circles with his finger in the mat of brown needles to indicate how Sterl had traveled around and around. It was a humiliating thing to have verified, although he had been afraid of that. Sterl did not choose to betray his fear that he might never have gotten out. But that had been very possible.

"Boss track cassawary," said Friday.

There could not be any possibility of hiding physical things from this black. "Cassawary? All same like emu?"

Friday nodded. "Horses close up alonga water. Jester. King. Lady Jane. Black fella findum." This was such a matter of relief to Sterl that it assuaged his mortification. He finished eating the strip of meat in silence, then the damper, and arose from the ground with a handful of dried fruit.

"Come, Friday. Go alonga camp," he said. The black leaped to his lofty height, and strode off in exactly the opposite direction to that which Sterl had been traveling, so determined and sure he was right. Sterl could not withstand a shudder. Another night and another day, heading the wrong way, getting deeper and deeper into this bush and jungle maze, would almost certainly have ended in death.

At ten o'clock that night Sterl limped behind Friday into sight of a welcome campfire, where Slyter and his wife, Leslie and Red and Larry, kept a vigil that had only to be seen to realize their anxiety. The moment was more poignant than Sterl would have anticipated. Red, the sharp-eared fox, heard them coming, and, as he turned to see them emerge from the gloom, he let out his stentorian: *"Whoopee!"* That had scarcely ended when Leslie's cry rang out. Slyter burst out in agitation that surprised Sterl: "It's Sterl! Bless our black man!"

Leslie flew at Sterl, met him before he reached the fire, enveloped him with eager arms, crying out indistinguishable, broken words.

"Hazelton, I couldn't be any gladder, if you were my own son," Slyter said heartily. His wife at his side added: "Thank God you are safe, Sterl!" Then she addressed Leslie. "Girl, are you mad?"

"Yes, Mum. Mad with . . . joy!" cried Leslie as she turned her face, wet with tears, shining in the firelight.

Sterl bent his cheek to hers, then gently released himself.

Chapter Twelve

When the trekkers made several days' camp in comfortable spots where water and grass were abundant, they gradually worked back into something approaching congeniality.

The late October halt, after Sterl had come safely out of the jungle, seemed more than ordinarily marked by pleasant relations among all concerned. But there was one exception. Sterl, going to the stream for a bucket of water, encountered Ormiston and Beryl some rods away from the camp. The girl, sitting high upon a fallen gum tree, made a most attractive picture. She had a hand on Ormiston's shoulder, who stood leaning against the log and facing Sterl. She had not seen the cowboy. Sterl did not deviate from his course on account of them, though he usually avoided meeting the drover when possible.

"Hazelton," spoke up Ormiston, when Sterl drew abreast, in a derisive and taunting voice, "I'd never be afraid of being tracked by you."

Sterl was so dumbfounded that he passed right on without a word, although he flashed a searching glance at the drover. He heard Beryl ask: "Ash, whatever made you say that?" If Ormiston replied to that query, Sterl did not hear, although Ormiston's laugh rang unpleasantly like his remark. But Sterl resented that taunt. Beryl had evidently been puzzled and astounded, which was little to what Sterl felt. Ormiston had not appeared to be under the influence of liquor. He was not much of a drinker. Sterl could not come to any conclusion other than that Ormiston hated him so deeply that the opportunity to insult had been irresistible.

Back in camp Sterl related the incident to Red. The cowboy swore long and loud. "Thet's what's on the son-of-a-bitch's mind. He's gonna slope sooner or later."

"Right-o. But if he's secretive and close-mouthed, as we know, why did he make that crack?"

"Pard, it was a slip. Some men air so governed by passion thet they come right out with things."

"Yeah? There's going to be a reason for us to track him."

"Shore. That's in his mind, but I reckon it'll never come to an actual fact. I'm glad Ormiston busted out with thet. We've all been kinda forgettin', you know, like folks do when there's plenty of action an' little time to brood."

"Beryl had a hand on Ormiston's shoulder. And she didn't withdraw it, when I passed," Sterl said casually.

"Hell, thet ain't nothin'," returned the cowboy gloomily.

"No? Well, spring it, pard!" Sterl shot back, no longer casual.

Red appeared bitter and ashamed, but he did not answer Sterl's gaze. "I've seen Beryl in his arms . . . an' kissin' him back to beat hell."

"Where?"

"By thet big tree where you jest met them. You see, since the Danns throwed together with Ormiston an' Hathaway in one camp, Beryl an' Ormiston have been thick as hops. Slyter's camp is close this time, an' I couldn't help seein' them. But I got sore, an' jealous, an' played Injun on them. I sneaked up on them at night. An' I'm gonna keep on doin' it."

"Red, has Beryl ever kissed you?" Sterl asked seriously.

"Hey, pard, what's your idee? Want me to kiss an' tell?"

"Nonsense. This is different. I like Beryl. I've a queer faith she'll turn out OK. Red, has she?"

"Wal, yes, a coupla times," admitted Red. "Not the devourin' kind she gave Ormiston. Gosh, how she must like his brand! All the same what she did give me was enough to make me leave home."

"Red, your little finger is worth more than a wagonload of Ormistons," stormed Sterl. "And by heaven she'll find it out."

"I reckon . . . if only it ain't too late!"

"What you mean?"

"You savvy what I mean. Sterl, don't blame the girl. Hell, you know girls, an' what this wild livin' does to them. Ormiston is a handsome cuss. You remember Leslie sayin' he fascinated her. An' you an' me know only too well thet a man bein' bad is an urge to a woman's love, not a hindrance."

"Yes. But I can't forgive Beryl," Sterl returned with passion. "Listen, pard, I can pick a quarrel with Ormiston. Any day. It'd be murder, sure, but these people won't know that it'd be a fight. And he'd be out of the way. Lord knows what that might save the Danns."

"Right-o, Sterl," Red rejoined, cool of voice and dark of brow. "I've reckoned on thet myself. But shore as Gawd made little apples, if either of us bored Ormiston, it'd queer us with these drovers. We jest cain't afford to risk it on account of a girl."

"Let him hang himself, huh?"

"Thet's the deal. But it's long in comin'. Besides, Sterl, I'm good an' sore at Stanley Dann an' Slyter for not seein' the game this *hombre* plays."

"So am I," declared Sterl.

"All right, then. We can stand this trek longer than any of them, unless it's your black man. Gosh, what a guy! An' Sterl, leave Beryl's affair to me. I don't mean thet to apply to Ormiston. I'll spy on them. If Beryl doesn't give him away, Ormiston will himself."

"OK, Red. At that, I guess I have my own hands full."

"Ha! You had yore arms full the other night," Red declared with a short laugh. "Aw, Sterl, how thet kid worships you! It jest did my pore old battered heart good."

"Red! You . . . it's . . . only this infernal trek," burst out Sterl, as if stifled.

"Shore. Thet's the whole trouble. This trek! This . . . almighty trekkin' across the whole wide world till we die or turn into a boss!"

Stanley Dann sent word to all his company that, as he had decided to break camp at dawn the next day and continue the trek, he wished to see everyone at his campfire for a conference and to have dinner afterward.

An hour before sunset that afternoon, when the heat still lingered, all the invited were present except Larry and Cedric, and Henley—one of Ormiston's drovers—who were on guard with the mob. In the shade of a great spreading gum tree, the trekkers sat and reclined and stood around in a half circle before the leader. Sterl had an intimation that conference might become historical. It certainly showed a striking group of people. Leslie and Beryl, naturally, had put on bright colors, and their beauty graced the occasion. Brown, slim, strong, clear-eyed, and shining of hair, they attested to the beneficence of the sun and the rigors of the trek. The drovers matched any bronzed and bearded outfit of hard-riders Sterl could recall. The big men, like Stanley and Slyter, had trained down and did not show a pound of superfluous flesh.

Stanley Dann got up from his table with a paper in his hand, his eagle eyes alight, the goldness of him, the magnificence and virility impressively outstanding. "Well, here we are, family and partners and drovers," he began, in his rich, resounding voice, "at this pleasant camp, and it is an occasion to thank God, to take stock of the present, and renew hope for the future. We are one hundred and fifty-seven days and nearly six hundred miles on our great trek. It seems hardly possible. Barring the unfortunate and tragic loss of our partner, Woolcott, we have been wonderfully blessed and guided by Providence. There have been only minor injuries and accidents and illnesses, which, indeed, is remarkable. Our losses have been insignificant. We have lost only fourteen horses . . . a remarkable showing. And two hundred head of cattle, including, of course, those we needed for beef. Let me say this company upholds the prestige of Australians as meat-eaters!"

Dann consulted the paper in his hand, and then went on. "We have consumed one fourth of our flour. Too much, but it cannot be put down to extravagance or wastefulness. Tea we have, of course, an abundance left. Also salt and sugar. One fifth of our stock of dried fruits is gone, and that is our worst showing. We depend upon fruit to keep us well, and it must be conserved. There is a ton or more of canned goods left, which is luxury, and no doubt will not last long after we get into hard trekking. So much for all that. . . . By the grace of God we are going to win through to the Kimberleys, I hope and pray, some time towards the end of next year. In view of our good luck so far, and my faith in what is to come, I think it well to have everyone present speak out how they feel about the trek. If it is favorable, and I believe that will be true in every case, such open expression here before all will have been splendid spiritual reaction. Make us happier, stronger, more hopeful, more unified in faith. Because we have burned our bridges behind us. We cannot go back. Now Sister Emily, will you be the first to speak out?"

One by one all the women—Emily Dann, a sturdy little woman of forty, Mrs. Slyter of the weather-beaten face, Leslie with her wonderful eyes flashing, Beryl whose beauty graced the occasion—expressed their hope for the future, their determination not to turn back on Stanley Dann, and it was plain to all that what Beryl felt meant a great deal to him.

If Beryl had come on this strenuous trek to find a golden beauty, she would already have her reward. A red silken scarf enhanced the gold-tan of her face and the fairness of her hair. But if she had possessed only her eyes, blue-black with excitement, she would have looked her father's daughter.

"This trek is grand," she said. "I believe now in my father's vision. We trek on to seek and find, and never yield. We are empire builders. We will be remembered when Australia comes into her own. I idled away the days in Sydney. At home I vegetated. On this trek I am living."

The tall Hathaway had a tribute for their leader, and a courageous look forward. Slyter spoke brief, eloquent words about their progress and the surety of success. Eric Dann said: "It has been far better than I believed possible. I have been wavering on my chosen plan to stick to the old Gulf trek." Stanley Dann let out a roar of approval and called lustily upon Ormiston. Sterl, skeptic as he was, admitted the drover's forceful and convincing presence. His former, darkbrowed, sullen passion appeared in abeyance.

"Friends, I have not yet recovered from the loss of our partner, Woolcott," he said in a deep voice. "But still I see our unexpected and marvelous success so far. If it lasts, I will be hard put to make a decision when we come to the headwaters of the Diamantina. Far be it from me to cast cold water upon this meeting. Yet, there should be one voice of warning . . . one voice lifted against an over-confidence that might lead to fatal blunders. . . . It is absolutely certain that this incredible good luck will not last. But we will trek . . . and on!"

Red Krehl nudged Sterl as if to confirm a disappointment that had formed in Sterl's mind. Stanley Dann betrayed a disappointment that he harbored only a moment. Next he called upon the drovers, and they, apparently united, lustily vented their enthusiasm.

"Hazelton, you, being an American trail driver, long versed in this business of cattle and horses and men against the cruel and rugged ranges, you should have something unforgettable and inspiring to say to us novices at the game."

"I hope I have," rang out Sterl. "Stanley Dann, you are the great leader to make this great trek. On to the Kimberleys! No heat, no drought, no flood, no desert . . . no man can stop us!"

Of all those who had spoken thus far only Sterl appeared to

strike fire from their leader. He expanded his wide chest, his face flushed, he raised a prophetic hand and held it aloft. But if he had meant to respond to Sterl's eulogy and dynamic force, he thought better of it. Then he called to Red. "You, cowboy!"

"Dog-gone it, boss," Red drawled, "I had a helluva nifty speech, but I've clean forgot it. . . . However, enough has been said for us to trek on for another hundred an' fifty days. I've the same hunch as my pard heah. We cain't be licked. The thing's too big. It means too much to Australia. If Gawd is really guidin' us, as there seems some sense in our believin', little troubles like water an' blacks an' heat an' dust . . . an' the contrariness of men thet always bobs up . . . these can't swerve us from the great issue. Fork yore hosses, an' ride!"

Stanley Dann possessed the unquenchable ideal and courage and faith and zeal of the explorer-pioneer who stamped his name upon an unknown wilderness or left his bones to bleach there. He imbued his followers with a passion that kept pace in leagues and trials. All on that trek, except Sterl and Red, seemed to be overcome by that powerful personality, and even the brooding Ormiston reacted to the subtle influence. If Ormiston had not been in his heart all that he pretended not to be, he would have capitulated to this great leader.

But Red claimed he had caught limits and intimations which, pieced together, presented a certainty that Ormiston would not go beyond the headwaters of the Diamantina. Hathaway and Eric Dann believed the contrary drover would try to persuade them to make the longer trek by way of the Gulf to the Kimberleys. They were deceived. Ormiston had no communal interests. Sterl and Red, in their talks on night guard, were divided between a suspicion that Ormiston plotted to go on with Eric and Hathaway, if he could engineer the split with Stanley, in order to get possession of all their stock, or cut off from all of his partners to drove on alone to some unknown destination. The former was Red's opinion, the latter Sterl's. And there they were deadlocked.

"Pard," Red concluded somberly, "mark what I tell you . . . I'm gonna kill that slick devil. There are reasons enough, heaven knows, but the one that boils in me comes from heahin' him make love to Beryl."

"Red, every night when we come on guard you tell me that," replied Sterl impatiently. "Why, in the name of heaven, do you lay yourself open to it?"

"No sense a-tall in it. I jest love Beryl so orful!"

"I'm moseying," was Sterl's only reply.

He rode back to his post, and, finding Friday, he talked to the black a while, trying as always to pierce the veil of the aborigine's mind. But Friday forever eluded any deep penetration. That did not convince Sterl, however, that the black man did not understand him. Nevertheless, Sterl sensed a closer communion, if not understanding, as the nights multiplied.

Several series of two- and three-day treks without water marked the approach to the Diamantina River. The cattle did not suffer dangerously from thirst until the last arid spell. Then with two hot dry days and no prospect of relief, the drovers faced their most serious predicament.

That second night all the drovers went on guard duty. Sterl had observed the absence of game and birdlife, always an indication of the lack of water. Friday encouraged Sterl with a hopeful—"Might be water close up." But close up for the black could have a wide range. It was early in the evening when the riders went on guard at this camp. A full moon was rising. The cattle were restless, bawling, milling, and the guards had their work cut out for them. Sterl approached Red.

"Pard, Friday says there might be water close up. What do you say to my riding ahead on a scout? If I find anything wet around twenty miles, I'd advise Dann to trek clear through tomorrow and tomorrow night."

"Wal, it's a hell of a good idee," declared the cowboy. "Go ahaid. Thet is, if you reckon you can find yore way back!"

Red had never ceased to plague Sterl about getting lost. The opportunity for a cowboy was too good to resist. "Say, you could joke on your grandmother's grave!" Sterl retorted. "I've a notion to bat one. This scout job isn't funny. It's something Dann should have thought of."

"I should smile, pard. We gotta find water, or else. . . . I reckon we're workin' out on a plateau. Not one stream bed today. Rustle, pard, an' ride till you find water."

Sterl turned away toward the remuda to change horses. He wanted to save King. As he rode off, Red called after him: "If you figger the moon, you can find yore way back!"

The horses had been in need of water, but always after dark, when the dew was wet on the grass, they slaked acute thirst. Sterl changed to the big rangy sorrel, an animal he had not been able to tire. Then he set out, taking his direction from the Southern Cross.

Heat still radiated from the ground. But the night was pleasant. For two weeks and more the trek had been through open country, with the ranges fading gradually in the rear. The heave of the land suggested a last mighty roll toward the interminable level of the interior. Sterl rode at a brisk trot through bleached grass, silver in the moonlight. Stunted gum trees reared spectral heads; there were dark clumps of mulga scrub and bare, moonblanched spaces, across which rabbits scurried. Birds of prey whisked low over the ground. When at length the glimmer of campfires failed to pierce the blackness, Sterl halted his horse for a moment.

There was no hum of insects, no bark of dingoes, no sound that Sterl could distinguish. The silence seemed eternal. The solitude magnified anything of that nature that Sterl had ever encountered. It had a solemn and grand quality, a relentless aloofness to the state of man, that repudiated his little struggles, his ambitions, his brief days on the earth. Sterl could have loved it had not his mind cried out, like a child lost in the dark. He did not halt again to listen.

Two hours and more of steady riding brought Sterl to the edge of an escarpment which fortunately presented no steep step down from a level. Declivities always meant difficulties for the trail driver, especially when they were not discovered until too late. The void beneath Sterl appeared majestic in its immensity. Apparently land and sky never met. The slope was gradual. Far below a shining ribbon of a river made Sterl's heart leap. It could not be sand or a strip of grass or rock. It was water, and surely the long-hoped-for Diamantina River. But how far? At home on the western ranges Sterl had often distinguished water from land at considerable distances under similar circumstances. In that rarified atmosphere, under a soaring full moon, this river might be a few miles away, and it could be a dozen. But it was within reach of a twenty-four hour trek.

Some time after midnight Sterl arrived back at his starting point to find the mob somewhat quieted and snatching much needed sleep. Red received his good news with characteristic expression, after which he appended: "Wal, pard, you was gone so dog-gone long thet I was about to say hell with the cattle an' go hunt you."

Before dawn the cowboys and the black had a couple of hours' sleep. At daybreak the drovers came riding in by threes to get breakfast. Sterl lost no time telling Slyter the good news. The drover and Red accompanied him to Dann's camp. The partners had just finished their morning meal. Here was evidence that water or no water the trek had to go on. But dark grave visages attested to the heavy burden of worry.

"Boss, I rode ahead last night. Found water," Sterl announced bluntly.

"You did? Good-o, Hazelton," boomed Stanley Dann with joy, as he jumped up.

The others all asked questions in unison. Sterl waved them quiet. "It's a big river. Surely the Diamantina. I couldn't tell how far. Twenty miles, at the most."

"Twenty miles? Two days' trek?" Eric Dann ejaculated, disheartened. "We'll have a big loss."

Ormiston cursed roundly, apparently venting his rage at Sterl, as if he could be blamed for a dire calamity. Sterl deigned not to notice him, and addressed their leader: "We can make it in one trek."

Stanley Dann appeared checked by Sterl's terse speech. The other drovers united in negative calm.

"Keep quiet. Let me talk to our boss," shouted Sterl. "Dann, we can make it."

"All right. We'll have to," agreed the drover, and he swallowed hard.

"I've made worse drives than this will be," went on Sterl. "Ranges where there was little dew, but not so hot as this. . . . We must drive straight through to water."

Ormiston headed a furious opposition, in which, however, Stanley Dann did not concur. Sterl endeavored to convince the disgruntled and almost hopeless drovers, silencing all except Ormiston. He let Ormiston have his say out.

"Ormiston, you're a disorganizer," Sterl flashed steely and cold. "You're glad of anything that hinders us! You shut up, or I'll shut you up as I did once before."

Ormiston took the threat sullenly, but it was obvious that he was mostly concerned with what Sterl had called him.

"Boss, listen," went on Sterl. "We can make this drive. We could do more if we were called upon."

"I like your talk. How should we make this long trek to water?"

"Take it slow all day. Ease the mob along. Careful during the hottest hours. Then, after sunset, push them. When the dew falls, they can travel without breaking down."

"You heard Hazelton," Dann thundered. "His plan is sound. We'll adopt it. Tell every drover. Wagons to go ahead and make camp. Trek through to water!"

On Sterl's return to Slyter's camp, Red appeared supremely elated. "Pard, did you see Beryl?"

"No. Was she there?"

"I should kiss a pig she was. All eyes. Jest as if she never seen you before. Sterl, she'd like you, if it wasn't for Ormiston. Mebbe she does anyhow. But she's scared of thet geezer. Wasn't he sore as a stubbed toe? It was hard for him to swaller what you called him. Disorganizer? Fits him to a T."

"Red, will that showdown with him ever come?"

"Not any even break meetin', as we're used to in Texas. But it'll come! Be shore you have eyes in the back of yore haid."

Leslie was at her morning chore of feeding her pets. Jack, the kookaburra, and Gal were jealous of the new bird pets, and Cocky squalled from the top of the canvas-covered wagon.

"What was going on over there at Dann's camp?" she asked keenly.

Sterl told her of his trip during the night and his report to Dann. "We nearly had a row. But the boss accepted my plan to drive all day and all night. You go with the wagons."

"Umpumm. I'm good for twenty-four hours, and then some."

"But I'd rather you'd take it easy, whenever possible. You're in grand trim, Les. . . . Still, you go with your dad."

"Are you my boss, Sterl Hazelton?" she retorted rebelliously.

"Not yet. . . . But considering the remote possibility of my becoming that . . . and your cantankerous disposition . . . don't you think it'd be a good idea to get some practice?"

Her smooth nut-brown face grew suffused with a coursing red blood, and her wide eyes fell. She was tongue-tied. Her breast was swelling. Then Red's vociferous mirth did not appear conducive to a recovery of her equilibrium.

"Haw! Haw!" laughed Red. "Dog-gone, Les, thet was a jaw-breakin' speech. You got it on him now, if you play yore cairds. He cain't back out of thet if. . . ."

"Shut up, you cowboy devil," Leslie interrupted, and she fled, leaving her pets in noisy clamor.

"Always tickles me, the way a girl falls down over a crack like thet, if she's stuck on you," observed Red. "Why, when Beryl is so uncommon sweet, which does happen, I can trip her up."

"So you are progressing, Red? Go on. Faint heart never won fair lady! But, honestly, the only way I can offset Leslie's temper, or make her do something she ought to do, is by some crazy, high-handed speech like that."

"Wal, you can always add more, when it's necessary. Women air weak on thet one question. Pard, what hoss will you ride?"

"King. You fork Jester. We'll need shod horses, maybe." Then Sterl approached Slyter to tell him there was a break in the plateau about ten miles from camp and from there a grade down to the river. "And say, there's something I forgot to tell Dann. When you reach the river, be sure to drive to either side of the trek for camp, because this mob of cattle are liable to stampede when they smell water."

"Hold them back till daylight," replied the drover.

At sunset that day Sterl sat astride King on the rim of the plateau not far from where he had seen the valley by moonlight. Close at hand the front of the great mob of cattle, like a dust-clouded flood, was pouring wearily over the brink. As Sterl had hoped and predicted, they had ended the day's trek with some-thing to spare. Downgrade, in the night, with the dew falling, the beasts could plod away until the scent of the water energized them. And then, if they were at all like cattle of the Western ranges, they would stampede for the river. Sterl had seen ten thousand buffalo pile into a river to enact a spectacle he had never forgotten.

The basin beneath Sterl lay clear in his vision, as far as the river. The slope down to it showed no serious obstacle that he could see. What a sigh of relief he heaved! If the mob and re-muda belonged solely to him, he could not have taken their safety and well-being more to heart.

Weeks on end, almost every sunset, a different spectacle had spread out before his tireless gaze. This one was sublime. The basin was a red world with a black-bordered, ragged line of fire that was the river, winding away to the north. If all his vision en-compassed was the whole of Australia, it would have been vast and grand enough. But Sterl knew, though he could not grasp, that it was but a grain of sand in the immensity of this conti-nent.

Red rode along to upset his reverie and its parallel trance.

"Howdy, pard. Where the hell you been all day?" he drawled as he bent his hawk-like, red head over a cigarette, and straightened to flash his blue-flame eyes over cattle, descent, and basin. "A-huh. Pretty dog-gone-good! I'm handin' it to you, pard. There's the river, shinin' away in our direction. Water for many a long day!"

"Is that all you can say for this?" Sterl queried with an Indian gesture which embraced the void below.

"Wal, not so bad, now you tax me. End of the world! Fierce an' flamin' as the hell we're both slated for! How's that?"

"Not so good, pard," returned Sterl with a tinge of disappointment.

"All right, if you must drag a fellow's gizzard. It's this sort of night thet has made me love Australia an' reconcile me to the loss of Texas."

"Red, in a pinch you never let me down."

The cowboys rode down the slope as red dusk mantled the scene. Then, as night fell, they drifted apart, yet within calling distance. Friday for once had ridden on a wagon. Larry was ahead, at the left of the mob, and Drake was behind Sterl. The moon came up to lighten the shadows, and the dew fell. As that was the salvation of the trekking stock, so was it of that grassy land.

Downgrade, through thick grass, dew-laden, the mob labored and the trekkers followed. King had a liking for grass that did not appear so bleached out and dry. But then he was thirsty, too, and that accounted for the fact that Sterl had to dismount twice to loosen the saddle girths. By midnight the fairly steep slope had begun to level out. Kangaroos, wallabies, rabbits, emus were roused from their beds, to scamper away. King jumped out of his tracks more than once at the hiss of a snake. Only the tedium of that trek down into the valley wore on Sterl. There was nothing to do but sit his saddle. King did not need direction or urge. He had become like a shepherd dog. Often Sterl fell asleep for a few moments. Two nights without rest or sleep reminded him of the Texas cattle trail when the rivers were up.

The hours wore away, the stars grew wan, the bark of dingoes that followed the herd grew desultory, the warm air, a radiation from the heated earth, gradually grew cool. But the bawling of cows and calves, the bellowing of steers augmented as the miles grew unbearable and the mob had to be driven. Then followed the dark hour before dawn, with its ebbing vitality of man and beast.

Sterl huddled in his saddle, half asleep, his eyes closed, his mind almost a blank. A yell from Red, however, the old Comanche war whoop, brought him erect and startled. Daylight had come. He had slept some. A ruddy glow colored the eastern sky. Red was waving his sombrero. Spurring his horse, Sterl quickly reached his comrade. Red pointed toward the river, marked by a line of timber.

"Look, pard! Leslie ridin' down on us hell-bent for election! Larry's meetin' her."

Chapter Thirteen

Leslie pulled Lady Jane to a halt beside Sterl. The horse was dripping water in little streams. Leslie was wet to her waist. Her eyes glowed dark with excitement. Larry, who had accompanied her, reined in alongside.

"Girl, you didn't swim that river for fun?" demanded Sterl.

"Dad sent . . . me," panted Leslie. "Roland was . . . with me. . . . There he goes . . . making for the far side of . . . the mob."

"I seen him, pard," Red interposed.

"We're camped on this side . . . down there," went on Leslie, pointing with guantletted hand. "We couldn't cross. River too deep . . . with steep banks. Dad said we'd have a job. Stanley Dann's orders are to hold the mob on this side . . . to drive them that way . . . two miles up, where the banks are not so steep."

"Leslie, you should have met us five miles out, at least," Sterl rejoined seriously. "These cattle are thirsty. They're tired and cross. If they smell water. . . ."

"*When* they smell it," interrupted Red. "Rustle, Sterl. Tell the drovers. They gotta be quick. Come, Larry. We'll try to turn the leaders upstream."

Sterl urged King into a gallop to the rear, with Leslie racing beside him. They passed Cedric, Heald, and Monkton, to whom Sterl yelled Dann's orders in warning voice. The next guard was Drake. "Come with me!" shouted Sterl. They rode on swiftly to meet a bunch of Dann's drovers.

"Dann's orders. Push the mob upriver. To the east. High banks! When they smell water, we'll have hell!"

Between the larger mob and Ormiston's there were four drovers, two on each side, far up the wide lane. In the rear rode Ormiston and Hathaway. Far on the right side Sterl recognized Jack and Bedford, who had been stopped by Roland. The cattle plodded along, heads down, as if every step would be their last. The dust was caked on their wet flanks. Sterl caught the hot odor of the herd. He ran down on the partners, with Drake and Leslie at his heels.

"We've orders from Dann. Cattle must be turned upstream. River deep. High banks. Get your drovers out from between."

Ormiston added a dark frown to his forbidding expression. "We won't have our mob mixing with Dann's."

"You can't help it," Sterl declared curtly.

"That's what you say, Mister Cowboy. We *will* keep them separated."

"Hathaway, you have some sense, if this man hasn't," went on Sterl, trying to keep his patience. "This third dry day has been hot. Cattle are parched. When they smell water, they can't be held or turned. They'll stampede!"

The drover, impressed by Sterl's force, turned to his partner and spoke with hesitation. Roland came galloping up, red-faced and sweating. He called on Ormiston to drove his mob to the east. Then Drake added his voice.

"Mind your own business!" he shouted. "We'll take care of our own mob."

"You will like hell!" returned Sterl. "Rollie, ride through and warn Dann's drovers to rustle out of there. Back this way!"

Sterl wheeled King and was away like the wind. Leslie came along on her fleet Lady Jane. It was a race without intention. Drake followed, slowly losing ground. Halfway round the bigger mob, Sterl waved the drovers on that side to ride up toward the front. They strung out after Drake. Soon Sterl, accompanied by Leslie, came up with Larry and Red.

"Stubborn as mules!" shouted Red.

"No wonder. But we've got to push them, or they'll dam up the river. How far, Red?"

"A good coupla miles. But too close. An' downhill at thet."

"Ormiston doesn't know cattle, Red. He refused to help. Said he wouldn't let his mob mix with Dann's."

"Haw! Haw! Shore this's gonna be orful funny. About as funny as death for them drovers between."

"Roland rode through to tell Dann's. . . ." Sterl stood up in his stirrups to gaze across the mob. "Good-o! They're riding out. The last two of Ormiston's men. But that fellow up front. . . ."

"We cain't wait, pard," Red yelled, pulling his gun. "Leslie, keep back a little."

Then Red rode up to the herd, gun high over his head, to yell and shout. Larry took his cue from that and did likewise. Sterl, riding back a hundred feet, followed suit. Cedric and Drake, with the drovers farther back, let loose with guns and lungs.

The front of the great mob, like the sharp end of a wedge, roused to lunge and thud away from the din. It headed away from a direct line toward the river. That relieved Sterl exceedingly. The turn was not enough, but it had started. Cattle, like sheep, blindly followed the leaders. Every few seconds Sterl would fire his gun and whoop. Dust clouds began to lift. The trampling of many hoofs, the knocking of horns, the increase in hoarse bawling, indicated the start of the milling Sterl was so keen to accomplish. He had his doubts. The herd was too big, too immobile, too ponderous. But he hoped. The cattle had quickened out of their weary walk. Something like a current ran all the way back to the rear. That frightened Sterl. He yelled and fired and waved his sombrero. The way Red worked corroborated Sterl's fears. They had the apex of the mob quartering away from a direct line to the river bed. But the river took a bend to the east there, and looked less than two miles away!

Suddenly from the far side of the herd waved a trampling roar that drowned yells and gunshots. Sterl's piercing yell was a whisper in his ears. He had heard that kind of roar. His blood ran cold. Icy thrills chased up his spine. Standing in his stirrups, he saw Ormiston's mob charging straight ahead to meet the milling front of the vast wedge of cattle. The sight made Sterl curse. Ormiston's mob would all but defeat the work Sterl and his allies had started.

Then Sterl espied the one drover trapped in the swiftly narrowing space. The man saw his peril, but made the mistake to dash to the fore, hoping to get out of the closing gap. He should have gone back down the wider end of the space. This drover made a frantic break to escape. His calculation, however, did not allow for the curving front of the larger mob and the speed of the smaller mob. He was headed off, hemmed in. A moment later there was a terrific impact—a head-on collision of these two fronts. Sterl saw the white horse and its rider go down in a sea of horns and heads. Dust clouds hid the scene.

An increasing rattling crash of Ormiston's mob, colliding with Dann's all down the line, drowned the trample of hoofs. Still, only the head of Dann's mob and the far edge appeared to be affected. A smash-up like that did not necessarily mean a stampede. What had started Ormiston's mob? Sterl hated to admit this suspicion to his consciousness.

The clashing of thousands of horns merged with the pounding of hoofs. For the first time on that great trek nearly eight thousand cattle mingled in one mob. Sterl thought derisively of the bull-headed Ormiston. He was the one who would suffer most. His mob of branded cattle were taking the lead. They would be the first to run over the river embankment. It would serve him right, thought Sterl with accompanying curses, but what a pity so many cattle must be drowned and trampled! Sterl's hopes would not down. He kept at his job, as he saw his comrades doing. There remained still a chance of the main herd holding to their blind action.

Half of Ormiston's mob were in the lead, straight for the river, on the angle to which they had been deflected. That pointed a mile or less up the river. Let them pass! Sterl ached to see them win what must fatefully be a race for the water.

It came to him then that Ormiston's mob, on the farther upstream side to windward, had caught the fatal scent. After three days of heat and dust without a drink, they smelled the river. Water! If they had the scent in their dry nostrils, Dann's herd would catch it soon. But despite Sterl's readiness for the inevitable shock, when Dann's mob leaped into swift action and an appalling thunder boomed and the ground shook as if in earthquake, Sterl screamed with all his might and never heard his own voice.

He threw up his hands, a gun in one and sombrero in the other. And he sat King stricken and riveted by twice as many cattle as he had ever seen in stampede. The thunder was the thunder of stampeding buffalo. Mushrooming yellow clouds of dust rolled back over the mob, moving as one animal, covering them, swallowing them up. For a cowboy, it was a terrific and heart-rending spectacle.

But that awesome sight did not detract from Sterl's vigilance. His eyes veered everywhere, like a compass needle. And he was the first to see that a spur of the herd had shot out below him, between him and the other riders, and swung out in a swift, enveloping sweep.

In the tense excitement Leslie had gotten away from Sterl. Lady Jane wanted to tear along with the mob. Between holding her and watching the tremendous stampede, Leslie had no attention for anything else. Red and Larry had gone on. Sterl had to get to her in quick time, and, if he had had a cannon to shoot, she could not have heard it. With that thought he had King racing down the line. Lady Jane was fast. Sterl had no fear she could not outrun the wildest of cattle. But being a mare of great spirit, she might act up at the crucial moment, when she should be running stretched out for safety.

For Sterl this was the first time King had ever been extended. Fleet? He was like the wind. Fortunately, Leslie saw him coming and then the spur of cattle that had split away from the main herd. She did not lose her head. Quick as a flash she jerked Lady Jane around away from the sight of that frightful oncoming rush of hoofs, heads, horns. Released from strain and plunging under surprise and pain of the jagged spurs, Lady Jane leaped like an arrow from a bow.

At this juncture King caught up with her. Sterl thought he would pass the bay, but he did not. The two horses closed in. Sterl pointed to Leslie's stirrups. She was keen to grasp his intent—to slip her feet almost out and ride on her toes, so that in case Sterl saw fit he could lift her out of the saddle.

Sterl's terror left him. The girl could ride, and she could be trusted. Only an accident now was to be feared. He gazed back. The front of the outswinging spur of cattle had almost come up even with them. But this gain must mostly have been made before Sterl had espied the split. Downhill, however, these cattle would run. Sterl led Leslie off to the left, cutting off as much as he dared. The speed of the horses blurred Sterl's eyes. But he saw when they flashed ahead of the pointed column of maddened steers. A narrow shave for Leslie, thought Sterl. Lady Jane kept on while Sterl was pulling King. He broke from level run to plunge and halt, prancing, his ears erect.

The terrible rumble of the stampede still held Sterl earshocked. Down the line, Drake and four drovers were riding madly to push the offset of cattle back to the main mob. Larry and Red came sweeping in a wide curve around to the left. Leslie, no longer in danger, was pulling Lady Jane out of her stride.

Then Sterl urged King to the fore again, with the object of

turning the leaders of that spur to the right. The black was magnificent in action. He drove right to the front. A lean, rangy steer, red-eyed and wild, led that mutiny from the main herd. Four abreast his followers came, widening their number to the rear.

Sterl shot the leader. The great steer plunged to plow the earth. The others overran him, leaped and swerved. Larry and Red came up with flaming guns. The drovers behind were lost in dust. The cowboys and Larry turned that spur back toward the main herd, and in less than a quarter of a mile the split had closed up. To the left, scarcely farther than that, Sterl saw the timber belt and the shining river. It was wide, and the opposite bank looked steep and high. Farther upstream the bank appeared to slope gradually. As the mob was headed quarteringly up the river, there was hope that a major catastrophe might be averted.

The stampede had a half-mile front. Part of that front, clear across the flood of bobbing horns and heads and backs, moved in plain sight, unobscured by the dust that rolled back to hide the majority of the mob. All that could possibly be done by Sterl and his comrades, and the drovers sweeping from behind, had been accomplished, and it was a good job that saved thousands of cattle.

Sterl, never forgetting Leslie, gazed back to espy her trotting Lady Jane at a goodly distance behind. He waved his sombrero, but was not sure she saw him. He had no doubt, however, that she would give the mob a wide margin. Red was riding ahead toward a ridge under which the stampede was rolling. Sterl, and all the others, joined him on this vantage point. Their yells to one another were meaningless, so far as hearing was concerned. Even the stupendous roar had apparently ceased. But Sterl felt the vibration of the earth under King.

The climax of the stampede engaged the riders in rapt and fascinated attention. Just under the watchers swept a mighty torrent of beef, indistinct through the streaming dust. Following that flood forward, Sterl's sight came to the front of the mob. It rolled on, swallowing up the green, headed for the bend of the river, the steep bank of which could be seen by the watchers. The conformity of the land had something to do with the turn of the stampede which, like water, followed the line of least resistance.

The vanguard of the mob rolled out of sight to reappear in a moment, splitting around trees, and like a juggernaut, rolling the brush flat, to plunge over the bank in one long cascade of cattle distorted in the air. In concerted fall they hit the water in a tremendous splash. The bank was steep with a drop of twenty feet. And as the continuous steam of cattle poured over it, there ensued an appalling, threshing mêlée. The foremost line had no chance to rise under the shock of following lines. But presently out of the spouting, muddy splashes, heads of swimming cattle appeared. They milled around in bewilderment while the ghastly downpour of heavy bodies piled into the river. Some cattle struck out for the opposite shore.

The stampede rolled by under Sterl and his horrified comrades. Long as that tragedy seemed, it must have taken only a few moments for nearly eight thousand cattle to run down the slope. After the mob passed them, the tremble of the earth ceased, the roar again permeated deafened ears. It lessened in volume. It changed into that other sound—the incessant crash of water in a maëlstrom and the long-drawn, horrid bawl of frenzied cattle, that gradually overcame the lessening roar.

Back to the plunging waterfall of cattle Sterl's gaze swept. The river now was full of horned heads, moving, milling, cracking in collision, making for the opposite shore. The bank of that side appeared to be low, and wading cattle proved there was a bar.

Sterl saw the last quarter of the stampede run and roll and plunge down a bank, the steepness of which had been cut and plowed on a slope to the water's edge. Strangest of all this strange spectacle was the sudden cessation of rolling, trampling roar.

The imperturbable Red was the first to recover from that sight. He lighted a cigarette.

"Not too bad! Gawd A'mighty shore is on Stanley Dann's side! I wouldn't have given a handful of Mexican *pesos* for thet herd.

An' lo an' behold, heah they air, most of them, swimmin' acrost, wadin' out."

"Men," Drake ejaculated, "a bridge of cattle saved the mob!"

"Yes! And that bridge was Ormiston's! He wasn't going to let his mob mix with Dann's!"

"Haw! Haw!" rolled out the red-headed cowboy's caustic mirth. "Wal, fellers, Ormiston's cattle got the start an' cut in ahaid. An' am I tickled! It shore was a sight for sore eyes."

"Who was the drover that got trapped and rode down?" queried Larry.

"One of Ormiston's," Sterl replied. "The other bolted with Roland."

"Yeah? We can plant him in the mawnin', if there's any of him left," said Red. "Come on. It's all over but the shoutin', except we've got a hell of a job yet."

As they turned away from the riverbank to find a place to get down to the water, Sterl happened to think that Leslie had told him camp had been pitched on this side.

"Can the wagons be driven over?"

"No, indeed-ee. But up there the approaches are easier. Rollie said we could get them over somehow."

"All right. Drake, you heard Leslie," Sterl went on to Drake, who rode beside him. "What'll we do?"

"Looks like a river drove. What do you say?" rejoined Drake.

Sterl surveyed the river again, which certainly presented a colorful and animated scene. "Let me have Larry, Red, and Cedric. There's a good many crazy cattle swimming downstream. And in the middle there's an unholy mess milling around. We'll turn them upstream. Some of them are going to drown, Drake. You see that. Take the rest of the men and rustle up to where the cattle can wade out."

"Fellers, I see Ormiston's outfit up there," Red interposed, pointing his cigarette. "Trailin' up his mob! I'd like to heah him, when he sees thet animal bridge of cattle wearin' his brand."

"I don't like that idea, but I'll have to go," returned Drake, and he galloped off, accompanied by the other horsemen.

"Ormiston will be cry-eyed," Sterl said. "I'm sorry for the cattle. But I'm tickled. He swore he wouldn't let his mob mix with Dann's."

Presently Sterl found a ravine that opened at the edge of the water. "Leslie, this will be work. Won't you go back to camp?"

"Of course, if you say so. But can't I help? Sterl, you are always trying to save me from . . . from everything. It's kind of you. Only I want to ride and take my medicine, as Red calls it. Pretty soon I'll have to. You'll have to let me."

"Right-o," Sterl declared heartily. "You've got more sense than I have. And I've more sentiment than you."

"So you say, cowboy."

They reached the river where the ravine ended level with the water. "Load your guns, boys," advised Sterl, suiting action to words. "It'll save swimming your horses to shoot in front of a steer or cow. Bullets will turn them."

"Pard, this heah river is deep, but it ain't runnin'," Red observed.

"Stagnant! Gosh, I hadn't noticed that. . . . Look at the highwater marks on the banks!"

"In flood time the water runs over these banks," added Red.

"Yes, and the rainy season is not so far away," Larry said.

"Aw, hell, it ain't nothin'," drawled Red, "nothin' a-tall, as Dann says."

King did not require to be urged into the river, as the other horses. Red called the black a duck. Sterl surveyed the wide channel where just above them thousands of cattle were swimming.

"Red, I don't like this," Sterl called.

"Neither do I. But we gotta take to the water. Once that mess gets haided over, we'll be OK."

"But it's a long swim. If a horse gave out, it'd be good night. For the horse, anyway. Leslie, stick close to me. We must keep out of the mess."

Cedric and Larry were already out in the river where stragglers from the herd were swimming aimlessly. On the opposite side, above them, hundreds of cattle were pawing at the steep bank, lunging up to plunge back, and floundering. Some of them were wading, too, which indicated a strip of shallow water under that bank. Red swam his horse to a point one-third the way across, while Sterl with Leslie divided the rest of the width of the river between them.

They headed up the river in the face of as remarkable a conglomeration of animals as Sterl had ever been witness to. And the bawling clamor equaled the scene. The swimming horses and the yells and shots of their riders soon had all the stragglers headed in the right direction. Sterl made a hasty judgment that there were five thousand cattle in the river. A long string was wading out above. The danger point appeared to be less than a quarter of a mile beyond—and consisted of a mass of cattle twisting, plunging, in an intricate tangle. It relieved Sterl to see Drake and the other riders pile into the river at that point and make for the great maëlstrom. It was a risky job, if they got too close.

"Sterl, look on the bank!" shrieked Leslie.

Then Sterl espied Ormiston with Hathaway and the other drovers on the shore above the yellow, trampled slope which the cattle had cut through the bank. Below them stretched a long line of dead and dying cattle—the bridge of death—across which the main mob had poured into the river. Heads and horns and legs stuck up out of the crushed and trampled mass. No wonder the drovers sat their horses, appalled at the ghastly sight. But Ormiston, on foot, raged to and fro, flinging his arms, stamping and lunging. The roar of his fury sounded above the bawl of cattle. Sterl cupped his hands around his mouth and yelled in stentorian voice: "Hey, you dumbhead! Shoot the dying cattle!"

Ormiston heard, for he roared curses back at Sterl. The keen-eared Red heard, too, because his wild Comanche whoop pealed across the water.

"Yes, nice disposition Ormiston has," Sterl called. "Beryl has a sweet future ahead, if she marries that *hombre*."

"We'll never let her," Leslie returned hotly.

Some of the drovers with Ormiston heeded Sterl's humane suggestion, and began to shoot the crippled and drowning cattle. Sterl made for a strip of sandy bank beyond the bend and on the far side, Leslie following close behind.

They were making progress very carefully, when Leslie cried: "Sterl! Some horrid beast! There!"

An alligator, small in Sterl's estimate, being less than ten feet long, was sliding off the bar into the water. Sterl did not waste any seconds in sending a bullet into the reptile. It threshed, whirled, and sank. Lady Jane lunged out on the bar. Sterl quickly had King beside her.

"What . . . was that?" panted Leslie.

"Alligator. Didn't you hear that war whoop of Red's? All in the day's ride, Les."

"Yeah? Well, I've had enough . . . for this day. Lady Jane is winded."

"She is, at that," replied Sterl, noting the bay's heaving sides. "Rest here, Les, and then keep to this bar. Look out for more varmints."

King gave a huge heave, and then appeared to breathe normally again. Water and land were the same to him. Sterl rode up the sandbar to a point even with the upper edge of the mob. Then he surveyed the scene. The river was full of cattle so closely packed that steers and cows would lunge up on others and sink them. Across, nearer the other side, Red and his two comrades had their contingent of cattle headed out. Red, in fact, was making for the milling mob on the far side. On second glance, Sterl saw that the dozen or more drovers strung out behind the great mob, shooting, yelling, making splashes, had turned the line in that quarter. The rear and center areas of cattle were headed across but could not make much headway owing to the eddying mass of animals beyond.

Sterl let King go, and soon he was swimming gallantly to join the other horses. Sterl saw now what the daring cowboy was up to, and the old thrill coursed over him, recalling the numberless exploits of his comrade.

Red had untied his lasso. Cedric and Larry, who followed him closely, had exchanged their guns for ropes. Red was mounted on Jester, and that horse appeared to be some relation to a fish. He passed the end of the mob, the quarter, and, when he reached the center, Red whirled the loop around his head with that old trenchant cry—"*Ki-yi! Yippi-yip!*"—and let it fly to rope a big steer around the horns. Turning Jester toward the bank, Red literally dragged that steer out of the wheeling circle. It made a break. And a break like that was a crucial thing for a herd of stampeded cattle. Below Red a few rods, Larry roped another steer and turned shoreward. Cedric followed suit. Then one steer and cow and another and another got into those openings, until the wheel of twisting horns and snouts broke and a stream of cattle, like oil, flowed away from the mob. It took less time for the whole mob to be on the move across the river than it had taken for Red and his followers to break the milling mass.

The Diamantina was two hundred yards and more wide there, and it appeared narrow because the width and half a mile of its length had been full of cattle. But once the mob had caught the instinct of the leaders and had gotten headed right, the drovers had a reprieve from their strenuous labors. Sterl had no accurate account of the time it took to get the cattle across, after they had stampeded into the river, but he was amazed to find it afternoon.

Red, with Larry and Cedric, had long disappeared over the far bank. If there was grass on that side, the chances were greatly in favor of the stampede being over. But Red would have that in mind and would stop any flurry of the leaders, before the main mob had mounted the bank.

Nevertheless, Sterl experienced a vast relief when he, the last of the drovers to mount the bank and go through the trampled muddy belt of brush and timber, saw the great mob quietly grazing, as if no untoward event had come to pass.

Drake said: "I call for some volunteers to stand guard till supper time."

They all volunteered, so he had to make a choice from Slyter's drovers and those of the other partners.

"This cain't be the place to ford the wagons," Red observed.

"Farther up," returned Sterl. "I see the low banks and bars. It'll take time, but be easy. Dann will hardly order us to cross today."

"Well, you fellows will find out. And we'll be over there," concluded Drake.

Gazing across the river, Sterl espied Leslie sitting her horse on the opposite bank, somewhat aside from a group of horsemen. Stanley Dann, his brother Eric, and Slyter had ridden out to join Ormiston and Hathaway.

"Come on, Red, and fellows. Let's mosey across," Sterl said.

"Dog-gone, pard, if one of them damn' alligators didn't scare the daylights out of me," complained Red. "I kinda have a notion to stay heah."

"Me, too. But we must go. I shot one over there. Gave me the creeps. And Leslie, for once, yelled murder."

"Wal, pard, these hosses air grand, an' the drovers ain't so pore. I jest had a picnic, outside of thet scare."

They crossed the river without incident, to be met by Leslie. Stanley Dann called them over to his group. Ormiston, despite his tan, showed an unusual pallor, and his big eyes, with their lurid light, would have warned any man of his truculent nature. Sterl made a mental reservation that this queer composite of fool and villain would have blamed the stampede upon his partners and their drovers, if there had been any possible excuse.

"Men it is our first major disaster," boomed Stanley Dann. "That stampede could not have been avoided. I commend you all for right heroic work. Hazelton, I commend you particularly, with Krehl and Larry and Cedric. You saved the main mob twice, first when you turned the head of the mob up this way, and secondly when you got them out of that whirlpool. I never saw the like."

"Thanks, boss. Thet last was jest a little mill. All in the day's ride," Red said.

"Dann, we lost one man," added Sterl, wanting at once to give his version of that tragedy.

"Yes. Ormiston's drover, Henry Ward. He was warned. But he was over-bold or befuddled. Poor fellow!"

"Who warned him?" Beryl queried bluntly.

"Why, Ormiston said he sent a drover," returned the leader.

"Ormiston did nothing of the kind," Sterl denied. "When we rode around to the rear of the herd to give your orders, Ormiston grew furious. He said he wouldn't let his mob mix with yours. I told him he couldn't help it. Then he replied for me to mind my own business. But Drake sent Roland Jones to ride between your mob and Ormiston's, to warn the drovers to come out. Roland, back me up here."

"Yes, sir. Hazelton is right," Jones replied frankly. "I rode in, called off your two drovers, and yelled to Ormiston's. But the other drover, Ward, did not start out in time."

"Ormiston, this report hardly agrees with what you said," declared Dann. "If it is true, you are responsible for Ward's death."

"What do I care for these lying mongers?" Ormiston stormed, his bold eyes popping. "I gave you my version. Believe it or not!"

Roland Jones thrust forward a reddening visage. "See here, Mister Ormiston, don't you call me a liar."

"Bah, you big lout! I called you a liar. What are you going to do about it?"

"Men, the situation is bad enough without making it worse," said Stanley Dann calmly. "I'll not permit fighting. We've had a trying day, and we're upset."

They all heeded the leader's wisdom and patience, except Ormiston. Not improbably he saw opportunity to flay without risk to himself, or else at times his temper was ungovernable.

"Dann, this is insufferable. These riff-raff drovers of yours haven't a pound to their names. They can't pay for the loss of my cattle. I demand that of you!"

"Very well. I'll be glad to make up for your loss. It was my gain. Your cattle saved mine," boomed the leader, with a magnanimity and generosity that equaled the other's selfish greed.

Red Krehl let out a sibilant hiss. The drovers were simply stupified. If Hathaway did not look ashamed, he was endeavoring to hide it. The malignant Ormiston had not expected such a big-hearted restitution for his loss. His rolling eyes lighted avari-

ciously. Sterl interrupted his reply to Dann. He spurred King into
a jump to confront the drover.

"Ormiston, you go to hell!" Sterl said with a stinging, cold
contempt that a whole volley of epithets and statements could
never have equaled. It was not a challenge, because its very effrontery precluded any belief in the drover's manliness. Ormiston was not the kind of man to quail, but for once his ready
retort failed. But his visage expressed all that revolved in his
mind. With a gesture to his lieutenants, Bedford and Jack, he
wheeled his horse and rode toward camp.

"Pard, Dann's gonna ask you to make a count of the daid cattle," whispered Red. "An' you lie like a trooper."

Sterl made no reply, although he received that suggestion
most sympathetically. As they were about to turn off and ride
down to the scene of the massacre, Sterl turned to Leslie.

"Les, it'll be a dirty bloody mess. Don't go."

"Why not, Sterl?"

"Why! Heavens, you're a girl! Not a hard, callous, blood-
spilling man used to death!"

Leslie's look, the darkening flash of her hazel eyes, prepared
Sterl for a jolt. "Yeah?" she said, flippant as cracking ice. "Well,
I've a hunch there'll be another bloody death around here
pronto . . . and I'll be tickled pink."

Sterl gaped at her in silence, then turned to ride down the
trampled slope. Leslie's retort had not been a rebuff, but a
woman's passionate scorn, couched in Red Krehl's picturesque
vernacular. It was a repudiation of Sterl's softer side. It verified
his judgment of what this savage wild country, and the contact
with men who hated, would do to women. And despite the
shock of his intelligence and sensitiveness, he positively tingled
with the girl's taunt, hinting at, inciting Ormiston's death by his
hand.

Stanley Dann rode along the hoof-torn slant of recently
plowed earth, gazing down at the mashed bloody bodies of cattle,
at the grotesque horned heads pointing to the sky, mouths open,
tongues sticking out, staring dead eyes. In the center of that

bridge of massed flesh, dead cattle were so thick that there was really no water around them.

"Sterl, what is your count?" the leader asked tersely.

"Boss, I'd rather not say," replied Sterl with a deprecatory spread of his hands. "I'm only fair on the count, no better than Larry or Cedric. Red has always been the most accurate and reliable counter of stock we ever had on our ranges. In fact, while we were all trail driving, different trail bosses used to send for him after a flood or a stampede. And when they got to Dodge or Abilene, his tally was always close."

Thus, Sterl shifted the responsibility on his cowboy comrade. This time, wonderful to see, Red reveled in the prestige and trust.

"Very well, Red. I'm sure you could have no higher recommendation. I'll rely upon you. How many?"

"Wal, boss, I'm shore surprised," returned Red, strong-voiced and sincere. "I was afeared we'd lost a damn' sight more'n we really have. . . . Thet water was shallow all along heah. I seen the steers pitchin' up the mud. But they're layin only about three deep heah. Yeah, sir! We're darned lucky. I been countin' all along, an' allowin' the same for thet little distance below us . . . thet is, the same count I made before we got to his heah mess, my tally is just three hundred an' thirteen. Preecislee. An' I'll gamble on thet."

Sterl had not the slightest doubt in the world that a count of the dead cattle in sight would bear that estimate, and he knew there were layers and layers of cattle underneath.

"Is it possible?" the drover boomed, elated. "I am poor in calculation. I thought we had a thousand head."

"No, indeed-ee, boss," Red returned emphatically. "You take my tally. I'm kinda proud of my gift."

"Right-o. It's settled. How fortunate we are, after all. I have been blessed with my faith in divine guidance. We shall go through. Back to camp. We will forget this tragedy."

Sterl had despaired of picking out one camp that excelled the last. But this first one on the Diamantina halted him to a long, silent survey. Leslie came bounding over to where Sterl and Red were unsaddling behind their big wagon.

"Red, you terrible liar . . . you adorable cowboy . . . you friend in need," she began eloquently, her eyes steadfast and her breast swelling. "May I kiss you?"

Red regarded her dubiously, but he was alive to her youth and charm, as indeed Sterl was, too. "What for?" he asked.

"Because you convinced Stanley Dann our misfortune was not so bad."

"Wal, if thet's it, an' pard Sterl won't be sore, I reckon I can stand to have you kiss me," he drawled with that rare smile which so seldom shone to beautify his lean red face.

"Sterl! What has he got to do with my kisses?" she demanded, and then, with pink vying with the brown of her face, she put her hands on his shoulders and lifted her face to kiss Red warmly, if not right on his lips, then very closely.

He regarded her with tremendous interest, as Leslie drew away, and a feeling of emotion, the depth of which amazed him. He was falling in love with her more all the time, a fact that troubled yet elated him all at once.

Chapter Fourteen

Guard duty was split that night, half the drovers on from dark till midnight, and the other half from then till sunrise. It was a needless precaution, as Sterl told Slyter, for the cattle spent the quietest night since leaving Downsville. They were almost too tired to graze.

That morning Friday greeted Sterl with an enigmatic—"Black fella close up."

"Bad black fella, Friday?"

"Might be some. Plenty black fella."

"How do you know?" Sterl queried curiously.

"*Lubra* tellum."

From that Sterl knew the black had been in contact with aborigines. He told Slyter, who burst out vociferously that it was about time. "Except for once," he went on, "we've had no trouble with aborigines. And we expected that to be the worst of our troubles."

"All same a-plenty bimeby," put Friday with his air of mystery.

"Aw, what the hell do we care?" Red drawled, behind a puff of smoke. "We got wagonloads of shells. Mebbe we can use some."

"What's the orders, Slyter?" asked Sterl.

"Transport wagons over the river."

"Transport! Reckon you mean by thet cross the river, huh?"

"That's what I meant, Red."

"Wal, it'll be one sweet job. Whereabouts?" Red asked.

"Somewhat above where we droved the mob yesterday."

"Look aheah, boss. Thet's an orful place. No ford a-tall. We oughta go up the river a ways. This is just a big pond. Shore as shootin', this river ain't runnin'. I'll bet we could find shallow ford. Lemme ride up an' see."

"Dann's orders, Red. And he's mad this morning."

"Mad? Good heavens! Thet's somethin' to celebrate. Fust time, or I'll eat my sombrero. Gosh, I'm glad he's human, ain't you, Sterl?"

"It is sort of gratifying. What's the big boss mad about?"

"I'm not certain, but I think it's Ormiston. Anyway, he ordered his drovers to burn Ormiston's brand on three hundred odd cattle, as soon as we get the wagons across today."

"Today? Haw! Haw! Gosh, you Australian trekkers air a cockshore lot of gazabos. But I kinda like it, at thet. How to be cowboys."

"Slyter, does Dann really expect to get across today with this outfit?"

"By noon, he says. Eric tried to argue with him, but to no avail."

"It'll be the damnedest job you ever tackled."

"Boss," chimed in Red, "it'll take two whole days of orful work."

"With all our men and horses?" Slyter ejaculated, astonished. "Ridiculous!"

"Wal, I reckon it is, at thet," returned Red, and went his way.

Nevertheless, Sterl had to admit that Stanley Dann's enterprise and energy matched his optimism. He simply did not know. Perhaps, even if he had known, that could not have hindered him. By a half hour after sunrise he had all the wagons packed, ready to drive up to the place he had elected to ford. They soon started, with Slyter's remuda following in charge of Larry and the cowboys. Dann, who drove the leading wagon, halted on the bank of the river some distance above where the stampede had crossed the day before. He sent for Sterl, who reached him, presently, patiently listening to Eric's argument. Ormiston stood by, taciturn and brooding.

"Hazelton," boomed the leader. "This is the place we're going to cross. Eric is against my judgment. Ormiston swears he'll drove his mob back to this side. We have no time for argument. We cross here. Will you take charge?"

"Yes, sir. But it is a hard job and can't all be done today," Sterl answered earnestly.

"Very well. How do you propose to do it?"

"It's a pack job. Give me twenty riders. Five changes of horses. We'll empty the wagons and drays. Each rider will pack over what he can carry safely and keep dry. Flour and food to go first. All goods to be crossed today, because there will be aborigines here by night. Wagons and drays to be lifted off and dragged across by ropes. Same with wheels. Two of Slyter's wagons can be floated over, about half empty. I think that covers it, sir."

"That covers more than you think, Hazelton," boomed the leader, his amber eyes glinting with warm light upon the cowboy. "Men, you all heard Hazelton. Take orders from him. Let's unhitch and get at it!"

"Dann, I want a word in edgewise," demanded Ormiston.

"Ashley, I heard you. No more. I forgot to tell you that I ordered your brand burned in three hundred odd of my cattle, as soon as we cross."

Ormiston had no reply for that. But his surprise knew no bounds. It was Sterl's opinion that Stanley Dann had about reached the end of his rope with this drover. No doubt the last straw was his daughter's attachment. But even that would break eventually. Sterl's regard for the big Australian added another cubit to its stature.

Red had already made for Roland's wagon and dismounted there to begin unloading. Sterl joined him. Leslie was putting her pets in cages, much to their vociferous disgust.

"Sterl, I've a hunch Stanley Dann will ride rough-shod over our friend Ormiston one of these days," said the cowboy.

"You haven't a corner on all the hunches," retorted Sterl. "I had that figured long ago. Beryl now is the last connecting link."

"Bet yore life, pard. An' I'll bust that."

"Whatever are you two idiots talking about?" Leslie inquired, bobbing up from her tasks.

"Idiots? That's OK for Red, but not for me, lady. . . . I'm the big boss today."

"Really? Oh, that's dinkum. But not my boss."

"Yes, yours. For today, anyhow. And I'll bet that'll be enough. Red, go over to Beryl and tell her I sent you to pack her and her treasures across the river. Savvy?"

"Dog-gone yore pictoors!" Red exclaimed rapturously. "I never thought of thet. Watch me!" And he strode away to find the girl.

"Les, are your things all packed?" asked Sterl.

"Yes. Can I help, Sterl?"

"Help? Say, I'll work you to a frazzle. Rollie, let you and Larry and me pack all Slyter's load. We'll leave the bottom layer in, and float the wagon bed over. Unload now, while I go get the drovers started on the flour."

Sterl encountered Red. Never had he seen that cowboy in such a transport. "A-huh. I see. Must have worked dinkum, as Les says."

"Pard, bless yore heart, Beryl's jest about eatin' out of my hand," Red whispered huskily. "She'd been cryin'. I reckon her dad must have hopped her. What do you think she said? Wal, she said . . . 'Sterl is a big help to Dad. He'd be a good sort, if he wasn't hipped over thet chestnut-haired kid!' Can you beat it, pard? Hipped on Leslie! Beryl wanted to know how I'd get her across, an' I said I'd pack her in my arms, if she was afraid to ride. She said thet would be nice, but it would make her look a little coward, which she swore she was. An' she said she'd ride, if I came along close to her. I reckon I'll take her and Missus Dann together."

"Right-o. I'll send Friday across to watch the stuff."

In short order Sterl had twenty riders, not including Leslie and himself, swimming their horses across the river with packs in front, and on their shoulders. Leslie carried a precious bundle that she would not let Sterl touch. Mrs. Slyter elected to attend to a number of tasks while waiting for her husband to remember she also had to cross. Friday waited for Sterl, and, wading in, he grasped King's long tail and held on, to be dragged over. From bank to bank it took fresh horses ten minutes to make the crossing. On the return Sterl met Ormiston and Hathaway in midstream, and farther on, the Danns. All had become infected with Stanley's zeal and the novelty of the crossing.

It required twenty trips for each rider to unload Slyter's wagon to where it would be safe to ferry it across. Then ten men lifted the wagon bed off the wheels and carried it down to the river and set it in the water. It floated. It was a boat. It did not leak. With the use of long ropes and a team of horses on the far bank the start was made. Sterl swam King on one side, and Larry his horse on the other. There was no mishap. The heavy wheels, which went under, gave a good deal more trouble. But they were soon across, carried up the bank to where the wagonload had been left under some spread trees. In a few more moments the wagon was set up and reloaded. Leslie was as happy as her birds, and they squawked their glee.

"You were fine, kid," complimented Sterl. "That'll do for you. This hot sun will dry you *pronto*."

"But the water felt so nice and cool. I'm good for twenty more trips. But I'll rest Lady Jane."

"We'll see, later. Reckon King has done enough. One more trip. I'll fetch Duke over, or Sorrel."

"Plenty smokes, boss," Friday said, who sat in the shade, whittling on a new boomerang. Sterl saw them far off on the horizon.

"Watchum close, Friday."

Sterl enjoyed the strenuous labor. It was free of the peril that the trail drivers of Texas incurred crossing flood rivers. This fording supplies and belongings across the Diamantina was a colorful, noisy, mirthful, splashing procession. Red's war whoop pealed above the shouts and songs of the drovers. But by noon-tide the labor ceased to be fun. The only pleasure about it was the feel of the cool water under that broiling sun. By mid-afternoon the riders were sagging in their saddles, wet with sweat and water, dirty and unkempt. When drays and wagons were emptied, they began the harder job of getting them across. Sunset found the drovers with most of their outfit on the right bank of the river, but half a dozen wagons left behind, with harness and tools and much paraphernalia that had to be guarded from a raid by the aborigines who had appeared in the background.

Supper and bed were welcome that night. Red drawled wearily—"Pard, all same like old times."—and then he sank in to sleep. Sterl was not long behind. They were called at two o'clock to go on guard. Red's language might have been picturesque and reminiscent of trail driver days, but it was terribly profane.

All during their hours on watch, big fires burned on the other shore and hordes of blacks murdered the night silence with their *corroboree* over the dead cattle.

"Gosh, what a fiesta, pard," Red said. "If them cannibals don't eat themselves to death, they'll foller us till hell freezes over, an' thet ain't gonna be soon in this heah hot country."

At sunrise they rode into camp for breakfast and a change of horses, then to continue the river fording. With all hands and the partners doing their share that toilsome job was completed by mid-afternoon. Then the implacable and imperturbable Stanley Dann had his drovers brand cattle to make up for

Ormiston's loss. That drover might not have been squelched, but for the time being he made no more ado and manifestly chose to stay on Dann's side of the river. The leader ordered one day's halt in that camp to rest and dry out things. He said to Sterl: "Hazelton, I know more about cattle rushes and crossing rivers, thanks to you."

There had been very little loss and breakage and only superficial injury to men and horses on that first ford of the Diamantina. It was significant that Eric Dann did not remember this river, although the trek he had been on had undoubtedly crossed it surely farther up. Sterl strolled out in the open late that day, to take a "look-see," as the Indians used to call it, and stretch his cramped and bruised legs. Across the river he saw hundreds of blacks, like a swarm of ants, noisy and wild. From noon that day birds of prey had appeared in the sky, and by dusk dingoes were making the walking ring.

Sterl was impressed by the riverbottom valley. Despite the heat and dry spell, grass was abundant and luxuriant. Water fowl swept by in flocks, and the sandbars were dotted with white and blue herons. When he went to bed, which was early after dark, he heard them flying overhead, uttering dismal croaks.

Next day was a restful one with the cattle content to graze a mile or two up the river. The sky was black with buzzards, flocks of which spiraled down to share the feast with the aborigines. Kangaroos, wallabies, emus, rabbits were more abundant than at any camp for weeks. They were tame and approached to within a few rods of the wagons. Parrots and cockatoos colored the gum trees along the riverbanks. It was a camp that would be hard to leave, although Friday said it would be: "Same all alonga ribber."

At this Diamantina camp Leslie made several notations in her journal. **Stampede. Bridge of cattle. Packed across river. Flies something terrible!**

And so they were. Used as Sterl had gotten to these various pests—the invisible little demons and the whirling dervishes—they drove him crazy, here, if he did not cover his face. In the heat that was vastly uncomfortable. But it was the trekkers' misfortune to fall afoul of a bigger and meaner fly—a bold, black, green-winged fellow that could bite through shirts and pants. Red had been the first to discover this species to which Slyter could not give a name. Friday said—"Bite like hellum."—and no doubt he emulated Red in that nomenclature.

It chanced that Sterl came upon Red in the shade of a gum, where he had been working on a leather job. The cowboy had fire in his eye, as fierce as when Sterl had seen him bent on shooting some *hombre*.

"Pard, have you been bitten by one of these big flies heah?"

"Not yet, not by any big fly. But these little ones can bite big," replied Sterl.

"Hell, no. You haven't been bit a-tall. I got it twice through my shirt. By gosh, I thought some aborigine had speared me. Then right through my pants! Am I whoopin' mad? I heahed him buzzin' around, so I sat quiet, waitin' for him. Shore enough, he showed up, to light on my knee. Damn near the size of a hummin'bird! He was black, except for greenish or grayish wings. He must have had a proboscus like an augur. Wow! He went through my pants, right heah. I whaled away with my sombrero . . . knocked him flat. Bounded like a rock hittin' the ground. I reckoned I had done for him, an' wanted to pick him up so I could see what the hell he had stuck into me. He began to buzz like a threshin' machine, an' then he was off like a bullet. If I get bit by another one of them Outback flies, I'm gonna walk home."

Sterl had not long to wait for a visitation from one of Red's discoveries. And he decreed that his comrade had not done the new fly justice. Resignation was of no avail. Every time one of these insects bit Sterl, he set out on the warpath, or sought the cover of the tent.

It turned out that leaving that camp was a matter of rejoicing. While on the move, only the smaller species of flies irritated the riders, and that was enough.

Travel was slow but easy up the Diamantina. Eric Dann had

missed the road of the earlier trek, but that was not serious because it followed the river to its headwaters. Red had been right in his opinion that the river had stopped flowing. Two miles above the first camp the trekkers could have crossed dry shod. It must have mortified Stanley Dann, for at the next camp he took the trouble to tell Red that he would listen to him next time.

Ten days along this river bed of water holes and dry stretches tallied about a hundred miles, not good going to the cowboys, but satisfactory to their serene leader. The grass did not fail. Trees appreciably lessened in size and number. In some deep cuts verdure of tropical luxuriance marked advance toward eternal summer. The old monotonous trek set in for Sterl every day after the fresh morning hours. But from dawn until a while after sunrise the waterfowl and animals, making colored circles around the water holes and clouds of various hues above them, and the leagues of grass of white and green, the clumps of pandamus, the flowering gums of rose—all these afforded Sterl a pleasure that not even his sober mood could nullify.

But when the sun grew hot and the myriad of flies beset him, then the trek became a matter of grim endurance. He covered his face with his scarf and let King or Sorrel or Duke or Baldy graze along behind the remuda at will. Hours on end without one word spoken! Friday stalking along, carrying his weapons, tireless on bare feet, ever watching the tell-tale smoke signals on the horizon. Red, slumped in his saddle or riding sidewise, smoking myriad of cigarettes, lost in his unthinking enchantment. The wagons rolling along, creeping like white-spotted snakes, far to the fore. The mob of cattle grazing on contentedly. The horses, lazy and fat, sometimes nipping the grass, often asleep as they walked. The drovers, lost in habit now, nailed to their saddles, indifferent to leagues and distances.

Sterl marveled at Leslie Slyter. She rode with the drovers all the way. So sun-browned now that the contrast made her hair golden. She was the most wide-awake, although she sometimes took catnaps as they trekked on. How many times Sterl saw her flash in his direction! Ever she turned to him, to see if he was there, absorbed in her dream.

The great trek rolled on. The long hot days slow, golden, full to every moment, with their millions of humming pests that still could not quite make life unendurable, wore on to the short, solemn, starry nights, packed with dread of the unknown and the possible, separated from unreality and dream by the howls of wild dogs and the strange, wailing chant of the aborigines.

The water in the Diamantina failed gradually as the trek added to its leagues. There were fewer ponds, farther apart, smaller in size. But the myriad of birds and hordes of beasts multiplied because there were fewer watering places for them. Each camp presented a marvelous spectacle of wildlife and color.

Droving cattle along the course of this river was slow work, owing to sand and ruts in the soil, but it was no hardship, apart from the flies. The cattle grew fat on abundant grass and pure water. They waddled along, slowed up by the plodding wagons. Sometimes it took hours to fill the ruts in the dry soil.

Again Sterl grew conscious of the strange recurrence of the unthinking side of his dual nature. But for the passion in him, the love of Leslie, the hate of Ormiston, the hope that Beryl would go through the fire of this crisis to come out pure gold, the loyalty to Dann, the intense and unabatable desire to make this almost impossible trek a success—but for these Sterl could never have kept himself from reverting to the savage. "Gone bush," these Australians called that. For Sterl it meant merely the return of man to his age-old natural environment and state. He would have loved to do it. There were many of the drovers, most of them, in fact, who were too stolid, too unimaginative to have gone bush. But a year or two of this would make them clods, mere eating, drinking, fighting, self-preserving beasts. Perhaps that was a wise provision of nature for their survival.

Each day Sterl caught himself drifting many a time, and always he could rouse out of that sweet lull by gazing across at pensive Leslie as she rode along, at the cowboy who had abandoned home and range for love of an outcast, at the great mob of cattle, and the heat-veiled smoking hinterland, stretching away to purple nothingness.

This trek was enough romance and adventure and strife for one man in one lifetime. Sterl grew more obsessed, as the days passed, to make good his faith in the power of man to conquer nature at its worst. Where did he get that faith?

One night, at the camp Leslie had named Oleander, Sterl strolled with her to the bank of the river, where it was narrow and the bed full of water. At this sunset hour the bird and beast life was something to conjure with, entirely aside from its color and beauty. When dusk fell and the discordance subsided, and the endless string of kangaroos silhouetted black against the gold of the horizon had passed by, there began a *corroboree* of the aborigines on the opposite bank. The distance was not far; in fact, the closest these natives had been into a camp. By their bonfires, Sterl and Leslie could see the wild ceremony. Their chanting was not unmusical; their black shadows, grotesque and spectral, passing in front of the fire, fitted the primitive sound and background.

The heat of the day was lessening its hold on the land, moving away on a slight breeze. Mosquitoes were not in evidence here, and that alone would have made the hour unusually pleasant. Besides, Leslie had grown dependent upon Sterl, or thought she was, for the strength to resist all that bore down heavily. And this sweet dependence worked upon him as deeply as her youth and charm.

They must have sat there on the big log for an hour or more when the cat-eyed Red came along the bank, walking as easily as if it had been day.

"Howdy lovebirds!" he drawled. "I been lookin' for you. Gee! This ain't so bad for spoonin'."

"Say, you cowboy maniac on love," Sterl retorted, "we've been listening to the *corroboree*. Not spooning!"

"No offense, pard. Reckon I jest seen enough spoonin' to make me a maniac," Red rejoined with pathos.

"Yeah? Well, we forgive you. Who and where?"

"Sterl, besides us, there couldn't be anybody but Beryl and Ormiston . . . or . . . or some other fellow," interposed Leslie, who had taken Sterl literally.

"Shore, it was Beryl. An' Leslie, I happened to run into them back heah. But I didn't stay long. They was too het up for me."

"After all, pard Red, what difference does it make?" asked Sterl philosophically. "All we can hope for is to get out of this alive."

"No difference a-tall. Thet's all I hope for . . . gettin' Beryl out alive. An' leavin' thet slicker heah daid!"

Sterl felt Leslie quiver, and her hand tighten on his arm. Red's tone then had a hint of the inexorable justice and ruthlessness of the Western cattle trails.

Red put his arm around Leslie. "Les, you're gonna come out of this trek with a big brother, an' a sweetheart. Do you savvy thet?"

"Oh, Red! I . . . I hope so," Leslie faltered, disturbed and softened.

"Wal, it's a cinch. . . . Now, would you mind runnin' back to camp an' let me have Sterl a bit?"

"Red!" protested the girl. "You bet I'd mind. I won't do it. This is the first time I've had him this way for ages. Let me stay, Red. I don't care what you talk about. I won't listen."

"All right, honey. I guess I was pretty mean. We have no secrets from you. Shore you can be trusted. But I'm sorta upset."

"Red, get it off your chest," Sterl rejoined grimly. "Sometimes I help you a little in the way you always help me a lot."

"I been spyin' as usual," went on Red. "Hasn't been much good lately, till tonight. But I always keep sayin' it'll come some day. An' we got nothin' but time on our hands. Gosh, Leslie, what date is it, anyhow?"

"My journal says December fourth."

"Jumpin' Jehosaphat!" ejaculated Red, astounded. "Near Christmas! Oh, Lord, I shouldn't have said thet."

"Pard, you must be upset," Sterl replied kindly. "Maybe it'll please you to know that this Christmas I can remember last Christmas . . . and be far happier."

"Please me? Wal! All I can think of now is Gawd bless Leslie!"

"Me! Why should God bless me?" Leslie inquired very curiously. Intuitively she divined that she had taken the place of another woman.

Red gave her no other satisfaction than a hug. Then seriously: "Sterl, I was snoopin' about early after supper, an' I heahed Ormiston talkin' low to Bedford. Wait. I forgot to tell Friday gave me the hunch where to find them. We're all camped together heah, an' I slipped up on them. Ormiston first . . . 'Tom, I tell you I won't go any farther with Dann than the forks of this river.'

"'An' why not?' asked Bedford.

"'Because I don't know the country across toward the Warburton River. It's two hundred-odd miles from the head of the Diamantina through the mountains to my station. If the rains don't come, we'll lose all my cattle.'

"'Why not go on with Dann till we make sure of Hathaway's mob? An' also till the rains do come?'

"'I'll have his mob an' some of Dann's . . . you can lay to thet.'

"'In thet case it's all right. Jack an' Morse have been ill-satisfied. They want to make sure of more drovers an' more cattle. They came in on this because of a stake worthwhile . . . something thet they could end this bush-rangin' on.'

"'Sshh,' whispered Ormiston. 'You talk too much an' too loud around camp.'"

Red hesitated a moment, and concluded. "Thet *hombre* grumbled a bit an' then shut up. An' thet was all as Ormiston left, an' as I told you I seen him later with Beryl. Wal, pard, is thet a load to get off my chest?"

"You bet your life!" Sterl exclaimed.

"How you figger it?" demanded Red impatiently.

Sterl turned to Leslie. She clung to his arm with both hands. Her face was pale and her eyes unnaturally big in the starlight.

"Leslie, you heard?"

"Oh! How could I help it? I'm sorry. But Red didn't whisper!"

Sterl's speech flowed like running water. "Ormiston and his drovers have been rustling in a two-bit way, until this Dann trek. Now they're playing for big stakes. Ormiston is the boss, but not so clever as he thinks he is. But he fooled the Danns. His drovers are all in it, aiming to lead some of Dann's men to their side. Old stuff. You remember how cheap easy-going cowboys used to fall. How many have we seen hanged? They murdered Woolcott, got his mob. They have Hathaway's and will do for him sure as I know rustlers. Ormiston has a range somewhere over the mountains east of the head of the Diamantina. He doesn't want to risk going farther with the Danns. And there he figures right. The pot will boil over up at the forks of this river. Ormiston means to get more cattle by hook or crook. That's how I see it, Red."

"Pretty bright boy, but you haven't seen it all."

"Suppose Ormiston can persuade four or five of Dann's drovers to go in with him. Whew! What a hell of a fight there'd be. And we don't know the rest of these drovers would stand up under fire. Red, you and I, we could hardly stand off a gang as big as that, unless we had the drop on them with rifles from behind a wagon, or something. . . . Damn it, the thing looms bad!"

"Pard, I should snicker to snort. We've never met its equal, let alone its beat. . . . Bet you haven't figgered Beryl. Where's she come in?"

"Thunder and blazes! I forgot Beryl."

"Yeah. But I haven't. An' I say she's the pivot on which this deal turns. Ormiston's outfit haven't thet hunch yet, I reckon. But we have."

"You bet. Red, that *hombre* will persuade Beryl to go with him . . . or he'll take her anyway."

"Do you reckon he can persuade her?"

"I hate to think so . . . but I do."

"Wal, there we differ, pard. If Beryl is thet low-down, she'll deserve all she'd get, if we don't spoil Ormiston's plans."

"We'll probably find out," Sterl returned gravely. He had his doubts of Beryl.

"You can gamble on it, an' thet'd be a good thing. Some hell to pay might dig into the conceited, flattery-lovin' little hussy!"

"Oh, Red! Don't you call Beryl a hussy. She's not . . . she's not," Leslie declared spiritedly.

"I see someone comin'," Red's voice sank to a whisper. He peered like a nighthawk into the gloom up the riverbank. "Holy Mackeli, talk about the devil! It's Beryl and Ormiston. Let's hide. No, not by this log. . . . Heah, under the bank."

In another moment, Red had himself and comrades under the bank where a ledge ran out a few feet and some long-plumed grasses obscured it from sight above. Sterl sat with Leslie clinging to him on one side, while he clutched the cowboy on the other. Lights of the *corroboree* gleamed and danced on the dark water; weird chanting wailed from the opposite bank; black forms moved mysteriously around the smoking fires; the savory odor of roasted beef scented the air.

A rustle of weeds above, a footfall, and then Beryl's rich voice: "Here, Ash, this is far enough. I'd like to hear the *corroboree*."

"Yes, you like those damned niggers. . . . I smell cigarette smoke! Somebody has been here," came in Ormiston's voice, guarded and low. "Hazelton has been here with the damned little baggage," he growled. "Neither her father nor mother has sense enough to see. . . ."

"Of course, they see. But it's something beautiful, not what you see."

"Hazelton is no good. Like as not, he's one of those Western outlaws."

"No . . . no! Oh, Ash, darling, that would be . . . horrible!"

"Hazelton is one of those American gunmen. A killer! Jack has been abroad. He knows. He saw six notches cut on Hazelton's gun. That means the blighter has killed six men, at least. I'm no gun thrower. I'd be a fool to provoke him further."

"Indeed, you . . . would be, Ash," she said, checking her sobs. "He has made himself valuable. I'd like to see you strike him! But not to kill. Dad has come to rely upon him."

"The Yankee is a help, I'm bound to admit that. But, Beryl, I can't stand your praising him. I'm jealous. I see him watching you. He is as fascinated by your beauty as I am. He's got it as bad as that red-headed chum of his. Their eyes just gloat over you. . . . Beryl, you are so lovely. I'm mad over you. I love you beyond reason."

"Oh, Ash . . . do you, darling?" she murmured. "And am I so . . . so lovely?"

"Beryl, you are now the loveliest creature I ever beheld," he replied passionately, and his kisses rang softly. "You were pretty enough in Downsville to distract any man. But how you have improved on this trek! Such beautiful color! Such glorious eyes. You've gained. You were too thin. But now you've filled out. . . . You luscious creature. . . ."

"Ash! . . . you . . . must not . . . ," she remonstrated, but it was the remonstrance of love, that invites rather than repels. That next tense moment, with its kisses, its gasps, its murmurings, must have been a dreadful ordeal for Red Krehl. Sterl's heart was heavy for his comrade.

"Ash, darling, we came away to talk seriously," Beryl said, evidently regaining composure. "The dew is falling. It is warm, and I'm only lightly clad. I must not stay much longer. Tell me."

"Yes, we must settle it," he rejoined in a deep, low voice, without a trace of hesitation. "Beryl, I am not going on with your father, or with Eric Dann, even if he does take the Gulf road. I'm splitting off at the head of this river, not many days from here."

"Ashley! Not going? Oh!"

"No. We can't get along. Your father will never cross the Never Never! Not up in this northern half of Australia. He will be lost."

"We dared that risk," replied the girl. "Somehow father has imbued me with his wonderful faith. We'll win through."

"I doubt it. I almost know it. This interior Outback grows impossible west of the Warburton. I want to live . . . to love and be loved. I'm no pioneer . . . no empire builder. I'm a man who ran off from home as a boy . . . and who has lived the bush life."

"Ash, I promised to marry you. I will. But come with us to the Kimberleys. Make a home there."

"No. You come with me. Stanley Dann will go on that interior trek without his brother and Hathaway and me and some of his drovers. It will be suicide. . . . Beryl, come. Elope with me."

"Oh-h, Ash! How I would love to! That calls to me . . . to my soul. But I daren't listen. I will not betray my father. I will go on, even if they all desert him."

"They all will, sooner or later."

"Never! Not Hazelton! Not that droll Red Krehl! If ever a man rang true, he does! Not Leslie, or her family. They will go. And I will go, Ash." Her voice had begun low and rich with emotion, lingering over the first statements, then gathering power and passion, to end with the ring of a bell.

"But Beryl . . . you love me!" he cried huskily.

"Yes, I do. I do! But I would not betray my father. Ash, I beseech you . . . give up this selfish blind purpose of yours. It frightens me. You were not like this at first. You were so . . . so wonderful . . . for my sake, Ash, reconsider!"

"Darling, I will, despite my better judgment," Ormiston made haste to reply. And he fell to kissing her again. Presently she was whispering brokenly, won over anew, if not to compliance, then surely to belief. They moved away from the log.

Not for a long moment did Red let go of Sterl's hand. Then he sat with drooping head. He heaved a long sigh. "Pard, in the pinch heah she saved me my belief in her honor," he said, his voice trembling.

"She did, Red, she did, and I feel like a coyote . . . like a low-down idiot. But she had me buffaloed."

"Me, too. But my hunch was true. Sterl, Leslie, if it wasn't for you both, an' a hell-bent somethin', I'd walk right in this heah river!"

But Leslie was in no condition to answer. She clung to Sterl, weeping convulsively. Sterl held her closely.

"We gotta get outta heah," spoke up Red. "Gosh, I jest found we're bein' eaten alive by muskeeters."

"There weren't any a while back, I only just noticed them. Light a cigarette, Red, and smoke them out. We better not go back yet. Now, what to do, old-timer."

"Lord! We got the cairds. But how to play them? I say lay low, wait an' watch. If we'd tell all this to Dann, we'd bust the trek wide open right heah. I'm a dumbhaid, though. I cain't think of anythin' but thet pore misled girl. Pard Sterl, it's up to you to plan!"

Chapter Fifteen

On the morning of December Twenty-Fourth, the day before Christmas, Stanley Dann's trek toiled and limped into camp at the forks of the Diamantina, there to be stranded until after the rainy season.

The last fifty miles of that trek—owing to water holes lying in deep cuts almost inaccessible to the cattle, and dragging sand and terrific heat—turned out to be an all but insurmountable distance. Smoke signals preceded the drovers, and aborigines still followed them.

Dann selected his permanent campsite on the west side of the river above the junction of the several branches, which were steep-banked, deep, dry beds of rock and sand, with water holes dispersed at widely separated points, and where the heat was fast absorbing the water. Animals and birds ringed these spots in incredible numbers. Those water holes would be dry in a few weeks. But below this junction the main water hole of the Diamantina was a mile-long, narrow, partly shaded pool that would last until the next rainy season, even if that took a year in coming. Except in sandy patches, grass grew abundantly. Dann was assured of these cardinal necessities for man and beast for as long a spell as they were compelled to wait there.

Dann ordered camps pitched on the left bank in a grove of blossoming eucalyptus, standing far apart in stately aloofness from each other, spreading giant branches over a grassy, flowered bench where there were no marks of floods reaching that high.

The pitching of this camp registered for the trekkers an immense relief and joy, but it had some significant features, the most potent of which was Ashley Ormiston's refusal to camp on that side of the river. He drove his cattle and Allan Hathaway's, which together constituted a mob of about three thousand head—according to Sterl's calculation—across the dry streambeds to the farthest bank. Grass appeared more abundant on that side, and a shadier grove offered more comfort—two facts Ormiston gave as reasons for his choice. As a bird flew, however, the distance between the two camps was scarcely a quarter of a mile. Dann stood on his bank and for a long time watched Ormiston's mob trekking across in detour, raising clouds of dust, and scattering flocks of birds. No one knew what was in his mind, but Sterl thought he could make a fairly accurate guess. He knew this action of Ormiston's was a split, and not a procedure prompted by grass and shade, or more privacy for him and his drovers. The significance was ominous. He wanted to be on that side of the river, when the floods rolled down.

All hands worked hard that day at pitching permanent camp, while a few riders guarded the mob and remuda. The latter task was merely a matter of method and habit. Neither cattle nor horses would actually need guardianship for many a day.

Sterl and Red pitched their tent in a clump of pandamus trees which grew in a circle so closely that all their tops commingled, forming a dense canopy. The great seeds, somewhat resembling small pineapples, clustered aloft amid the foliage. Pandamus leaves covered with a ground canvas furnished a thick and soft carpet for the tent. Their nets promised protection from mosquitoes and flies. But nothing could save them from the heat. They worked naked to the waist, and the sweat poured off their bodies. Friday built himself a bark shack in back of the tent, and Roland and Larry elected to stay with the wagon, which had been drawn up near the clump of pandamus.

Slyter's wagon, some fifty rods or more distant, was sheltered by the largest gum, or at least one with the bushiest foliage on the bench. Near at hand, Bill was working hard to establish a comfortable cooking unit. The camps of the Danns were lower down, nearer the riverbank, and most picturesquely located among the gums.

Not until late in the afternoon did Sterl feel free to change his wet and dirty garments. He decided to get the lay of the land in his mind, and to that end sought out Leslie to accompany him. But she was an extremely warm and wet and bedraggled young person bent over a washtub.

"Leslie!" Sterl ejaculated. "Have you been all day washing?"

"Howdy, Sir Galahad! Where have you been all day? Have you anything you need washed?"

"Yes, thanks, gobs of them. But Red and I are used to doing our own. Les, it looks like a grand camp."

"I haven't looked. Oh . . . the heat . . . and the flies! Hell!"

"Right-o! But Red says, if we don't croak, we'll get used to it. See you at supper."

"I'm croaking now," Leslie sent after him.

Sterl went back to his camp. "Come on, Red, let's take a look at the scenery."

"Wha-at? To hell with the scenery!" growled the cowboy. "I wanna rest an' there ain't none."

Then Sterl turned to the never-failing black, Friday, who was always there when wanted. "Come, Friday. Let's go look-see."

With rifle and spear the two crossed the grassy flat back of camp, and climbed a low ridge that in ages past had been the bank of a vast river. From this point Sterl expected to get in his mind's eye the lay of this upper Diamantina land. But the blazing sunset and the appalling grandeur of that country drove from his mind at first any thought of topography. One glance at the fiery sun blinded him for moments.

"Good camp place, Friday?" he asked.

"Plenty wood, plenty water, plenty meat. All same bad," replied the black.

Sterl made for a big, flat rock, to use as a seat, while Friday stood beside him, resting his tall spear.

"Why all same bad?"

"Plenty black fella, plenty *lubra*, plenty fly. Eatum up alive. No rain long time. Big water bimeby."

"One thing at a time, Friday. Why plenty black fella bad?"

"Some black fella good. No good alonga here. Eat . . . steal. More come all time. Eat . . . steal. White fella like *lubra*. That bad."

Sterl reflected upon the intimation in the black's words. Perhaps Stanley Dann's fine mind had never been troubled by such a contingency.

"What black fella do about young girls, I mean *lubra*?"

"Mebbe stickum white fella spear."

"Not so good. But I hope our friend Ormiston runs true to type, and gets speared," muttered Sterl half to himself.

"Friday spearum 'im bimeby."

The black had said that once before, months back. Gazing up at him, Sterl thought his native ally was not one to forget.

"Save Red or me the trouble. . . . Friday, what you mean, no rain long time?"

"Black fella tell all about," Friday replied, making one of his eloquent gestures. It seemed to include the sun, the land, the growths, the living things within its compass. The black man was a part of all this. He had senses utterly beyond the white man's ken.

"Would you stay here till rain come bimeby?" went on Sterl.

"Yes, boss. Good."

"Then it's both good and bad," Sterl mused. "I just about figured thet myself. Friday, why bad when rain comes bimeby?"

"Big water. All alonga. Ribber washum away. Cattle stuck." Friday's gestures here were more indicative of drastic calamity than his specific words. Sterl conjured up a mental picture of floods that were frightful in the extreme. But he knew that he could not imagine how terrible they might be.

"Friday, how longa stay here?"

The black opened and spread his wonderful hands, enumerating with his fingers. "Moons. Plenty moons. Friday no tell. Mebbe plenty more."

Strangely enough Sterl became alive to the fact that such a prospect was dreamingly good. He was glad without thinking of the cost in the end. There was rest, rest from that infernal trek, water, plenty of water to drink and bathe in, food enough, and unlimited meat, protection from the flies, Leslie to ride and walk and hunt with, and this glorious place. Sterl awakened to the fact that this last, which included Leslie's part in it, too, held the significance of his unconsidered content. Therefore, he climbed up on the rock to grasp to his mind and heart the reason for such a devastating and ruthless forgetting of the meaning and success of this trek. And he found the same old thing facing him—the ever-new, strange, and stupendous nature of this Australian wilderness.

A sheen of gold illumined the sky and enveloped the land. The three forks of the Diamantina, dry watercourses, white and glaring by day, now wound away like rivers of golden fire. That afterglow of sunset left the league-wide areas of green grass faintly suffused with its hue, but the riverbeds of rock and sand took on a phenomenal and supernatural intensity of color. There was a deeper tinge of gold on the canvas wagon tops, the tents, and a flock of white cockatoos, covering the branches of a dead gum tree, appeared transformed birds of paradise of that hue. Below camp to the right, where the water of the river gleamed through the trees, there was a flickering, twinkling myriad of golden facets.

But this peculiar glow and glory of the scene over which Sterl's gaze roved from place to place was only physical beauty, not by any means the dominating, compelling force that he felt, yet had not grasped. All he could do in those moments of fading effulgence was to drag his gaze from the scene at his feet, and face the wilderness into which these three spreading river courses wound away into mere threads of fire, to become lost in magnificent and illimitable purple haze.

In his helplessness, as if he had been lost again and starving,

Sterl appealed to the black man—the evolved product of this boundless country.

"Friday! What see? How far? Where?"

The aborigine understood him. Sterl had absolute assurance of that, as also conviction that the black could see clear to the horizons and beyond them. Friday's long spear described a grand curve impressively holding the height of the arch toward the west, where the golden luminosity still emphasized a silhouette of ragged mountains.

"Never Never Land!" said Friday in the white man's language.

Sterl was answered, and, although that answer seemed inexplicable, he felt satisfied. He would have to live a lifetime in this country to understand and assimilate it—a lifetime which he thought would be well-spent.

From the Diamantina's three-pronged fork the land spread away with grassy plain and rugged bush, a level land that never appeared to end, yet rose to long, heaving ridges with wide valleys between, and low ranges leading westward, and on and on over never-ending blank spaces of purple, toward a horizon-wide portal between black domes and gold-rimmed peaks, far within this gateway there lifted an upflung spectral range, like a mirage in the moon, that beckoned and called with never-ending lure and promise.

Dusk fell while Sterl made his way by easy stages back to camp. Every part of him except his mind felt tired. What an adventure he was living! What a pity it could not last. How hateful to contrast all he had just seen with the hate, greed, lust he knew existed in this camp!

Red sat with his back to a tree, his hands spread listlessly. The cowboy was too tired to care about anything. "Pard, I seen you up there, like an Apache scout. Pretty nifty, huh?" he drawled lazily.

"Red, I've no regrets, any more."

"Wal! Not a-tall?"

"Not a-tall, old friend."

"Thet's dog-gone good! Neither have I, Sterl. Couldn't we jest be happy but for thet bastard Ormiston?"

"Ha! We could be, and almost are. . . . Maybe, in spite of him."

Leslie approached, for once not running or even showing any of her usual energy. She had changed her rider's ragged garb for a light cotton dress, and, as she came into the circle of Red's little fire, both cowboys were struck by the difference.

"Gosh, Les, you look sweet. I'd jest like to hug an' kiss you," drawled Red.

"Why don't you, then?"

"Wal, I have two good reasons. One is, I want to preserve my life, an' the other is I kinda want to be true to Beryl."

Sterl laughed. "Leslie, I dare say wholesome flattery like Red's rings sweet in your ears. But such invitation as you offer him is rather risky."

"Do you boys know what day tomorrow is?" she asked wistfully.

Sterl knew, but he remained thoughtfully silent.

"It's Christmas. . . . I'm going over to see the Danns. Mum is there. Won't you come?"

"Les, I'm too dog-gone daid tired even to see Beryl, or to care whether it's Christmas or the Fourth . . . days thet used to be red letters in a cowboy's life."

"Me, too, Leslie. You see, we've let down. I did have the strength to climb the hill back here. And it was worth the pangs."

"I watched you, Sterl. Oh, that color . . . the light on everything! Glorious!"

When Leslie left, Sterl sat down heavily beside his comrade. "Any 'skeeters, pard?"

"Nary one yet. Gosh, wouldn't it be grand, if this heah camp was minus moskeeters? But thet'd be too good to be true."

"No. Might be, as Friday says. You know we've had camps where there weren't any. It's open here, even along the river."

"Wal, I hope so. If we had the early mawnin's an' late evenin's free from blood-suckers, we'd live through this wait."

"Red, you remember that day in Brisbane when we spent so much money?"

"Hell, yes. But it seems years ago."

"Well, I flatter myself I'm a pretty wise *hombre*, if I do say it myself. I bought Christmas presents for you and myself. And as we heard there were to be a couple of girls with us, I took a chance and bought some for them."

"Aw, pard!" wailed Red. "But I didn't. I never thought of thet. What a pore muddle-haided cowboy I am! Gosh, what a chance I missed! Ormiston is too selfish an' stingy to buy nice things for girls."

"Umpumm, Red, you haven't missed it. I bought enough for you to give Beryl and Leslie, too."

"Sterl, you were always the finest gazabo who ever forked a pony!" ejaculated Red, elated. "Spring it on me, *pronto*. What kind of presents?"

"Candy, for one thing."

"Naw, not candy! Why, pard, you're loco. Heah we been trekkin' a thousand miles under this hot sun . . . candy would melt!"

"I'm sure this hasn't melted. It's hard candy in tin boxes. Then I bought some pretty handkerchiefs and sewing kits. Leslie, two leather cases full of toilet articles you know, the kind of things girls like. I found that out long ago. But out here in this country, after seven months of travel . . . gee . . . these things imported from England, mind you, make a hit."

"Sterl, you're shore a Mackavellian . . . or whoever that guy was! It jest fills me full of tingles. Not only to make Beryl happy, but to make that black-browed geezer sick!"

"Maybe that will make me feel good, too! All right . . . tomorrow morning we'll unpack the stuff and plan our surprise. How about guard tonight?"

"Dann sent word by Slyter thet you an' me could lay off tonight. But I said nix. Anyway, it's only two hours on, an' Larry will call us. Let's roll in, pard, an' go chasin' dreams. Night before Christmas? My Gawd, I was a boy once!"

Broad daylight had come when Sterl and Red were called to take their turn at guard from four o'clock until six. Friday went with them. There were not many cattle standing, and the whole mob needed no watch. The Slyter remuda, having formed a habit of grazing alone, kept aloof from Dann's several hundred horses.

The early morning was not cool, but it was delightfully pleasant. Not one single drawback. Kangaroos and emus dotted the grassy level and were outlined black against the skyline of the hill. A thousand parrots of all sizes and hues murdered the early morning serenity, and ten times that many waterfowl filled the air and littered the water holes.

Breakfast was called at sunrise. Both Sterl and Red beat Leslie and her parents in hearty Christmas greetings. The Downsville folk might have felt the significance of this Christmas Day, far from home, and with only uncertainty in the future, but the cowboys were happy to be right there in the Australian hinterland.

"Dann wants us all present after breakfast," announced Slyter.

Sterl and Red appeared mysteriously from their tent, each carrying a canvas knapsack on his shoulder. It had developed in the tent, a little before this exit, that Sterl's prodigality had made it possible to save some presents for a future surprise. "Dog-gone it!" Red had exclaimed, "I'm whole hawg or none. Mebbe we'll never live till another Christmas. Or our outfit will be lost or stolen. Let's give all the presents right now."

"Umpumm, pard. And I'll bet you see why *pronto*," responded Sterl.

Leslie caught up with them on their way to Dann's camp. Her bright simple garb graced the occasion. She appeared mightily curious about the contents of the knapsacks. Upon trying to feel what was in Sterl's, only to be severely rebuffed, she grew suspicious.

"I'll bet you Yankees are up to something," she said.

Neither cowboy gave her any satisfaction whatsoever. They were the last to arrive at the Dann encampment. All of the trekking party were present except Ormiston's drovers and several of Dann's. Stanley Dann stood up, bareheaded, to read a passage from the Bible. After that he offered up a general prayer, commemorating the meaning of Christmas, of peace on earth and good will to man, and ended with a specific thankfulness to God for their good fortune, and his unshakable faith in all to come.

Beryl, looking lovely in a blue gown that had evidently been donned for this occasion, was holding a little court all her own in the shade of a tree near her wagon.

"Tip off your mother an' dad to rustle over heah *pronto*," whispered Red to Leslie.

"Tip off?" queried Leslie, mystified but intensely eager. "Talk English, you funny fellow."

"Wal, no matter. I see everybody trekkin' over heah to Beryl."

"Oh, Red! What have you got up your sleeve?"

Even then Sterl felt certain that Leslie did not guess the truth. They approached Beryl at her court in the rose shade of the tree, where Cedric and Larry and the younger drovers were offering felicitations of the day. Ormiston, shaven and in clean garb, occupied what looked like a privileged place close to Beryl. His handsome face and person were strikingly in evidence, and his manner was one of assurance and civility.

Suddenly Beryl espied Sterl and Red. Her pleasure was evident when they made their gallant bows and wished her the greetings of the season. She kissed Leslie in sincere gladness. But her attention deepened into sparkling-eyed delight and anticipation when the cowboys unlimbered their knapsacks, to set them down with a flourish in front of Beryl and Leslie.

"Wal, folks, me an' Sterl heah air playin' Santa Claus," drawled Red, with his smile that made him boyishly good to look at. "But he is a modest gazabo, so I have to do the honors."

Beryl let out a shriek of delight. Leslie, blind to the issue until that moment, flushed with amaze and rapture. The Danns and their company looked on with smiles.

Then Red and Sterl, acting with the accord which, indeed, had been rehearsed, reached into the knapsack, with the air of magicians, to fish out a small box of cigars for Dann and his partners, some brightly wrapped gifts for Emily Dann and Mrs. Slyter.

"My word!" boomed Stanley Dann. "I haven't had a smoke for months. . . . Well, well, to think these Yankees could outdo English people in memory of Christmas!"

The donors gave Beryl and Leslie handy little sewing kits which were received with deep appreciation. Then came the two handsome leather cases which evoked cries of delight.

"Out here in the Never Never!" exclaimed Beryl incredulously.

"Sterl Hazelton," cried Leslie, with glad eyes upon him. "When all my things are gone or worn out. . . . Aladdin!"

"Girls, thet ain't nothin' a-tall," beamed Red. "Come on, pard, all together."

Then in slow deliberation, purposely tantalizing to the quivering girls, each cowboy produced two boxes—one of goodly size, the other small—both wrapped in shiny paper and tied with colored ribbons.

"What in the world?" cried Beryl, her eyes shining in purple eagerness.

"Oh! Oh! Oh!" burst out Leslie, reaching brown hands for her boxes. "What? Oh, what?"

"Candy!" Sterl shouted triumphantly.

"Red Krehl . . . not candy? Not ever," whispered Beryl. "You could not guess how I've missed that . . . but . . . but candy would be too much!"

"Wal, Beryl, it is candy," drawled Red happily.

Evidently Leslie had been rendered mute, but she bestowed upon Sterl's cheek a kiss that left no doubt of her unspoken delight.

Beryl scrambled to her knees, unmindful of the dainty gown, and she held all her presents in her arms.

"Leslie, you shall not outdo me in thanks," she cried with spirit. "Red Krehl, come here! I would knight you, if I were a queen. I am glad that *somebody* remembered me on Christmas Day." And as the awkward cowboy, impelled beyond his will, stumbled to his knees before the girl, she lifted a lovely rosy face and kissed him.

Sterl, glancing at Ormiston, saw his face grow ashey and a glare of terrible jealous hate light his prominent eyes. Then Ormiston turned on his heel and strode away, an erect, violent, forbidding figure.

Ash Ormiston, after leaving Dann's camp in high dudgeon on Christmas morning, did not return the next day or the next. Beryl palpably chafed and worried at this evidence of his resentment, but, so far as Sterl could see, her pride upheld her. His conviction was now that Ormiston, having arrived at the scene of his intended split with Dann, had another arrow to his bow besides persuasion.

A different kind of fight had begun for Stanley Dann's trekkers, a fight not against distance and time, rough land, treacherous water, but against heat and flies and what was worst of all, the peril of the idleness of waiting and of their effect on the mind. Each day—between the blazing sun and the thirst of thousands of cattle—saw the water in the long water hole recede inches down the sand and rock. One night from Ormiston's side of the river gunshots and shrill yells of aborigines startled the campers on Dann's side. There was no *corroboree* that night.

Next morning a drover reported to Dann that Ormiston's men had shot five blacks. No reason was given. It was well known how Ormiston hated blacks. Stanley Dann was overheard to express the opinion that his surly partner had sought to drive thieving natives away from camp. But Sterl, after talking with Friday, came to the conclusion that Ormiston wanted to drive the aborigines across the river. At any rate that was what had happened. The several hundred blacks had congregated in a grove at the lower end of the long water hole.

By way of reparation and kindness Dann ordered crippled cattle shot and dragged down to the aborigine camp. Blacks, *lubras*, *gins*, pickaninnies deserted their camp while this restitution took place. But later, after Friday had visited them, they gradually approached nearer and nearer to Dann's camp. Dann argued for pursuing any course that would keep the blacks friendly, and

Slyter agreed with him. Friday might have influenced Dann in this attitude, but Sterl thought that their leader, in any case, would be generous and the opposite of hostile. When Sterl asked Friday what he had told Dann and Slyter, the black replied: " "Plenty black fella good. Mebbe steal bimeby. No fightum."

"Wal, I'd rather stand for thet," asserted Red, "than rile them into slitherin' spears about. I've an orful dread of one of them things through my gizzard."

It appeared that Beryl weakened in the end, to send a note by one of the drovers across the way to Ormiston, and that evening he came to see her. Thereafter, he appeared at Dann's camp every evening, exactly as Red had predicted to Sterl. Beryl Dann would need a terrible lesson before she began to react from her infatuation and then it might come too late. More obviously than any other of Dann's trekkers, she was responding to the wild environment.

The trekkers settled down to suffer and to wait. The second hour after sunset usually brought a night breeze that gave welcome respite to the torrid heat of the day. Sterl devoted himself to Leslie at this time, and they seldom remained in camp. Leslie felt alienated again from Beryl, and did not like to see the girl and the drover together. Sterl strangled his disgust for Beryl, and tried to emulate the patient, long-suffering Red. As he did not have the motive which sustained Red, he found patience difficult.

The morning hours, from daylight until an hour or more after breakfast, were the most supporting and profitable of the day. Sterl made use of this time, often with Leslie or Friday. He soon learned, however, that the middle of the day was intolerable in the sun and just endurable in the shade. The cattle needed no watch then—although Dann maintained a short one for two drovers—as they sought the shade of the trees where they lay down or stood resting.

The sun grew hot enough almost to drive a man crazy, and the ever-increasing flies made existence well-nigh unbearable. During this period, when it was possible, all of the trek kers kept under cover of the tents or wagons or mosquito nets, where they shut the flies out. The constant humming and buzzing outside, like that of a great hive of bees, made this protection so welcome that the stifling heat was endurable.

The days wore on endlessly, each one hotter than the last. The small water holes dried up. All living creatures were dependent upon the long water hole. No cloud appeared in the sky. No hope of rain, although hope would not die. At midday rocks were so hot that they blistered a naked hand, the cattle ceased to bawl, the birds to scream, the aborigines to move about. The whites lay prone, enduring, unless forced to some task. Sterl had always thriven on hot weather, likewise Red. They could sleep, but they would awaken wringing wet with sweat. But when the mercury rose to a hundred and ten degrees, then the cowboys were hard put to endure it.

When Friday was asked if the rains were ever coming, he would reply: "Might be, bimeby."

When Sterl made signs to any of the other blacks, he would be invariably answered by indistinguishable talk accompanied by gestures almost as unsolvable. But Friday would translate.

"Black fella say plenty rain someday."

"He might mean another year," expostulated Sterl.

"Might be," said the imperturbable black.

But the bearable hours always renewed interest in things of the moment and hope for the future.

Sterl never tired of the aborigines nor of his efforts to observe and understand them. His first contacts were productive only of awe, nausea, bewilderment. These blacks seemed far below Friday in development. But they belonged to the same age as Friday, and that was the Stone Age.

Friday could not name this tribe of natives, but he understood their language well enough to interpret, and it was through this that the overtures of Stanley Dann and Sterl counteracted the fright and hostility for which Ormiston and his drovers were responsible.

Sterl learned that, when a death occurred in a camp of theirs, they moved away at once. Ormiston's ruthlessness, apparently, was exercised merely to get rid of the aborigines. They had fled across the river, far below the forks, but later, after their fears had been allayed, they moved closer to Dann's camp. Every day newcomers arrived, and still the smoke signals continued to rise above the horizons. Some of these smoke signals could be seen fifty miles and more distant.

They went stark naked except for a breechcloth of woven grass or hair. The men were tall, lean, although muscular, black as coal, with broad faces and large heads covered by a mop of tangled black hair. The troops of pot-bellied youngsters, upon being approached, scattered like a flock of frightened quail. The women, or *gins* as Slyter called them, were such monstrosities of human creatures that Sterl had to force himself to glance at them. For the most part the *lubras* were not good to look at either, although they were young, sturdy, chattering, shining-eyed girls. Some few of them, however, were prepossessing and far from averse to making eyes at the younger drovers. One of the tribal customs was the punishment of adultery by death. This was identical with a law of some of the Indian tribes Sterl had known.

It was a singular thing for Sterl to realize he had little interest in the religion, if they had one, the strange age-old customs, and the mental evolution of these primitive people. To him they seemed the lowest order of human beings on the face of the earth—not only had their development from the dark ages been incalculably slow, but they appeared to have been arrested in the Stone Age at this period. Doubtless before they could evolve much further, civilization would wipe them out.

This was a pitiful, astounding tragedy, but aside from Sterl's awe and sadness over such a fate, he did not delve deeply into the spiritual mystery. To him they were not far removed from their ape ancestors. They could never change and grow, unless left to themselves. Contact with the white man would only hasten the inevitable dissolution. They should be left alone in their fight with Nature.

At this stage the aboriginal's life consisted of preservation and reproduction. The latter took care of itself, and, if there was no birth control, there certainly was an elimination of the unfit and the encumbrance. Babies born during nomadic wanderings, if they were in the way, or retarded progress, were sacrificed. But preservation filled every hour with its ceaseless demand. The problem of the aboriginal was to eat, and he ate everything from dirt and grass and seeds and fruit to all living creatures, including his own species.

The black man was a hunter, no doubt a descendant of the greatest hunters that ever lived, the cavemen. He made his own weapons, very few in number, and these he carried. The *gins* and *lubras* were the beasts of burden.

Friday told Sterl that the people caught live fish underwater with their hands. Sterl saw these black men at Dann's camp swim underwater, and drag down ducks beneath the surface, and stay under so long that Sterl feared they were drowned. He saw them mash up ants' nests, made of leaves stuck together, and devour with a relish a mess of ants. He saw them eat every last vestige of a bullock, meat, entrails, and even pound up the horns. He found *lubras* and children out on the plain, digging for roots, herbs, lizards, eggs, and one of their reptile luxuries, the goanna.

Red Krehl called the natives a lousy bunch. They roused no sentiment whatsoever in him. One morning Red accompanied Sterl and Leslie, with the inseparable Friday, on a visit to the aborigines. They came upon two blacks, both mature men, tall and lean, who fastened ghoulish eyes upon Leslie's supple and brown bare legs, and then shifted their black gaze to the cowboy's red head. One of the natives held a most striking posture which certainly produced an effect. He stood on one lean, long leg, leaning on his spear, while his other leg was bent at right angles, with his foot flat against the inside of his thigh. He stood at ease.

"What'n'll is the matter with this gazabo?" inquired Red.

"Nothing. He's just resting. I see a good many blacks stand like that," replied Sterl.

"Looks like a big, sandhill crane."

The aborigine, evidently impressed by Red, spoke to him in his native jargon.

"Yeah?" drawled Red, and then added sonorously: "Holy Mackeli . . . Kalamazoo . . . Raspatas . . . Mugg's Landin'. You one-laiged black giraffe!"

Whereupon the aborigine, tremendously impressed, let out a flow of speech that in volume certainly matched Red's.

"A-huh? Thet didn't sound so good to me. Friday, what did he say?"

Friday indicated Krehl's red head and replied: "Makeum frun alonga you."

"Hell he did?" roared Red. "Hey, you! I'm from Texas, an' I'm liable to shoot thet one laig out from under you."

Upon their return to the Dann encampment Slyter called Red and Sterl to him, and informed them that Stanley Dann wanted to see them promptly.

"Now, what's up?" queried Sterl impatiently, quick to catch Slyter's sober mood.

"I'd rather Dann told you," returned the drover. "There's been a fight, and the drovers are upset."

"Yeah? Wal, if you ask me thet ain't nothin' new these days," drawled Red with a bite in his tone.

Slyter accompanied them the few rods under the trees to the bright campfire where Stanley stalked to and fro. He was bareheaded, in his shirt sleeves, a deep-eyed giant who stood erect under obvious burdens. Beryl was there in the background, with her Aunt Emily and Mrs. Slyter. A group of men, just visible near one of the tents, stood and conversed low. Their posture, with heads together, sent a shiver over Sterl.

"You sent for us, sir," spoke up Sterl quickly.

"Yes, I regret to say. But the tragedy that has dogged our trek broke out again tonight. Harry Spence has been shot. The drovers just fetched him in. He died without regaining consciousness."

"Spence? That is regrettable, sir. But it can hardly have anything to do with us," returned Sterl. He had not thought much of Spence or several other of the rougher element among Dann's drovers. Spence, to judge from his tattoo marks and his foul language, had been a sea-faring man. And plenty tough, to quote Red Krehl.

"Only indirectly," rejoined Dann hastily. Sterl's stilted response had reacted subtly upon him.

"Boss, who shot Spence?" interposed Red coolly.

"Ormiston's drover, Bedford. Tom Bedford. He was badly wounded in the fight, but will recover."

"Wal, beggin' yore pardon, boss, an' if you ask me, there ain't much love lost in Spence's case, an' if Bedford croaked, it'd be a damn good night's job," Red replied in cold deliberation.

"I'm not asking you for your judgments, Krehl," said the leader tersely.

"I'm sorry, boss, but you gotta take them just the same."

Sterl put a placating and persuasive hand on Red's shoulder. But all the same he was glad the cowboy had spoken out. He, too, was sick of subterfuge and concealment.

"Sir, what has Ormiston to do with this . . . that you approach us?" Sterl inquired quietly.

"Boys, it is only that I preferred to tell you myself, rather than have you hear it from others. I want to persuade you to see it my way. I have come to rely upon you both. I have come to have a personal regard for you. Can I exact a promise from you both . . . not to shed blood . . . except in some drastic case of self-defense?"

"Yes, sir, you can from me," declared Sterl, instantly rallying to his sympathy for this great and trouble-besieged man. "Red, you'll give that promise, too, won't you? Remember, whatever you do for him, you'll be doing for Beryl."

"Pard, I ain't so shore about Beryl," the cowboy rejoined bluntly. "Boss, you ain't askin' me to make a promise like thet an' keep it forever. I'd have throwed my gun long ago but for you."

"Krehl, don't misunderstand me," Dann returned in haste. "I

would not presume to have you deny your creed, your honor. I beg this promise only for the present, because I still hope and pray we can go through this trek without undue strife among us drovers . . . at least without bloodshed."

"Wal, boss, as I see it, you ain't," flashed Red. "It wouldn't be natural. You've got some low-down *hombres* mixed up with you on this trek. An' everyday the strain grows wuss. All the same I'll give you my promise thet I won't raise a hand against Ormiston, or anyone, except in self-defense . . . or, let me say, to save somebody's life."

"Thank you, Krehl. I begin to appreciate what it means for you to give such a promise," replied Dann. "Don't think I fail to see the growing complexity of this trek. If I'd let myself believe, it'd be appalling. But we shall succeed. Now, for the detail that will be as offensive to you as it was to me. This morning a new contingent of blacks arrived. It seems there were some unusually comely *lubras* among them. Ormiston propitiated them with gifts . . . an action Slyter and I are strongly opposed to. But Ormiston did it, and took some of the *lubras* to work around his camp. Spence and Bedford quarreled over one of them. It was obvious that all the drovers had been drinking. The two men fought, with the result I told you. Ormiston sent the report to me. And I at once ordered him here. I took him to task. We had bitter words, that might have led to worse but for Beryl. She came between us, and in part, when Ormiston maligned you boys, she took his side. She believes him. I do not."

"Thanks, boss. But spill it. What has Ormiston said now?" retorted Sterl harshly.

"In the first place, he was extremely ruffled at my censure," continued Dann. "Then he ridiculed my offense at the idea of his drovers making up to the *lubras*. And the part applicable to you is this, in his own words . : . 'Look at your Yankee cowboys . . . Hazelton, posing as a gentleman, and Krehl as a comedian . . . to please the ladies! They go from their soft speeches to Beryl and Leslie to the embraces of these nigger *lubras!*' "

If Stanley Dann expected the cowboys to arise in rage to disclaim against their traducer, he reckoned without his host. Nothing Ormiston might do or say could surprise them any more.

As fate would have it, Leslie had followed them over, and Beryl with the two women, evidently wishing to intercept her, had all come within range of Dann's stern voice, as he quoted Ormiston's vituperation. Sterl threw up his hands. He sensed events. What was the use? He knew these things would happen. Let them happen. However, Red tenaciously held onto something akin to ideals. Stanley Dann threw fuel upon the fire by reprimanding the feminine contingent for listening to what was none of their business. Mrs. Slyter attempted to drag Leslie away. The girl, not only would not leave, but she came up to the camp-fire and Beryl was at her side. Sterl, with an inward groan, felt at once contempt for Beryl and a saving pity. She could not be held responsible for any silly or mad thing she might do or say. That responsibility rested upon the head of her pioneer father.

Red, keen as he was, did not fortify himself with subtle knowledge and bitterness, as Sterl had done. But his innate chivalry permitted no intimation that these girls could believe such vile slander.

"Beryl, you needn't look so orful bad," he said gently. "Leastways not on my account. I jest promised yore dad I wouldn't throw a gun on Ormiston for what he said."

"You don't deny it, Red Krehl?" Beryl cried passionately, beside herself.

"Deny . . . wh-what?" stammered Red.

"You know. Your ready wit and humor fail you here."

"Wal, there's more than thet failin' me, I reckon. What you mean . . . I don't deny?"

"Ormiston's accusation that you cowboys go from me and Leslie . . . to . . . those *lubras*," rang out the outraged girl. She was pale under her tan, and her big eyes strained with horror.

Red twitched as if he were about to draw a gun. His red visage lost its ruddiness then. "Me deny thet? Hell, no! I'm a Texan, Miss Dann. You English never heahed of Texas, let alone know what a Texan stands for in regard to women. What you've got in yore mind, Beryl Dann, what you think of *me*, is what's true of yore rotten lover. An' by Gawd, someday you'll go on yore knees to me for thet!"

The girl recoiled. She gasped. Her eyes dilated. But she could not cope with passion and jealousy and hate—those primitive emotions that this trek had increased by leaps and bounds. Her intelligence, that faculty of hers which governed affection and faith, grasped the distortion of some insanity or injustice here. But she let Red stalk away without another word.

Sterl saw with a pang this calamity fall upon the loyal and devoted head of his friend. He felt Red's hurt so keenly that it seemed almost his own.

"Sterl! Sterl!" Leslie burst out wildly. "You deny . . . that . . . that. . . . Or I'll hate you!"

"Leslie, it is a matter of supreme indifference to me what you believe," returned Sterl, cold and aloof, without scorn. Then he addressed the parents of the girls. "Dann, Slyter, and you, Missus Slyter, you all can't fail to see what your wilderness outback has done to your precious offspring. Next, they'll condone in Ormiston and his bunch the very thing they insult us with now!"

Chapter Sixteen

As for Leslie, who met him that morning at breakfast as if awakening from a nightmare, and who appeared stunned to bewilderment that he did not notice her, Sterl felt that she, the same as Beryl, must learn her bitter lesson. Until that time she would not exist for him, so far as intimacy and friendly contact were concerned. He was deeply hurt, but not resentful. She was only a young girl, sentimental, wayward, passionate, placed in a terrible situation, to which she had reacted as might have been expected. Sterl felt sorry for her. Little by little his love had grown until it had almost made him forget that he was an outlaw who, if he considered marriage, must find himself in a grave plight. Sterl had been hurt before by love. He could not kill this new love, but he put it aside. Krehl's love affair with Beryl, however, had a fair chance to survive. Sterl seemed to feel something deep and latent in this Dann girl. She was blindly in love with this dark-browned bush-ranger. But when she learned the truth about Ormiston, as must inevitably happen, it was Sterl's opinion that the girl would hate him more than she had loved him.

January blazed to its end, but the rains did not come. They might skip a year. The heat and the flies had become insupportable. Yet human life lived on, although in each and every person's being there were signs, even in himself, revealing to Sterl's keen eyes that white people could not live there for long. The days were terrible; the sky was a vast copper dome close to the earth; the night hot even till dawn. Work and meals were undertaken before sunrise and after sunset. The mob of cattle grazed slowly by night and rested by day. The flies were harder on them than the sun. Hundreds of calves were born. Stanley Dann had now more cattle than when he had left Downsville.

Bedford, being a tough and phlegmatic man, recovered from his serious wound. Hathaway came down with some kind of fever which neither Ormiston nor Dann could alleviate. Emily Dann was a woman unused to life in the open, and, despite what had appeared at first a certain robustness, she began to fail. It was mental, Sterl thought, more than physical. She simply dried up into a shadow of her former self, and met death with a wan and pathetic gladness.

Eric Dann presented a problem to Sterl. The man had something on his mind, either a cowardice he could not beat, a gnawing indecision about splitting with his brother, or something secret. Sterl had seen criminals not big enough to stand up under the adversity that tried men's souls, and it seemed to him there was a furtive similarity between their moods and Eric's. Ormiston had turned gaunt of visage, hollow-eyed. But for that matter, all the drovers lost flesh, hardened, tanned almost as black as Friday, and, if they ever smiled, Sterl did not see it. It was in Ormiston's eyes, however, that the difference lay. He never met Sterl's scornful gaze. He ceased to eat at Dann's table, but at sunset and dusk he haunted Beryl, and kept her up late. Beryl Dann could not lose her grace of form or beauty of profile, but she grew thin, and her large, violet eyes had a wild look.

Leslie bore up surprisingly well under this oppression and travail. She lost weight, but very little. The sun burned her very dark. She grew quieter, less cheerful, far more considerate and helpful. She was growing older. She had courage, and despite an apparent realization of tragedy she carried on in a way to win Sterl's respect more than ever. But she had not yet betrayed a spiritual awakening to the wrong she had done Sterl. At times she was childish, wistful, appealing. She missed his help, his encouragement and stimulation. She approached Sterl endlessly with subterfuges, innocent advances, unthinking expectations which were never realized, and which left her pondering and sad.

Stanley Dann proved to be the great physical and spiritual leader Sterl had imagined he would be. Dann did not change, except to lose a few pounds in weight. He remained imperturbable, cheerful, confident, and active during the hours that activity was safe. He seldom talked to his brother, he never voluntarily addressed Ormiston; he often came to Slyter's camp to smoke and talk a little. Unconsciously he relied upon the cowboys more than upon his other drovers. Slyter and his wife were admirable helpmates to this great pioneer. They had faith in him and in the future he had planned. They had also the unimaginative and plodding natures, coupled with physical stamina, to endure to the limit with this trek and its awful wait.

Always when Sterl watched these people, with whom he had cast his fortunes, and whose hopes and lives had become as his own, he ended by going back to study Friday, the aborigine, who day by day loomed greater in his sight. Here was a man. His color mattered little. His hair must have been white, if that meant anything. He worked every day. He was always on guard with Sterl and Red. He had made their lives his life. He asked nothing for his allegiance. He must have understood them. Separated from them by inestimable ages, by aboriginal mystery and darkness of mind, he yet felt for them, for their trials and sorrows and terrors. It was something Sterl felt and could not explain, although more than once Friday had electrified him with divination of his depressed moods.

"Bimeby rains come. All good," he said on several nights. And once, as if the question of rain was not altogether the trenchant thing, he wagged his black head, and gazed at Sterl, his great black eyes unfathomable, yet strangely intelligent in the starlight. "Black fella savvy Ormiston tinkit he get cattle, Missy Dann, eberyting. But no, boss Hazel, nebber!"

Sterl lifted his gaze to the stars and thought of things unsolvable but inspiring and strengthening. In the lonely hour, out on that forbidding veldt, he believed the black man. He felt the brotherhood of man in him that once he had known in an Indian he had befriended, and who had never failed him. There was something omniscient in this, something which made him hate the elemental pressure all around, of the human and the inarticulate.

Days back Sterl had taken the journal from Leslie's listless hands, and was not surprised that she had missed many recordings of late. He filled these in from memory, and, thereafter, wrote the daily report himself, knowing full well how valuable it would be when the trek was ended. There would be other treks, other brave pioneers like Stanley Dann, to whom such a journal would be priceless, even if it chronicled privations and tragedies without end.

Sterl once had a look into Dann's journal, to find it a compendium of dates, miles, camps, hopes and faiths, with a woeful lack of practical details. The leader was a dreamer.

On Friday, February Thirteenth, the limit of heat was reached—a hundred and twenty-five—in the shade. It had to be the limit because Dann's thermometer burst as if the mercury had boiled. Red said it was a good thing. They had all been asking how hot it was, watching the instrument, wondering how much hotter it would get, and if they could live through it. But now there would be no way to learn.

Still the next day was worse. The early sun looked like molten metal; the noonday sun would have burned the eyeballs sightless. Sterl and Red waded into the river a dozen times without bothering to remove their garments. On the way back to camp those wet garments dried, except the leather boots, and they did not remain wet an hour.

Sterl seldom visited the aborigine camp now, and only because he scorned to substantiate Ormiston's blackguard slander by staying away altogether. But perhaps that lingered only in his own mind. Everybody seemed to be concerned with keeping alive, and not drying up to blow away in the hot breeze.

Nevertheless, Sterl had been both drawn to these blacks and repelled by them. Some of the naked children had come to run to him, shy, bright-eyed, trusting. The half dingo dogs had learned to stop barking at him. The hideous old *gins* and the withered old men had smiles for him. Only the bold *lubras* eyed him askance.

The birds and beasts and reptiles he encountered in his morning walk did not trouble to move out of the way. Almost he could pet the gray, old kangaroos; the wild owl would peck at him, but not fly. The parrots and cockatoos knew him as well as Gal and Cocky and Jack. There was a goanna that he had saved from the ravaging black boys, and even it seemed to know him without fear. At least it did not run from him. There were compensations, Sterl thought, for the excuses some of the partners evidently made for him, and for the dislike of Yankees that had to crop out in these troublesome times. Stanley Dann, however, always had a niche in Sterl's mind, apart from his lesser companions. And as the days wore on, burned on toward an end that must come soon to annihilation or salvation, Sterl pitied the girls more, and forgot his hard protective indifference long enough to sorrow for them.

Hathaway's death, coming one night when he was unattended, shocked everyone, even the cowboys, out of the abnormal unfeeling stages. For days he had been delirious and burning up with fever. He had been a sorry, dread burden, and it seemed that he should pass on. They buried him beside Emily Dann, and erected another cross. Stanley Dann, in his faltering prayer, committed his soul to rest, and freedom from the plague of unsatisfied life.

Sterl wondered if the great leader was breaking. Then he reproached himself for such disloyalty. That very night, when Ormiston, who had not attended the funeral, presented himself at Dann's camp, professing grief for the loss of his friend, the leader delivered himself of a significant and far-reaching speech.

"Ormiston," he boomed in his sonorous voice, "you need not demean yourself to tell me that you won *Hathaway's* cattle at cards, or that he otherwise owed you money."

That staggered the bush-ranger for a moment, perhaps because both the cowboys and Beryl were present. It penetrated the hide of his monstrous conceit. It struck deep into him and disrupted thoughts and doubts that had become allayed. His dark gaze, questioning, scarcely veiling malignancy, would have warned a man less noble than Stanley Dann. The drover dropped his head and went his way.

"Dad!" exclaimed Beryl petulantly, "anyone would think you doubted Hathaway owed Ash money. I knew it ages ago."

"Yes, Daughter, *anyone* who hasn't a mind would think that," returned her father, and left her to find consolation with Leslie. The cowboys sat staring into the fire, enduring its smoke to insure a relief from the pest of mosquitoes that had been recently added to the tribulations of the forks.

Sterl revolved Dann's caustic speech in his mind. Their leader was not such a fool, after all. He was merely greater than most men. But what did it signify beyond a hint that Ormiston was greedy? It was not inconceivable for Dann to believe Hathaway had owed Ormiston money. Hathaway liked games of chance, and the hellish hold-up of the trek could account for any weary seeking of distraction. Still, Dann might have divined more than that. *When would this game stamp upon the viper?*—Sterl wondered and kept thinking, although his brain felt confined under a red-hot skull.

Sometime during that night Sterl opened his eyes, wide awake instantly. It was pitch dark, stifling hot, still as the grave. His long training in the open had magnified his sensorial perceptions. In a flash his consciousness told him that he had been awakened by something unusual. He listened. Friday, the faithful black man, lay just outside the tent. There could be no danger.

He thought while his keen ear, his instincts were strained to the uttermost. A cowboy learned to awaken at the slightest jar, sound, touch. A drop of rain on his face, a rattlesnake slipping under the edge of his blanket, a tarantula crawling across him, any unusual sound—these had hundreds of times brought Sterl out of slumber, on the *qui vive*.

He was wringing wet with sweat. The heat of the day always lingered until after midnight, often till dawn. But despite the heat and the burning sweat, a queer little chill ran over him. What had awakened him? It struck him presently that he could not hear Red's regular deep breathing when he slept. Still he felt that Red was there.

Suddenly that painful silence broke to a long, low, rolling rumble. *Thunder!* Had he gone mad with the heat? Was he dreaming? It sounded again, like the distant roar of stampeding buffalo. Yes, it was thunder!

Sterl sat up, transfixed and thrilling. His heart thumped audibly. His breast swelled. He had a dry mouth and a constriction in his throat.

"Red . . . Red," he panted huskily.

"Hell, pard. I heahed it. Thunder."

There came a soft tapping on the tent outside, then Friday's voice.

"Boss, bimeby rain!"

"Yes, Friday. Yes, we heard," replied Sterl, and he groped with trembling hand for his boots. "My God! Red, it's coming."

"Funny, pard, I was layin' heah, after I heahed it, thinkin' I hadn't never appreciated rain before. A feller always learns. Life cain't be too long fer thet."

They pulled on their boots, crawled from under their nets, and out of the tent. There was starlight enough to see Friday's tall, black image, the pale wagons, the spectral trees. The air was sultry, oppressive, heavy, strangely different. Then on the moment a flare of lightning ran along the eastern horizon. How exceedingly beautiful, beneficent, overwhelming! With bated breath Sterl waited for the thunder, to assure himself, to enable him to judge how far distant. Would it never come? That storm was far away. Then—low rumble, continuous, swelling rumble—the gods of the elements were rolling clouds on high!

"Aw!" Red's expulsion of breath told his acceptance, his relief. "The real old thing, pard. Thunder! Deep an' heavy! I reckon I'm orful glad."

"Friday, it's a storm . . . lightning . . . thunder . . . rain!" burst out Sterl. "How far . . . when?"

"Alonga ober dere," replied the black, with his slow gesture. "Rain bimeby. Mebbe soon . . . mebbe no."

Slyter came stamping from the direction of his wagon. Leslie's rich glad voice rang out. Stanley Dann boomed to his brother. The drovers were calling one to another. Across the river lights flashed at Ormiston's camp, and answering yells resounded. They had all heard. They were all astir. Their shouts had a ringing note. Everybody seemed excited, exultant.

Slyter's thought was for his horses. Dann boomed to his drovers that thunder and lightning, after so long a dry spell, might stampede the mob. In short order all the drovers and partners, even Leslie, were mounted and on guard.

But the storm passed by to the southward. Soon, however, the disappointed trekkers thrilled to more thunder, low and long, rolling far away, but coming. In due course that storm, too, passed by the forks, but closer, heavier, longer. Even the most pessimistic knew that these two storms were the forerunners of the belated rainy season. They rejoiced. Red Krehl's piercing Comanche war whoop rang out to make the welkin ring. Larry tried to imitate it. From the aborigine encampment there came proof that even the blacks felt the saving promise of rain.

The day broke just the same. The sun rose just the same, fiery red, burning to molten steel. The birds and wildfowl, in flocks and flocks, came in to water. The slopes and flats were black with kangaroos and wallabies. Again the heat blazed down; again the infernal hordes of whirling, humming, biting, blood-sucking flies settled down around man and beast.

After breakfast Stanley Dann assembled all his trekkers, to the last one, to hear what Sterl anticipated was to be a startling address. The leader towered before them, his gold hair rumpled like the mane of a lion, his amber eyes shining with a wondrous light.

"Friends, countrymen, my brother, my daughter," he boomed, "my prayers have been answered. The wet season is at hand. We are saved, and we lift up our voices in thanksgiving to Him, in whom we have never lost faith. When the rains cease, or when it has rained long enough to fill the rivers and creeks and lakes and water holes, we shall proceed on our trek. But with this change, we will go by the Gulf route, and on to Darwin, and from there to the Kimberleys. A year longer in my calculation! But that is better than to split up our party, our cattle, our strength, our harmony. Eric has traveled this Gulf route. We are off it now, but surely it is close to the Forks, and we can find it. Ormiston, you who have been even more stubborn than my brother in refusal to cross the Never Never, you can rejoice now that I have changed my mind, have waived my wishes, even my judgments, to keep the peace and join up all together, to trek on and ever on to victory."

Sterl had fastened searching eyes upon Ormiston during this address, and he saw, perhaps, what was not visible to others, that not only was the truculent drover amazed, but secretly chagrined and perplexed. But that passion did not last. Ormiston quickly grasped, that vital as this decision was to the Danns, it meant nothing at all to Ormiston, so far as his plan was concerned. In any event he was not going on with them.

A loud hurrah from a half dozen lusty-throated drovers broke up the silence following Dann's address. The leader waited, naturally, anticipating a response from Ormiston. But none came. The drover turned away his dark face and mingled with the others. Then Sterl averted his gaze in time to see Beryl drop her head as if stupefied, and make for her wagon. Eric Dann, however, received the news with a blank visage, then a gradual breaking expression which Sterl interpreted as extreme consternation. He, too, shouldered his way out of the circle, a man haunted by something.

Leslie, in the stress of the hour, forgetting the estrangement she had caused between herself and Sterl, met him with eyes darkly excited, to grasp his arm with the old familiar intimacy.

"Oh, Sterl! I'm glad . . . glad in a way. But I did want to cross the Never Never. Didn't you?"

The answer that sprang to Sterl's lips was both cruel and insulting, but somehow he could not hold back the words. "Yes," he said caustically, "I sure hate the idea of having to spend a year longer in the society of two shallow, mindless girls like you and Beryl."

Her face turned red, her eyes blazed with passion, and there was little doubt that but for Red's intervention she would have struck him. As it was, she gave him a start and a shock not wholly unpleasant. She might have been a little fool—she certainly had responded unthinkingly to the vile camp gossip—but she had nerve and spirit, she was a fighter, and she was honest. These qualities Sterl respected. He went on his way, deeply disturbed by the encounter. Red caught up with him.

"Say, pard, the kid would have smacked the daylights out of you but for me," he said.

"That didn't escape me, Red."

"Mad as hell. An' I left her cryin'. That was a mean kind of speech you gave her, Sterl."

"Agree with you," Sterl snapped. Then after a pause: "Did you look at Beryl while her father was blowing up?"

"Shore. I knowed you'd have yore lamps on Ormiston. Beryl

was surprised at their dads' change of heart. We know thet she knows Ormiston ain't goin' no farther. But what struck me deepest was mebbe she's not so true to them noble idees of bein' true to her dad. Mebbe she's been talked into elopin' with Ormiston."

"Ah, I had that thought, too. Red, I hoped I was wrong . . . doing Beryl an injustice. But how can a man think right in this hellish hole? It's hard enough to live . . . to fight the things you don't think about."

"Wal, we not only have to think but figger pretty darn *pronto*."

"It's welcome. Anything for action. Red, Eric Dann was sunk at his brother's decision. Sunk! That's all I can call it.

"Hell you say?" ejaculated Red. "Now isn't thet another sticker? He oughta be overjoyed. If he ain't . . . why ain't he?"

"Give me an easy one."

"Paid, this feller Eric always struck me kinda phony. Aw, I don't mean crooked. But he's weak or somethin', not even a shadow of his brother."

"Red, what will Ormiston's next move be?"

"I cain't say. I ain't givin' a damn. He shore thinks he's ridin' high, wide, an' handsome. But he's ridin' for a fall. Gosh, ain't it hot again? Thet false alarm last night made us expect this . . . sun wouldn't shine no more."

"But the air feels different."

Indeed, there was an infinitesimal humidity in the atmosphere that morning. But the sun and the dry, hot earth soon dispelled it. That day white clouds, like ships at sea, sailed over the ranges to the northeast. They were good to see. They seemed to soothe seared eyeballs. Before they crossed the zenith the heat had dissipated them. The sky took on a brassy hue. Trekkers suffered that day to exhaustion, because their hopes kept them out from under shelter.

Nevertheless, although night seemed never to come, that day ended. The sunset was ruddy, dusky, smoky. A sultry mantle covered the parched earth. The cattle lowed. There was an uneasy activity among the birds and kangaroos. Nature had a way of telling them what it was going to do. Friday talked to the old men among the aborigines, and he returned so uncommunicative, that Sterl dared not ask him questions. It could not be that there would be no rain. Madness surely would follow such failure.

Sterl wrote in Leslie's journal by firelight. Red nudged him. In the gloaming Ormiston led, almost dragged, Beryl away from Dann's campfire.

"Watch a while, pard. It won't be long now," said Red, getting up to glide off like an Indian on Ormiston's trail.

Friday sat with his legs under him, smoking, wrapped in his prehistoric thought, his long spear standing high, resting on his shoulder. A murmur of Slyter's conversation with his wife came to Sterl's ears. Leslie hovered about the tiny fire, resentful at Beryl's desertion. Out of the corner of his eye Sterl watched Leslie, and knew she would approach him. At last she did.

"Beryl has gone off with Ormiston," she announced.

"So I observed," rejoined Sterl.

"Red has followed them. What's he going to do? Kill that blighter? I wish to God he would."

Sterl did not deign to answer this outburst. But it reached a response deep within him. Leslie would break down sooner or later. She had to talk, to rid herself of suffocating thoughts, fears, hopes, griefs. Sterl felt sorry for her, but he did not soften outwardly.

"Eric Dann has got the willys, whatever Red means by them," went on Leslie restlessly, edging closer.

"Yes? That's interesting," Sterl returned just a bit encouragingly.

"He acted queer. And he was drinking whiskey. In this heat!"

"How do you know?"

"I saw him. I smelled it. Sterl, the rains will come?" she asked imploringly.

"Friday says bimeby. Mebbe soon. Mebbe no."

"I thought I'd die last night, hoping, waiting. But the storm went by. It'll never rain. We'll all dry up and blow away."

Sterl allowed silence to intervene after this passionate speech.

Leslie came closer, and suddenly, desperate, she sat down beside Sterl.

"You hateful, callous, unforgiving cowboy," she whispered huskily.

"Leslie, how very unflattering," he rejoined mildly.

She appeared tense, quivering, bursting with emotion. "I hate you!" she went on.

"That is only natural, Leslie. You are a headstrong child, wholly influenced by. . . ."

"Headstrong, yes, but I'm no child. I'm not even a girl any more. I'm a woman. I'm old. I'll be like these *gins* presently."

"Very well, then, you're old. What of it?"

"Oh, I don't care. Nobody cares. You don't. I . . . I wish I'd thrown myself away on Ormiston."

"Yeah? Is it too late?"

"Don't be a damned fool," she flashed. "It's bad enough for you to be a monster of indifference. A man of rock! I'm sick. I'm wild. I'm scared. I'm full of . . . of. . . ."

"You must be full of tea, darling," interposed Sterl lightly.

"Sterl Hazelton, don't you dare call me that . . . that . . . when you're making fun of me. I'm so miserable. And it's not all about myself."

"Who, then?"

"Beryl. She's strange. She was lovely to me for a while. Now she's changed. She's sort of numb, thick. It's that cad Ormiston's fault. Sterl, you must do something, or she'll go away with him."

"What could I do?" Sterl asked wearily.

"You can kill the blighter! Dad should do that, but he won't. Red ought to, but something holds him back."

"Why should Dann or my friend Red kill Ormiston on Beryl's account?" asked Sterl constrainedly.

"Because he's got the best of her," wailed the girl.

Sterl did not want to hear that ambiguous assertion made clear; he did not want to know any more; he did not want to think any further than the stand Beryl had taken that night by the river.

"Les, hadn't you better go to bed?" he queried gently.

"Yes. I'm weak as a cat and wet as water. But, before I go, I want to tell you something I overheard Mum say to Dad. It made me sick. They were talking. They didn't know I was around. Mum said . . . 'I see Hazelton doesn't go to the *lubras* any more.' And Dad replied . . . 'I hadn't noticed. But it's none of your business, woman.' Then Mum snapped out . . . 'Bingham Slyter, I didn't hold it against Sterl. I'd do it myself, if I were a man! In this horrible hole, where God only knows what keeps us from going mad! The Danns rely on the bottle. You drink, too. But these cowboys don't.'"

"Well, well!" ejaculated Sterl, taken aback and flustered. "Then what did your dad say?"

"He swore terribly at Mum."

Sterl relaxed into the flimsy protection of silence. All these good people, and the hard-driven drovers, even Ormiston and his bush-rangers, might be forgiven for anything. It was a diabolical maëlstrom—this trek.

"That . . . distressed me . . . Sterl," Leslie went on falteringly. "I'm as crazy as Mum, or any of them. I . . . I lied when I said I hated you. I worship you, Sterl Hazelton. It hurts me . . . that about you . . . and the *lubras*. But I forgive you. I . . . I don't care. I'll never think of it again. There! I've told you. Maybe I now can sleep."

She ran off sobbing, leaving Sterl prey to somberer thoughts than ever. It was well, he reflected, that Leslie had fled. A kind word, a tender touch from him at that crucial moment would have fetched the distracted girl into his arms. Fortunately she had missed what surely he would have said and done. In the future he would not risk any contact like that again. There could never be anything between them. He could keep the secret that made him a man without a country.

Friday sat there, immobile and passive, his head bent, the dim red glow from the embers shining upon him. He had heard, undoubtedly. How much of Leslie's poignant disclosure had he understood?

Sterl sat there a long time. The fire died down, and Friday crossed a couple of sticks over the ashes. Mosquitoes began to snarl around. Red returned, dragged his feet, his gait like that of a whipped cur. A furious flame of passion waved over Sterl. That this cowboy, as keen as flint, a man who had laughed and drawled in the very face of death—that he should crawl back to the firelight, ashamed and abased, crushed at the weakness or perfidy of a girl, was too revolting to withstand. Sterl leaped up, muttering: "I won't endure it!" Then a deep low roll of thunder stilled his passion.

Chapter Seventeen

Thunder! Deep, detonating, long-rolling, it caused Sterl to catch his breath. The rains must come, perhaps this very night, if not, then on the morrow—in any event, soon. That would alleviate this hell on earth; it would precipitate the crisis, the fight which hung in the air like a sword of Damocles.

Krehl approached the burned-out campfire, his head lifting like that of a listening deer. Again the heart-shaking rumble, booming, thundering over the ramparts of the desert.

"You heah, pard?" he queried.

"You bet. It goes clear to my boots. Deeper, heavier tonight, Red."

"Rings to me like a great bell."

Friday loomed out of nowhere, soft-stepping, black as the night.

"Rain!" he said impressively.

"Red, that means tonight or tomorrow. We must sleep. When that storm breaks, there'll be no rest till God only knows when."

"Right-o. Let's hit the hay. But I reckon I'll never sleep no more."

Friday replenished the fire with two sticks laid crosswise. He squatted down, rested his weapons, and became as a statue of black marble. Sterl watched him a moment while Red made for their tent. Friday could sleep in any position, at any time. Sterl had caught him asleep, standing on one leg like a sandhill crane. To Sterl he was a never-ending source of delight, knowledge, courage.

Inside the tent, pulling off his boots, Sterl said: "What kicked you in the middle, pard?"

Red heaved a sigh. "Somethin' wuss tonight, Sterl. Don't ask me. I had my gun out to murder Ormiston, when that first clap of thunder fetched me to my senses."

"A-huh! I'm sorry it thundered just then. But there's an end to the longest road, old friend. I've a hunch it's near. Leslie told me things while you were out there. But wait. Maybe I'll forget them. Ah-h! Listen, Red! Did you ever hear thunder as strange and deep and angry as that?"

"Nope, I reckon not. But we never been in such a strange, big, an' mad country as this heah Outback of Australia. Gawd, but I'd love it . . . if I didn't want to die!"

Sterl cursed his friend lustily. It silenced Red and relieved his own overwrought feelings. Then he stretched out on the hot blankets to rest if not to sleep. As on the night before, this thundering forerunner of the season's storms passed by the Forks, booming on, rolling on to rumble and mutter and die away in the distance. But it did not leave Sterl with the sickening sense of disappointment and dismay he had suffered previously. He now felt sure that the rains would come; besides, he had unabatable faith in Friday.

Sterl went to sleep, and was called a few hours before daybreak. He and Red rode out upon the heat-blanketed veldt. They had little to say before they parted on guard. Red mentioned that the stars looked queer to him. To Sterl they appeared less pitilessly white and immutable.

The cattle were quiet, not even one of the calves bawling. A brooding, dreaming, terrible silence lay on the land. Nature was about to check up on its waste and tardiness. There seemed to be a strange soundless voice abroad. No stir from the herd, no nighthawk crying, no wail of wild dog, no cowboy or drover brave enough to break the eternal silence and defy the solitude. It was uncanny. It portended evil. Sterl's senses, attuned to an exquisite keenness, caught the faint swish of grass. No animal, no black, no white man could slip up behind him. But this was Friday, and his advent made the weirdness endurable.

The hours passed. Day broke. The east flung up a crimson that spread to the zenith. The endless leagues of grass took on the hue of fire. When the sun rose, fire again possessed the sky and earth.

At breakfast Larry told how three thunderstorms had passed about midnight, and the last had gone by to the west of the Forks.

"We'll get socked right in the eye tonight," he said cheerfully.

"Folks, am I gettin' balmy, or is it hot sooner an' wusser than yestiddy mawnin'?" inquired Red.

"Feels hotter."

Slyter interposed to inform them that the last day of a hot spell was the hottest. The temperature this day would top one hundred and thirty degrees. If the Forks had been a dusty place, with hot gales blowing, life would have been impossible.

"It's that way Outback in the Never Never, they say," he concluded.

"Say, boss, I reckon you have one of them red-hot camp kettles over yore skull, huh?" drawled Red. "Wal, to hell with the heat. Let's take to the water like the blacks. Then we cain't get sunstroke."

Sterl seconded the motion, and Slyter's drovers agreed to become amphibian during off hours. The listlessness, the skepticism that had prevailed, seemed to have vanished in the prospect of rain. Slyter warned against too much moving about. It would be safer to lie down in the shade and give up, rather than fight the heat. Beryl had fainted already that morning. Leslie, however, the youngest of the trekkers, did not go around gasping, with oppressed breast.

"As long as your face is wet, you're all right," said Slyter, including everybody. "But, if it gets dry and hot, look out. Keep in the shade with a bucket of water and bathe your head."

Sterl's attention was called presently, when Sterl followed Red to their tent, by Friday pointing to Eric Dann's crossing the main fork of the dry riverbed toward Ormiston's camp. In the mornings and evenings someone was always crossing to and fro. But in this instance Sterl had a premonition. Very likely this was the last of the dry spell. Momentous thoughts must be revolving in Ormiston's mind, and in anyone who knew his plot. Sterl was certain that Eric Dann did not share Ormiston's confidence.

"Red, I've got a hunch," said Sterl, and proceeded to get his field glass from under a flap of the tent. "Friday just tipped me off to that." Sterl indicated Dann's plodding across the soft sand, scattering the birds in a colorful shower.

"A-huh. Reckon he's gonna persuade Ormiston to drive his herd back on this side, before the river rises. Haw! Haw! Like hell . . . he will!"

"Red, Eric Dann is either out of his head or crooked," averred Sterl. "Let's find a place where we can watch them through the glass."

"Good idea. Pard, last night I heahed Beryl tell Ormiston that her dad wanted Eric to get Ormiston to drive his mob over heah."

"What else did Beryl say?"

"A hell of a lot. But not pertainin' to this deal we know is comin' off. Beryl thinks Ormiston will stick to her dad, for her sake. Of all the gullible. . . ."

"Here by this log," interrupted Sterl. "Nobody can see us. Now!" He adjusted the glass and, leaning upon the huge trunk of a fallen gum, he rested on his elbows and peered at Ormiston's camp. At first glance he saw that it was a pretty busy place, considering the torrid heat. Drovers naked to the waist were passing to and fro, packing things from one wagon to another. Ormiston paced a short beat under the shelter of palm and pandamus leaves. His right-hand man, Bedford, sat on the ground, mending harness. Both of them watched Eric Dann, plodding up the sand of the river slope, and their remarks must surely have fitted their malevolent looks. The magnifying glass brought the drover as close as if he had been right there in front of Sterl. In a moment more his visage underwent a remarkable change, and he was again the smiling Ormiston, greeting his visitor agreeably.

Eric Dann wiped his pallid face. His shirt was wet through with sweat. He accepted the drink Ormiston offered him. Dann seemed a harassed man in a grip of contending tides. They talked, and Sterl did not need to hear them to know that Eric Dann never delivered his brother's message.

"Lemme have a look, you hawg," spoke Red impatiently.

Sterl relinquished the glass to the cowboy, and pondered dubiously over the situation.

Red glued his eyes to that glass and remained rigid for a long time. "Wal, thet's over, whatever it was," he said presently. "Dann is comin' back. He's carryin' the world on his shoulders, if I know a sucker when I see one. He doesn't know Ormiston is goin' to double-cross him, any more than does Stanley Dann. Ormiston drinks out of thet black bottle. His big weakness for a bad *hombre*. He an' Bedford understand each other, I'll tell the world. Gosh, I can hardly wait to bore thet beady-eyed bastard! I shore ain't a-gonna be sick to my stummick after I kill him. There goes Ormiston back to thet wagon they're packin'. Cain't see very good through the branches of thet tree. Reckon I've seen enough."

He handed the glass back to Sterl and stood erect, to wipe his red and sweaty face. His blue-ice eyes glinted like gunmetal steel as he faced Sterl.

"All over but the rain . . . an' the shootin', pard," he rang out.

"Well, dammit, suppose you go over there and do the shooting before it rains," declared Sterl impatiently.

"Umpumm. There ain't no motive yet thet'd go far with Stanley Dann. We gotta have thet. Why, what've we been waitin' for all these months? Use yore haid, pard."

"Lord, how can I, when it aches like a toothache and burns like fire?"

"Wal, so does mine. But, pard Sterl, it's comin' off, this deal, pretty *pronto*. I figger Ormiston will throw Eric Dann down, mebbe after gettin' his hosses an' cattle. I wouldn't be in Eric's boots then for a million."

"Neither would I. But, Red, oughtn't we tell Stanley?"

"Hell, no! Not before, an' ruin our chanct to bore them *hombres*. Afterward it'll all be plain as print. We won't have to talk. Ormiston will raid the boss' mob an' remuda, shore as you're born."

"Yes, I got that, too. But is he such a fool as to think we won't be on the lookout for it? Or to track him, if he gets away?"

"Sterl, he's jest thet big a conceited jackass," Red bit out contemptuously. "He figgers this river in flood will keep us from getting acrost after him. Hell! If he only knew what little we care for flooded rivers!"

"OK, then. But one last point. Where does Beryl come in?"

"Pard, that stumps me, too. Beryl thinks Ormiston will take the Gulf road, now thet Stanley has given in to go thet way. But Ormiston isn't takin' it, as we know. An' I'm about shore there's no hope of Ormiston persuadin' Beryl to elope, as he tried so hard. Mebbe he jest don't want her."

"Red! The man was mad over her."

"Shore. But thet was months ago. An' long months in which he has been with her some part of every day, an' hours of every night. Mebbe he has had enough."

Sterl let that tense conjecture sink in, trying to think away any hasty conception of his whirling consciousness.

"You see, Sterl," went on the cowboy, "Ormiston is far from the kind of a man who'd risk much for a woman, let alone go to hell for her, an' get himself shot full of holes. Shore, you've seen how Beryl has failed lately. Why, she's only a shade of thet lovely girl we met back in Downsville. She's goin' downhill. She'd be a burden. I reckon he's gonna let Beryl go. What he wants air hosses an' cattle."

"Red, you're overshooting the deal here, I swear," declared Sterl with passion. "Ormiston is low-down enough to do anything.

Beryl's physical condition wouldn't deter him one single whit, if he *wants* her. He has to travel with wagons. She can be packed like a bag of flour. If she dies on the way, what the hell? If it's conceivable that she would hold up his trek . . . which it isn't . . . well, I am pretty sore, pretty tough these days. Perhaps I'd better not say more about that. We'll hope that, when it comes to the break, Beryl won't go with him. I've forgotten how she said that she wouldn't betray her father. Red, there's still something soft left in me that this damned desert hasn't hardened."

"Wal, there ain't in me," Red cut in wearily. "Let's wait for the showdown. It's a cinch Ormiston will try to steal some of Dann's hosses an' cattle. Mebbe some of Slyter's, too. But if he's as pore a bush-ranger as he is everythin' else, why, hell, it'll make us laugh. I'd like to laugh in his teeth, when I'm shootin' hot bullets through his guts! Let's make for the river. It's shore too hellish hot to live."

Stanley Dann sent orders by Cedric for everyone to lie quiet that day, protected from the direct rays of the sun. Before that order was issued the cattle had strung out for two miles in the shade of trees along the riverbanks. There was little movement among the colored strings of birds. Kangaroos kept to the brush. The whirling hordes of flies were out early, but they soon vanished. The sun was too hot for them. The younger blacks stayed in or by the water; the older ones did not move from their shelters.

Sterl and Red submerged themselves in the river until the hot water and green floating scum sickened them and drove them back to their tent. But they found the inside of the tent unendurable. They could not breathe. Red said the top of his skull would fly off, like the lid of an over-boiled coffee pot.

Almost naked they lay under their wagon on the grass. There they faced torrid hours, conscious of the fact that life depended upon the least exertion possible. The air was blisteringly hot. Sterl kept track of each sensation, true to that ruling passion of his, a twist of curiosity as to the effect of outside things upon him. His brain seemed to be confined inside a binding band of hot metal. His pulse beats, his panting breaths labored as after strenuous, unusual exertion. As long as his skin continued to be moist, he was not alarmed. The difficulty was to force his mind to accept the idea that he could stand it. If it was so racking for him, how could those drinking trekkers keep from going mad?

At long intervals Sterl would open his eyes. Krehl lay prone, his arms outspread, his brick-red visage covered with beads of perspiration, his breast heaving slowly, his posture one of extreme relaxation and calm. This cowboy, who had crossed the Texas *Llano Estacado* in mid-summer, would see this day through. Sterl knew he would, also, but the ordeal was hell multiplied.

Nothing stirred, not a blade of grass, not a bleached plume, not a slender eucalyptus leaf. The heat bore down with leaden weight. Heat veils, like transparent smoke, poured off the earth, to rise swiftly upward. The sky was like a shield of shimmering brass reflecting the sun. That arched dome was all sun.

Friday lay in the shade of the big gum tree. That was the only time Sterl ever saw the black incapacitated. He, too, being human, and as perfect an engine to resist the elements that evolution had ever turned out, had to fight for his life.

Sterl's temerity resulted in reddened eyesight. Bending over a bed of burning coals was nothing compared to exposing his eyeballs to that noonday glare. He did not repeat his rash act. He felt a queer little boil of the blood in his brain. And he knew when he began to have flighty spells. He would recognize when he was out of his head. The trick resembled somewhat the dreams he used to have of falling from a height, and yet, notwithstanding the vividness of his perception, he had always known he would wake up before he struck. He was not going to go mad over one day's onslaught of the remorseless sun. The tension upon his nerves and blood vessels reached its peak—only perceptible to Sterl afterward, when his mind cleared, and there came a diminishing of the various pangs that had prostrated him. Sweat dripped from his brow again, and there was a pound in his breast, and the palms of his hands were wet.

Red called out: "Pard, air you daid or in the land of dreams or burnin' to beat hell?"

"Gosh! I guess I've . . . been all of them," gasped Sterl, and opened his eyes to a dusky golden effulgence. The sun had set. That awful door of the blast furnace had closed. In the west, colossal thunderhead clouds loomed halfway to the zenith. Low down over the horizon their base was a dusky purple, but as they billowed and mushroomed upward, the darkened hues changed to rose and gold, until their rounded tops were pearl white. All the way across the western horizon on around into the northeast these marvelous signs of a transformed desert lifted exquisite crowns on high.

"Look at them thunderhaids, pard!" exclaimed the prosaic Red, when he stood upright again and reached to the wagon wheel for his shirt. "Did you ever see the beat of them? All same Staked Plain to make up for a dry spell!"

"They are grand, Red. At the end of this torturing day they are like God's promise in the rainbow."

"Wal, I shore hope Gawd keeps his promise, Sterl," drawled the cowboy. "Let's look an' see how many of us croaked. Wal, there's Leslie, bless her game heart! She can still smile. An' Bill is gettin' supper. I see others movin' about. And the cattle air workin' out on the grass. How you feel, pard?"

"I think I'm all right."

"Wal, I'm sorta daid on my feet, or in my haid, I don't know which. Shore it must be hot as hell yet, but it doesn't feel hot."

Friday appeared, stalking under the gum trees. He came directly to them.

"Howdy," he said, using the cowboy greeting Sterl had taught him. Accompanying it was a transfiguration in the black visage that Sterl recognized as Friday's exceedingly rare smile.

"Boss, rain come," he said, as if he were a chief addressing a multitude of aborigines who had prayed for rain.

"Bimeby?" Sterl asked huskily.

"Alonga soon night."

Red expanded his chest to ejaculate. "Aw, Friday, our trouble's over."

"Trubble come. Rain like hell."

A call to supper disrupted this interesting conversation. While the cowboys forced themselves to partake of the eternal damper, meat, and tea, the magnificent panorama of pillared cloud pageant lifted perceptibly higher and changed its hue as well as form. The bases closed the gaps between and turned to inky black. The purple deepened and encroached upon the gold, blotting it out, as if by magic, and, while the trekkers forgot to eat and sat gazing upward spellbound, the darkening transformation went on until the sculptured scalloped crowns lost their pearl and white. From glorious clouds of liveliness they changed to menacing clouds of storm.

Friday ate his meat, standing, while he watched the sky. Presently he strode out to where he could have an unobstructed view. Upon his return he informed Sterl the rain would come soon. Slyter, and all at his camp, heard the good news, and liberated their taut apprehensions in various kinds and degrees of unprecedented rejoicings. One of Slyter's manifestations was to run across the way to tell the Danns. Red whooped and hobbled after him, evidently to inform Beryl that the rains were coming.

"I'm going to ride guard tonight," Leslie announced brightly, approaching Sterl.

Her face showed the havoc of these torrid weeks less than that of anyone, Sterl had observed, but that was enough to give him a pang.

"Yeah. You look like it," he rejoined dubiously.

"How do I look," she retorted hastily.

"Terrible."

"So do you. So does Red. I saw Beryl a minute ago. Oh, if I took terrible, you should see her. . . . What do you mean by terrible?" She was apprehensive and startled, if not actually over her looks, then because of Sterl's aspersion.

"Eyes hollow, blue veins at your temples, lines you didn't used to have."

"Oh, Sterl! I hate my mirror, because it says just that. Am I pretty no longer?"

"You couldn't help being pretty, Leslie. You have grace, line, contour, color, spirit that you can't lose while you're young, if ever," replied Sterl, yielding as always to the appeal which destroyed his relentlessness.

Grateful and happy again, she glanced around. "Too many people," she said, significantly. "Then I'm not to ride guard with you tonight?"

"I didn't say so."

"But you're my boss."

"Long ago, Leslie, when we were full of fun and dreams and sentiment, before this trek had made me old and you a little savage . . . then I might have called myself your boss. But no more."

"What if I *am* a little savage?" she asked wistfully. There was wisdom in her query. If nature had made her that, it was to enable her to endure. Sterl did not want her in the least different. She shamed him with the truth that was not in him.

Red and Slyter returned from the Dann camp, and Slyter said: "Saddle up, all hands. Stanley wants the mob driven into that basin out there, and surrounded."

Sterl went on with Red. They gathered up bridles, saddles, and blankets, and, thus burdened, made for the open. Friday appeared to relieve Sterl of his saddle. The afterglow of sunset shone over the land. The vast mass of merging clouds shut out the northeast. The two seemed to be in conflict.

"I seen Beryl," Red was saying, his voice deep with pain. "She lay on her bed where the canvas had been rolled up. When I called, she didn't answer. I stepped up on the hub an' then on the wheel, so I could look down on her. My Gawd, if I only knowed what made her look like that! This orful day, I reckon. I hope. . . . I spoke, an' she whispered 'Red,' with a heartbreakin' ghost of a smile. But it was her eyes thet got me, as she whispered more. 'Bury me on . . . the lone prairie. . . .' You know, I used to sing thet to her . . . before Ormiston. Sterl, *could* Beryl Dann look at me like thet, smile like thet, say thet to me, if she meant to run off with this black-faced rustler?"

"Red, give me something easy," replied Sterl grimly. "Back

home, or back in Downsville, I'd swear to God she couldn't. But out here, after what we've gone through, I say, hell yes, she could. Take your pick."

"Pard, my faith dies hard. An' thet's because I've a love that cain't die. If you was me, would you watch Beryl's wagon tonight, instead of guardin' herd?"

"No! Red, you might kill Ormiston, and kill him too soon. Let these Danns find out what we know. Then you can break loose, an' I'll be with you. Man alive, she can't get away . . . Ormiston can't get away . . . not with her or his stolen cattle or his life. If he took Beryl on horseback, we'd run him down and kill him in a day. Red, old man, come to your senses!"

"Thanks, pard. Reckon I . . . I was kinda queer. Mebbe the heat. . . . Heah's the hosses."

"What'll you ride?" asked Sterl, as he looked the remuda over. The horses were fat, lazy, tame. King whinnied and thudded toward him.

"Leslie's Duke. He's a big water-dog. An' mebbe there'll be a flood. Them clouds all same Red River color, pard."

Sterl threw his bridle over King's neck. "Well, King, I've never forked you in thunder and lightning with a stampede on. But I'll gamble you'll be as good as you look."

Mounted, the cowboys headed for the grassy basin already half covered with cattle. From the riverbanks strings of the big mob wagged in to the call of the drovers. Sterl made out Stanley Dann on his white charger. Slyter came pounding along to join the cowboys, and he expressed anxiety for his horses. Red said he was sure they would stand, unless run down by a frightened mob. The peril lay with the cattle. But the drover claimed that after these torrid weeks it would take the eruption of a volcano to start the mob. Already many of the cattle were lying down. The calves were bawling. The usual crowding was not manifest.

The afterglow still lingered when the mob had been pressed into the shallow basin half a mile back from the river. A wide swath of bare ground led into it from the river, where during former floods the water had overflowed into this depression. It had already been grazed over, but there was still plenty of grass, bleached white during the hot spell.

Stanley Dann rode around the mob, hauling up last where Sterl and Red had been joined by Larry and Roland. "Station yourselves at regular intervals. Concentrate on the river and camp sides," said Dann. "Probably the mob won't rush. If they do, keep out of their way. They won't run far, and we can drove them back. From the looks of it, we are in for a rip-roarer of a storm."

"She can't rip and roar too hard for us, Mister Dann," asserted Larry, as the leader wished them luck and rode away.

"Boys," went on Larry, "Rollie and I will hold down this corner. You take your stand farther toward camp. Don't expect to see anything after this storm bursts. Keep up the slope a little way."

"Wal, if you cain't see a-tall, what the hell's the use of us guardin'?" asked Red caustically.

"Rollie and I say there isn't any sense in it at all. But that's orders, and we'll do our best," returned Larry. Then he and his partner turned away, while Red and Sterl rode back as they had been directed.

"Let's stick pretty close together," suggested Sterl.

"You cain't lose me, pard. I jest wonder what'n'll's comin' off. Look at them clouds! An' the sky over heah! There ain't no such things."

"Still hot as blazes, Red, but somehow not the same," rejoined Sterl. "The air's stirring. Smells dusty."

"Pard, them high clouds air comin' faster. But it's them low clouds thet holds the storm. God, but they're black."

The last of the afterglow of sunset brightened to flood the landscape with a dusky, ruddy gold. In the west a broad belt of sky remained clear, losing its golden effulgence. The wild ranges stood up stark and ragged, silhouetted in ebony. Down the river, a lane of shining water, between its borders of trees, shimmered to show the flight of waterfowl, winging away toward where the sun had set. Stormward, however, the scene was majestic and awe inspiring in the extreme. The columnar towers of clouds had joined only at their lower half, an inky blank space, horizon wide, which lighted up every second with fitful flashes. On the summits of the clouds the pearly white had turned to sinister red. Then the first deep, detonating rumble of thunder rolled toward the waiting drovers. The tired, heat-dulled cattle gave no sign of uneasiness.

"Bet you they won't stampede," called Red, some yards to Sterl's right.

"They're English cattle. They cain't be scared, maybe," Sterl returned jocularly.

Thunder boomed over the battlements of the ranges north and east. Flashes of lightning flared from behind these mountains. The first breath of moving air struck Sterl in the face, hot like the breath of fire, and laden with dry scents of the desert. It came in by puffs. It strengthened. Sterl coughed and strangled against its impact. A shining, darkening wave rippled across the grass, and the lacy foliage of the eucalyptus trees began to toss against a sky still clear. The front of it had rolled over the ranges. Zigzag ropes of lightning shot down at wide distances and minute intervals.

"Whoopee!" yelled Red. "She's a-comin' an' a humdinger!"

The onslaught of this storm—end of the long dry spell had a thundering vastness and weird magnificence that fitted the boundlessness of the country. It had been brewing for months. It meant to make amends for the devastation of the sun. It came rolling on like an avalanche. Sterl conceived the impression that this storm had started on the Gulf or even the distant coast, and gathered volume and momentum as it fed its furnace with the fuel of torrid air over the grassy barrens.

When the hot gale struck Sterl, he turned his back and felt that he was shriveling up like leather in a flame. The gum trees bent away from its force; streaks of dusty light sped along the ground; the afterglow faded into a gloaming that was a moving curtain before the wind. Dusk mantled the scene. Leaves and grass and bits of bark whipped by Sterl, and King's mane and tail stood straight out. Behind Sterl the thunderbolts grew sharper, and flashes of lightning illumined the dusk.

Night still held aloof, with fading light in the west. Against that western sky the tossing treetops resembled specters dancing through the air. A ghastly unreal phantasmagoria of shadows and gleams preceded the storm, racing on a gale too hot to face. Sterl listened for the cattle to rush. King did not like this thing, and had to be held with an iron hand. That freakish, flitting dance of shadows along the grass, now on fire with lightning and again blacker than the dusk, worked upon Sterl with its unreality. Strange country, forbidding and inhospitable—strange visitation of blasting sun—strange storm that threatened destruction with its salvation.

All at once Sterl's senses awakened to a startling fact. The hot furnace blast had gone on the wind. The acrid, dusty, sulphuric smell was lessening its strangling grip. The air was cool, damp! He cried aloud to the darkening skies his gladness that the heat which had nearly driven him mad was gone.

Then Sterl faced the storm, exultant. Red sat his horse close by, a dark figure, bent forward and to one side, as if listening, and he held a hand aloft. His wild yell came splitting Sterl's ear. And with it pierced a roar, steady, gaining, tremendous—the roar of rain.

The cattle were huddled in one vast mob, densely packed, now dark, now gleaming, according to the flashes of lightning. Dusk had given place to night. Peering into the wind, Sterl could make out the closer half of the mob, when a broad flare illumined the sky. Beyond, the rest was black.

But above the ground and the mob, Sterl's keen eyes made out the storm almost upon them, a colossal octopus of black arms and black body, huge as the north, alternately revealed by the dazzling, blue-white streaks of lightning, and hidden by the blank contrast, and rendered appalling by the jarring thunder of the storm gods and the deafening roar of the rain.

The pall bore down upon them, steel-gray in the blazes of white fire, a wall of rain like an engulfing sea, to swallow up earth and night and lightning and thunder. Sterl felt that he would drown, sitting astride his horse. He could not see a hand before his face. But how he reveled in that drenching—how King stood there with bowed head and minded not the deluge!

It swallowed up time, too, and he almost forgot the great mob of cattle. But to think of them was futile. Red, his comrade, an arm's length away, was as invisible as if he had been leagues distant. Sterl shut his eyes, bent his head, and thanked heaven for every drop of that endless torrent. The rains had come; Stanley Dann's faith and prayers were justified; the trek was saved; long leagues of grassy plains and filled creeks and water holes awaited them for months ahead. It was something to have suffered, this arid and terrible spell of heat, and to have lived through it. The stupendousness of the deluge did not frighten Sterl—almost he would have welcomed the great deluge.

That rapt enchantment made the moments or hours as naught for Sterl Hazelton. He was wrapped in thoughts and feelings that did not record time. But a rough hand on his shoulder roused him instantly. He opened his eyes. The lightning flashes were far in the west, and the thunder rolled with them. The rain was pouring down, but not in a solid sheet. He could see indistinctly.

"Pard!" yelled Red close to his ear. "Cattle Stampede! Feel the ground shakin'?"

Chapter Eighteen

King's nervous stepping turned out to be caused by a vibration of the ground under his hoofs. Above the roar of the rain swelled the trample of cattle running.

"Stampede shore. Jest started," shouted Red. "Let's find the break. You ride. I'll ride ahaid, meet heah, if we can make it."

Turned away from the pelting rain, Sterl could see a little better, enough, at least, to locate the darker line of cattle against the white grass. Riding closer, he failed to make out any action. They were not moving on this side. He checked King to listen again. There was a decided roar of hoofs, but it was lessening in volume. He failed to detect further vibration of the ground.

These facts allayed the strain and excitation under which he labored. He walked King farther on. Perhaps a spur of cattle had broken out of the main mob. But in a lull of the heavy downpour, he caught a trampling roar again. Gunshots. They were muffled, dull, just audible. Turning to peer back, he saw dim flashes away across the herd. Dann's drovers on that side were trying to hold the mob and prevent a rush. Presently Sterl made out the dark shape of a horseman. Riding close, he shouted and got an answer. This rider was Roland.

"Rush on over there, but they're quiet here," yelled the drover. "They'll hold now. If they were going to rush, it's strange they didn't when the storm was fierce."

"Strange at that," replied Sterl. "Where's your next guard?"

"Not far along. Drake. He rode up here, got my report, and told me Slyter was fussing about his horses."

"Small wonder. I'll ride back to Red."

The wind and rain came in violent gusts, during which Sterl could not hear anything else. He saw dim flashes from guns either farther away or obscured by the rain. Sound of reports did not reach him. Wet to the skin, Sterl had not felt so cool and comfortable at any other time on this trek. The rain poured down with intermittent heavier bursts. He had sent Friday back to the camp before the break of the storm, which fact he recalled when he was unable to locate the black. And he did not feel sure just where he and Red had parted. He halted in a couple of places, and on the last stop he found the cattle jostling and pressing one another. To his dismay the roar seemed to have grown louder. In the gray gloom the mob moved and swayed as if from irresistible pressure from its center.

Sterl trotted King a hundred yards farther around that corner of the herd. Two riders emerged from the impenetrable black.

"Heah you air," shouted Red, as the three met.

"All jake down the line on this side, according to Rollie and Drake," replied Sterl.

"Wal, it shore ain't 'round on the other. Tell him, Larry."

Larry leaned to Sterl and told him that before the storm broke there was a line of guards, Dann's drovers, spread beyond his point all the way around the herd on that side and that on his last ride that way, before he met Red, these drovers were all gone.

"Gone?" echoed Sterl. "They must have worked around. Cattle busted out somewhere. We heard them."

"Cattle rarin' to slope around there," interposed Red. "It ain't safe, but we might stop a stampede."

"Where's Cedric?"

"He was number six or seven beyond me," rejoined Larry. "The mob is unguarded from his post to mine."

"But those guards will be back unless. . . ."

Red interrupted: "Like hell they will! Pard, we had it figgered. Some of them drovers, in cahoots with Ormiston, have cut out a bunch of cattle. It wasn't no stampede. But I reckon they hoped to start one. An' there will be yet, if we don't stop it. Let's mosey."

The three riders loped their mounts through the driving rain and lashing grass for perhaps a quarter of a mile around the curving line of cattle.

"Ride up an' down heah," shouted Red, pointing to the surging mob. "Blaze away with yore guns. Mebbe we can hold 'em. But if there's a break anywhere, run for yore lives."

They separated. Sterl rode back along the way they had come. Close to the herd he made out their unrest, and he heard the bawling. At intervals he fired his gun. Turning back, he would retrace his steps until he met either of his two comrades. Along Sterl's line of progress the restive cattle finally settled down and stood. But soon he found that in the other direction Red and Larry were encountering extreme difficulty in preventing a break. A bulge of cattle was crowding out. Sterl joined the boys at the crucial point, and for a few moments it seemed vain to attempt blocking the cattle. But the intrepid riders, with a gun in each hand, spouting fire, stubbornly contested the charge, and at the expense of great risk, and practically all their ammunition, they finally held the animals in check. Then it was a matter of taking advantage of the good work by persistent riding to prevent a new charge. At last the excited fringe of the mob on this side quieted down.

"Jest luck an' you . . . cain't beat it," panted Red, as the three reined in together.

"I'd call it some work, too," averred Sterl.

"Boys," said Larry, "I'll tell the Danns who saved their mob. New work to me, and my heart was in my throat half the time. Where are those drovers?"

"Haw! Haw! Yes, shore, where in the hell air they. Heah! Listen. . . . What's thet roar?"

"My God, they're on the rampage again!"

"On the other side. Bad!"

"Umpumm, boys," yelled Red. "Thet's not cattle. No stampede. I know thet roar, by heaven! It's the river!"

Sterl marveled that he had not been as quick as Red to recognize the low, steadily increasing roar which had filled his ears. All in a flash he was back along the Cimarron, the Purgatory, the Red, the Brazos—all those Western rivers that he had known and battled in flood. His hair stood up stiff under his hat.

"Fellers, thet big dry wash has been a river, raisin' all the time we been buckin' this storm an' herd. But thet roar you heah now is a flood."

"Red, we've seen driftwood in the trees along the bank ten feet above our heads. We'd better pull leather out of here."

"I should smile. It's good the camp is on that high bench. Gosh, do you heah her comin'?"

A mighty, seething, crashing, bumping roar bore down from the black night. The rain had let up somewhat so that it was possible again to hear it distinctly. The riders loped their horses back toward the far side of the basin, intent on reaching higher ground. They encountered a two-foot wall of water, rushing in at that end. Somewhere above the basin an overflow from the river had met it head on. They waded their horses through to the rising slope beyond, from which vantage point they halted to listen to the flood roll on, and perhaps to see the mob of cattle swamped. At first the three riders shouted to each other, but presently gave up the attempt at being heard. The deafening crest of that flood could only be calculated to have passed by when once again it was possible to hear.

Gray dawn broke hours sooner than Sterl had imagined it would. The rain had ceased except for a drizzle, but the overcast sky predicted more and continuous downpour. The mob of cattle stood heads down, knee-deep in the overflow. The stream that had half filled the basin had dwindled to a ribbon of muddy water. Across the basin and the flat beyond, the main stream raced by full from bank to bank. Green trees and logs floated by. In the middle of the river huge waves curled up to break back upon themselves. A solemn splashing roar seemed to glide on and on down the valley.

It was a changed world, drenched to the bone. No vestige of the dry hot spell remained to give its evidence. The wildfowl and four-footed rivals for the water holes were conspicuous for their absence.

"Red, give us a count," Sterl said grimly.

"Wal, I was jest about to," replied the cowboy. "About four thousand haid there now. Ormiston an' his bush-rangers have sloped with half our cattle."

"Bush-rangers!" yelled Larry. "Good grief! Last night I thought you were off your heads."

"Shore, we were. Let's ride in an' check up. All the rest of the drovers have ridden in for tea, or they're drowned . . . or gone."

"Gone?" Larry echoed, furious and baffled.

Sterl kept his gloomy calculations to himself. The worst was yet to come. He dreaded it.

They rode into camp. Friday met them and took Sterl's horse. The aborigine's blank visage and silence were ominous. Sight of half a dozen of Leslie's Thoroughbreds, haltered to trees, reminded Sterl that he had not seen Slyter's horses on the way in. Bill had a fire going, with tea brewing. The smell of fried bacon permeated the damp air. No womenfolk were in sight. Over at Dann's camp there was less activity, but a group of drovers stood as if stunned.

Slyter passed to and fro like a maniac confined in a cell. Some of Leslie's best race horses were gone, including Lady Jane and Jester.

"What the hell you beefin' about, boss?" queried Red curtly. "Thet ain't nothin' a-tall. Wait till you get the load."

Sterl, still silent, hurried to change into dry clothes, refill his belt with shells, and get out his rifle. He made sure that the oil-skin cover was tight.

Red came in, cursing Slyter through his clenched teeth. "What you think, Sterl? Thet hoss-mad geezer doesn't even know about the loss of cattle. An' damn little he'd care if he did. Pard, we gotta hand it to Ormiston. It's a cinch he stole those race hosses."

"But you swore that wasn't anything at all," rasped Sterl. "Rustle. We've got a job. And my God, am I ready for it!"

They hurried out to the fire where Bill gave them hot damper, tea, and bacon. They ate standing, eyes alert, thinking hard, waiting for the denouncement. Larry came running awkwardly on his bowlegs. His face was gray, and his eyes popped.

"Hey, wait a minnit, you!" Red ordered sharply. "Get yore breath. An' drink somethin', whiskey preferable, before you spring anythin' on us. Slyter, come heah."

The drover, gloomy-faced and disheveled, stamped to the fire almost belligerently.

"How many hosses missin'?"

"Five! Leslie's!" He repeated what he had groaned out before. "I knew that storm would rush them. But Dann ordered to concentrate on the mob. We can't track those racers, not after this deluge. And I'll lose them. It'll about kill Leslie."

"Yore hosses were stole, Slyter."

The drover might have doubted such a statement, if it had not come from Red Krehl.

"Who? Who?" gasped Slyter, staggered.

"By thet bush-ranger you an' Dann have been harborin'."

Sterl broke his silence. "Keep it from Leslie, boss, if you can. Bill, rustle me some meat and bread."

"Wal, Larry, if you can talk now, come out with it," said Red, and he appeared to shrink as he faced the young drover.

"Two thousand head and five drovers gone! Eric Dann gone! Beryl gone!"

"A-huh. How about Ormiston's outfit?"

"Gone, too, so Drake said. Wagons not where they were. Mob not in sight. Moved out of the way of the flood, so they say."

"So they say!" ejaculated Red sarcastically. "Rustle, Sterl. Let's see what Dann says."

"Come, Friday," called Sterl.

They hurried toward Dann's camp, followed by the others, even the cook. Dann turned from the group of drovers. He appeared deeply concerned, but compared to Slyter his demeanor was strikingly tranquil.

"Pard, you start the palaverin', an' I'll finish," suggested Red.

"Bad going, boss. What's your angle?"

"There was a rush during the storm. My drovers followed, but they are not in sight. Eric and Beryl must have crossed to Ormiston's camp last night before the storm. They got held up. No doubt Ormiston moved his camp and mob back out of sight."

"How do you account for five of Slyter's Thoroughbreds being gone?"

"That's more news to me. They must have rushed in the storm."

"Mister Dann, it is our opinion that they were stolen," returned Sterl bluntly.

Dann took that as Sterl imagined he would have taken a blow in the face—without the bat of an eyelash. "Stolen? Preposterous. Who would steal horses, when there are cattle to eat?"

Drake intervened with concern: "Boss, I forgot to tell you that the blacks, too, are all gone."

"Good riddance. But they would not steal horses."

Red Krehl had listened attentively to this interview, while his blue eyes, clear and piercing, had been covering the whole camp and the open beyond. They flashed back to fix upon the leader.

"Dann, I'm orful sorry I have to hurt yore feelin's," he bit out, cool and bitter. "You been too friendly with a bushranger who turns out to be a slicker *hombre* then we savvied. Name of Ormiston, which I reckon ain't his real name by a damn' sight. He stole Slyter's racers. He corrupted yore drovers an' raided yore mob. He made a sucker out of yore weak-minded brother. He. . . ."

"You blasphemous Yankee lout . . . to whom not even blood relation is sacred!" boomed the leader, manifestly a preface to a mighty wrath.

"Save yore wind, boss," snapped Red. "I've had real shore to Gawd bad *hombres* riled at me. An' I'm pretty gawd damned riled myself! Mebbe it might help for you to see that Eric Dann's wagon is gone."

It was, indeed. Sterl knew exactly the gum tree which had shaded Eric's canvas-topped wagon. His dray was there, its cover dripping with rain. Drake burst out to corroborate Red's statement. The other drovers wonderingly conceded the point. That crushing blow, which obviously mystified and staggered Stanley Dann, did not by any means convince and prostrate him.

"Dann, there's a lot to tell, when I got time," went on Red. "I heahed Ormiston say he was a bush-ranger. An' Jack an' thet *hombre* Bedford were his right-hand men. I knowed they all was rustlers before I'd been a month on this trek. Sterl, heah, knowed it, too."

"Suspicion I don't listen to," thundered Dann. "If you had facts, why didn't you produce them?"

"Hell's fire, Dann! No man could tell you something, much less a Yankee lout. But you gotta heah this. Ormiston is gone! An' yore daughter went with him, either willin' or by force . . . an' so help me Gawd, I still reckon it was force!"

"Proofs, man, proofs!" raged the giant, overwhelmed by the implacable cowboy.

"Come on out along the river," retorted Krehl. Then he whipped a strap of his open bridle around Duke's neck, and mounted to his saddle in one long step. "Come, pard, fetch the black man. Drake, Slyter, all of you get in on this."

Sterl surveyed the scene on all sides. The main fork of the

river, some two hundred yards wide there, ran like a millrace, a yellow turgid torrent, full of driftwood and débris. From upriver sounded the dull roar of threshing waters. Below the bench upon which the camp stood, the flood had crept up over the bank. Some of the eucalyptus trees were standing in the water. Across the river, under the trees, Sterl espied one wagon, from the blackened and dismantled top of which thick smoke rose aloft through the rain. Pieces of canvas flapping from branches, boxes and bales littered around, even at that goodly distance attested to a hastily abandoned camp. Sterl did not even look for cattle.

The day was warm, muggy, but far cooler than the preceding ones. Even with tragedy uppermost in mind, not one of the trekkers, Sterl thought, could fail to feel glad for that wet, forbidding, sinister day.

A mile up the river, Red halted his horse to wait for the others to come in. At this point the grassy flat ran to the bank of the river. There was a break along here in the border of trees. Above, a constriction in the riverbed marked the rough center of the current where backlashing waves made turmoil and clamor.

As Sterl and the others reined in to line up back of the cowboy, he swept a fierce hand at the plowed-up ground and the deep trough that had been cut in the bank. This muddy swath, where grass had been trampled flat, extended fully a hundred yards up the river. A big herd of cattle had been run, densely packed, along this course, to go over the bank. Across the flood the opposite bank was sloping, and the center of its sandy incline showed a deep, broad trail of tracks where the cattle had climbed to a level. A novice at the cowboy game could have read that telltale track. Resourceful and intrepid drovers had seized a timely period during the storm to cut out a couple thousand head, and cross them before the flood had arose.

"Mister Dann," spoke up Drake, hollow-voiced. "I never trusted Ormiston and his drovers. They weren't friendly with us. They had a set plan, and it must have worked out true to the day they plotted it."

Others of the drovers corroborated Drake's opinion. All eyes

turned to Stanley Dann at that moment. It had to be a realization of betrayed trust.

"It could have been a rush," he boomed. "A rush in the storm!
My drovers are with them."

"Dann, you shore die hard," drawled Red, halfway between
admiration and contempt. "But, by Gawd, I gotta hand it to you
for thet, an' I like you the better. Only look heah . . . down the
track aways. . . . There's a daid hoss, an' a daid drover. I've a
hunch it's Cedric. If yore eyes air keen, you'll see his bright hair,
almost the color of yores, Dann."

Sterl was the only one to speed after the cowboy. But the others followed slowly, no doubt actuated by Dann's tardiness. Some
terrible thing was being beaten into his dense and trusting brain.
Red had dismounted beside the prone drover, when Sterl came
up, having a bit of trouble handling the iron-jawed King. Sterl
did not recognize the dead horse, but horror and sorrow fastened
upon him as he reined in some paces from the dead man and dismounted. He knew that wavy, tawny hair, even though it was
sodden with blood and sand.

"Pard, it's Cedric, all right, pore brave devil," said Red, as he
knelt beside the prone figure. "Herd ran him down. Trampled to a
pulp, all except his haid. Look heah! So help me Gawd. Sterl,
heah's a bullet hole. Cedric was murdered before he was run down!"

Sterl likewise knelt to verify Red's stern diagnosis. He saw
plainly the hole in the back of the young drover's head. Then he
looked up to meet the flinty eyes of his comrade. His passion
burned out the nausea caused by the ghastly remains of the fine
boy. Then he espied the butt of a gun almost concealed under
Cedric's side. Sterl pulled it out, shook off the sand, opened the
chamber. Six empty shells dropped out.

At this juncture the others, surrounding Dann, arrived to confront the cowboys, and to bend dark, fearful gaze upon the corpse
before them.

"It's Cedric, my friend!" cried Larry, leaping off his horse. He
slumped down beside Sterl, wringing his hands. That was surely
the first dead comrade Larry had ever seen.

"Aye, Cedric it is, poor boy!" burst out Dann, his sonorous voice full of grief. "The mob rushed over him. He died on guard!"

"Dann, a blind man could see thet," drawled Red, whose habit was to grow cooler and deadlier as a hard situation tensely worked to its close. "It's a cinch Cedric died on guard. But how? Thet herd run over him . . . trampled him flat . . . shore as he lays heah. But he was shot in the back of his haid . . . murdered . . . before the herd run over him."

A hastily stricken silence fixed upon Red's listeners.

"Dann, it is true," put in Sterl sternly. "Here's the bullet hole."

"Larry, you examine thet hole," suggested Red, as he rose to draw a scarf and wipe his bloody hands. "I don't want no one heah to take my word. Nor Sterl's."

Larry, Drake, and Slyter in turn minutely studied the wound in Cedric's skull, and then solemnly averred the boy had been murdered. Stanley Dann, with corded brow and clouded eyes, listened to them, responded as they in horror and grief at the tragedy, but he did not share their conviction of murder. He maintained that it must have been an accident, that his empty gun indicated he and the other drovers had been firing to hold the cattle back, that in the blackness and strife of the storm anything could have happened.

Red eyed the leader with amazing tolerance and respect for that hard cowboy to exhibit at such a difficult time.

"Dann, from yore side of thet fence thet is good figgerin', an' givin' the benefit of a doubt," Red said with finality. "But I know Ormiston either shot Cedric or put somebody up to it. Let's don't argue any more. We're wastin' time, an' we'll know for sure pretty *pronto*."

"Men, fetch shovels and a ground cloth," ordered Dann. "We'll bury poor Cedric here on the spot of his brave stand. Keep it from the women!"

A shrill aborigine yell startled the group. Friday appeared on the highest part of the bank, gesticulating violently, in marked contrast to his usual deliberate actions.

"What the hell?" muttered Red. Then he mounted a fraction of a second behind Sterl. They raced for the black man, while the drovers pounded behind.

King covered those few hundred yards at such a pace that he passed Friday before Sterl could haul him to his haunches, sending the sand flying. Red thudded to a halt behind him. They both shouted grim queries to the black who had a long arm and spear pointing across the river. Sterl located an object crawling down a slight sandy slope. His eyes blurred. He took the object for a crippled kangaroo. But Red let out a piercing cry, terrible in its significance to Sterl.

"Man! White fella! Boss's brudder!" called Friday dramatically.

Sterl wiped his eyes with steady hand.

"Look, pard. Make sure," he said coolly. His faculties were swiftly settling for action.

"Friday's right," declared the cowboy. "It's Eric Dann. Bad hurt! Face all bloody!"

Larry and Roland galloped up, with Dann and the others close behind. Friday repeated his words, as well as his dramatic pointing with his spear. Sterl, gazing across the river, had no time to look at Stanley Dann. The man across the river flopped down a sandy slope, crawled, got to his knees to wave weakly. His face and head appeared bloody, but Sterl recognized Eric Dann.

"Boss, it's yore brother," Red was saying curtly. "Bad hurt . . . probably dyin'. Ormiston has done for him."

Stanley Dann roared out a mighty curse of mingled horror and wrath. Behind him the drovers uttered loud outcries. But so far as action was concerned they were paralyzed.

"Red, strip King's saddle," flashed Sterl, leaping down to sit flat and tear off spurs and boots. Just as swiftly Red threw the black's saddle and blanket. "I can land here, some place, if you rope me."

"I could rope yore cigarette. Rustle."

"Hazelton, what do you intend doing?" boomed Stanley Dann.

Sterl had no time for the leader then. Leaping upon King, he seized the bridle and wheeled the black up the river. At a hard gallop he covered the few hundred yards of open bank and hauled up short of a heavy growth of brush through which he did not choose to ride. The flood here came swirling to the edge of the bank. At the plunge the water would be deep. A few yards of the current ran swiftly. Farther on the yellow waves curled back, crashing upon themselves. Logs and brush went sweeping by. They constituted the menace of swimming that river. Sterl gazed upstream to pick out a place less thick with driftwood. The river curved beyond a short distance, at a point where the rapids began. The muddy torrent appeared criss-crossed with débris, logs, and brush.

King champed his bit and snorted. He knew what he was in for and wanted to go at it. The drovers, led by Red, arrived at this juncture. With them was Leslie Slyter, riding bareback. Her big eyes resembled burnt holes in a sheet. Red looked up the river.

"Hazelton, I cannot let you do this thing. It's suicide," shouted Dann, above the noise of the flood.

Drake yelled: "The rider doesn't live who can get across here!"

"Look at the drift, Sterl!" cried Larry. "It'll drag you down!"

Red leaned close to Sterl. "You can do it, pard. But wait. Let me pick out a slatch for you."

Again the leader intervened, distressed, terribly torn between what he must have felt his love for his brother and duty to a man about to imperil his life.

"My son, listen! Eric looks wounded unto death. You cannot save him. Don't imperil your own life!"

Apparently the cowboys did not hear him. They bent keen eyes of experience upon that surging flood of turgid waters. Red pointed to a live gum tree that had been uprooted and was rolling in the current, tossed like a cork, its green branches now high out and again sinking under.

"You gotta dodge drift like thet," Red was shouting. "No hurry, pard. Hold thet hoss! I tell you, let me pick the time."

"OK. But I don't see any slatches."

"It's shore black. An' all bad, but some places will be safer. Hell! Ain't she travelin'? Wuss than the Brazos, pard."

Stanley Dann thundered: "Hazelton, don't throw your life away. It's my order!"

Slyter could see only death for man and beast in that racing whirlpool of flood and driftwood. Drake added his terse opinion. The other drovers exclaimed against the mad intention.

Sterl was deaf to them all. And Red confronted the men to yell: "Shut up! We want to save Dann's life in any case. But if he's gonna croak, we gotta find out about Ormiston *pronto*."

"Krehl, are you cowboys mad . . . or do you know. . . ."

"Hell, yes!" interrupted Red. "Thet'll be duck soup for Hazelton!"

"Go, Sterl! Go!" cried Leslie poignantly.

Sterl was not deaf to that. He turned long enough to give her a piercing look and a word: "Thanks for that, kid."

"*Now!*" pealed out Red Krehl.

Sterl released his strain on the bridle and thumped King hard in the flanks. The black sprang into action and took off in three jumps. He plunged clear under, taking Sterl up to his shoulders. His momentum carried him yards, and he was swimming with powerful strokes when he came head and shoulders out.

As they hit the current, Sterl turned King downstream, quartering for a point far down on the opposite shore. Then Sterl turned keen gaze upstream. If he could see bad pieces of drift in time, he could avoid them. But that had to be before King got into mid-stream. Logs moved faster than the current. He passed the lea of the point of land above and in a moment entered the zone of waves. Again and again, the backlash of the waves crashed over the heads of horse and rider. They were strangled, submerged, tossed. Logs grazed them, a huge piece of driftwood rolled over them, a great gum tree bore down on them, upending now its blunt trunk and now its roots. But just as it was about to fall, the roots caught momentarily on the river bottom, and the tree landed just behind them with a great splash and heave that submerged horse and rider again. The wave carried them on, swept them up, and left them safely out of the worst of the current. As they went on, Sterl pushed log after log away from the horse. Brush drifted around and upon them, but the stouthearted King drove through the tangle into the clear. Two hundred yards and more below the jump-off King struck bottom, and with a tremendous heave and snort he waded out on that shallow side ahead of where Sterl had aimed to reach.

Ringing yells from the drovers on the opposite bank brought back to Sterl the issue for which this battle with the flood had been undertaken. He had forgotten Eric Dann. When King emerged from the river to shake himself like a huge dog, Sterl searched the sandy slope for the wounded man. He did not locate him at once because he looked too far up river. Red's piercing yell and outstretched arm gave him a clue, and presently he saw Dann sprawled upon the sand. Riding up the slope, Sterl dismounted and ran to him.

Dann lay flat on his back, arms wide, eyes open. At first glance, Sterl thought he was dead. That part of his visage not covered with dirt and blood was ashen white and clammy. His hair, matted with blood, failed to hide contusions. As Sterl bent over to scrutinize them more closely, he quickly recognized wounds made by the butt of a gun.

"Dann, you've been beat up," cried Sterl anxiously. "Have you been shot, too?"

"Not that . . . I know of," replied the man in faint, hoarse tones. "Must have . . . been unconscious some time."

Sterl gave him a hasty examination for bullet wounds, but failed to find any. "Ormiston's work?"

"Yes. Bedford, too . . . set upon me."

"When?"

"About daylight."

"Then they left?"

"Yes. But I didn't know that . . . till I came to."

Sterl, lifting the drover to his feet, found that he could not walk even when supported. So Sterl heaved him up to straddle the horse and, holding him there, urged King up the river. Sterl did not like the leaden glaze in Dann's eyes. Still he might not be fatally injured. He wanted to question the man further, but decided that was not best, considering that Stanley Dann would interrogate him. Sterl confined himself then to consideration of getting across the river again. That was serious enough without being burdened by a helpless man.

The bed of this fork of the river widened upstream, with a correspondingly flatter bank. Sterl turned to look across. Red sat his horse in the middle of the open space, where the cattle had run. He waved his lasso. Leslie was close, and she fluttered something white. The others walked their horses up the river, keeping even with Sterl.

One thing of decided advantage to Sterl was unobstructed sight of the river above this bend, around which the current raged. He could pick out a time when there was less driftwood. Also he calculated that he could strike the swift current at the quartering angle. These two fortunate things almost counterbalanced the added risk of dragging Dann across.

Finally Sterl decided upon the point from which to start. It was somewhat above where he had leaped off to come over. Surveying the scene, he knew that King could cross again, if there was no accident. He waded the black into the shallow water up to his haunches.

"Slide off Dann. I don't want double weight on the horse. I'll drag you."

"But it . . . it looks impossible," panted the drover, terrorstricken.

"Not so bad as it looks. This is a great horse, Dann."

"Can you . . . make it?"

"Yes."

"If you're not sure . . . I'd like to confess . . . something you can tell Stanley . . . in case. . . ."

"If you drown, so will I," interrupted Sterl. "But we'll make it, Dann. All in the day's work."

He helped Dann to slide off feet first and let him down up to his shoulders. Then Sterl took a strong hold of his shirt, high up in front. He had to keep Dann's head out of the water when that was possible. Even with good fortune and management, it would be underwater to the suffocating limit. To hold Dann and climb on King without stirrups or saddle at one and the same time was a job that made Sterl pant. After he did get up, he watched the river for a slatch. An endless procession of drift came swirling down. Sterl chose the first comparatively open stretch, and, timing so as to meet its forward, he urged King into deep water. Resting Dann's head on his leg, he floated him along on the downstream side of the horse.

Sterl's first break of emotion into his hard mood came as King breasted that flood, held his black nose high, parted the mass of débris, and, striking the current broadside on, sheered into the crested waves, magnificently powerful. Sterl thought then of other grand horses. Horses with fighting hearts. Horses that would die for their masters. King was another—surely the greatest—so great that he would save Dann's life and his own.

The last of the heavy driftwood, in front of the open space, caught the horse and bore him on, submerged him, almost rolled him before he extricated himself. Then they were in the thick of the crashing turmoil, as wave on wave curled back to bury Sterl beneath its yellow crest. For the first time Sterl hauled on the bridle with that rigid right arm. King responded and swam out of the rough water, while they were swooping downstream. Sterl feared his charge might have drowned. Blood and sand had washed away to leave Dann's face livid. He hung limp, like a sack, in Sterl's grasp.

A ringing yell awakened Sterl to the proximity of the bank. He looked up. Red was riding Duke at the water's edge, swinging a loop of the lasso round his head. They were fifty feet from the shore, drifting swiftly toward the lower end of that bare place. If King passed that, he would be lost.

"He's founderin', Sterl," Red yelled at the top of his lungs. "Beat him on! Only a little farther!"

The black had almost cracked. He had spent himself. Sterl

knew he never needed to beat that horse. But he bent low and screamed: "On, King! On! You can make it! Only a little farther! Oh, King!"

The gallant horse responded to that piercing call. A last violent spurt, a last plunge, when his head rose high—then that lasso whipped out and spread to hiss and tighten with a crack round horse and rider.

Red dragged them ashore. Strong hands pulled Sterl and his burden up on the bank. Sterl was fast in the loop that likewise passed around King's neck. The cowboy leaped off to come bounding back. He released Sterl from the noose, and then he yelled for help to pull the horse up. Drovers ran to his aid. In a moment more King, pawing the earth and strangling, was dragged up on the bank. Red's brown hands flashed to spread the noose. King stood there on wobbling legs, his noble head bent, his tongue out, his eyes wild, and his beautiful body in convulsions. But spent, beaten, he did yet not collapse.

"King, that was a grand job, for a grand hoss!" rang out Red.

Sterl was almost on his knees while the drovers resuscitated Dann. He had almost drowned. But expelling the water from his lungs, rubbing and manipulating, brought him to. Then a drover put a black bottle to his lips.

"Boss, he's been beaten up on the head . . . with a gun," said Sterl, panting for breath. "No other wound . . . that I could see. Told me Ormiston and . . . Bedford did it. About daylight. Then they left."

"Hazelton, it goes without saying, that I will forever be in your debt," boomed Dann, his big voice singularly rich and deep.

"Forget it," Sterl returned tersely. "Get his story . . . if he's able to tell it."

"I can talk," spoke up Eric huskily.

"But not now, brother. Your wounds must be dressed. You must rest," Stanley Dann said.

"Boss, get his story," cut in Red, cool and hard. "He might have a fractured skull or internal injury. Let him talk before he croaks or goes out of his haid."

"But now that his life is saved," remonstrated the leader.

"Hell's fire!" flashed the cowboy. "We're goin' after Ormiston. Hurry! Let him talk. Help us thet much."

"Eric, tell me," interposed Sterl. "It may help. Answer my questions . . . short, to the point. When did you drive your wagon across to Ormiston's camp?"

"Last night . . . at dusk . . . before the storm broke," whispered Dann.

"What for?"

"I wanted to be . . . on that side . . . to go with Ormiston."

"Did you know he didn't want you?"

"Not till daylight. Then I realized . . . what he was. Bush-ranger! Ash Pell! That's his real name. Notorious Queensland bush-ranger. We've heard of him. I heard Jake and Bedford call him Pell. I found out they had rushed . . . our mob . . . stolen our horses. I confronted him . . . with these facts. Then they beat me down."

"Did you know he had Beryl there?"

"He told me. She had come willingly."

A groan emanated from Red Krehl's lips. The muscles rippled on his bare arm. His jaw bulged. But he kept silent.

"Do you know any more?" went on Sterl, rising.

"When I came to . . . my senses . . . they were gone. My wagon was smoking. They had rifled it . . . then burned what they . . . didn't take. I crawled down . . . to the bank."

Stanley Dann lifted his hands high as if to invoke a curse upon his head. He swayed like a great tree uprooted, about to fall.

"God forgive my ignorance . . . my stubbornness! God forgive me for all except my faith in man! Shall that fail because some men are evil? Oh, my daughter! My daughter! Oh, my little Beryl!"

Sterl forgave him then.

"Dann, we'll fetch her back," he said. "Red, look King over. Saddle him, if he's all right. Somebody get my saddle, boots, and spurs."

"Pard, King was only strangled."

"Friday, will you come?" queried Sterl, addressing the black.

"Me go alonga you," he replied inscrutably.

"Good. Red, we've got some meat and bread. Dried fruit, too. They'll get wet, but no matter. Dann, how many of your drovers carry rifles on their saddles?"

"Not one of those drovers who . . . deserted me . . . turned bush-rangers . . . perverted by that villain's promises."

"Red, I remember Ormiston had rifles in his wagon."

"Yes. Small bore. An' he couldn't hit a barn door with them."

"Ormiston and his outfit depended on this flood. That and nothing else! They all make mistakes, these *hombres*."

"Sterl, let me go?" entreated Larry. "They murdered my friend. Let me go."

"You bet," retorted Sterl. Larry might not ever have ridden a deadly chase, but he had a light in his hawkeyes that was sufficient for Sterl.

Drake addressed himself to their leader. "Mister Dann, I couldn't let these boys go alone. What Hazelton has done we can do . . . or try, at least. I've already learned some lessons from these cowboys."

"Drake, you're on," rang out Sterl. "One more man. Rollie, are you game to go? There'll be some hard riding . . . and a little gun play."

"Hazelton, I was about to ask you," returned Roland, pale and resolute.

"Here, fellows!" ejaculated Sterl, as the other drovers chimed eagerly, although plainly aware of the deadly nature of that pursuit, and the braver for knowing. "Three men are plenty. Thanks, though. You're real pards, when the going gets bad. Mister Dann, I'd advise packing your brother back to camp. I think he'll pull through."

Dann gave the order to his drovers. Then he addressed the cowboys—not with his usual direct assurance. "If you will come up with Ormiston and his drovers. . . ."

"If?" flashed Red, disrupting the other's speech. "We'll ride down thet outfit before noon!"

"Then . . . there will be violence?" went on Dann, swallowing hard. He was on strange ground here and was treading upon it with uncertainty.

"For cripe's sake, boss!" burst out the cowboy, utterly incredulous. "Ormiston has damn' near croaked yore brother! He has corrupted yore drovers an' raided yore cattle! An' as for Beryl . . . I swear to you, it's wuss than if she *did* elope with him. I swear she never did. But he's got her, an' he'll ruin her, if we don't save her *pronto*. An' you ast me if there'll be violence!" Red halted to gain wind and find adequate expression for his amaze, his scorn and fury. "Hell, no!" he exploded. "There won't be any violence! We'll catch up with Ormiston, pay our respects, drink some tea with him, an'. . . ." Here Red lost his voice.

"What will you do?" thundered Dann, roused by the cowboy's stinging irony.

Sterl, having gotten his boots and spurs on, rose to face their leader. He was as cool as Red had been hot.

"Dann, we will hang Ormiston, if possible. It will be pleasant to see him kick. But kill *him* in any event! And his right-hand men. Your drovers will make a run for it . . . which may save them. With Beryl to care for we can't chase a lot of white-livered suckers all over the place. You may expect us back with Beryl by nightfall, or tomorrow sometime, at the latest."

"My God! What manner of men are these? You petrify me, Hazelton. But you have never failed me. Nor has Krehl. Go! Bring back Beryl. I leave the decision to you."

He stalked away, leading his horse, in the wake of the drovers who were carrying Eric back to camp. Red, with Larry and Roland, had galloped ahead of them.

It was then that Leslie, who had evidently kept well in the background, stole up to Sterl, and hung weeping to him.

"Cry baby! Didn't you tell me to go, to take that plunge on King, when your dad and the others were scared stiff?" asked Sterl.

"Yes, I did. I'm not . . . crying . . . a-about you."

"No? Well, I was conceited. You're not afraid I'll drown or be shot by Ormiston?"

"Hell, no! You can do . . . anything. You're wonderful. I knew there . . . must be something . . . I loved you so! My heart's broken . . . over Beryl. I know it's worse than you made out."

Chapter Nineteen

The five white avengers, picking a relatively calm stretch, swam their horses across the river. Friday crossed by holding onto King's tail and floating behind. King did not need to be urged. He did not like those other horses ahead of him. He waded in and went off the bank into deep water without going clear under. While Sterl's activities had gone on, brief as the time had been, the river had come up another foot. Ormiston, Sterl reflected, had probably assumed that the flooded river was an insurmountable barrier to pursuit.

There came a slight change in the temperature, the cool air moderating, and the drizzle increasing to rain. The gray overcast sky darkened. The five riders emerged from the river near the spot where Sterl had found Dann. They moved over the sandy stretch, and into the deserted camp, where the one wagon left was still smoking. Under the shelter Ormiston had used, the sand was still dry, and it was easy to read the signs where Dann had been struck down and had lain in a pool of blood.

Owing to the heavy rain, Dann's wagon had not burned up. The canvas cover was partly destroyed, and some of the contents. Half of the load had evidently been stolen and carried away, but part of Dann's supplies and effects had been overlooked or rejected. There was no sign of his team or harness.

"Ormiston was kinda rarin' to leave, huh?" drawled Red.

"Wal, I don't see where a few more miles was so all-fired good for him."

"Boys, pile off and let's run the wagon under that shelter," suggested Sterl. "Lots of stuff worth keeping dry."

With that accomplished they mounted again to ride out of the timber. Broad wheel tracks curved away to the east.

"Three wagons," said Red, thinking aloud. "All loaded heavy. Ten or twelve miles a day over good ground is about all they could do. Three drivers, which I reckon will be Ormiston, Jack, an' Bedford. They'll drive ahaid of the cattle."

"Right-o, Red. Say they left camp an hour or so after daybreak," rejoined Sterl, looking at his watch. "Dog-gone, it's stopped. Water leaked in. Anybody got the time?"

"Half after nine," replied Drake.

"They'd be six or seven miles at the most," pondered Sterl.

"Pard, wait till we see them an' the lay of the land. Then we'll deal the cairds. But be shore the deck is stacked against Ormiston, the . . . fool!"

"Friday, here, climb up behind me," called Sterl to the black.

"Me tinkit run alonga."

Sterl and his riders set off at a lope, with the aborigine running along easily. He had a marvelous stride, and he covered ground as smoothly as an Indian. Red followed the wheel tracks for a mile out on the grassy level, until they disappeared under the trampling hoofmarks of the cattle. Presently the broad, heavy track of the herd that had been raided across the river joined the main mob.

"One of them there little ridges ahaid will. . . . Look heah!" Red leaped out of his saddle to hit the ground with a jingling thud. He bent to pick up something. How curiously he bent over it. And when he held it up for Sterl to see, what blue lightnings flashed from his eyes. The object was one of the handkerchiefs Red had given Beryl for Christmas. Soiled, trampled, it yet was a poignant reminder of the girl who had either run off with the man she still believed in, or had been carried off by him. Sterl made no comment. But he felt deeply, and, when he carefully stowed the handkerchief away inside his leather coat, Sterl thought he would not have been in that bush-ranger's boots for anything in the whole world.

They rode on to where the mob track curved to the left away from the first ridge. Once beyond that the country opened out much the same as that on the west side of the Forks. It was open bushland, grassy plains, patches of scrub, scattered gum trees all over, with rolling, ridgy country beyond. The rain fell incessantly, sometimes heavily, and again in a more or less light drizzle. This and the dark overcast day made it difficult to see far ahead.

Sterl took note of their three Australian companions. Drake was the only one who was not over-excited. Being a mature man, evidently used to drover life, he had probably seen some hard days. But Larry and Rollie, stalwart and grown, young outdoor men though they were, had certainly never shot at a man in their lives. Sterl knew how they felt, for that had happened to him before he was sixteen. Red Krehl was just the leader to rouse followers to stand up under anything. Sterl himself felt the terrific passion of the cowboy. In any case, Red was one to be cool and provocative in the face of a fight, but here he was fierce and relentless.

With him in the lead they rode at a brisk trot several miles into the bushland before any more words were exchanged. Then Red swerved to ascend the first rather high ridge. Upon arriving at the summit, he said: "Spread out, fellers, an' see what you can see."

Sterl rode to the edge of a bluff and peered out over the rolling land. In spite of the rain and leaden sky he could see several miles. Widening valleys and higher ridges indicated an approach to the big, rough range country Sterl had seen clear from their first lookout; he studied it carefully from different angles. In that open timber not even a deer could have eluded his sharp eyes. Meanwhile, Friday caught up with them. The rain had let up to a fine mist. They climbed the rocky ridge, the summit of which was several hundred feet above the valley.

Distance, heights, lowlands preserved their gray-green monotony, but all were magnified. In the center of a long valley the
mob of cattle stood out strikingly clear for so dark a day. The var-
iegated patch of color crawled across the green. The pursuers
gazed in silence, each occupied with his own thoughts, until Red
spoke: "Four or five miles, mebbe. They're pushin' the herd. Not
grazin' a-tall."

"They're sure covering ground," replied Sterl.

"I can't see any wagons," Larry added.

All of them, except Red, made similar statements. "I ain't so
damn shore I cain't," said Red slowly. "On a clear day it'd be
duck soup."

Friday touched Sterl's arm. He extended his bundle of long
spears.

"Wagons. Alonga dere."

"A-huh! I'd gambled on it! How far, pard?"

Sterl thought surely that was the only instance in Red Krehl's
life when the Texan had called a black man his partner.

"Close up," replied the black.

"Red, for him that means a few miles, at least," interposed
Sterl. "The wagons are that far in front of the cattle."

"Jest too bad. Mister Bush-Ranger Ormiston shore figgers
things good for us," returned the cowboy. Then he bent a keen,
calculating gaze upon the herd of cattle in its relation to landmarks on each side. "Reckon there's plenty of cover all along
heah to the left. Come on, fellers. It's gettin' kinda hot."

They descended the ridge on its steep side. Here Red told Friday to get up behind Sterl. The black understood. He stared,
then shook his head. "Friday, you may be a hell of a runner, but
we're gonna cut loose, an' we need you."

"Come, Friday," called Sterl, and extended his hand. "Look
out! For cripe's sake, don't stick me with your spears!" He helped
the aborigine to a place astride King behind the saddle. "Hang
onto me," concluded Sterl.

Red led off at a gallop, due west from that ridge. They crossed
the flat to find a pass between two low ridges, then turned east

again. It was thicker bushland, through which the cowboy led in a zigzag course. The ride must have been uncomfortable for Friday, but in Sterl's opinion he did very well, indeed. King showed no sign that he was carrying double. But the long, slender black man was not much of a burden. Five miles, more or less, of this zigzag gallop, through brush, over logs, under low-branching gums, the cowboy led, and finally halted to the left of another ridge.

"Reckon this heah is ahaid of the herd an' drovers. You can wait heah, while I take a look-see," Red said, and took a slanting course up the ridge. Friday had slid off King at once, and, if his dark visage could have expressed distaste, it did so then.

"Me tinkit hoss no good," he said.

Sterl's grimness broke to this, but the perturbed drovers did not even crack a smile.

"What will we do next?" asked Larry, his voice not quite natural.

"I don't know what Red will advise. Depends on the lay of the land. But if there's any chance for a fight, he'll have us in it *pronto*."

"We . . . we'll attack them?" added Rollie.

"I rather think so."

Red appeared, riding down in what seemed a surprisingly brief time. Sterl watched the cowboy, as he came on at a lope, seemingly a part of the horse, and tried to imagine what the sensations of Larry and Rollie might be. Drake wore a reassuringly stern and resolute expression. Red reined Duke in, and, as was characteristic of the cowboy, he lighted a cigarette before he spoke.

"Jest couldn't be better. Herd about a coupla miles below us, close to this side of the valley. Bunch of hosses behind. All the sly drovers ridin' behind, bunched close, as if they had lots to talk about, an' they're goin' to pass less'n a hundred yards from a patch of brush right around this corner of ridge." He paused, puffed clouds of smoke that obscured his lean, red face and fire-blue eyes, and presently resumed, this time cooler and sharper.

"Heah's the deal. This set-up will be duck soup. It's jest a shame to take the money. Sterl an' me, with Friday, will ride ahaid, hell-bent for election, an' get in front of the wagons. They're about three or four miles up from heah. Drake, you take Larry an' Rollie, ride around this corner, then lead yore hosses back of the thicket you'll see. Keep out of sight. Crawl through thet brush to the edge, wait for the herd to pass by, an' the drovers to come up even with you. I reckon thet's about all."

"All right, Krehl. We'll do it," Drake declared firmly. "Looks a great deal luckier than I hoped for."

"You'll have to give us the time it takes for the herd an' drovers to come up. Thet'll be between a quarter an' a half. But we gotta rustle. Let's don't argue. I've had a deal of such work. An' thet's my idee of what's best. Sterl, what say?"

"Made to order for us," returned Sterl darkly.

Larry burst out: "Let's not waste time. We'll do it, Krehl!" This young man had not the least recklessness in his make-up. He had never shot at more than a kangaroo in his life. But he realized that he was going out to shoot at his fellow men, and be shot at, perhaps killed. He was pale, trembling, but courageous to a degree.

"Wait!" ejaculated Rollie hoarsely. "What will we do?"

Red eyed the big drover in supreme disdain. Then he spoke with a deadly softness. "Wal, Rollie, you might wave yore scarf an' call woo-hoo!"

"Don't cast aspersions upon me, you cowboy blighter!" Rollie retorted angrily.

"Hell's fire, then! Come out of yore trance. This is a manhunt. These drovers you've hobnobbed with mebbe air traitors . . . cattle an' hoss thieves! I've had to help hang more'n one cowboy friend thet I reckoned was a clean, honest chap, when he'd come to be a low-down rustler. Same, mebbe, between you boys an' Dann's drovers. It'll be tough. But it's gotta be done."

"Krehl, I can take orders. Stop ranting in your lingo, and give orders."

"Short an' sweet. Think of yore pard Cedric. Think of Beryl

Dann, who's in Ormiston's hands. An' they're dirty, bloody hands! Cut loose with yore rifles an' *kill* them drovers. If you cain't down 'em *pronto*, fork yore hosses an' ride them down."

"Thanks. I understand you a little better," returned Rollie, gray of face.

Without another word the three drovers rode toward the brushy slope.

"Sterl, I had to rake them, but I reckon now they'll give a good account of themselves. But Drake is no tenderfoot," said Red, as he watched them ride away. "Rustle now. Get Friday up an' hang onto him."

Unwilling or not, the black had to get up behind Sterl. "Hold those spears low, like that," shouted Sterl, and he reached around with right arm to clasp Friday. "OK, pard, see if you can run away from King."

The cowboy led off, and Sterl knew what he had suspected would be a fact—that he and Friday were in for a ride. Another hard downpour, right in their faces, made accurate vision difficult. It was not possible to bend heads low to shield faces behind broad-brimmed sombreros. But that did not deter Red Krehl. He ran Duke on the open stretches, galloped him through the brush, jumped him over logs, and cut a zigzag course over uncertain and rougher ground. Friday had a bear-clutch on Sterl, yet, even with Sterl's iron hand holding him, the black all but fell off several times. The slapping of wet branches and the cracking of saplings added to the pain and discomfort, if no more. At the end of what was a hard five-mile run Red pulled Duke to a slower gait and headed to the right. Evidently they had reached beyond the head of the long, open flat and had come into bushland again. Red did not halt until he got to the edge of the timber. The three wagons were in plain sight out upon the open, the first about a mile distant, and the other two farther out, but still separated.

"Haidin' almost straight for us," soliloquized Red.

Friday laboriously fell off from behind Sterl, undoubtedly pretty much knocked up. He rubbed his lean, wet legs. His great black orbs, unfathomable as they were, appeared to hold contempt for the horse.

"Tinkit hoss damn' bad!" he cursed for the first time in Sterl's presence. At any other time that would have earned a hearty laugh.

"Pard, we'll get farther back in the bush, an' make our plan as the wagons come up."

Friday took a long look at the three wagons. Then he pointed. "Ormiston wagon dere farder. Hosses alonga 'imm," he said.

"Thet *hombre* last, huh? Wal, I guess I recognize him, but I cain't quite make out the hosses. Come on, Sterl."

Red rode over to line up with the wagons, then turned back into the bush, keeping out of bare ground and away somewhat from the course he decided the first wagon driver would take. The rain lessened again. The clouds at one point lightened and appeared about to break. Perhaps two miles back from the open Red halted again.

"Far enough, I reckon, pard," he said, "now. . . . Say, where in the hell did Friday go to?"

"By thunder! He's gone. I never noticed. But he won't cramp us, Red. Don't worry."

"All I'm worryin' about is thet he'll get to Ormiston before I do," ground out Red.

"If he does, that's to the good. It'll save your killing him."

"Ha! Then I'd never rest in my grave."

"Spring your plan. We've got the line up."

"Wal, simple enough. If I wasn't so . . . mad, I'd laugh at this set-up. We shore never had nothin' so easy back in Texas."

"Right-o. But let's take it on as if it was as tough as any rustlers ever put up to us. Hurry. What's your plan?"

"I'll ride back a ways. Let the first wagon go by me, unless it should happen to be Ormiston. You wait about heah someplace. An' when thet wagon comes up, introduce yourself either to Jack or Bedford. Then you rustle back after me."

"You'll time it to meet that second wagon just about when the first one gets up to me?"

"I reckon. But it's all over 'cept the fireworks."

Red rode off under the dripping gums, keeping to the left of the expected wagon line, and soon disappeared in the gray-green bush. Sterl searched about for a suitable cover where he could hide until the leading wagon reached him. There did not happen to be a thick clump of brush near at hand. And he did not want to go far aside from that imaginary line. At length he chose some gum saplings, close together and leafy enough to make a comparatively safe shelter. Any sharp-eyed man, however, on the lookout, could have espied the horse through them. Sterl dismounted, and, drawing his rifle from its saddle sheath, he removed the oilskin cover and put it in his pocket. Then he leaned the rifle against the largest sapling, and, with a quieting hand on King, he peered back through the drenched bushland.

With a tense wait like this involved, it was almost impossible not to think. Sterl preferred quick meetings, if he were ready, to ones of prolonged suspense. But even confronted by the introspective habit of his mind, he had no dislike for this job and no compunction. In any case, he would not shoot a man from an ambush, although he had retaliated upon Indians by that very act. Here he wanted to face Jack or Bedford.

Naturally, however, he had concern for his comrade. Red could be trusted, especially in this case, to be really superhuman. But Sterl would have preferred to be with Red, for more than one reason. Beryl's life might be at stake. Because of that Red could be capable of any rash act, even to a sacrifice of himself. Then again, Sterl wanted powerfully to see Ormiston meet the cowboy. It would be something to experience.

The minutes dragged by with Sterl's mind active, and his senses of sight and hearing strained. After what seemed a long time, King suddenly vibrated slightly and shot up his ears. He had heard something.

"Quiet, you son-of-a-gun!" exclaimed Sterl in a loud whisper, and he patted the wet neck. "What you want to do . . . spoil the party?"

More moments passed before Sterl's alert ear caught a creaking of wheels. King threw up his head. The sagacious animal had been well trained, but not to stand still and keep silent. Sterl stepped to his head and held him. A thud of hoofs sounded through the silent bush. At last a sight of four horses, plodding along, then a canvas-topped wagon, then a burly driver, reins and whip in hands. It was the drover, Jack. A slight cold chill quivered over Sterl. But he thought fast. He would wait until the drover had reached an angle almost even with him, then step out, confront him, and force him to draw.

A distant gunshot rang out, spiteful, ripping asunder the bush-land silence. Red's .45 Colt speaking. Almost at once a duller, heavier shot boomed.

The drover, Jack, hauled his four horses to a dead stop and dropped the reins. He was in the clear, with the wagon on level and bare ground. Sterl saw the man sweep out a hand to grasp a rifle, then peer all around with black, wild eyes.

At this instant King let out a loud neigh, and the other horses answered. Jack's gaze fixed upon King. Sterl should have shot the drover then. Quick as thought Jack leaped out of the wagon. As Sterl plunged to get low down behind a log, the drover fired from behind the left front wheel. The bullet whistled closer to King than it did to Sterl. Fearful that Jack might kill the horse, Sterl took a snap shot at the only part of that wheel he could see—the under rim and a section of spokes. His bullet struck with a thud, to spang away into the bush. It must have stung the drover's foot, or come too close, for he leapt away to the rear end of the wagon. Evidently the wagon was so fully loaded that he could not lean upon it. His boots were in plain sight down between the two right wheels. Sterl's second shot hit one of them. The drover flopped down like a crippled chicken, bawling frightfully, and he crawled behind the only gum tree near. The trunk was not wide enough wholly to protect his body. But he knelt low, risking that. He had Sterl located but could not see him. Sterl tried an old ruse, common on the frontier. He stuck up his sombrero. Jack fired, and then again. His second shot knocked Sterl's sombrero flat. Then the drover rashly stood up and stuck his rifle, his shoulder, and half of his head out from the tree. Probably he believed that he had shot this adversary. Sterl drew a careful bead on the one baleful eye visible, like a hole in a mask, and shot. Jack pitched to one side of the tree, and his rifle flew to the other.

Sterl worked the lever of his rifle, waited a moment, then snatched up his sombrero, and leaped on King. The excited horse was hard to hold. Sterl rode by the wagon. With one grim glance at the drover, lying on his back, with one eye blank and the other set hideously, Sterl took up the wheel tracks and raced through the bushland.

It grew more open as he progressed. In less than half a mile he sighted another wagon, standing still, the foremost team of horses plunging. Sterl drew closer to the wagon and was pulling King to a slower gait, when again he heard gunshots, and not far away. Two guns of different caliber. No rifle shot. Throwing caution to the winds, Sterl struck the steel into King's flanks. As the black tore on at top speed and reached the wagon, Sterl saw the drover, Bedford, hanging head first over the right wheel. His feet had caught somewhere. In the middle of his broad back his gray shirt showed a huge, bloody patch. Red had shot him through from front to back.

The third and last wagon! It had been pulled half broadside across the line of wheel tracks. Horses had been tethered to the rear. They were plunging, and on the moment one broke away. Sterl recognized Leslie's Jester even at that distance through a drizzling rain.

The driver's seat was vacant. No one in sight. But another shot cracked and that from Red's gun. The cowboy was alive! Sterl's heart leaped out of its petrifaction. Sterl drove King down upon the wagon with tremendous speed. The trees blurred.

Suddenly to Sterl's right and ahead his strained sight caught the gleam of something white, something red, something black. There was a bare glade close ahead—a huge gum towering over the wagon—a low branch sweeping down. Through the thin foliage that white thing moved. A woman's scream, high-pitched, piercing, rent the air.

Sterl lay back with all his might upon the bridle. King broke his gait, flashed by the brush, and plunged to slide on his haunches into the glade.

Red, his temple bloody, was lying in the middle of the bare spot, raised on his left elbow, his gun extended, his posture unnatural. In a flash Sterl was out of his saddle, his gun leaping as his feet thudded the earth.

The white thing was Beryl Dann, half nude, in the grasp of Ormiston. A black blanket had slipped to her knees. Ormiston crouched behind her, left arm around her middle. In his right he had a gun leveled at Red. As he fired, the girl pushed his arm. She shrieked in terror, in fury. And she fought the drover like a panther. The red thing near them was Leslie's horse, Sorrel, saddled and bridled. Ormiston had tried to get away on that horse.

"Kill him . . . Red . . . don't mind me!" panted the girl wildly.

Chapter Twenty

Sterl leveled a cocked gun, but dared not risk firing. Only a portion of Ormiston's body projected from behind the desperately struggling girl.

She hung onto Ormiston's rigid arm as he lifted her in an effort to align his gun upon Krehl. He fired. Dust and gravel flew up into the cowboy's face. Red rolled convulsively over and over, as if struck. Sterl, stricken at that terrific instant, just barely held himself back from a rash onslaught at the drover. But Red came out of that roll to lie flat with his gun forward.

"*Hurry, St-erl!*" shrieked the girl frantically.

Then the drover espied Sterl, and struggled to aim at him. Sterl leaped to dive behind a rock. His momentum carried him almost beyond it. Swift to get on his knees, he thrust his gun over the top. He was in time to see Beryl's last frenzied struggle to destroy the bush-ranger's aim. Then she collapsed, arms, head, and shoulders hanging down supported by Ormiston's clutching clasp. But this caused him to crouch lower to hide his head. Sterl all but shot at it on that instant. Ormiston's further stooping caused him to bend his left leg, and his knee became exposed. Red's gun cracked. Sterl heard the bullet thud into flesh. The bush-ranger yelled in agony. That shot of Red's had broken his aim. Cursing savagely, he gathered his forces for another attempt.

Sterl screamed like a Comanche at Ormiston; his finger quivered on the trigger in the act of imperiling Beryl's life to save Red's. Behind Sterl a strange yet familiar tussling sound checked his firing. *Whizz!* A dark streak flashed across his line of vision. *Chuck!* Sterl's taut senses registered the sickening thud of something rending flesh.

Ormiston uttered a strangling, inhuman yell and sprang up as if galvanized. His gun went flying to the ground and exploded. Beryl dropped from his hold like an empty sack. Ormiston's hands were up, clutching at something, as a drowning man might at straws. His powerful physique strained and reeled accompanied by unnatural cries. An aborigine spear stuck out two feet beyond his throat. Its long end still quivered with the tremendous force that had impelled it. Ormiston's hands tore at it, broke the long end square off.

"Friday!" yelled Sterl as he leaped from behind the rock. "Look, Red, look! Friday has done for him!"

Red got up, bloody-faced and grim as death. He had been shot over the right temple and in the left shoulder. But he showed no weakness. As he strode toward the whirling Ormiston, swift footfalls thudded behind Sterl, and Friday came leaping with savage mien and energy.

"Hold on, Friday!" yelled Red, blocking the aborigine. "No go with thet. You're gonna help me with a little necktie party."

Sterl could not have unrivetted his sight from the terrible spectacle of the doomed Ormiston. He reeled and swayed like a drunken man, his hands still tearing at that shaft. No blood showed on his brawny neck, but a red-tinged froth issued from his mouth with his awful cries. He fell only to bound up again with marvelous agility and strength. He was a conscious madman, still capable of destroying his foes, if he could find a way.

Sterl kicked Ormiston's gun into the grass. Again his trigger finger pressed quiveringly, as the bush-ranger roared and plunged like a wounded bull.

"Bore him, Red! Put him out of it!" shouted Sterl.

Red's jangling footfalls sounded behind Sterl, just as Ormiston's protruding eyes fell upon Beryl. She was on her knees, trying to pluck up the blanket over her bare shoulders. He made at her, insane to drag her to perdition. But before Sterl could shoot, still waiting for the expected shot from behind, a hissing lasso shot out. The noose fell over Ormiston's head, to be stopped by the spear through his neck. Red gave the rope a tremendous pull. Ormiston lunged backward, to fall face forward, his arms upflung, and that queer vociferation ended abruptly.

"Lend a hand, Friday," shouted the cowboy. "Don't forget how this white trash treated you!"

Probably without that ruthless urge the black would have lent a hand. As it was, he leaped to Red's assistance. They dragged the bush-ranger under the spreading arm of the huge gum tree. The cowboy paused there to gaze down at his victim. Sterl had seen Red, after the custom of gunmen on the frontier, bend such a look upon an expiring foe who had provoked the old, even-break encounter. It seemed more terrible here, yet Sterl could not find voice to interrupt retribution and ruthless justice.

"Rustler, you swing! Jest the same as any cattle thief in my country! But bad as they came, I never seen one as low-down as you!"

Evidently Ormiston was still conscious, although choked beyond the power of speech. Red threw the free end of his lasso up over the low end branch and caught it as it fell.

"Lay on, Friday! Pull, you black man who's shore no nigger! All my life I'll love you for this day's work. Ha! There you air, Ormiston! Swing an' kick! An' . . . yore black soul!"

Sterl wrenched his fascinated gaze from that gruesome spectacle and wheeled to Beryl. He was startled to see her on her knees, the blanket slack in her nerveless hands, wholly oblivious to her nudity, her big, blue eyes fixed in horror upon that frightful execution. No doubt she had seen it all.

"Beryl! Don't look!" cried Sterl, sheathing his gun and rushing to her. In a second he had flung the blanket around her and obstructed her sight by lifting her to her feet, into his arms. "Shut your eyes, Beryl. It's . . . all over. You're saved. And he . . . it's justice, Beryl, no matter."

But he realized that she had fainted. He carried her to the wagon and laid her up in the seat, out of the rain, and tucked the blanket around her bare feet. Her eyes fluttered open. "OK, now?" inquired Sterl. She nodded. "Then lie here a while, until you get yourself together. No more danger." And he drew away.

How long he leaned there he did not know, but a jingling step aroused him, and he turned to see Red approaching. Beyond the cowboy, Friday appeared, silhouetted against the green, gazing fixedly up at the limp figure, grotesque and strangely still, in dark relief against the gray sky.

Warmth rushed over him at the sight of his cowboy friend. Red had come through another appalling crisis, and here he was again, blood and dirt all over him, the passion and fire that had sustained him gone, as if by magic.

"Close shave, pard," he said just a little huskily, as he wiped his bloody hands with his scarf, and glanced up to see Beryl's pale, quiet face.

"Gosh! I don't recall a closer!" ejaculated Sterl.

"Reckon I cain't, either. But wasn't Beryl the game kid? My Gawd, who'd ever thought she'd fight like thet? For me . . . against him? She kept him from borin' me a second time. An' I reckon she saved yore life, too."

"Like as not, Red. I was afraid to shoot, for fear I'd hit her."

"She fainted, I see. Wal, it was about time. I'm glad she didn't see the end of it."

"But she did, Red. She did! When I could look away from you and Friday, I found Beryl on her knees, eyes wide as doors, staring right at you. She saw it all, believe me."

"Aw, thet's too bad. Pretty tough, considerin' how she must have loved. . . . But, pard, did you get it? Beryl had on only her nightgown. Thet *hombre* stole her from her bed. She didn't run off with him!"

"Yes, I savvied that, Red, and I never was any gladder in my life. But you're all shot up. Let me see."

"Nothin' a-tall, pard."

"You're a liar."

"Wal, they'd have to be a hell of a lot wuss than they air to croak me now. Let me tell you. When I ran down on Bedford, he saw me comin', an' he was ready for me. I bored him, but damn if he didn't hit me heah in this shoulder. Ormiston heahed all the shots, I reckon, for he was trying to get away with Beryl on the sorrel when I run in on him. Beryl was fightin' him. But for her, I'd shore have bored him before he got in thet first shot. It knocked me flat, but not out, an' I was tryin' to get a peg at him behind her when you got heah."

"Red, didn't you take an awful chance?" Sterl queried gravely.

"What the hell else could I do? Them drovers were separated. Ormiston had Beryl."

"We can always tell better after it's over. But we should have . . . both of us . . . gone after Ormiston first."

"I reckon. We didn't have any too much time to figger. Great, wasn't it . . . Friday ringin' in there with that spear? Jest great! Better look these bullet holes over an' tie them up. This one on my haid hurts like hell."

Examination disclosed a painful, although not serious, wound in Red's head, a groove that cut through the scalp, but had not touched the skull, and another in his left shoulder, high up, where the bullet had lodged just under the skin on the far side. It would have to be cut out, but Sterl left that operation for camp and bound his scarf tightly around under his arm.

"We'd better leave the other one open," said Sterl. "It's not bleeding much. Besides, we haven't anything clean to tie round it. Your scarf is. . . . Hello, what's that?"

"I heahed it. Reckon we forgot about the cattle, an' the job we left three pardners to do. Gosh, Sterl. Thet's cattle aplenty an' hoofin' it for fair."

"Fag end of a stampede. Look to Beryl. I'll wrangle the horses. Come, Friday."

The black ran off under the gums to get Duke, while Sterl drew King and the sorrel back away from the open. Two of Leslie's Thoroughbreds, haltered to the wagon, were released and put with the other horses. Red had been standing by Beryl, in case she had to be moved, and waiting to see when and where the mob would appear.

A bobbing line of cattle soon hove in sight down through the brush, loping along wearily.

"Wal, they might have started wild, but they're bein' chased now," said Red. "Get the rifles heah, pard, an' if it happens to be any of Ormiston's outfit, they'll never get nowhere. Gosh, I hope Larry an' Rollie didn't get wiped out. New to them . . . such a deal."

On a front perhaps a quarter of a mile wide, so wide in fact that Sterl could just make out the far end, a herd of cattle came loping past, scattered and bawling, almost ready to drop. The trampling roar swelled and receded. No stragglers ran close to the wagon. It did not take the herd more than five minutes to pass.

"Lot of cattle, but not all Ormiston had, do you think, Red?"

"Coupla of thousand haid, shore as you're born. Thet's sort of queer. I recognized one of them steers. Couldn't have been Ormiston's, for I seen him jest lately. Pard, thet was the bunch raided out of Dann's last night."

"Might be."

"Heah comes some riders. Two! Thet's Larry's hoss . . . an' Rollie's, too. OK, Sterl, it's our friends. But Drake ain't with them."

The two riders had checked their approach upon sight of the wagon. When they recognized the cowboys, they came on again. Some hundred paces distant they espied the hanged bush-ranger swinging with horrible significance, and this brought them up into a quick halt.

"Come on, Larry. It's all over heah but the shoutin'," called Red.

Then the drovers rode slowly up, their eyes gleaming, their lips tight.

"Rollie, that's Ormiston!" ejaculated Larry in awe, and forced his gaze ahead. But Rollie appeared divided between curiosity and shock. He rode closer, exclaiming incoherently. He pointed to the spear.

"Beryl?" Larry queried hopefully.

"She's heah on the seat, in a daid faint. Ormiston stole her out of her bed. She was daid game. Fought him to a standstill heah, when he hid behind her. Saved us both. She spoiled his aim, an' we couldn't shoot," declared Red, and it seemed more than evident that he was elated to give this information.

Larry slumped out of his saddle to sit down like a man whose legs were wobbly.

"Then Friday slung thet spear through the dirty dog's neck an' the fight was over. But you should have seen the show."

Sterl did not like the looks of either of the drovers.

"Where's Drake?"

"He wouldn't shoot bare-faced that way from ambush," replied Larry tragically. "Rol and I didn't know it though, till right at the last he ran out, yelled at Anderson and Henley, then, as they jerked their guns, shot them both off their horses. I . . . I killed Buckley . . . and Rol did the same by Smith. Herdman and Smith had begun to shoot. It was Herdman, I think, who hit Drake. Rol's horse was shot from under him. The mob rushed, ran us back into the brush. They split. Part of the mob headed back. Herdman and Smith had to ride hard. But they got around them and headed off to the east. We couldn't chase them until the cattle had run by. Then it was too late. They got into the brush. We'd have caught up with the wagon sooner, if we could have got around the other half of the mob that rushed this way."

"A-huh. Too bad about Drake. Air you shore he was daid?"

"There was no doubt of that."

"It's orful tough, Larry. I reckon Sterl an' me feel for you. But the fact is, we got off lucky."

"Jack and . . . Bedford?"

"They beat Ormiston to hell pretty considerable. Pard, them two *hombres* thet got away . . . they'll hang back in the bush to see what we do . . . an' thet's somethin' to figger on."

"Easy, Red. There's only one thing," returned Sterl. "Take Beryl back to camp *pronto*. You're all shot up, too. We've got to cross that infernal river before dark."

"I agree, pard. Spring yore idee. My haid is kinda thick."

"Larry, stay here with Red. Keep your eyes peeled sharp. Those two drovers might sneak up for a shot, although that's doubtful. Red, get a dry blanket to wrap Beryl in. Search Ormiston. That *hombre* was heeled. Rollie and I will ride up to search Jack and Bedford."

"Rustle a-back. I ain't so keen on bein' left heah."

"We won't go. It'll be little enough that those *hombres* will have. But Ormiston. . . ."

Sterl found a money belt upon the bush-ranger. Heavy and full it had lent Ormiston a corpulence that he really did not possess in flesh. Sterl also took his watch and a pocketbook full of papers. He carried these to where King stood and buckled them inside his saddlebag.

Meanwhile, Red had wrapped Beryl in a couple of dry blankets, and he was folding a third. Beryl had come to, and sat hunched in the driver's seat, with great, dilated eyes staring out of her pallid face.

"Pard, I was plumb worried about her nightgown," said Red. "I feared it'd be wet. But only a little. She'll be warm."

"That's good. Let's get to it."

They approached the river and again were astounded, especially by its speed and big waves. Sterl waded King some yards before the horse had to swim. Friday, preceding him, waited and got his tow. Rollie followed a rod behind. For Sterl, so far as he was concerned, this crossing did not rouse acute sensations of apprehension, as he had felt before. King was surely a magnificent horse in the water as well as on land. Striking the mid-current, they were swept down and soundly threshed, but that lasted only a couple of tense moments, then they were out of the bad water. Stanley Dann, the Slyters, with Heald and Monkton, and one of Dann's drovers awaited their landing visibly laboring under extreme excitement and fear.

King made the shore fifty feet above his former landing, but he had to be helped in climbing the steep bank. Rollie landed safely behind, to be hauled up. Friday chose a less steep place to get up.

"My daughter?" asked Dann, almost voiceless.

"Safe," replied Sterl, not looking at him and leaping to the ground. He waved his sombrero to Red and Larry, still on the other side of the river. They returned the wave, then waded in.

Sterl untied his lasso. "Get your rope ready," he said to Rollie. "We might need it."

Sterl had been aware of Leslie's presence close beside him and a little back. Once she touched him with a timid hand, as if to see if he were really back in the flesh. They were all talking except Leslie. Finally she spoke in her deep contralto: "Sterl! Sterl?"

Then he looked around and down upon her, meaning to be kind, trying to smile as he said—"Hello, Kid!"—but she instinctively recoiled from his face. Sterl did not marvel at that. It had happened before to girls who approached him after a hard job. But how could he help it? Men had to kill other men. The wonder in him was that it made any difference in his face and look.

Sterl turned to watch the swimming horses as they entered the current. Sorrel, and Leslie's other horses, hesitated but finally followed.

"Rollie, go below me. Everybody get back so I can swing this rope."

Red and Larry were ten feet apart, heading evenly into the

current. On account of Beryl, the crossing was more frightening than productive of thrills. If Red suddenly collapsed, which was unlikely, he would get Beryl to Larry in time. Sterl's common sense asserted there really was no peril. Still accidents so often frustrated well-laid plans. It was just as well that the four rider-less horses were far back.

They hit the current. All save the rider's heads and that of the horses disappeared under the frothy upflinging waves. Duke, be-ing a heavier horse, carrying a heavier burden, was swept down-stream right upon Larry's mount. For a moment it looked bad. But the lean noses came on abreast, and the shoulders of the rid-ers rose higher—into plain sight. The onlookers watched an-other moment, tense and breathless, while the horses swept down with the current, at last to forge out of it, and again come straight for the bank. A cheer of released emotions rent the air. Duke, as powerful as if he had not performed miracles that day, waded out in King's tracks. To make sure, Sterl roped Duke and hauled lustily to help him pound up the bank. Rollie helped Larry. No one thought of Leslie's four horses, now making for shore.

Sterl held the heaving horse's head and swiftly loosened the lasso noose. Stanley Dann crowded close, his eyes streaming tears, his bearded jaw wobbling, his great arms outstretched. With one shaking hand Red unfolded the dripping slicker and let it fall away from Beryl's white face. If her eyes had not been wide open, wonderfully awake to that moment, she would have looked like a drowned girl.

Red lifted her form in front of him and bent down to yield her to her father's eager arms.

"Dann, heah's yore girl . . . safe . . . an' sound," Red said in a queer voice Sterl had never heard before. "An' thet lets me out."

What did the fool cowboy mean by that speech? wondered Sterl. Red had settled some strict deal to himself, not to anyone else there.

"Ormiston?" boomed the drover.

"Wal, the last we seen of thet bush-ranger, he was dancin'."

Dann evinced an incredulity he did not voice, but all the others were audible and curious enough.

"Yep, dancin' on thin air!" hissed the cowboy, and, with that, passion appeared to have spent its force, as well as his strength. "Where the hell air . . . you . . . pard?" he went on, in a strangely altered tone. "I . . . cain't . . . see you. It's . . . all dark! Aw, I . . . get it. Heah's where . . . I cash!"

His staring blue eyes, as blank as dead furnaces, his tortured lean, gray face under the dripping bloody bandages told their tragic story as well as his words. He swayed and fell into Sterl's arms.

Chapter Twenty-one

Larry helped Sterl carry Red across to Slyter's camp and into their tent. For Sterl all this slow walk was fraught with icy panic. He forgot even a word to Rollie and Friday who followed with the horses. It might well be that Red had been more severely wounded than a superficial examination had shown. Absolutely he had overtaxed his strength. How like Red Krehl to have such a finish. It was wonderful. The fool cowboy would have died at Beryl's feet to give the vain beauty everlasting remorse and grief. But Sterl suffered anguish at the mere thought of losing his more than brother, no matter how noble that end. Both of them had entered upon this ghastly trek with eyes wide open, boldly aware of a hundred desperate perils; they were young and supremely confident in powers that had brought them through the hard tests of the Texas frontier. Notwithstanding this, when Sterl faced his friend, lying so pale, so still, scarcely breathing, the moment was one of heart-wrenching torment.

"Get hot water . . . Larry," faltered Sterl, flinging off some of his wet and bedraggled garments. Then he got out his kit from a grip. Larry returned, with Bill peering anxiously over his shoulder.

They undressed Red, finding no more than the two wounds. They rubbed him dry, soaked his cold extremities in hot water, forced whiskey between his teeth. Then Sterl unbound the wounds, washed them thoroughly, and ruthlessly cut open the one on his back, and extracted the heavy bullet. It had gone under his collar bone, to spend its force, and stop just beneath the surface. No wound to bother Red Krehl! But the one Beryl Dann had done to his soul—to his intense and vivid love of life and her—that might be the serious one. Sterl dressed the shoulder injury, bandaged it, and went on with steadying hands to that bullet groove in Red's scalp. Sterl could not be fearful over this, either. He had seen the cowboy laugh at scratches like this. But Sterl found evidence that Red had bled freely all during the ride back to the river. The water had washed him clean. But one of Red's boots, however, had been half full of blood, very little diluted with water. There lay the danger. Drained of half his life's current, that intrepid and vain-glorious and love-struck cowboy had worked a miracle. Too glorious for that heartless little flirt.

"Larry, I reckon we . . . can't do more," panted Sterl. "Give these wet things to Bill to dry out, and change yourself. It's been a day."

"The most terrible and wonderful of my life!" exclaimed Larry.

Sterl took a long pull at the flask Larry offered. It burned the coldness out of his vitals. Then he rubbed himself thoroughly and got into dry clothes.

"I'd feel all right, if only Red . . . ," he choked over the hope. But again his intelligence, his experience told him Red would live. He went out. It was almost dark, and the rain fell steadily. Under Bill's shelter a bright blue blaze gleamed with shining rays through the rain. Bill had steaming vessels upon the gridiron.

"Eat and drink, lad," said Slyter. "We have to go on, you know. How is Red?"

"Bad. Bled almost to death. But I hope . . . I . . . I believe he'll recover."

"And you?"

"Oh, I'm jake. Tired, though, I guess. Where's Leslie, and the wife?"

"They're still with Beryl. But they should be back any minute now."

"How did the kid take the return of her horses?"

"Sterl, you wouldn't believe it . . . the way that girl went over them. But it was a breakdown, from all this day's strain, and the tremendous relief of your return."

"Of course, that accounts for any violence. Leslie is deep . . . not one to crack easily."

"My son, I very much fear Leslie is in love with you."

"Slyter, I fear that, too," Sterl replied ponderingly, a little bitterly. "I hope, though, that isn't quite so bad as what happened to Beryl."

"My wife says it's good. Ormiston was after Leslie. So were the drover boys. We have trusted you, Hazelton."

"Thanks, my friend. That'll help some."

The return of Slyter's womenfolk put an end to that intimate talk, much to Sterl's relief. Yet, still Slyter's kindness had touched him. They threw off wet coats and stood before the fire, Leslie with her back turned and her head down. Mrs. Slyter appeared cheerful as she asked Bill if supper was ready. "Come, Leslie, you haven't had anything but a cup of tea all day. Look at Sterl. If he can eat and drink!"

"I assure you it's an effort," said Sterl. Leslie turned then to flash a wholly inscrutable look upon Sterl from eyes wonderful and deep. "Leslie, how is Beryl?"

"I don't know. She . . . she scared me," replied the girl strangely.

"Shock and exposure, Sterl," interposed Mrs. Slyter. "There didn't appear to be any injury. She comes of good healthy stock. She'll stand it. How is your friend Red? He looked terribly the worse for this day's work."

Sterl briefly told them his hopes for Red, omitting his fears. But that sharp-eyed psychic, Leslie, did not believe him. When Sterl looked at her, she averted her piercing gaze. Then Larry and Rollie came, with Benson, to stand back of the fire to await their turn.

"Leslie and I will take turns tonight, sitting up with Beryl," said Mrs. Slyter.

"I'll look after Red," rejoined Sterl. "Reckon I can't stay awake long. But I'd hear him. He never moved after we laid him flat."

"Who shot him?" Leslie rang out suddenly.

"Les, you'll have to be told, I suppose," returned Sterl, in sober thoughtfulness. "Bedford shot Red first in the shoulder . . . and then Ormiston shot him in the head. Not serious wounds for a cowboy. But Red lost so much blood."

"I heard Red say to Mister Dann . . . that about Ormiston dancing on thin air. I know . . . but Bedford?"

Slyter interposed: "Leslie, wait until tomorrow. Sterl is worn to a frazzle."

Sterl wanted to get part of it over with, and he bluntly told Leslie that Red had killed Bedford.

"What did you do?" queried this incorrigible young woman unflinchingly.

"Well, I was there when it happened."

That seemed to be all the satisfaction Sterl could accord the girl at that time.

"Thanks, Sterl. Please forgive my curiosity. But I must tell you that I asked Friday."

"Oh, no. Leslie!" Sterl exclaimed, taken aback.

"Yes. I asked him what happened to Ormiston. He said . . . 'Friday spearum. Red shootum. Me alonga Red hangum neck. Ormiston kick like hellum. Then imm die!'"

It was not so much Friday's graphic and raw words that shocked Sterl as the girl's betrayal of the elemental. For once her parents did not reprimand her for indecorum, or whatever they might have deemed it. They were obviously too shocked themselves.

"Retribution," Mrs. Slyter added in a moment. "That bastard stole Beryl from her bed. I'll never forgive myself for believing she ran off with him."

"Neither will I, Missus Slyter," said Sterl, in poignant regret.

"I was afraid of it. Beryl was sweet again on him, lately," replied the girl frankly.

"Sterl, Dann will want to see you. Let us go now, before Les and Mum loosen up," suggested Slyter.

Glad to escape, although with a feeling for Leslie that he did not wish to analyze, Sterl accompanied the drover through the dark and rain. They found Dann at his table under a lighted shelter. Before him lay papers, watches, guns, money, and money belts.

"Hazelton, do I need to thank you?" queried Dann, his rich voice thick.

"Indeed, no, boss. I'm too happy to care for praise or reward. All I pray for is Red's recovery." And he told Dann of the cowboy's wounds and condition.

"Please God, that wonderful cowboy lives! Slyter, our erstwhile partner, had thousands of pounds, some of which I recognize had belonged to Woolcott and Hathaway and are now put aside for their heirs. I appropriated what I consider fair for my loss. Do you agree that the balance should go to the cowboys, and Larry and Roland?"

"I do, most heartily," rang out Slyter.

"Not any for me, friends," interposed Sterl, as the leader held out Ormiston's still bulky money belt. "But I'll take it for Red. He deserves it. He uncovered this bush-ranger. He made our plan today, saved Beryl . . . and hanged Ormiston."

"Terrible, yet . . . yet. . . . I'll want your story presently. I've heard that of Larry and Roland. But they, of course, did not see your fight. Poor Drake! Too brave, too rash! Too . . . what shall I call it? You may not know that Drake was friendly with both Anderson and Henley. That may account . . . what a pity he had to find them unworthy . . . to see them seduced by a notorious bush-ranger, as I, too, was seduced . . . and kill them! Yet how magnificent!"

"It was, indeed," replied Sterl, suddenly seeing Drake's strange recklessness stand out illumined.

"Take this belt, Sterl, and give it to Red," went on the leader.

"Not as a reward, but as wages earned. Slyter, divide the rest of that with Larry and Roland."

"Boss, if you don't mind, I'd like to have Ormiston's gun," said Sterl restrainedly.

"You're welcome to it. Now for your story, Sterl."

Sterl told it as briefly as possible, but not slighting one single detail, even at the end. But Dann surprised him by the way he took the raw narrative. He flinched at Sterl's graphic portrayal of the moment Friday's spear sped through Ormiston's bull neck, surely saving Red's life, and perhaps the girl's. And when Sterl told of the hanging of the bush-ranger—that brought the cold, clammy sweat to Dann's brow and a convulsion to his huge frame. Otherwise, he took the narrative as one who had at last recognized the villainy of evil men and the righteous and terrible wrath of hard avengers whom he understood.

"I'm not one to rail at the dispensation of Providence," said the leader at length. "How singularly fortunate we have been! I've a mind to let well enough alone, except to try to save the mob that rushed to its old grazing ground across the river."

"That can be done, Dann, as soon as the river drops. But I think you're wise not to attempt mustering the cattle that stampeded by us up there. Those two drovers, Herdman and Smith, will get away with one wagon, no doubt Ormiston's, although we hid the harness, and some of Ormiston's horses. If that herd bunches again and keeps along with the wagon, which is possible, those drovers might control them, a part of them anyhow. Let them go, Dann. We have more cattle now than we can handle. And seven less drovers."

"Right-o, Hazelton. But I'll send Larry and four men up there tomorrow to fetch back two of the wagons, if possible, and any horses available. Later, as you say, we'll cross that mob which obligingly rushed back to us. They won't leave that fine grazing over there."

Sterl and Slyter left the chief, to return to their camp.

"He was hit below the belt, Hazelton," said Slyter, "but never a word!"

"He took it fine, for a big cattleman who trusted friends and enemies alike, and never had any experience with thieves and murderers. But that sort of men are common on our frontier. Outside of Beryl's abduction, I think Dann was hurt most by his own drovers double-crossing him."

"Yes. I wonder what will happen next?" Slyter rejoined morosely.

"All our troubles are not over, boss, you can swear to that. Red would say . . . 'Wal, the wust is yet to come!' By the way, how is Eric Dann?"

"Bunged up pretty badly, but he'll be around in a few days. Wonder if he will be cured?"

"I have my doubts."

"Good night, Sterl. It has been a day. Never mind guard duty while Krehl needs attention. I hope to heaven he pulls through."

"Amen, boss."

Friday loomed up in the dark, evidently thoughtful of Red during Sterl's absence.

"Has he been quiet, Friday?"

"All same imm like dead. But imm strong, like black fella. No die."

"Bless your heart, my aborigine pard," returned Sterl gratefully. "You ought to be tired. Get some rest."

Sterl struck a match in the darkness of his tent and lighted his candle. Red looked like a corpse, but he was breathing, and his heart beat faintly. "If he only hangs on till tomorrow," Sterl whispered fervently, and that was a prayer, indeed. Sterl undressed, which was a luxury that had been difficult of late, and, when he stretched out, he felt as if he would never move again. His last act was to reach for the candle and blow it out.

Stress of emotion, no doubt, had more to do with his prostration than the sleepless night and strenuous day. He caught himself listening for Red's breathing, and he could not hear it. The rain pattered ceaselessly on the tent, and the river roared sullenly. Dingoes barked dismally. Sleepy as he was, he could not arrive at the point of oblivion. Despite his confidence in Red's recuperative powers, he suffered from dread. That speech of the cowboy's when he delivered Beryl into her father's arms—that haunted Sterl. He mulled it over and over in his mind. It meant, he deduced, that Red had withstood love and shame and insult and humiliation and torture for willful and vain Beryl Dann; in the face of opposition and antagonism he had uncovered Ormiston's villainy, and had killed him to save the girl. And that had let Red out. If Sterl knew Red Krehl, that retort Beryl had goaded him to, weeks past—"Someday you'll go on yore knees to me for thet!"—would never be enough to reconcile the cowboy. Yet Red was tender-hearted to a fault, and never had Sterl, in their twelve years of trail driving, seen him so terribly in love before. But then they had never had such a terrible experience before.

The rain lulled to patter on the canvas and then swelled to pelting force. The river roared on, sullen and menacing. Above the tent a swish of wattle branches and a moan of night wind in the gums helped keep Sterl awake. But outworn nature conquered at last, and he felt himself fading perceptibly into sleep.

When Sterl awakened, he heard the ring of Bill's axe. The blackness of the tent had turned to gray. Day had broken, and the rain had ceased temporarily. In the gloom he saw Red lying exactly as he had seen him hours past. But so pale, so silent. It was impossible for Sterl to stand the torture of uncertainty. Yet it was equally a torture to crawl out of bed to bend over his friend. Sterl's acute sensibilities registered a perceptibly stronger heartbeat. That drove Sterl's sluggish blood gushing through him. He dared to believe that Red would live. But was that love and hope? Fever must be reckoned with, and pneumonia, diseases likely to fasten upon a man so wounded and exposed.

Sterl got out in time to see five horsemen across the river, riding at a brisk trot to the east. They were, of course, the drovers Dann had sent after the wagons and horses. The sky was dark, except for some broken rifts, low down in the west. A wet drab landscape offered another cheerless day. The river had fallen a couple of feet; driftwood had ceased to pass by, and the muddy water was clearing.

While Sterl ate breakfast with Slyter, and Friday stood by Bill's fire, meat and drink in hand, Mrs. Slyter approached from Beryl's wagon. Her usual brightness was lacking.

"Mum, you don't look reassuring," Slyter said anxiously. "I was up at midnight with Leslie. We had a cup of tea. She said Beryl was sleeping, when she left her."

"Beryl has been shocked beyond her strength . . . any sensitive woman's strength," returned Mrs. Slater gravely. "She's violently delirious. I fear she'll go insane or die."

Leslie came in then, pale but composed, to take a seat at Bill's makeshift table.

" 'Mawnin'. What'd you fear, Mum?"

"That Beryl would go crazy from shock, or die."

"How awful! Oh, no, Mum, let's not give in to that! What do you think, Sterl?"

"Well, it's the cold gray dawn after two terrible nights with an awful day between. We can at least think clearly. Of course, I don't know what Beryl had to endure before we appeared on the scene, but it probably was enough to tax any girl's strength." Here Sterl described Beryl's fight with the bush-ranger, her fierce effort to keep him from killing Red. "Beryl was game, and she went the limit. She wrestled with Ormiston, kicked and bit him, spoiled his aim every shot. Well, then, Friday ended that fight by spearing Ormiston through the neck. He knew where he was sending that spear and had no fear of hitting Beryl. I don't believe I ever lived the equal of that few moments. If Beryl had only fainted then, as any soft creature like we thought her would have done, it would not have been so bad for her. But she didn't faint. She saw Ormiston roar and plunge around, like a mad bull. She saw Red rope him, around his . . . neck, over that spear he was tearing at. Saw Red hdrag him under the tree, and yell for Friday to help. They hanged Ormiston! I could hardly tear my eyes away from that kicking wretch. But when I did, it was to see

Beryl on her knees, staring in transfixed horror at him. I ran to cover her . . . shut out that sight. And it was then she did faint."

"Mercy!" gasped Mrs. Slyter.

"So that was how it happened?" ejaculated her husband, spellbound.

"I'd like to have been there," Leslie declared, with an unnatural calm that was belied by the piercing glint in her hazel eyes. .

"Talk sense, you wild creature," returned her mother impatiently.

Sterl had not at all intended such a disclosure and felt at a loss to understand why he had yielded to the impulse. If it was to see Leslie's reaction, however, he had been strangely justified.

"And your patient, how is he?" Mrs. Slyter asked anxiously.

Sterl expressed his hopes for Red and retained his morbid fears.

"Oh, I pray that he will recover," sighed Mrs. Slyter. "What a story we are living! It can never be told because no one would believe us."

"Mum, have you observed that I'm growing gray before my time?" Slyter queried in grim jocularity.

It rained on and off all day. During the intervals Sterl left his vigil by Red's bedside to walk out, stretch his cramped legs, have a bite to eat and a cup of tea, and always to watch the falling river. Toward what would have been sunset, if there had been any sun, he admitted Dann to the tent. The leader bent over the cowboy, listened to his breathing and heart, studied his stone-cold face. Then he said: "I've played many parts in my time, including both minister and physician. I'm happy that I shall not have to administer pontifically to our valiant cowboy. Be at peace, Sterl. He will live."

"Ah! I had almost dared to believe that myself."

"Come out with me," added Dann, arising. "The drovers have returned. I see one wagon and probably two score horses."

They went out, to be followed by Friday. Rain had set in again, and the air was muggy. Sterl sighted a large wagon, which he recognized as Ormiston's, rolling into the timber toward the old camp across the river. Four riders were driving a bunch of horses down to the shore. By the time Sterl and Dann had arrived at the landing point above camp, Larry had led off into the river, with the four riders behind urging and whipping the extra horses ahead of them. With the flood down six feet and no driftwood running, Sterl anticipated no difficulty in their crossing. So it proved to be. Neither riders nor unsaddled horses required any help at the landing. Dann expressed satisfaction upon seeing the best of his horses returned.

"Well done, Larry," said Dann, as the young drover rode up to make his report. "I'm glad, indeed, to see my saddle horses brought back."

"We got them all, I think," was the reply. "Herdman and Smith left last night, soon after our departure. They took the four teams, but only one wagon . . . the food supply wagon driven by Jack. They either buried Jack and Bedford or took them away in the wagon. Ormiston's wagon had been fired, but its contents were so wet it wouldn't burn. We erected a cross over Drake's grave."

"That was well," replied Dann, as Larry hesitated. "But what about Ormiston?"

"They left him hanging. So did we."

"Indeed! That seems strange. But they were hurried. You, of course, gave Ormiston decent burial."

"We did not, sir. We, too, left that bush-ranger for the buzzards!"

There was flint in Larry's eyes and words. Stanley Dann, seldom at a loss for words, found none to say here.

"Larry, sure you fetched Red's lasso?" Sterl asked laconically. "It was his favorite . . . too good a rope to waste on such a skunk as Ormiston."

"Sorry, Sterl. But we didn't. We left Ormiston hang!"

"Dog-gone, Larry, you're going Western, and maybe bush, too!" exclaimed Sterl mildly, when he would have liked to whoop.

"Any more orders, sir?" Larry asked of their leader.

"Not tonight. Change your wet clothes, and come to my tent for whiskey before supper," answered Dann gruffly.

That night at supper there was a release of tension as to Red's condition, but not for Beryl's. She had raved half the day, then fallen into a lethargy that preceded the sinking spell Mrs. Slyter had feared. Eric Dann, too, according to Slyter, was either a very sick man or pretended to be. Red was running a high temperature that night. He showed no symptom of having caught cold, however, and that eased Sterl's mind of one serious possibility.

Again it rained, hard and softly, on into the night, subsiding at daybreak. That morning Red came out of his stupor, or unconscious spell, and he whispered almost inaudibly for whiskey.

"You son-of-a-gun!" cried Sterl in delight, as he dove for a flask. "Easy now, old-timer! You had fever last night . . . and your head is not well still."

Red did not hear Sterl's advice. A tinge of color showed in his gray cheeks. "How . . . long?" he asked in a husky whisper.

"This is the third day. How you feel, pard?"

"Orful! Air you . . . shore . . . I'm not daid?"

"You're not lively, but you're shore no corpse."

"Got anythin' . . . back from . . . ?" He moved his thumb to indicate across the river and eastward.

"One wagon, Ormiston's twenty-odd horses . . . and this." Here Sterl picked up Ormiston's bulky belt to shove it front of Red. "He sure was heeled, pard. Dann took out what was due him, with Woolcott's and Hathaway's. The rest is yours. Wages justly earned, the boss said."

"Hell . . . he did. How much?"

"I was afraid to count it. But I took a peep. Plenty mazuma, pard."

"I'm gonna . . . get drunk. Never be sober . . . again."

"Is that so?"

"Sterl, give me . . . another pull at . . . thet."

"Umpumm. You're a sick man."

"Gimme a . . . cigarette."

"No. But I'll see what Missus Slyter advises in the way of grub."

Red was forced to swallow some gruel, which he would never have done had he not been too weak to lift his hand. The fever augmented again, accompanied by throbbing pains. Sterl sustained anxious hours that night before Red found relief in sleep. He did not awaken until late the next day, and that day turned out to be a terrible one for the cowboy. Sterl seldom left his bedside and then only to eat. He scarcely saw Leslie, who was in faithful attendance upon Beryl. She was in a far more precarious condition than Red.

Still the sky stayed drab and gloomy, shedding copious rains at slowly widening intervals. On the fifth day there came a break in Red's favor and a lessening of his pain. It seemed a definite crisis passed. At supper that night Bill told Sterl the river had fallen low enough for the drovers to pack Ormiston's supplies and wagon across, piece by piece. And the next day or so the cattle on that side were to be swum across. Eric Dann was up and about, moody and strange, which hardly seemed unnatural for a man who had been severely beaten over the head by a supposed friend. That eventful fifth day, however, showed no improvement in Beryl's mental or physical condition. Her father averred that she would pull through. Red knew nothing of this. He had not mentioned Beryl, except during some of his deranged flights, and Sterl did not vouchsafe the information.

After that day Red began to mend. He was as tough as wire, young and resilient, and, as soon as his depleted blood began to renew, his complete recovery was only a matter of days. On the tenth day of the rains he sat at table with Sterl and complained to Bill about fare not fit for a grub-line cowboy. On the twelfth he had Larry fetch Jester in. Red saddled his favorite and rode around the camp, out to see the mob, a full five thousand strong again. And on the fifteenth he told Sterl: "Wal, if the sun would only come out, I'd be rarin' to go."

"Go where, pard?" retorted Sterl.

"Hell, I don't know. Anywhere away from this heah doggone hole."

Red Krehl was himself again almost—lithe and lean, blue fire-eyed, drawling in his speech, vital once more with that spirit which upheld Sterl and had come to galvanize the drovers to whom he had become a hero. But not even to the persistent and sentimental Leslie did he ever ask about Beryl or hear, apparently, her disclosures and confidences. The only thing Sterl ever heard him say to Leslie that might have had, and probably did have, some bearing upon Beryl was: "Wal, darlin', a burnt child dreads the fire!" And Leslie retorted: "Darling, nonsense. I'm not your darling, and I wouldn't be if you wanted me . . . you heart-less, soulless Yankee cowboy!"

During the last few days of this period there were encouraging signs of the rainy season loosening its grip. It still rained, but far less frequently. The flat, dull sky broke at intervals, showing the first rifts of blue sky for over weeks. Still the sun did not show.

Stanley Dann sent Sterl and Larry across the ridge and flat to have a look at the west branch of the river. Smaller than the main fork, it ran swiftly and almost clear. Birdlife, with its color and melody, predicted a return of good weather; kangaroos and wallabies, emus and aboriginals appeared in increasing numbers. The last, Friday claimed, were different black fellas from those who had crowded at the Forks before the flood. The great triangle of grassland, which had its apex at the junction of the river forks, waved away, incredibly rich with new grass, and everywhere on the miles where the riders covered there were pools of water. Larry and Sterl reported to the leader that the trek could be re-sumed, rain or shine. But the patient Dann stroked his golden beard and said: "We'll wait for the sun. Eric is not sure about the road. He thinks it'd be more difficult to find it in wet weather."

"Then you'll keep to this Gulf road, if we find it?" queried Sterl quietly.

"Yes. I shall not change my mind because Ormiston is gone."

"Mister Dann," Larry ventured with hesitation, "the creeks, water holes, springs will be full for months."

"I am aware of that. But Eric has importuned me, and I have decided."

Dann might have been actuated to delay because that would be better for Beryl. She had come to herself, and only time and care were necessary to build up the flesh and strength she had lost.

When one night the stars came out, Dann said. "That rainbow today is God's promise. The wet season is over. Tomorrow the sun will shine. We go on and on again with our trek."

Chapter Twenty-two

Sunrise next morning was a glorious burst of golden light. The joyous welcome accorded to this one-time daily event seemed in proportion to that of the Laplanders after their six months of midnight. Even Beryl Dann, from under the uprolled cover of her wagon, gazed out with sad eyes gladdened. By the exultant cheer and hope the agony of that endless enforced wait and the trial of the rainy season with its tragic ending could be measured. How they had prayed for the coming of the rains and how they prayed now because of the sun and the bright face of the trek again!

Breakfast was almost a hilarious event. The drovers whistled while they hitched up the teams to the packed wagons; they sang and called to one another as they mustered the mob for the trek.

Sterl, keen to see and share all this excitement, was perhaps the only one to observe that Eric Dann was not in accord with it. It struck Sterl that Dann would have felt the exhilaration of the hour, if they had been headed homeward. The man had never felt the greatness of this trek as had the others. He did not have his pioneer brother's soul. He was afraid. But he was the first to start, driving his own wagon. Stanley, driving the big canvas-covered wagon that carried Beryl, sent his trusted drover, Bligh, ahead with the second wagon, and followed it, calling lustily for the others to come.

Sterl, mounted on King, and, as eager as the horse, waited with Friday for the other wagons to get under way. But Slyter was detained by Leslie's pets. At the last moment Cocky had betrayed that the freedom he had been trusted with at this long camp was too much for him. Leslie had not even clipped his wings. And when he flew up to join a flock of screeching, white cockatoos, he became one of many. Gal, sitting on top of the wagon, exhibited a tremendous squalling and flapping joy at Cocky's base desertion. Leslie gave up trying to call Cocky back.

Laughing Jack, the tame kookaburra, also turned traitor. He sat on the branch of a dead gum tree with three of his kind and helped in an uproarious concatenation of raucous jackass mirth. When they paused for breath, Leslie called: "Jack! Jack! Come down here, you rascal! We're leaving!" Jack led another outburst of deafening clatter, he bobbed up and down, he ruffled his feathers, and he laughed hoarsely and derisively at the mistress who had been so kind to him. But he would not come down.

"Imm go alonga kookaburra," said Friday.

That filled Leslie with anger and despair. She called furiously. In vain! Then she used some of the profanity she had heard from Red's careless lips. Red laughed, and Leslie's mother reproved her. All to no good. Jack had tasted the sweetness of utter freedom.

"Les, he's gone bush," said her father.

"Back to the wild!" Sterl added. "Leslie, would you ever be content to live with us again, after nearly a year on this free trek?"

"No, but I . . . I always lose everything I love," wailed the girl, and, mounting Lady Jane, she rode out under the trees and did not look back.

Sterl was the last to leave the Forks. He was glad to go, because that was imperative, yet he felt a strong and inexplicable regret. He was the last to look at the crosses of the trekkers who had perished there. What lonely graves! The full-banked river ran swiftly and green; the wattles and gums were bright with colorful blossoms and wildfowl. On the opposite bank a line of blacks stood at gaze, motionless, wild, locked in their mystic thoughts. Blue and white herons lined the sandbars. Turning away, Sterl loped King out of the timber upon the level, to pass the line of wattles, and go on over the grazed and trampled grass to his old position at the left end of the mob.

On their way—on the great trek again—with the unknown calling! Sterl felt the swell of his heart. But his emotion was not all exultance. Many cattle and horses, several wagons, and fourteen dead men and one woman had been left behind. Slyter's five drovers, not including him and Red, and four of Dann's, remained to handle that mob and three hundred horses, and six heavily laden wagons, across the endless leagues. The trek assumed more monumental risks and travails than ever.

Yet the start, the fact, the fate seemed unutterably inspiring. *Why was it*, wondered Sterl, *so soul-stirring, so pulse-ringing?* The answer was romance, adventure, the call of the unknown, the unconquerable spirit of man to roam, to seek, to find, and never to yield. Stanley Dann and Slyter might think in terms of new grassy downs, perennial springs and rivers, and multiplying cattle, an empire of their own, but that was not their ruling passion. They were the explorers, the doers, the finders. Even Ormiston must have been actuated by the spell of the bushland. And Eric Dann had succumbed to it without the courage to carry on like a man. Never in all Sterl's life of riding ranges had his sight been assailed by so much brightness.

The sky was deep azure, floating a few silver-white clouds. The sun appeared no relation to that molten copper disc of a few weeks past. And the waving, rippling, shining landscape, in all its infinite variety of brilliant hues, stormed and assailed Sterl's beauty-loving and color-worshipping senses.

King's mane and smooth hide were a dead black, yet somehow they shone. Friday, stalking beside Sterl with his spears and *wommera*, naked except for the loincloth he wore, presented another kind of black, a glistening ebony. The mob of cattle appeared to consist of a hundred hues, yet there were really only very few. It was the variation of them that gave the living mosaic effect. They looked as clean and bright as if they had been freshly scrubbed.

Compared to one of the trail driver's herds in Texas, the long-horned, moss-backed, red-eyed devils that were the bane of cowboys' lives, this mob of five thousand bulls and steers and cows and calves were tame, lazy, fat pets. The slow trek, the widely separated frightening situations, and the kindness of the drovers accounted for this. Sterl had never seen a bunch of cattle like it, especially in this atmosphere which made them look as if they were painted.

This new golden sun, shining down upon everything living and inanimate, gave all a supernatural touch of infinite loveliness. Stanley Dann had predicted this as God's promise in the rainbow.

Ahead of the leisurely moving mob the grass resembled that of the Great Plains in thickness and height, but in its richness of color and multitude of flowers it could have no comparison. Out of that eight months' baked soil, by the magic or rain, had sprung up above and around the bleached and dead grass an abundant growth of green and gold and purple. When King bent his spirited head to tear off a long tuft of blossoms and grass, it gave Sterl a pang.

In the distance all around loomed purple bush-crowned hills, and to the north, far beyond, lilac ranges hung to the fleecy clouds like mirages right side up. If there could be enchantment on earth, here Sterl rode amidst it. That he seemed not the only one under its spell he proved by glancing at his companions on the trek, trying to pierce their minds. Every one of them rode alone, except Friday, who stalked lost in his own lonely, impenetrable thought. The drovers sat their horses and gazed, no doubt, at things that were only true in dreams. Red Krehl had forgotten his cigarette. Leslie rode far behind lost in her world. The wagon drivers rolled on from time to time, and halted between whiles. Nothing about them suggested the stern labor of the trek.

So the long bright day, like one endless golden afternoon passed without Sterl realizing where the hours had gone. At sunset, Larry, who had been sent on ahead to locate a camp near water, rode back to halt the herd and direct the teamsters to a wattle-bordered stream that meandered away to join the middle fork of the river.

A thousand white cockatoos swooped out of the trees, screechingly resentful of this invasion. Kangaroos dotted the level, standing head and shoulders above the grass. These live creatures and the physical attributes of their environment were part and parcel of the trek.

At this place Stanley Dann inaugurated a new order of arrangement whereby supplies and cooks and trekkers were consolidated into one camp. Red Krehl grumbled about eating with the Danns and Slyters, but Sterl's curiosity as to the reason was wasted. He had known sooner or later that even such a big company must settle down into one family. Their members and supplies were being reduced, which fact had its advantages as well as drawbacks.

The exhilaration of the morning had carried through to evening. A sudden change from dark to bright, from gloom to hope, from stagnation to activity, from one terrible camp to a new one without terrors, from torrid heat and drenching rain to pleasant warmth and fragrant air, where, marvelous to experience, flies and mosquitoes were conspicuous by their absence—these facts could not help but be gratefully, almost rapturously, received. Only Sterl, perhaps, bothered to think that they would not last, that he must make the uttermost of them while they were present.

"Pard, it's kinda good to be alive at thet," Red drawled.

"Red, you've never fooled me about your indifference to beautiful places any more than to girls," replied Sterl satirically.

"Yeah? Wal, mebbe Les was right, when she said once thet I wore my heart on my sleeve."

"Red Krehl," spoke up Leslie, "if you *have* a heart, it's an old boring bag stuffed with grass and what-not."

Leslie had come over to where Sterl sat writing in the journal, and Red was smoking. Friday, as usual, had made a little fire. The day was done, and the darkness was descending. A multitude of insects had begun night music.

"Gosh, am I thet bad?" rejoined Red mildly.

"Why wouldn't you come with me to see Beryl, when I asked you before supper?"

"Wal, I reckon I didn't want to see Beryl."

"But she begged to see you. She looks better today. Glad for such perfect weather . . . and to leave that horrid Forks. I made sure you'd come with me, Red. And I was embarrassed. I lied to her."

"Shore, you always was a turrible liar."

"I was not. Red, you're so queer. You never were hard before. Why, you stood positive cruelty from that girl, when she was a devil! And now, when she's such a shadow of her once lovely self, she needs to be cheered, fussed over . . . loved."

"A-huh. That weakness got her into a pack of trouble, Les Slyter. But would you mind shettin' up, onless you want me to go out an' commune with the kangaroos?"

"You mean the aborigines, Red Krehl," Leslie returned spitefully. She was disappointed.

"Wal, I would at that, if there was any about."

Leslie plumped down beside Sterl, and, pretending to peep at the journal, which he believed was only a ruse to get close to him, she asked to see it.

"I'm busy, Leslie. 'Way behind. Will you slope off to bed, or somewhere?"

"No, I won't slope off to bed . . . or to hell, as you hint so courteously," she retorted petulantly, but she left them.

"Pard, what'd she mean by that crack about aborigines?" asked Red.

"I think it was a dirty crack. But don't ever overlook this, old pard. Every dirty crack a woman makes, every mean or rotten thing she does, every terrible blunder, like Beryl's for instance, can be blamed on some man."

"Aw, hell! You've said that before. It ain't so. What did you ever say or do to make Nan Halbert double-cross you, an' send us off to this turrible Australia?"

That blunt query pierced like a blade in Sterl's heart. Not only was he amazed at Red, but the sudden opening of a healed wound flayed him. Still it drove him to be honest.

"Red, I flirted with Nan's best friend . . . that damned, little, black-eyed hussy who wouldn't let any man alone."

"Hell you say! You mean Flo, of course. Wal, so did I! But what you mean by flirtin'? Thet ain't nothin' a-tall."

"Well, it was enough to make Nan furious. Proud and jealous, you know. We quarreled. She smacked me something fierce. Then to hurt me she went hot foot after Ross Haight. And there she made her terrible blunder. It was my fault."

"But, you locoed two-faced Romeo, you never told me thet. You swore Nan liked Ross best."

"I lied, Red," returned Sterl somberly, closing the journal. He would write no more in its pages that night.

"Wal, I'm a son-of-a-sea-cook! If you'd told me that back home, Ross Haight could have gone to jail for his little gun play. An' we wouldn't be heah!"

"For me, Red, it is better so. Only I grieve for what I led you into."

"Funny how things come about. But you needn't grieve too hard. I'm not sorry we're heah."

"Honest, Red?" Sterl appealed earnestly.

"Honest to Gawd. This trek is right down my grub-line trail. 'Course, I've had an orful blow in the gizzard. But if I get over it, an' we get through. . . . Wal, wherever we end up, I'm bound to make some punkins of a man."

"Red, you're a good many punkins of a man right now. The best cowboy . . . the best friend I ever knew!"

"Wal, I can return thet compliment," replied Red feelingly. "Heah we are throwin bouquets at each other! I call thet fine. Nobody else has a good word for us. That crack of Leslie's. . . ."

"Red, she loves Beryl, and she's hurt that you wouldn't go with her to see Beryl. You ought to have gone. That surprised me. You used to be kind to anyone sick, even a no-good cowboy or a horse."

"Mebbe I was. Mebbe I've changed a lot," Red rejoined bitterly. "I wouldn't want to see Beryl, if she was like she used to be before that hot spell, but let alone now, after. . . ."

"Red! You're here!" exclaimed Sterl sharply.

"Shore. Harder than the hinges of the gates of hell. But, if you cain't see thet I've had a-plenty to make me hard, wal, you're as blind as a bat, an' gettin' further an' further from yore old thinkin' self."

"I deny that, Red Krehl," flashed Sterl. "Sure you've had enough to make you flint. But you're not flint. . . . Are you keeping something secret from me?"

"No. Jest the same I cain't go around barin' all my pore thoughts to you."

"Red, you haven't told me everything about Beryl."

"Hell's fire, man, you can think, cain't you?" Red cut in with that icy edge in his voice. "An' let's change the subject, before we say things you an' me never was guilty of."

"Red, I beg your pardon," said Sterl, astounded into contrition. "I didn't mean to hurt you, old man. Let's forget it, and go to bed."

But Sterl, however loyal he wanted to be, could not forget it. Long he lay awake, thinking. Red had said—*Hell's fire, man, you can think, cain't you?* And Sterl certainly indulged in that faculty. But what he eventually deduced—the one fatal thing that all threads of memory and significance led to—his consciousness refused to accept, although it substantiated insupportably the truth of his theory that nature in the raw and wild reduced human beings to its level far oftener than it exalted them.

In another day the trek fell back into its old leisurely time-effacing stride. What would have been spring back on Sterl's range was autumn here in Australia, but the elements of the perennial renewal of the earth and its creatures and plants was just the same, only its beauty and freshness and bloom more joyous and vivid.

One day's trek was like another, although every league of that lonely land had infinite variety as well as endless monotony. The blaze of a benign and pleasant sun lay over all. With the increase of miles there was increase in every detail of beauty that had marked the entrance to this level, rolling hinterland. Sterl had his surfeit of loveliness. It had passed into his being. At last seas of green and golden grass, islands of flowers, kangaroo-dotted plains, flamboyant bushland, a myriad of birds, flocks of emus, mile-wide ponds where the mob splashed across, scattering the flocks of waterfowl, winding tiny brooks and still reed-bordered streams, and always, every hour of the long day, that illusive beckoning haunting purple mountain range—at last Sterl Hazelton's soul was everlastingly filled to the brim with these physical things which he divined were rewards in themselves, and which gave him fleeting, vague visions of the long ago, of other sons of time and their abundance, back in the arid ages, and the ice, and the volcanic, from which by some omniscience life and beauty and spirit had evolved.

The trek along the middle fork continued for seventeen days, to where its headwaters sprang from the tropic verdure of the foothills. This swiftly flowing, gradually narrowing stream had sheared to the northwest for many days and leagues, so that the purple mountain range lay in the eastward, beyond the foothills that rolled down from it.

"Camp here two days," boomed Stanley Dann. "We will rest the stock, make repairs, and scout abroad for this Gulf road. Eric has not found it yet."

Leslie named the place Wellspring. It was felicitous because the splendid volume of water sprang as from a well, deep under the shadow of a bold, dark green foothill. The cattle trooped for a mile along the stream that rushed from this spring. Three hundred horses frolicked in a pasture behind the camp, a level flower-spangled meadow of grass half surrounded by hills. Camp was pitched in the open within sound of the babbling of the brook. Soon fires sent columns of blue smoke curling upwards; the ring of axe kept the parrots squalling. Bill, with Scotty, the other cook, prepared for the best meal they could devise, in honor of Beryl Dann's first attendance for many weeks.

Sterl and Red had heard this announcement before Leslie came to tell them. They had finished their camp tasks and, as Red put it, had shaved and spruced up a bit. Just before Leslie's arrival, Sterl had had some words with his friend.

"Pard, you will be decent to Beryl? You have not spoken to her since . . . since that . . . mess."

"Umpumm," drawled Red.

"Say, do you see that?" rang out Sterl, extending a big fist.

"Shore, I ain't blind."

"You know where it used to hurt you to be hit?"

"A-huh. My belly. An' I ain't recovered yet, either."

"That's dinkum. If you don't swear to be nice to Beryl, I'll lam into you right now. And I'm not fooling."

"Yeah? Wal, I choose the wusser of two evils. I'll speak to Beryl an' be as . . . as nice as I can. It's gotta be done sometime, jest for appearances. An', after all, what the hell do I care?"

"Thanks, Red. That's more like my old pard," rejoined Sterl dubiously.

Then Leslie arrived. Once again, after so long an interval, in feminine apparel, a flowered gown in which she looked extremely pretty. One glance at Sterl was sufficient for her to see that he meant to grace the occasion of Beryl's return to their circle. But at Red she gazed most appealingly and fearfully.

"Red, you'll . . . come?" she asked falteringly.

"No, Les," he said, contriving to wink at Sterl. "Umpumm, now, nix come the weasel!"

That he could jest at such a moment, certainly poignant and important to Leslie, called to all that was spirited in her.

"You ornery, bull-headed, low-down . . . ," she burst out, choking over the last two words, which, like those preceding, were from Red's vocabulary, only they were indecorous and scandalizing on a girl's sweet lips, although most eloquently forceful. Then as quickly as the flare-up of her tongue, she broke into sobs.

"Aw, now, Leslie, don't cry, please," begged the cowboy, who could not bear to see a girl cry. "I didn't mean it a-tall. You see I'm all spruced up. I'll go with you an' do the elegant."

"Hon-nest, Red? You're such a . . . a brute. You might be . . . teasing."

"No, I mean it. Thet is I'll go, if you stop cryin'. Why, the idee! Spoilin' thet happy face! An' you did look the prettiest I ever seen you."

The magic of his words cured that crying spell. Leslie came out of it like the sun from behind a rain cloud. "Oh, it was so . . . so silly of me! Thanks, Red, you can be a dear. Sterl, have I . . . do I look terrible?"

"Personally I prefer you in tears," said Sterl with a laugh. "Come, let's go before our pard changes his mind."

The Danns' three wagons were only a few rods distant, and between two of them, a canvas shelter had been erected on poles. A large ground cloth table and chairs gave an air of comfort. The Slyters were there, also Larry and Rollie, and Stanley Dann, from whose knees Beryl arose to greet her visitors. The blue gown, which she had worn at one other time, hung loosely upon her slender form, yet not at the expense of grace. Every vestige of the golden tan had vanished from her face, the whiteness of which accentuated the loveliness of her violet eyes and fair hair. Her beauty struck Sterl with great force, and suddenly he understood both Ormiston and Krehl.

Beryl advanced a few steps to meet them. Leslie had been hanging onto Red, who was behind Sterl. Now she ran to Beryl. "Oh, it's so dinkum to see you out again!" Beryl returned her kiss and greeting, then offered her two hands to Sterl. "Now, Mister Cowboy, what do you think of me, up and well . . . and rarin' to go?"

"I think it's great," Sterl responded heartily, as he took her hands. "Beryl, you look just beautiful!"

But she did not even get that last. Red stepped out from behind Sterl, and then Sterl, with a pang, saw what a terrible moment this was for both of them.

"Beryl . . . I . . . I'm shore dog-gone glad to see you out again," Red said huskily, and he was both gallant and self-possessed. One of his long strides bridged the distance between them.

Her eyes dilated and turned black. "Red . . . Red," she whispered as she put out quivering hands. But this meeting was not what she had anticipated. None of those present, except Red, had any idea what that meant. She was facing the cowboy whom she had lured to a love beyond belief, who had passed by slight and indifference and insult, who had withstood jealousy in the front of monstrous and just trial. She was facing the cowboy, the stranger, the alien, the common uncouth man whose ruthlessness had saved her from the ruin only she and he knew. It was too much for the girl. Her groping hands missed his, to clutch his blouse. She fell against him with a gasp and fainted in his arms.

A shocked silence held all of the witnesses mute. Then Red cried hoarsely: "My Gawd! Too much for her!"

"It was, indeed," replied Dann reproachfully. "She is not as strong as she thought. Let me have her." Dann took her from Krehl and sat her gently down in the one rocking chair, which he tipped back somewhat. "Missus Slyter . . . Leslie!"

Sterl could not withdraw his gaze from Beryl's face. Her eyes were closed, long fair lashes on her white cheeks. Had the shock hurt her? Sterl turned to Red and forgot his concern for Beryl in the dumb misery of his friend. He kept his mouth shut, by biting his lips, but he clutched Red with lean strong hands until he recovered. Dann's hearty voice attested to the fact that Beryl had regained consciousness.

"I fainted," she said weakly. "How stupid. But all went black. . . . I'm all right now. Dad, let the rocker down. Why, Leslie, you are as white as a sheet."

"No wonder! Beryl, I thought you'd gone to join the angels."

"No such luck for me. Boys, come back. I promise you, I won't be such a weakling again."

Sterl, with his arm through Red's, dragged the hesitant cowboy to the small circle of which Beryl was the center. She had color in her cheeks. Apparently she was all right. The cowboys found seats. Dann boomed out his admonition for her not to let herself become excited again. Mrs. Slyter insisted that Beryl sip the cup of tea proffered her. Leslie hovered over her, wide-eyed and loving. And the strain passed. Sterl tried to ease it away with reference to the beautiful campsite, and to turn Beryl's mind away from its evident channel of poignant memories. It developed that he failed to do that.

"Red, perhaps I fainted because sight of you brought you back . . . as you looked when I last saw you . . . how long ago? Ages ago?"

"I forget. It shore was an orful long time," drawled Red. "An' about thet faintin'. I knowed a girl once who could faint . . . or let on . . . whenever she wanted to knock the daylights out of a feller. So you see, Beryl, I been educated."

"Did this girl faint in your arms?" asked Beryl, her speaking eyes on him.

"Wal, thet was one way she had of gettin' into 'em. An' once she got there, she'd come to orful quick."

Presently Beryl's nurses fed her sparingly, then, despite her protests, they led her away to her wagon and bed. The look she gave Red as she bade him good night was not lost upon Sterl. Beryl's eyes were always dark and proud, because that was their peculiar property, but Sterl thought, if he had been Red, he could never have resisted that look.

At this juncture Eric Dann entered the shelter, greeted the cowboys, and drank with Stanley. The younger brother had never recovered from the shock of being beaten by Ormiston. Physically he had mended, but he never seemed the same mentally. He had one bad livid scar on his forehead, a gun butt mark that he would carry to his grave.

Sterl took advantage of the opportunity to question the drover.

"Dann, if I remember correctly, we lost the Gulf road halfway or more down the Diamantina from the Forks?" queried Sterl.

"Somewhere back there. It didn't concern me then, because I expected to come across it any day," returned Dann.

"We haven't crossed it. Roads and trails, as well as horse tracks, have been a specialty of mine. I kept a sharp lookout for wheel tracks, such as our wagons make. On level ground half a dozen wagons would leave a rut that would last for years."

"Surely. We have just missed them, unless, of course, they have washed out."

"Eric, it was less than two years ago when you returned from the Gulf," interposed Stanley. "Hazelton's contention is plausible."

"Did you return on your back track?" went on Sterl.

"Part way. I don't recall just where we made short cuts."

"Some of these landmarks along here, if you ever saw them, you couldn't forget."

"That depends on the angle from which we saw them. For my part, all landmarks meant very little to me."

"Hmm, it's unfortunate you did not have an instinct for such things," said his brother. "You said you knew the way, Eric."

"I've told you a thousand times that I thought I did," Eric replied impatiently.

Sterl made note of the shifty eyes and the beads of sweat coming out on Dann's brow under the livid scar. Sterl's dubious conjectures about this man became definite doubts. Sterl could never swallow Dann's relation to Ormiston. It had not been open to the light.

"Mister Dann," drawled Red, lifting his drooping head behind a puff of cigarette smoke, "if you come back along heah a-tall, you had to cross this middle fork somewhere in the hundred-odd miles we've traveled it. Cain't you remember crossin' it somewhere?"

"No. We crossed several strong streams as big as this."

"Eric! It was in the dry season you got back," expostulated the leader. "I've never forgotten one single reference of yours to this trek. Some of your statements are inconsistent."

Red fixed his piercing eyes upon the drover. "Dann, we're all in the dark. If you don't know this country a-tall, you oughta tell us damn' *pronto*."

"But I do know it, in general. I've recognized a good many places we passed at a distance from this trek. I'd like it understood that I'll not be put on the carpet by you Americans," declared Dann with signs of nervousness and heat.

"Wal, we Americans ain't puttin' you on nothin', except yore word," rejoined Red coolly. Then he asked Dann bluntly: "Have you ever been through this Diamantina country?"

"Stanley, will you allow this . . . this blighter to insult me?" demanded Dann.

"But, my brother, no insult is intended," Stanley remonstrated, perturbed.

"No insult meant, Dann," spoke up Red for himself. "We jest gotta get somewhere."

Dann made what appeared to be a powerful effort to control unstable nerves and fight down some fear or doubt that the cowboy had stirred. Nevertheless, he did not reply to Red's query, giving the impression of offended dignity.

"Wal, heah's one you can answer, Mister Dann, onless . . . ?" Red did not complete his dubious inference. "This heah range we've come to an' have seen for so many days, makes a cross-section of this country. A fair estimate could be thet it runs fifty miles or so to the east and some more than that to the west. There's a pass that nobody could miss seein'. If yore trek or any other trek climbin' a little all the time, travelin' north from Cooper Creek up the Diamantina, you or they'd have to go through this pass. Ain't that figgerin' reasonable?"

"Yes, it is, Krehl. They'd have to," replied Dann readily.

"All right. Then what kind of country will we find on the other side of this range?"

"It will be practically the same as this."

"Thanks, Dann. We'll remember thet," returned Red caustically. It was plain he had not the slightest faith in Stanley Dann's brother as a guide, or for that matter as a man. Then he addressed Sterl: "Pard, do you reckon I oughta shet up now or relieve my mind to the boss?"

"Speak out, Red," advised Sterl.

"By all means, Krehl," boomed Stanley. "I'd be a poor leader, if I did not want my drovers, especially such capable and experienced men as you and Hazelton, to give their opinions, and advice, too, when asked for it."

"Wal, I wouldn't presume to advise you heah. I'm no Australian. But I've known open wilderness country since I was knee-high to a grasshopper. This heah country has been changin'. It's altogether different from the Forks. Grass shorter an' not so rich. Trees fewer an' smaller an' different, too, except the gums an' wattles. Bare patches aplenty, when back aways there wasn't any. These foothills air covered with ferns an' palms an' vines, an' stuff I never seen. Wal, back of these foothills is a pretty high range for this country. It won't be a cinch to cross. An' when you do cross it, if you ever do, you'll find the stream runnin' the wrong way for us. Thet's my hunch, boss. Take it or leave it."

Turning on a jangling heel, Red stalked away from the Danns with a mien that left little to the imagination. Dann, so seldom perturbed, was bewildered and excited by what was evidently a new aspect to him.

"Incredible!" he ejaculated. "We should be still hundreds of miles from the watershed that sends its streams into the Gulf. Eric, you substantiate this, do you not?"

"Absolutely. We'll find rivers on the other side as scarce as they are on this," answered Eric Dann with no hint of uncertainty. "Northeast of this range, when we pass it, we will reach the headwaters of the Warburton River. That runs westward. Beyond that, we will come to the headwaters of rivers emptying into the Gulf."

"That agrees with our map. I am sure Krehl has miscalculated. What do you think, Hazelton?

"It'd be only natural, if he did miscalculate. And wonderful if he didn't. All I say is, I'm sorry we are not trekking west."

"If we should make a blunder now . . . and go the wrong way . . . ," boomed the leader, halting before he allowed himself to predict dire disaster. But he trusted his brother. He was too great in hope. Sterl, in his old hard, bitter skepticism, heard the leader's voice ring and break, but he made it his business to be watching Eric Dann at that critical moment, and either he was prejudiced against this man's vacillation and incompetence, or he saw through him with Red Krehl's lynx eyes.

Chapter Twenty-three

Wellspring Camp multiplied all the properties that the trekkers had found on the way up the middle fork, to make in the sum of them a place of extraordinary comfort and pleasure. But after that conference with the Danns a premonition of evil took possession of Sterl, and he could not shake it. That Red Krehl shared it, probably more somberly, intensified the haunting significance. That neither of them reopened the subject while there argued for a sinister dread they wanted to forget.

On the morning of the third day Sterl sat his horse and indulged in something he seldom if ever yielded to. The trek was under way again, on the upgrade, making for that pass. He looked back. Wellspring shone dazzlingly colorful under the early morning sun, a lonely and beautiful place where only the aborigines would gather. If Sterl could have stayed there to settle on a ranch—a station, these Australians called it—he would have been content. Long he gazed and then turned reluctantly away, somberly sure he was seeing the last of something clearly defined in its beauty, richness, and solitude, and as well something vague, fading to its close. But Sterl was destined to forget that place and its portent in the immediate toil and difficulty of the trek.

At a break in the foothills, apparently leading to the pass through the range, Eric Dann asserted that he was sure he had been through there, going or coming, and the mob was driven into narrow defiles between the foothills. Larry had reported dubious ground ahead; Slyter broke his rule to ask their leader to investigate before proceeding. Red Krehl had climbed to a hilltop to reconnoiter. Upon his return he said to Dann in no uncertain terms: "Cain't see far. But no country to drive cattle, let alone wagons."

Stanley showed his usual thoughtful consideration. He held up the trek for the purpose of a conference.

"No hurry, friends, we'll climb to look the ground over. Krehl should know where, and where not, to drove a mob."

But Eric Dann leaped from his wagon seat to confront his brother in a terrific fury.

"First it was Hazelton! Now it's Krehl . . . Krehl . . . Krehl! I'm sick and tired of having my judgments ruled aside by these blighters. I won't stand it any longer."

"Eric, you've lost your temper," replied Stanley severely. "Calm yourself before you say something you might regret. These cowboys have been a help to me, not a detriment . . . as Ormiston, Woolcott, Hathaway, and you have been."

Eric Dann's visage grew purple, and the cords of his neck bulged. He appeared a victim of insane and unjustified rage. "By God, I'll turn back!" he shouted.

"Eric! Are you mad? You couldn't turn back alone."

"Henry will go with me. He's my man, not yours."

"But that wagon and team are mine," rejoined Dann, controlling evident heat.

"I don't care. I'll take them. I've earned that much on this infernal trek."

"Out of the question!" boomed the leader.

"I tell you I'll go back!" yelled his brother.

Red Krehl slid off his horse and entered the scene. Sterl's impulse was to halt him, until he saw that it would be impossible.

"Bah! It's a bluff, boss. He hasn't got the nerve."

"Wait, Krehl," ordered Dann, suddenly apprehensive. He sensed something about this cowboy, if his brother did not. "Eric, I cannot allow you to do any such foolhardy thing. Control yourself. What is it you want?"

"You brought me on this trek as partner and guide," Eric shouted hoarsely.

"Yes, I did."

"Then hold to that contract, or I'll leave you!"

"Eric, I was not aware that I had broken it. . . . Very well, I will hold to it . . . come what may," returned the leader, with a finality that asserted his honor if not his heartfelt assurance.

"It's understood that I am the guide?"

"Yes. But you must *guide* us."

"I'll brook no further interference from these meddling cowboys."

"Brother, I don't agree with you about them. But let that pass. We must preserve amity. Let Bligh drive your wagon. You take to your saddle, and get us somewhere. Once more, for the last time, do you *know* this country?"

"Yes, I do," rasped Eric passionately, yet haltingly, and he gulped as if something had stuck in his throat. "In a general way, I mean. I can't recognize every river and gum tree and anthill we see, as those intolerant cowboys expect. This is not a pasture land, such as they must be used to riding. It's an enormously vast country."

"Yeah, an' you *know* it?" interrupted Red with stinging scorn.

"Yes, I know it, you . . . you . . . !" burst out the goaded drover.

"Dann, you're a . . . a . . . liar!"

"Wha-at? Insolent rowdy! Stanley. . . ."

"Shut up! Stop bellerin' for yore brother! Go for yore gun . . . if you got the guts!"

"*Krehl!*" thundered the leader.

"Too late, boss. Stay where you air. Buttin' in heah might be risky. Come on, Mister Eric Dann. . . . Gawd only knows all you really air! But it's a cinch you're a fool, an' a two-faced double-crossin' liar! Come on, throw yore gun!"

Eric Dann revolted from that challenge. Pale-faced instead of red now, gasping and speechless, he turned to spread wide his hands, appealing to the leader.

"Let this end here!" commanded Dann.

"All right, boss, it's ended," replied Red curtly. "But I'll bet you live to see the day you wish it'd ended my way. I won't open my trap to him again. Thet's all. We better be movin', 'cause you're shore gonna need a coupla months to get through."

Days without end before what seemed to be the pass; Sterl lost track of days. By now, Slyter, beating down the opposition of Eric Dann, had insisted that the wagons go ahead—for in places they had actually to improvise roads. Sometimes three miles a day were good going. The cattle found little grass and took to browsing. Many of them strayed. The drovers rode hard at night in five-hour shifts. Slyter's second wagon, with Roland driving, went over a steep bank. He escaped, but the horses had to be shot. Often at night Sterl and Red could find no level place to pitch their tent. They would drop on the ground, cover their heads against mosquitoes, and sleep like logs nevertheless. More and more, Sterl inclined to the truth of Red's caustic forecast.

They came to a V-shaped valley, which led up to the deceiving pass. It was short as actual miles went, but long on labor to progress up it. The wagons had to follow a rocky streambed where stone bridges needed to be laid over deep channels. The mob split to follow the rough slopes where it required hours to drive them a mile. Rounding up cattle in Arizona cañons had been easier than this. Slyter loomed ahead of all the others in this toil of getting wagons and mob through rough going. He had been used to that in the hills back of Downsville. His judgment stood the trek to good stead here. This keen ability of his matched the leader's resistless passion to go on, and the magnificent horsemanship of the drovers. This was driving cattle and wagons through country where no cowboys would have ventured, because it was country no herd of horses should have been put to.

Ten nightmare days up this V-shaped valley. And then the trek seemed halted for good. Eric and Larry and Slyter returned in defeat from their scouting. But Friday, last to get back, galvanized their low spirits and energies.

"Go alonga me," he said, and the black had never failed them yet.

They hitched six horses to a wagon, and with a drover on each side, pulling with a lasso and whipping the teams, they hauled that wagon over the saddle. It took all the rest of that day to get the other wagons over. The mob had to be left behind in the valley until the morrow.

Riding across that saddle, Sterl, seeing the lay of the land ahead, groaned his disappointment at the apparently impenetrable labyrinth of jungle and rock-ribbed confines ahead. And he cursed in his bitterness the man accountable for this. Ten miles or more of incredibly tough going stretched ahead—a distance that might as well have been ten times that—and then a gap and a blue void.

"We will go on," declared Stanley Dann.

"We can't get through," averred Slyter.

"I've missed the way," added Eric Dann, aghast and faltering. No one paid any attention to him.

"Larry, Bligh, what do you say?" queried the leader.

They replied practically in unison that it looked very bad, well nigh impossible.

"Hazelton?" he boomed.

"Boss, we can't go back," said Sterl.

"Krehl!"

"Yes, sir," retorted the cowboy.

"What do you think?"

"Me? Wal, I ain't thinkin' a-tall," drawled the cowboy.

"Don't bandy your ridicule with me!" roared the leader. "If I'm still the leader of this trek . . . if you have any respect for me as such . . . think!"

"All right, boss. Excoose me. I ain't no mule-haid . . . I think we must find a way out thet we cain't see from heah."

"Right-o! Men, look for a place we can camp."

Sterl detained Friday on the ridge. "Friday, you've been looking all alonga here. What say?"

"Bad, boss," replied the black, shaking his ragged head.

"Can we get through?"

"Might be. Bimeby me go see."

They camped on the right side of the saddle at the base of a rugged slope. Firewood and water had to be picked up—a job Red and Sterl took upon themselves. There were not any idle hands any more. Even Beryl helped Mrs. Slyter at tasks to assist Bill. The other cook had been incapacitated.

"Sterl, don't forget Leslie is still down there," said Beryl appealingly. "Those horses will be the death of her yet."

"Les is all right, Beryl. Standing this trek as well as any of us. But you, girl, you've only begun to pick up. Please rest."

"Sterl, I'll do my bit," replied Beryl, smiling up at him. She might not have realized that she was telling him she had begun to learn a great lesson of life. How frail she looked, yet her sad face seemed lovelier than ever. She had courage—that thing Sterl respected more than all else in man or woman. If she lived, she would come through this fire pure gold. If! Sterl had a melancholy regurgitation of old emotions. They did not last. He went out along the saddle to look for Leslie. He could see the colored splashes of cattle along the green slopes. And in a fertile corner under the saddle he espied the horses.

There was gold in the hilltops in the distance—the last steps of dying day. Dully he comprehended that the scene might be grand, but he had no interest in it. He was tired. Depression gnawed at him, spiritually and physically. Then he espied Leslie climbing the slope on foot, in the track of the wagons. Presently she saw him and waved. Lithe and supple, browned by exposure, clear-eyed as a falcon, her drover's garb ragged and soiled, she always dragged a meed of praise from him.

"Howdy, Sterl. Been worrying about me?" she panted, a gauntletted hand at her full breast.

"No, Les. Only King and the remuda."

"King, Jester, Duke, Lady Jane, all tiptop. Sorrel is lame. Count is fagged out . . . oh, Lord! Is that what . . . we climbed out . . . to see? Sterl, will we ever, ever get through this Deception Pass?"

"I don't know . . . and don't care much."

"Sterl! . . . that's not like you. Oh, dear boy, you're worn out. You and Red have done the work of two men. So has everybody! After all, it's something to fight."

"Fight! What for?"

"To beat this trek."

"Les, you and Beryl make me a little ashamed," replied Sterl.

"Sterl, you and Red all through this terrible year . . . almost a year . . . have filled my heart, and Beryl's, and Mum's with courage to carry on. Small wonder that you lag a little now. But don't fail me, Sterl. And don't let Red fail Beryl. It is he who has saved her . . . who is changing her very soul. Oh, I know he seldom looks at her . . . never speaks to her. But no matter. She sees, she feels, she thinks. . . . Sterl, would you mind . . . holding me for a bit . . . like you used to?"

But Sterl evaded that, despite the warmth she stirred in his cold heart, and made excuses, and, talking kindly to her, he led her to camp. In the dusk they sat on the ground to eat and drink—not that they had appetite for the eternal fare which had become tasteless, but because of the need for strength. Darkness fell upon silent trekkers, some going to their beds, and others about their jobs, and all with plodding spirits, bowed but not broken.

It took all the next morning to drive the mob up over the saddle. Friday had returned from his scout below. To Stanley Dann he spread his wonderful, sinewy black hands, fingers wide. "Boss, might be cattle go alonga dere," he said, and manifestly he meant they should separate, as his fingers indicated, and streak through various channels to whatever lay at the end of that green maze.

Like a great waterfall the mob poured off the saddle, to roll and wag and clatter down, to disappear at will in the jungle. It was Sterl's opinion that they could not have followed the wagons, and perhaps that was what Friday had intimated. Nor could the drovers leave the wagons to try to hold the mob. But the horses were kept back to go with the wagons.

Then began a feverish and ceaseless labor of fourteen men to

chop and build a road for six wagons through ten miles of wilderness jungle. It was a Herculean task. It dwarfed all their former
labors put together. At first it was fraught with worry about the
cattle. After five days of digging, chopping, carrying rocks, packing supplies, wading all day long in mud and water and grass, all
the toilers except Stanley Dann and Slyter forgot about the cattle and horses. Every day Friday, whose duty it was to report on
the mob, as well as ferret out the best way through the jungle,
would say—"Cattle along dere farder."—and that day when he
said—"Cattle gone!"—there was not one of the trekkers who betrayed grief. It was now a battle for their lives. Without wagons
they could not freight supplies for so large a band, and without
supplies they would starve.

Their beef gave out, and two drovers, mounted on horses,
could not find even a crippled steer to shoot. Slyter swore he
would starve before he ate horseflesh, but the other men ate it,
and the women did so without being aware of the fact. Slyter
and Red and Sterl toiled all day at road making, and droved the
horses near camp at night. Leslie kept track of them by day.

During the daylight hours the flies were almost as fierce as at
the Forks, and at night the mosquitoes were so thick and blood-
thirsty that they would have killed an unprotected man. The
second cook practically died on his feet, sticking it out with fever
and dysentery, and then collapsing finally, after all. Monkton
was bitten by a death-adder, and for days his life was despaired of.
Injuries multiplied as the men grew so weary that they could not
be vigilant.

In the middle of that jungle Eric Dann made a startling pro-
posal. "We've got to abandon the wagons and pack out!"

It was midday, hot and muggy, when the men had halted a
half hour for tea and damper. Stanley Dann, dirty and sweaty
and bedraggled, gazed at this blood kin of his with great amber
eyes that had not lost their magnificent light.

"How about the women?" he asked.

"They can ride horseback. I asked Beryl. She said she could,"
Eric returned eagerly.

"We are two thousand miles from anywhere. Beryl would die."

"If she gave out . . . we could pack her," exclaimed this extraordinary man.

The giant shook his shaggy golden head wearily, as if it was useless to listen to his brother.

"We can't get through," bawled Eric Dann, his voice rising high. "I climbed up to see. We're not halfway! Man, would you sacrifice us all for your worthless daughter?"

When Stanley Dann rose to that jibe, all the mildness and weariness of him appeared never to have been. The swelling of his wide chest attested to what his outburst would be.

"Oh, I know," shouted Eric, yielding to the fear that was his major failing. "I've heard Ormiston's brag. Beryl was a fool over him . . . a vain, brazen. . . ."

Red Krehl leaped upon Dann and felled him. He would have killed the man, too, but for a sharp cry. Beryl and Leslie, coming from Beryl's wagon to the cook shack, had heard and seen. That cry and Beryl's presence obviated further violence on Red's part. But it could not silence him.

"I'm gonna kill this brother of yore's yet," bitterly predicted the cowboy. "Ain't it enough thet he got us into this hellhole . . . that he proposed we pack out of heah to save his own yellow hide? Ain't thet enough without his lowdown . . . ?"

"Red, don't kill Uncle Eric. Not for me!" cried Beryl passionately. "I'm not worth it. I *was* a fool. I *was* vain, brazen, mad! But Eric only knows the half. I plotted with Ash Ormiston . . . that he steal me from my bed. I was to go with him willingly. He meant to rush Dad's mob . . . to kill anyone who opposed him . . . especially to kill Eric, with whom he had plotted. I agreed to go with him to save Uncle Eric's life, and Dad from ruin, if not worse. But Ormiston betrayed me. He stole Dad's cattle. He would have murdered Uncle Eric but for me. He . . . he. . . ."

She broke down then. Leslie led her away from the stunned group of men. Eric Dann heard that denunciation, for he slunk away under a tree. Of all present, Sterl thought his friend Red seemed the most staggered by Beryl's revelation. But it was not in his case, as with the others, that Beryl's participation in Ormiston's plot had come to light. Red had known that. He had kept it secret from Sterl. And he knew now why the girl had betrayed him and her father and all of them. What a pity she had not remained there to see Red Krehl in that moment.

After what seemed a long silence, Stanley Dann said: "Men, we are being sorely tried, but let us not lose our faith in God and in each other. Krehl, I thank you for withholding from your creed. But I disagree with my daughter. She *is* worth all she disclaimed she was not."

"Wal, boss, if you ask me, I kinda reckon so myself," returned Red Krehl ponderingly.

"All of you back to work. We are going through!" boomed the leader.

Sterl bent for his shovel and whispered to his friend. "Pard, now another job of mine is to keep you from being shot in the back."

Before many more hours passed that break in their toil, with its resurging of lulled passions, was forgotten in the sheer physical prostration of effort that could not have been prolonged if life itself had not been at stake.

This was the only period so far on the trek that Stanley Dann neglected his record of travel. If they ever got through this fight with nature, it must be a black memory, a blank page.

When, at last, the implacable trekkers reached the end of that impasse and were sunk to their lowest ebb, the black man Friday found a gateway for them out into the open.

The hour came when they faced vastly different country from that which Eric Dann had pictured to them. No one except Sterl, perhaps, thought of Dann's mistake or falsehood.

A few miles below a gentle green slope, out upon a velvet green down, Stanley Dann's mob of cattle grazed in a great colorful patch. Beyond them spread endless green downs dotted with clumps of pandamus and palms, on and on, apparently forever, streaked by black fringes of trees, and bisected from league to league by shining water, and bordered by what resembled limitless purple horizon. That was what Sterl's eyes beheld, and that was why Stanley Dann boomed his prayer of gratitude to heaven. They were also so overjoyed to get clear of that awful jungle and the awful toil, to see the cattle peacefully grazing, that no one of them asked audibly where they were. They did not care. They were again delivered. Only Sterl thought of what Eric Dann had sworn, that the country beyond the range would be the same as the headwaters of the Diamantina.

Chapter Twenty-four

Days of leisurely and comfortable going now, over level downs with grass and water abundant. But one jarring fact—in a week's trekking, they reached a point opposite the flattening out of that range whose crossing had cost them so many supplies, so much toil and life. By a week's detour, they could have gone around it. Six weeks more than lost.

With firewood so scarce, whenever they found any dead wood Bill insisted on packing enough for the next camp. Flocks of wildfowl were seen in flight, but only herons and cranes were met on the downs. One flock of emus rewarded Sterl's unflagging gaze. Kangaroos were scarce. A number of small streams were forded every day; they ran every whither, but offered no obstacle to the trek.

Then, one afternoon late, the black, ragged line that had gradually grown for days turned out to be a good-size river. It flowed north. It presented a problem, not only to cross, but because the water, flowing the wrong way, upset their calculations. The Warburton, for which Dann thought he was trekking, would have flowed due west. According to the leader's rude map, when they crossed it, they would be headed north between the Never Never Land and the Gulf. They would head all the streams flowing into the Gulf. Sterl and Red agreed that this was good calculating on their leader's part. At Dann's conference, the first for a long time, Red and Sterl agreed with Slyter that they would like to get back along the fringe of these boundless downs, instead of crossing them.

"This is the Flinders River," asserted Eric Dann positively. "I remember it. Probably we are two or three hundred miles from the Gulf"

"Flinders River? Gulf?" Stanley echoed aghast. "That means salt-water, crocodiles, and cannibal aborigines!"

"Gosh!" ejaculated Red Krehl. A mention of those threats corroborated his doubts. "Boss, of course, hunches mean nothin' a-tall to you. But let's follow mine an' rustle back onto dry land."

Any suggestion of the cowboy's was to Eric Dann like waving a red flag at a bull.

"Stanley, it's along the fringe of the Never Never that bad blacks are to be encountered," he said impressively. "If we cross here and continue northwest, we'll avoid them."

"How do you know that?" demanded the leader intensely.

"I know it," returned Eric stubbornly.

"What *is* your objective?"

"Southeast of the Port Darwin," answered the brother glibly. "There are fertile ranges. We can choose to stop there, if you like, and send in to Darwin for supplies. I think you will decide for them, instead of the Kimberleys."

If Eric Dann was capable of absolute sincerity, here seemed to be the moment when he adhered to it. Perhaps this had been his scheme all along, since Ormiston would have none of him.

"Yes, true enough," mused the leader. "We have that information from more than one reliable source. It appeals to me for reasons of salvation. I could always move on to the Kimberleys. Eric, one more word before I say the die is cast. I never expected you to travel straight as a beeline to our objective. You have made mistakes . . . this last one, terrible! You will make more. But in your heart, are you honest?"

Before the stern and just leader, the hawk-eyed cowboys and

the dubious Slyter with his drovers, Eric Dann solemnly asserted his truth. But to the soul-searching Sterl, used to watching men where greed and hate and life and death hang in the balance, the man was a liar.

Four days were consumed in crossing this river; and it turned out that Dann's elaborate plans were unnecessary. The maintaining of a camp on each side, so as to guard both cattle and supplies seemed a wise move. But no aborigines appeared, and the cattle were too tame to get out of their own tracks, except to graze.

The river, which Leslie called the Muddy, appeared to be fresh-water, although it had a weedy taste, and the middle channel had to be swum. Neither accident nor injury marked the crossing of the wagons, although it took dragging and persistent labor. Friday had averred—"No croc' along here."—which good news of the absence of the fearful twenty-foot crocodiles of the Northland was received with gratification.

Early on the fourth day, with four wagons and the horses safely across, the mob of five thousand cattle was started. All the drovers took part in this. They expected any and all kinds of trouble. But they had none. The mob waded and swam across in an hour, a record job, with one drawback only, which was that they spread nearly a mile along the far shore.

Dann's big wagon, which was Beryl's domicile, presented a problem. The drovers, particularly Eric who had come to regard himself as more than a guide, wasted time arguing. Finally Stanley Dann took Red's advice. The wagon was driven out until the water was over hub deep on the wheels, and from there ten men on horseback packed the contents piece by piece. Then the big wagon was ferried across the deep channel with ropes and horses. By noonday it had been safely crossed and repacked.

Leslie and Beryl, with Friday, had been left to the last. Then Stanley Dann sent the cowboys, Larry and Rollie, back to fetch the girls.

"Where's a horse for me to ride?" demanded Beryl, as the bedraggled riders waded their horses out on the bank.

"Boss's order is for us to pack you over," Larry replied quite uneasily.

"Oh . . . so I'm a sack of flour . . . or maybe an empty one?" asked the girl sarcastically.

"Your dad didn't think you were quite strong enough to ride," went on Larry.

To Sterl's surprise, and certainly to Red's, Beryl acquiesced without further remark. Sterl thought he could guess the reason.

"Sterl, will you pack me on King?" asked Beryl, turning away a little from the others. Certain it was that she winked one of her big violet eyes at Sterl.

"I couldn't think of it, Beryl," replied Sterl mildly.

"Beryl, I'd be afraid to risk you on this nag," put in Larry.

"I'll take you," interposed Rollie, who was as dense as he was kind.

"Pooh! On that horse? No, indeed," returned the young lady whose eyes had begun to sparkle.

Leslie, who had been about to protest with spirit and perhaps berate those drovers, happened to meet Sterl's glance, and then she bit her tongue.

"Red, I'd feel safer with you on Duke. He's so big," said Beryl casually, with downcast eyes. "Besides, you have packed me before."

"Yeah? Wal, why didn't you wear yore pants?" returned Red, far removed from gallantry in this instance.

Beryl flushed vividly at that blunt query. "I haven't worn my riding clothes for a long time."

"You cain't straddle a hoss in thet dress."

"I couldn't, Mister Krehl . . . and look decent," retorted Beryl, whose temper was seldom proof against Red.

"Wal, you might have thought to put on yore nightgown," drawled Red, as deadly cool as if he were facing a man who had provoked him.

"*Red!*"

"Come on. Gimme yore hand . . . stick yore foot in my stirrup. Aw! . . . so Mister Hazelton has to butt in!"

Sterl had leaped off to help Beryl up in front of Red. She was so slim that she fitted across his knees. Red put his left arm around her, and Beryl put her right arm about his neck. Anyway Sterl looked at the position, it was an embrace—reluctant on Red's part, subtly willing on Beryl's. She laid her head back and looked up at him.

"Red, it won't take long," said Sterl in cheery significance. But he did not mean the trip across.

"I don't care how long it takes ... if only ... ," murmured Beryl, with a hint of her old audacity.

There was nothing revengeful or unresponsive in Red Krehl. Sterl caught a fleeting glimpse of the soft yearning glow in Beryl's violet eyes. There would not have been any use or any sense in trying to resist that. Sterl dated his faith in Beryl Dann's awakening from that moment. How could she help but love the cowboy? But Red's reaction was as natural as his sincerity was hidden.

"Slope along, Duke," he drawled. "Pick out thet deep hole, fall in, an' never come up!"

Red entered the river with Larry close on one side and Rollie on the other. Leslie waited for Sterl, who watched the trio for a moment before he started. Then he became aware of Leslie's poignant joy at sight of Beryl in the cowboy's arms. It amused him, yet somehow he liked Leslie the better.

"Oh, Sterl! Isn't love wonderful!" she sighed dreamily.

"It must be. I can't speak from personal experience, as evidently you can, but real love must be wonderful."

"That's true, you devil!" flashed Leslie, disrupted from her sweet trance, and she rode out ahead of him, splashing the water in great sheets.

Sterl idled along, reflecting sadly that this little byplay had been the first pleasantry, the first lessening of the raw tension, for many a week.

Dann's caravan covered in five days some fifty miles of green downs, not one long or short stretch of it differing noticeably

from any other. Its beauty palled; its sameness irritated the
nerves; its monotony grew unbearable. Level as it was, its coars-
ening grass, its creeks and ruts, made hard going. A scarcity of
bird and animal life gradually augmented an impression of barrenness.

But on that fifth day darker and apparently higher ground broke
the level horizon. Sterl feared it was a mirage. Two more days'
travel proved this broken land consisted of low ridges and round
areas covered with dense but scrubby timber. The hope of everyone was that this change in the monotony of the downs heralded
higher and drier land beyond. No blue foothills, however, loomed
above the wandering black line of scrub. And the day came when
Sterl, gazing backward, could no longer see the shadowy purple
ranges. They kept on the northwest, traveling by compass.

"Slyter," said Sterl, at Blue Grass camp, "if we are trekking
through this country to get to the headwaters of the Warburton . . . it's all right. But if we are trekking *deeper* into these
downs. . . ."

"Good heavens, Sterl . . . that's on my mind, too!" exclaimed
the drover, when Sterl paused.

"Aren't you afraid of it?"

"I am. And you?"

"It's beginning to get me. Friday says . . . 'Tinkit allsame
alonga bimeby water plenty.'"

"And there's no smoke signals of the blacks."

"Red says if we follow this four-flush Eric Dann much farther,
we'll be lost."

"We're the same as lost now, Sterl. But I won't nag Stanley any
more. He's set. We're going through, he swears. Says to remember the bad times before . . . how we always came out."

"What season is it?"

"Autumn. Some time ago, when I asked Stanley, it was late in
May. We've been gone long over a year."

"Is that possible? But time means little to me any more."

"But, Sterl, we must keep hopeful, for the sake of the women.
They are standing this hellish trek better than we men."

"They are! Only yesterday Red said to me . . . 'Pard, I gotta hand it to these females. Talk about them bein' the weaker sex. Haw! Haw! They got us men skinned to a frazzle.'

"Slyter, human nature can stand only so much. Still we have no idea how much that is. . . . I'm tired. Something is happening to my mind. It's sick, maybe. I find it hard to think. But, my friend, I can swear for Red and me . . . we haven't begun to fight."

"Bless you both, son. You've had a great training for such a trek as this. But I'm fighting. And so is Stanley."

"A-huh. What is Eric doing?"

"Lord save us! I don't know. But he thinks he's guiding us right."

Days and days and days! And dark, cool, dewy nights, when the stars blazed white, the bitterns boomed from the reed-bordered lakes and streams, and the owls hooted dismally to the pandamus scrub. The moon soared in the sky, blanching the endless downs. Solitude reigned. The loneliness was terrible. Sterl fought a feeling that they had reached the end of the world. Insupportably slowly the trek went on into this forbidding land of grass.

They came at length into a stranger, blacker, wilder country. The dense growth of bush denoted a river—a river somewhere beyond the dark fringe of giant ash trees and bloodwoods and enormous big trees with their multiple trunks, grotesque and gnarled.

Camp was pitched where the wagons halted at the edge of the forest, where a huge, wide-spreading banyan afforded thick, green canopy for the whole caravan. A boiling spring of sweet water ran away from the bank of bushland, forming a little stream that meandered away toward a pale lake, black and white with waterfowl. Birds of species known to Slyter and many he had never seen enlivened the scene, but did not dispel its sinister mood.

Stanley Dann christened this camp. He sat at the driver's seat of his wagon and gazed at the gloomy, impenetrable bush.

"'In the midway of this, our mortal life, I found me in a gloomy wood, astray,'" he quoted sonorously, then added: "Doré's Bush."

"Wal, who in the hell was this guy Doré?" drawled Red.

"Pard, according to his pictures, he's been in hell all right, so as usual your guess is correct," returned Sterl.

Friday completed the mystic picture as, with long spear forward, he stalked under the green canopy.

But for that dismal mood of bushland, its forbidding aspect, this camp would have been ideal. The grass was rich and abundant, and the mob bunched out in the open, contentedly grazing. Kookaburras flew under the trees, perched on branches to watch the intruders, but they were silent. That strange feature alone affected the morbid trekkers. The sun slanted in what appeared the wrong direction. Sterl was completely turned around. Red wearily said he did not give a damn, and that he wished what was going to happen would come *pronto*. The lean, bronzed drovers performed their tasks and stood around Bill's campfire with hungry eyes. Some of them helped. Eric Dann sat apart, burdened by whatever he had on his mind. Stanley wrote in his journal. Slyter and Leslie mustered their horses on the green between the mob and the bush. Beryl leaned back in the seat of her wagon with the flap rolled up, and her big eyes, dark, brooding, fixed intently upon Red Krehl. Sterl cursed under his breath and yearned passionately for something to happen to break this spell which had fixed upon all with a deadening clamp.

Bill beat upon a tin pan to call them to supper. Parrots and cockatoos flocked squalling out of the trees. Friday appeared, glistening in the sinister rays of the sunset. Always impressive, there was that in his mien to induce awe. All the trekkers mutely interrogated him, then the leader boomed: "What ho, Friday?"

"Plenty bad black fella alonga dere. Big ribber. Plenty croc'. Plenty salt."

They were crushed. Stanley Dann sat with his elbows on his knees, his broad hands over his golden beard. The corded veins stood out upon his bronzed brow. His huge frame writhed as if to release itself.

"Lost!" he ejaculated in a hollow voice. "Hundreds of miles out of our way."

"Salt water!" burst out Slyter appalled.

"It must be the Flinders River," croaked Eric Dann hopefully.

"Wha-at?" roared the giant. "According to you, we crossed the Flinders weeks back!"

"But, afterward, I remembered it was not. This is the Flinders. Near its source, hundreds of miles in winding course from the Gulf. We are right. Once across we will find higher ground."

He seemed so fired with inspired certainty that his listeners, grasping at straws, sustained a renewal of hope. Even Sterl. But Red eyed the pallid and shaky-handed drover with a fixed glare of derision. Stanley Dann, quick always to rise above doubt, called them all to eat. He might as well have boomed out: "This Doré's Bush is the end of another phase of the great trek . . . tomorrow will begin a new day, a new trek toward the promised land. Carry on!"

In the gray of the cool dewy dawn the guards rode in; the ring of axes awoke the bush echoes; the camp stirred to life. The sun rose bloody on the wrong side, and the lonely, melancholy day began.

"Spread along the river to find a place to cross," ordered Stanley Dann to his drovers.

Below camp some distance, Sterl and Red and Larry found an opening in the bush where the mob could be driven to the river, and where a road could be opened for the wagons.

"Look dere," called Friday, who strode beside Sterl, and he pointed to smoke signals, rising beyond the break in the bush. "Imm black fella know."

"Wal, they wanna steer clear of this outfit," returned Red grimly. "Fellers, I cain't figger it a-tall, but I got goose pimples."

They rode through the opening, along with Friday in the lead, scaring the tiger snakes out of his path with his long spear, and presently emerged upon the low bank of a wide river. It differed greatly from streams the cowboys had ever seen. Slopes of yellow mud ran a hundred yards out to meet a turgid channel of muddy water about the same width, and from a far edge the opposite slope ran a farther distance up to the bush.

"Tide running out. Swift, too," observed Larry.

"Gosh, you mean this heah is tidewater?" queried Red.

"It must be. Friday said it was salt water. If that mud is soft, we're in for a cropper."

"Friday, go alonga, see how deep mud," said Sterl.

Ankle-deep the black waded some rods out, and then began to sink in deeper and deeper until he was over his knees. From his exertions wading back Sterl concluded that mud would be a sticky and dragging medium for cattle.

"Not so good," averred Red.

"In fact, it is rotten," added Sterl.

"Even with the tide in full, the mob would have to wade a bit, at least close to shore," observed Larry seriously. "And the wagons. That will be a job to cross them here."

"Right-o. But it can be done. We'd cut poles and brush to make a road. Thet channel buffaloes me, though. What say, Sterl?"

"Boys, without the menace of crocodiles, which Friday mentioned, we'd have a killing job here."

"I don't see any of them damn' varmints. Do you?"

"Not looking for them."

"But, pard, suppose this . . . mud hole is full of crocodiles?"

"Heavens, Red! Haven't we enough to worry about? Say, Larry, how big do these Gulf crocodiles grow?"

"Up to twenty-five feet, I've heard. They can break a man's leg with one whack of their tails."

"Holy Mackeli!" ejaculated Red. "I oughta go back an' bore Eric Dann before some big croc' plays Jonah an' the whale with me."

"Fellows, I'll bet you Dann cracks before we get across this river," asserted Sterl.

"Wal, thet won't do us any good now. But I hope he croaks."

"Red, *how* will we get the girls across?"

"Aw, that's a sticker. I was thinkin' about it. If we only had a boat! Mebbe we could build a raft. In a pinch we might use the bed of our wagon . . . but I wonder . . . should we go across?"

"Red, we can't help ourselves."

"Shore we cain't. But we can wonder. Somehow I've a hunch this river will bust us. Gets my nerve, somehow. I'd as lief face the Brazos in flood with a band of Comanches on the other side."

"Yeah? Well, I'd a damn' sight rather, too. This has got me stumped. Let's ride back. Maybe somebody has found a better crossing."

They rode to camp as had Slyter and Benson and the other drovers who had ranged still farther up the river. They reported no possible crossing. Stanley Dann, dark of visage, turned to Sterl and his comrades.

"Boss, there's a ford below. But it looks awful tough."

Red added: "It'll be tougher than it looks."

Larry corroborated these statements and enlarged upon them.

"Mister Dann, cain't we get out of tacklin' this heah river?" Red queried anxiously.

"Impossible! I'm surprised you ask, Krehl," exploded the leader.

"But, sir, if you'll excuse me, I cain't see no reason for it, except to keep on this wild goose chase. It might be better to travel up this river two hundred miles to haid it rather than try to cross heah."

"Krehl, this is the first instance you've shown hesitancy in the face of an obstacle," declared Dann testily.

"Yes, sir, thet's true," returned Red, remarkably mild for him. "I'm shore hesitatin'. But the reason is, I'm not quite bughouse, as this two-bit guide of yores is."

"Bughouse? Will you please be explicit. Speak English. If you know how."

"Wal, boss, I don't speak your language a-tall," retorted Red, now cool and biting. "But all the same I feel beholden to you. Only this heah last job yore brother has hipped on is the wust."

"Krehl, I'd go look the ford over, but what good would that do?" returned the chief patiently.

"Hell, no! We can go back a ways, an' thet'd save an orful job, a lot of cattle, an' somebody's life shore as Gawd made little apples! You're a great guy, Dann. Yore a cattleman as big as all this heah outdoors. You've been a great leader in every way but on these rivers. But a dry land drover. It's the rivers thet have stuck you. An' as you don't savvy rivers, I was hopin' I could turn you back from this one."

Perhaps no man of the open could have heard unmoved this simple, forceful plea of the cowboy's. Certainly Dann and Slyter, the drovers and Sterl himself did not. But Eric Dann's abnormal and malignant obsession again protruded its hydra-head.

"Krehl is afraid," he shouted hoarsely. "Once and for all, I demand to be heard! I will not stand any more opposition, especially from such a source. Who could have helped but make mistakes on this trek? Nevertheless, no foreigner is going to upset my plans to make me ridiculous."

"Brother, there is more than your plans upset," rejoined the leader darkly. "I ask you once more and for the last time . . . do you know what you're doing to put us against this river?"

"Yes, I know. I know, too, that Krehl is afraid. Ask him yourself. I'll ask him. See here, cowboy, are you man enough to confess the truth . . . that you *are* afraid? I see it in you."

Red Krehl gave the drover a long, uncomprehending gaze. Dann was, indeed, a new one for the Texan. Then he spoke: "Hell, yes. I shore am afraid of this river, the croc's, an' the aborigines. But I reckon I oughta be more afraid of you, Mister Dann. Because you're a queer mixture of fool, liar, an' crook."

Sterl felt hot under the collar through all this argument, but he restrained himself until it ended, then he addressed the leader. "Dann, I want you to know and to remember . . . that I strongly advise against the attempt to cross this river."

Dann threw up his hands at this stern and inflexible speech.

He was influenced, although not deeply enough. There was no telling what he thought, but his immutability was manifest. "Sorry, but we cross!"

But the river and the tide had something to say about that, and, when they were right, as nearly as the drovers thought they could be, then the cattle had the last word. This mob had been extraordinarily docile and easily managed as the cowboys knew cattle. Many of the bulls and cows that had distinguishing spots or horns or habits that brought them into daily notice had become veritable pets. Toward the end of that first day, however, they manifested evidences of the contrary dispositions which Australian cattle were noted for in the bush. About mid-afternoon, they stopped grazing and became uneasy. Friday was the first to report this. It corroborated the feeling of the drovers. Slyter went out to observe the herd for himself. Upon his return he announced: "For some reason or other they dislike this place."

"Ha! Our feeling has been communicated to the mob. But the water is sweet, the grass rich. Surely they will settle down presently."

"If they don't, we are in for a night of it. I wouldn't care to try to stop a rush in this bush at night."

The cattle did not settle down. They bawled and stirred and pressed away from the river bush. They had to be held by the drovers.

"Might be smellum croc's," said Friday.

"Umpumm," averred Red. "I can't smell an alligator as far as a polecat. But there's shore somethin' round heah that smells queer."

Flying foxes had appeared during the afternoon, great, wide-winged, grotesque bats, flapping out of the bush over the cattle, and their dark number increased toward sunset. It developed that this dark bush was the home of thousands of these strange flying mammals, and, as night approached, they increased in numbers. Out of the huge fig tree right over camp the uncanny, slinky, silky creatures emerged to flap swishingly away out over the herd. From all along the edge of the bush they streaked out.

"Shore, it's them dinged bats thet have the herd buffaloed, an' they're gonna get us, too," said Red. But Slyter and Dann did not agree with Red.

"You can never tell what will start a mob," declared Dann. "Often the cause of rushes is never known. But there's something here that worries them."

"Wal, I should snicker to snort there is," drawled Red pessimistically. "If it ain't bats, it's alligators, an' if it ain't them, it's thet cussed river, an' if it ain't thet, it's jest a feelin' they've gone far enough."

"Krehl, I agree with you," returned Dann. "But as it is something we cannot help, we must meet it."

Here was one camp where a fire did not flame brightly. The wood burned as if it was wet, and the smoke was acrid. The girls particularly exclaimed against it. They hated the big bats, too, and added materially to the evil impression of Doré's Bush. Then night settled down black, with the stars obscured by the foliage on three sides. Sterl was not the last to wish they were out of there. Mosquitoes were not abundant, but they made up in ferocity for what they lacked in numbers.

Supper had been eaten and five drovers had ridden out on guard, when all left in camp were startled by a low, weird sound off in the bush, apparently across the river.

"Black fella *corroboree*. Imm no good," said Friday, his long black arm aloft.

The trekkers stood and sat around the fire, listening, not one in a mood to ask questions or tell what they felt. Eric Dann, sitting with his head drooped, manifested extreme depression. Stanley paced to and fro. The women left off their tasks and instinctively pressed close to the others at the campfire. The black bush, the dank odor, the moaning across the river fell heavily and dishearteningly upon all.

This fearful silence, that was accentuated by the low chant, suddenly broke into a trampling roar of hoofs. The cowboys were as quick to leap up as Larry and Rollie. Slyter came thudding from his wagon. Eric Dann lifted a pale and haggard face. Stanley Dann swore a great oath.

"Aw, I knowed it," Red said grimly. "Come on, Sterl. Let's rustle our hosses."

"Wait, you cowboys," ordered Dann. "Some of us must guard camp. Larry, Roland. Call Benson and join the drovers out there."

Slyter made off with the hurrying drovers, shouting something about his horses. Those left at the campfire were joined by Bill and Mrs. Slyter, and all stood listening to that stampede. Friday, at the edge of the circle of light, turned to the others and yelled: "Tinkit mob run alonga here!"

"My God!" boomed Stanley Dann, lifting his great arms in a gesture of horror. "Will they rush camp? Stand ready, all! If the mob comes this way, take to the trees!"

The increasing roar, the quaking sound, held all those listeners fraught with suspense and panic for an endless moment.

"Stampede'll miss us!" yelled Red Krehl.

Friday stooped to make violent motions with his right arm, indicating that the herd was rushing in that direction. It sounded close, but really was not, although it certainly came toward the river. Gunshots banged faintly out of the black, to leave it blacker. That mob of cattle had evidently rushed straight for the river. The camp happened to be located a little below the point for which they were making. But the terrified women could not yet be sure of that. They clung to the men.

"*All right! We're safe!*" yelled Sterl, and then felt himself sag under the release of tension. It had been a terrible few moments of uncertainty.

Then a crashing augmented the trampling roar. The stampede had run into the bush, evidently pointed up the river. What a knocking, cracking, continuous crash! The noise lasted for minutes before it began to lessen in volume. Soon the cattle ran on out of hearing.

"Providence saved us again," rang out Stanley Dann in immense relief. "But this rush will be bad for the mob."

"Dog-gone bad for the drovers, too, I'd say," declared Red.

"You may well think so. One of the worst things a drover can experience is to stop a rush at night in the bush. I've known drovers to be killed. But usually a mob does not rush long. I am hopeful."

"They might stampede into the river," interposed Sterl.

Eric Dann sat down again and bent his gaze upon the ruddy fire embers. Sterl did not desire to know that man's thoughts. The mosquitoes buzzed around like dragonflies. Again the mournful wail of the aborigines at their chant became audible and haunting. The flying-foxes swished overhead; up in the trees they rustled and squeaked. In the dim firelight their black grotesque shapes could be discerned, hanging heads and wings spread from the branches.

Someone had thoughtfully rolled a short log to one side of the fire and placed some packs on the other side for seats. It was necessary to sit close to the heat and smoke to be even reasonably safe from the mosquitoes. Eric Dann, however, sat back in the shadow. Not improbably he had too much on his mind to feel bites. The rush of the mob had apparently interested him. Stanley Dann stalked in and out of the circle of light. Presently Slyter returned to camp.

"Horses all right, nothing to worry about there," he was saying to Dann as they approached the fire. "The rush was bad. But half the mob was not affected."

"That was strange. Usually cattle follow the leaders like sheep. Uncanny sort of a place."

"Right-o. I jolly well wish we were out of it. Hello, Mum. You and Les should be in bed."

"I see ourselves, with the mob threatening to run us down. And Stanley calling to us to climb trees!" retorted his good wife. "But we'll go now."

"Beryl, that would be a good idea for you," said her father.

"I'm afraid to go to bed," replied the girl petulantly.

"Me, too," added Leslie. "These sneaky, furry bats give me the creeps. I just found one in our wagon. Put my hand on it in the dark. Ugh!"

"Well, as long as Sterl and Red have to sit up, waiting, I suppose it's all right for you girls, too. But it's not a very cheerful place for courting."

Beryl let out a scornful little laugh. "Courting! Whom on earth with?"

"Sometime back it was royalty condescending. Now it's how the mighty have fallen," returned Mrs. Slyter subtly, and left them to join her husband and Dann for a cup of tea.

"Leslie, whatever did your mother mean by that cryptic speech?" asked Beryl, annoyed.

"Oh, Mum's got softening of the brain," returned Leslie, and she dropped down on the log very close to Sterl. He could not move over for her, because he was at the end. Red, who sat across the fire from them, gave them a glance and then looked up at Beryl, who was standing. In the firelight against that eerie background with her fair hair and her great, dark eyes, she made an arresting picture.

"Say, all you women have softenin' of the brain," he drawled.

"Yeah?" queried Leslie.

"Is that so, Mister Krehl?" added Beryl.

"Yes, it's so. Take thet crack of Leslie's mother, for instance. She meant spoonin', didn't she?"

"That's what you crude Yankees call it," Beryl retorted, spoiling for a fight.

"Beryl, haven't I told you lots of times that Sterl an' I air not Yankees?"

"You have. But I don't care."

"Wal, Les's ma an' you girls air of one mind, I reckon, so far as men are concerned. The idee is to collar a man, any man temporarily, till you meet up with one you aim to corral for keeps."

"That's true, Red. Disgustingly true," admitted Beryl, suddenly frank and earnest. "But Les and I are not to blame for this female of the species business."

"I reckon not, Beryl," returned Red, conciliated by her sincerity.

Leslie laid her head back on Sterl's shoulder, and he, sympathetic as well as devilish, put his arm around her. Both actions were plain to Beryl and the cowboy, and seemed, in fact, like waving a red flag at belligerents.

"Go on, Red. You *were* going to say something," went on Beryl.

"I was, an' though mebbe I'm kinda ashamed of it, I won't show no white feather," rejoined the cowboy, ponderingly for him. "It seemed to me kind of far-fetched an' silly . . . thet sentimental yearnin' of yores, if it *was* thet. Heah we air lost in this gawd-forsaken land. Aw, I know Eric there swears we ain't lost, but that doesn't fool me. An' this hole is as spooky an' nasty a place as I ever camped. It's more. It's a darned dangerous one. We jest escaped somethin' tough. Thet stampede might jest as well run over our camp. Shore we'd all got safe up in trees, but no matter. What might had happened to our supplies an' belongin's? I hate to think of it, because I've been in camps thet buffalo stampeded over. Bad enough without girls on yore hands! What with that an' the alligators an' the blacks, why, we'll have the wust hell yet. An' thet's why I jest wondered at you womenfolk, feelin' thet soft, sweet, mushy sentiment in the face of hell, an' mebbe death."

"Red Krehl, that's the wonder of it . . . that we *can* feel and need such things at such a time," returned Beryl eloquently. "I left such things behind, to come with my father, to help make a new home for him. I could have gone to live in Sydney. I could have married there in Downsville. But I came with Dad . . . with you. And you've seen something of what I've suffered. But you have no appreciation of how I feel. Even if I were the most selfish girl, which I am not, I could have not deserved the misery I've already endured. This hard experience has not wholly destroyed my sensitiveness, my former habits. I can see the point of Sterl's old argument about us going bush. I can see that we'll turn into aborigines, if we're stuck here forever. But just now, I'm a dual nature. By day I'm courageous, by night I'm cowardly. I can't sleep. I'm afraid of noises. I lie with the cold chills creeping over me. I am morbid and fearful. I conjure up the most horrible imaginings. I can't forget what . . . what has already happened to me. I nearly went mad, you know. It was this sensitive side of me I'm trying to explain about . . . Red Krehl, you said you wonder at me. But I say it's a wonder you cannot see how I'd welcome any kindness, any attention, any affection, any boldness, even from *you at least*, to keep me from thinking."

It was a long speech, although quickly spoken, one that Sterl took to his heart in shame and self-reproach. He was intensely curious to see how Red would take it, and somehow he had faith in the cowboy's greatness of soul, if not intelligence.

"Come heah, girl," said Red gently, and held out his hand. Beryl stepped to him and leaned, as if compelled. He drew her to a place beside him on the narrow pack, and he put his arm around her to draw her close. "Now, look at them silly fools acrost there an' think all the dreamy things you can about them. I'm sorry I made all them hard cracks about this place. Only I'm glad, 'cause I understand you better. But Beryl, I reckon you cain't figger me out. When all was goin' fine back on this trek . . . it seems long ago now . . . you gave me plenty bad times. I don't forget them, as you seem to have done. Thet's *one* reason why I cain't help you not to think. On the other hand, this trek has worked deep on me. I've seen all along what was comin'. I see it heah, an' wuss than ever. I'm a queer duck thet way. Sterl calls me psychic, whatever thet is. But I do have queer hunches. So, even if I wanted to be sweet an' soft about you, which I shore cain't after the way you treated me, I couldn't be on account of what this damn' trek has made me. All thet's opposite to soft an' sweet, Beryl! I've saved yore life a coupla times, an' I reckon I'll have to do thet a heap more. If I wasn't a hard-ridin', hard-shootin' cowboy, a killer, grim an' mean, I couldn't do thet much for you. Thet ought to make you see me clear, and be glad that I am as I am."

"Oh, Red," Beryl cried poignantly, as she gazed up at him in the fading light, "I don't want you any different."

They had forgotten Sterl and Leslie, and Eric Dann back in the shadow, and the others. For Sterl it was sweet and exalting to see Beryl leaning to his friend, yearning to be forgiven and taken in his arms, to see Red shaken by his Homeric mood, yet still proof to her allurement. The thud of hoofs disrupted this scene with its potentialities, and in another moment Larry rode up to the fire. Friday came running to throw brush upon the blaze. The cowboys disengaged themselves to leap to their feet. Larry almost fell off his horse. Slyter and Dann came thudding out. The fire blazed up brightly.

"Larry, you're all bloody!" exclaimed Sterl.

"What came off, you?" added Red, taking Larry's arm. "Have you been speared?"

"No. Just ran into a snag," panted the drover. "Let me sit down."

Dann arrived to bend over Larry. "Bad scalp cut. Girls, fetch water and linen. Larry, are you all right?"

"Yes, sir . . . except played out."

"Where are the other drovers?"

"Back with what . . . was left of the mob. That rush got away, sir."

"How many?"

"I don't know. Benson said one third of the mob. They rushed into the bush. We drove after them . . . hell for leather! They were a crazy lot of cattle. They crashed through the bush . . . some into the river. We drove them by sound. It was pitch dark. Bad going. We couldn't hear them. They got away. So we yelled to come together . . . then rode back. That mob will work out of the bush by morning. Maybe we can ring them then."

Meanwhile, Dann had unwound the bloody scarf from Larry's head and began to dress the wound. Slyter told the girls to go to bed, and this time they obeyed. Red was sent off to take Larry's place with the drovers, and Sterl told to stay in camp. It developed that the night was far spent. Sterl sat beside the campfire while the black stalked into the bush and out again, listening, peering. He did not trust the place. All sounds but those of the flying-foxes ceased, and the silence seemed more pregnant with the meaning of Doré's Bush.

When toward dawn Red and Rollie came in, relieved by two of Dann's drovers, Sterl lay down beside the cowboy. They got a couple of hours' sleep. The sun was up, when Friday called them.

"Where's black fella, Friday?"

"Alonga dere. No good. Hidum about. Watchum white man."

"Sterl, these aborigines up heah 'pear to be a different breed. All same Comanche Injuns," said Red.

"I'd rather they came out in the open. What will Dann do to-day?"

"Hah! Thet guy will do things. Take it from me."

"And if we judge from how Larry was cut up, all those drovers will be crippled."

"Right-o. Did you ever see a rider as ragged as Larry was?"

"Game fellow, Red, and don't you forget it."

"I ain't forgettin', pard. Nor am I forgettin' about those girls."

"Oh, Lord! I never saw their beat. Beryl, used to luxury, comfort, adulation . . . fighting all this bush life! Leslie, girl of the open, horse-lover, game as any man, and almost as strong!"

"Yeah? I reckoned thet much wasn't left in you, pard. So what the hell will we do?"

"Red, you ask me that . . . for the hundredth time?"

"Shore I ask you . . . you aborigine."

"I don't know. You tell me."

"Wal, we gotta get madder'n hell. Madder'n we ever was. Full of thet somethin' which keeps Dann an' Slyter up."

"Red! How can we? They are Australians. Their incentive is great. We're only a couple of adventure-seeking outcasts."

"Hell, no! We ain't nothin' of the kind. These people shall be our people . . . their ways our ways . . . their cause our cause."

"Red, you have me tied to a hitching post for being a real man," returned Sterl with a sigh.

"I ain't so damn' shore. Come on. It's another day."

They found the drovers straggling in. Benson reported two thirds of the mob left. With ragged garb, scratched hands, bruised faces they gave evidence of what strenuous effort had been given to heading that rush. Bligh and Derrick were the last to come in. And their torn and blackened appearance spoke eloquently.

"We headed the rush, five miles west," reported Bligh wearily. "They're out in the open, not many on their feet. De-horned, crippled, snagged . . . a sorry mess!"

"Bligh . . . Derrick!" exploded the leader. "What can I say?" Obviously there was nothing to say. But it did not seem an anti-climax for Dann to offer them a choice between whiskey and tea, and that they chose the latter.

Friday appeared carrying a kangaroo that he had speared.

"Plenty 'roo," he said. "Ribber full up. Plenty croc'."

"What's he mean?" queried Red anxiously. " 'Gators or croc's?"

"Both species in these northern rivers," replied Slyter. "But only the crocodiles are big and dangerous."

"Friday, see any more blacks?" asked Sterl.

"Black fella imm alonga bush. Bimeby."

"Men, eat and drink all you can hold," said Stanley Dann. "Stuff your pockets full of damper and meat."

That order elicited no reply. Manifestly Dann had made his plan, and the suggestion was ominous. One by one the drovers gorged themselves, and then waited for they knew not what. Eric Dann moved among them, yet strangely did not see any of them. At length they were all through, waiting fatefully upon their leader's words.

"Listen sharp," he began, and his voice rang. "We'll leave those cattle that rushed last night until the last. If they stray too far or scatter, we'll abandon them. Our mob has been too large . . . we'll break camp now. Move all the wagons and horses to the open break in the bush below. Then drove the main mob closer. Two guards on and off for two hours. We'll ford the river with the wagons, split up our party, and camp on each side until the last job, which will be to drove the mob across."

It was a bold and masterly plan, Sterl conceded, as far as purpose was concerned. The execution remained to be an inspiration of genius and an heroic job. They mounted and rode away.

In less than two hours the wagons had been hauled to the new campsite. The cowboys and Leslie drove Slyter's horses. The Dann horses, still a hundred odd in number, were moved by two of his drovers, and then all, except Larry and Sterl, mustered the mob and drove it within sight of camp.

The day was perfect. Wildfowl, parrots, cockatoos, flocks of other birds, and kangaroos everywhere, enlivened the scene, and robbed the bush and downs of the menace that abided there by night.

But the river! The drovers, even their leader, had only to go within sight of that reed-bordered, mud-sloped, yellow-swirling tide to be affronted by seeming impossibilities. These, however, had no place in Stanley Dann's lexicon. The courage of men could accomplish what their doubts and fears made hopeless.

"Friday, where are the crocodiles?" boomed Dann.

"Alonga here," replied the black, his spear indicating the river and the margins of reeds.

"Slyter, do they hide in the grass?"

"Yes, indeed. These big croc's live on animals. This water is brackish. I tasted it. Kangaroos, wild cattle, brumbies would drink it. I've been told how the croc's lie in wait and with one terrific lash of their tails knock an animal or an aborigine into the water. They will snap at the nose of a drinking or swimming animal and drag it under."

"They may not be plentiful. But all of you use your eyes. Have you guns ready. Slyter, you will drive your wagon in first. Send a drover ahead to test the bottom. Larry, Krehl, Hazelton . . . help Bill pitch camp while Friday keeps an eye on the mob. The rest of you make ready to go with Slyter. Unhitch his teams. Drove them across. Pack ropes and tackles. Come back to unload his wagon. Make haste, while the tide is in."

They all watched Heald wade his sturdy horse into the river. They were all fearful of the unseen perils. But nothing untoward transpired. Heald waded perhaps a hundred steps, before his horse got up to his flanks. Then he returned to say: "Mud bottom. Soft. But not quicksand. If you keep your horse moving, you can make it."

"What will a heavy wagon do?" queried Slyter dubiously.

"It'll stick, but not sink," Dann declared. "We have heavy ropes and strong horses. We can pull out. Come on, Slyter."

Stanley Dann was the first to lead off in that uncertain venture. Sterl had always respected their leader as a man who would not order anyone else or ask any of them to do what he would not do himself. In a moment more Slyter drove the big teams into the river, accompanied by Dann and six drovers.

Slyter did not get quite so far out as Heald had waded. The wheels stuck. Two of the drovers leaped out of their saddles to unhitch the teams. Dann lifted a pack out of the wagon to his shoulder and waded his horse beyond its depth. That was one quarter of the way across. Bligh and Hod dragged the teams out. Rollie, with a bag in front of him and a cracking stock whip in hand, kept abreast of the teams. Soon they were swimming. Four drovers followed, carrying packs. Slyter stood up in his wagon, rifle in hand, watching vigilantly.

Sterl saw the reeds shake and part. "Grab your rifle, Red," he shouted, and then to Slyter: "Look out, boss. We'll watch the bank. You watch the water."

Suddenly on the opposite bank there was a loud rush in the reeds and then a *zoom*, as a huge reptile appeared quick as a flash, to leap off the bank and slide upon the narrow strip of mud. But it was not quick enough to escape Red's shot.

Sterl heard the battle thus, and then the huge reptile flopped up and flashed into convulsions. Sterl let out a yell as he drew a bead upon it and pulled the trigger. The distance was nothing to a marksman. His bullet, too, found its mark. The crocodile sent sheets of water and mud and blood aloft. Red fired another slug into it, as it slid off the slope. The bullet glanced with a spang.

"Ahaw! Look at thet bird," yelled Red, pointing up the bank to the left of the swimming horses. "Wants to know all about what's comin' off! Did you ever see such impudence? Wait, pard, till he comes all out."

Sterl had seen the reeds part and an ugly snout emerge followed by an immense head, with jaws wide, and a mud-colored, wide-shouldered crocodile crawl down the bank until all of his tremendous proportions were in sight.

"Now, pard! Bust him! Right in the middle!" shouted Red. Another four shots left that reptile rolling in the mud, snapping terrific jaws, lashing to and fro with its powerful tail. Its back must have been broken, for it made no progress into the river.

"Dere, along dere!" shrilled Friday, pointing below.

Slyter was shooting at another one, smaller and nimbler. But there was another rush and *zoom* as a big one catapulted off the bank to meet a hail of lead. Crippled and slow, he got into the river.

"Good work, boys," shouted Slyter. "We got some lead into them."

"Pard, I heah another one somewhere," said Red, peering up and down the river.

"I heard a splash. Might have been on this side," rejoined Sterl.

"Gosh! I reckon the critters air up an' down this river. Holy Mackeli! The size of them! Why, they could eat all our Texas alligators an' still be hungry."

Stanley Dann's horse appeared, wading out, laboring in the mud. But he made the low bank. Dann cheered his followers on. The drovers dragged and yelled at the teams, while Rollie cracked his long whip from behind. The issue was no longer in doubt, unless the beasts that infested the river halted their progress. Those few moments were tense for the watchers, and no doubt infinitely more so for the waders. But they got across and climbed the low bank, evidently to deposit the packs and find a place to land the wagon.

Then, Leslie and Beryl appeared to catch their breath and find their voices. But they did not get their color back. Mrs. Slyter shook an avenging finger at her husband.

"Bingham Slyter, if one of these beasts gets you, it'll be what you deserve for dragging us on this trek."

"Oh, Mum, how dreadful!" cried Leslie. "Sterl, here's one place I won't ride Lady Jane!"

"I should say not. Makes my hair stand up."

"Mine, too," drawled Red. "But I reckon it all depends on how many of them varmints there air."

Dann and his six drovers piled into the river pell-mell, keeping close together, some of them with drawn guns held high.

Slyter yelled: "Make all the commotion possible."

They crossed in short order and, loading heavily, turned back in haste, crossed again. It was skittish work while they were in deep water. Sterl was more than relieved to see them wade out again.

Suddenly Friday screeched out something aboriginal. Then Slyter roared unintelligibly, and began to pump lead into the water. A thumping splash followed, then a vicious churning of the surface, yellow and red mixing.

"I got him!" shouted Slyter, peering down. "Right on top of me. Longer than the wagon. Never saw him till he came up!"

"How terrible!" cried Beryl, shaken anew. "Red, what can we do?"

"I haven't an idee, Beryl. You girls might pray for me."

When the drovers arrived at the wagon again, Stanley Dann called out lustily: "Boys, that was splendid work. I heard your big bullets hit. It's not so bad having Yankee gunmen with us!"

"Oh, Dad, come ashore," Beryl cried appealingly.

He waved a reassuring hand, and heaved a load to his shoulder. The drovers did likewise. They made that trip uneventfully, and the tension relaxed somewhat. During nine more trips, while the cowboys with Slyter, Larry and the black kept vigil from several points, nothing untoward happened. Dann, with three of the drovers, then remained on the far side with the teams backed out into the shallow water, while the other three, dragging the tackle and ropes, swam their horses back to make fast to the wagon. They made it.

"Tramp all around!" shouted Slyter. "I shot a big croc' right here. Look out, for heaven's sake."

Bligh slid off his horse and, waist-deep, groped about with his feet to find the wagon tongue. To watch him thus exposed made the cold sweat ooze out all over Sterl. Bligh found the tongue, and went clear under to lift it up. In a moment more, the heavy tackle was fast. He yelled and waved to Dann. The two teams sagged down and dug in; the drovers in front of the wagon laid hold of the thick rope. Slyter lifted his arms on high, swung his rifle, and added his yell to that of the others. A moment of strain and splash—then the wagon lurched and began to move. It gathered momentum. Soon it was moving and sinking below the wheels. Then as luck would have it, the empty wagon half floated. Slyter stood up on the driver's seat, balancing himself, still peering into the water for crocodiles. The two teams and the six single horses dragged the wagon across the deep channel and did not slow up until the wheels touched bottom again. But there was no halt. In a very few moments the wagon was safely up on the bank, and yells heralded the success of the drovers. Despite the crocodiles, the achievement augured well for the success of the operation.

Chapter Twenty-five

All this time the tide was slowly going out. The channel split wide, bare stretches of mud. Sterl observed that the big crocodile he had thought surely killed had disappeared from the bank opposite. It seemed reasonable, however, to believe that a mortally wounded or crippled crocodile would not attack. The one Slyter had shot lay on its back, claw-like feet above the shallow water. Its dimensions, added to its hideous appearance, might well have shaken the stoutest heart. But these drovers were desperate and invincible.

Some of Dann's party repacked the wagon, others cut poles and brush to lay lengthwise on the mud over the plowed-up tracks of wheels and horses. Bill sat about erecting a canvas shelter to work under; Larry limped out to have a look at the mud. Sterl, Red, and Friday hurried at camp tasks the crossing had halted. The womenfolk could not remove their fascinated eyes from the river. Their movements in fighting the flies appeared mechanical. Time flew by. Presently, Dann's drovers, all except Roland, who had been left on the far side of the river, arrived muddy and wet, noisy and triumphant, back in camp. Slyter had returned on Roland's horse, and he had considerable to say about the huge reptile he had killed.

"Bing, stop looking at the beast," boomed Dann. "After all, we are only human."

"It'll be harder work, but safer to cross while the tide is out," replied Slyter.

"Volunteer wanted to drive the small dray," called the leader.

They all wanted that job. Dann chose Benson, the eldest. Six men cut slim brushy trees while two riders snaked these down to the river. Dann and Slyter built the corduroy road. Eric Dann lent a hand, like one in a trance. Larry returned to report the mob not so restless as on the preceding day. Friday pointed to aborigine smoke signals far back in the bush, and he shook his shaggy head. These signals were calling aborigines far and wide.

Many energetic hands made short work of the road on the camp side of the river. It was significant that Slyter covered his dead crocodile with brush. Then Benson drove the one-team dray off the bank. The brush road upheld both horses and wheels as long as they moved. Once in the channel, however, both sank in the mud until the wagon stopped, wheel-deep. The drovers un-hitched the team and started it across. They each got a sack of flour from Benson, and, packing it on a shoulder, they yelled and drove the team into deep water. A yelling, splashing mêlée ensued. The cowboys and Friday kept sharp lookout for crocodiles. The black man espied one far down the river. Fear, no doubt, spurred the drovers on. They emptied that dray of sacks and bags in what seemed to Sterl a short and trying hour. When the dray was dragged into the channel, it sank. Benson stood knee-deep in the water, and, when it got to his waist, he climbed on the driver's seat. It was a grotesque sight to see him crossing without effort of his own, both ropes and wagons out of sight. Soon the dray was hauled high up on the bank. A fire was built and the wagon re-loaded. Then Dann left Roland and Bligh over there, and re-turned to camp with the others. By this time the afternoon was far spent, and Bill had supper ready. Benson volunteered to pack sup-per across to the two drovers, and remain over there with them.

"Keep your fire burning," said Slyter, "and take turns on guard. But get away from the wagons a bit. Better to risk mosquitoes, snakes, and crocodiles than blacks!"

The drovers were spent, bedraggled, a slimy mess from the river mud. They ate like wolves, but were too tired to talk. Not even Dann or Slyter changed wet clothes, but hung around the fire until their garments dried and caked upon them. Friday and Larry were given the job to guard camp. Sterl and Red went out on duty with the mob.

Again the night was uncanny, dark and silent, except for the bark of dingoes far away and the silken swish of flying-foxes overhead. But the mob appeared to be free of the fears of the night before. They grazed and rested by turns. Sterl and Red kept together, and after a few hours, when all was quiet, one of them would watch while the other slept. Thus, the night did not seem interminably long. But Sterl's wakeful intervals were fraught with the same sinister sense which had settled upon him at Doré's Bush. He could not rid himself of misgivings. They had been wonderfully fortunate so far at the crossing. But still something cold clutched his vitals. His watch fell through the darkest hour before dawn, and of all the innumerable times he had held that watch, this one seemed the strangest, the most haunted and inscrutable with fantasies and phantoms. He listened and he observed as the blackness slowly paled to gray. Kangaroos and owls and bats could not get by him unnoticed. A stir in the mob brought him up alert. But his mind worked beyond all these things, and it conjured up fateful events for which there seemed no reason.

At last the dawn came, from gray to daylight, and then a ruddiness in the east. He awakened Red from his hard bed on the grass. The cowboy sat up, haggard and blinking, his red beard and red hair a queer combination. "Aw, my Gawd! Why was I borned?" he groaned, yawning wide.

"Surely not to waste your life following an outcast cowboy all over the earth," rejoined Sterl bitterly.

"Say, what ails you? Why, pard, I jest eat this up. An' I'll bet my spurs, it'll come off today."

They rounded up the remuda, and changed their mounts for King and Duke.

"Red, it's dirty business to risk Leslie's horses in that river," said Sterl, as they rode campward.

"Wal, I was thinkin' thet same. We won't do it, 'cept to cross them. We'll fork two of these draft horses. But, Holy Mackeli, *they* cain't keep one of them croc's away! I swear, pard, I never had my gizzard freeze like it does at thet thought."

"Nerve and luck, Red?"

"Them drovers shore had it yestiddy."

They met some of the drovers mustering horses from Dann's herd. Camp was astir. The fragrance of frying ham—seldom encountered these rationing days—greeted their nostrils. The girls were up, slim and dark in their boys' garb, their eyes fearful, yet somehow strangely keen for the day's adventure. Stanley Dann boomed hopefully. Friday stood high, watching the river. Mrs. Slyter had slept in Sterl's tent and looked none the worse for the night's dread. Halloos came from across the river. Rollie and his comrades waved all was well. Breakfast was over at sunrise. Friday approached the fire to get his fare.

"Alligators alonga eberywhere," he announced.

That shut down upon the trekkers like a clap of thunder. Slyter, the cowboys, and the drovers followed the striding Dann out to view the stream. The river area was flooded except for a fifty-foot lane of bare mud along each bank. A dead steer floated by in mid-channel, gripped by several crocodiles. Downstream a cow or steer had stranded in the shallow water. Around it ugly snouts and notched tails showed above the muddy water. Crocodiles were trying to drag the dead animal into deep water. Upstream on the far side a third cow had stuck himself in the mud and was surrounded by the reptiles.

Larry explained: "Night before last a number of cattle rushed into the river. We heard them bawling and plunging."

Slyter said: "Blood and meat scent in the river will have every croc' for miles down upon us. . . . Stanley, it looks worse than ever this morning."

"But it may not be as bad as it looks," replied the leader. "Let's cross Bill's dray at once. Tell Bill to keep out food and tea for to-day and tomorrow."

"Bill has to butcher fresh beef," said someone.

"We have 'roo meat ready," added Larry. "Friday fetched that in yesterday . . . or was it the day before?"

"Enough. I'll have him broil it all. One of you remember to put tucker on the dray for Bligh and the other boys across there. A kettle of hot tea! Who'll drive Bill's dray?"

Red Krehl elected himself for that job. But Dann preferred to have the cowboy on shore, rifle in hand. Before Sterl could offer his services, Dann selected Heald for this office.

They lost no time. The feverish energy of the drovers attested to their desire to have this job over and done with. Heald drove in until the water came almost to the platform of the wagon. Then the procedure that had proved so successful the day before was followed and carried out with even more celerity. It struck Sterl that in their hurry and fury of labor the drovers were forgetting about the crocodiles, which might have been just as well. The peril for them lay more in the shallows than in the channel where the violent actions of hoofs and the splashes might hold the brutes off.

Nevertheless, when this big job terminated, the drovers took time out for a cup of tea. That inevitable gesture amused Sterl. He wondered if these drovers would pause in a battle with murderous aborigines to indulge in their favorite brew.

"Ormiston's wagon next," boomed Stanley Dann. "It's evident the former owner cannot very well drive so that duty falls to Eric."

Dann's brother made no comment for or against the duty. He seemed thick of comprehension or at the end of his rope. Yet Sterl's penetrating gaze delved into the man's desperation.

The drovers hitched two teams to the wagon, while others, at the leader's order, unpacked a goodly half of its contents. Flour in special burlap sacks and other food supplies came to light. These were deposited upon a ground cloth and covered with canvas.

At the take-off the leading team balked, and upon being urged and whipped they plunged and gave Eric a bad few minutes. No doubt a scent of the dead crocodiles came to them. Drovers on each side slapped their haunches with whipping bridle ends. Eric laid on the stock whip. The horses plunged and reared, nearly upsetting the wagon. It was a scene of great excitement. Shouts and yells rang in the air. Stanley Dann boomed orders that Eric did not hear or could not obey. About a hundred steps out was as far as either of the other wagons had been driven. But Eric drove as if he meant the teams to wade the river. At length they halted of their own volition, with the front team submerged to their shoulders. This was extremely bad, because it was immediately evident that the team was sinking in the mud. Half a dozen drovers urged plunging horses to the rescue.

At that critical moment Friday hit Sterl and let out a wild stentorian yell. Sterl saw a dead steer, surrounded by crocodiles, drifting down upon the teams.

"*Back Heald! Back Hod!*" shouted Sterl, at the top of his lungs. "*Croc's!*"

Then the drovers and their horses, too, saw this mess drifting down upon them. Snorting, lunging, the horses wheeled and sent mountains of water flying. They reached the shore just as the dead steer drifted upon the teams and lodged. Pandemonium broke loose then, on shore and in the water. Even Stanley Dann's big voice could not be distinguished. But he was yelling for his brother to climb back over the wagon and leap for his life. Eric might have heard, as well as have had sense enough to think of that, but shrieking in terror, his gaze was glued to the mêlée right under him.

At the first contact the screaming horses had reared high, pawing the air. The dead steer drifted in between the two teams to lodge against the wagon tongue. And the great reptiles attacked the horses. They made a tremendous commotion, completely obscuring themselves and the front horses with churning splashes. The snap of huge jaws, the crack of teeth, the rend of flesh could be heard amid the roar of water and the clamor of the drovers.

It was an unprecedented and terrible situation. No one knew what to do. Eric pulled his gun and shot. Not improbably he hit the horses instead of the crocodiles. The left front horse reared high with a crocodile hanging to its nose. Sterl sent a bullet into the head of this beast, but it did not let go. It pulled the horse under. The right front horse was in the clutches of two crocodiles. The open jaws of one stuck beyond the neck of the horse. Blood streamed to redden the water. Krehl's rifle cracked. Sterl shot to kill a horse, if he missed a crocodile. The second team had been attacked by half a dozen of them.

At that awful moment for Eric Dann, horses and wagon were pulled into deep water. The wagon sank above its bed and floated. Between the threshing horses the dead steer rolled and rocked with four legs standing up. Eric leaped to the driver's seat and held on. As he turned to those on shore, his visage appeared scarcely human. If from his open mouth any sound issued, no one could hear it. And the crocodiles, probably a dozen or more, were tearing the horses from the wagon as it drifted down the river.

"Fellers, fork yore hosses!" yelled Red. Leaping on Duke, his rifle aloft, he raced into the bush to catch up with the drifting wagon. Sterl was quick to follow, and he heard the thud and crash of the drovers at his heels. But Sterl lost sight of Red and had to trail his passage through the thickets and between the trees. The bush proved to be dense. Red had gone through it at breakneck speed. There was no opening along the bank to see out into the river. And not for a good long run did Sterl break out into the clear.

A low bank afforded means to get down to the river. It made a bend there. Sterl yelled to those behind and sent King tearing through the brush. He came out at the edge of the mud. Sterl saw Red and the wagon in one glance. The cowboy had Duke in the mud, wading out. The wagon had lodged in shallow water. It had turned around with the horses toward the shore. A horrible fight was going on there. Beyond it several other crocodiles were tearing at a horse that had been cut adrift. Eric Dann clung to the driver's seat. The tips of lashing waves splashed over him. One huge, slimy reptile slithered in front of the wagon and gave it a resounding smack with his tail.

Stanley Dann and his followers arrived on the scene. For once, the leader's booming voice was silent at a crisis. Even Sterl could not yell to the daring cowboy.

Red had thrown aside his rifle. He held his gun in his left hand and a lasso in his right. On the moment, a lean, black-jawed crocodile stuck his snout and shoulders out of the water and, reaching over the wagon, snapped at Eric. He missed the cowering man, but not by more than two feet. It had been plain to the cowboy, and it now became to Sterl and the others, that Eric would not last long there.

The horses had ceased to struggle. Sterl could not locate the dead steer. What with the tugging and floundering of the crocodiles, the wagon appeared about to tilt over. That meant instant end to Eric Dann. It would all be over with quickly, if the brutes did not tear the horses free.

Red sent that grand horse plunging into the water. Duke's ears stood up; his piercing snorts made the other horses neigh wildly. Red was taking a chance that the crocodiles would be too busy to see him. Sterl's breast caved in with relief, when he saw that the cowboy had the terrible situation in hand. When Duke was up to his flanks and the curdled, foamy maëlstrom scarcely a lasso's length distant, Red yelled piercingly: "*Stand up, Eric!*"

The man heard, for he tried to obey. But he must have been paralyzed with horror.

"Stick out yore laig . . . yore arm!" shrieked the cowboy, in a fury, and he shot the outside crocodile, sliding into view.

But Eric was beyond helping himself. Again that ugly brute lunged out and up, his corrugated jaws wide, and, as they snapped like steel, he missed by only a few inches.

"Rope him, Red!" yelled out Sterl.

Then the lasso, like a shiny striking snake, shot out, and the noose cracked over Eric's head and shoulders. Red whirled the big horse and spurred him shoreward. Eric was jerked off the wagon, over the very backs of those threshing crocodiles. One snapped at him too late; another cracked at him with a mighty tail. But Red dragged him free, through the shallow water, up on the mud. Red leaped off, to run and loosen the noose. Eric's head had been dragged under through the mud. Then Stanley and two others were off, lifting the half dead man, and packing him ashore. Sterl sat his horse, his throat constricted, his tongue falling from the roof of his mouth. He had not cared much about Eric Dann, but the mad risk that intrepid cowboy had run!

"He ain't . . . hurt none," Red panted, coiling the muddy rope. "I was afraid I'd get the noose around his throat. But it was a narrow shave."

They washed the mud from Eric's face. He coughed and spat. His breath wheezed. He was unable to stand alone, but it appeared fairly evident that he was not injured.

Red led Duke out on the grass, and looked up at Sterl. His fireblue eyes were full of dancing, devilish little flecks. "Not so pore . . . huh?" he asked huskily.

Sterl could hardly curse his friend before these men, so he remained silent and took it out in looking.

"Pard, thet's one hoss . . . in a million," he said, drawing Duke's head close. "By Gawd, I was scared he wouldn't do it. But he did, he did!"

They laid Eric Dann on the bank to let him recover. Then they attended to the battle of the leviathans. Sterl dismantled with his rifle, and every time a head or a body lunged up, he met it with a bullet. But the angle was bad. Most of the bullets glanced singingly across the river. One by one the horses were torn loose from the traces, and dragged away, a ghastly and gory spectacle, until they were taken under the deep water. The heavy wagon had remained upright, with the back end and wheels submerged. The tide was falling.

"Miraculous, any way you look at it!" exclaimed Stanley Dann. "One more lunge by that black crocodile would have reached Eric! Red Krehl, as if my debt to you had not been great enough!"

"Hell, boss. We've all been around yestiddy an' today, when things came off," dragged on the cowboy.

"Yes, but in this case. . . ." He paused eloquently. "Some of you take Eric back to camp. Fetch my teams harnessed."

At low tide Ormiston's wagon was hauled out and back to camp. Nothing perishable had been left in it. The contents were unloaded and laid out to dry. During this latter procedure the girls clamored for the story. Red laughed at them, but Sterl told it, not wholly without elaboration. He wanted to see Beryl Dann's eyes betray her quick and profound emotions. If he had ever seen anything lovelier than her eyes, he did not remember.

"Beryl, all in the day's ride," drawled Red, but he was gratified at her reaction. "Now if you was only like Duke!"

"Red, I am not a horse. I am a woman," she rejoined with no response to his humor.

"Shore, I know thet. I mean a hoss, if he's great like Duke an' cottons to a feller, as he shore has to me, why he'll do anythin' for you. Beryl, I'd die for him, an' I'm shore he'd die for me."

"I'd like you to feel that way for me," she returned vibrantly. "I would die for you."

"Wal, yore wants, like yore eyes an' yore heart, air too big for you, Beryl."

Leslie let go of Duke's neck to face Red. She appeared almost as deeply moved as Beryl. "Red, I give Duke to you. And you can return jester to me," she said.

"Well, dog-gone it, Les, you hit me below the belt. No cowboy could turn a deaf ear to thet, much less me."

"It'll make me happy. And Beryl, too. Sterl, do you approve?"

"Les, since I can't have Duke, and you in the bargain, I'd love to see Red get him."

Leslie blushed furiously, as she was wont to do when off her guard and suddenly shocked. But she rallied: "Sterl Hazelton, you can have all my horses, and . . . and. . . ."

Stanley Dann broke in upon them with his booming order. "Cut more poles. The tide will be low enough. We'll relay the road and cross my wagon before this day is done."

While his drovers worked like beavers, he had Beryl's bed and baggage unloaded from his wagon. The bed was put in Sterl's tent. The baggage was packed down to the edge of the mud, ready to be moved. When the brush road was done, Dann said to the cowboy: "You and Friday make sure of the time for me to take to the river."

"It'll be safer now the tide is low," averred Slyter.

Stanley drove his big wagon and changed from the seat to his saddle, and cheered and helped the drovers in their strenuous labor. Friday sighted crocodiles, but none came near. Load and wagon were crossed in record time, after which six drovers carried Beryl's belongings across in two trips.

The sun set red and evilly upon that eventful day. The trekkers ate, and tried to be oblivious to the aborigine signals, the uncanny bats, the howls of the dingoes, and the unseen menace that hovered over Doré's Bush.

Sterl was not subject to nightmares, but that night he had one. An enormous crocodile had hold of his boots. He could not kick the beast free, nor rise up to shoot, nor yell for help. A terrific wrench of some kind broke that dream. It turned out to have been delivered by Red.

"For cripe's sake, stop diggin' me with them bear claws of yours," growled the cowboy.

They were sleeping in the open, beside a fire that had burned out. The Danns and Slyters, and some of the drovers, lay under the wagons. Sterl and Red had been on guard for three hours, after which they rolled on their ground cloths, covered their heads, and sank into the slumber of exhaustion. After the nightmare Sterl lay awake. That hour at the low ebb of vitality was no time to think. He tried not to think, but he could not help feeling. The dew, the silence, the oppression weighed upon him. All around and over him swished the uncanny and infernal flying-foxes. They squealed like fighting rats. The river made a low, somber, gurgling sound, as if it were strangling life out of something. Once he raised up to peer around. Red, Friday, Larry lay prone, dark faces indistinct in the paling starlight. Was it a shadow or a kangaroo that moved across his vision? Wearily, he fell back.

Stanley Dann roused them all in the gray of dawn. It was wet and chill. Dingoes bayed dismally in the bush. Bill appeared slow at his tasks in this camp. He did not whistle while he worked. Sterl chopped wood until his lethargic blood awakened in his veins. Red Krehl, the indefatigable, the unconquerable, sat staring into gray space, his mop of tangled red hair hanging over his drawn face. When the crippled Larry crossed his sight, Red came to himself.

"Lay off them bridles, you geezer. Don't you know when you're knocked out? Me an' Sterl will wrangle the hosses."

They found two of Dann's drovers mustering horses for the day. The cowboys bridled Duke, King, and Lady Jane, and drove the rest of Leslie's horses into camp. Stanley Dann's hearty voice, his spirit, the drab gray dawn lighting ruddily, the hot breakfast—all seemed to work against the gripping, somber spell.

"Men, this is our big important day," boomed the leader. "Roland's wagon first. Unload all the heavy stuff. Pack these bags of dried fruit Ormiston had . . . unknown to me. Carry all this cowboy junk down to the river."

"Boss, I reckon we're gonna need all thet junk," remonstrated Red.

"Those heavy packs! Slyter, will you drive Roland's wagon?"

"Yes," replied Slyter. "Mum, here's where you ride with me."

"Husband, I pray it will not be our last," responded Mrs. Slyter cheerfully. This sturdy little woman was far from being a drawback.

"With Beryl and Leslie, that will be a load," went on the leader.

"Dad, I won't cross in the wagon," spoke up his daughter decidedly.

Leslie interposed to say: "I'm riding Lady Jane."

The leader gazed at these pioneer daughters with great, luminous eyes, and made no further comment to them. He hurried the unpacking and the hitching of two big draft horses to Roland's wagon. The sun came up gloriously bright. Shining river, shining green bush, sailing waterfowl, clamor of cockatoos all seemed to give the lie to that forbidding night spell. When Slyter mounted the high wagon seat, ready to drive, shouts from across the river told him that the drovers there were ready. Roland straddled one of the lead horses of the teams. Bligh and

Hod sat their horses. The tide was on the make, wanting a foot in height and a dozen yards up the mud bank to fill the riverbed.

"Friday! Everybody watch the river for croc's," ordered the leader.

Leslie sat her horse, beside Sterl on King. The girl looked pale, resolute. She knew the peril. At this juncture Beryl emerged from the tent, slim in her rider's garb. She had not forgotten or neglected to brush her fair hair. It rippled and blazed in the sun. She carried a small, black bag. She walked quickly, graceful and erect.

"Red, will you carry me across?" she asked simply. Her darkly dilated eyes betrayed her terror.

"Shore, Beryl, but why for?" drawled the cowboy.

"I'd feel safer . . . and . . . and. . . ."

No man then could have refused Beryl Dann anything she might have asked for.

"What you got in thet bag?" queried Red.

"My few treasures and keepsakes."

"Wal, dog-gone! Let me get hold of you. There. Put yore foot on my stirrup. . . . Up you come! No, I cain't hold you thet way, Beryl. You've gotta fork Duke. Slip down in front of me. Sterl, how about slopin'?"

"Friday grins good," replied Sterl grimly. "Les, keep above me close. Larry, keep upstream from Red. Idea is to move *pronto*."

The four plunged in as Stanley Dann boomed to Slyter and the drovers. Loud thumping splashes attended the onslaught upon the river. Roland and his comrades cheered. Friday appeared leaping through the shallow water, his spears and *wommeras* aloft. He added sinister reality to that scene. Duke and King, slightly ahead, sent the yellow splashes flying. The other two horses leaped not to be left behind. Then the four passed Slyter's teams and the drovers, and plunged into the deeper water.

"Fellers, get ready for gun play!" shouted the hawk-eyed Red. "Shet yore eyes, Beryl!"

Across the river from the reedy bank above Roland's position came a crackling rush, a waving of reeds, then a *zoom*, as a big crocodile took to the water and slid along with surprising speed. The guns of Roland's group banged, and the mud spattered all around the reptile.

"Larry, watch out for thet bird," yelled Red. "I reckon he won't come, but he might."

Farther upstream, muddy-backed crocodiles, as huge as logs, piled into the river. The drovers were clamoring in fright and excitement. Slyter had driven his teams in up to their flanks. One drover was unfastening the traces, while two others were ready to drag the teams into the channel. Sterl spared only a glance for them. Roland and his men came pounding through the shallow water. All seemed to work with machine-like precision. Halfway across—two-thirds! Bligh's horse was lunging into the channel above Larry, carrying the tackle and rope for the wagon.

Suddenly, almost in line with them, an open-jawed, yellow-fanged monster spread the reeds, and *zoomed* off the bank. He moved across the slippery mud into the water. Red was shooting. But the crocodile came on, got over his depth, and disappeared.

"Watch for the wake!" called Red. "Thet feller is mean. We gotta hit him, pard. Watch!"

All Sterl's nerves were on edge. In any event that situation was terrible, but with the girls. . . .

"Heah he comes! See them little knobs. Thet's his haid!"

Sterl espied them, along with the long chain of tiny, ragged notches weaving to and fro. He regretted having left his rifle in the wagon.

"Drop behind me, Leslie," called Sterl. "Don't weaken. We'll get him!"

It was impossible to tell whether or not the crocodile meant to attack. The chances were that he would, unless the commotion in the water turned him. Sterl did not fire because he did not want to drive the brute underwater again. Evidently Red had the same thought. The cowboy headed Duke quarteringly away from the long ripple, and he leaned far forward, gun extended. His left arm held the drooping girl. At the right instant he spurred Duke.

It must have come at the instant when Duke struck bottom, because he lunged, powerfully. The crocodile was less than six feet distant, when Red turned his gun loose in a volley. The bullets splashed and thudded. But they did not glance. With a tremendous swirl the reptile lurched partly out, a ghastly spectacle. Sterl sent two leaden slugs into it. Falling back, the monster began to roll over and over, his ten-foot tail beating the water into foam. Sterl and Leslie waded out below, while Red and Larry waded shallow water above.

"Hey, Rollie," yelled Red, "don't worry none about this bird!"

They waded past the teams and waiting drovers, out on the bank to the wide path trampled up the slope. The drovers cheered. Sterl, with Leslie behind him, followed Red up to a wide, level spot, where wagons and packs marked the camp.

Red slid off and laid his gun on the grass. Beryl swayed in the saddle, her eyes tightly shut, her fingers in her ears.

"Wal, Beryl, come out of it," shouted Red, and he tugged at one of her arms. She opened eyes as black as night. Her arms fell weakly.

"I won't faint! I won't," she cried, still with passion left in her weak voice.

"Who said you would?" drawled Red, as he helped her off. "Beryl, you're gettin' to be a pretty dog-gone good cowgirl. If you jest wasn't so sentimental. Come, let me help you off."

It was Beryl's prerogative then to fall into Red's arms, but she did not take advantage of the moment. Red helped her off, and steadied her a moment to see if she could stand.

"Girl, I never gave you credit," flashed Red. "Set down, an' if you faint now, you'll spoil it all."

Leslie, who had dismounted, came to Beryl. They clung together, a gesture more eloquent than any words.

When they rode out on the mud flat again, Sterl was amazed to see Friday dragging what evidently was the monster crocodile into the shallow water. A long spear sticking in the reptile spoke for itself. A yelling, splashing mêlée distracted Sterl. The two teams were straining on the ropes, plowing through the mud. Be-

tween them and the wagon, the drovers were yelling and hauling. Sterl observed that this wagon, the one in which he had
caulked the seams, floated almost flat. Mrs. Slyter stood behind
her husband, hanging onto the seat, while he made ready for the
waiting teams. Once the wagon was in shallow water, they unfas-
tened the ropes and tackles, hitched the two teams, and gave
Slyter the word to drive out.

Sterl and Red followed the muddy procession up the bank.
The unhitching and clamor of the drovers were halted by Stanley Dann's booming voice from the opposite bank: "Good work!
Rollie, Larry, Friday, stay there to guard camp. Rest of you hurry
back to drove the mob."

Friday said to Sterl and Slyter: "Tinkit more better boss wait
along sun. Croc's bad."

"We can't stop Dann now," Slyter said grimly. "Come all
who're going back."

"Wal, if you ask me, we oughta load our guns," drawled Red.

Chapter Twenty-six

The tide had turned to ebb, and the strip of muddy riverbed
had widened. On the flat lay the enormous crocodile that
Red had shot and Friday had speared. It was over twenty feet
long, a yard wide, and would have weighed a hundred stone and
more. It lay on its back, exposing the gory hole where Red's bullets had torn through, and the broken shaft of Friday's spear.

Five drovers crossed the river with Sterl and Red. Dann met
them like a general, greeting a victorious army.

"We've time to drove Slyter's horses across, and pack these
loose things," he said. "Ormiston's wagon can be left till last."

The cowboys unsaddled King and Duke, changing to two of
Slyter's draft horses, and it was a pleasure to see how Leslie's
great favorites raced across the river, leading the other horses.

Without riders and saddles to weigh them down, these iron-shod horses would have given a crocodile a hard fight, even in the water.

Slyter and Stanley Dann helped pack the loose supplies across. Bill Simpson, the cook, went with the first trip. But Eric Dann stayed on the seat of Ormiston's wagon, gloomy, dead to the excitement of the great ford. His saddled horse remained tethered to the wagon. Nine men on fresh horses, all spurred by the never-failing danger of that crossing, transported bags, supplies, tents, beds, utensils, saddles in a dozen trips, averaging ten minutes to the trip, without an attack from the river saurians. But as the tide ebbed, they sighted more reptiles than upon any other occasion.

Stanley Dann roused his brooding brother with a curt command. His patience and kindness might not have been exhausted, but this was a stern hour.

"Men, this is the great job," he boomed. "If it is successful, to-morrow we will muster the cattle that rushed, and drove the mob."

Sterl estimated that there was three thousand head, more or less in the mob, and they were tractable. Slyter had charge of the drive. His idea proved to be a gradual moving of the cattle down the river in the open, leaving an unguarded end of the mob at the lower side, through which they could string out. It worked. Red spoke well of the plan, and also of the very slow driving. But he had his doubts about that river.

"OK, if a big bunch of leaders gets started," he ejaculated. "But if they buck at sight or smell of them ugly, stinkin' varmints . . . *whoopee!*"

Sterl felt the reverse of optimistic. But even in his doubts he had to think of Stanley Dann's magnificent and immutable spirit. He would drove that mob across, despite almost insurmountable obstacles. He would end this trek successfully or die trying.

When the drovers had the big herd lengthened out to perhaps

half a mile, the front end and the hundred or more extra horses were driven in from behind. At a signal from Dann the widely separated drovers opened fire with their guns and charged. The fifty-yard-wide belt of cattle headed for the river and piled over the low bank. Across the river crocodiles basked in the sun. The odor of the reptiles was thick on the air. The first line had slid off the bank into the mud before they took fright and balked. Then it was too late. The pushing, bawling lines behind forced them on. Some of them were bogged, to be trampled under. But almost miraculously the whole mob was driven into the mud before they could attempt a rush back.

The point of least resistance lay to the fore. The leaders had to gravitate that way. From the opposite bank crocodiles slid down and shot across the mud into the shallow water. Sterl had no time to count, but he saw many. Red saw, too, for he shouted to Sterl: "Mebbe the herd will trample the gizzards out of them."

A plunging line leaped headlong into the channel. Released from a wall in front, the mass behind piled frantically into the river. As if by a miracle, then, hundreds and thousands of horned heads breasted the channel. In several spots swirling, churning battles ensued, almost at once to be overridden by swimming cattle. Sterl, from his position behind the center of the advance, could not see what was going on at each end of the mob. But it appeared a marvelous, progressive movement, losing its raggedness as more and more cattle reached deep water. Then they were all in, except the dozens of mired and trampled ones that had fallen before the onslaught. Swimming cattle in large numbers always fascinated Sterl. He sat his horse on the bank, thrilled to the core of his being, and tried ineffectually to take in the whole spectacle. The wide channel was full of bobbing, horned heads. As the front line struck bottom, the stench of the crocodiles and their furious, charging attack, precipitated a rush that was obscured in flying spray.

"Come on, pard!" yelled Red from below. "We wanna be close behind that stampede or the croc's will get us!"

All the drovers were in the mud, some at the heels of the mob, others shooting crippled and smashed cattle. The big herd, in the wake of the mob, excited by the roar, had made frantic efforts to get ahead. Soon they lunged into deep water. Sterl spurred the big draft horse under him. Compared to King, it appeared to stand still, yet Sterl was glad he was not astride the black. His gun held ready, Sterl peered into the murky, swirling water. Red did likewise on one side of him, and Benson on the other. That was a heart-racking, stomach-collapsing ordeal which seemed not to have an end. Nevertheless, it eased its sickening clutch on into shallow water. Then Sterl looked up.

A sea of glistening, bobbing backs sloped up to a fringe of bobbing horns which fell out of sight all along the line. In each direction the long belt of cattle was moving with amazing speed. A thousand crocodiles could not have halted that stampede. Sterl gazed back and up and down the mud bank. Everywhere, mired cattle dotted the river. Squirming crocodiles attested to the trampling they had received. Only one horse was down, and it appeared to be struggling to rise.

"Laig broke!" yelled Red, close to Sterl's ear. "Saddled, too! By Gawd, pard, thet's Eric Dann's hoss! An' if he ain't lyin' there on the mud, my eyes air pore!"

The long mob poured up the bank and over it, out of sight. The roar ceased markedly. Drovers all along mounted the incline. Stanley Dann and two others appeared, galloping. The leader was pointing to the fallen horse and rider. Sterl and Red had already headed in his direction.

"So help me!" panted Red. "Pard, I wouldn't give a goose pimple for thet man lyin' there. You've seen 'em, Sterl, flat as empty sacks!"

"But Red, whoever that is, was behind the herd," protested Sterl. "He couldn't have been run over."

"Thet's Eric Dann's hoss, I tell you," flashed Red. "He's bogged down or his laig's broke."

"Look! A croc' slipping off into deep water," shouted Sterl.

Stanley Dann reached the prostrate man and horse ahead of

Bligh and Hod. Sterl and Red got there as the drovers were dismounting, to sink ankle-deep in the mud.

"It's Eric!" boomed the leader, as he leaned over. "Dead . . . or . . . or . . . no! He's still alive!"

"Horse's front leg's broken," reported Bligh tensely.

"Shoot it! And help me, the two of you."

They lifted him across Bligh's saddle. How limp he hung! What a slimy, broken wreck of a man.

"Hazelton, you and Krehl and Hod follow the mob," ordered the leader harshly. "That rush will end soon."

From the height of the bank Sterl looked over bushland and green downs which led to higher and denser bush. Smoke signals rose in straight columns and separate puffs. In the foreground, the mob of cattle had halted.

"All the stampede is out of them," said Red.

"Crocodile stampede. New one on us, Red," rejoined Sterl.

"Cost Dann and Slyter plenty. Hundreds of cattle down, daid an' dyin'. What a mess there'll be, when the hot sun has a chance at them."

"Aborigines, croc's, dingoes, and buzzards! In two days this camp won't be livable."

"A-huh. You're thinkin', too. If Eric Dann is bad hurt, we cain't leave."

"He was bad hurt, somewhere."

"Laigs looked busted to me. You saved his life onct, an' then all same me . . . to no good. We might have saved ourselves the risk. I hope he croaks!"

"Red, your bark is always worse than your bite."

"Yeah? I shore am the champeen sucker. But you're kinda easy yourself. Sterl, about Dann's drovers, after this last shuffle, what's the deal gonna be?"

"You mean if Eric Dann holds up the trek?"

"I shore mean thet little thing."

"Damn' serious, pard."

"Serious? Well, old man, what's it been all along? It'll be orful. If Bligh an' Heald an' the others stick it out, I'd say it'll be a damn' sight more than any Americans would do. 'Cept a couple of dumb-haid, lovesick suckers like us. But they're as game an outfit as we ever seen."

The drovers had turned the long right wing of the mob back upon itself. When the cowboys arrived, the cattle had begun to lie down, too exhausted even to bawl. They would not need any guarding that night. There was a creek meandering through the downs toward the river, but obviously it had no outlet except during high water. The reed border along the river, where the crocodiles lay in wait, did not extend far back. Sterl found the sun hot, the flies bothersome, the scene unwholesome despite the flocks of colored parrots and ducks, the cranes, and the myriad kangaroos.

The horses had scattered off to the left toward camp. Sterl and Red helped muster them and drove them within sight of the wagons.

"What held up the boss?" inquired Bligh, as the drovers collected again, their tasks ended for the present. Bligh was a young man, under thirty, gray-eyed and still-faced, a man on whom the other drovers leaned.

"Eric's injured. Legs broken, I think," replied Sterl. "They had to shoot his horse."

"We got off lucky at that. How bad was he hurt?"

"Other than his legs, I don't know, Bligh. Looked bad. Red thinks it was bad."

Bligh exchanged apprehensive glances with his intimates. It was natural that they should take this news amiss, as, indeed, the cowboys had done. Finally Bligh turned back to Sterl: "If the boss's brother is unable to travel, it'll precipitate a most serious situation."

"We appreciate that. Let's hope it's not so bad he cannot be moved in a wagon."

"Yes. You hope so, but you don't believe it," said Bligh brusquely.

"Right!"

"Hazelton, we all think you and Krehl are wonderful drovers, and, what is more, right good cowboys," said Bligh.

"Thanks, Bligh," returned Sterl heartily. "Red and I sure return the compliment."

"For us this trek seems to have run into a forlorn cause. It is keeping us awake at night."

"Well, Bligh, I'm bound to agree with you. But it's not a lost cause yet."

The drover shook his shaggy head and ran skinned, dirty fingers through his scant beard. "Friend, it's different with you cowboys, on account of the girls, if you'll excuse my saying so."

"Different? Maybe you pay us too high a compliment."

Here Red interposed. "Bligh, you all savvied my case, an' thet's OK with me. But don't think I've got any high-falutin' ideas."

"You boys are both too modest," returned Bligh with a smile. Sterl felt the warmer for that little exchange of words. They rode into camp. Rollie and his mates had put up the cook's shelter and table, and the tents. They had split a pile of red hardwood and collected a lot of the kind of bark that burned well. Friday had evidently come back to camp with Dann. Sterl felt reluctant to ask about the injured man. Weary as he was, Sterl followed Red's example of discarding wet, slimy clothes, washing and shaving with hot water, and getting into dry things. That made a considerable difference in mood, for the time being.

Neither Beryl nor Leslie put in an appearance. Dann seemed for once a forbidding and unapproachable figure. Slyter conversed in low tones with his wife, and once Sterl saw him throw up his hands in a singular gesture for him. Red stayed in the tent. Friday kept gazing fixedly at the smoke signals, as if reading their strange omens. The seven young drovers remained in a group at the other side of the camp, where Bligh appeared to be haranguing them. Sterl had seen numberless conferences of both honest and evil men out in the open, faced by momentous issues, and in this instance he drew a dismaying conclusion.

Sterl felt a helpless, sinking sensation. He could not control his own thoughts or emotions, much less events. All leading up to the event of Doré's Bush, all the events that had happened there down to this hour, presaged a tragic climax, the uncertainty of which added to the resistless portent. All the eyes Sterl had caught a glimpse into, except Red Krehl's, had a furtive, hunted look. Then, the instant the sun set, all that had been bright and gold underwent a change. Sterl imagined that it emanated from his mood, but he could not hold that thought. The dark, still bush, secretive, pregnant; the fading drifting smoke signals, proof of the mysterious aboriginal menace; the gliding river, between its yellow mud borders; the wide-winged buzzards sailing around and around, dropping down to the gnarled branches of a dead gum tree—all these were physical facts that pressed to be felt. They strengthened the dread oppression that seemed to lend weight to the very atmosphere.

Sterl turned away from his prolonged scrutiny of the river, the bush, the downs, all that constituted this place. And he sustained a galvanizing shock that this was the moment. Suddenly, Bligh, leading Derrick, Hod and Heald, rose and started toward Stanley Dann's shelter. Pale despite their tan, resolute despite their fear! It did not seem a coincidence that Beryl and Leslie appeared from nowhere; that Slyter came out, his hair ruffled, his gaze fixed; that Red emerged from his tent, his lean hawk-like head poised; that Friday hove into sight, lending the stark reality of the aborigine to the scene.

Under Dann's shelter it was still light. Mrs. Slyter stood beside the stretcher where Eric Dann lay, his head and shoulders propped up on pillows, fully conscious and ghastly pale. His lower extremities were covered with a blanket. The drovers halted just outside the shelter. Bligh took a further step.

"Mister Dann, is it true that Eric is badly injured?" burst out Bligh, as if forced.

Dann gave a violent start, and rose to his full height to stare at his visitors and from them to the cowboys, the girls, and Slyter. He stalked out then, like a man who faced death.

"Bligh, I grieve to inform you that Eric is badly hurt," he boomed.

"Just how badly, sir?"

"The bones of his legs broken as if they had been clay pipe-stems."

"We are terribly sorry for him and for you," rejoined Bligh huskily.

"I'm sure of that, Bligh."

"Will it be possible to move him? In a wagon, you know, to carry on our trek?"

"No! Eric cannot be moved. He has sustained terrible compound fractures of both legs. Even with proper setting of the bones, he may be a cripple for life. To move him now, over rough ground, would be inhuman. He would suffer excruciating agony. The broken bones would not knit."

"What do you intend to do?"

"Stay here until he is mended enough to travel."

"That would take weeks, sir. Perhaps more."

"Yes, weeks. There is no alternative. On the moment I am confronted with a situation as grave as that. Eric would not let me reset his broken bones. When I moved his legs, he suffered torture. We have no chloroform. He must be bound and held while I work on him."

Bligh made a gesture of inexpressible regret. He choked. He cleared his throat. "Mister Dann, we feared this very thing. We talked it over, hoping against hope. But we can't . . . we won't . . . stay here . . . and go on with this wild goose trek. You started all right. Then Ormiston and your brother put us in all wrong. No sense in crying over spilled milk. We've stuck to the breaking point. And that's right here. We four have decided to trek back home."

"Bligh! *You*, too?" boomed the leader. Sterl saw him change as if he had shriveled up inside. His eyes were great, pale furnaces. He was taking the brunt of another almost mortal blow.

"Yes, *me!*" rang out Bligh. "You ask too much of young men. We built our hopes on your promises. One of us planned to have his girl come by ship to Darwin. To marry her there! Hod has a wife and child. Derrick is sick of this. We are going home."

The leader thrust aside his selfish feelings and saw the stand of these young drovers as if he were one of them. "Bligh, I have exacted too much of you all," he returned with a sonorous tone in his voice. "I'm sorry. It cannot be undone. If I had it to do over again . . . you are welcome to go, and God speed you. Take two teams for Ormiston's wagon. It is half full of food supplies. Bill will give you a box of tea. And, if you can muster the cattle that rushed up the river, you are welcome to them."

"Boss . . . that is big and fine of you," returned Bligh haltingly. Manifestly it griped him to fail this man. "We meant to ask only for horses and a little food. But this . . . . Honestly, sir."

"Don't thank me, Bligh. I am in your debt."

Eric Dann called piercingly from under the shelter. "Bligh . . . tell him . . . *tell him!*"

The listeners all appeared impelled to press closer, to see that wan visage standing out from the shadow of the darkening shelter. Sterl felt that the gathering suspense could grow no more before the break.

"No, Eric," returned Bligh sorrowfully. "I've nothing to tell."

"Tell me what?" boomed the leader, like an angry lion aroused. "Bligh, what have you to tell me?"

"Nothing, sir. Eric is out of his head."

"No, I'm not," yelled Eric, and his attempt to push himself higher on the stretcher ended in a shriek of pain. But he did sit up, and Mrs. Slyter supported him.

"Eric, what could Bligh tell me?" queried Stanley Dann.

There ensued a silence that seemed long to Sterl. It was terrible. Every moment added to the torment of coming terrible disclosures. Eric Dann must have been wrenched by physical pain and mental anguish to a point beyond resistance. "Stanley, we are lost!"

"Lost?" echoed the giant blankly.

"Yes . . . yes. *Lost!*" cried Eric wildly. "We've been lost all the way! I didn't know this bushland. I've never been on a trek . . . through outback Queensland!"

"Merciful heaven!" boomed the leader, his great arms going aloft. "Your plans? Your assurances? Your map?"

"Lies! All lies!" wailed Eric Dann. He was stricken with horror at some perfidy and by a horrible need to unburden himself. "I never was inland from the coast. I met Ormiston. We talked cattle. He inflamed me about a fabulous range in the Northern Territory . . . west of the Gulf. Gave me the map we've trekked by. I planned with him to persuade you to muster a great mob of cattle. I didn't know he was the bush-ranger Pell. But I found out too late . . . . That map is false. We are lost. We must be way south of the Gulf . . . instead of west. I couldn't confess! I couldn't! I kept on blindly. We're lost! Bligh knows that. Ormiston could not corrupt him. Yet he wouldn't betray me to you. We're lost . . . irretrievably lost, and I'm damned to hell!"

Stanley Dann expelled a great breath and sat down on a pack as if his legs had been chopped from under him. He whistled with an intake of breath. "Lost? Yea, God has forsaken me," he whispered.

Bligh was the first to move after a stricken silence. "Boss, you've got to hear that I didn't know all that Eric confessed."

"Bligh, that is easy to believe, thank heaven," Stanley Dann said presently, his voice gaining timbre. He wrestled with himself, as if to shake off a demon. "We'll thresh it all out right now. Somebody light a fire to dispel this hateful gloom. Let me think a moment." And he paced somberly to and fro outside the shelter.

"Listen, all of you," he began, and again his voice had that wonderful deep roll. "I see it this way. I cannot desert my brother. Nor can I stay here alone. Whoever does stay must carry on with me and the trek, when we are able to continue. You are all free to decide for or against me. I have exacted too much of you all. I grieve that I have been wrong, self-centered, dominating. Beryl, my daughter, will you stay?"

"Dad, I'll stay!" There was no hesitation in Beryl's reply, and, to Sterl, she seemed at last of her father's blood and spirit. "I don't want to go back. My place is with you. Don't despair. We shall not *all* betray you!"

A beautiful light warmed his grave visage as he turned to

Leslie. "Child, you have been forced into womanhood. I doubt if your parents should influence your decision here."

"I would not go back to marry a royal duke!" she replied.

"Missus Slyter, your girl has, indeed, grown up on this trek," went on Dann. "But she will still need a mother out there across the Never Never. Will you stay?"

"Need you ask, Stanley? I don't believe whatever lies in store for us could be so bad as what we've lived through," rejoined the woman calmly.

"Slyter, how about you?"

"Stanley, I started the race, and I'll make the good fight," replied the drover.

"Hazelton!" demanded Dann, without a trace of doubt. His exclamation was not a query.

"I am keen to go on," answered Sterl, finding simplicity in the turmoil of his feelings. But these were for others. If he had only this great pioneer to consider, he still would have chosen to go on, knowing beforehand what his cowboy friend would do.

"Krehl!"

The cowboy was lighting a cigarette. Beryl was hanging to his arm. He puffed a cloud of smoke which hid his face.

"Wal, boss," he drawled, "it's shore a great privilege you've given me. Jest a chanct to know an' fight for a man. I've rode for a coupla men like you, an' I reckon thet's why I'm Red Krehl. It's shore a tough jam for you. I cain't be sorry for Eric, but I am for these other fellers who show yellow in the pinch!" His last words of that vow of allegiance had a stinging bite.

Bligh betrayed it most. Larry, Rollie, and Benson, almost in unison, hastened to align themselves under Red's banner of heroism.

Bill, the cook, stepped forward and unhesitatingly spoke: "Boss, I've had enough. I'm getting old. I wouldn't mind dying so much, if I had some peace and rest. But this trek is more hell than I've earned. I'll go home with Bligh."

"Bingham, put it up to our Friday," said Dann.

Slyter spoke briefly in the aborigine's tongue, or in that jargon which the black understood.

Friday leaned on his long spear and regarded the speakers with his huge, unfathomable eyes. Then he swerved them to Sterl and Red. He was weighing whatever might be in the balance. He understood. There was not the least doubt of that. His dark face included Beryl and Leslie.

Friday tapped his broad black breast with a slender black hand. "Imm no fadder, no mudder, no brudder, no *gin*, no *lubra*," he said, in slow laborious dignity. "Tinkit go bush alonga white fella cowboy pards!"

At another time Sterl would have shouted his gladness, but here he only hugged the black man. And Red clapped him on the back. Friday astonished them at infrequent times with expressions he had absorbed. Always he seemed to divine what he did not wholly understand. Here had been evidence of loyalty and friendship, if not almost a sense of humor. Friday would carry on with his white friends, see them through. Sterl accepted the magnificence of his own conceptions.

Suddenly a heavy gunshot boomed hollowly under the shelter, paralyzing speech and action. The odor of burnt powder permeated the air. There followed a queer, faint tapping sound—a shuddering quiver of hand or foot of a man in his death throes. Sterl had heard that too often to be deceived. Mrs. Slyter uttered a low cry. The girls had frozen in their grips upon the cowboys. Stanley Dann broke out of his rigidity to wave a shaking hand.

"Go in . . . somebody . . . see," he whispered.

Benson and Bligh went slowly and hesitatingly under the shelter. Sterl saw them bend over Eric Dann on the stretcher. They straightened up. Bligh drew a blanket up over the man's face. The pale blot vanished under the dark covering. The drovers stalked out. Bligh accosted the leader in hushed voice: "Prepare for a shock, sir."

Benson added gruffly: "He blew out his brains!"

"My God!" gasped Stanley, and staggered away to lean against the wagon. Slyter followed to lay a hand on him. Bligh, with his companions, groped away into the dark, and presently their low voices came to Sterl's ears. The other drovers eyed each other in the firelight, awed and tight-lipped. But their gaze flashed the intelligence of deliverance. Swiftly upon a consciousness of tragedy had followed for everyone there, possibly except their leader, a sense of release.

Red Krehl was the first to speak, as he drew Beryl away from that dark shelter with its dim still image, prone on the stretcher, and the smell of brimstone.

"Pard," he ejaculated with that low voice of surprise, "he's paid! By Gawd, he's shot himself . . . the only good thing he's done on this trek. Squares him with me."

Chapter Twenty-seven

No man ever again looked upon the face of Eric Dann. The agony of his last moment after the confession which had plunged his brother and the drovers into tragic catastrophe was cloaked in the blanket that had been thrown over him. Stanley Dann gave that order. An hour after the deed which was great in proportion to his weakness, he lay in his grave under a gum tree, with no sign to mark his last resting place. Stanley Dann most surely prayed for his soul, but no one heard that prayer. Sterl helped dig the grave by the light of the torch Friday held.

Night had fallen then—black, starless, with its haunting sounds. They were called to a late supper. Bill, actuated by a strange sentiment at variance with his abandonment of the trek, excelled himself on this last meal for Dann and those he would never cook for any more. The leader did not attend that meal. Mrs. Slyter and the girls had to force what little they ate. But the drovers were all of a mind with Krehl's philosophical remark: "Wal, it don't 'pear human. But we're a pore starved outfit . . . an' there's hard work an' more hell ahaid. Come an' get it, fellers!" Sterl was famished, and he ate his fill. The same old fare, this time embellished by a few little sweets and luxuries Bill had contrived to hang on to.

No orders to guard the mob were issued that night. But Sterl heard Bligh tell his men they would share their last watch. The girls haunted the bright fire, which Friday kept burning. They were wide-eyed and sleepless. They did not want to be alone. Mrs. Slyter finally dragged them off to Beryl's wagon. Sterl and Red sought their own tent, and removed only their boots.

"Hard lines, pard," said Red with a sigh, as he lay down. "It's turrible to worry over other people. All my life I been doin' thet. But mebbe this steel trap on our gizzards will loosen now that Eric at last made a clean job of it. You never can tell about what a man will do. . . . An' as for a woman . . . didn't yore heart jest flop over, when Beryl answered her dad?"

"Red, it sure did! And the crack of Leslie's . . . that she wouldn't go home to marry the Prince of Wales!"

"Wal, she's got a prince. I told her you was a prince. I reckon you've been one to me."

"Oh, she's mad and so's Beryl. You're mad, and I'm going."

"It'd be kinda sweet, bein' thet way, but for all this work an' pore grub, an' those crocodiles, an' the bloody mess we never get jest free of. . . . Gosh, I'd like to be like Friday."

"I'd like that, too, Red. But it can't be. Try to sleep, old man, and don't think of tomorrow."

Sterl could give sage advice that he could not live by himself. In a few moments Red was asleep. And Sterl lay awake, grateful for the flimsy sheet of canvas that shut out the light and counterfeited protection. Once he got up noiselessly to peep between the flaps. Friday sat by the fire, propped against a pack, his spear over his shoulder, his head bowed. How did he know that the aborigines would not prowl during the early hours of night? Sterl returned to bed and at last fell asleep with the howling of dingoes in his ears.

Awakening brought a vague sense of unutterable relief. It puzzled Sterl. He had to inquire into that. His unconscious mind had cast off a dread. They were across the crocodile-infested river with horses and cattle. Eric Dann's malignant influence had passed. Sterl had been lost many times, and for him another time held no fears. Dann would turn his back on the endless north-ward trek this very day. The gray light awakened Red. And a bustle outside attested to the drovers' activity.

"Bingham, we break camp at once," said Stanley Dann as he met Slyter at breakfast. "What do you say to trekking west along this river?"

"I say good-o," replied the drover. "What do you say to split-ting the load on the second dray? There's room on the wagons. That dray is worn out. It retards our progress. Leave it here."

"I agree," returned the leader. Already the tremendous incen-tive of getting on a new trek in the right direction had seized upon them.

"My wife can drive any wagon. So can Leslie, where it's not overly rough. We'll be shy of drovers, Stanley."

The leader nodded a realization of increased obstacles. Yet, that silent gesture was far removed from a doubtful shake of his head.

"Plenty bad black fella close up," Friday broke in upon them, and his indication of the absence of smoke signals was far from reassuring.

Rollie tramped up to report that the mob was still resting, but that the larger herd of horses had been scattered. Larry and Ben-son, helped by Bligh's drovers, had them mustered now just out of camp.

"We found one horse speared and cut up. Aborigine work," added Rollie.

"Could these savages prefer horseflesh to beef?" queried Dann, incredulous.

"Some tribes, so I've been told. Bligh heard blacks early this morning," asserted Slyter. "We cannot get away from Doré's Bush any too soon now."

Bligh and his three dissenters drove a string of horses across the river. Bill, the cook, had slipped down the bank, under cover of the brush, to straddle one of those horses. He did not say good bye or look back. Heald waved his hand to the cowboys. Hod and Derrick packed bags across on their saddles. They left Heald to hitch up two teams to Ormiston's wagons while they returned with Bligh for their bags and beds. On, their trip back through camp Sterl saw that Bligh hung back somewhat, and seemed possessed. Still, he overcame his weakness and followed the drovers down the path and into the river.

"Queer deal, thet," spoke up the ever valiant Red, who sat by the fire, oiling and loading his rifle. "Bligh was sweet on Beryl there at first. It seems years ago. An' the damned little jade encouraged him! You'd reckon he'd say good bye an' good luck to her, if not the old man. Wal, men air queer ducks."

"Red, he'll come back," said Sterl. "Bligh is a real guy. He rings true."

"Yeah? You heahed him say he had a girl back home," Red replied sarcastically. "Mebbe to save his face. But if he's smart, he won't say good bye to Beryl Dann. Not after failin' her dad at the crisis of his life!"

"I'll bet you two bits Bligh comes back."

"Gosh, I hope he does. I like the fellar. But I jest feel sorry for him, as I shore do for the other geezers who got turribly stuck on Beryl Dann."

"Um . . . oh!" warned Sterl too late.

Beryl, running about at the tasks she and Leslie had undertaken, had passed Red to hear the last of his scornful remark to Sterl. Beryl was lovely when in one of her sweet and appealing moods, with her better side uppermost, but Sterl was most moved by her when, as now, she was furious and her wonderful eyes blazed purple fire.

"You're sorry for whom, Red Krehl?"

Then Red was in a bad predicament, because his remark could have been and had been taken for an insult. Red had been hard, unforgiving, cold to this girl who had played with him and flouted him, but he had always been a gentleman.

"Beryl, I was sorry for Bligh," drawled Red coolly. "Me an' Sterl air gamblin' on his sayin' good bye to you. I'm bettin' thet, if he's smart, he won't try. Sterl bets he will."

"And if Bligh's smart, *why* won't he try to say good bye to me?" retorted Beryl.

"Wal, he'll get froze for his pains."

"He will, indeed . . . the coward! And now what about the *other* geezers who're stuck on Beryl Dann?"

"Aw, jest natoorally I feel sorry for them," returned Red with his easy, cool nonchalance. But there were dancing flecks in his blue eyes.

Sterl would have taken another gamble, then—that Red would not fail to rise to the occasion. But Beryl exemplified the fury of a woman scorned.

"Wal, Miss Dann, it so happens thet I'm one of them unfortunate geezers who got turribly stuck on you," returned the cowboy.

The bitterness of his sarcasm was wholly lost upon Beryl Dann. It was the deliberate content that struck her overwhelmingly.

For Sterl it was remarkable to see her, all in one moment, transformed from a desperately hurt woman, passionately furious, to one amazed, struck to the heart, bluntly told the truth that she had yearned for and ever doubted, robbed at once of all her blaze, to be left pale as pearl.

"Mister Krehl, it's a pity . . . you never told me!" she cried. "Perhaps the *geezer* who's so terribly *stuck* on me might have found out he's not really so unfortunate, after all."

Red, spirited and ready-tongued as he always was, could hardly have responded adequately to the feminine unanswerable retaliation. Sterl understood how Red could have gotten the best of her once and forever, and that would have been—right there before him and Leslie and others—to hold out his arms to her. But Red was a long way from that capitulation. Sterl saw signs of it that the suddenly humble girl could not grasp.

The situation was disrupted, however, by the appearance of Bligh.

"Come out of it, kids," whispered Sterl. "Here comes Bligh, and I win the bet."

The young drover faced Beryl to remove his sombrero and

bow. Water dripped off him from the waist down. He smelled of river ooze, but he appeared a handsome, manly fellow, uncertain of his reception, but sure of his feeling and duty.

"Beryl, I hate to go like this," he said huskily. "But when I came on this trek, I had hopes of . . . of . . . you know what. I must leave . . . and this is the time. I pray your dad gets safely through. And I wish you happiness . . . prosperity in the future. If it is as we . . . we all guess, then, indeed, the best man has won."

"Oh, Bob, how sweet of you!" cried Beryl radiantly, and all the pride and scorn of her were as if they had never been. "I'm sorry for all . . . that you must go. Kiss me good bye!" And giving him her hands, she leaned on him and lifted a scarlet face. Tears streamed from under her closely shut eyelids. Bligh kissed her heartily, but not on her lips. Then, releasing her, he turned to Sterl.

"Hazelton, it's been dinkum to know you," he said, extending his hand. "Good bye and good luck." They shook hands.

"Red Krehl, you are the damnedest fellow, the greatest fellow I ever drove with. Put her there, as you Yankees say."

"Wal, Bligh, I always kinda wanted to punch you on the nose," drawled Red, gladly accepting the proffered hand. "But I was way off. I'm sorry. I reckon you're some punkins of a fellar yoreself."

"Thanks, Red. Good bye, Leslie. You're one real Aussie lass. And now to part with our great boss. That'll be hard." He moved away from them, gazing about for Dann. Beryl averted her face and covered it with her hands. Leslie, taking her arm, led her away.

Then Bligh espied Dann, coming from his wagon, and strode to intercept him.

At that instant Red leaped like a panther. "Injuns!" he yelled fiercely. "Run! Run!"

Sterl ducked instinctively, his swift gaze taking the direction of Red's leveling rifle. He was in time to see a magnificent naked savage in the very action of throwing a spear. He heard the tussling sound as the spear was launched. Then Red's rifle cracked.

The aborigine's tremendous energy ceased as bluntly as if he had run into a wall. He fell back out of sight on the ridge.

Sterl heard, too, almost simultaneously, the chucking thud of that spear entering flesh. Wheeling, he saw the long shaft quivering in the middle of Bligh's broad back. The drover emitted a mortal groan. As he swayed backward, Sterl espied the red spear point sticking out of his breast. It had passed through Bligh almost to penetrate Dann. That last stride of Bligh's had intercepted the spear, evidently intended for the blond giant standing in the sunlight.

"Get down behind something!" Sterl yelled at the top of his lungs. He ran for the rifle leaning against the wheel of his wagon. Friday came running under the trees, his *wommera* held aloft. He must have thrown his spear, for he had none.

He reached the cover of the wagon just as Sterl got his rifle. The *whizz* of spears went by, but Sterl could not see any. Dann's roar of rage and his thumping boots relieved Sterl's fears for him.

"Plenty black fella . . . close up," panted Friday, and pointed to the low rise of brushy ground just back of camp.

Sterl peeped over the top of the wagon, but could not see any blacks. Red's rifle cracked again, accompanied by a hideous screech of agony.

"Friday, they better keep out of that red-head's sight," declared Sterl in his grim satisfaction. Then he looked around. Dann and Slyter had taken refuge behind Slyter's wagon. The drover was hurrying the women inside it. "Lie down!" Slyter commanded. "Stanley, here's one of my rifles. Watch sharp . . . along that bit of bush!"

Yells of alarm from the drovers across the river drew from Dann a booming order: "Stay over there! Hide! Abo' attack!"

Sterl swept his glance around in search of Red. It passed over Bligh, who on the moment was lying on his side, in a last convulsive writhing. The spearhead protruded from his breast. Blood poured from his mouth. The sight recalled to Sterl the work of Comanches on the plains.

"Pard," shouted Red from behind the dray a dozen steps away, "they sneaked up on us from the left. Bunch of big yeller devils! They'll work back thet way 'cause it's open below. An' I seen Larry an' Ben ridin' hell-bent for the riverbank. We'll heah them open the ball *pronto*. Where's Friday?"

"He's with me. They just missed getting him."

Red's rifle spoke ringingly. "Ha! These abo's ain't so careful as redskins."

"Where's Rollie?"

"To my right heah, back of thet log. But he's only got his six-gun. Pard, put yore hat on Friday's *wommera* an' stick it up, all same old times."

Sterl complied. The ruse drew whistling spears. One stuck the wagon seat; the other pierced Sterl's hat and jerked it away, twenty feet beyond.

Again Red shot. "I got thet bird, pard. Seen him throw. Aw, no, these blacks cain't throw a spear a-tall!"

Friday touched Sterl and pointed. It was evident that he sighted an aborigine, but Sterl could not discern any color save green. He did see the brush move, and he fired low under that place. The shot brought results in shape of a wild yell. Then the drovers across the river entered the engagement, and, following a volley from them, Larry and Benson began to shoot from behind the bank down the river below camp.

"They must be slopin', pard, but I cain't see any," called Red. "Coupla of our outfit acrost the river climbed up trees, which was a helluva good idee. I heerd lead hittin' flesh. You know thet sound."

The firing ceased, and there followed a period, tense and watchful. One of the drovers across the river hailed Dann: "Boss!"

"Hello," yelled Dann.

"They broke and ran. About a hundred or so."

"Which way?"

"Back over the downs, toward that big strip of bush where we saw smoke signals."

"You drovers take advantage of that," yelled Dann. "Clear out! Bligh's done for!"

"Right-o. Good luck!"

After a moment, Slyter called: "Blacks can't stand rifle fire. But wait . . . Hazelton, send Friday out to make sure they're gone."

But Friday had anticipated such an important move and appeared, darting from tree to tree, until he disappeared. Sterl waited anxiously. Red came running to join Sterl.

"All over 'most before it started," he said. "Did you bore one, pard?"

"I'm afraid not. But I made one yell."

"Wal, I made up for thet. They was great, tall fellers, Sterl, wonderful built, an' not black a-tall. Kinda a cross between brown and yeller. Wild? Holy Mackeli!"

"Can you see Friday?"

"Shore. He's comin' back from the ridge there. Gosh! He's heeled, too. Packin' spears an' *wommera*. So we must have bored a few."

Presently the black strode back into camp. The cowboys met him, and Slyter and Dann followed in haste. Rollie was next to arrive.

"Black fella run alonga here," said Friday. "All guns. Come back bimeby."

"We must not lose a moment," boomed the leader.

Red gazed down at the dead drover: "My Gawd, ain't thet tough? Jest a second quicker an' I'd have saved him! I saw somethin' out of the corner of my eye. Too late."

"Bligh stepped in front of me in time to save my life," rolled Dann tragically. "That black was after me! I saw him rear back and throw. Paralyzed me!"

"Damn sad, boss. But not for us. We was losin' Bligh anyhow. I reckon we oughta slope *pronto*."

Larry and Benson came panting up on foot. They stared in horror at Bligh. It had appeared they were eager to speak, but sight of the speared drover inhibited them for the moment.

"Slyter, we must muster and drove out of here in double-quick time," declared Dann.

"Right-o. They might track us. But maybe not."

"Friday, will those aborigines track us?" queried Dann.

"Might be. Pretty cheeky."

"Let me see," pondered the leader. "The horses are close. We'll abandon another wagon. Pack . . . Hazelton, you and Krehl go with Larry Benson. Drove the mob up the river. We'll follow behind the horses . . . Slyter, you and Friday help me bury this poor fellow who had to say good bye to me . . . which saved me and cost him his life."

Riding out with the drovers, the cowboys had a look at the several dead aborigines. There were evidences that the fleeing natives had taken their wounded with them. Sterl rode straight to the place where he had fired at one through the foliage. He found blood, but no body.

The savage who had murdered Bligh lay in the grass on the open ridge where Red had espied him. The aborigine did not resemble Friday in any particular. He was taller, more slender, more marvelously formed. The color appeared to be a cast between brown and red. Perhaps the thin red hair covering the body accounted for that tinge of color. The matted mop of hair had a tinge of red in its black. His visage was brutish and wild, scarcely human.

"Wal, I shore didn't hit the bastard where I aimed, but I bored him all right," declared Red. "Gosh, he's long-laiged! Reckon I don't want one like him chasin' me on foot. I'd be a gone goslin'.'"

Only the physical signs about that aborigine appeared to interest the cowboy. He was, however, tremendously wrathful over the fine horse the aborigines had slaughtered and cut up. "Hossmeat eaters! When there was daid beef for the takin'!"

The mob had moved away of its own volition, but as the direction was upriver, the drovers were gratified about it. They caught up in short order and were again on the trek. The ground was hard and level, the grass luxuriant, and clumps of brushland widened away to the north. Sterl kept looking back for the wagons, and, while doing so, he could not help seeing the smoke signals in the distance. The cattle were fresh, restless, and eager to hurry along, although part of the mob grazed intermittently.

"Hosses comin', pard," Red said over his shoulder. "Leslie an' Friday herdin' them. Two wagons an' a dray behind! If you ask me, we're an outfit shore smothered with luck."

"Bad or good?" queried Sterl.

"Good, you locoed gent!"

"But we're lost. Too many cattle and horses. Too few men."

"Bet you we get along better."

"It's a bet."

Sterl looked back. The sky was black with circling, drooping birds of prey. What a relief to get away from the stench! The larger gum trees were white with birds. Beyond them the smoke signals thinned out. Ahead of the mob, kangaroos dotted the rippling downs. In the west only faint shadowy lines of clouds or ranges hovered in the air.

The horses came trooping up in two bunches, one large on the left, and that on Sterl's side numbering perhaps a hundred. These were Slyter's horses, and included the five Thoroughbreds that were left of Leslie's band. But she rode Lady Jane, and Red was on Duke, and Sterl on King. Considering everything, it was a remarkable achievement of Slyter's to have still nine-tenths of the horses he had started with. Once behind the mob, the horses slowed down to their leisurely grazing gait. Leslie kept behind them. The wagons caught up, then slowed to a walk. Sterl espied Beryl, sitting beside her father. Mrs. Slyter was with her husband. Friday shifted over to Sterl's side. There was a tomahawk stuck in a belt round his waist, and he carried two *wommeras* and a bundle of spears. Rollie brought up the rear.

The trek was on again. Sterl hardly realized it. He felt the old instinctive reactions tugging at his tragic mood. Brief as the last few days had been, they were crowded with so much stern labor and so many incidents that they seemed to cover a long period.

Friday gazed often back over his shoulder. It must have been to read the smoke signals, not to see any signs of pursuit. But it was not possible to believe they had seen the last of this strange and war-like tribe of aborigines. According to Slyter, a daylight attack was extremely rare. The earliest dawn hour had always been the most favorable for the blacks to attack, and perhaps the worst for the drovers. Tired guards were likely to fall asleep at the last. Sterl hoped for the best, but his fears could not simmer down.

At intervals the trek crossed small, fresh-water streams that showed no evidence of tides. The line of travel was a mile or thereabouts from the bush that lined the river. Toward sundown Slyter left his wife to drive his wagon, and, mounting a horse, he rode ahead, obviously to pick out a campsite. Besides grass, water, firewood, there was now imperative need of a camp which the aborigines could not approach under cover.

Sunset had come when Slyter finally called a halt. Three gum trees marked the spot. One of them was teak and would supply the necessary firewood. A running stream was adjacent. Off toward the river a hundred rods grew a dense copse fringed by isolated bushes. The rest was level, grassy downs. All of these features had figured in Slyter's selection.

"From now on everyone does two men's work," boomed Dann. "Missus Slyter and the girls take charge of rations and cooking. We men will all take turns at supplying firewood and washing up after the meals."

An anxious, hurried, mostly silent attack upon camp tasks followed. Supper was disposed of while there was still daylight. The level downs shone gold, apparently clear to where the sun set.

"An important thing now is to sleep away from the fire and the wagons," asserted Slyter. "It is good to keep a fire burning all night. Blacks often spear men while they are asleep. That's why we must all hide."

"Old stuff for me an' Sterl, boss," drawled Red. "We're used to sleepin' with one eye open. An' heah, why we can heah a grasshopper scratch his nose."

But none of the trekkers laughed any more, nor smiled. That climax at Doré's Bush had been like a great mace, beating into them a final sense of the fatal chances against them. Even Stanley

Dann saw at last the futility of relying solely upon hope, faith, courage. These would help, especially the last, but the issue depended upon sight and hearing, and the instinct to fight. Red Krehl was throwing a bluff. It was well known to Sterl that the narrower a margin of safety, the cooler and more deadly nonchalant this Texas cowboy grew. For himself, Sterl could only gird up his loins and set himself bitterly against catastrophe.

The cowboys helped Dann and Slyter carry ground cloths, blankets, and nets over to the fringe of brush near the copse. That appeared to be an impenetrable thorny brush—*A favorable place*, thought Sterl. Beds were laid under the brush. The three women were to sleep between Dann and Slyter. The mosquitoes were terrible, but they had become a secondary trial. Presently Red came over, escorting the girls, who were frightened.

"Do you really think the aborigines will come tonight?" asked Beryl apprehensively.

"Wal, there's no tellin'. Let's expect the wust. An' it might not come."

Leslie said: "Oh, I'd just as lief be speared by aborigines as speared by those mosquitoes!"

"Crawl in, both of you," ordered Slyter. "Don't take off even your shoes. There! Now, Red, tuck that net around their heads, but not flat."

While Red carefully arranged the net, Beryl gazed up at him with eyes unnaturally large and dark in the starlight.

"Just to think, Red, I could have escaped all this . . . if I had married one of those nice Sydney boys, or even a Downsville merchant!" she exclaimed wonderingly, yet not without subtlety.

"Shore you could, you darn little fool," drawled Red. "I told you that the day I met you."

"If I remember rightly, you did not," she retorted.

"Sterl, we're supposed to sleep . . . and lie quiet, no matter what happens?" asked Leslie.

"We'll be reasonably safe here," interposed Slyter. "Come on, Mum, get in next to the girls. I'll be along presently. Go to sleep.

If you should hear aboriginal yells, gunshots, or anything . . . don't be unduly frightened."

The men returned to the fire. Friday was splitting quantities of wood.

"It will be bright moonlight presently," Dann said. "That's in our favor. Benson, take Larry and Roland on guard. I needn't tell you to be vigilant. Don't be separated for more than a moment at a time. Stay off your horses unless there's a rush, or something unusual. Come in after midnight to wake Hazelton and Krehl."

"Hazelton, where will you sleep?" asked Benson.

"What do you say, Red?" returned Sterl.

"Something pretty close to these trees . . . on the side away from the open. We'll heah you, when you call."

No more was said. The drovers led their horses away toward Dann's band to change to fresh mounts. Slyter went out to have a look at his band, in plain sight under the rising moon. Dann tramped off to bed. Friday dropped his axe to replenish the fire.

"I'm not sleepy a-tall," said Red, rolling a cigarette. "Air you, pard?"

"Nope."

The hungry horde of mosquitoes were outwitted so long as the net was away from his face. The dew fell almost like mist. Water-fowl winged swift flight over the downs. A heavy splash attested to some creature that was not a bird. The moon shone so brightly that Sterl had to turn his eyes away from it. He wished the night was over. To wait, to listen, to be in suspense seemed harder than actual combat. No sound from horses or mob. He was listening when he went to sleep.

When a gentle hand fell on his shoulder and Friday's voice followed, Sterl felt that he had not had his eyes closed longer than a moment.

"All well, Friday?" he asked.

"Everything good. But bimeby bad," replied the black.

Red had sat up, putting on the coat he had used for a pillow. Everything was wet with dew. The moon had soared beyond the zenith and blazed down with supernatural whiteness. The downs resembled a snowy range. A ghastly stillness reigned over the wilderness. Even the mosquitoes had gone.

At the refreshed campfire the three drovers were drinking tea.

"How is tricks, Ben?" asked Red.

"Mob bedded down. Horse quite quiet. Not a move. Not a sound. It was as if we were in another world."

"Boys, have another cup of tea while I muster your horses," said Larry.

"Heah comes Slyter," added Red.

The drover appeared, a dark blot against the moon-blanched grass. He asked anxiously about the horses, and then the mob.

"Lucky it's so bright. Almost like day," he replied in relief. "Roland, give me a cup . . . Let's see, it's half after midnight. Boys, look sharp for three hours . . . then sharper."

The cowboys left camp, leading their horses, accompanied by Friday.

The mob could be seen for a long distance. It was like a checkerboard on the silvery downs. They passed the two herds of horses, the larger of which—Dann's—were grouped between the cattle and the camp.

Red chose a position near a single tree on that side from which they could see both the mob and the herd. They remained on foot. Friday made off until he vanished in the ghostly brightness. Red and Sterl smoked, walked to and fro, talked but little, listened intensely. Nothing happened. Friday returned to squat under the tree. His silence seemed encouraging.

"Let's take turns dozin'," suggested Red, and proceeded to put that idea into execution.

Sterl marked a gradual slanting of the moon and a diminishing of the radiance. But a good while elapsed before the silver turned to gray. Red fell over his knees to awaken, and then to insist that Sterl take a nap. Long habit made this easy, unless there was strong mental opposition. But Sterl fell into a half slumber. When he awakened, the moon was far down and weird. The deep boom of a bittern broke the dismal silence. The stars were wan. The hour before dawn was close at hand.

"Pard, there's no change in the herd, but Dann's hosses have worked off a bit, an' Slyter's air almost in camp. One of the boys just threw wood on the fire," said Red.

Sterl got up to stretch his cramped legs. "Red, you said no change. Why this isn't the same night at all."

"It's mawnin', pard, an', if all of us air gonna be murdered, it's shore about time."

"Shall we ride around a bit?"

"No good a-tall, an' it might be bad. Let's hang heah an' listen. It's a cinch we cain't see much longer."

"*Shoosh!*" hissed the black, and that from him froze the cowboys. If he had heard anything, he did not indicate what or from whence. Rifles in hands, the cowboys stood motionlessly in the shadows of the trees. The horses drooped their heads. But as the moments passed and nothing broke the unbearable stillness, and the grāy shadowy mantle spread uncannily over the downs, Red and Sterl moved about a little. Several times Friday laid his ear to the ground, an action remarkably similar to that of Indian scouts the cowboys had worked with. It was so still that any slight sound would have carried far. The gray gloom encroached up the downs, hiding the mob, and then the horses, and at last made the campfire fade into a ghostly flicker.

The moment arrived when Sterl made sure that no sensorial perception of any kind had given rise to his feeling that they were not alone out here. Red's posture added to the strength of his stimulus. The aboriginal's positively confirmed it. Possibly the black man was responsible for this strange effect. It was impossible for Sterl to remain longer motionless and speechless. He stepped to Red's side and whispered.

"I'm buffaloed, pard, an' skeered clean out of my skin," replied Red.

Sterl asked Friday the same question.

"Smellum black fella!"

So it was scent! Like a hound, his keenest sense was in his nose. Sterl might have been so affected, but he could not tell if that were true. They waited, Red and Sterl, strangely reverting to physical contact in their intense suspense. Their guide and comrade, an aboriginal himself, smelled the approach of his species on the down. They could not be seen or heard. A white man could not have scented them, to know it.

"What do?" whispered Sterl hoarsely, leaning to Friday's ear.

"Tinkit more better alonga here." Undoubtedly the black advised staying right where they were.

The ensuing minutes were fraught with almost insupportable strain. Sterl thanked heaven for this black man. Without him they would have been lost in that Outback wilderness, as so many Australian explorers and pioneers had been.

"Pard, I cain't smell a damn' thing," whispered Red.

"I'm glad I can't. If we could . . . these abo's would be close. Red, it's far worse to stand than a Comanche stalk."

"Hell, yes! Oughtn't be, but shore is. All the same, Sterl, they cain't sneak right up on top of us. I'm scared they'll stumble across the girls."

"Stumble? Say, if Friday can scent them, you bet they can scent us."

"Aw! I reckoned it was the stink of some of these aborigines."

"Shooosh!" The black added a hand to his caution. Again the cowboys became statues. This kind of menace seemed peculiarly horrible. Sterl felt he could not long suppress a fierce yell of mingled rage and fear.

"Obber dere," whispered Friday. And to Sterl's great relief he pointed away from camp in a downriver direction. Dann's herd of horses had vanished in that direction. Although Sterl strained his ears to the extent of pain, he could not hear a sound. The way Friday turned his ear, however, proved that he had heard something in that direction.

Suddenly the speaking and sinister silence broke to a thud of hoofs. Sterl jerked up as if galvanized.

"Skeered hoss. But not bad. Reckon he got a scent, like Friday," whispered Red.

Another little run of hoofs on soft ground.

"I heahed a hoss wicker," whispered Red intensely. Friday held

up his hand. Events were about to break, and Sterl greeted the
fact with a release of tension. But he found his mouth dry and
swallowing difficult and breathing oppressive.

Whang! On the still air sped a strange sound, familiar, although
Sterl could not place it. Instantly there followed the peculiar
thud of bullet or missile entering flesh. It could not have been a
bullet, for no report followed. Hard on that sound pealed out the
shrill, horrid, unearthly scream of a horse in mortal agony. There
came a pounding of hoofs, a trampling, and a heavy body, thudding the ground. The herd took flight, snorting and whistling.

"You savvy *wommera?*" asked Friday in a whisper.

"I shore did. An' you bet I shivered in my boots," replied Red.

Then the strange sound, almost a twang, became clear to
Sterl's mind.

"Black fella spearum hoss," added Friday.

Red broke into curses. "They're butchering one of our hosses.
I heah the rip of hide! Let's sneak over an' shoot the gizzards out
of them!"

Chapter Twenty-eight

Sterl gave grim acquiescence to Red's bold suggestion that
they stalk the aborigines. But Friday whispered: "More better
black fella go alonga bush *corroboree.*"

The cowboys weighed that advice. And as the entering wedge
of caution penetrated their hot anger at the slaughtering of
horses, they saw the wisdom of it.

"Pard, he talks sense. It's more better we let the abo's gorge
themselves on horse meat, an' dance an' sing, than for us to run
the littlest risk."

"Right, Red. But it galls me," rejoined Sterl, and lapsed into
silence again. New, faint sounds reached their ears—what must
have been a rending of bones. The aborigines were dismembering

the horse they had speared. Splashing sounds succeeded these, and then the keenest listening was in vain.

Meanwhile, the gray lightened; the birds began to sing. At last day broke, an infinitely relieving event. The ring of an axe signified activity in camp.

Slyter's horses grazed along the streams beyond camp; Dann's horses had worked toward the river; the mob had begun to stir. All appeared well with the stock.

Daylight made a vast difference in the feelings of the cowboys. While Friday went on into camp, they took a short cut to change horses. King and Duke were saddled and led on in. King had a loose shoe that Sterl wanted to renail. Red said he would ride out and see what signs the marauding aborigines might have left. Then Sterl returned to camp.

All the men were up, and Slyter was helping his wife get breakfast. His eyes questioned Sterl in mute anxiety. But, upon hearing Sterl's report, he was far from mute. Dann, too, ground his teeth.

"We could spare a bullock, but a good horse. . . ."

Rollie had just come in with a team. Sterl helped him hitch them to the wagon. Larry and Benson led the other teams and saddle horses in. Last to arrive, as Mrs. Slyter called to breakfast, was Red.

"Boss, I reckon Sterl has told you what come off this mawnin'," he said, looking down from his saddle. "I found where them abo's had killed an' butchered yore hoss. Nary hide nor hair nor hoof left! They packed all of that hoss away. Grass all trampled an' gory. Must have been a hundred abo's in thet outfit!"

"They will dog our trek," boomed the leader tragically.

"Rode across to the river," added Red. "Could see the plains on the other side. No sign of cattle or drovers."

"We will never see them again."

Slyter added pessimistically: "No one will ever see them again."

The girls appeared at breakfast, betraying the havoc of an uncomfortable and wakeful night. But their demeanor augured well. They all ate breakfast together, even Friday, sitting with them on the ground. Leslie had learned to imitate the cowboys who sat Indian fashion, their feet tucked under them. Beryl was valiant, but she had not managed it yet. While eating thus, one of the drovers let out what Sterl and Red had desired to keep from the girls—the butchering of the horse. Beryl contained her disgust and anger, but Leslie burst out with profane words she had learned from the cowboys. Mrs. Slyter did not reprove her.

By sunrise the trekkers were on their way, with the sun warm on their backs. The pace of the cattle was tediously slow, but that could not be helped. Mile after mile and league after league failed of that tranquil restoration to peace which had been the good fortune of the trekkers on the earlier stages. Behind them rose the yellow smoke signals, and far in advance floated the same strange menacing telegraphy of the aborigines.

For ten nights that band of aboriginals, reinforced at every camp, hung on the tracks of the trekkers. Nothing was ever seen of them but their haunting smoke magic. The silence, the mystery, the inevitable attack on the horses in the gray dawn, wore increasingly upon the drovers. The savages never chose to kill a beef. They were horse-meat eaters. The horrible fear they impressed upon the pursued was that, when they tired of horseflesh, they would try to obtain human flesh. For Slyter averred that they were cannibals. Friday, when asked about this dire possibility, looked blank and did not answer.

Stanley Dann bore the brunt of the loss in horses. Slyter's blooded stock was herded into the best available spots, while Dann's was left free to roam with the mob. His contention was that to make it difficult for the aborigines to butcher horses increased the peril of his drovers.

"Wal, mebbe, when they get done feastin' on hossflesh, they'll try beef," drawled Red. "An' as we're drivin' about twenty-five hundred haid, we got enough meat to feed them for eight more years."

But no one laughed any more at Red's caustic humor, or at anything else.

Twelve days' trek from Doré's Bush, which seemed ages and thousands of leagues back in the past. Now the trekkers approached the end of the downs. The river had diminished to a creek. Long had they passed by the zone of the tides. Day by day the patches and fringes of bush had encroached more upon the green, shining monotony of the downs. Vague blue tracery of higher ground hung over the horizon. The waterfowl, except for cranes and egrets, had given way to a variable and colorful parrot life. And, once more, kangaroos became too numerous to count.

A western horizon, clear of smoke signals for several days, raised the hope that the haunts of this particular tribe of aborigines had almost reached a limit. But Slyter averred that the Australian blacks knew no limit to their wanderings. They ranged where food and water were to be found.

"Makes no difference, if we do pass the happy huntin' ground of this breed of abo's," said Red. "We'll only run into more. They're as thick as kangaroos. This heah bunch has got me buffaloed. You cain't see them. A coupla more hosses butchered will put me on the warpath, boss or no boss."

"Krehl, thet's not like you," reproved Dann. "Seldom do you forget our womenfolk."

"Hell, boss! I ain't forgettin' them," protested Red. "I figger these abo's up heah air yeller clear to their gizzards. They shore ain't like Friday. An' I figger that killin' some of them would stop their doggin' us. Thet used to be the case with the plains redskins."

The leader shook his shaggy, golden head. The problem was growing beyond him. Slyter seemed inclined to side with the cowboy.

As the bush encroached more upon the downs, *corroborees* were held nightly by the aborigines. The wild revels and the weird chantings murdered sleep for the trekkers. Always over them hovered the evil portent of what the cannibals had been known to do in the Australian remote wildernesses.

One gray morning dawned with bad news for the Slyters. Leslie's Thoroughbred, a gray roan stallion of great promise, which the girl called Lord Chester, was missing from the band. Red and Sterl made this discovery, but were loath to tell her. They scoured the downs and nearby bush in hope that he had strayed. Then Red ran across the spot where he had been killed and butchered. Upon their return to camp, Leslie was waiting in distress.

"Les, we cain't find him," confessed Red. "An' I jest reckon he's gone the way of so many of Dann's hosses."

Slyter admitted that he had expected this very disaster and had been prepared for it. But that did not help Leslie. She broke down and wept bitterly.

"Leslie, we're dog-gone sorry," Sterl said. "It's sure hard to bear. But you've been lucky." That solicitude only added fuel to the fire of Leslie's grief.

"Say, cain't you take yore medicine?" queried Red, always prone to hide his softer side under a cloak of bitterness or scorn. "This heah trek ain't no circus parade. What's another hoss, even if he is one of yore Thoroughbreds?"

"Red Krehl!" she cried in passionate amaze at his apparent callousness. "I've lost horses . . . lost Duchess and never whimpered. But Chester . . . it's too much. I loved him . . . almost as I do Lady Jane!"

"Shore you did. I felt thet way once over a hoss, though out heah it's hard to remember. Chester is gone. It's tough. But don't be a baby."

"Baby? I'm no baby, Red Krehl! It's Dann and Dad and you . . . all of you who've lost your nerve! If you and Sterl and Larry and Rol . . . if you . . . any one of you . . . had any courage, you'd *kill* these abo's!"

The girl's passion, her rich voice, stinging with scorn, appeared

ZANE GREY®

to lash the cowboy. No one could have doubted what she would have done had she been a man.

"By gosh, Leslie, you're right," he replied. "I shore deserved thet. No excuse for me, or any of us, onless we're jest plain worn to a frazzle."

Beryl, listening intently, her dark eyes on Red, evidently interpreted him in like manner with Sterl.

"Red Krehl, what do you mean by that speech?" she demanded.

"Never mind what I mean. Leslie hit me one below the belt."

"That is no reason for you to concoct some blood reprisal of revenge."

"Dog-gone it, Beryl, if you cain't talk English I savvy, try abo' lingo, will you?" Red complained evasively.

"Red, loss of that lovely gray horse has hurt Leslie unbearably," went on Beryl eloquently. "It has made her a selfish hurt child again. Leslie is a grand girl. She has proved that to me. But she's like you . . . a savage. She forgets."

"Yeah? Forgets what?" drawled the cowboy, fascinated by the beauty and appeal of this young woman.

"That her loss was only a horse. That her grief and scorn might influence you to revenge upon these aborigines. If you and Sterl and Larry and Rollie should be killed or badly wounded, our trek is doomed."

"Beryl, I shore like you a heap more for your talk," returned Red, evidently profoundly stirred. "You're smarter than any of us, an' you've gone less savage. But heah we air. Mebbe Leslie's ravin' is more sense than yore intelligence. It's a hard nut to crack. . . ."

"Girls, you are both right," Sterl replied earnestly. "We can gain much from what you said. The thing to do is to act upon Leslie's rage with all the caution that your reason suggests."

"Right, pard," said Red gratefully. "Beryl, we'll pay these abo's in some bloody coin without undue risk to ourselves. Will thet rest yore mind?"

"Yes, thank you, Red. I have faith in your promises," Beryl returned gravely.

A hundred times that day Sterl saw Red turn in his saddle to look for the smoke signals of the aboriginals rising above the bush horizon to the north. Toward noonday, they dispursed and vanished. No more were any seen to the west.

But that night in camp, when Larry, Rollie, and Benson were about to go out on guard, Friday held up his hand: "*Corroboree!*" They listened. From the darkness wailed a chant, as of the savages. The festivity might have been a reveling in fresh meat, but the sound seemed one of lost souls, bewailing their fate. It rose on the night wind.

"How far away, Friday?" asked Red tersely.

"Close up."

"How many?"

"Plenty black fella. No *gin*. No *lubra*."

Red swept a blue-fire glance all around to see that he would not be overheard by the women. "Fellers, it's a hunch. Grab yore rifles an' extra cartridges. We'll give these abo's a mess of lead."

Friday led the way beyond camp. Out in the open the sounds of the *corroboree* became more pronounced. A slight breeze wafted the mournful chant distinctly to their ears. With all its pathos and strange mystic rhythms, it had an unparalleled savagery. It curdled the blood. These aborigines had chanted that way over a feast of human flesh. It was that conviction that served to inflame the stalkers.

As they neared the bush, the chant swelled to a pitch indicating many voices. Lights of fires glimmered through the trees. Soon dark, dancing forms grotesquely crossed the lights. Friday led a zigzag way through the bush and brush, and at last he crawled. Every little while Sterl put out a hand to detain him. The black seemed keen to visit disaster upon this tribe of his people.

They were halted by a stream or pond.

"About as far as we can get," whispered Red. "Let's take a peep. When I get the lay of the deal, I'll talk turkey. Careful now!"

Silently the five rose from behind the fringe of brush to peer through rents and over the top. Sterl was surprised to see a wide stretch of water, mirroring three fires and fantastic figures of dancing aborigines. The camp was fully two hundred yards distant. There were three fires around which a hundred or more moved in strange gyrations, filling the air with solemn and discordant chant. Yet it had a peculiar rhythm. It was symbolic. The smell of roasting meat pervaded the atmosphere, and did not divert the attention from movement and music that must have been ritual. They were wild men. That they were not actually beasts—that there was hope for their dark and undeveloped brains lay in the presence of Friday, the black man, who had led the white avengers to the attack. The distance was about a hundred yards.

"Plenty black fella," whispered Friday in tense excitement. "Big *corroboree!* Full debbil along hoss meat! Bimeby bad!"

"I should snicker to snort," whispered Red. "Mebbe he means thet hossflesh has gone stale. They want long-pig! Let's frame it thet way."

Sibilant whispers attested to the three drovers, roused to grim, death-dealing mood. Sterl said: "It's a cinch they'll roast us next!"

"All right, heah's the deal," whispered Red tensely. "It's a long shot. But we're bound to pile some of them. Make shore of yore first shot. Then empty yore rifles *pronto*, reload, an' we'll slope. Ben, take the extreme right. Rollie, you next. Then Larry . . . pard Sterl, forget yore Injun-lovin' weakness, an' shoot like you could, if one of us was in there roastin' on the coals."

They cocked and raised their rifles. Sterl drew down upon a dense group of dark figures huddled together, swaying in unison.

"One . . . two . . . three . . . *shoot!*" hissed Red.

The rifles cracked. Instantly there ensured a terrific scene of terror and shrieking activity. Pandemonium broke loose. The aboriginals knocked against each other in their mad rush. And a merciless fire poured into them. Sterl's ears dulled to the cracking volleys. On each side of him flame and smoke belched forth. Sterl aimed and shot as swiftly as his faculties permitted. When his rifle was hot and empty, he peered through the smoke. Red was still shooting, using his shotgun now. One of the drovers was doing likewise. From the circle of light, gliding black forms vanished. But around the fires lay prone aborigines, and many wrestling, writhing, shrieking.

"Slope . . . fellers." Red ordered huskily, and they turned away on the run. Friday led the way. Sterl followed closely. The drovers thudded behind. They ran swiftly at first, then gradually slowed down. The grass tripped them. Red fell headlong. Larry followed suit. At length, the cowboy halted from exhaustion.

"Reckon we're out of reach of them spears," he gasped. "I ain't used to runnin'. Wal, did it work?"

"Work? It was a massacre," declared Benson in hoarse, broken accents.

"Ground was . . . covered with abo's," added Larry.

Rollie exclaimed in deep, inaudible words that were eloquent without being distinguishable. Sterl kept his thoughts to himself. Such liberation of passionate deadly instinct had its reaction. "Let's rustle for camp," added Red. "They'll all be scared stiff."

His premonition had ample vindication. There was no sight of anyone in camp until Friday ran into the firelight. Then they all appeared from under the wagon.

"What the hell?" boomed Dann, rifle in hand, as he stalked out.

"Were you attacked?" Slyter queried sharply.

Beryl ran straight into Red, to throw her arms around him, then sink limply upon his breast. Red upheld her, while he looked over her head at the frightened drovers.

"Boss, the abo's didn't stalk us," he said. "We went after them. It jest had to be done."

Red appeared to realize that he had a girl in his arms. She had not fainted, as was manifest in her movement, when she gazed up at Red and slipped her hands down to his coat. She was beyond thinking of what her actions betrayed.

"We blasted hell out of them," declared Benson. "And it was a good thing."

"Hazelton, are you dumb?" asked Slyter testily, his strain relaxing.

"Wholesale murder, boss," replied Sterl. "But justifiable. When we saw them dancing 'round their fires. . . . Well, Friday intimated that we might be roasting next on their spits."

"Oh, Red!" cried Beryl. "I thought you had broken your promise . . . that you might be. . . ."

A heart of flint would have melted at her faltering voice, so pregnant with love, if it could have withstood the white face and darkly dilated eyes.

"Umpumm, Beryl," Red returned, visibly moved as he released himself and steadied her on her feet. "We was shore crazy, but took no chances. Mebbe we done them pore devils wrong when we figgered them cannibals. But, honest, I had thet hunch. . . . Beryl, you an' Leslie can feel shore thet bunch of abo's won't hound us again."

Red's prediction turned out to be true. There were no more raids on the horses, no more smoke signals on the horizon. But days had to pass before the drovers believed in their deliverance.

They trekked off the downs into mulga and spinifex country, covered with good grass, fairly well watered, and dotted with dwarf gums and fig and pandamus trees. The ground was gradually rising, but the low hills that had been seen from the downs could not be sighted.

They came next into a region of anthills. Many a field of these queer, earthier habitations had been passed through, but this one gave unparalleled and remarkable evidence of the fecundity and energy of the wood- and leaf-eating ants. The hills shone gray and yellow in the sunlight. They were of every conceivable size and shape, up to the height of three tall men, and broad in proportion. In shape they were round, domed, fluted, or square. Each one had been built around and over a stump. They did not stand close together, yet they appeared to be as numerous as the gum trees they subsisted on. At night they shone ghostly in the starlight. Sterl found that every dead log he cut into was only a shell—that the interior had been eaten away. And from every dead branch or part of a live tree poured forth an army of black or red ants, furious at the invasion of their homes.

At last Sterl understood the reason for Australia's magnificent eucalyptus trees, predominating everywhere in greater or lesser degree. In the ages past, during the evolution of this oldest continent, nature had developed the gum tree with its many varieties, but all secreting the poisonous eucalyptus oil, as defensive a characteristic as the spines on a cactus. Other trees had developed a hardness of fiber that was impervious to the ravages of ants.

In due course, the trekkers camped on a range of low hills, with a watercourse which gave them an easy grade. Followed to its source, that stream led to a divide. Water here ran toward the west. That was such a tremendous circumstance, so significant in its power to stir almost dead hopes, that Dann called a halt where the pass widened out. They pitched camp to rest, to recuperate, to make much needed repairs, and to try to recapture something of that spirit which they felt had been blunted, if not broken.

The highest hill near that camp was not a mountain, but from its summit, four or five hundred feet up, next morning Sterl and Slyter, accompanied by Friday, gazed out to the west with awe and fear.

Down in camp the last preparations for a start were being made. Dann was waiting for a report on the land ahead. The trek had achieved another crisis, perhaps the most important of all. If any direction for the drovers could be more unknown than another, this west was it.

"It is that unknown country beyond Outback Australia!" exclaimed Slyter, and there was awe in his tone.

The black man, Friday, made a slow, grand gesture which seemed symbolic of the infinite. Indeed, this abyss resembled the void of the sky. Sterl had feeling enough left in him to be deeply moved. But not by appreciation of beauty! It was an appalling vision of immensity and endlessness.

The early morning was hot, clear, windless. No dust or haze obstructed his view. Beneath and beyond him yawned what seemed a thousand leagues of green-patched, white-striped slope, leading down, down to a nothingness.

That emptiness out there struck at Sterl's intelligence. It was nature's secret. It did not mean to be solved. It was the last stronghold of the elements. It had taken hundreds of millions of years to evolve into what it was, and it seemed to flaunt a changeless inhospitality in the face of man.

But if it was not verdant, it certainly was not barren. Sterl could make sense of the land that his gaze commanded. The stream which flowed out of the pass meandered through a park-like bushland. It shone like a waving ribbon in the sun. Sterl made sure of it for twenty, thirty miles, then it faded into the green that had become gray and the gray that ended in blue. The widely separated gum trees looked like tufts of weeds; the pale patches might have been bleached grass; the roll of land resembled a rippling sea.

An austere and terrific loneliness infested that boundless area. It was the other half of the world. It dreamed and brooded under the hot sun. On and on forever it spread and sloped and waved away into infinitude, its monotony inscrutable and insupportable.

"Never . . . Never . . . Land!" gasped Slyter.

Sterl had not needed to be told that. But he faced his aboriginal comrade.

"White fella go alonga dere nebber come back!" said Friday.

Sterl's mood augmented rather than quieted as they approached the blond giant who awaited them. At camp, Slyter reported simply and truthfully that the trek had passed on to the border of the Never Never Land. No need to repeat the aborigine's warning.

"Good!" boomed Stanley Dann. "The promised land at last! Roll along, you trekkers!"

Red Krehl averted his gaze from the dark eyes of havoc that spoke so eloquently from Beryl's small, brown face. Sterl had no word for the tragic question in Leslie's hazel eyes. These young women had passed beyond filial duty. It was primitive love, born of the travail, the agony, the terror, that upheld them. But Sterl accorded them the highest meed of reverence that was in him. A thousand to one were the chances against their ever crossing the Never Never. Yet, as they rode out of the wide portal into the unknown, with the dry eucalyptus fragrance closing their nostrils, with the wagons rolling ahead of the wagging mob, for Sterl the moment was grand in the extreme.

Midsummer caught Dann's trek out in the arid interior. They knew it was midsummer by the heat and drought, but in no other way, for Dann had long forgotten his journal and Sterl had long since tired of recording labor, misery, fight, and death. Always he imagined events would be recorded upon his memory in letters of fire, yet all had become effaced except the unforgettable few.

They had followed a stream for weeks. Here and there, miles apart, they found clear pools in rocky places. The bleached grass had grown scant, but it was nutritious. If the cattle could drink every day or two, they would survive. But many of the weak dropped by the wayside. Cows with newly born calves had to be driven from the water holes, and, when the calves failed, the mothers refused to leave them. Some mornings the trek would be held up because of strayed horses. Some were lost. Dann would not spare the time to track them. The heat was growing intense. If the duststorms came, a halt would have to be made.

The trek had become chaotic when the drovers reached a zone where rock formations held a succession of pools of clear water, one that amounted to a pond.

"Manna in the wilderness!" sang out Stanley Dann joyfully. "We'll camp here until the rains come again!"

To the girls that meant survival. To the drovers it was exceedingly joyous news. The water was a saving factor, just in the nick of time. Sterl and Red welcomed that reprieve. Rest seemed a heavenly thing. Hope and faith were hard to eradicate from the human breast. Long reaches of scant, bleached grass waved away under the hot sun. Dead, gnarled gum trees vied with the live ones and gave the veldt a forlorn appearance. The only kangaroos they saw were dead ones that Slyter said had traveled too far for water. The omnipresent parrots, cockatoos, and magpies were remarkable for their absence.

Everywhere were evidences of a long cessation of rain in these parts. In good seasons the stream must have been a fair little river, and during flood time it had spread all over the flat. Birds and animals had apparently deserted the locality. The grass was bleached white; the plants had been burned sere by the sun; trees appeared to be withering.

Dann gave orders to the drovers to unhitch, and unpack, then bury the putrefying and sun-dried bodies of birds and kangaroos that lay scattered about to poison the air and water.

There was a deep pool of pure water in a shaded pocket among the rocks; there were many other pools, and one long pond, all of which would provide drink for man and beast over an indefinite period until the rains came. This fortunate circumstance and the miles and miles of spare grass solved the drovers' critical problem.

Dann said philosophically to Slyter: "We have water enough and meat and salt enough to exist here for five years." That showed his trend of thought. Sterl heard Slyter reply that the supply of water would not last half as long as that. "We'll have to build a strong brush roof over that pond, in case the duststorms begin," he added.

The most welcome feature of this camp was the cessation of haste. For days and weeks and months the drovers had been working beyond their strength. Here they could make up for that. The horses and cattle, after a long, dry trek, would have to be driven away from this sweet water. Very little guarding would they need.

Sterl and Red, helped by Friday, leisurely set about selecting a site, pitching their tent, making things comfortable for a shady, though sparsely timbered, bench just above flood-water stage. The cowboys selected their location on the edge of the high bank with huge rocks adjacent. They put up the tent and a canvas shelter. They hauled out the hammocks which had not been unrolled since the Forks. They improvised a table from the wagon seat and placed boxes to sit upon. This work gave Sterl and Red a peculiar feeling, verging upon pleasurable sensation. It took them back to boyhood camping days. They snaked into camp dead trees to be chopped up and split at leisure. A permanent camp without a plentiful supply of firewood was unthinkable for a cowboy. Friday, too, liked his little fire of faggots laid crosswise on red embers.

Working at these tasks, which were interspersed with rests in the shade out from under the hot sun, took up the whole first day. Everyone else had been very busy likewise. At supper Sterl gazed around to appreciate a house-like camp. But if, or when, it grew windy in this open desert, he imagined they would have more to endure than even the scorching heat of the Forks camp.

"Wal, I don't give a damn about nothin' a-tall as long as my cigarettes hold out," drawled Red as they were hunting through their packs. But his most pessimistic talk could usually be discounted.

After sundown they were called to supper. The labor of the drovers accounted for a wide shelter with rock-walled fireplace built high, so that the women need not bend over while getting meals, a wind-break, rude table and benches made of poles, a well-screened meat box, and other conveniences which had long been wanting.

Mrs. Slyter laid out the same old food and drink, but almost unrecognizable as such because of her skill in cooking and serving. As for Beryl and Leslie, their help was not inconsiderable. Red summed it up in his inimitable way: "Wal, dog-gone it, I reckon a cowboy could stand a grub line forever with two such pretty waitresses. Heah you air, girls, thin as beanpoles an' burned brown as autumn leaves . . . and yet you shore make a feller glad jest to see you!"

"Red, that is sweet flattery from *you*," retorted Beryl. But she was pleased.

"We're not as thin as beanpoles," asserted Leslie. This epithet of Red's was not wholly true, yet how slim and frail Beryl was, and how slender the once sturdy Leslie!

But, indeed, few and far between were the relapses into the old badinage and pleasantry which had once been so marked. They were a sober group. The womenfolk, having served the supper, joined the drovers at the table. Afterward, Larry and Rollie cleared away the utensils and washed the dishes. The drovers sat and smoked a while, conversing desultorily.

"No flies or mosquitoes here," said Dann.

"Flies will come bye and bye," replied Slyter.

"There'll be a good few calves dropped here."

"And colts foaled, too. But we have lost so many!"

"We'll make up for all that here."

"If pulero does not break out in the mob."

"Well! Well! Sufficient unto the day is the evil thereof!"

"Boss, where did you figger we air?" asked Red.

"Somewhere out in the Never Never Land. Five hundred miles Outback, more or less."

"An' about what time of year?"

"It is summer, early or late . . . I don't know."

"Dann, I'll catch up with my journal now," interposed Sterl. "I can recall main events, but not dates."

"Small matter now. Keep on with your journal, if you choose. But I've changed in that regard. I don't care to recall things. No one would ever believe we endured so much. And I would not want to discourage future drovers. The details of our trek will never be history."

Slyter remarked reflectively: "If, in case, you know . . . we left records in sealed tins or boxes nailed on trees, we'd have hardly a hope of their ever being seen by white people. The abo's would find and destroy them."

"Yes, yes. But I have cut my mark on a thousand trees along this trek."

Red puffed a cloud of smoke to hide his face, while he drawled: "Girls, you're gonna be old maids shore as shore can be, if we ever get out alive."

"You bet we are, Krehl, if help for such calamity ever depended on Yankee blighters we know," cried Leslie with spirit.

Beryl's response was surprising and significant. "We are old maids now, Leslie dear," she murmured dreamily. "I remember how I used to wonder about that. And to . . . to pine for a husband. But it doesn't seem to matter now."

"Beryl, even if we are trapped here until we die, we can't

become exactly abo's," rejoined Sterl, not quite sure why he said that.

"But it would be well, if we could!"

Stanley Dann said: "As God gave us thoughts and vocal powers, we use them, often uselessly and foolishly. You young people express too many silly ideas. You girls are not going to be old maids, or are you cowboys ever going to be old bachelors. Or will we be trapped here! We are going through."

"Shore we are, boss," flashed Red. "But if we all could forget an' face this hell like you an' also be silly an' funny onct in a while, we'd go through a damn' sight better!"

Dann slapped his knee with a great broad hand. "Right-o! You Yankee sage! I deserve the rebuke. I am too obsessed . . . too self-centered. Never mind my cross-grained temper. But I do appreciate what I owe you all. Relax, if you can. Forget! Play jokes! Have fun! Make love, God bless you!"

As Dann stamped away, Sterl remarked that there was gray in the gold over his temples—that his frame was not so upright and magnificent as it had once been. And that saddened Sterl. After all, the trek had been Dann's responsibility. How all the dead must haunt him.

"Red Krehl, your bluff has been called," said Beryl sweetly.

"Dog-gone it! Thet wasn't no bluff, Beryl," complained Red, disconcerted.

"Very well, show me! I'm from Missouri, as you say so often."

"Yeah? Wal, I reckon you're from heaven, too, but you shore got a little hell in yore make-up."

"That goes for the other star-eyed member of this quartet," said Sterl with a laugh. "I feel compelled to tell you that all of a sudden this little argument has revived my gladness to be alive. But just yet I'm not quite able to relax . . . play jokes . . . have fun . . . and make love!"

"Whoopee!" drawled Red with mild elation. "Pard, you saved my life. Girls, listen. All the rest of my days I'll hand it to yore sex for courage an' sacrifice, for somethin' upliftin' an' great.

An' also for thet cussed, everlastin', infernal, sweet, an' wonderful passion you have to rope an' corral some pore fool man!"

The abrupt change from excessive labor, sleeplessness, and fear to rest, ease, and a sense of safety reacted on every one of the trekkers. It took several days for them to become wholly rational again. They had one brief spell of exquisite tranquillity before the void shut down on them with its limitless horizon lines, its invisible confines, its heat by day, its appalling solitude by night, its dread sense that this raw nature had to be fought.

Nothing happened, however, that for the time being justified such fortification of soul and body. If the sun grew imperceptibly hotter, that could be gauged only by the touch of bare flesh upon metal. The scarcity of living creatures of the wild grew to be an absolute barrenness, so far as the trekkers knew. A gum tree blossomed all scarlet one morning, and the girls announced that to be Christmas Day. They had long memories in one regard and an ulterior motive. Sterl and Red seemed blind to sentiment and deaf to innuendo until the day was far spent. Then they found the last of the gifts they had brought on the trek. Candy and nuts were dug up. At supper, presentations followed. The result was not in Sterl's or Red's calculations. From vociferous delight Beryl fell to hysterical weeping, which even Red could not assuage. And Leslie ate so much of the stale candy that she grew ill.

"Girls, the evils of civilization were behind us," said Stanley Dann. "And look at you! Dragged from your serene primitive state back to Christmas gifts and sweets! Still, have we forgotten what Christmas commemorates?"

One day Friday sighted smoke signals on the horizon. He pointed them out to the drovers, shook his shaggy head, and said: "Black fella close up!"

At once the camp was plunged into despair. Dann ordered fortifications thrown up on two sides. Peace had been theirs only long enough to realize its preciousness. Before supper Friday called the drovers' attention to a strange procession filing in from the desert. Human beings that did not appear human! They came on, halted, edged closer and closer, halted again, paralyzed with fear yet driven by a stronger instinct. First came a score or less of males, excessively thin, gaunt, black as ebony, and practically naked. They all carried spears, but appeared the opposite of formidable. The *gins* were monstrosities. There were only a few *lubras*, scarcely less hideous than the *gins*. A troop of naked children hung back behind them, wild as wild beasts, ragged of head, and all remarkable for their huge pot-bellies.

Not much was said by the drovers as this procession lined up outside of camp. At first glance panic had been the order of the moment. But somehow that oozed out.

Friday advanced to meet them. Sterl heard his voice, as well as the low replies. But sign language predominated in that brief conference. The black came running back.

"Black fella starbin deff," he announced. "Plenty sit down die. Tinkit good feedum."

"Oh, good, indeed, Friday," boomed Dann gladly. "Go tell them white man friends."

"By Jove!" ejaculated Slyter. "Poor starved wretches! It's a wonder we couldn't see it. But we were frightened. That puts a different complexion on this visitation. We can feed them. We have crippled cattle that it will be just as well to slaughter."

Benson had butchered a steer that day, of which only a haunch had been brought to camp. The rest hung on a branch of a tree a little way from camp down the river course. Head, entrails, hide, and legs still lay on the rocks, ready to be burned or buried. Dann instructed Friday to lead the aborigines to the meat. They gave the camp a wide, fearful berth. Slyter packed down a small bag of salt, of which the drovers had abundance. Larry and Rollie built a line of fires. Sterl and Red, with the girls, went close enough to see distinctly. It was an opportunity not to be missed, despite something repellent. The aboriginals crouched and stood around the beef and watched the drovers with ravenous eyes. Larry pointed to a big knife and cleaver on a log, then joined Rollie to one side. Sterl wondered what would happen. Red made fantastic speculations.

All of them expected a *corroboree*. But this tribe of aborigines had evidently passed beyond ceremony. They did not, however, act like a pack of wolves. One tall black, possibly a leader, began to hack up the beef into pieces and pass them out to his fellows and *gins*. While they sat down to devour the beef raw, the children were given generous slices. Sterl did not see one aborigine place a piece of meat on the fire. They were too hungry. When, presently, the blacks attacked the entrails of the beef, Beryl and Leslie fled. The cowboys watched a while longer, intently curious and glad to see the famished wretches eat. But a call to supper hurried them away to camp, mindful of their own hunger and the need of sustenance. Relief and gladness were expressed at the table. It was well to feed some famished aborigines from whom hardly more than thieving proclivities need now be anticipated.

When darkness fell the little campfires flickered under the trees, and dark forms crossed them, but there was no sound, no chant. Next day discovered the fact that the aborigines had disposed of the entire carcass, and lay around under the trees asleep. More arrived that morning as famished as the first ones. Toward the end of the afternoon a number came in, evidently hunters who had been out scouring the desert for food.

Friday had some information to impart that night, when he returned. These aborigines he called some name no one could quite understand. They lived in that country from the hills to the hills, and for two years of drought had been a vanishing race. The birds and beasts, the snakes and lizards, the goannas and rabbits had all departed beyond the hills to a lake where this weak tribe dared not go because they would be eaten by giant men of their own color. Friday said that the old aborigines expected the rains to come after the wind and the duststorms.

The drovers took that last information with dismay and appealed to their black man for some grain of hope.

"Blow dust like hellum bimeby!" he ejaculated solemnly.

Days passed, growing uncomfortably hot during the noon hours, when the trekkers kept to their shelters.

Dann fed the aborigines. They turned out to be good people. Day after day the men went out to hunt game and the *gins* to dig weeds and roots. The children rolled naked in the dust and sported in the pond. They grew less fearful of their white saviors as time passed. Presently it became manifest that the aborigines had recovered and were faring well. The suspicion of the drovers that they might reward good deeds with evil thefts had so far been wholly unjustified. The blacks never came into the camp.

In the morning Sterl and Red tramped around the country with their guns, but they never saw anything to shoot, and the monotony of the still bushland, everywhere open, vistas all alike, leading nowhere, was far more oppressive than laziness in camp. In the evenings after sunset they usually took the girls out to see the horses and walk a little for exercise. Both girls improved during that enforced idleness.

One night the sharp-eyed Leslie called attention to a dim circle around the moon. Friday shook his head gloomily, but offered no explanation. His silence was foreboding. Next morning the sun arose overcast, with a peculiar red haze.

A light wind, the first at that camp which had been named Rock Pools by Leslie, sprang up to fan the hot faces of the anxious watchers, and presently came laden with fine invisible particles and a dry, pungent odor of dust.

Chapter Twenty-nine

Any of you folks ever been in a dust or sandstorm?" Red Krehl asked at breakfast.

The general experience in that line had been negative, and information meager. "Bushwhackers have told us that duststorms in the Outback were uncomfortable," vouched Slyter.

"Wal, if it blows, I'd say they'd be hell on wheels. This heah country is open, flat, an' dry for a thousand miles."

"Are they frequent on your Western ranges?" queried Dann.

From both cowboys there followed a long dissertation, with anecdotes, on the dust and sandstorms which, in season, were the bane of cattle drives in their own American Southwest.

"Boys, I've never heard that we had anything similar to your storms here in Australia," said Dann.

"Wal, boss, I'll bet you two bits you have wuss than ours," drawled Red.

"How much is two bits?"

"One bob."

"I think I might risk such an extravagant wager," Dann returned with a smile. "But upon what do you base your conviction?"

"Nothin' more than the heat. It's almost as hot heah as it was back at thet Forks camp. Only we've turned into blacks, an' we don't feel it so bad."

"Very well. We are forewarned. By all means let us do something to fortify ourselves. We have already roofed the rock pool. What else?"

Without more ado Sterl and Red put into execution a plan they had previously decided upon. They emptied their tent and repitched it on the side of Slyter's big wagon. While they were covering the wheels as a windbreak, Beryl and Leslie approached, very curious.

"Sterl, what in the world are you doing?" asked Leslie.

"Red, why this noble look on your sweaty brow?" asked Beryl.

"Don't be funny, Beryl Dann. This heah is one hell of a sacrifice. Dig up all your belongin's an' yore beds, an' put them in this tent."

"Why?" queried Beryl incredulously.

"'Cause yore gonna bunk in heah an' stay in heah till this comin' duststorm is over."

"Yeah? Who says so?"

"I do. An' young woman, when I'm mad, I'm quite capable of usin' force."

"I'll just love that. But it's one of your bluffs."

Red appeared checkmated for the moment. Leslie was less obdurate.

"Sterl, it's kind of you boys to think of our comfort, but really we can't accept it. We'll manage all right in the wagon."

"That is no protection. You'd stifle. And all your nice things would be loaded with dust. Leslie, please let me be the judge."

"Oh, of course, Sterl, I'll do as you wish," decided Leslie.

But Beryl was of a different mind. She stood before Red in her slim boy's garb, hands on her hips, her fair head to one side, her purple eyes full of defiance, and something else that was as fascinating as it was unfathomable. She was lovely and provocative. Sterl felt glad his comrade seemed not impervious to her mood.

"Beryl, I'll muss yore nice clothes all up," insisted Red.

"You will do nothing of the kind."

"But they gotta go in this tent an' so do you."

"Red Krehl, you are a tyrant. I'm trained to be meek and submissive, but I'm not your slave *yet!*"

"You bet you're not an' you never will be," said Red, hot instead of cool. "But thet talk is just ornery, Beryl. You meek an' submissive . . . my Gawd!"

"Red, I could be both," she returned sweetly.

"Yeah? Wal, it jest wouldn't be natural. Beryl, listen heah." Red evidently had reacted to this situation with an inspiration. "I'm doin' this for yore sake. Fact is, I hate to give up this tent. There's yore good looks to think of. Beryl, you air the damnedest prettiest thing in the world. Most yore hair an' eyes, of course, which wouldn't suffer. But yore face, Beryl, thet lovely gold skin of yores, smooth as satin, an' jest lovely. A dry duststorm will shrivel it up into wrinkles. Why, I've seen thet happen even to Injun girls. But it needn't happen to you. Pack all yore things in the tent. An' when the duststorm comes, get in heah with Leslie an' stay. Sterl an' me will keep a wet sheet over the door heah. Thet'll keep out the dust except what filters through the canvas. An' it'll be bad enough. You should use oil or grease on yore skin, but no water. Water will dry yore skin to leather. You girls will have to stay heah while the dust blows. All day long! At night it usually quiets down, at least where I come from. Then you can come out. Then we'll eat, if we *can* eat. If it's a bad storm you'll almost die, but you won't die. Please now, Beryl."

"All for my good looks!" murmured Beryl, with great, dubious eyes upon him. "Red, I'm afraid I don't care so much about them as I used to."

That might have been true, and again it might have been a bare-faced falsehood. Sterl could not tell, so bewildering were the transformations of this girl.

"But I care," rejoined Red.

"Then I'll obey you," she said. "You are very sweet to me. And I'm a cat! Come, Leslie, let's hurry before it gets too hot."

The cowboys helped the girls move their beds, blankets, and heavy pieces into the tent, and then left them to their own devices. For their own protection they packed their belongings under the wagon, then proceeded to fold and tie canvas all around it and weight down the edges. The important thing was to make the improvised tent as dust-proof as possible. When this task was done, they were satisfied. They advised the drovers to do likewise, which advice was followed. Dann and Slyter had covered their wagons with extra canvases. Sterl, going to the rock-pool for water, saw that the aborigines were erecting little windbreaks and shelters. At this hour the sun had lost none of its heat but some of its brilliance.

Sterl and Red walked away from camp out into the open to the highest point nearby, which had no great altitude. There seemed to be fine, invisible fire embers in a wind that had perceptibly strengthened. Except for the rustle of leaves and grass there was absolute silence. Transparent smoke appeared to be rising up over the sun. A dry, acrid odor, a fragrance of eucalyptus and a pungency of dust, seemed to stick in the nostrils.

"There she comes, pard, rollin' along," drawled the Texan, pointing northeast, over the low ground where the bleached streambed meandered.

Sterl saw rolling, tumbling, mushrooming clouds of dust,

rather white than gray in color, moving toward them over the land.

"Dust all right, Red, and plenty thick," returned Sterl. "I hoped it might be a false alarm."

"Aw, hell, we cain't have no luck! Dann is Jonahed from A to Z. Thet may be jest a little blow. But all these days! An' the daid calm! An' the talk about rains! Makin' for a gale, mebbe. This heat has to blow off before cool air brings the rain. Feel this stone, pard. Hot as a skillet."

"It'll be the toughest yet on the girls."

"If we can only keep them in thet tent while the dust blows!" With incredible speed the duststorm appeared still a few miles distant, but it had now reached to the zenith, blotting out the sun, spreading gloom over the earth, bearing down in convolutions. Like smoke expelled with tremendous force, the front bellied and bulged and billowed, whirling upon itself and throwing out great rounded masses of white streaked by yellow, like colossal roses exploding, blossoming, to be sucked back into a vortex and then puffed out again.

Shadow as from dark clouds eclipsing the sun fell around the watchers. Every instant the spectacle grew more formidable and august. It had too much violence to be beautiful. It typified unrest, change, rage.

"You dog-gone, 'ory-eyed galoot!" ejaculated Red. "Come on."

"Red, your soul has atrophied."

"I reckon, but we gotta get in our cubbyhole before the dust blows in. Do you savvy thet?"

"It's monstrous, Red. Magnificent! One time I had Nan out riding. It was late fall. A snow squall was sweeping at us. I raved. What do you think that girl said?"

"I have no idee, pard, but I'll gamble it was smart."

"Nan was like you, Red. Soulless! She said . . . 'Ain't nature enough grand!' I never forgave her for that."

"Sterl, mebbe I'm not so daid as you fear. Leastways, I had enough soul to stick to you . . . you handsome, moon-gazin', no-good geezer!"

They ran back to camp, aware of thick streams of dust racing ahead of them. They wet two sheets and fastened one over the door of the girls' tent.

"Air you in there, girls?" shouted Red.

"Yes, our lords and masters, we're here. What's that roar?" replied Beryl.

"It's the storm, an' a humdinger. Don't forget when the dust seeps in bad to breathe through wet silk handkerchiefs. If you haven't handkerchiefs, use some of them folderol silk things of Beryl's thet I seen once."

"Well! You hear that, Leslie? Red Krehl, I'll wager you have seen a good deal that you shouldn't have."

"Shore, Beryl. When it was accidental on purpose shoved right under my eyes! Turrible bad for me, too. *Adiós* now, for I have no idea how long."

"Sterl, don't keep us caged up this way very long. Hang the storm," protested Leslie.

"Wait, child. You'll be glad to stay."

By this time the duststorm was almost upon them. Sterl saw the sweep of the tree boughs and the wave of the bleached grass. Sterl's last glimpse, as he crawled under the wagon, was the striated, bulging front of the dust cloud. Red seized the wet sheet and crawled under the wagon. Sterl was on his heels. They closed the entrance, and, tying the wet sheet, they weighted it with rocks and billets laid there for that purpose.

The storm enveloped them, and there was twilight in that canvas-enclosed space under the wagon.

"Roar an' be damned," drawled Red, as he began to divest himself of boots and shirt. "This is duck soup for us, pal. But it'll shore be harder'n hell on the girls."

"Maybe it'll be thick duck soup."

"Aw, hell! Always a killjoy! I know I'm gonna damn' near croak, an' I hope I do."

"Because I won't let you smoke?"

"Yass. It wouldn't be so bad, if you could croak while you're smokin'."

"Say, wonder where Friday is?"

"Search me. But I reckon thet old boy is snug as a bug in a rug."

"And now to wait it out," Sterl said with a sigh as he lay down on his bed. "We have a lot to be thankful for. Suppose we were out in it."

"Suppose thet mob rushes? There wouldn't be no sense in goin' out to stop them."

"I'm curious, too. But the drovers weren't worried. Let's not borrow trouble."

They settled down to endure. It was pretty hot inside. Sterl attended to the storm. The encampment had been enveloped in a freaky gale of wind, heavy enough to carry pebbles, sticks, and bits of wood, and a rustling, seeping, silken, sifting dust. After a while invisible dust penetrated the pores and cracks in the canvas. Red had covered his face with a wet scarf, and Sterl concluded he had better do the same. It was harder to breathe, but the dust did not penetrate the silk. Red promptly fell asleep. Sterl dozed, during which time he seemed to hear the roar of wind, the pelting of gravel, the threshing of boughs.

Patience and resistance, the experience that always held out however much worse anything could get, kept that long day from being unendurable. After sunset the wind lulled. The cowboys went out. An opaque gloom cloaked the scene. The dust was settling. The drovers were astir; a fire had been started. The Slyters were getting supper.

Sterl approached the girls' tent to remove the sheet. It was dry and caked with dust.

"Girls, if you're alive, you can come out now. It's not so bad."

They burst out of the tent with violence and vociferation that attested to much. They were disheveled, too.

"Sterl, it has been a perfectly detestable and horrible day," Beryl cried. "My nose and lungs are full of dust."

"Sniff a little, weak, salted water," advised Sterl. "And don't chafe so bitterly. We are stuck here. This ordeal may knock that one at the Forks into a cocked hat."

By supper everything had cleared a good deal and cooled off.

After supper, tasks that had been neglected during the day were attended to. Sterl and Red went out with the drovers to look for the horses and cattle. They had not strayed, but Dann ordered guard duty that night in three shifts. When they returned, Friday sat by the fire with a meat bone in one hand and a piece of damper in the other.

"How long the storm last?" asked Red.

"Mebbe day, mebbe more. I tinkit long," Friday replied.

"Friday, I wish the hell you'd be wrong once in a while," complained Red.

"Bimeby," said the black.

"Red, let's keep the girls up till we go on guard," suggested Sterl. "That won't be long. If this duststorm gets to hanging on at night, the girls will be stuck in that tent all the time."

"Shore. We'll drag them around, if they holler murder," agreed Red. "Plenty exercise, plenty water, an' only a little grub . . . thet's the ticket, pard."

"Girls, would you like the devotion of two cavaliers who know how to beat this duststorm?" asked Sterl.

"Would we? Rather! Just try us, Sterl!" cried Leslie.

"Another day like this will be my last," said Beryl.

"Humph!" ejaculated Red. "If you was gonna die so easy, you'd been daid long ago. Girls air tougher than they think."

"I could die of unrequited love," replied Beryl with no shadow of deceit in her.

"Wal, if you did croak for love, it'd only be squarin' up for the blasted hopes an' ruined lives you're to blame for."

"Monster! I tell you, Red Krehl, I'm not fooling."

"Wal, I'm in daid honest, too. Let's go peep at the abo's."

Sterl kept a smooth-backed piece of eucalyptus in his tent, and for every day that the dust blew and the heat grew more intense, he cut a notch. And then one day he forgot, and another he did not care, and after that he thought it was no use to keep track of anything because everybody was going to be smothered.

Yet they still carried on. Just when one of the trekkers was going to give up trying to breathe or go mad, then the wind would lull for a night, and they would recover. They could not eat any food to keep up their strength. Every morsel they ate was full of dust that gritted on the teeth. The drovers nightly circled the mob and horses, and butchered a bullock, now and then, for themselves and the aborigines. At night they had their meals and performed their tasks, but not every night. So much dust blew into the pools that they began to fill up. The situation grew terrible. The confinement in the heat, the clogged nostrils and lungs were harder to endure than hunger. Fortunately, their drinking water remained pure and cool, which was the one factor that kept them from utter despair.

Leslie, being the youngest and singularly resistant in spirit, stood the ordeal longest before beginning to go downhill. But Beryl seemed to be dying. On clear nights they carried her out of the tent and laid her on a stretcher. At last only Red could get her to eat.

Sterl considered it marvelous that she had not passed away long ago. But how tenaciously she had clung to love and life! *It must have been love,* Sterl thought, *that kept her from giving up.* At last, however, the spiritual succumbed to the elemental, as Sterl knew must inevitably happen to her, and to all of them, one by one. Shipwrecked men on a barren island never all died at once. The thing Sterl fought most bitterly and fiercely of all was the fading away in effort, the gradual alienation of thought, and, therefore, hope, faith, longing. Hours he would lie under their shelter as lethargic and inert as a hibernating animal. He had to drive himself to do anything. Red had become silent, grim, locked in his own thoughts most of the time, and then in his grief over Beryl. If they could only get out of their horrible prison, and breathe and start their sluggish blood again!

One night, after a scorching day that had been only intermittently windy, the air cleared enough to let a wan spectral moon shine down upon the camp. But the day had been so hot that all were practically prostrated. If it had been fiercely dusty as well, then the story of Dann's trekkers might have ended. That night, however, there was a difference that Sterl imagined to be only another lying mirage of his brain. Friday touched Sterl on the arm and pointed up at the strange moon with its almost indistinguishable ring, and said: "Bimeby!" Did he mean death? How soon that must surely come! But there seemed to be a hopeful portent in his posture, his meaning. The black man was beyond Sterl's ken at this critical hour.

In the pale moonlight Beryl lay on her stretcher, a shadow of her old self, her dark little face lighted by luminous, lovely eyes that must have seen into the infinite. She was conscious. She knew she was dying. And she seemed glad. Dann, in his indestructible faith, knelt beside her to pray. Red sat at her head while the others moved to and fro, silently, like ghosts. He held her hand and watched her. Sterl could not tear himself away, although the sight was torturing.

"Red, don't take it so hard," whispered Beryl almost inaudibly.

"Beryl, don't give up, don't fade away!" implored Red.

"Red, you'd never marry me . . . because of. . . ."

"No! Not because of thet. I'm not good enough to wipe your feet!"

"You are as great as my dad."

Sterl led the weeping Leslie away from there. He could endure no more himself. Red would keep vigil beside Beryl until she breathed her last. How insupportable to think of consigning those speaking, violet eyes, that shining hair, that lovely frail flesh which housed a spirit so imperious and sweet, so wayward, to a lonely grave in this Never Never Land. Sterl seemed to crack over that last torturing emotion. He had no feeling left, when he pulled the clinging Leslie from him and slunk back to his prison under the wagon, to crawl in like animal that hid in the thicket to die. He fell asleep.

He awoke in the night and felt that it was owing to the intense silence. The moan of wind, the rustle of leaves, the swish of branches, the seep of dust, sounds that had been indelibly stamped upon his memory for all time, were strangely absent. The stillness, the blackness were like death.

Then he heard a faint, almost imperceptible pattering upon the canvas. Oh! That lying trick of his fantasy! That phantom memory of trail nights on the home ranges, when he lay snug under canvas to hear the patter of sleet, of snow, of rain? He had dreamed of it here in this accursed Never Never Land!

But he heard the jingle of spurs outside, and the soft pad of Friday's bare feet.

"Pard . . . pard! Wake up!" That was Red's voice, broken, sobbing.

"I'm awake, old-timer," replied Sterl.

"It's rainin', pard! Beryl's gonna live."

The musical jingle of spurs moved away, leaving Sterl transfixed and thrilling. Emotion, life resurged. Friday shook the canvas flap, as was his wont to waken Sterl.

Then the pregnant silences of that night ceased. The drovers built fires and stayed up, with wild notes in their exultant voices. From the aboriginal camp came a low, rhythmic chant. The raindrops pattered softly, steadily. *What a heavenly sound,* thought Sterl. He opened the canvas door to let the cool air in, to hear the better. And sooner or later he fell into a slumber devoid of nightmare, of fevered blood, of gasping breath.

Morning disclosed many changes. The sky was dark, the air cool, the heat gone, the dust washed off trees, leaves, grass, rocks, logs, and, as Larry averred cheerfully, off the backs of horses and cattle.

What the weakened drovers lacked in strength, they made up in humble thanksgiving spirit. Dann, who had throughout been the least affected, nevertheless, seemed a changed man. Beryl could breathe and drink and smile. All, but she, went out into the rain to let it soothe their stiffened skins. Benson and Rollie killed a bullock, and Dann gave half of it to the aborigines. While the drovers sat at a merry meal, the aborigines had their first *corroboree* there.

"Old abo' say tinkit rain come bimeby," said Friday. "Black man say along all same. Bimeby rain come!"

It might have been a pathetic fallacy when Sterl imagined the trees, the grass, the pools shared the feelings of the drovers. But he swore he saw it.

For nineteen days it rained. At first it rained steadily, all day and all night. Before half that time was over the dry streambed was a little river, running swiftly. It had cleaned out the rock pools. No more dust-covered puddles! No more green scum! The dry odors and rank smells were gone.

After the steadiest downpour had ceased, the rains continued part of every day and every night. On the morning of the twentieth day since the fatal duststorm, the drovers arose to greet the sun again and gloriously saw a changed land.

"On with the trek!" boomed Stanley Dann.

He gave the aborigines a bullock, and steel implements that could be spared. Then the trek moved out of Rock Pools, and these black people, no longer scarecrows, lined up to watch the white men pass out of their lives.

The grass waved green and abundant, knee-high to a horse; flowers born of the rain bloomed everywhere; gum trees burst into scarlet flame; the wattles turned gold; kangaroos and emus appeared in troops upon the plains; and on all sides flocks of colored birds graced the scene. Water was omnipresent. It lay in league-wide lakes, with the luxuriant grass standing fresh and succulent out of it. Every depression in the land had its pond. Streams ran bank-full and clear, with flowers and flags bending over the water.

The Never Never Land stretched out on all sides, boundlessly. It was level bushland, barren in dry seasons, rich now after the rains. Eternal spring might have dwelt there.

Chapter Thirty

Only the black man Friday could tell how the trekkers ever reached Paradise Oasis, and his limited vocabulary did not permit a detailed description.

"Many moons," repeated the black perplexedly. "Come alonga dere." He pointed east and drew a line on the ground, very long, very irregular, with gestures that intimated incalculable things. "No black fella, no kangaroos, no goanna. This fella country no good. Plenty sun. Hot like hell. White fella sit down. Tinkit he die. Boss Dann an' Redhead fightum. Cattle no drink, fall down. Plenty hosses go. White missies sleep like imm dead. White fella sit down. No water, no tucker. Friday find water. One day two day alonga die. Imm waterbag. Go back. Makeum come."

That was a long dissertation for the black. Sterl pieced it together and filled the interstices. His mind was not a blank or a void. It seemed to be a labyrinthine maze of vague pictures and sensations made up of hot sun and arid wastes, of wheels rolling, rolling, rolling on, of a thousand camps all the same, of ghostly mirages, and forever the infernal monotony of distances, of water holes, and finally fading faces, fading voices, fading images, a horrible burning thirst and a mania for water.

He had come to his senses in a stream of clear, cool, running water. Gray stone ledges towered to the blue sky. There were green grass, full-foliaged trees blossoming gold, and birds in noisy flocks. Once more the melodious *cur-ra-wong* of the magpie pealed in his dulled ears.

Dann and Red and Slyter had not been quite so badly off as Sterl. But they, too, had only irrational and dim recollection of what this last and most terrible ordeal had been. Friday had saved the lives of the girls with a waterbag—and the drovers, the horses, and cattle by leading them to this oasis.

"God and our black man have delivered us once more. Let us pray, instead of thinking what has passed," said Stanley Dann through thick, split lips from which the blood ran. All seemed said in that.

As great a miracle as the lucky star that had guided the trekkers here was their recovery through sweet, fresh, cool water. Even its music seemed healing. It gurgled and bubbled from under the ledges in many places to unite and form a goodly stream that sang away through the trees to the west. That place was the birth of a river which ran toward the Indian Ocean. It sprang from a range of hills and a high plateau. For Sterl—and surely all of them—it was the rebirth of hope, of life, of the sense of beauty, of an exquisite return of pleasure. On the second morning Leslie staggered up to gaze about, thin as a wafer and dark as a savage. She cried: "Oh, how lovely! Paradise Oasis!"

Beryl could not walk unaided, but she shared Leslie's joy. How frail a body now housed this chastened soul. Hammocks were strung for them in the shade, and they lay back on the pillows, wide-eyed, while the drovers passed to and fro at their renewed tasks.

Wild berries and fruit, fresh meat and fish, bread from the last sack of flour added their wholesome nourishment to the magic of the sweet, crystal water.

"Let me stay here forever," pleaded Beryl.

Leslie added: "Oh, Sterl, let us never leave!"

The drovers were content to bide there a while. A rich grass spread out over the rolling country. Soon the cattle would be restored. Already the gaunt flanks of the horses had filled out. No pests or vermin so far fouled the sweet air of this pleasant oasis. The haggard drovers took on a new lease of life.

One morning Friday sought out Sterl. "Boss, come alonga me." And he led Sterl away from camp to the base of a high hill.

"What see, Friday?" queried Sterl eagerly.

The black tapped his broad breast with his lean, virile hand. "Black fella tinkit see Kimberleys!"

"My God!" gasped Sterl, suddenly pierced through with vibrating thrills. "Take me!"

Whereupon Friday started to climb the hill. Sterl saved his breath and tried to go slowly. The black halted here and there to rest. Sterl gazed back down at the camp. What a sparkling, gorgeous place! To his right, other hills, growing higher, scaled up a gray escarpment. At length they surmounted the foothill.

"Boss, look dere," said Friday.

Sterl's gaze, intense and keen, followed the impressive long arm of the black man. It seemed he looked far across a warm and colorful plain to an upflung purple range that rolled and billowed along the Western horizon, as far as he could see from north to south.

"The Kimberleys!" shouted Sterl in a frenzy of joy. "So help me heaven! We trekked far north . . . and then straight west. It has to be the Kimberleys!"

Then he wrenched his gaze from the haunting vision of dim blue domes and peaks to the plain beneath him. The shining stream wound away between green and gold borders out across the undulating desert; trained eyes traced it for a hundred miles, straight toward the mountains. He stood another long moment, his hand hard on his black comrade's shoulder, his heart too full for utterance. If he had not loved this aborigine long before, he would have done so now.

Turning toward camp and looking down, Sterl cupped his hands and loosed a wild and stentorian yell that pealed in echo from hill to hill, rolled afar, clapping along the ramparts, to die away. He waited long enough to see the drovers run out into an open space to look up. He waved his sombrero. The girls waved something white in return. Then Sterl ran down the hill, distancing the bare-footed black.

The drovers waited for him, as he slowed up, panting and hot. They faced him, fire-eyed and mute. Leslie was the first to move. She ran to meet him, her heart in her eyes. But Sterl saved his speech and his eyes for that gaunt, golden-bearded leader. The moment was so great that he heard his voice as a whisper.

"Sir . . . I . . . report . . . I sighted . . . the Kimberleys!"

Ten days down the stream from that unforgettable Paradise Oasis the trek came out of a bushland into more open plains where rocks and trees and washes were remarkable for their scarcity. The Kimberleys did not become nearer, but they appeared to tower higher. Sterl conceived the idea that the range was closer than he had calculated.

The trekkers had been reduced to a ration of meat and salt with one cup of tea and one cup of stewed fruit each day. They thrived and gathered strength upon it, but Sterl felt certain that the reaction came as much from the looming purple range, beckoning them on, mysterious, the promised land. The horses followed the wagons. The cattle were as tame as sheep. Many of them were pets and answered to names. Twenty-two hundred strong, the mob had improved since they struck good water, and every day calves were born, as well as colts. No smoke signals on the horizon.

One day Sterl rested a lame foot by leaving his saddle for Slyter's driver seat. The mood that had come to him at Paradise Oasis not only had persisted, but it had clarified and possessed him. Slyter's good wife lay asleep back under the canvas, her worn face betraying the trouble that her will and spirit hid while she was awake. Sterl talked to Slyter about the Kimberleys, the finding of suitable stations, the settling, and the plan for getting supplies at the seaports, all of which led up to what was in his mind—the future.

"Slyter, would it interest you to learn something about me?" asked Sterl.

"Indeed, it would, if you wish to tell," returned the drover. "But, Sterl, you need never tell me anything."

"Thanks, boss. It's only that I'd feel freer and happier, if you knew," rejoined Sterl, and then he told Slyter of the girl with whom he had been involved and of the man he had killed because he deserved killing; that, if he had remained at home, the risk he would have run was more gun play with the man's relatives and friends. "In cattle towns of my West, it is nothing to kill a man. But one meeting always led to another. Red and I were glad to shake the bloody dust of the Texas trails for a new country. And we'll never go back," he concluded.

"After this awful trek, you can't still like Australia?"

"I'm mad about it, Slyter. I'm a lover of the wild, of the color and beauty of the open. And Outback Australia is glorious."

"You tell me this, your story, because of Leslie?"

"Yes, mostly. But if there had been no Leslie, probably I'd have told you anyhow."

"She loves you."

"Yes. And I love her, too. Only I have never told her that or the story you've just heard."

"Sterl, I could ask little more of the future than to give my daughter to such a man as you, or Krehl. It seems I have known you both a lifetime. We have been through the fire together. As for you, young man, Australia will take you to its heart, and the past will be as if it had never been."

"I see that, Slyter. I see, too, that you drovers are as big as your country. I'm happy and fortunate to be able to cast my lot with you."

"Right, and here comes sharp-eyed Leslie. Sterl, I think I'll get off and straddle a horse for a while. You drive and talk to Leslie."

Almost before the heavy-footed drover was on the ground, Leslie was out of her saddle to throw him her bridle reins.

"How jolly!" she cried in gay voice, as she leaped to a seat beside Sterl. "Months, isn't it, Sterl, since I rode beside you like this?"

"Yes, years, I think."

"Oh, that long, long agony. But I'm forgetting it. Sterl, *what* were you talking to Dad about? Both of you so serious!"

"I was telling him what made me an outcast . . . drove me to Australia."

"*Outcast?* Oh, Sterl! I always wondered. Red, too, was so

strange. But I don't care what you've ever been in the past. It's what you are that made me. . . ."

When she choked up, Sterl told her the story of his life and its fatality.

"How terrible! Was Nan very pretty?"

"Yes, but not so pretty as you, Les."

"Oh! You are nice, unless you're a liar! But that's like Beryl. I take it back . . . did you love her very much?"

"I'm afraid so," he said.

"I'm sorry. Oh, it is sad . . . what you have been through. No home, no friends! This far-away Australia . . . so hard and bitter. Love is a terrible thing."

"Les, that gives me an idee, as Red would say," Sterl spoke up. "Let's get the best of this old terrible love."

"Sterl, it can't be done. I know."

"Les, it can. Listen. All's fair in love. You get hold of Red the very first chance tonight in camp. Tell him you can't keep it secret any longer. That Beryl is dying of love of him. That she dreams of him, babbles in her sleep, calls out . . . 'Oh, Red, I'll go on my knees to you . . . I will!' That she begs for his kisses . . . that now we are nearing the end of this trek, she can't live without him. All that, Les, and anything more you can make up."

"Sterl Hazelton, I wouldn't have to lie, as you're coaxing me to. That is all absolutely true," returned Leslie, somber golden fire in her eyes.

"You don't say? That bad? Then all the better. Leslie, I'll get hold of Beryl at the same time, and tell her what a state Red is in over her. I'll lay it on thick. Will you do this for me?"

"Is it true? Does Red care that much?" Leslie queried doubtfully.

"Yes. I don't think it's possible to exaggerate Red's love for that girl. But he feels he is a no-good cowboy, as he says. Red really comes from a fine old Texas family. He never had any schooling to speak of."

"Sterl, are you sure it's that, instead of Beryl's affair with Ormiston?"

"No, I'm not," returned Sterl, unable to lie under the piercing gaze of those hazel eyes. "That . . . whatever it was . . . mortally hurt Red. But he's big . . . he's splendid. If only we can do some drastic thing to throw them into each other's arms. Les, I beg of you . . . help me."

"You bet I'll help you," she flashed, suddenly sparkling. "It's one glorious idea. We'll carry it out, very soberly, as if the whole world depended upon it. But . . . but . . . Sterl. . . ." Under the dark tan of her cheeks and temples a dusky scarlet waved up.

"But what?" he queried, apparently blind, and he changed the long reins from one hand to the other.

"But who is going to . . . to tell you . . . about me?" she faltered, hardly able to get it out.

"Oh, that? Well, darling, if you think it's necessary, you can tell me yourself."

She fell against him, quivering, her heavy eyelids closed, with tears welling from under them to stain her dark cheeks. Sterl's conscience smote him. But he discovered a happiness deeper and sweeter than any he had ever known. Then he wrapped his long arm round her and drew her close.

At this juncture Mrs. Slyter's voice came to them mildly. "I've been listening to some very interesting conversations."

"Oh . . . Mum," faltered Leslie aghast, starting up.

But Sterl held her all the closer. Presently he said: "Well, then . . . Mum . . . we have your blessing, or you would have interrupted long ago."

"Bless you, indeed. It makes me happy. Why, you young people have kept Slyter and me alive. All's well that ends well! If we only get somewhere!"

"We are. Look at that purple range. Not so many days away. I hope you approve of our plan for Beryl and Red."

"Plan? I didn't hear it. But, assuredly, I'd approve of anything to cure that lovesick couple."

Every camp along the stream appeared to grow more beautiful and pleasant. Flowers and blossoming trees, birds and falling water, a sickle moon that blanched a track upon the pool, the song of late thrush and magpie, and the almost complete departure of the mood of nature which had seemed inimical to the trek, here struck Sterl anew with the revivifying current which sang along his nerves. He had contrived to get Red and the girls out away from camp along the stream, and here, at a murmuring waterfall, he put his arm around Beryl and led her away from their companions.

"Beryl, I want to talk to you," he said simply, and pressed her slim form to him.

"Yes?" she murmured wonderingly, and Sterl saw her glance down at his encircling arm, and then up at him.

"I'm terribly fond of you, Beryl."

"I am of you, too, Sterl."

"We've been thrown through hell together. It'll be grand to look back at some day. Very much too close now."

"You and . . . and Red will be leaving us to become wanderers again . . . seeking adventure . . . ? I wish I were a man."

"Who told you we'd be doing that?"

"Red."

They paused beside a rock, upon which Sterl lifted Beryl to a seat, and he leaned against it to face her. The moon shone upon her fair head and lighted the dark, proud eyes. He took her slim hands in his, to feel the callous little palms and the rough fingers, and all that he sensed welled up from his heart, making it difficult for him to speak.

"So that geezer has been hurting you again? Dog-gone him! Beryl, I'm going to double-cross him, give him away."

"You mean betray him? Don't, Sterl. I . . . I wasn't badly hurt to hear you would leave us. I . . . I always expected. . . ." Here her soft voice failed.

Sterl was utterly unable to carry out his plan to make her suffer a little more before he made her happy. Red, with that incredible jealousy of a lover, might still want to do so in proud reprisal for the many slights and insults she had visited upon him. But Sterl saw her clearly as she sat there in the moonlight, saw through the transparent shell to her heart—as well as the beauty the sun and the privation and the tragedy could not destroy. She was the lovelier for those haunted eyes and dark little face and the thin hands that plucked at him.

"Umpumm. We're not . . . leaving," he said, making a break so that his voice would lend him courage. "I wouldn't leave Leslie and. . . ."

"Oh, Sterl! Then . . . then . . . ?"

"Yes, then! And Red would never leave me. For why? Well, I'll tell you, but you mustn't tell him very soon." Here Sterl related again for the third time that day the story of his exile.

"How very wonderful of Red! Oh, he is wonderful! Sterl, you have suffered. I always felt it. But this Aussie lass will never be like Nan. She will make up for all you've lost."

"That I know . . . and Beryl, I'd be happier than I ever was, if only you and Red. . . ."

"If only he could see!" she interrupted passionately. "If only he were not so hard! If only he could forgive and forget Ormiston . . . what I . . . what . . . he. . . ."

Sterl grasped her slim shoulders and drew her down until her face was close and her wide eyes dilated in the moonlight.

"Hush! Don't say that . . . don't ever think of that again!" he said sternly. "Forget it! That is absolutely the only obstacle between you. Red feels it. The jealous fool in his bad hours thinks you regret . . . I won't say it, Beryl Dann. And for Red's sake and yours, and ours . . . Les's and mine, who love you both . . . forget. Forget! Because Red Krehl worships the ground you walk upon. He has loved you from the first. Oh, yes, even while you flouted him one moment and were sweet another. Don't I know? For months . . . years on this terrible trek, I have been with him . . . I have seen him suffer. I've heard him in his delirium . . . in his dreams. Beryl . . . Beryl . . . always Beryl! Beside my love for that little flirt of the past . . . Nan . . . even beside this bigger, finer love I have for Leslie, why his is this blazing sun we know so well, compared to that wisp of a moon there, or one of these pale stars. I swear to you that this is true, Beryl. I swear that you can overcome his queer obsession. Don't grieve another single hour. Don't let him hurt you. Don't believe in his indifference. Break down his armor. Oh, child, a woman can, you know. You don't have to be brazen. You don't need to fall into his arms, although that might be a last card. The past is dead, Beryl. This will be a new life for us four. It looks bright to me. Why . . . why, Beryl. . . ."

She slid off the rock into his arms, blind, weeping, torn asunder, her slender hands clutching him. "No . . . more," she sobbed. "You break . . . my heart . . . with bliss. I . . . I had . . . despaired. . . . Twice I have . . . nearly died. I knew . . . the next time. . . . But this . . . this will save me. Oh, Sterl, my friend! I will . . . obey you. Tell me what to do."

"Well . . . stand up if you can," replied Sterl huskily, as he put her down and supported her. "Stop crying. You can cry all night after we go back. Red mustn't know. Don't betray me, Beryl. He's proud . . . why, as proud as you. I think the thing for you to do is to be this . . . this sweet new self, without the old sadness. Loving . . . irresistible! Oh, you know a woman's wiles. You used to practice them, when you didn't care a damn. Now it's love, Beryl . . . and life or death. Choose life, Beryl. . . . I see Red and Leslie coming. We'll walk ahead. See that you compose yourself. Wipe your tears away. How sweet and lovely you are, Beryl! If I didn't love Leslie, really I'd be fighting my only friend over you. So terrible is beauty. There! Why, you're smiling. That is just fine."

Thus Sterl, talking swiftly, eloquently, saying he knew not what, led Beryl back to camp, to find her the woman he had sought to inflame and inspire, star-eyed, wearing a tranquil mask through which love shone. He left her at the campfire and rushed away to be alone. He watched the thin disc of moon go down, and, justifying his duplicity if it were such, he achieved serenity and gladness.

Day after day the purple range loomed closer. It was a lodestone, a fulfillment. If the drovers were starved, they did not feel it.

Every day the richness of the land magnified. The days were hot, and the nights grew cold. This last condition they attributed to the proximity of the mountain range.

And one day the eagle-eyed scouts saw that the stream they had followed for so long was presently going to join another, which from its course they judged would be a river. That green and gold line disappeared around the northern end of the range. Beyond this river line the land began to slope toward the foothills, losing their blue haze of distance for the gray of grass and the green of bush.

The next day, the leader of the drovers, for once actuated by haste, made for the junction of stream and river. The point seemed a magnet. Blue smoke rose about the big trees. Smoke that was different from the dread smoke signals that had haunted them on the trek. It must come from aboriginals, but was not hostile. Friendly aborigines could communicate to Friday where the drovers had come. But those beautiful mountain domes, widely separated, aloof from each other in purple majesty, could belong only to the Kimberleys.

"Boss, plenty smoke dere. I ben tinket no black fella," said Friday to Sterl.

With that tremendous information Sterl rode ahead to tell Dann. The possibility of meeting white men again seemed something only second to the end of the trek, to have crossed the Never Never, to ride down into a lovely land of milk and honey.

Sterl told the leader.

"Aye, my boy, I guessed that," he beamed. "We have fought the good fight. With His guidance! Look around you, Sterl. Richest, finest land I ever saw!"

Sterl had looked around, and he did so again. A great wedge of range pointed at the junction of the two streams. It widened and extended back as far as the eye could see. Dann drove on, and Slyter gained from behind. At length, horses and mob made for the shallow, sparkling stream, drank their fill, to climb up the wooded bank and out to the grassy level. Here the young drovers left them to gallop ahead and join the wagons. Excited and intense, all the trekkers gazed ahead. They saw teams grazing and huge wagons.

"Ha! A road . . . a ford!" boomed Dann, and pointed with long arm. He had, indeed, come to a road that sloped down under the giant trees to the shallow stream. His followers all saw, but none could believe their eyes. A road? In the land of the Never Never? But they had traversed that unknown and terrible void.

A shrill shout preceded the action of three white men coming out in the open, halting to stare. They pointed. They gesticulated. They gazed from one to another, plainly nonplused. They saw Dann's wagons, the women on the driver's seats, the mounted drovers, the big band of horses, the great mob, and they were as astonished as the drovers were enraptured. Then the campers ran to meet the trekkers. Dann halted his four horses, and Slyter stopped beside him. The mounted drovers lined up, a lean, ragged crew, with Leslie conspicuous among them, unmistakably a girl, bronzed, and beautiful.

"Good day, cobbers!" boomed Dann, his voice singularly deep.

"Who may you be?" replied one of the three, a stalwart man with clean-shaven, rugged face and keen, intelligent eyes. He addressed Dann, but these eyes enveloped the group.

"Are those mountains the Kimberleys?" asked Dann intensely.

"Yes. The eastern Kimberleys. Drover, you can't be Stanley Dann?"

"It really seems I can't be. But I am!" declared Dann.

"Great Scott! What good news, if true! Dann was lost two years and more ago, according to reports at Darwin."

"Lost, yes, though not to life and use. Two years!"

"If you are Dann, it has taken you two years and five months to get here!"

"God above!" cried Dann incredulously.

"It was summer, two years ago, when news of your death reached Darwin. I was there at the time."

"My death was grossly exaggerated," returned Dann. "But death visited and dogged our trek, alas."

"You trekked across the Never Never?" asked the other wonderingly.

"We trekked to the Gulf and then across the Never Never. And we lost drovers, five thousand head of cattle, and a hundred horses on the way."

"My word! Incredible! Dann, I congratulate you. What great news for Western Australia! I see you have a mob of cattle left. I'm glad to be the first to tell you good news."

"Good news?" boomed Dann in echo.

"Well, rather. Dann, your fortune is made. Cattle are worth unheard-of prices. Horses the same. Reason is that gold has been discovered in the Kimberleys."

"*Gold?*"

"Yes, gold! There's been a rush in for months. Mines south of here. Trekkers coming in from Perth and Freemantle. Settlers by ship to Darwin and Wyndham. These ports are humming. I am engaged in freighting supplies in to the gold fields. My name is Horton. We camped here on the return trek. Tomorrow you would have missed me."

"Do you hear, all?" boomed Dann to the rapt-eyed girl on the seat beside him, to the Slyters, to the drovers. "What have we come into? Not only the promised land of the Kimberleys, but to gold fields, seaports . . . the beginnings of the empire I envisioned."

"We all hear, Stanley, and our hearts are full," replied Slyter.

"What river is this?" queried Dann, shaking off his bedazzlement to point to the shining water through the trees.

"That is the Ord. You have come down the Elivre," replied Horton. "The three high mountains nearest are Timerley to the south, Mount Bradley, and Mount Barrett. I don't know the names of the other peaks in sight, if they have names. Dennison Plains are in sight to the south. The finest country, the finest grazing for stock in the world!"

"Aye, friend. It looks so. But this road? Where does it lead and how far?"

"Follows the Ord to the seaport, Wyndham, a good few miles

less than two hundred. Darwin farther northeast. There are a few cattle stations near the ports. Sheep drovers working in to the southward. You are in on the ground floor, Dann. The government will sell this land to you or any land you agree to develop so cheap it is unbelievable."

"Ha! This land?" called Dann, his voice rolling as he waved his whip to encompass the river junction and the great wedge. His great eyes were blazing gold.

"Yes, this land here. And to my mind it couldn't be bested in all Australia."

"Dann's Station!" rang out the leader. What a moment that must have been for him! Sterl's breast seemed to cave in with his own emotion. "Slyter, come out of your trance. We have reached the Kimberleys. This will be our range. Beryl, do you like your new home?"

"Lovely beyond compare, Dad," cried the girl. "If only I am not dreaming."

"Stanley, we must send at once for supplies," said Slyter, rousing.

"Horton, do we look like starving trekkers?"

"Indeed, you do. I never saw such a peak-faced ragamuffin lot of drovers. Or ladies, so charming despite all."

"They have lived on meat and dried fruit. And for days now wholly upon meat. I am famished for a cup of tea."

"Forgive me, Dann, for not thinking of that. But who could think, meeting you like this? Sam, run and boil the billy. Dann, I can let you have some tea, fruit, sugar, canned milk, and. . . ."

"Enough, man! Do not overwhelm us! Slyter, what shall we do next . . . that is, after that cup of tea?"

"Stanley, we should thank heaven, pitch camp, and plan to send both wagons to Wyndham for supplies."

"Right-o. But I'd make it two cups of tea."

"Wal, air you gonna ask us to get down an' come in?" drawled Red. "I shore could guzzle a big pull at red likker. But I reckon I can stand tea."

"American!" called out Horton with twinkling eyes.

"Savvied again. The name is Krehl. An' heah's my pard Hazelton."

Gaiety, delight, hospitality prevailed for a blissful few moments. Dann could not be expected to rest long with the tired horses in harness and camp to pitch. When he interrogated Horton again about sending his wagons and drivers to Wyndham for supplies, Sterl took occasion to wink at Red and say: "Boss, Red and I want to take that trip. How about it, Red?"

"I shore had thet very idee," drawled Red. "Gosh, won't it be grand to see people again an' stores, an' places to eat? An' drink! An' girls? Whoopee, pard!"

Consternation in Leslie's look and the absolutely crushed appearance of Beryl induced Sterl to relent in his little joke. "Boss, on second thought, I'll take that back. It is very evident my friend Krehl could hardly be trusted in a civilized community so soon after the long trek."

Beryl turned an eloquent and grateful glance upon Sterl, then fastened those speaking, violet eyes upon Red.

"He might not come back," she said intensely, for the instant seeing no one else.

"Wal, shore, if you're all against me," drawled Red coolly. "I had kind of a notion thet I'd fetch a parson back with me. But if he ain't needed a-tall. . . ."

A burst of merriment, in which Beryl, scarlet-faced under her tan, joined unreservedly, interrupted Red's droll turning of the tables.

Then Dann said: "I'll send Benson and Roland. There will be a stupendous list to make out. Everybody make theirs out by tonight, so as to insure an early start. . . . And now to unpack and pitch temporary camp."

But there were frequent rests and much conversation and many visits of the girls to Sterl and Red before sunset ended a momentous day.

The cook for the freighters served supper for all that evening, and the guests were saved from gastronomic disaster only because of a limited quantity of delicious and forgotten dishes.

Speech burst out intermittently and irrelevantly, betraying incredulity, rapture, and gratitude. After supper, Beryl and Leslie went into ecstasies and perplexities over the innumerable things they wanted bought. Sterl and Red sat beside a box in the light of a little fire and racked their brains to think up necessities to have purchased in town.

"Strange, Red, just think!" ejaculated Sterl. "We don't really need anything. We have lost the sense of need."

"But, pard, there's things to wear. Why, I haven't had socks for so long I forgot. An' other things, if you'd only figure 'em out."

"Red, I didn't mean clothes. Of course, we can't go quite naked, although I'd like that. You'll find we have learned a great deal from the aborigines. I meant other things."

"Yeah? An' what?"

"Toothbrushes, powder, soap, towels, iodine, glycerin, combs, scissors to cut hair, and a whole pack of things to wear."

"Help! Thet shows how you've gone bush, I don't think."

"Red, honest, I'd just as lief go without them all. I've been washing my teeth with a rag! How many times have I seen you roast a piece of beef on a stick, salt it, and eat it just like any abo'?"

"Pard, I don't know how many. About a thousand times, I reckon. Will we ever get over thet trek?"

"No, never. And something tells me that is well, although I can't explain. But it's on account of the girls that we must get over, if not forget, all these savage habits."

"Wal, the girls have shore upset us," said Red ponderingly. "An' now we're heah, on the outskirts . . . within drivin' reach of towns an' people, we gotta face things."

"Have you made up your mind about Beryl?" asked Sterl soberly, averting his eyes.

"Pard, she cared more about me than I deserve . . . than I ever had a girl care for me before. I tried an' wanted to doubt thet, but I cain't."

"Well?"

"Wal, lately, I don't know for how long, she's been different.

All thet misery gone! She's forgot Ormiston an' every damn' bit of thet . . . thet. . . . An' she's been happy. Jest the sweetest, softest, lovingest creature under the sun. An' I'd be loco, if I didn't see it's because of me . . . thet she takes it for granted. Oh, hell, you know what I mean! She gets hold of my torn clothes . . . mends them. She's proud of her needlework. She waits on me. She makes the weak kind of tea I can drink. I've caught her tryin' to make me eat things she should eat herself. An' every night, when we walk out to see the sunset, an' come back in the dark, she hangs back, an' slips close to me into my arms . . . close an' warm . . . an' lifts her mouth without a word. Never a word, pard! My Gawd, what can a pore feller do?"

"I should think you'd be the happiest man in the world," declared Sterl feelingly. "I am."

"Wal, I'm glad you air, an' I reckon I'd be, too, if I'd jest give up."

"Red! Then right this minute . . . give up . . . for Beryl's sake . . . for mine . . . for Leslie's!" rang out Sterl.

"Holy Mackeli! Don't knock me down. Words can be as hard as bullets. All right, old pard, I knuckle, I show yellow, I give up! But there's a queer twist in my mind. I've forgiven an' forgotten all Beryl's slights to me. Only she always got the best of me. If I could jest think up one more word to get the best of *her* before, or mebbe better *when* I tell her how I love her an' want her . . . then I'd match you for who's the luckiest an' happiest man."

"You son-of-a-gun! You same old Red Krehl . . . cowboy and devil! But big as that Never Never Land we crossed! Grand idea, pard. I'll think of something."

"Make it good an' *pronto*. I cain't stand Beryl's eyes much longer. Eyes of a lost fawn! Eyes of a dove thet was bein' starved an' beaten. My Gawd, what a load off my mind! Sterl, you're a real friend. I'm glad I ran away from home with you. Now let's look at practical things. You remember we always wanted to be cattlemen . . . to own a ranch an' oodles of hosses? We always had dreams we knew would never come true. We always reckoned on a last trail . . . gun play, an' a grave on the lone prairie.

Wal, it's not gonna turn out thet way. Have you looked over this range we been ridin' for days? Grandest I ever seen! Cattle an' hosses will multiply heah. The soil is rich an' will raise anythin'. No droughts where these two rivers meet! Wal, think! I've got more money in my kick than I ever earned in my life. An' you bet I reckon I earned thet. An' you had a small fortune when I seen yore belt last . . .'way back there in thet town where we bought out the store. You haven't lost it, have you, pard, or lighted cigarettes with some of those big bills?"

"Red, I've thought of that at long intervals. Yes, I have it all packed in my bag."

"Good-o! Wal, bright prospect, huh?"

"Bright? It's glorious!"

"We've had about enough wild adventure?"

"*Si, señor.*"

"An' jest 'cause we liked thet sort of thing, an' cottoned to a grand guy an' fought for him . . . we've found the pot of gold at the foot of the rainbow."

"Yes, pard. Adventure, romance, love, fortune . . . a story to dream over all our lives!"

Although Sterl conjured up a number of coups calculated to devastate Beryl for good and all, not one of them did Red care to accept.

Meanwhile, the October days warmed on, hot in the sun, pleasant in the shade. If there were flies and mosquitoes in this locality, they did not put in an appearance. The nights were cool, starry, still, unbroken by the dingo howl or wild *corroboree*. It was good to wear a coat, and a campfire added to the charm of this new country. The drovers claimed the mob had reached its home and knew it. The animals waxed fat and increased their numbers with frolicsome calves. Dann counted over a hundred horses, and Slyter seventy-nine. Leslie was happy with the five Thoroughbreds the trek had left her. Lady Jane, King, and Duke had the run of the camp like pet dogs.

On the eighth day on which Benson and Roland were expected to return with the wagons and supplies, Sterl and Red had progressed well with their cabin building. The site Sterl had selected was one of unbelievable loveliness. It was on the Ord River side of the wooded point, high up on a grassy, flower-spangled bank, shaded by grand trees from the morning sun and facing across the river to the Kimberleys.

The cabin was to have thatched roof and walls, for which Friday scouted out a wide-leafed palm, perhaps a species of pandamus. Slyter designed the framework, which consisted of long round poles carefully fitted. Larry, who was a good carpenter, often lent a helping hand, while Sterl and Red got in each other's way in their enthusiasm. Friday's job was a skillful plaiting and weaving of the long, wide, tough leaves, and it appeared he was a master at such craft. According to Slyter the aborigines were nomads and seldom or never made permanent homes. But this black could lay his sinewy hand to anything. Sterl had specified a solid floor high off the ground. It required a day's labor to ride up the stream, cut long poles, and snake them down to camp, where one round side had to be rough-hewn with an edge. Very often he halted to rest, wipe his sweaty face, and talk with his helpers, and always look at his surroundings, as if to make sure they were reality.

The side point sloped very gradually to the junction of stream and river. Trees huge and small, plain and showy appeared to have been especially planted for Sterl's delight. There were crimson flowering gums and other blossoming trees which Slyter could not name, and giants that towered high without a branch for seventy feet. The drover thought this species was the great jarrah. The wattles were there, showering gold amid the green. And Sterl's favorite gum—the opal-barked monarch with the grand, spreading branches and lacy foliage. Five of these gums grouped around Sterl's cabin, and these had scaled the balance in his difficult choice of a site. Next in order was the murmur and music of the Elivre as it poured over rocks into the river. The Ord was neither wide nor deep, but it was a gliding stream of crystal water, rocky-banked and bedded, and full of fish, and

frequented by flocks of waterfowl. The sunlit bush on the point
appeared to be the home of innumerable birds unknown to Sterl.
There were kookaburras with blue on their wings, and they were
remarkable for their curiosity and friendliness. But they did not
chatter and laugh like the laughing-jackass. Other birds, however, filled that grove with melody. Last charm of the place was
the view across the river to the bright trees, the sloping, gold-
tinged land, and the foothills that led up to the purple range.

While the cabin was in process of erection, the girls visited
there many times a day. They did not like this, and they suggested that, and they were enthusiastic over the beauty all
around. They brought tea to the workers and partook of a cup
themselves. Red, who was unusually mild and sweet these days,
made one characteristic remark.

"Say, anybody would think you girls expected to live over
heah with us fellers!"

That sally precipitated blushes and a rout, and also, from a little distance, very audible giggles.

"Red, that was a dig," remonstrated Sterl. "You are a mean
cuss. If you would only take a tumble to yourself, the girls *could*
come over here to live."

"Hell! I've shore tumbled. What do you want for two bits?
Canary-birds? An' why don't you figger out thet trick for me to
play on Beryl? I cain't last much longer. Why, when she comes
near me, I go plumb loco. You notice I shy away from them little
walks we used to have. Fact is, I know I'm a goner, an', wal, I
want to grab her an' kiss her half to death!"

"*Whoopee!* That's talking. You must give in to it, Red. But not
till after the deal I've planned."

"Yeah? What's it this time? Wuss than ever, I'll bet my spurs.
You gotta recollect, pard, thet Beryl is a proud little lady."

"I haven't forgotten. But she just can't be hurt or shocked or
shamed over this one, Red. Oh, it's clever. Even Dann thought
so. He agreed. And he was tickled!"

"You double-crossin', two-faced, Arizonie geezer!" ejaculated
Red. "You told Dann before me?"

"Sure. I had to get his consent, or there wouldn't be any sense in telling you at all. Listen, pard. . . ."

Whereupon Sterl briefly confided his newest and profoundest scheme to subjugate Beryl, beautifully and blissfully, while incidentally working the same miracle on Leslie.

Red appeared stunned, and then frightened, and presently, after he could collect his scattered wits, most tremendously elated.

"Holy Mackeli!" he babbled, blazing at Sterl. "What an idee! Best you ever figgered out in yore whole life! Nice, too, an' surprisin, an' everythin'. So Stanley Dann consented to help us put up thet job on his own daughter? If I've only got the nerve! Aw! I swear I'll do it, Sterl, cool as a cucumber."

Excited cries broke in upon their colloquy. The girls appeared off at the edge of the grove, waving and calling. Then Leslie cupped her hands to her lips and shrieked: "Boys! Wagons back! Come!"

"Gosh, heah thet, pard? Ben an' Rollie back. Let's rustle."

"You hobble-footed, hoss-ridin' *hombre* . . . I can beat you," taunted Sterl. They raced like boys, fell headlong to scramble up, and thump over the ground, to draw up abreast and panting before two huge, bulging, canvas-covered wagons and their excited comrades.

Surely no two freighters in all the annals of Outback Australia's pioneering days ever received the ovation accorded Benson and Rollie by those with whom they had trekked and suffered for long over two years.

The wagons were driven into the shade of the great gum tree that sheltered Dann's camp. The drovers and the women all talked at once, giving the smiling Benson and Roland no chance to reply. But Dann boomed them momentarily quiet.

"Welcome to Dann's Station, men," he called, when he could make himself heard. "Get down and unhitch. Larry, water these teams. Slyter, you and the boys untie these wagon covers. Are you crazy, you womenfolk? Contain yourselves."

"Boss, boss," shouted Benson, beaming. "Ten days going and coming. Fair to middling road. Plenty abo's, but friendly. One wagon loaded with food supplies, milk, sugar, vegetables, fruit, everything. Other wagon full of personal effects for all. Bought all lists complete. Four freight wagons following us with lumber, mattresses, staples . . . the biggest order ever filled in Wyndham!"

The ensuing scene of wild animation among the young people and the eager gladness of their elders could never have been rendered, except by a company who had known the long, long trek with its sacrifices and privations, and who had learned through bitter travail the value of things.

While the big wagons were being unpacked and the ground all about littered with boxes, bags, sacks, and packages, while the cowboys whooped and the girls squealed, and the drovers searched for tags and hefted this and that, a steady, voluminous stream of questions poured into the bewildered ears of Benson and Roland, these fortunate ones who had been to town, to a seaport, who had seen people and been in stores and heard news of the world and of the old home.

Sterl could not catch and catalogue one tenth of all the wonderful information Benson and Roland had fetched back.

Gold had, indeed, been discovered in the south and west of the Kimberleys. Ships and prospectors, sheepmen and drovers, trekkers and adventurers were coming north from Perth and Fremantle and points far to the south. On the other side of the continent, at Sydney and Brisbane, Australians were awakening to the El Dorado in the northwest, and ships plied regularly to Darwin. Stanley Dann and his company had come in on a rising tide. His trek across the Never Never Land was the wonder of two busy seaports, as soon it would be for the whole of Australia.

Most amazing facts of all, and yet wholly natural, were the letters for all the company, except Sterl and Red. Somehow that silenced the drawling Red and struck a pang to Sterl's heart. Now eager-eyed these trekkers opened letters with shaking hands! What ghosts in Beryl's dark eyes as she recognized the handwriting of friends, relatives, suitors long ago forgotten! They were voices out of the past. Stanley Dann read aloud in his booming voice a communication from Heald. He had gotten out safely with his comrades and the mob of cattle Dann had told them to drove, if they could. Heald had taken Ormiston's trail from the Forks, and they had worked out toward the coast into fine grazing country where he and his partners established a station. Ormiston's three escaping bush-rangers had been murdered by aborigines. News of Dann's trekkers perishing on the Never Never had preceded Heald's return to Queensland. But he never credited the rumor and chanced a letter to prove it. Another gratifying bit of news was that the government offered to sell hundred-mile-square tracts of land in the Outback for what seemed little money.

"Gosh! A hundred-mile-square ranch for nothin'!" drawled Red. "I reckon I gotta buy myself a couple of them."

"A hundred square miles?" mused Sterl. "Strange how that seems so small beside the Never Never Land."

"Wal, pard, we shore trekked a grub line for three thousand miles. An' thet's the champeen record ride for any cowboy."

Stanley Dann boomed out: "Let us halt these proceedings for a cup of tea, and try to think of something joyous to commemorate the end of our wonderful trek."

They settled themselves in the pleasant shade. Mrs. Slyter and Leslie served tea. Beryl sat pensive and abstracted. On that auspicious morning, when all had been gay, Red had not deigned her even a smile or hardly a word, that the watchful Sterl had observed. What a capital actor Dann was! To all save Sterl and Red he appeared only the great leader, glad and beaming, for this simple occasion. But the cowboys shared with him the thrilling fact that this hour was to see a great occasion, a fulfillment of the trek, a promise that his young folk were to carry on his work.

Presently Stanley Dann produced a little black book, worn of back and yellow of leaf. He opened it meditatively. "Beryl, will you please come here," he said casually. "In this new and unsettled country I think I may be useful in other ways besides being a pioneer . . . cattleman. I shall need a little practice to acquire a seemly dignity and a clarity of voice." He did not look up and continued to mull over the yellow pages.

Sterl saw the big fingers quiver ever so slightly. He was quaking inwardly himself.

Beryl, used to her father's moods, came obediently to stand before him. "What, Dad?" she inquired curiously.

"Sterl, come here and stand up with Beryl," he called. "No, let Krehl come. In the light of possible future events he might be more fitting."

Red strolled forward, his spurs jingling, his demeanor as cool and nonchalant as it ever had been.

"I've observed you holding my daughter's hand a good few times on this trek," Dann said mildly. "Please take her hand now."

As Red reached for Beryl's hand and clasped it, she looked up at him with a wondering smile and her color deepened. Then Dann stood up to lift his head and expose his bronze-gold face, which appeared a calm and profound mask, except for the golden lightning in his amber eyes.

"What's the idee, boss?" drawled Red.

"Yes, Dad, what is . . . all this?" faltered Beryl, confused, her ready intuition at fault at such an unusual procedure before all the others.

"Listen, child, and you, Krehl," replied Dann. "This should be for you, and surely for the others. Please watch me. Criticize my ministerial manner and voice. It's been a long time. Trekking, I find, does not improve even the civilized and necessary graces. Well, here we are. . . ." And in a swift resonant voice he ran over the opening passages of the marriage service. Then, more slowly and impressively, he addressed Red. "James Krehl, do you take this woman to be your lawful wedded wife . . . to have and to hold . . . to love and to cherish . . . until death do you part?"

"I do!" replied Red ringingly.

The leader turned to his daughter. "Beryl Dann, do you take this man to be your lawful wedded husband . . . to have and to hold . . . to love, cherish, and obey . . . until death do you part?"

"I . . . I . . . I do!" gasped Beryl faintly.

Dann added sonorously: "I pronounce you man and wife. Whom God has joined together, let no man put asunder!"

Beryl stared up at him, visibly a prey to conflicting tides of emotions. It had been a play, of course, but to her the mere recital of the vows, the counterfeit solemnity had torn her serenity asunder. When her father embraced her, thick-voiced and loving, she appeared further bewildered. Not one inkling of the truth had yet pierced her mind.

"Daddy, what a . . . a strange thing . . . for you to practice that . . . on me!"

"Beryl, it is the most beautiful thing of the ages. Krehl, I congratulate you with all my heart. I feel that she is safe at last."

Sterl dragged the astounded and backward Leslie up to the couple. "Red, old pard, put it there!" he cried, wringing Red's free hand. "Beryl, let me be the first to kiss the bride. I always wanted to kiss the girl!" And he availed himself gallantly of that privilege. But Leslie could only stare, her lips wide.

"But . . . but it was only a play!" flashed Beryl, rising to a hint of her old fire. Then Red kissed her lips with a passion of tenderness and violence commingled. Beryl loosed herself partly from that embrace, the scarlet wave receding to leave her pale.

"Wal, wife, it was about time," drawled Red.

That word unstrung Beryl. "Wife?" she echoed almost inaudibly. A woman would have to be mad, indeed, to have failed to divine Krehl's masterful and adoring gaze. "Red! You . . . you *married* me . . . really? It wasn't . . . just fun?"

"Wal, darlin', it shore was fun. But I was kinda scared. I came near slopin' for the Never Never."

"Father! Have I been made a . . . fool of?" cried Beryl tragically. "Could you perpetrate such a trick on me? Oh, I've been so horrid . . . always. I deserved nearly anything. But this . . . this farce. . . ."

"My daughter, compose yourself," returned Dann. "We thought to have a little fun at your expense. But you are Krehl's wife. I'll find a marriage certificate somewhere in my luggage, and make it out for you."

She swayed back to Red. Sterl, at sight of her lovely eyes, that had always stormed his emotions, swallowed his fright and gloried in what he had done. She could not stand without support. She lifted frail brown hands that could not cling to Red's sleeves. "Red! You never *asked* me!"

"Wal, honey, the fact was I didn't have the nerve. An' Sterl heah, an' Les most, jest made me believe you cared for me. So Sterl an' I went to yore dad an' fixed it up. Beryl, he's one grand guy."

"Why . . . why did you . . . ?"

Red snatched the swaying girl to his breast. Her eyelids had fallen. "Beryl!" he shouted in fear and remorse. "Don't you dare faint! Not heah an' now of all times in our lives! I did it thet way, because I've been dyin' of love for you. Since thet . . . thet orful time, I've been shore you cared for me, but I never asked, I never risked you outwittin' me. I swore I'd fool you once an' then go on my knees the rest of my life. Forgive me, Beryl, an' don't faint, for then I'd never forgive myself!"

"My Never Never Man!" she whispered, suddenly shot through and through with revivified life. She did not see any others there. And when she lifted her lips to Red, it was something, the look of them then—that dimmed Sterl's eyes.

"Come, Sterl and Leslie," Dann boomed. "I require more practice. Here, before me, and join hands. . . . Our bride and groom there may stand up with you." Almost before Sterl realized anything except the shy and bedazzled girl beside him, clutching his hand, he was married to her and receiving the clamor of his friends.

Not the least happy were the words of Friday. That black fella knew what it was all about. He wrung Sterl's hand. No intelligence could have exaggerated what shone in his eyes. "Me stopum alonga you an' missy. Me be good black fella. No home, no fadder, no mudder, no *lubra*. Imm stay alonga you, boss."

"With all my heart, Friday, my black brother. If you left us today, that would be the one bitter drop in our sweet cup!"

Sterl and Red walked by the river alone. It was sunset. The heat still lingered. The bees hummed. The stream murmured, and the melodious *cur-ra-wong* was sweet on the still air.

"Pard, it's done," said Red. "We're Australians. Who would ever have thunk it? But it's great. All this for two no-good, gun-slingin' cowboys?"

"Red, it is almost too wonderful to be true. We're lost . . . we're gone! Better so than the old trails . . . the end of which we couldn't escape. New faces, new people, new life! God, I hope we can be worthy. But in our hearts we will never forget."

It was as Stanley had said of them all: "We have fought the good fight." In that moment Sterl saw with marvelous clarity. Even the black man symbolized the use and reward of noble life. It had taken a far country and an incomparable adventure with hardy souls to make men out of two wild cowboys. He would not have changed past or present one single iota. How he had been transformed, what had been flayed into his blood and bone and brain by the wilderness, only time could tell. But part of it was that which he peered at now—the purple land, the sunset-flushed slope, the bright trees and shining river, the many-hued, singing birds, the kangaroos and emus coming down to drink, the whole of an alien country which had absorbed him, and the primal nature that he had not worshipped in vain.

About the Author

Zane Grey was born Pearl Zane Gray at Zanesville, Ohio in 1872. He was graduated from the University of Pennsylvania in 1896 with a degree in dentistry. He practiced in New York City while striving to make a living by writing. He married Lina Elise Roth in 1905 and with her financial assistance he published his first novel himself, BETTY ZANE (1903). Closing his dental office, the Greys moved into a cottage on the Delaware River, near Lackawaxen, Pennsylvania. Grey took his first trip to Arizona in 1907 and, following his return, wrote THE HERITAGE OF THE DESERT (1910). The profound effect that the desert had had on him was so vibrantly captured that it still comes alive for a reader. Grey couldn't have been more fortunate in his choice of a mate. Trained in English at Hunter College, Lina Grey proofread every manuscript Grey wrote, polished his prose, and she effectively managed their financial affairs. Grey's early novels were serialized in pulp magazines, but by 1918 he had graduated to the slick magazine market. Motion picture rights brought in a fortune and, with 109 films based on his work, Grey set a record yet to be equaled by any other author. Zane Grey was not a realistic writer, but rather one who charted the interiors of the soul through encounters with the wilderness. He provided characters no more realistic than one finds in Balzac, Dickens, or Thomas Mann, but nonetheless they have a vital story to tell. "There was so much unexpressed feeling that could not be entirely portrayed," Loren Grey, Grey's younger son and a noted psychologist, once recalled, "that, in later years, he would weep when re-reading one of his own books." More than stories, Grey fashioned psychodramas about the odyssey of the human soul. They may not be the stuff of the real world, but without them the real world has no meaning—which may go a long way to explain the hold he has had on an enraptured reading public ever since his first Western romance in 1910.

☐ **YES!**

Sign me up for the Leisure Western Book Club and send my **FREE BOOKS!** If I choose to stay in the club, I will pay only $14.00* each month, a savings of $9.96!

NAME: _____

ADDRESS: _____

TELEPHONE: _____

EMAIL: _____

☐ I want to pay by credit card.

☐ **VISA**   ☐ **MasterCard**   ☐ **DISCOVER**

ACCOUNT #: _____

EXPIRATION DATE: _____

SIGNATURE: _____

Mail this page along with $2.00 shipping and handling to:
Leisure Western Book Club
PO Box 6640
Wayne, PA 19087
Or fax (must include credit card information) to:
610-995-9274

You can also sign up online at **www.dorchesterpub.com**.
*Plus $2.00 for shipping. Offer open to residents of the U.S. and Canada only. Canadian residents please call 1-800-481-9191 for pricing information.
If under 18, a parent or guardian must sign. Terms, prices and conditions subject to change. Subscription subject to acceptance. Dorchester Publishing reserves the right to reject any order or cancel any subscription.

GET 4 FREE BOOKS!

You can have the best Westerns delivered to your door for less than what you'd pay in a bookstore or online. Sign up for one of our book clubs today, and we'll send you 4 FREE* BOOKS, worth $23.96, just for trying it out...**with no obligation to buy, ever!**

Authors include classic writers such as
LOUIS L'AMOUR, MAX BRAND, ZANE GREY
and more; plus new authors such as
COTTON SMITH, JOHNNY D. BOGGS,
DAVID THOMPSON and others.

As a book club member you also receive the following special benefits:
- **30% off all orders!**
- **Exclusive access to special discounts!**
- **Convenient home delivery and 10 days to return any books you don't want to keep.**

Visit **www.dorchesterpub.com**
or call
1-800-481-9191

There is no minimum number of books to buy, and you may cancel membership at any time.
*Please include $2.00 for shipping and handling.